HELLBENT

This Large Print Book carries the
Seal of Approval of N.A.V.H.

HELLBENT

GREGG HURWITZ

THORNDIKE PRESS
A part of Gale, a Cengage Company

Farmington Hills, Mich • San Francisco • New York • Waterville, Maine
Meriden, Conn • Mason, Ohio • Chicago

LIBRARY OF CONGRESS CIP DATA ON FILE.
CATALOGUING IN PUBLICATION FOR THIS BOOK
IS AVAILABLE FROM THE LIBRARY OF CONGRESS.

ISBN-13: 978-1-4328-4740-1 (hardcover)

Published in 2018 by arrangement with Macmillan Publishing Group, LLC/St. Martin's Press

Printed in the United States of America
1 2 3 4 5 6 7 22 21 20 19 18

To Gary and Karen Messing
and
Darra and Zach Brewer.
You don't get to choose your family,
but sometimes you luck out.

"And now that you don't have to be perfect, you can be good."

— John Steinbeck, *East of Eden*

Evan's scuffed knuckles, a fetching post-fight shade of eggplant, ledged the steering wheel. His nose was freshly broken, leaking a trickle of crimson. Nothing bad, more a shifting along old fault lines.

He inspected his nose in the rearview, then reached up and snapped it back into place.

The Cadillac's alignment pulled to the right, threatening to dump him into the rain-filled roadside ditch. The seat springs poked into the backs of his thighs, and the fabric, dotted with cigarette scorch marks, reeked of menthol. The dome light housed a bare, burned-out bulb, the brake disks made a noise like an asphyxiating chicken, and the left rear brake light was out.

He should have stolen a better car.

Rain dumped down. That was Portland for you. Or — if he was being precise — a country road outside Hillsboro.

Big drops turned the roof into a tin drum.

Water sluiced across the windshield, rooster-tailed from the tires.

He sledded around a bend, passing a bill-board. A moment later smeared red and blue lights illuminated the Caddy's rear window.

A cop.

The broken brake light.

That was inconvenient.

Especially on this car, since a BOLO had likely been issued. The cop would be running the plate number now if he hadn't already.

Evan blew out a breath. Leaned harder into the gas pedal.

Here came the sirens. The headlights grew larger.

Evan could see the silhouette of the officer behind the wheel. So much like a shooting target — head and chest, all critical mass.

Hillsboro prided itself on being one of the safest cities in the Pacific Northwest. Evan hoped to keep it that way.

As he popped the brakes and jerked the wheel, the heap of a car rocked on its shocks, fanning onto an intersecting road.

Two more cop cars swept in behind him from the opposite direction.

Evan sighed.

Three patrol cars lit up like Christmas, sirens screaming, spreading out across both lanes and closing in.

That was when the thumping from the trunk grew more pronounced.

1
No Version of Being Too Careful

Evan moved swiftly through the door to his penthouse suite at the Castle Heights Residential Tower, his RoamZone pressed to his ear. The phone, encased in hardened rubber and Gorilla glass, was as durable as a hockey puck and essentially impossible to trace. Every incoming call to 1-855-2-NOWHERE traveled in digital form over the Internet through a labyrinth of encrypted virtual-private-network tunnels. After a round-the-world tour of software telephone-switch destinations, it emerged through the receiver of the RoamZone.

Evan always answered the phone the same way.

Do you need my help?

This time, for the first time, the voice on the other end was a familiar one.

Jack Johns.

Jack had plucked Evan from the obscurity of a foster home at the age of twelve and

13

placed him in a fully deniable black program buried deep inside the Department of Defense. Jack had turned Evan into Orphan X, an expendable assassin who went where the U.S. government would not and did what the U.S. government could not. Jack had fought for Evan to stay human even while teaching him to be a killer.

The only father Evan had ever known was calling this line now, a line reserved for those in mortal danger. And he had answered Evan's question — *Do you need my help?* — with a single syllable.

Yes.

Evan and Jack had an elaborate series of protocols for establishing contact. Never like this.

For Jack to call this number meant that he was up against what others might consider world-destroying trouble.

All Evan had gotten over the phone so far was that one word. Static fuzzed the line infuriatingly, the connection going in and out.

He was gripping the phone too hard. "Jack? Jack? *Jack.*"

Eight years ago Evan had gone rogue from the Orphan Program. At the time he'd been the Program's top asset. Given the sensitive information in his head, the bodies he'd put in the ground, and the skills encoded into his muscles, he could not be allowed to exist. The most merciless of the Orphans, Charles Van Sciver, had taken over the Program and was hellbent on tracking down and eradicating Evan.

Vanishing was easier when you already didn't exist. The Orphan Program lived behind so many veils of secrecy that no one except their immediate handlers knew who the Orphans were. They were kept in separate silos and deployed through encoded comms that preserved plausible deniability at every level. Double-blind protocols ensured that even the handlers' whereabouts were often unknown by higher headquarters.

And so Evan had simply stepped off the grid, keeping only the operational alias he'd earned in the shadow service, a name spoken in hushed tones in the back rooms of intel agencies the world over.

The Nowhere Man.

He now helped the desperate, those with no place left to turn, people suffering at the hands of unrepentant and vicious abusers. His clients called 1-855-2-NOWHERE. And their problems were solved.

Antiseptic. Effective. Impersonal.

Until this.

15

Evan's tense steps echoed around the seven thousand square feet of his condo. The open stretch of gunmetal-gray floor was broken by workout stations, a few sitting areas, and a spiral staircase that rose to a loft he used as a reading room. The kitchen area was equally modern, all stainless steel and poured concrete. The views up here on the twenty-first floor were dazzling, downtown Los Angeles shimmering like a mirage twelve miles to the east.

Despite all that space, Evan was having trouble breathing. He felt something wild clawing in his chest, something he couldn't identify. Fear?

"Jack."

The reception crackled some more, and then — finally — Jack's voice came through again. "Evan?"

It sounded as if Jack was in his truck, an engine humming in the background.

"I'm here," Evan said. "Are you okay?"

Through the receiver he could make out more road rolling beneath Jack's tires. When Jack spoke again, his voice sounded broken. "Do you regret it? What I did to you?"

Evan inhaled, steadied his heart rate. "What are you talking about?"

"Do you ever wish I'd never taken you out of that boys' home? That I'd just let you live an ordinary life?"

"Jack — where are you?"

"I can't tell you. Dollars to doughnuts they've got ears on me right now."

Evan stared out through the floor-to-ceiling, bullet-resistant Lexan windows. The discreet armor sunshades were down, but through the gaps in the woven titanium chain-link he could still see the city sparkling.

There was no version of being too careful.

"Then why are you calling?" Evan said.

"I wanted to hear your voice."

Over the line, tires screeched. Jack was driving fast, this much Evan could glean.

But he couldn't know that Jack was being pursued — surreptitiously, yet not so surreptitiously that Jack didn't notice — by five SUVs in rolling surveillance. Or that a Stingray cell-tower simulator was intercepting Jack's signal, capturing his every word. That within five minutes the *thwap-thwap-thwap* of rotor blades would stir the clouds and a Black Hawk attack helicopter would break through the night sky and plummet down, fanning up dust. That thermal imaging had already pegged Jack in his driver's seat, his 98.6-degree body temperature rendered in soothing reds and yellows.

All Evan knew right now was that something was terribly wrong.

The static rose like a growl, and then, abruptly, the line was as clear as could be. "This is looking to be my ninth life, son."

For a moment Evan couldn't find his voice. Then he forced out the words. "Tell me where you are, and I'll come get you."

"It's too late for me," Jack said.

"If you won't let me help you, then what are we supposed to talk about?"

"I suppose the stuff that really matters. Life. You and me." Jack, breaking his own rules.

"Because we're so good at that?"

Jack laughed that gruff laugh, a single note. "Well, sometimes we miss what's important for the fog. But maybe we should give it a go before, you know . . ." More screeching of tires. "Better make it snappy, though."

Evan sensed an inexplicable wetness in his eyes and blinked it away. "Okay. We can try."

"Do you regret it?" Jack asked again. "What I did?"

"How can I answer that?" Evan said. "This is all I know. I never had some other life where I was a plumber or a school-teacher or a . . . or a dad."

Now the sound of a helo came through the line, barely audible.

"Jack? You still there?"

"I guess . . . I guess I want to know that I'm forgiven."

Evan forced a swallow down his dry throat. "If it wasn't for you, I would've wound up in prison, dead of an overdose, knifed in a bar. Those are the odds. I wouldn't have had a life. I wouldn't have been me." He swallowed again, with less success. "I wouldn't trade knowing you for anything."

A long silence, broken only by the thrum of tires over asphalt.

Finally Jack said, "It's nice of you to say so."

"I don't put much stock in 'nice.' I said it because it's true."

The sound of rotors intensified. In the background Evan heard other vehicles squealing. He was listening with every ounce of focus he had in him. A connection routed through fifteen countries in four continents, a last tenuous lifeline to the person he cared about more than anyone in the world.

"We didn't have time," Evan said. "We didn't have enough time."

Jack said, "I love you, son."

Evan had never heard the words spoken to him. Something slid down his cheek, clung to his jawline.

He said, "Copy that."

The line went dead.

Evan stood in his condo, the cool of the floor rising through his boots, chilling his feet, his calves, his body. The phone was still shoved against his cheek. Despite the full-body chill, he was burning up.

He finally lowered the phone. Peeled off his sweaty shirt. He walked over to the kitchen area and tugged open the freezer drawer. Inside, lined up like bullets, were bottles of the world's finest vodkas. He removed a rectangular bottle of Double Cross, a seven-times-distilled and filtered Slovak spirit. It was made with winter wheat and mountain springwater pulled from aquifers deep beneath the Tatra Mountains.

It was one of the purest liquids he knew.

He poured two fingers into a glass and sat with his back to the cold Sub-Zero. He didn't want to drink, just wanted it in his hand. He breathed the clean fumes, hoping that they would sterilize his lungs, his chest.

His heart.

"Well," he said. "Fuck."

Glass in hand, he waited there for ten minutes and then ten more.

His RoamZone rang again.

Caller ID didn't show UNIDENTIFIED

20

CALLER or BLOCKED CALLER. It showed nothing at all.

With dread, Evan clicked the phone on, raised it to his face.

It was the voice he'd most feared.

"Why don't you go fetch your digital contact lenses," it said. "You're gonna want to see this."

2
DARK MATTER

Five Days Earlier

The burly man forged through fronds and the paste of the jungle humidity, his feet sinking into Amazonian mud. A camouflaged boonie hat shadowed his face. A cone of mosquito netting descended from the hat's brim, breathing in and out with him. The ghostly effect — that of an amorphously shaped head respiring — made him seem like a bipedal monster flitting among the rotting trunks. Sweat soaked his clothes. On his watch a red GPS dot blinked, urging him forward.

Behind him another man followed. Jordan Thornhill was gymnast-compact, all knotty muscle and precision, his hair shaved nearly to the skull, a side part notched in with a razor. He'd taken off his shirt and tucked it into the waistband of his pants. Perspiration oiled his dark skin.

They'd left the rented Jeep a few miles back, where dense foliage had finally smothered the trail.

They kept on now in silence, mud sucking at their boots, leaves rustling across their broad shoulders. Strangler vines wrapped massive trees, choking the life from them. Bats flitted in the canopy. Somewhere in the distance, howler monkeys earned their names.

Thornhill kept tight to the big man's back, his movement nimble, fluid. "We're a long way from Kansas, boss. You even sure this dude has it on him?"

The invisible face beneath the boonie hat swiveled to Thornhill. The netting beat in and out like a heart. Then the man lifted the netting, swept it back over the brim. Surgeries had repaired most of the damage on the right side of Charles Van Sciver's face, but there remained a few feathers of scarring at the temple. The pupil of his right eye was permanently dilated, a tiny starfish-shaped cloud floating in its depths.

Souvenirs from an explosive that had been set by Orphan X nearly a year ago.

As the director of the Orphan Program, Van Sciver had the resources to eradicate most of the physical damage, but rage endured just beneath the skin, undiminished.

Thornhill grew uneasy under Van Sciver's gaze. That shark eye, it had an unsettling effect on people.

"It was on his person," Van Sciver said. "I have it on good authority."

"Whose authority?"

"Are you actually asking me?" Van Sciver said. The scars didn't look so bad until he scowled and the skin pulled taut, stretching the wrong way.

Thornhill shook his head.

"The real question is, is it still there?" Van Sciver said. "For all we know, it could be riding in the belly of a jaguar already. Or if there was a fire — who the hell knows."

"Sometimes," Thornhill said, "all a man needs is a little luck."

Yes, luck. For months Van Sciver had lived inside a virtual bunker built of servers, applying the most powerful deep-learning data-mining software in computational history to finding some — *any* — trace of Orphan X. The recent directives from above had been clear. Van Sciver's top priority was to stamp out wayward Orphans. Anyone who'd retired. Anyone who hadn't made the cut. Anyone who had tested questionable for compliance.

And most important, the only Orphan who had ever — in the storied history of the Program — gone rogue.

The Program's large-scale data processing had at last spit out a lead, a glimmer of a fishing lure in the ocean of data that surged through cyberspace on a daily basis. Even calling it a lead, Van Sciver thought now, was too ambitious. More like a lead that could lead to a lead that could lead to Orphan X.

The story behind it had quickly become legend in the intel community. It went like this: A midlevel DoD agent had once, through a labyrinthine process of extortion and blackmail, acquired a copy of highly sensitive data pertaining to the Orphan Program. A few aliases, a few last-known addresses, a few pairings of handlers and Orphans. These key bits and pieces had been captured from various classified channels outside the Orphan Program in the seconds before they autoredacted.

The agent had hoped it would hasten his rise inside the department but quickly learned that he'd caught a hot grenade; the data was too dangerous to use. He'd kept it as an insurance policy despite standing orders to the contrary that originated from Pennsylvania Avenue that any and all data pertaining to the Orphan Program *must* be expunged. Rumors of this shadow file persisted over the past months but had remained only rumors.

Until the powerful data-mining engines at Van Sciver's disposal had caught the scent of this shadow file and verified its existence by shading in bits of surrounding intelligence — like gleaning the existence of invisible dark matter by observing gravity effects around it. The midlevel agent had sensed the crosshairs at his back and had gone to ground.

In more ways than one.

In the end it hadn't been an Orphan or a fellow agent who had brought him down but an unexpected trade wind.

Van Sciver had promised himself that when the time came, he'd leave his bunker and get his boots muddy for a lead that might bring him to Orphan X. So here he was, squelching through the boggy muck of another continent, reaching for that shiny lure.

They smelled it before they saw it. A slaughterhouse stench lacing the thick, heavy-hanging air. They crested a slope. Up ahead the snapped-off tail rotor of a Sikorsky S-70 was embedded in the trunk of a banyan, cleaving the massive tree nearly in half.

Thornhill waved a hand in front of his face. "God*damn*."

Van Sciver drew in a lungful of aviation fuel and rotting flesh, a reek so strong he could taste it. They shouldered through a tangle of underbrush, and there it was. The downed fuselage rested on its side, nudged up against an enormous boulder like a dog trying to scratch its back. A tired seventies army-transport chopper repurposed for private charters, sold and resold a dozen times over, now being slowly devoured by the jungle.

The pilot had been thrown through the windscreen. His body, held together by the flight suit, was cradled tenderly upside down in the embrace of a strangler vine twenty feet off the ground. His flesh seemed to be alive, crawling with movement.

Fire ants.

A rustling came from the fuselage, and then a desiccated voice: "Is someone there? God, please say someone's there."

Van Sciver and Thornhill drew close. Van Sciver had to crouch to see inside.

The NSA agent hung lifeless from the sideways seat, his arms dangling awkwardly, a roller-coaster rider in the twist of a corkscrew. The shoulder harness bit into a charcoal suit jacket and — given the heat — seemed to be making some headway through the underlying flesh as well.

The agent's fellow passenger had managed to pop his own seat belt. He'd landed with his legs bent all wrong. A shiv of bone jutted up through his pants at the shin. The skin around it was puffy and red.

Tears glistened on his cheeks. "I thought I was gonna die here. I've been alone with . . . in the middle of . . ." His sobs deteriorated into dry heaves.

Van Sciver looked past him at the dead agent and felt a spark of hope flare inside his chest. The body looked reasonably well preserved hanging there. Van Sciver forced his excitement back into the tiny dark place in his chest that he reserved for Orphan X. He'd been close so many times, only to have his fingertips slip off the ledge.

"The harness kept him off the ground," Van Sciver said to Thornhill. "Away from the elements. We might have a shot."

The passenger reached toward Van Sciver. "Water," he said. "I need water."

Thornhill darted inside, hopping gracefully through the wreckage until he stood beneath the agent, practically eye to eye.

"He's fairly intact," Thornhill said. "Not

gonna place at the Miss America pageant, but still. We got us a good-looking corpse."

The passenger gave with a dry, hacking cough. "Water," he whispered.

"Let's get the body out," Van Sciver said.

"I'll unclip the harness," Thornhill said, "and you ease him down. The last thing we need is his festering ass disintegrating all over the fuselage."

"Please." The passenger clutched the cuff of Van Sciver's pants. "Please at least look at me."

Van Sciver removed the pistol from his underarm tension holster and shot the passenger through the head. Taking hold of the passenger's loafers, he dragged the man clear of the fuselage. Then he returned to the downed helo, and he and Thornhill gently guided the agent down. It involved some unpleasant grappling. The stench was terrible, but Van Sciver was accustomed to terrible things.

They carried the corpse gingerly out into the midday blaze and laid it on a flat stretch of ground. Thornhill's eyes were red. Choking noises escaped his throat. They took a break, walking off a few paces to find fresh air. When they got back to civilization, Van Sciver realized, their clothes would have to be burned.

By unspoken accord they reconvened over the body. They stared down at it. Then Van Sciver flicked out a folding knife and cut the clothes off.

The bloated body lay there, emitting gases. Thornhill was ordinary-looking by design, as were most of the Orphans, chosen so they could blend in, but his smile was unreasonably handsome. He flashed it now.

"This shit right here? We are livin' the dream."

Van Sciver reached into his cargo pocket, removed two sets of head-mounted watch-repair binoculars, and handed one to Thornhill.

"Any idea where it would be?" Thornhill asked.

"Fingernails, toenails, hair."

They tied their shirts over their mouths and noses like *bandidos,* got down on all fours, and began their gruesome exploration.

The first hour passed like a kidney stone.

The second was even worse.

By the third, winged insects clustered, clogging the air around them. Shadows stretched like living things. Soon it would be nightfall, and they could not afford to wait another day.

Thornhill was working the agent's hair,

picking through strand by strand. Finally he sat back on his heels, gulped a few quick breaths, and spit a wad of cottony saliva to the side. "Are we sure it's on him?"

Van Sciver paused, holding one of the agent's jaundiced hands delicately. It was goosenecked at the wrist, ready to receive a manicure. The skin shifted unsettlingly around the bone.

Sweat trickled down into Van Sciver's eyes, and he armed it off. He could still see through his right eye, but after so much meticulous concentration the blown pupil and bruised retina gave him trouble focusing. He could feel the muscles straining. He did his best to blink free the moisture.

Then he froze, seized by a notion.

Leaning forward, he parted the dead man's eye. Its pretty blue iris had already filmed over. He thumbed at an upper lid, splaying the lashes. Nothing. He checked the lower lid next.

And there it was.

A lash hidden among others. It was glossier and more robust, with a touch of swelling at the insertion point.

It was a hair, all right. Just not the agent's.

With a pair of tweezers, Van Sciver plucked out the transplant and examined it more closely.

The lash was synthetic.

This was not the future of data storage. It was the *original* data storage. For billions of years, DNA has existed as an information repository. Instead of the ones and zeros that computers use to render digital information, DNA utilizes its four base codes to lay down data complex enough to compose all living matter. Not only had this staggeringly efficient mechanism remained stable for millennia, it required no power supply and was temperature-resistant. Van Sciver had reviewed the research and its big claims — that one day a teaspoon of synthetic DNA could contain the entirety of the world's data. But despite all the outlandish talk of exabytes and zettabytes, the tech remained nascent and the costs staggering. In fact, the price of encoding a single megabyte with digital information was just shy of twenty grand.

But the information on this single eyelash was worth more than that.

To Van Sciver it was worth *everything*.

It contained nothing directly related to Orphan X — Evan was too adept at covering his trail — but compared to the expansive data Van Sciver had been sifting through, it held a treasure trove of specifics.

Holding the lash up against the orange

globe of the descending sun, Van Sciver realized that he had forgotten to breathe.

He also realized something else.

For the first time he could recall, he was
smiling.

3
EVERYTHING HE HELD DEAR

Venice was a beautiful city. But like many beauties, she was temperamental.

Furious weather kept the tourists inside. Rain hammered the canals, wore at the ancient stone, bit the cheeks of the few brave enough to venture out. The storm washed the color from everything, turning the Floating City into a medley of dull grays.

Nearing the Ponte di Rialto, Jim Harville spotted the man tailing him. A black man in a raincoat, bent into the punishing wind a ways back. He was skilled — were it not for the weather-thinned foot traffic, Harville never would have picked him up. It had been several years since he'd operated, and his skills were rusty. But habits like these were never entirely forgotten.

Harville hiked up the broad stone steps of the bridge, the Grand Canal surging furiously below. He reached the portico at the top and cast a glance back.

Across the distance the men locked eyes.

A gust of wind howled through the ancient mazework of alleys, ruffling the shop canopies, making Harville stagger.

When he regained his footing and looked back up, the man was sprinting at him.

It was a strange thing so many years later to witness aggression this naked. Instinct put a charge into Harville, and he ran. Vanishing up a tight street, he took a hairpin left between two abandoned palazzos and shot across a cobblestone square. He had no weapon. The man pursuing him was younger and fitter. Harville's only advantage was that he knew the city's complex topography as well as he knew the contours of his wife's back, the olive skin he traced lovingly each night as she drifted off to sleep.

He shouldered through a boutique door, overturned a display table of carnival masks, barged through a rear door into an alley. Already he felt a burning in his legs. Giovanna liked to joke that she kept him young for fifty, but even so, retirement had left him soft.

He careened out onto a *calle* at the water's edge. Across the canal a good distance north, his pursuer appeared, skidding out from between two buildings.

The man saw him. He flung his arms

back, and his jacket slid off gracefully, as if tugged by invisible strings. Rain matted his white T-shirt to his torso, his dark skin showing through, the grooved muscles visible even at this distance.

The man's eyes dropped to the choppy water. And then he bounded across, Froggering from pier to trash barge and onward, leaving two moored gondolas rocking in his wake.

Dread struck Harville's stomach like a swallowed stone. He registered a single thought.

Orphan.

The man was on Harville's side of the canal now, but propitiously, a wide intersecting waterway provided a barrier between them. As Harville began his retreat, the man vaulted over an embankment, rolled across a boat prow, and sprang up the side of a building, finding hand-and footholds on downspouts and window shutters. Even as he went vertical, his momentum barely slowed.

That particular brand of obstacle-course discipline — parkouring — had come into popularity after Harville's training, and he couldn't help but watch with a touch of awe now.

The man hauled himself through a third-story window, scaring a chinless woman smoking a cigarette back onto her heels. An instant later the man flew out of a neighboring window on Harville's side of the waterway.

Harville had lost precious seconds.

He reversed, splashing through a puddle, and bolted. The narrow passages and alleys unfolded endlessly, a match for the thoughts racing in his head — Giovanna's openmouthed laugh, their free-standing bathtub on the cracked marble floor, bedside candles mapping yellow light onto the walls of their humble apartment. Without a conscious thought, he was running away from home, leading his pursuer farther from everything he held dear.

He sensed footfalls quickening behind him. Columns flickered past, lending the rain a strobe effect as he raced along the arcade bordering Piazza San Marco. The piazza was flooded, the angry Adriatic surging up the drains, blanketing the stones with two feet of water.

Quite a sight to see the great square empty.

Harville was winded.

He stumbled out into the piazza, sloshing through floodwater. St. Mark's Basilica tilted back and forth with each jarring step.

The mighty clock tower rose to the north, the two bronze figures, one old, one young, standing their sentinels' watch on either side of the massive bell, waiting to memorialize the passing of another hour.

Harville wouldn't make it across the square into the warren of alleys across. He was bracing himself to turn and face when the round punched through his shoulder blade and spit specks of lung through the exit wound as it cleared his chest.

He went down onto his knees, his hands vanishing to the elbows in water. He stared dumbly at his fingers below, rippling like fish.

The voice from behind him was as easy-going as a voice could be. "Orphan J. A pleasure."

Harville coughed blood, crimson flecks riding the froth.

"Jack Johns," the man said. "He was your handler. Way back when."

"I don't know that name." Harville was surprised that he could still form words.

"Oh. You mistook me. That wasn't a question. We haven't gotten to the questions yet." The man's tone was conversational. Good-natured even.

Harville's arms trembled. He stared down at the eddies, the stone, his hands. He wasn't sure how much longer he could keep his face out of the water.

At some point it had stopped raining. The air had a stunned stillness, holding its breath in case the storm decided to come back.

The man asked, "What are your current protocols when you contact Jack Johns?"

Harville wheezed with each breath. "I don't know that name."

The man crouched beside him. In his hand was a creased photograph. It showed Adelina nestled in Giovanna's arms, feeding. She was still wearing her pink knit cap from the hospital.

Harville felt air leaking through the hole in his chest.

He told the man what he wanted to know.

The man rose and stood behind him.

The water stirred around Harville. He closed his eyes.

He said, "I had a dream that I was normal."

The man said, "And it cost you everything."

The pistol's report lifted a flight of pigeons off the giant domes of the basilica.

As the man pocketed his pistol and forged his way through the floodwater, the hour sounded. High on the clock tower, the two

39

bronze forms, one old, one young, struck the bell they'd been ringing across these worn stones for five centuries and counting.

4
ARE YOU READY?

Back to the Present

Evan was still sitting in the kitchen, the Sub-Zero numbing his bare back, the glass of vodka resting on his knee. The phone remained at his face. He felt not so much paralyzed as unwilling to move. Movement would prove that time was passing, and right now time passing meant that bad things would happen.

He reminded himself to breathe. Two-second inhale, four-second exhale.

He reached for the Fourth Commandment: *Never make it personal.*

Jack had taught him the Commandments and would want — no, *demand* — that Evan honor them now.

The Fourth wasn't working, so he dug for the Fifth: *If you don't know what to do, do nothing.*

There was no situation that could not be

made worse.

The vodka glass perspired in Evan's hand.

The phone connection was as silent as the grave.

Van Sciver said, "Did you hear me?"

Evan said, "No."

He wanted more time, though for what, he wasn't sure.

"I said, 'Go fetch your digital contact lenses. I have something you want to see.' "

Two-second inhale, four-second exhale.

"Let me be perfectly clear," Evan said. "If you do this, nothing will ever stop me from getting to you."

"But, X," Van Sciver said pleasantly, "you don't even know what I have planned."

The line cut out.

Two-second inhale, four-second exhale.

Evan rose.

He set the glass down on the poured-concrete island. He walked out of the kitchen and past the living wall, a vertical garden of herbs and vegetables. The rise of greenery gave the penthouse its sole splash of color and life, the air fragranced with chamomile and mint.

He headed across the open plain of the condo, past the heavy bag and the pull-up bar, past the freestanding central fireplace, past a cluster of couches he couldn't remember ever having sat on. He walked down a brief hall with two empty brackets where a katana sword had once hung. He entered his bedroom with its floating Maglev bed, propelled two feet off the floor by ridiculously powerful rare-earth magnets. Only cable tethers kept it from flying up and smashing into the ceiling. Like Evan, it was designed for maximum functionality — slab, mattress, no legs, no headboard, no footboard.

He entered his bathroom, nudged the frosted-glass shower door aside on its tracks. It rolled soundlessly. Stepping into the shower, he curled his hand around the hot-water lever. Hidden sensors in the metal read his palm imprint. He turned it the wrong way, pushing through a slight resistance, and a hidden door broke free from the tile pattern of the stall and swung inward.

Evan stepped into the Vault, the nerve center of his operations as the Nowhere Man.

Four hundred square feet of exposed beams and rough concrete walls, crowded from above by the underbelly of the public stairs leading to the roof. An armory and a workbench occupied one side. A central sheet-metal desk shaped like an L held an impeccably ordered array of computer towers, servers, and antennae. Monitors filled an entire wall, showing various hacked security feeds of Castle Heights. From here Evan could also access the majority of law-enforcement databases without leaving a footprint.

The door to the massive gun safe hung ajar. Beneath a row of untraceable, aluminum-forged, custom-machined ARES 1911 pistols, a slender silver case the size of a checkbook rested on a shelf.

Evan opened it.

Ten radio-frequency identification-tagged fingernails and a high-def contact lens waited inside.

The device, which Evan had taken from the dead body of one of Van Sciver's Orphans, served as a double-blind means of communication between Evan and his nemesis.

Evan applied the nails to his fingertips and inserted the lens. A virtual cursor floated several feet from his head.

He moved his fingers in the space before him, typing in thin air: HERE.

A moment later Van Sciver's reply appeared: EXCELLENT. ARE YOU READY?

Evan took a deep breath, wanting to hold on to these last precious seconds before his world flew apart.

He typed: YES.

Jack finally decided enough was enough and pulled his truck over onto a broad dirt fire road that split an endless field of cotton. Dust from the tires ghosted its way down the deserted strip of road. He couldn't see the chopper in the darkness, but he heard it circling high overhead. He threw the truck into park, kept his eyes pegged on the rearview, and waited, his breath fogging in the winter chill.

Sure enough, SUV headlights appeared. Then another set. The vehicles parked ten yards off his rear bumper. Three more black SUVs came at him from the front. He watched them grow larger in the windshield until they slant-parked, hemming him in.

He traced his fingers absently on the driver's window, drawing patterns. Shot a breath at the dashboard. Then, groaning, he climbed out.

The men piled out of the vehicles in full battle rattle, M4 carbines raised. A few of the men held AK-47s instead. "Both hands! Let's see 'em."

"Okay, okay." Jack wearily patted the air in their direction, showing his palms.

He was still pretty goddamned fit for a

man in his seventies, but he'd noticed that his baseball-catcher build had started to soften over the past few months no matter how many push-ups and sit-ups he did each morning. The years caught up to everyone.

He breathed in fresh soil and night air. The cotton stretched out forever, dots of white patterned against brown stems, like snow melting on a rocky hillside. It was Thanksgiving Day; the harvest looked to be running late.

He watched the men approach, how they held their weapons, where their eyes darted. They moved well enough, but two of them had their left thumbs pointing up on the magazine well grips rather than aligned with the AK barrels. If they were forced to switch shooting sides, the charging handles would smash their thumbs when they cycled.

Freelancers. Not Orphans. Definitely not Orphans.

But there were fifteen of them.

A few grabbed Jack, patted him down roughly, and zip-tied his hands behind his back.

One man stepped forward. His shaved head gleamed in the headlights' glow. The plates of his skull ridged his shiny scalp. It was not a pretty head. It could have used a bit of cover.

He raised a radio to his lips. "Target secured."

The others shifted in place, boots creaking.

"Relax, boys," Jack said. "You did good."

The guy lowered the radio. "You're finished, old man."

Jack pursed his lips, took this in with a vague nod. "He'll come for you." He cast his eyes across the freelancers. "With all the fury in the world."

The men blinked uncomfortably.

The door of the closest SUV opened, and another man stepped into view. Compact and muscular. He threw his sculpted arms wide, as if greeting a long-lost relative.

"You're a hard man to track down, Jack Johns," he said.

Jack took his measure. "Jordan Thornhill. Orphan R."

Surprise flickered across Thornhill's face. "You know me?"

"*Of* you anyway," Jack observed. "When you live as long as I have, son, you have eyes and ears in a lot of places."

"You're fortunate," Thornhill said, "to have lived so long."

"Yeah," Jack said. "I was."

The whooping grew louder. A Black Hawk banked into view over the hillside and set down before them. Dirt and twigs beat at them. Jack closed his eyes against the rotor wash.

As the rotors spun down, a pair of geared-up men emerged. They wore flight suits and parachutes and looked generally overprepared. Three more men and the pilot waited inside the chopper.

Jack shouted, "A bit of overkill, don't you think?"

Thornhill shouted, "We owe a debt of gratitude to helicopters this week!"

Jack didn't know what to make of that.

"Well," he said, "let's get on with it, then."

The two men in flight suits took Jack by either arm and conveyed him over to the helo. The others hauled him in. As they lifted off, Jack caught a bird's-eye view of Thornhill vanishing back into the SUV as smoothly as he'd appeared. Two freelancers headed to search Jack's truck, and the others peeled off to their respective vehicles and drove away.

The helo rose steeply and kept rising. Black Hawks have an aggressive rate of climb, and the pilot seemed intent on showing it off. This wasn't gonna be a joyride. No, this trip had another purpose entirely.

Jack had done more jumps than he could count, so he knew how to roughly gauge altitude by the lights receding below.

They passed ten thousand feet.

Fifteen.

Somewhere north of that, they stopped and hovered.

One of the men donned a bulky headset and readied a handheld digital video camera.

Another slid open the doors on either side.

Wind ripped through the cabin, making Jack stagger. Given his cuffed wrists, he couldn't use his arms for balance, so he took a wide stance.

The cameraman shouted, "Look into the camera!"

Jack did as told.

The cameraman listened to someone over his headset and then said, "What are your current protocols for contacting Orphan X?"

Jack shuffled closer, the wind blasting his hair, and squinted into the lens. "Van Sciver, you can't honestly believe this will work on me."

The cameraman listened again and then repeated his question.

Jack's shoulders ached from his hands being cinched behind his back, but he knew he wouldn't have to bear the pain much longer.

49

"There is nothing you could ever do to make me give up that boy," Jack said. "He's the best part of me."

The cameraman winced, clearly catching an earful from Van Sciver over the headset, then squared to Jack with renewed focus. "I'd suggest you reconsider. We're at sixteen thousand feet, and you're the only one up here without a parachute on."

Jack smiled. "And you're dumb enough to think that puts you at an advantage."

He bulled forward, grabbed the cameraman's rip-cord handle between his teeth, and flung his head back.

There was a moment of perfect stunned silence as the parachute hit the cabin floor.

The wind lifted the nylon gently at first, like a caress.

And then the canopy exploded open, knocking over the men in the cabin. The cameraman was sucked sideways out the open door. The Black Hawk lurched violently as first the chute and then the cameraman gummed into the tail rotor.

The Black Hawk wheeled into a violent 360. Jack gave a parting nod to the sprawled men and stepped off into the open air. On his way out, he saw the powerful ripstop nylon wrapping around the bent metal blades.

By instinct Jack snapped into an approximation of the skydiver's stable position, flattening out, hips low, legs spread and slightly bent. His hands were cuffed, but he pulled his shoulders back, broadening his chest, keeping his hanging point above his center of gravity. The wind riffled his hair. He watched the sparse house lights wobble below, like trembling candles holding strong in a wind. He figured he'd have hit 125 miles per hour by now, terminal velocity for a human in free fall.

He'd always loved flying.

Jack thought of the malnourished twelve-year-old kid who'd climbed into his car all those years ago, blood crusted on the side of his neck. He thought about their silent hikes through the dappled light of an oak forest outside a Virginia farmhouse, how the boy would lag a few paces so he could walk in the footprints Jack left shoved into the earth. He thought about the way his stomach had roiled when he'd driven that boy, then nineteen years old, to the airport for his first mission. Jack had been more scared than Evan was. *I will always be there,* Jack had told him. *The voice on the other end of the phone.*

The ground was coming up fast.

I will always be there.

Jack shifted his legs and flipped over, now staring up at the night sky, letting gravity take his tired bones. The stars were robust tonight, impossibly sharp, the moon crisp enough that the craters stood out like smudges from a little boy's hand. Against that glorious canopy, the Black Hawk spun and spun.

He saw it disintegrate, a final satisfaction before he hit the ground.

Evan stood in the darkness of the Vault, breathing the dank air, watching the live feed with horror.

The dizzying POV of the camera flying haphazardly around the cabin, banging off tether straps, jump seats, screaming men. And then airborne, free of the cabin, spinning off into the black void. The only sound now was the violence of the wind.

Evan's brain was still stuck thirty seconds back when Jack had walked out the cabin door as calmly as if he were stepping off a diving board.

The virtual ground came up and hit Evan in the face.

Static.

Evan's last panicked text to Van Sciver remained below: NO WIAIT STOP I'LL TELL YOU WHEREWW I AM

His next exhalation carried with it a noise he didn't recognize.

The cursor blinked.

Van Sciver's response finally arrived: TOO LATE.

Evan removed his contact lens and fingernails and put them back in the case.

He walked out of the Vault, through his bedroom, down the hall, and across the condo to the kitchen area.

The glass of vodka waited on the island.

He picked it up with a trembling hand.

He drank it.

5

COMMON INTERESTS ARE IMPORTANT

For the first time in memory, Evan slept in. "Slept" wasn't quite right, as he was awake at five. But he lay in bed until nine, staring at the ceiling, his mind re-forming around what he had witnessed, like a starfish digesting prey.

At one point he sat up and tried to meditate, but every breath was punctuated not with mindfulness but a red flare of rage.

Finally he went and took a shower. He soaped his right hand and ran it up and down the tile, leaning his weight into the arm to stretch his shoulder. It had been recently injured, and he didn't want the tendons and ligaments to freeze up.

Afterward he got dressed. Each bureau drawer held stacks of identical items of clothing: dark jeans, gray V-necked T-shirts, black sweatshirts. This morning in particular, it was a relief to move on autopilot, to not make any decisions. Clipping a Victo-

54

rinox watch fob to his belt loop, he padded down the hall into the kitchen.

The refrigerator held a jar of cocktail olives, a stick of butter, and two vials of Epogen, an anemia med that stimulated the production of red blood cells in the event of a bad bleed. Three contingency saline bags stared back at him from the meat drawer.

His stomach reminded him that he hadn't eaten in almost a day. His brain reminded him to make a sweep of his various safe houses scattered across L.A. County to take in the mail, change the automated lighting, alter the curtain and blind positions.

He had never wanted to leave his condo less.

There is nothing you could ever do to make me give up that boy.

Behind his front door, he took a deep breath, preparing himself to transition modes. Here at Castle Heights, he was Evan Smoak, importer of industrial cleaning products. Boring by design. He was fit but not noticeably muscular. Neither tall nor short. Just an average guy, not too handsome.

The only person who knew that he was not who he seemed was Mia Hall, the single mother in 12B. She had a light scattering of freckles across her nose and a birthmark on her temple that looked like it had been applied by a Renaissance painter. Because all that wasn't complicated enough, she was also a district attorney. When it came to Evan's work, they had settled on an unspoken and uncomfortable policy of don't ask, don't tell.

He pressed his forehead to the door, summoning greater resolve.

He's the best part of me.

He stepped out into the hall, got on the elevator.

On the way down, the car stopped and Lorilee Smithson, 3F, swept in. "Evan. It's been a while."

"Yes, ma'am."

"Always so formal."

The third wife to an affluent older gentleman who had recently left her, Lorilee was a vigorous practitioner of cosmetic surgery and body sculpting. She'd been beautiful once, that much was clear, but it was increasingly unnerving how her forehead remained frozen in an approximation of surprise no matter what the rest of her features were doing. She was fifty years old. Or seventy.

She wove her arm through Evan's and gave it a girlfriendy shake. "There's a craft class right now — scrapbooking. You should really come. Preserve those childhood memories."

He looked at her. She had three new lines radiating out from her eyes, faint wrinkles in the shiny skin. They looked pretty. They made her face look lived in. Next week they'd be gone, her face ratcheted even tighter, a tomato about to burst.

He contemplated the least number of syllables he could make that would get her to stop talking.

He said, "I'm not really a big scrapbooker."

She squeezed his arm in hers. "C'mon. You have to try new things. At least that's what I'm doing. I'm going through a transition right now, as you might have heard."

Evan had heard but had absolutely no idea how to reply to her. Was this one of those times that people said, "I'm sorry"? Wasn't that a stupid thing to tell someone whose asshole husband had left her? "It'll get easier" sounded equally platitudinous.

Fortunately, Lorilee wasn't much for silences. "I'm getting out there again, you know? Been seeing a new guy — a wedding photographer. But it's hard to tell if he really likes me for me or if he just likes my money."

She pursed her inflated lips and gave his

57

arm another little shake.

He patted her wrist, using the gesture as subterfuge to disentangle himself from her. But when he did, his hand came away powdery with tan dust. He looked down at her arm and saw the bruise marks she'd tried to conceal. Three finger-size marks from where someone had grabbed her.

She covered her arm with her purse, looked away self-consciously. "He's okay," she said. "You know how those artist types are. Temperamental."

Evan had no reply for that.

It was none of his business. He thought of Jack walking into space as if stepping off a diving board. Evan needed to get food, and then he had people to kill.

Her smile returned, though it labored to reach her cheeks. "That's why I'm scrapbooking. They say common interests are important."

A sudden dread pooled in Evan's gut. "Where did you say the scrapbooking class was?"

The elevator doors parted on the lobby to reveal a bustling crowd of Castle Heights residents massed around various craft tables that had been erected for the event.

Every head turned to take in Lorilee and Evan.

Evan made a snapshot count. Seventeen residents, including HOA president Hugh Walters. They all looked eager for small talk.

Evan finally made it into the subterranean parking garage, closed the door behind him, and was about to exhale with relief when he noticed Mia and her nine-year-old son sitting at the bottom of the stairs.

Mia shot him a tentative glance. He couldn't blame her for looking hesitant. He'd gone to her last night, ready to leave behind his aliases and untraceable help line to see what it might be like to attempt a normal relationship. In the wake of Jack's call, he had left her — and the conversation — hanging.

Peter craned his neck, his charcoal eyes staring up. "Hi, Evan Smoak."

Evan said, "What's new?"

Peter said, "Braces suck."

"Language," Mia said wearily.

"What're you doing down here?" Evan asked.

"Mom's hiding out from the scrapbooking lady."

"That's not true," Mia said.

"Is too. You called her 'pathologically chipper.' "

"Well, she is." Mia's hands fluttered, then

59

landed in her chestnut curls, a show of exasperation. "And I just needed a moment away from . . . chipperness."

Peter's raspy voice took on a mournful note. "I wanted to see, is all. Plus, she had a bowl of Hershey's Kisses."

"Okay, okay," Mia said. "Go ahead. I'll be up in a sec."

Peter scampered up the stairs, paused before Evan, gave a chimpanzee smile to show off the new hardware. "Do I have anything stuck in my braces?"

"Yeah," Evan said. "Your teeth."

Peter smirked. Then he fist-bumped Evan and shot through the door into the lobby.

Mia stood. She did a slow half turn, stretching her arms, letting them slap to her sides. "That was an odd conversation," she said. "Last night."

He came down the stairs. It was hard to be this close to her and not want to move even closer. She was the first person he'd ever met who'd made the notion of another life appealing. He'd had to overcome a lifetime of instinct and training to summon the courage to go to her door last night.

It felt like a decade ago.

He said, "I'm sorry."

"I'm not looking for an apology," she said. "Just an explanation."

Evan thought of a digital video camera hurtling around the cabin of a plummeting helicopter.

He cleared his throat, a rare nonverbal tell. "I'm afraid I can't give one."

She tilted her head. "You look terrible. Are you okay?"

That image flashed through his mind again: Jack stepping out of the Black Hawk, vanishing into the void. It seemed like a dream remnant, resonant and unreal.

"Yes," he said.

"Are we gonna talk about what happened?"

"I can't."

"Because of whatever . . . things you're into."

"Yes."

She looked at him more closely. In his childhood Evan had endured countless hours of training at the hands of psyops experts, training that involved brutal interrogation that lasted hours, sometimes days. To ensure he gave nothing away with his body language or facial expressions, they'd monitored everything down to his blink rate. And yet today emotion had left him loose and vulnerable. He felt as if Mia were looking right through his façade. He stood there, exposed.

"Whatever happened this time," she said, "it hurt you."

Evan locked down his face, held a steady gaze.

She gave a concerned nod. "Be careful."

As he walked past, she caught him around the waist. She hauled him in and hugged him, and he felt himself tense. Her cheek was against his chest, her arms wrapped tight around the small of his back. He breathed her scent — lemongrass lotion, shampoo, a hint of perfume redolent of rain. He wanted to relax into her, but when he closed his eyes, all he could see was a Black Hawk spiraling out of control against a backdrop of stars.

He tore himself away and headed to his truck.

6
THE BRINK OF VISIBILITY

His tasks for the day completed, Evan sat at his kitchen island before a plate of steaming mahimahi, seasoned with thyme from his living wall. The plate was centered precisely between knife and fork. Offset symmetrically beyond the plate were two bowls, one filled with fresh pomegranate seeds, the other with cherry tomatoes, also plucked from the vertical rise of vegetation. His vodka tonight, shaken until bruised and served up, was 666 Pure Tasmanian, fermented in barley, single-batch-distilled in copper pots, and filtered through highest-grade activated charcoal. Ice crystals glassed the top.

He'd prepared the meal with focus.

And he didn't want any of it.

He wondered what Mia and Peter were eating in their condo nine floors below. Their colorful home with action figures on the floor, dishes in the sink, messy crayon drawings magneted to the refrigerator. When he'd first visited them, the disorder had made him uncomfortable. But he'd learned to understand it differently, as an affirmation of lives being fully lived.

He forced a bite. The flavor was good and told his body it was hungry. He reminded himself that no matter what emotions were cycling through him, he was a machine bent to a single purpose and machines required fuel.

He ate.

When he was done, he scrubbed the plate, dried it, put it away atop a stack of others. It struck him that only the top plate ever got used.

He took the vodka over to the big windows stretching along the north wall and stared out at the Los Angeles night. He could see clearly into the building across from his, like peering into a dollhouse. A man emerged from an elevator, scrubbing furiously at his collar with a handkerchief. The fabric came away lipstick red. He folded the handkerchief into his pocket, walked down the hall. Evan watched his wife react happily to the door's opening. They embraced. Three floors up, a family quartet lay on their stomachs on the living-room carpet, playing a board game. Next door to them, a woman sobbed alone in a dark bedroom. An older couple on the top floor practiced ballroom dancing. The woman had a flower in her steel-gray hair. They both smiled the entire time.

All that humanity in motion. Like observing the inside of an intricate clock, gears and cogs and hidden machinations. Evan could tell the time, but he would never fully grasp the inner workings.

His gaze returned to the woman crying in the dark. As he watched her, he felt something inside him twist free, a fresh shoot of grief rising up to match hers. He'd never lacked sympathy — no, that he'd always had in spades. But he'd protected himself from empathy, had withdrawn here to his Fortress of Solitude and taken up the drawbridge.

He watched the woman sob and envied her ability to release so powerfully and so well.

His release would be paid for in blood.

He took a sip of his drink, let it slide across his tongue, cleanse his throat. Hint of dark chocolate, touch of black-pepper heat.

He dumped out the remaining vodka, then crossed to the Turkish rug near the fireplace, sat crossed-legged, and rested his hands gently on his knees. He straightened his vertebrae and veiled his eyes so they were neither open nor closed.

He dropped beneath the surface of his skin and focused on his breath, how it moved through him, how it left his body and what it took with it.

He felt the grief and fury inside him, a red-hot mass pulsing in his gut. He observed it, how it crept up his throat, seeking egress. He breathed through it, even as it raged and fought. He breathed until it dissipated, until he dissipated, until he was no longer Orphan X, no longer the Nowhere Man, no longer Evan Smoak.

When he opened his eyes sometime later, he felt purified.

He set aside his grief. He set aside his fury.

It was time to get operational.

The high-def contact lenses had their own data storage and as such could be rewound and replayed. Evan watched the footage dispassionately, a bomb investigator searching a blast site for clues.

The POV blinked on, a shuddering view of the Black Hawk's interior. Evan ignored the handcuffed man it was pointed at. Instead he watched one of the captors slide open the cabin doors to reveal paired slices of night air.

It was too dark to pick up any surface bearings. Evan could not determine how high the helo was, though one of the captors had mentioned sixteen thousand feet. As the wind whipped through and ruffled the hostage's hair, the moon jogged into sight in the corner of the open door. If Evan had a team of NASA astronomers at his disposal, perhaps he could determine the chopper's location based on star position.

But all he had in the Vault was himself and an aloe vera plant bedded down in a dish filled with cobalt-blue glass pebbles. She was named Vera II, and while she made for excellent company, she lacked the computing power of a team of NASA physicists.

He'd already done an extensive news search online and had not been surprised to find that there was no report of a Black Hawk's crashing anywhere in the world last night. Van Sciver's non-fingerprints were all over it. If Evan wanted to pick up the trail, he'd have to shine a light in the shadows.

He focused on the footage as the freelancers in flight suits positioned themselves around the Black Hawk's cabin.

Someone off-screen shouted, "Look into the camera!"

The hostage obeyed.

Evan searched the captors for identifying

tattoos, insignias, but they were geared up from their boots to their necks, only their faces showing. These freelancers loved their apparel. Evan studied their comportment, their builds, their postures. The men not in motion stood like they had two spines. Their boots were straight-laced, the preferred style of hipsters and ex-military.

Evan presumed they were not hipsters.

Van Sciver liked to use spec-ops washouts as his guns-for-hire, dishonorably discharged men who had all the training but were too brutal or unruly to stay in the service.

A voice came from off camera: "What are your current protocols for contacting Orphan X?"

The hostage kept his feet wide for balance and talked to the lens.

As the back-and-forth continued, Evan's eyes picked across the scene for any telling details — a Sharpied nickname on a rucksack, a serial number on a gun, a map with a cartoon red X on it. No such luck. They'd done a superb job of sterilizing the visual field.

The hostage squared to the lens, gave his line: "And you're dumb enough to think that puts you at an advantage."

The ensuing commotion, if viewed with

detachment, bordered on comedic. The calmness of the hostage, such a contrast to the terror of his captors.

As the digital camera flew around the cabin, Evan worked his RFID-covered fingernails, bringing up virtual settings that shifted the footage to slow-motion. In the chaos perhaps something would be revealed.

He watched the scene through five, six times to no avail.

Then he changed his focus to a later segment of the footage, when the camera sailed free of the failing helo. He put on a night-vision filter, hoping to identify something on the ground, but it was whipping by too fast. Even when he moved to frame-by-frame, all the flying lens caught were blurs of occasional lights, tracts of what looked like farmland.

He was about to give up when he caught a glimpse of a bigger earthbound splotch, less illuminated than the other lights. He reversed and freeze-framed. It was darker because it wasn't in fact a light. The night-vision wash had picked it up, lightening it to the brink of visibility.

He rotated forward one frame. Back one frame. That was about all the space he had. He returned to the middle frame, squinted, instinctively leaned forward. Of course, the virtual image moved with his head, holding the same projected distance.

Fortunately, Vera II didn't judge.

Evan grabbed the splotch, enlarged it, squinted some more.

A water tower.

With a hatchet cut into it? It looked like an apple.

No — a peach.

A peach water tower.

There was one of those, all right. He'd seen it on a postcard once.

He was already scrambling to free himself of the contact lenses. Off with the new tech and in with the old.

A Google search brought up the Peachoid, a one-million-gallon water tower in Gaffney, South Carolina. It was located just off Interstate 85 between exits 90 and 92 on the ingeniously named Peachoid Road.

It wasn't a big red X on a map.

But it was pretty damn close.

7
TWO GRAVES

Evan's Woolrich shirt sported fake buttons hiding magnets that held the front together. The magnets gave way easily in case he needed to go for the holster clipped to the waistband of his tactical-discreet cargo pants. Right now the holster was empty. He wore lightweight Original S.W.A.T. boots that with his pant legs down looked like boring walking shoes. The boots would be a pain to unlace at airport security.

In his back pocket, he had one of many passports gorgeously manufactured by a gorgeous counterfeiter, Melinda Truong.

The matter was too urgent to wait for a cross-country drive.

It was oh-dark-hundred, and the elevator was empty this early — thank heaven for small mercies. As the doors zippered shut behind Evan, he smelled a trace of lemongrass. On the floor was a pea of balled-up tinfoil, the Ghost of a Hershey's Kiss Past.

Or maybe *he* was the ghost, drifting invisibly among the living, following in their wake.

The ride down was quiet. He enjoyed it.

Evan carved through the whipping desert wind and ducked into the armorer's workshop. Lit like a dungeon, it was off the Vegas Strip and off the beaten path. Evan checked the surveillance camera at the door, verified that it had been unplugged before his arrival, as was the standing arrangement.

He smelled gun grease and coffee, cigarette smoke and spent powder. He peered through the stacks of weapon crates, across the machines and workbenches that were arrayed according to some logic he'd never been able to decipher.

"Tommy?"

The sound of rolling wheels on concrete presaged the nine-fingered armorer's appearance. And then there he was, sliding in from stage left in a cocked-back Aeron chair, welder's goggles turning him into some kind of steampunk nightmare. Beneath the biker's mustache, a Camel Wide crackled, sucked down to within a millimeter of the filter. Tommy Stojack plucked out the cigarette and dropped it into a water-filled red Solo cup, where it sizzled out among countless dead compatriots. Given the ordnance in evidence, a misplaced butt would turn the shop into a Fourth of July display.

Tommy slid the goggles up and regarded Evan. "Fifteen minutes prior to fifteen minutes prior. I could set my watch by you."

"You have it?"

"Of course I have it. What's with the ASAP?"

"I'm on something. It's highly personal."

"Personal." Tommy plucked out his lower lip and dropped in a wedge of Skoal Wintergreen. "Didn't know that word was in your lexicon. You threw in an adverb and everything."

Evan could count the people he trusted on the fingers of Tommy's mutilated hand, with digits to spare. Since the Black Hawk's disintegration, Tommy was one of the few remaining. Even so, Evan and Tommy knew nothing of each other's personal lives. In fact, they knew little of their respective professional lives either. From the occasional dropped tidbit, Evan had put together that Tommy was a world-class sniper and that he did contract training and weapons R&D for government-sanctioned black-ops groups that were not as dark a shade of black as the Orphan Program.

Tommy supplied Evan with his firepower, too, and made each of Evan's pistols from scratch, machining out a solid-aluminum forging of a pistol frame that had never been stamped with a serial number — a ghost gun. Then he simply fitted a fire-control group and loaded up the pistol with high-profile Straight Eight sights, an extended barrel threaded to receive a suppressor, and an ambidextrous thumb safety, since Evan preferred to shoot southpaw. He ordered all his pistols in matte black so they could vanish into shadows as readily as he did.

As Evan entered the heart of the lair, Tommy used a boot to shove himself away from a crate of rocket-propelled grenades, conveying himself over to a workbench where he at last creakily found his feet.

Laid out on a grease-stained silicone cloth were a laptop and a narrow pistol that looked like one of Evan's 1911s that had gone on a diet.

"I skinny-minnied this little lady up for you," Tommy said. "What do you think?"

Evan picked it up. It fit oddly in his grip. His usual pistol, sliced in half. It was barely wider than the 230-grain Speer Gold Dot hollow points it fired. He turned it over in his hand and then back. "The weight'll take some adjusting to."

"That's your way of saying, 'Thank you, brother. You're PFM. Pure Fucking Magic.' "

Evan eyed the sights. "That, too."

Tommy slung an altered holster across the workbench. "And here's a special-sauce high-guard Kydex to fit it."

Evan hefted the weapon a few more times. "To be honest, I wasn't sure how you'd pull it off."

"Pull it off?" Tommy's head drew back haughtily. "Boy, I've been calibrating a laser gun for the navy that can knock drones out of the sky. I've been field-testing self-guided fifty-cal sniper rounds for DARPA that change direction in midair. Fine-tuned a smart scope that *doesn't let you* shoot a friendly target." He crossed his arms. "I think I can handle smuggling a handgun past a few mouth-breathing TSA agents." He snapped his fingers, pointed to a sticky coffeepot gurgling behind Evan. "Fetch."

Evan poured a mug for Tommy, had to wipe his hands on the gun-cleaning cloth. Tommy slurped the coffee across his packed lower lip. Then he lit up another Camel. Evan figured the only reason Tommy didn't smoke them two at a time was that it hadn't occurred to him yet.

Tommy pulled three Wilson eight-

75

rounders from his bulging shirt pocket and offered them up. "Test-drive it."

Evan slotted in the first mag, put on eye and ear pro, and walked to the test-firing tube. He ran through all twenty-four rounds without a hitch. Then gave a faint nod.

He came back over to the workbench. "How's the A-fib coming?"

Tommy waved him off. "I'm getting extra beats in between my extra beats. I figure I speed shit up enough, I'll go full-tilt Iron Man." He jabbed the stub of his missing finger at the arrayed items. "Let me break it down Barney style. Same everything you're used to but skinnier. 'Why skinnier, Chief Stojack?' you may ask." The finger stub circled. "Witness."

Tommy took the skinny gun and slid it into the laptop's hard-drive slot where some hidden mechanism received it. "All they'll see on the X-ray is the solid block of the hard drive. I had to go thirteen-inch screen on the laptop to make the specs fit, so they might make you take it out, power it up, all that security Kabuki-theater bullshit, but you'll be GTG. Obviously you gotta clean the piece so there's no residues that'll ring the cherries in a puff test. As for the laptop, I filled it with bullshit spreadsheets, generic documents, a few stock photos." He picked up the laptop, showed off its slender profile. "High speed, low drag." He made a production of handing it off to Evan, a waiter displaying the Bordeaux. "Go forth and conquer." He gave his gap-toothed smile. "Fair winds and following seas."

Evan took the laptop and started for the door.

"Hey."

Evan turned back.

"You're not exactly a barrel of belly laughs generally, but you seem decidedly more somber. This 'highly personal'? It's *actually* highly personal?"

"Yes."

Tommy studied him, tugging at one end of his horseshoe mustache. The crinkles around his eyes deepened with concern. "You get in a jam, send up a smoke signal. I'm not too old to cover your six, you know."

"I know. But it's something I have to handle alone."

Tommy nodded slowly, his gaze not leaving Evan's face. "Remember what Confucius say: 'Before you embark on a journey of revenge, dig two graves.' "

"Oh," Evan said, "I'm gonna dig a lot more than that."

8

SERVE WITH GLADNESS

It had all been for shit.

Evan stood in front of his rented Impala on the side of Peachoid Road, staring at the street's namesake, which he had grown to despise. He held the giant fruit monstrosity personally responsible for the stagnation of his pursuit.

He didn't know precisely what he was looking for, but some indication that Jack and a ten-ton Black Hawk helicopter had struck the earth in this vicinity would have been a start.

Van Sciver's Orphans were a conspiracy theorist's wet dream. Not just at killing — they were good at killing, very good, but humans had been killing one another for a very long time. No, *this* is what they did best — erased any trace of their actions from the official world everyone else lived in. Nothing for the media, local PD, FBI, even CIA to grab hold of. They moved with the fury of a hurricane and didn't leave a dewdrop in their wake.

Evan had driven the frontage and access roads, carved through the checkerboard plots of farmland, housing, and forest surrounding the novelty landmark, searching for that dewdrop to no avail. There was no wreckage, no scorched earth, no Jack's truck abandoned at the side of a road.

The flight from Las Vegas, with a layover in Houston, had taken seven hours and seven minutes. Driving fifty-three miles from Charlotte Douglas International had tacked on another hour and twenty. A long way to come for a whole lot of nothing.

They say that revenge is a dish best served cold, but Evan preferred to serve it piping hot.

He took in a deep breath and a lungful of car exhaust.

The Fourth Commandment: *Never make it personal.*

He repeated it over and over in his head until he almost believed it.

Then he got into his Impala and drove off. He took a final loop upslope, winding through thickening forest that coaxed a distant memory of the trees surrounding Jack's farmhouse.

He checked his RoamZone. Even after a

long day, the high-power lithium-ion battery kept the phone's charge nearly full. He wondered briefly what he would do if the next Nowhere Man case rang through — a *real* Nowhere Man case as opposed to the personal mission he was on now. After he helped his clients, he asked them to find one — and only one — person who needed his help and to pass on his untraceable number.

He had a rule, encoded in the Seventh Commandment: *One mission at a time.*

For Jack he was willing to make an exception.

He pulled over to get a bottled water at a convenience store. As he headed back to the car, chugging down the water, he caught a chorus of singing voices on the breeze.

Only when he turned and saw the open front door of the Baptist church across the parking lot did he realize that it was an actual choir. Drawn by the music, he walked over, climbed the stone steps, and entered. The pews sat empty, but the singers were in place in the choir stand, decked out in royal-blue gospel gowns. They were working on an a cappella hymn, practicing beneath a stark wooden cross flooded with light from behind. The choir conductor, an older man, directed from a podium. The voices rose pure and true.

Evan's form in the doorway cut the light, and the director half turned, his hands still keeping time for the singers. He gave a welcoming nod in the direction of the pews.

Evan felt the habitual pull to withdraw, but there was a power in the joined voices that hit him in the spine, made it thrum like a guitar string. He took a seat in the last row and let the hymn wash over him.

With the harmony came memories. Waking up in the dormer bedroom in Jack's farmhouse that first sun-drenched morning. Walking behind Jack in the forest, filling those boot prints with his own small shoes. The cadence of Jack's voice, how it never rose above a measured pitch during their nightly study sessions. Jack had taught him everything from Alexander the Great's battle tactics to basic phrases in the Indo-Iranian languages to toasting etiquette for Scandinavian countries — nothing was too trivial. The smallest detail could save Evan's life in the field.

Or kill him.

He thought about an Arab financier peering through raccoon eyes, wearing a half-moon laceration from Evan's garrote like a necklace. A fat man, bald as a baby and clad only in a towel, staring back at him lifelessly through the steam of a bathhouse, blood drooling from a bullet hole over his left eye. A man slumped over a table in a drab Eastern European kitchen, his face in his soup, the back of his head missing.

He thought about what he was going to do to Van Sciver and every one of his men he came across along the way.

The choir finished. Before they could disperse, the director cleared his throat to good dramatic effect and said, "Now, when you get back out there with your car pools and your grocery shopping and your punching the clock, you take a little time to think about the works you do and the life you lead. When you're back in this here church one day boxed up in a coffin, that's gonna be all that's left to speak for you." With a crinkled hand, he waved them away. "Go on, now."

The singers filed out, joking and gossiping. A few glanced Evan's way, and he nodded pleasantly. People forget anything that's not a threat, and Evan had no intention of being remembered.

He lifted his eyes to the glow behind the altar and wondered at the beliefs men held and what those beliefs drove them to do. In his brief time on the planet, he'd seen so many dead stares, so many visages touched with the gray pallor of death. But he'd never blinded himself to the humanity shining through the cracks of those broken guises. Jack had made sure of that. He'd lodged that paradox in Evan's mind and in his heart. It had saved him, in a manner of speaking. But it came with a price.

Evan started to rise when the director turned and caught his eye. The old man limped up the aisle toward him. "Our altos are flat and our tenors are sharp. You'd think it'd even us out some."

"It sounded perfect to me," Evan said. "But I've got an untrained ear."

"You must." The man sat heavily in the pew next to him, let out a sigh like air groaning through a bellows.

"I'll let you get on with your day, sir," Evan said.

"Minister."

"Minister. Thank you for letting me listen."

"A man doesn't stumble into a church for no reason."

Out of deference Evan didn't take issue with him.

The minister sat back, crossed his arms, and gazed at the vaulted ceiling. Evan felt a familiar tug to leave but realized that for the moment he had nowhere to be. The minister scratched at his elbow, clearly in no rush.

Evan considered the man's words again. Decided to rise to the challenge.

"Which matters more?" he asked.

"Which *what* matters more?"

"At the end. Which matters more? The works we've done or the life we lead?"

"Say 'I,' son. First person. You'd be surprised at how powerful the change is."

Evan took a pause. "Which matters more? The works I've done or the life I lead?"

The minister was right. The words felt different in Evan's body and behind his face.

"You assume they're different," the minister said. "One's works and one's life."

"In some cases."

"Like yours?"

"That remains to be seen."

The minister gave a frown and nodded profoundly. It took a good measure of dignity to manage a profound nod, but he managed it just fine. "Do you follow the Commandments, son?"

Evan nearly smiled. "Yes, Minister. Every last one."

"Then there's your start."

Evan held a beat before switching tracks. "I'd imagine that few people are woven into this community as well as you are."

"I'd say you imagine right."

"Has there been any word about government folks coming through town, a helicopter, a fire?"

The minister arched an eyebrow. "There has not."

"Suspicious flurry of activity down by the" — he hesitated slightly before naming his nemesis — "Peachoid?"

"No."

"How about alien spaceships cutting crop circles?" Evan countenanced the man's watery glare. "Kidding."

"What's all this hokum about?"

"I was supposed to meet a friend at the peach water tower."

"Why don't you call him?"

"Long-lost friend. We'd arranged a meet online."

"Hmm." The minister mused a moment. "You sure you got the right one?"

A jolt of anticipation straightened Evan up slightly in the pew. "The right friend?"

"The right Peachoid. Same folks built a smaller one down in Clanton, Alabama."

Evan had not in fact been following all the Commandments. He'd overlooked the first one: *Assume nothing.*

He rose. "Thank you, Minister. I can't tell you how useful your guidance has been."

"I serve with gladness."

Evan shook the proffered sandpaper hand. "As do I."

9
FROM BEYOND THE GRAVE

Five hours and thirty-eight minutes later, Evan was standing on the side of I-65 between Birmingham and Wetumpka, gazing up at a five-hundred-gallon version of the same eyesore.

Twenty-seven minutes after that, his headlights picked up Jack's truck parked at the edge of a fire road running between two swaths of cotton that stretched into the darkness, maybe forever.

He climbed out of the Impala, unholstered his slender ARES pistol for the first time, and approached the truck tentatively. It was cold enough out to be uncomfortable, but he didn't have any interest in being uncomfortable. He shone a key-chain Maglite through the windows and took in the damage. Slashed seat cushions, scattered papers from the glove box, holes punched through the headliner. They'd searched as well as he'd expected they would. They'd have been looking for anything that might point them to Evan.

His breath fogging the pane, Evan stared at the defaced interior and considered how many years Jack had polished this dash-board, vacuumed the seams, touched up the paint. Anger and sorrow threatened to escape the locked-down corner of his heart, and he took a moment to tamp it back into place.

He walked around the truck, searched for booby traps. None were visible.

The truck was unlocked. It was two de-cades old, but the hinges didn't so much as creak when the door swung open. Jack's hinges wouldn't dare.

Evan sat where Jack used to sit.

Do you regret it? What I did to you?

He put his hands on the steering wheel. The pebbled vinyl was worn smooth at the ten and two. The spots where Jack's hands used to rest.

I wanted to hear your voice.

Out of the corner of his eye, Evan caught a gleam from the molded map pocket on the lower half of the door. He reached down and lifted Jack's keys into the ambient light.

Odd.

Jack never left his keys in the truck.

He was a creature of habit. The Second

Commandment had always been his favorite: *How you do anything is how you do everything.* He had drilled it into Evan's cells.

There was a likelihood, of course, that Van Sciver's men had taken Jack's keys when they'd grabbed him so they could search his truck. But if that were the case, once they were done, wouldn't they just have tossed the keys back on the seat or dropped them into the cup holder? Placing them in a map pocket low on the door took consideration and a bit of effort.

It's too late for me.

Jack had known he was about to get grabbed.

This is looking to be my ninth life, son. Dollars to doughnuts they've got ears on me right now.

And Jack would've controlled the terms. Evan guessed he would've gotten out of the truck under his own power. Left it unlocked for the search. Placed the keys carefully for Evan to find.

But why?

Sometimes we miss what's important for the fog. But maybe we should give it a go before, you know . . .

Jack had known he was about to die.

I guess . . . I guess I want to know that I'm

89

forgiven.

Evan looked through the dirty windshield. The night swallowed up the land all around. Sitting in the cab of Jack's truck, Evan could just as well have been floating through the black infinity of outer space.

"We didn't have time," he told the dashboard. "We didn't have enough time."

I love you, son.

"Copy that," Evan said.

He pondered the darkness, his breath wisping in the November chill.

Before he died, Jack had wanted to set things right with Evan — he'd made that much clear. But maybe his words held a double meaning. What if there was something else he was looking to set right? He'd known that Van Sciver was listening. He would've spoken in code.

Evan replayed the conversation in his head, snagged on something Jack had said: *Sometimes we miss what's important for the fog.*

The turn of phrase was decidedly un-Jack. Jack had a down-to-earth, articulate speaking style, the patter of a former station chief. He was not flowery, rarely poetic, and tended to make use of metaphors only when undercutting them.

Evan looked down at the keys in his hand.

miss what's important for the fog

The realization dropped into his belly, rippling out to his fingertips.

He zippered the key into the ignition.

The well-maintained engine turned over and purred.

Evan sat.

He leaned forward so that his mouth would be that much closer to the cooling windshield. And he breathed.

A full minute passed. And then another.

Fog started creeping in from the edges of the windows. He shifted in the seat, watched the driver's window.

As fog crept to the center of the pane, a few streaks remained stubbornly clear. They forged together as the condensation filled in around them, finally starting to resolve in the negative space as letters.

In his final minutes, Jack had written a low-tech hidden message for Evan with the tip of his finger.

Evan stared at the window, not daring to blink.

At last the effect was complete, Evan's orders standing out in stark relief on the clouded glass.

GET PACKAGE
3728 OAK TERRACE #202

HILLSBORO, OR
Jack had given him a final mission.

10

A GOODLY AMOUNT
OF DAMAGE

The apartment complex was so sturdy that it bordered on municipal. Ten-foot security gate, metal shutters, callbox with buzzer. Evan had approached the target slowly, winding in on the address block by block like a boa constricting its prey. Then he'd parked behind the building in the shade of a tree — Hillsboro was lousy with trees — and surveilled.

The rented Toyota Corolla reeked eye-wateringly of faux new-car smell, courtesy of an overly exuberant car washer. Evan had been watching for three hours now, which was a lot of new-car smell for a man to take.

Traffic ran past steadily. A Tesla Model S flashed by, and more Priuses than he could count. Buses creaked to a stop across the road at intervals approximating ten minutes and disgorged various domestic workers and floridly bearded young men. Evan used the reflection off the bus's windows to observe the wide parking lot enfolded in the horse-shoe of the three-story complex. People came and went, and they looked ordinary enough.

Then again, so did Evan.

The same HILLSBORO HOME THEATER IN-STALLATION! van drove by two times, a half hour apart. A half hour was an eyebrow-raising interval, though it was plausible that the driver had bid a job or had completed a small repair and was returning to the shop.

Evan didn't like vans.

He gave it another hour, but the van didn't reappear. Besides, what idiot would put an exclamation mark on an undercover vehicle?

He reapplied a thin layer of superglue to his fingertips. Superglue was less conspicu-ous than gloves and left him with full tactil-ity. He pressed the fingers of his left hand to the window. They left five printless dots.

A rickety old Cadillac coasted to the curb across the street from Evan at the rear of the complex. An elderly man emerged, the strains of a Beethoven piano concerto still drifting through the open windows. He began to unload from the trunk various canvases, which he propped against the wall of the building. They featured cubist takes on musical instruments — a deconstructed trumpet, a piano turned inside out. There was a flair to his artwork, an inner life. The canvases kept coming. They lined the base of the building, filled a blanket he spread on the sidewalk, peered from the jaw of the open trunk. The man sat creakily, adjusted his herringbone flat cap, and nodded to the music.

Evan listened along with him. It was Concerto No. 3, one of Jack's favorites. He remembered Jack's saying that it owed something to Mozart, how all things should honor what preceded them and inspire what is to come.

He wondered how he could best honor Jack.

The question of inspiration was even thornier.

He remembered Jack's message scrawled on the foggy window. He wondered what the hell the package was and why Jack had hidden it all the way across the continent. Something essential. A long-buried secret from Jack's past that would lead to Van Sciver? Maybe even a torpedo that would sink him.

Evan checked his gun. Along with the skinny 1911, he'd smuggled one extra go-to-war magazine in the laptop. He'd validated the mag at a range, making sure it dropped clear. That gave him seventeen rounds, which was less than he was comfortable with. Then again, he could do a goodly amount of damage with seventeen rounds.

He heard an echo of Jack's voice: *Just don't put all the holes in the same place.*

He got out of the car. Scanning the traffic, he walked around the east wing of the building, tucking quickly into the horseshoe. At the edge of the parking lot, the callbox sprouted from the metal mesh of the security gate. It was a serious gate with a serious double-keyed lock. Another metal gate guarded the stairwell, which was itself caged.

Fire hazards to be sure, but this was a bad section of Hillsboro — whatever that meant — and the folks who lived here cared more about day-to-day safety than about the sliver percentage of a fire-induced stampede.

Jack had chosen a good place to hide the package.

On the directory, number 202 was blank. Evan scanned the other names. Given the security concerns of the residents, a button-pushing deliveryman ruse wouldn't likely get him far.

He'd bought a rake pick and a tension wrench at a hardware store and was about to get busy when a guy yammering into a Bluetooth headset clanged out of the stairwell gate. As the man strode up the corridor toward the front, Evan pretended to punch a code into the callbox's keypad.

"I heard this new ramen place is *sick,*" the guy told his interlocutor and anyone else in the vicinity who might have been interested. "They have, like, a hundred flavors of shōchū."

He shoved his way out the front gate, ignoring Evan and the rest of the world, and Evan slipped through. In case he had to beat a hasty retreat, he wedged a quarter between the latch and the frame so the gate wouldn't autolock.

At the stairwell he finally got to use his pick set. He engaged a second quarter to keep that gate from locking also.

A fine fifty-cent investment.

He crept up to the second floor and down the corridor. Apartment 202 had a peephole. He ducked beneath it, put his ear to the door. Heard nothing inside.

Though the building was late-afternoon quiet, he couldn't risk creeping around the corridor for long.

The apartment lock was also double-keyed. With the rake and wrench, he jogged the pins into proper alignment and eased the door silently open.

The place was dimly lit and smelled of

carpet dust and greasy food. A brief foyer led to a single big studio room. No furniture.

He made out a faint scraping sound.

Pistol drawn, Evan eased through the foyer, heel to toe, minding the floorboards. More of the studio came into view. A bare mattress. A mound of fast-food wrappers. A geometric screen saver casting a striated glow from an open laptop. Then an over-stuffed rucksack.

The scraping grew louder.

He eased out a breath, peered around the corner.

A girl crouched, facing away, her forehead nearly touching the far wall. She had a mane of dark wavy hair, torn jeans, a formfitting tank top. It was hard to gauge from behind, but he guessed she was a teenager. She was bent over something, and her shoulders shook slightly. Crying?

The closet and bathroom doors were laid open, and there was no furniture for anyone to hide behind. Just her.

He thought about the double-keyed locks and wondered — was she being held captive?

He aimed the ARES at the floor but didn't holster it. Stepping clear of the foyer, he lowered his voice so as not to startle her.

"Are you okay?"

She jumped at the sound, then glanced tentatively over her shoulder. Her back curled with fear, her expression vulnerable. She looked Hispanic, but he couldn't be sure in the dim light.

"Who are you?" she said.

"I'm not gonna hurt you."

"Why are you here?"

He drew closer slowly, not wanting to scare her. "It's a long story."

"Can . . . can you help me?"

He holstered the pistol but stayed alert. "Who put you here?"

"I don't know. I can't remember. I . . . I . . ."

Her posture suddenly snapped into shape, a bundle of coiled muscle. She pivoted into a vicious leg sweep, leading with the hard edge of her heel, sweeping both of his boots out from under him.

As he accelerated into weightlessness, he saw the glint in her eye matched by the glint of the fixed-blade combat knife in her right hand. A sharpening stone lay on the carpet, the stone she'd been crouching over, scraping away when he'd walked in. Already she'd rotated, spinning up onto her feet, readying to drive the blade through his sternum.

He struck the floor, the wind knocking from his lungs in a single clump, and it occurred to him just how badly he had misjudged the situation.

11
ENEMY OF MY ENEMY

Evan's first focus was the knife.

Darting down at him like a shiv stab, all blade, nothing to grab.

Laid out on the carpet as if he were a corpse, he swept the bar of his forearm protectively across his chest, hammering the girl's slender wrist and knocking the knife off course just before it broke skin. The tip skimmed his shirt above the ribs, slicing fabric.

His second focus was her fist.

Which she'd cocked and deployed even while her knife hand had still been in motion. He had a split-second to admire the technique — knuckles following blade with double-tap timing — before she broke his nose.

He rolled his head with the punch, tumbled gracelessly up onto his feet. She grabbed the back of his shirt, but the magnetic buttons gave way — *click-click-click*

— and he spun right out of it. His eyes watered from the blow to the nose, but the escape bought him a much-needed second to blink his way back to some version of clarity. She flung the shirt aside and launched a barrage of kicks.

He parried, parried, parried, bruising his forearms and knuckles, holding his attention mostly on the knife.

She came at him again, a jailhouse lunge, but now he was ready for it. His hands moved in blurry unison, a *bong sau/lop sau* trap that simultaneously blocked and grabbed her arm. He clenched hard, slid his fist up the length of her forearm, and hit the bump of her wrist with enough force that her fingers released and the knife shot free.

They were nose-to-nose, her mouth forming an O of perfect shock. He had a wide-open lane to her windpipe — one elbow strike and she'd be over — but Jack's Eighth Commandment sailed in and tapped the back of his brain: *Never kill a kid.*

He barreled her over and pinned her with a cross-face cradle, a grappling move that left her locked up, her knee smashed to her cheek, arms flailing uselessly to the sides.

"Get off me!" she shouted. "I will kill you! I will fucking —"

He pressed his forehead to her temple, immobilizing her head and shielding his eyes. "Breathe," he said.

She inhaled sharply.

"Again."

She obeyed.

"Where is the package?" he asked.

"What?"

"What'd you do with the package?"

"The hell are you talking about?"

"You saw the message. You beat me here."

"Can you get your knee out of my ribs?"

Evan eased off the pressure. "What'd you do with it?"

She gave no answer. Each breath rasped through her contorted throat.

Blood was trickling from Evan's nose, tickling his cheek. "I'm gonna let you go, and we're gonna try this again, okay?"

Her answer came strained. "Okay."

"I'd prefer not to have to kill you."

"I'd like to say the same, but I haven't decided yet."

He released her, and they stood. They kept their palms raised, halfway to an open-hand guard. She drew in deep lungfuls, her cheeks flushed. She was expertly trained but still green.

He got his first clear look at her. Her hair fell to her shoulders, thick and dark and lush. The right side had been shaved short, but it was mostly hidden by the tumbling length of her locks, a surprisingly subtle effect. She was lean and fit, her deltoids pronounced enough to show notches in the muscle.

"I'm gonna put my shirt back on," he said. "If you come at me, it won't go well for you."

Keeping his gaze on her, he backed up and put on his shirt. Next to the rucksack, a ragged flannel rested on the carpet. He tossed it to her.

She tugged it on.

Keeping a bit of distance, they stared at each other. A wisp of agitated piano reached them from outside, the concerto hitting the third movement.

"Let's cut to it," Evan said. "I see how you move. I know you're an Orphan. I know who sent you."

"You don't know anything."

"What's the package?"

She answered him with a glare.

He risked a fleeting look at her rucksack. "Is it in there?"

"No."

He crouched over the rucksack.

"Don't touch my stuff."

He rooted around in it, sneaking quick

glances down. Clothes, a few toiletries, a shoe box filled with what looked like personal letters.

"Put those *down.*"

"Is there some kind of code in these papers?"

"No."

He armed blood off his upper lip. "Is the package something on the laptop?"

"No."

"If you're lying, I can hack into it."

Her mouth firmed into something more aggressive than a smirk. "Good luck."

As he started to reach for the laptop, it suddenly alerted with a ping, the screen saver vanishing.

Four surveillance feeds came up, tiling the screen. It took a moment for Evan to register that they were streaming different angles of the outside of the apartment complex.

The bottom-left feed showed two SUVs blocking the horseshoe of the parking lot. Teams of geared-up operators charged for the front gate.

"Your backup's here," the girl said. "What — you couldn't handle me yourself?" Her voice stayed tough, but her chest heaved with the words. She was scared, and this time he knew she wasn't faking it.

105

Evan stared at the screen. The operators displayed a similar military precision to that of the men in the Black Hawk. Evan counted six of them.

Seventeen rounds. Six men.

Just don't put all the holes in the same place.

On-screen the lead operator kicked the front gate, and it clanged open. Evan heard it in stereo, registered the vibration in the floor.

He and the girl watched as the men poured into the ground-floor corridor.

He said, "They're not with me."

His eyes met the girl's, and he saw that she believed him.

Her voice was hammered flat with dread. "You left the gates unlocked behind you."

Clang. The stairwell gate flew open, courtesy of Evan's ill-spent twenty-five cents.

The men throttled up the stairwell. The girl's eyes darted from the screen back to Evan.

"Enemy of my enemy," he said.

She gave a nod.

He drew his ARES. "Get behind me. Pick up your knife."

The girl moved, but not for the knife. She shot over to the mattress and lifted it, revealing a hatch cut through the floor. She looked at him, eyes wild, hair swinging. "My

106

stuff," she said. "Get my stuff."

The clamor of the men reached the second floor, spilled onto the corridor.

Evan snapped the laptop shut, rammed it into the rucksack, tossed the combat knife in after. She slipped through the hatch and disappeared. The mattress fell back into place, covering the hole. He didn't hear her land. He sprinted across the room.

As he yanked up the edge of the mattress, he heard the front door smash in. Snatching the rucksack behind him, he shoulder-rolled beneath the mattress, free-falling. A thump announced the sealing of the hatch above.

He rotated to break his fall, but a soft landing caught him off guard. His boots struck another mattress, positioned on the ground floor directly beneath the one above. He tumbled off the side onto the carpet.

He looked up.

The girl was waiting.

She wrenched the rucksack from his grip, pistoned her leg in a heel stomp directed at his throat. He caught her foot in both hands and twisted hard, flinging her aside. She bounced up off the floor like a cat, shot across the room, flung open the window.

As she leapt through, he grabbed a strap of the rucksack, halting her momentum. She jerked back and banged against the outside wall, one arm bent over the sill. She wouldn't let go of the rucksack. They were both off balance, caught in a ridiculous tug-of-war across a windowsill.

Boots drummed the floor above. It was only a matter of time before one of the men looked under the mattress.

Evan dove through the window, collecting both the rucksack and the girl in a bear-hug embrace. They sailed past the elderly artist, their fall cushioned by the blanket covered with his paintings. The Cadillac's radio blared away, the C-major coda galloping along in presto.

Evan hopped to his feet, broken frames falling away, the cubist pieces now cubist in three dimensions. Through the window Evan saw a beam of light appear, a golden shaft piercing the gloom of the ground-floor apartment.

The upstairs mattress, pulled back.

He looked helplessly across the street at his rental car.

Thirty yards of high visibility through traffic.

He'd never make it.

The artist rose from the sidewalk, his flat cap askew. "What kind of damn-fool nonsense is this?"

The girl thrashed free of Evan, landing on

all fours. She scampered across the blanket to get away, but it bunched beneath her knees, impeding her progress.

Evan grabbed her arm, spun her up and around, and dumped her into the Cadillac's open trunk, shattering her straight through a painting of a dissected bassoon. He slammed the trunk an instant before she started battering at it.

He snatched up the rucksack, slung it through the open rear window. "If they hear you, they'll kill you."

Her muffled shout came through the trunk. "How do I know *you're* not gonna kill me?"

"Because I would've done it already."

He hopped into the car. The keys waited in the ignition, enabling the radio and a pleasing whiff of air-conditioning.

As the concerto tinkled to a close, Evan looked out the open passenger window at the old artist. Through the window over the man's shoulder, he saw the first shadow tumble from the ceiling.

"Sorry about your art," Evan said, and peeled out.

He wheeled around the edge of the complex, blending into traffic, coasting past the open mouth of the horseshoe. He looked back at the building.

In the center of the parking lot, a man stood facing away, his head tilted up to take in the second floor. Waiting. He would have looked like an ordinary guy were it not for his posture; he stood with the perfect stillness of the perfectly trained.

Orphan.

One of the operators stepped out through the splintered door of 202 and gestured to the man with two fingers — *He's on the run, went down and out.*

The traffic light turned red, and Evan hit the brakes, peering back transfixed as the man in the parking lot sprang into motion. He hit the front gate with his foot, vaulted up, ran four pounding steps along the high fence top, then leapt onto the outside of the stairwell cage. With a series of massive lunging leaps, he scaled the cage and then swung around onto the third-floor corridor. He jumped up, grabbed the hanging roof ledge, and spun himself onto the roof, where he stood with the command of a mountaineer claiming an apex.

He'd parkoured his way up the entire route in under six seconds. Evan allowed himself to be impressed.

The man peered down, evidently picking up the commotion on the sidewalk outside apartment #102. He began a slow rotation,

pivoting like a weather vane, his eyes s
ning the streets below.

Evan turned back around in the driver's
seat, cranked the side-view mirror to a
severe tilt, and watched the man's reflection. The man finished his rotation, staring
down at the mass of cars at the traffic light.
It seemed like he was looking directly at
Evan in the Cadillac, but of course there
was no way it was possible from that distance.

The light turned green, and Evan drove
off.

12
INCREASINGLY RURAL TANGLE

Keeping the needle pegged at the speed limit, Evan drove a circuitous route to the nearest freeway and ran past four exits before hopping off and shooting west through an increasingly rural tangle of desolate back roads. Gray clouds pervaded the sky, heavy with the promise of rain. Sure enough, a few drops tapped the roof, quickening to a rat-a-tat, ushering dusk into full night. Decreased visibility was good; it went both ways. Local law enforcement had undoubtedly already issued a Be On the Lookout for the Cadillac.

He had to change vehicles, but first he needed to get a good distance between himself and the men who'd raided the apartment compound. Then he would regroup, determine what the package was, and deal with the problem in the trunk and the myriad questions that came with it.

He closed his eyes, inhaled deeply, settled

his shoulders. He blew out a breath, opened his eyes, and reset himself, assessing everything as if he were confronting it for the first time.

Jack's dying message.

A package.

An address.

A girl who was an Orphan — or at the very least Orphan-trained.

Who was hostile.

But not allied with the crew of men, led by another seeming Orphan, who had raided the apartment complex in pursuit of her, the package, or Evan himself.

A crew that had Van Sciver's fingerprints all over it.

Which left a whole lot of questions and very few answers.

The rain thrummed and thrummed. The girl in the trunk banged a few times, shouted something unintelligible. The windshield wipers groaned and thumped.

First order of business was to do a quick equipment appraisal.

Evan's scuffed knuckles, a fetching postfight shade of eggplant, ledged the steering wheel. His nose was freshly broken, leaking a trickle of crimson. Nothing bad, more a shifting along old fault lines.

He inspected his nose in the rearview,

then reached up and snapped it back into place.

The Cadillac's alignment pulled to the right, threatening to dump him into the rain-filled roadside ditch. The seat springs poked into the backs of his thighs, and the fabric, dotted with cigarette scorch marks, reeked of menthol. The dome light housed a bare, burned-out bulb, the brake disks made a noise like an asphyxiating chicken, and the left rear brake light was out.

He should have stolen a better car.

Rain dumped down. That was Portland for you. Or — if he was being precise — a country road outside Hillsboro.

Big drops turned the roof into a tin drum. Water sluiced across the windshield, rooster-tailed from the tires.

He sledded around a bend, passing a billboard. A moment later smeared red-and-blue lights illuminated the Caddy's rear window.

A cop.

The broken brake light.

That was inconvenient.

Especially on this car, since a BOLO had likely been issued. The cop would be running the plate number now if he hadn't already.

Evan blew out a breath. Leaned harder

into the gas pedal.

Here came the sirens. The headlights grew larger.

Evan could see the silhouette of the officer behind the wheel. So much like a shooting target — head and chest, all critical mass.

Hillsboro prided itself on being one of the safest cities in the Pacific Northwest. Evan hoped to keep it that way.

As he popped the brakes and jerked the wheel, the heap of a car rocked on its shocks, fanning onto an intersecting road.

Two more cop cars swept in behind him from the opposite direction.

Evan sighed.

Three patrol cars lit up like Christmas, sirens screaming, spreading out across both lanes and closing in.

That was when the thumping from the trunk grew more pronounced.

He checked the wheel, loose enough to jog two inches in either direction with no effect on the steering. He was going to have to attempt tactical driving maneuvers in a car that should not be highway-approved.

Evan had spent a portion of the summer of his fifteenth year on a specialized course in the sticks of Virginia with Jack in the passenger seat keeping one hand on the wheel,

steering him through everything from eva-
sive driving to acceleration techniques in
challenging traction environments.

Just another kid out with his old man,
learning to drive.

In their final conversation, he'd told Jack,
I wouldn't trade knowing you for anything. He
felt it now not as a sentiment but as a
warmth in his chest. He was glad he'd gotten the words out.

The Cadillac backfired. The motor
sounded like it had a marble loose in it.
Evan grimaced.

All right, Jack. Let's do this together.

He started to alternate brake and gas,
playing with the pursuing cruisers, forcing
them to alter their lineup. At last one
separated from the pack, moving bullishly
to the fore.

Evan held the wheel steady, luring the lead
car closer.

A crackly loudspeaker pierced the rain.
*"Pull over immediately! Repeat: Pull to the
side of the road!"*

Evan called back to the girl in the trunk,
"You might want to brace yourself."

The girl shouted, "Great!"

He unholstered his ARES.

Seventeen bullets.

The lead car crept up alongside him, nosing parallel to the Caddy's rear tires.

The PIT maneuver, or precision immobilization technique, was adapted from an illegal bump-and-run strategy used in stock-car racing. The pursuing car taps the target vehicle just behind the back wheel, then veers hard into the car and accelerates. The target vehicle loses traction and spins out.

The lead cop car was preparing for it now.

Unfortunately for him, so was Evan.

He waited, letting the cruiser ease a few more inches into position at the rear of the Caddy.

Then he hit the brakes.

He flew backward, catching a streak of the driver's *Oh, shit* face as he rocketed by.

The cars had perfectly reversed positions, the do-si-do taking all of half a second.

Evan crumpled the sturdy prow of the Caddy into the rear of the cruiser, steered into the crash, and stomped on the gas pedal.

The cruiser acquiesced to the laws of physics, sheering sideways. It wrapped around the grille of the Cadillac in a series of elegant mini-collisions before fishtailing off. As Evan motored ahead onto open road, he watched in the rearview as the cruiser wiped out one of its confederates, wadding

117

them both into the roadside ditch, where they steamed in a tangle of bent chassis and collapsed tires.

One set of headlights held steady, navigating through, sticking to the Caddy's rear.

A quarter mile flew by, then another, as Evan and the last cop standing gauged each other.

The cop finally feinted forward, trying to steer into position, but Evan held him off by veering squarely in front of him. They kept on that way, swerving unevenly across the sodden road, the cruiser coming on, Evan answering with avoidance maneuvers.

The Caddy was growing weary, the reaction time a little worse by the second. Evan was pushing it to the limit, but it was a low limit.

He eyed the mirror. The cruiser gathered itself on its haunches, readying to dart forward again to deal a decisive blow.

All right, Jack. What next?

First of all, get off your heels, son. The Ninth Commandment: Always play offense.

"Right," Evan said to the empty passenger seat.

He raised his 1911, turned away, and shot out the windshield. It spiderwebbed, but the laminate held it in place. With the heel of his hand, Evan knocked out the ruined

118

glass, and rain crashed in over him, a wave of spiky cold. Evan stomped the brake hard and whipped the wheel around. The boat tilted severely as the back swung forward, sloughing through mud. For a moment Evan thought it might flip.

But it righted itself into a sloppy 180, Evan jerking the transmission into reverse and letting the wheel spool back through his loose fists. Gears screamed.

So did the girl in the trunk.

Already he'd seated the gas pedal against the floor, capturing what forward momentum he'd had, except now he was driving in reverse.

Nose to nose with the cruiser, their bumpers nearly kissing.

The young cop at the wheel blinked at him.

They hurtled along the road, two kids in a standoff on a seesaw.

Except the seesaw was traveling fifty miles per hour.

Wind howled around the maw of the windshield. Driving backward protected Evan from the rain. He had a clear view over the top of his pistol and no bullet-deflecting glass between him and the target.

Before the cop could react, Evan jogged the wheel slightly, offsetting the vehicles, opening up an angle to the side of the cruiser.

He shot out the front tire.

Fifteen rounds left.

As the cruiser wobbled and lost acceleration, Evan braked in time with it, holding it in his pistol sights the entire way.

Both cars slowed, slowed, gently nodding to their respective halts. They faced each other about ten yards apart.

Pistol locked on the cop, Evan got out of the Caddy. His boots shoved mounds in the soggy ground. The rain had stopped, but the air still felt pregnant, raising beads of condensation on his skin. His shirt felt like a wet rag.

The cop was still buckled in, fingers locked on the steering wheel, collecting himself.

"Out," Evan said. "Hands."

The cop unbuckled and climbed out. Sweat trickled down his face, clung to the strands of his starter mustache. He stood in the V of his open door. Evan indicated for him to step clear of the car, which he did. He looked earnest and stalwart standing there before the block lettering of his cruiser: HILLSBORO PD. A holstered Glock rode his right hip. His hands were shaking, but only slightly. He wore a wedding ring.

A muffled voice yelled from the Caddy's trunk, *"Don't do it! Don't you hurt him!"*

The cop stiffened, licked his lips. "Who's that?"

Evan said, "I'm not sure yet."

The cop inched his hands down a bit.

"You have a family," Evan told him.

The cop said, "And you've got a girl in the trunk of your stolen vehicle."

"I'll admit there are rare occasions on which there's a reasonable explanation for that," Evan said. "This is one of them."

The cop did not look impressed with that.

"I'm not going to hurt her," Evan said.

"Forgive me for not taking you at your word."

The breeze swept a bitter-fresh scent of churned soil and roadside weeds. The cop's right hand twitched ever so slightly, raised there over the holster. He was the kind of guy who worked hard, helped his neighbors, stayed up late watching westerns on TV.

"Kids?" Evan asked.

The cop nodded. "Daughter. She's five." His Adam's apple lurched with a strained swallow. "I have to look her in the eye every morning and every night and know I did the right thing."

"Think this through," Evan said. "Do I

seem like a guy who doesn't know what he's doing?"

The cop's hand dove for his pistol.

It got only halfway there before Evan fired.

13
DYING ONLY MEANT ONE THING

Evan's shot clipped the rear sights of the cop's holstered Glock. The force of the round flipped the entire holster back off the cop's waistband. It made a single lazy rotation and landed in a drainage ditch with a plop, vanishing into the murky brown water.

Evan hadn't wanted to waste another bullet, but there it was. Down to fourteen.

When the cop blew out his next breath, he made a noise like a moan. He leaned over, hands on his knees.

"Couple deep breaths," Evan said.

"Okay."

"You're gonna radio in that you got me and you're taking me in."

"Okay."

"Right now."

The cops Evan had left in the wreckage several miles behind them on the road would have called in a rough location for backup already, which meant that Van

Sciver would hear, because Van Sciver heard everything.

As the cop leaned in for his radio, Evan stayed tight on him in case he went for the mounted shotgun. But the cop's nerve had deserted him.

"Unit Seventeen to Dispatch. I have apprehended the suspect and am heading home to HQ, over."

"Copy that, Seventeen. We will call off the cavalry."

Evan reached around the cop, yanked the transmission into neutral, and snatched the keys from the ignition. Both men jerked clear as the cruiser forged through the mud, bounced across the ditch, and plowed off the road. Bushes rustled around it, and then it was gone.

Evan said, "March."

At the point of Evan's ARES, the cop walked off the road, through a stand of ash trees, and onto the marshy land beyond.

"Kneel," Evan said.

The cop stopped on a patch of bluegrass. His knees made a sucking sound in the wet earth.

Evan stood behind him. "Close your eyes."

"Wait." The word cracked, came out in two syllables. "My daughter? The five-year-old? Her name is Ashley. She waits up, watches

for my headlights every night. Plays with her American Girl doll in the bay window by the kitchen. Won't go to sleep until I'm there." He choked in a few gulps of air. "I promised her I'd always come home. Don't make a liar out of me. Please. Don't make a liar out of me."

Silence.

"Do you have kids? A wife? Parents, then. Think about them, how they'd feel if you . . . you . . . Or if something happened to them. Think about how you'd feel if it was something someone did. Something that wasn't even necessary. If they were taken from you."

He fell forward onto his hands. His eyes were still closed, but he felt his fingers push into the yielding earth. He thought about his body landing here, taken in by the spongy ground.

He waited for the bullet. Any second now. Any second.

Would he feel it, a pinpoint pressure at the base of his skull before the lights went out?

He thought about the chewed corner of his daughter's blankie, the smell of her head, how when she was a newborn her feet used to curl when she cried.

He thought about his wife's face beneath

her white veil, how he couldn't quite see her, just a sliver of cheek, of eye, until the minister had said the magic five words and he'd lifted the soft tulle fabric and uncovered her beaming back at him.

He thought about how dying only meant one thing, and that was not seeing them again. How lucky he was to have been given that purpose. And how wretched it must be for all the lost souls out there who floated through their years, adrift and alone.

Twenty minutes passed, maybe more, before it dawned on him that he wasn't dead.

He opened his eyes, peered down at his hands, lost to the bluegrass.

He pulled back onto his haunches, moving as slowly as he'd ever moved, and turned around.

There was nothing there but wind shivering the leaves of the trees.

14
A Pang of
Something Unfamiliar

Evan stood at the trunk of the Cadillac. Golden light filtered through the high windows of the ancient barn, lending a fairy-tale tint to the hay-streaked ground and empty stables. He braced himself and opened the trunk.

The girl erupted from inside.

This time Evan was ready. He ducked, and the tire iron strobed by, fractions from his skull. She landed, spun, and came at him again, but it was halfhearted. She knew she'd lost her one good shot.

He stripped the tire iron from her hands and deflected her onto the ground. She lay there panting, a strand of glossy brown-black hair caught in the corner of her mouth.

"Well," she said, and spit out the strand. "Can't blame me for trying."

"No," Evan said.

She sat, laced her hands across her knees,

rolled back slightly onto her behind, and looked up at him. Broad cheekbones, long lashes, vibrant emerald eyes. The pose was youthful, disarming. She might have been watching a movie at a slumber party. But there was something haunted beneath her strong features. As if in her brief life she'd seen more than she'd wanted to.

"You killed him, didn't you?" she said.

"The cop?"

"No," she said. "Not the cop."

"Who?"

"I only had him for a few months," she said. "I finally had someone who . . ." Then she went blank, a screen powering down.

"Who?" he said.

Silence.

He tried a different tack. "What's your name?"

"Joey." Same empty expression.

"What's it short for?"

Her eyes whirred back to life, clicked over to him. "None of your business." She looked up at the high rafters. "Where the hell are we?"

"Off the beaten path."

"What's the plan?"

"Leave the Caddy here. There's a working truck outside a storage shed a klick and a

128

half north. I take that and leave you here. After."

"After what?"

"You give me the package. We can go through your things, piece by piece. Or you can tell me. But there's no way this isn't happening."

She just stared at him.

"Look, Joey, you know how this works. You are a classified government weapon —"

"No. Let's be clear." She stood up, half crossed her arms, one hand gripping the opposite elbow. Her shoulders tensed, rolled forward. Defensive. "I'm a defective model of a classified government weapon. I got pulled off the assembly line."

"Meaning?"

"I washed out, okay? I didn't make it."

"Who was your handler?"

"Orphan Y," she said. "Charles Van Sciver."

Hearing the full name spoken aloud in the muffled damp of the barn — it was a profanity. For a moment Evan was unsure if she'd actually said it or if he'd conjured it, spun it into life from the primordial soup of his own obsession.

He breathed the sweet rot of old wood. His throat felt dry. "He trained you?"

"Yeah," she said. "Until he didn't."

He fought to grasp the contours of this. "Van Sciver was neutralizing the remaining Orphans. Everyone that wasn't his inner cadre."

"Yeah, well, he decided to rev up recruitment again. More assets, more power."

A stab of eagerness punctured Evan's confusion. "So that's the package? Information on Van Sciver."

"No," she said. "I don't have any of that."

"Then what were you doing in that apartment?"

"I lived there," she said. "What were *you* doing in that apartment?"

"Jack Johns sent me."

Her stance shifted at once, forward ready. "Who the hell are you? How do you know Jack Johns?"

"He was my handler."

"Bullshit," she said. "Bullshit. Where is he?"

"He's dead."

Her eyes welled with an abruptness that caught him off guard, emotion rushing to the surface. "I knew it. You killed him."

"Jack was a father to me."

"No. *No.*" Her hands were balled up tightly. "If that was true, if he was your handler, you wouldn't have killed those cops."

"I didn't."

"Never let an innocent die."

"The cops are all —" He cut off in mid-sentence. "What did you just say?"

It seemed all the oxygen had gone out of the barn.

"Nothing."

"The Tenth Commandment," Evan said.

She glowered at him. And then her face shifted, just slightly.

No one would have gotten the Commandments out of Jack. Evan knew that. Which meant she knew it, too.

"The First," she said. "What's the First Commandment?"

" 'Assume nothing.' " He drew in a breath. "The Eighth?"

" 'Never kill a kid.' " She brushed her hair out of her face, her lips slightly parted, her expression heavy with something like awe. When she spoke again, it was a whisper. "You're Orphan X."

The wood creaked around them. Dust motes swirled, fuzzing the air. Evan gave the faintest nod.

"Evan," she said. There was something intimate in her saying his first name. "He told me about you."

"He didn't tell me about you."

"Jack saved me when I broke with the

Program."

"Saved you?"

"You know how it is with Van Sciver. Either you're with him. Or." She didn't have to complete the thought. "Look, I told you. I'm not a government weapon. I'm not an Orphan. I'm just a girl."

It dawned on him, a full-body shiver like a wash of cold water. He sat down against the Caddy's bumper. Tilted his forehead into the tent of his fingers.

"What?" she said.

"Jack wants me to look after you."

"Look after me?"

Evan gazed up at her, felt the blood drain from his face. "You're the package."

They moved beneath the bright moon, high-stepping through a field of summer squash, vectoring for the truck Evan had scouted earlier. Joey's bulging rucksack bounced on her shoulders, made her lean frame look schoolgirl small.

What the hell had Jack been thinking? Evan felt a pang of something unfamiliar. Guilt? He pictured Jack free-falling through the Alabama night and let in some rage to wash the guilt away.

"Let's be clear," Evan said. "I'm not Jack. It's not what I do. I'll get you to safety, square you away, and that'll be that."

Her face had closed off again. Unreadable. Their boots squelched. An owl was at it in one of the dark trees, asking the age-old question: *Who? Who?*

"How'd Van Sciver's men find my apartment?" she asked.

"They were closing in on Jack. They must've gotten the address somewhere, staked it out."

"You sure *you* weren't followed?"

"Yes."

"If they knew I was there, why wouldn't they just have killed me?"

"Because I'm more valuable to them."

"Oh. So they only let me live to lure you in."

"Yes."

A burning in his cheek announced itself. He raised his fingertips, felt a distinct edge. He picked out the safety-glass pebble and flicked it to the ground.

The girl was talking again. "Van Sciver had Jack killed."

He kept on, letting her process it. It was a lot to process.

She dimpled her lower lip between her teeth. "I can help you go after Van Sciver."

Evan halted, faced her in the moonlight. "How old are you?"

"Twenty."

"No."

"Eighteen."

"No."

She squirmed a bit more. "Sixteen."

He started up again, and she hurried to stay at his side. The only colors were shades of gray and sepia. The moonlight ripened the green squash to a pale yellow.

"How did you know?" she asked.

"When you lie, your blink rate picks up. You've also got a one-shouldered shrug that's a tell. And your hands — just keep your hands at your sides. Your body language talks more than you do, and that's saying something."

"God," she said. "You sound just like Jack."

He took a moment with that one.

They cleared the squash and came onto a stretch where something — pumpkins? — had been recently harvested. Hacked vines populated the barren patch, pushing up from the earth like gnarled limbs. An aftermath scent lingered, fecund and autumnal, the smell of life and death.

"It doesn't matter how old I am," she said. "I can help."

"How? Do you have locations, addresses for Van Sciver?"

"Of course not. You know how he is. Everything's end-stopped six different ways. I didn't even know where I was most of the time."

"Do you have any actionable intel on him?"

"Not really."

"Do you know why Jack was in Alabama?"

She colored slightly. "Is that where he died?"

"Joey, listen. You're raw, totally unbroken —"

"I'm not a horse."

"No. You're a mustang. You fight well. You have extraordinary coordination. But you're not finished, let alone operational."

"Jack sent you to me."

"To protect you. Not get you killed."

"I have training." She was angry now, punching every word. "I knocked you on *your* ass, didn't I?"

"You can't imagine the kind of violence that's coming."

"Did Jack advise you to just ship me off somewhere to hide for the rest of my life?"

The shed loomed ahead, a dark mass rising from the earth, the outline of the beater truck beside it. Evan quickened his pace.

"Jack died before he knew how this would all unfold. I have only one concern now, and that is finding Van Sciver and every person who had a hand in Jack's death and killing them." Evan pulled open the creaky truck door and flipped down the visor. The keys landed in his palm. He looked back at Joey. "What am I supposed to do with you?"

"I'm not useless."

"I never said that."

She came around the passenger side, got in, slammed the door. "Yeah," she said. "You did."

15
JUST GEOMETRY

The neon sign announcing the motel in Cornelius had lost its M and L, blaring a woeful orange OTE into the night. The place was rickety despite being single-story, tucked beneath a freeway ramp, the pitted check-in desk manned by a woman who smacked watermelon gum vigorously to cover the scent of schnapps.

It was perfect.

Evan checked in solo, prepaid in cash, and didn't have to produce any details of the alias he had at the ready. Not the kind of establishment that made inquiries of its patrons. The woman never looked him in the face, her attention captured by a hang-nail she was working to limited success with her front teeth. The security camera was a fake, a dusty plastic decoy drilled into the wall for show.

He signed the book "Pierre Picaud," took the key that was inexplicably attached to a duct-taped water bottle, and trudged like a road-weary salesman to Room 6.

As he opened the door, Joey materialized from the shadows and slipped inside with him.

She dumped her rucksack on the ratty carpet, regarded a crooked watercolor of hummingbirds at play. "Look," she said. "Art."

"Really spruces up the place."

She gestured to a corner. "I can sleep there."

"I'll take the floor."

"I'm younger. The bed looks shitty anyways."

"I want to be right by the door," Evan said.

She shrugged. "Fine." She fell back stiffly onto the mattress, a trust fall with no one there to catch her. There was a great creaking of coils. "I think you got the better deal."

"That bad?"

"It feels like lying on a bag of wrenches. No — not *quite* that bad. Maybe, like, rubber-handled wrenches."

"Well, then."

"And I'm used to some shitty places," she said.

"That's the biggest thing the Program has on foster-home kids," he said. "We think

138

wherever we're going isn't as bad as where we've been."

She lifted her head, putting chin to chest, the diffuse neon glow of the sign turning her eyes feral. "Yeah, well, foster homes are different for girls."

"Like how?"

"Like none of your fucking business."

"Okay."

"I never talk about it. *Never.*"

"Okay."

She let her head fall back again. Evan followed her gaze. The water-stained ceiling looked like a topographical map. He wondered if anyone ever knew what went on inside the mind of a teenage girl.

"Do you have a legend?" Evan asked her.

"Jack was getting me a passport, driver's license. It was still in process when . . ."

"Airport's out in that case. That's okay. They're expecting it anyway."

"What's the plan, then?"

"First train departs Portland at eight A.M."

"Okay. So a train. To where?" She waved a hand dismissively. "Doesn't matter."

"We'll make arrangements, make sure you're taken care of."

"Yeah."

"Anything I need to know about Van

139

Sciver, now's the time to tell me."

She sat up, crossed her legs. "I didn't interact with him privately much, if that's what you mean."

"Anything."

"He took me when I was fourteen."

"He's the one who found you?"

"No. It was a guy. Old as death. Gold watch, always smoking, wears Ray-Bans all the time, even at night."

Something crept back to life inside Evan's chest. Something he'd thought long dead.

Boys mass in a bedroom doorway at Pride House Group Home, Evan at the bottom, always the smallest. They peer down the hall at a man but can see only a partial profile. He is extending a solid black business card to Papa Z between two slender fingers. A gold wristwatch glints, dangling from a thin wrist.

"Mystery Man," Evan said.

She cocked her head.

Most of all he remembered the helplessness. Twelve years old, his fate in the control of forces so large and unseen they might as well have been ancient gods. Being asked to jump and jump again, never knowing if there'd be earth underfoot, if he'd ever land.

Until there was Jack, the bedrock to his life.

When Joey had landed, it was with Van Sciver.

Her upturned face waited for him to say something. He wondered how she had scraped her way through her sixteen years. That pang knifed through him again, but he ignored it, turned his thoughts to business.

"How did he choose you?" Evan asked. "The Mystery Man?"

"He watched us all at first, playing in the yard. Just . . . *observing.* For some reason he picked me out one day, drove me a good ways to a marine base. I don't remember which one, but I was in Phoenix, so I'd guess now it was Yuma? He walked me into a giant training facility. The whole inside of the building had been converted to an indoor obstacle course. It had everything — barbed-wire crawl, mud pits, rope climbs, tire pulls, traverse walls. The most stuff I'd ever seen, the place just crammed with it. At the end of the course, there was a bell, and when you finish, you know, you ring it. The old guy had a stopwatch. He said, 'The sole aim is to get from Point A to Point B in the fastest time possible.' I was wearing a dress and sandals. I said, 'The sole aim?' and he said, 'That's right.' "

She paused and again bit her plush lower lip. Her front teeth were slightly too big, spaced with a hair-thin gap. The imperfection was endearing. Without it her features would've been too smooth, too perfect.

"What'd you do?" Evan asked.

"I turned around and walked out," she said. "Then I circled the building from the outside, went through a service door by the end of the course, and rang the bell. I looked across at him, and he was still standing there, hadn't even started the stopwatch yet."

"Smart."

She shrugged. "It's just geometry."

"And then?"

"Two seconds later the old guy's cell phone rings. There must've been cameras there. By the time I'd walked back around, he had a syringe in his hand. I don't remember him sticking me or anything else." She paused. "I never saw anyone again."

"Where'd you wake up?"

"Maryland. But I didn't find *that* out until eleven months later when I escaped."

"Van Sciver kept you in a house for an entire year?"

"A house?" She coughed out a laugh. "I lived on an abandoned air-force installation. My bed was a mattress in a hangar. I ate, slept, trained. That's it. Usually with other instructors. Van Sciver only dropped by now and then to gauge my progress."

"Was he pleased with it?"

"Yeah. Until." She pulled in a deep breath. "One night I woke up. Heard noises. A man crying. I don't why it's worse than when a woman does, but it was. I crept over to the raised office area, you know, up a short set of stairs. It had the only window. I looked out and saw Van Sciver stuffing an unconscious guy into a duffel bag. Then they carried the duffel toward the hangar. I ran back, pretended to be asleep. Van Sciver came in, woke me. He handed me a Glock 21, you know — the Gen4?"

Evan was suddenly aware of how cool the room was.

She said, "I asked what we were doing and he said —"

" 'It is what it is, and that's all that it is,' " Evan said.

She stared at him.

"Cognitive closure," Evan said. "Van Sciver's mode of thinking. A strong preference for order which, okay, a lot of us have. But it's paired with a distaste for ambiguity. That's why Jack cultivated it in us. Ambiguity. That's the part that keeps you human."

"Question orders," she said, her voice a hoarse whisper. "The Sixth Commandment."

He nodded.

She swallowed, was silent a moment, then continued. "So I took the gun. I didn't feel like I had a choice. Van Sciver walked me over to the duffel, told me to shoot it. I asked why. He said it was an order and orders don't come with whys. I could see the guy's outline there inside the duffel."

In the neon glow, Evan caught a sheen on her forehead. Sweat.

She shook her head, breaking off the story. "We've all done shit we regret. I regret every day of my life what I did."

Sliding off the bed, she dug in her rucksack. She pulled out a few toiletries, which she shelved to her chest with an arm, and disappeared into the bathroom. A moment later the shower turned on.

Evan looked at the open mouth of her rucksack. A piece of paper had fallen out. He picked it up to put it away for her when he saw that it was a birthday card. Tattered envelope, no address.

The front of the card featured a colorful YOU'RE 16!, though much of the glitter had been worn off from handling. A well-loved card.

Evan opened it.

A pressed iris had been preserved inside, already brittle.

Know that I am proud of you, sweet girl. That I see the beautiful woman you have grown into.

Xoxo, M.

Evan stared at the scrawled feminine hand for a time, felt a stirring inside him. Was "M" the mom who had lost Joey into the foster system?

It certainly wasn't Orphan M; Evan had left his pieces scattered on a roadway in Zagreb.

But how would "M" have been in touch with Joey? Joey would have been taken off the grid when she was tapped for the Orphan Program. Jack must have arranged some way to reestablish contact between daughter and mother — mailbox forwarding or a dead drop. It would've been a lot of trouble to get done correctly, and Jack only did things correctly. Which meant that whoever "M" was, she meant a lot to Joey.

Evan put the card away, careful not to fragment the dried flower further, and found a plug to charge his RoamZone.

Crouched over the faint green glow, he pondered what he would do if a Nowhere Man call rang through right now. The missions formed an endless chain, each client passing on his untraceable number to the next. That was the only fee he charged for his services. He'd found that this simple act was also part of the healing process for clients, a first step on the road to putting their lives back together. What was more empowering than helping to rescue another person?

For the first time since he'd become the Nowhere Man, he felt unready to answer if the black phone rang. Holed up in a motel in Cornelius, Jack's death still unavenged, stuck with a sixteen-year-old who was at her best difficult to manage — he was in no state to handle a mission.

He reminded himself that six hours from now things would get drastically simpler. He just had to hold out until that first train pulled into Union Station. He'd have Joey off his plate.

Then he'd run Van Sciver to ground and put a bullet through his skull.

The shower turned off, and a few minutes later Joey emerged, towel wrapped around her. She gestured at the rucksack. "Do you mind if I, uh . . ."

"You change out here. I'll clean up."

They passed awkwardly, giving each other a wide berth. In the bathroom he leaned close to the mirror and studied his face, nicked in several places from the shattered

146

windshield. The sterile light caught a dab of dried blood at the corner of his mouth. Only then did he become aware of a throbbing above his right incisor. He lifted his upper lip, saw that the tooth was outlined in crimson. Above it a dot of safety glass speckled in his gum line. He worked it free with his fingers, dropped it in the trash.

Then he rinsed out his mouth and nose, brushed his teeth using Joey's toothpaste and his finger, and went back into the room.

She was in bed, facing away, her breathing already slow and steady. She'd left a pillow on the floor for him.

He lay down on the carpet near the door and closed his eyes.

He awoke to movement in the room. Stayed perfectly still. Kept his eyes veiled, mostly closed.

Joey continued to ease out of bed, moving so slowly she didn't even creak the hair-trigger coils.

Two silent steps, and then she hunched over her rucksack, reaching for something. She rose, turned. He watched her approach. Her hand passed through a fall of light from the window.

She was holding her fixed-blade combat knife.

She moved well, floating on bare feet. He read her posture. Her shoulders were hunched, her head lowered on her neck.

Nothing in it registered aggression.

Just fear.

She leaned over him.

He made the call to let her.

He felt the carbon-steel blade press against his throat.

He opened his eyes all the way.

Her own eyes were so large, the light coming through them from the side turning the irises transparent. The vivid green of them jumped out of the dark, the eyes of a great cat that no longer knew itself to be great.

"Don't hurt me ever," she said. "Please."

"Okay." He felt the word grind against the knife edge.

She nodded and then nodded again, as if to herself.

The pressure eased.

She withdrew as silently as she'd approached.

He lay there and stared at the water-stained map of the ceiling, the whole world laid out in its darkness and complexity.

16
THE TURN TO FREEDOM

A four-sided Romanesque Revival clock tower adorned with lit signage staked Portland Union Station to the west shore of the Willamette River. Evan hustled Joey beneath the GO BY TRAIN flashing sign and into the glossy Italian-marble waiting room, where he bought her a ticket under an alias on a train heading for Ashland, Kentucky, because the choice struck him as sufficiently random. The route ran through Sacramento and Chicago. Between travel time and layovers, that would keep her on the move for nearly three days.

He steered her out onto the chill of the platform, handed her the Amtrak tickets and a wad of cash.

"My email address is the.nowhere.man@gmail.com," he told her. "Say it back to me."

She did, her first words in nearly twenty minutes.

He took her gently by the arm, hustled

her down to the far end of the platform. "When you get to Ashland, log into my account." He told her the password. "Type a message to me in the Drafts folder. Do *not* send it. I will log in, leave you instructions in the same unsent email. If it doesn't ever travel over the internet —"

"I know the protocols," she said.

She turned and waited for the train. A limp wind fluttered her hair, and she hooked it behind an ear, exposing a swath of the shaved area.

Frustratingly, his feet kept him rooted there.

"Watch your back better," he said. "Use windows as mirrors — like there or there. The reflections off passing trains. Watch your visibility, too. You should be noting where surveillance cameras are, minding their sight lines, head down."

Her lower jaw moved forward, and he heard a clicking of teeth. "I know the protocols."

"Then move four inches back behind this post," he said.

She stepped beneath the metal overhang and shot him a glare.

He said, "If you don't know what you don't know —"

" '— how can I know what to learn?' "

she said. "Jack told me that one, too. Like I said. The protocols? I know them."

"Okay," he said.

"Okay," she said.

He left her on the platform. Staying alert, he carved his way back through the waiting room, scanning the crowd. His nose looked okay, but the break had left thumbprint bruises beneath his eyes, so he preferred to avoid looking anyone directly in the face. With each step he sensed the distance widening between him and Joey, between him and Jack's final, ill-considered wish. His boots tapped the cold, shiny marble. It felt like walking through a tomb.

He came out the front, hustled across the hourly-pay parking lot to a Subaru with a MY CHILD IS STUDENT OF THE MONTH bumper sticker. He'd swapped out vehicles early that morning in an office garage, taking advantage of a parking attendant's bathroom break to snatch a set of keys from a valet podium. Assuming the proud parent worked a full day, that gave Evan until five o'clock before the car would be reported missing.

He'd backed into the parking spot, giving him privacy by the rear bumper. He knelt down now and removed the license plate, switching it out for that of the Kia in the neighboring slot. One more layer of protection before he hit the road, free and clear to resume his pursuit of Van Sciver.

He got into the car and pulled out of the parking lot, eyeing the freeway signs.

He was just about to make the turn to freedom when he checked the rearview and saw the HILLSBORO HOME THEATER INSTALLATION! van turn into Union Station.

17
A SINGLE HUNGRY LUNGE

A Hertz rental sedan moved in concert with the van. They parked side by side at the outer edge of the parking lot, reversing into the spots to allow for a quick getaway.

Three husky men emerged from the van. They wore commuter clothes, Dockers and button-ups. Muscle swelled the fabric. There was no way around that. Loose-fitting jackets to conceal their builds and their pistols. They entered the waiting room and spread out immediately, fighter jets peeling out of formation.

The driver in the sedan stayed put, his head rotating as he scanned the parking lot and roads leading to the train station. The lookout.

The men streaked through the waiting room, sidling between passengers and heavy oak benches. They stepped out of three different doors onto the platform and into the shade of the overhang. In the distance a freight train approached, *woo-wooing* a warning, rumbling the ground.

The whistle would provide good audio cover for a gunshot.

The men looked through the clusters of waiting passengers on the side platform and the two island platforms beyond. One of the men spotted a rucksack tilting into view from behind a wooden post at the end. And part of a girl's leg.

His head swiveled, and he caught the eye of the man in the middle, whose head swiveled in turn to pick up the last man. They shouldered their way along the platform, closing the space between one another.

Woo-woo.

The freight train wasn't slowing. It would blow right through the station, giving even more sound cover. The girl was isolated there at the end of the platform. That provided relative privacy to get the job done.

Woo-woo.

They converged on her, now shoulder to shoulder, linemen coming in for the sack.

Fifteen yards away.

Woo-woo.

She saw them only now. Alarm flashed across her face, but even so she stepped back into a fighting posture, hands raised, jaw set.

The man in the middle reached inside his loose-fitting jacket.

They swept forward.

Ten yards away.

Behind them a form swung down from the metal overhang and crouched on the landing to break his fall, one hand pressed to the concrete.

Soundless.

Evan couldn't fire his ARES. Not with Joey in the background. But that was okay. He was eager to use his hands.

Joey spotted him through the gap between the advancing men. They read her eyes, the change in her stance.

They turned.

Three men. One pistol drawn, two on the way.

Evan moved on the gun first.

A jujitsu double-hand parry to a figure-four arm bar, the pleasing *snap-snap* of wrist and elbow breaking, and —

— *Jack sways in the Black Hawk, hands cuffed behind him, wind blasting his hair when* —

— the pistol skittered free across the tracks, the guy on his knees, his arm turned to rubber. The second man gave up on the draw and came at Evan with a haymaker,

155

but Evan threw a palm-heel strike to the bottom of his chin, rocking his head back. He firmed his fingers, drove a hand spear into the exposed throat, crushing the windpipe. The man toppled, crashing through a trash can, and made a gargling sound, his access to oxygen closed now and forever and —

— *Jack reeled back, a parachute rip cord handle clenched in his teeth, his eyes blazing with triumph, when —*

— the third man's gun had cleared leather, so Evan grabbed his wrist, shoved the pistol back into the hip holster, hooked his thumb through the trigger guard, and fired straight down through the tip of the holster and the guy's foot. The man was still gaping at the bloody mess on the end of his ankle when Evan reversed the pistol out of the holster, spun it around the same thumb, and squeezed off a shot that took off half the guy's jaw. Evan blinked through the spatter and the image of —

— *Jack's parting nod to the men pinballing around the lurching Black Hawk, a nod filled with peace, with resignation, before he stepped out into the abyss.*

People were screaming now, stampeding off the platform, the express train bearing down. Two corpses on the concrete, a glassy puddle of deep red spreading, smooth enough to reflect the clouds in the sky. The first man remained on his knees, straddling the yellow safety line on the platform, gripping his ruined arm as the hand flopped noodlelike on the broken stalk of the limb. Despite all reason he was trying to firm it, to make his wrist work again, when Evan wound into a reverse side kick, driving the bottom of his heel into the edge of the man's jaw and sending him flying over the tracks just in time to catch the — *woo-woo* — freight train as it blasted through, flyswatting him ahead and grinding him underneath in what seemed like a single hungry lunge.

Joey stared at Evan across the expanding puddle and the sprawled legs of the third man. Furrows grooved the skin of her forehead. She had forgotten to breathe.

The engagement had lasted four seconds, maybe five.

The other man had landed to the side, propped against the toppled trash can, one hand pawing the air above his collapsed windpipe. The motion grew slower and slower.

Joey looked at him and then back at Evan, her eyes even wider.

"He's dead," Evan said. "He just doesn't

know it yet."

She cleared her throat. "Thanks."

"Grab your rucksack. Let's go."

She did.

They barreled through the doors into the waiting room. Chaos reigned. People shoved and elbowed to the exit. A homeless man was bellowing to himself, stuffing his bedding into a shopping cart. Workers cowered behind counters.

There were sirens outside already, flashing lights coloring the parking lot. Lead responders spilled through the front entrance, bucking the stream of humanity.

"This way." Evan grabbed Joey's arm, ushered her up the corridor to the bathrooms.

They were halfway there when a service door swung open and two cops shouldered through. Their eyes lasered in on Evan and Joey, Glocks drawn but aimed at the floor.

Evan swung her around, reversing course. They didn't get three steps when, up ahead, responding cops filled the waiting room.

They were trapped.

18
SHORT ON TIME AND
SHORT ON CROWBARS

Behind them one of the cops shouted, "Wait! Stop right there!"

Evan and Joey froze, still facing away. The corridor was empty, squeaky clean save for a dropped newspaper and fresh plug of gum stuck to the wall.

"What now?" Joey said to Evan out of the side of her mouth.

"We don't kill cops."

Ahead, PD started locking down the big hall. Behind them the cops' boots squeaked on the marble as they approached cautiously.

"I know," Joey whispered. "So what do we do?"

"Get arrested. Face the consequences, whatever they are. We go down before we break a Commandment."

The cops were right behind them. "Turn around. Right now."

Joey reached up and flipped her hair over,

exposing the shaved side of her head in its entirety. She brushed against Evan as she pivoted around, and when he followed her lead, he saw that she had his RoamZone in hand.

"This is totally not fair," she said. "Some big guy ran past us, all freaking out, and *whammed* into me. I dropped my phone and it's, like, *ruined.*"

Her posture had transformed, shoulders slumped, twisty legs, head lolling lazily to one side, a finger twirling a tendril of hair — even her face had gone slack with teen-age apathy.

And she was chewing gum. With teenage vigor.

Evan shot a look at the spot on the wall where the fluorescent green plug had been a moment before.

Joey yanked on Evan's arm. "Dad, you are buying me a new phone. Like, *now.* There's no way I'm going to school with the screen all cracked."

Evan cleared his throat. "I'm sorry, Officers."

The cops looked behind them. "A big guy ran past you? This way?"

"Yeah. You, like, *just* missed him."

The cops exchanged a look and bolted back down the corridor to the service door.

Joey called after them, "If you find him, tell him he's paying for my new phone!"

The door banged shut after them. Joey swept her hair back into place, blanketing the shaved side. " 'Adapt what is useful, reject what is useless, and add what is specifically your own.' "

"Odysseus?"

She took the gum out of her mouth, stuck it back on the wall. "Bruce Lee."

He nodded. "Right."

They moved swiftly out through the service door, skating the edge of the parking lot just before more cops swept in, setting a perimeter around the building.

Evan peered across to the outer fringe of the lot. Even through the windshield glare, he could discern the outline of the man in the rent-a-car. He was trapped for now; the cops had blockaded the exits.

Joey took note of the man. "The lookout?"

"Yes."

Evan hustled her away from the commotion and into an employee parking lot shielded from view by a flank of the building.

"Is the car this way?" she asked.

"No. I parked it a block to the south."

"Then why are we here?"

He stopped by a canary-yellow Chevy Malibu.

"Evan, this isn't the time to swap cars again. We can't drive out of here anyways. You saw the exits."

Dropping to his back, he slid under the Malibu. He unscrewed the cartridge oil filter and jerked it away from the leaking stream.

He wiggled back out from under the car.

She saw the filter and said, "Oh." And then, *"Oh."*

He shook the filter upside down, oil lacing the asphalt at his feet. Then he examined the coarse threading inside. "Give me your flannel."

She took it off. He used it to wipe oil from the filter and then his hands. It wasn't great, but it was the best he was going to do. Holding the filter low at his side, he stepped over a concrete divider onto the sidewalk and started arcing along the street bordering the station, threading through rubberneckers.

"Why are we risking this?" Joey asked. "Right now?"

"Given their response time, these guys have some kind of headquarters in the area. We saw at least seven more men at your apartment building, including the Orphan. We find the HQ, we get answers."

"You think the guy's just gonna tell you? This place is swimming with cops. It's not like you can beat it out of him."

"Won't have to."

They came around the fringe of the parking lot. The lookout's car was up ahead, backed into its spot, the trunk pressed to a row of bushes. The majority of cops were at the main exits or across the lot at the station proper, scurrying around, gesticulating and talking into radios.

Evan removed his slender 1911. He knew that the threading of the oil filter would be incompatible with the threading of the barrel, so he tore a square of fabric from the flannel, held it across the mouth of the filter, and snugged the gun muzzle into place.

A makeshift suppressor.

They skated behind a group of looky-loos who had gathered by the main entrance and vectored toward the rise of juniper hemming in the parking lot.

Evan said, "Wait here."

He sliced through the bushes. Three powerful strides carried him along the driver's side of the sedan. The lookout picked up the movement in the side mirror and lunged for a pistol on the passenger seat. Evan raised his 1911 to the window, held the oil filter in place at the muzzle, and shot him through the head.

The pop was louder than he would have hoped.

Between the flannel patch, the oil, and the muzzle flash, the filter broke out in flames. Evan dumped it onto the asphalt and stomped it out.

He squatted by the shattered window and watched, but no one seemed to have taken notice.

He opened the door, releasing a trickle of glass. The lookout was slumped over the console. Evan wiggled the guy's wallet and Samsung Galaxy cell phone from his pocket. Then he lifted his gaze to the object of his desire.

The Hertz NeverLost GPS unit nodded from a flexible metal stalk that was bolted to the dashboard.

Evan tried to snap it off, but the antitheft arm required a crowbar.

He sank back down outside the car, re-shaped the flattened cartridge oil filter as best he could, and firmed it back into place over the muzzle. The sound attenuation of the first shot had been far from spectacular, and he knew that a makeshift suppressor degraded with every shot. But he was short on time and short on crowbars.

He took a few breaths. Juniper laced the

air — bitter berry, pine, and fresh sap undercut by something meatier.

He leaned into the car, aimed at the spot where the stalk met the dashboard, and fired.

The unit's arm nodded severely to one side. He glanced through the blood-speckled windshield, saw some of the cops' heads snap up. They were looking around, unable to source the sound. As Evan worked the metal arm back and forth, several cops moved into the parking lot, Glocks drawn.

They were moving row by row.

The stalk proved stubborn. He sawed it back and forth harder, polyurethane foam swelling into view on the dash.

A female cop worked her way up the line of vehicles directly ahead of Evan. In a moment she'd step around the end car and they'd be face-to-face.

The unit finally ripped free of the molded plastic above the glove box. Evan backed out of the car, already powering down the GPS so it couldn't be accessed remotely. Staying low, he reversed through the juniper. He saw the cop come clear of her row and spot the windshield an instant before the foliage wagged back into place, enveloping him.

He popped out the other side onto the

sidewalk, bumping into Joey. He handed her the NeverLost, unscrewed the filter from the tip of the pistol, and dumped it into a trash can. Then he holstered his 1911 beneath his shirt, took Joey's hand like a doting father. She understood, folding her clean fingers around his, hiding the oil smudges.

They crossed at Irving Street, blended into a throng of pedestrians, and headed for the family car.

19

MORE THAN A MISSION

November was a pleasant month in Alabama.

Van Sciver sat in a rocking chair, sipping sweet tea. On his knee rested an encrypted satphone, the screen dancing with lights even when it was at rest.

The plantation-style house wasn't so much rented as taken over. Though relatively humble compared to some of the mansions in the region, the place still showcased classic white woodwork, a formidable brick chimney, and an impressive pair of columns that guarded the long porch like sentries. It was a National Historic Landmark. Which meant that it was under federal jurisdiction — the Department of the Interior, to be precise.

The Orphan Program had a special relationship with the Department of the Interior. When the DoD required cash for Program operations, they made use of the bureaucratic machinery of Interior, figuring correctly that this was the last place that any inquiring mind would look for Selected Acquisition Report irregularities.

The money itself came straight from Treasury, shipped immediately after printing, which made it untraceable. And which meant that Van Sciver could quite literally print currency when he needed it. The life of an Orphan was not without hardships, but those hardships were cushioned by secret eight-figure bank accounts sprinkled throughout nonreporting countries around the world.

When forced to leave his data-mining bunker, Van Sciver didn't generally pull strings with Interior. But this mission was more than a mission.

It was a celebration.

So he'd made a single phone call, the effect of which had rippled outward until he found himself here, sipping sweet tea on the veranda, waiting for mosquitoes to stir to life so he could swat at his neck with a kerchief just like they did in the movies.

One of his men circled, his bushy beard and sand-colored FN SCAR 17S battle rifle out of place here among the weeping willows and lazy breeze.

"Perimeter clear," he said as he passed,

and Van Sciver raised his iced tea in a mock toast.

Jack Johns had been the number two on Van Sciver's list. But killing him was not what had given Van Sciver his current glow of contentment. It was the fact that killing him had made Orphan X hurt.

That alone was worth the cost of a Black Hawk and six men.

Van Sciver's history with Evan stretched back the better part of three decades to a boys' home in East Baltimore. Their rivalry at Pride House had been nearly as vicious as it was now. Van Sciver had been a head taller, with twice the brawn. He'd been the draw, the one they'd scouted for the Program, the one they wanted.

And yet Evan had squirmed himself into position, had gotten himself picked first. Now Van Sciver held the keys to the kingdom and Evan was a fugitive. Van Sciver had played the long game.

And he had won.

Yet even here, rocking soporifically on a centuries-old porch at a mansion requisitioned on a whim through the federal government, even surrounded by ranks of trained men ready to do his bidding, even with the levers of power awaiting the slightest twitch of his fingers, he knew that it wasn't enough.

It would never be enough.

The phone chimed, the call routing in through Signal, an encryption app developed by Open Whisper Systems. Every call, made over a Wi-Fi or data connection, was end-to-end protected, the only encryption keys controlled by app users. As he did with all security measures, Van Sciver had gone above and beyond, tweaking the code slightly, altering the protocols.

He eyed the screen, which displayed two words: ADDER LUSTFUL.

He thumbed to answer. "Code," he said.

He heard a rustle as Orphan R eyed the words displayed on his end. " 'Adder lustful.' "

The matching code verified that the call was secure; no man-in-the-middle attack had occurred.

Van Sciver said, "Is the package in hand?"

Orphan R said, "We didn't get her."

"Because?"

A hesitation spoke to Thornhill's dread. "X showed up. Took out four of my men."

Van Sciver found himself actually using his kerchief to mop sweat off his neck. "How many men did you have at the train station?"

"Four."

Van Sciver had no response to that.

"We thought it was just the girl. The surveillance cameras picked up only her. Alone. We thought it'd be a quick snatch-and-dash, and then we could use her to lure him in."

"Instead he lured you in."

"Seems that way."

Van Sciver leaned forward in the rocking chair, set his glass down on the uneven planks of the porch. "We have unfinished business here. I want you back."

"Shouldn't we stick around in case X rears his head?"

"Leave your team in place there. But you won't find him. He and the girl are gone. You missed your shot."

There was an even longer pause. "I'm on a plane."

Van Sciver hung up.

He picked up his glass and tossed the remaining tea into the hydrangeas.

The time for celebrating was over.

20
WAYWARD PIECES

It took some doing, but Evan found a motel on par with the beauty in Cornelius. Stale cigarette smoke oozed from the bedding, the towels, even the popcorn ceiling. The toilet was missing the tank lid. A pull-chain table lamp with a yellowed shade threw off a jaundiced glow. The comforter sported a stain the color of dried blood, which Evan hoped it was, given the less appealing alternatives. He'd rented the room for three hours, which explained everything worth explaining.

Now he sat cross-legged on the floor, the Hertz NeverLost GPS unit before him. Still attached to the metal stalk, it resembled a dismembered antenna. The lookout's wallet and Samsung were laid on the floor beside the stalk, parallel to each other, edges aligned.

Order helped him think.

Joey leaned her shoulders against the bed,

her hand working what seemed to be a steroidal Rubik's Cube that she'd produced from her rucksack. She spun it with the speed and focus of a squirrel stripping a walnut.

Evan opened the lookout's wallet. It contained four crisp hundred-dollar bills and nothing else. All the slots and crevices were empty. He set it back in its place.

Then he turned on the Samsung and checked the contacts. There were none. E-mail was empty, as was the trash folder. No recent calls. No voice mail.

The clacking of Joey's Rubik's Cube continued, grating on his nerves. Without looking up, she said, "No luck, huh?"

He ignored her, powering on the Never-Lost GPS. When he searched the settings, he saw that everything had been deleted from this device as well. No saved locations, no last destinations, no evidence that the unit had ever been used.

Clack-clack-clack-clack —

"Can you please stop that?"

She halted, cube in her hands. The thing had exploded outward into different planks and beams, an architectural scribble.

He frowned at it. "What *is* that thing?"

"This?" She turned the monstrosity in her hands, showing off its various dimensions.

"It's a three-by-three-by-five. Cubers call it a shape-shifter."

"What does it do?"

"Gives you a headache."

"Like you."

She flashed a fake grin. Let it fall from her face.

She returned her focus to the cube. Her hands moved in a flurry, whipping the various planes around. "You have to solve the shape first. Wait, wait — see?" She held it up. She'd wrangled it back into form. It looked like a miniature tower. "Then you solve the colors. This part's easier. There are algorithms, sequences of steps. . . ."

To him it was just a blur of primary colors.

"You have to look for the wayward pieces, find the patterns that make them fall into place. Like so."

She held it up, finished, gave it a Vanna White wave with her free hand.

"Impressive."

"They say girls suck at geometry, but they forgot to tell me that."

"You would've ignored them anyway."

She tossed the cube into her rucksack, flicked her chin at the GPS unit. "How's it going with that?"

"They wiped everything. Can I use your laptop? I need to get into this thing."

She shrugged. "Sure." She retrieved her laptop and a USB cable, watched him plug in the NeverLost. "Whatcha doing?"

"Even if they deleted everything, the GPS still has coordinates, destinations, and deleted routes stored internally somewhere." He set to work. "First step of a forensic recovery is to image the data. It's called mounting the file-storage system. Then you make a copy of the device's internal memory in your computer but contain it so it can't infect your own data. Then I'm gonna wade through it, determine the data structures, see where and how the data's stored, what kind of encryption I'm dealing with. Like jailbreaking a phone. Understand?"

She tilted her head at the screen, taking in his progress, then looked at him with an expression he couldn't read. "What grampa taught you to hack? You learn that when COBOL and IBM S/370 were state-of-the-art?"

This joke seemingly amused her.

He said, "What?"

"Maybe you could use a dial-up modem. Or, like, we could get a bunch of hamsters on wheels to power the software."

He stopped, fingers poised above the keys. "You have a better approach?"

"You're using a memory-dumper program," she said. "Why don't you spin up a new local virtual machine like any idiot would, image and then boot the virtual device inside it, use the Security Analysts desktop code to do the heavy lifting?"

Blowing hair out of her eyes, she spun the laptop around to face her. Her fingers moved across the keyboard, a virtuoso pianist hammering through Rachmaninoff. Then she flicked the laptop back around to him.

The screen was doing lots of things and doing them speedily.

She settled back against the bed again, as bored as ever. He read the coding here and there, catching up to it well enough to start directing the software.

"Lemme see the phone," she said.

"I already checked it. It's been wiped."

"Two sets of eyes are better than one. Especially when the second set is mine."

"Trust me. There's no point."

She plucked up the Samsung, started thumbing at it.

The laptop spit out some results. It took Evan a moment to decipher them.

"Shit," he said.

"Hmm?" The phone made little tapping noises, its glow illuminating her round face.

"Looks like they used a secure erase tool,"

he said. "Layered over the data with twelve hours of alternating ones and zeros."

"There is a shortcut, you know."

He closed the laptop a touch harder than necessary. "What's that?"

"Oh, I don't know, maybe the Waze app on his phone." She held up the Samsung to show the nav application lighting up the screen. "It shows where the cops are, accidents, traffic jams. You know, useful stuff for lookouts and getaway drivers. Why did you think he had a phone?"

Heat rose beneath Evan's face. "To make calls."

"To make calls," she said. "That's so cute."

"The app — it has all the routes?"

"Yeah. But we don't need them."

"Why not?"

"Because look what happens when you touch the smiley car." She pressed the icon. A column of recent destinations came up. The second one down, an address in Portland's Central Eastside, was labeled HQ.

"That's what we in the spy business refer to as a clue," she said.

Evan rubbed his eyes.

"You really need to watch your nonverbal tells," she said.

He lowered his hands to his lap. "You have

location services turned off on that phone, right?"

"Of course."

"Power it off anyway. Just to be safe."

She did. Then she tossed it back onto the worn network of threads that passed for a carpet. "When you said they could pick me up on the surveillance cameras at the train station, I thought you were being paranoid. But it's not paranoid when you're right, is it?"

"I need to get you far away from here before we put you on any kind of public transportation. I'm talking multiple states away."

"What about the headquarters?" She tapped the phone. "I mean, we're forty minutes away. You drive me to Idaho and come back, they'll be cleared out by then."

"What am I supposed to do with you?"

She just looked at him.

"No. No way."

"Give me your gun."

She stared him down, unblinking. Finally he unholstered the skinny ARES and handed it to her. She regarded the slender 1911 with amusement, turning it this way and that. "Nice gun. They make it in pink?"

"Only if you special order it."

"It goes well with your hips."

"Thanks."

"You should accessorize it with, like, a clutch purse. Maybe a string of pearls."

"Are you done?"

"Just about."

He waited.

She said, "If you pull the trigger, does a little flame come out the end? Or a flag that says 'Bang'?"

"Joey."

"Okay, okay," she said. "Go to the lamp."

He rose and walked over to the table lamp.

"Turn it off, count five seconds, then turn it back on."

He pulled the chain, the room falling into darkness. A five count passed, and he turned the light back on.

The 1911 rested in front of her crossed legs. It had been fieldstripped. Frame, slide, bushing, barrel, guide rod, recoil spring, spring plug, and slide stop. In a nice touch, she'd stacked the remaining four rounds on end on the magazine.

Her gaze held steel. "Again," she said.

He tugged the chain once more, counted to five, clicked the lamp on.

The pistol, reassembled.

She had a tiny dimple in her right cheek even when she wasn't smiling. She wasn't smiling now.

"You can be my lookout," he said. "But only because it's safer for you to be near me than on your own."

"Gee," she said. "Thanks."

She stood, twirled the gun on her palm, and presented him with the grip. He took the ARES and clicked it home in his high-guard Kydex holster.

"What if they're expecting you?" she asked.

"Even if they are," he said, "it won't help them."

21
QUICK AND EASY

Central Eastside was an industrial district checkered with low-rent housing. Evan coasted in the stolen Subaru with the switched rear license plate, watching a parade of radiator shops, commercial laundries, and wholesale construction-supply joints march by. The streets were pothole-intensive, shimmering with broken glass. A few spots had been taken over by brewpubs and distilleries, gentrification doing its cheery best, but they were out ahead of the curve here and — from the looks of the clientele and graffiti — in over their heads.

Joey took in the streets and seemed not uneasy in the least.

She wore a half squint, her taut cheeks striking, the youthful fullness of her face turned to something hard and focused. Evan found himself admiring her. She was a medley of contradictions, surprises.

They drove for a time in silence.

"I need a shotgun," Evan said.

"I'm sure we could rustle one up in these here parts."

"Last thing we need is to go down the rabbit hole dealing with local criminals and wind up with a rusty Marlin Goose Gun. We need something well maintained, and we need it quick and easy."

"Where you gonna find a shotgun like that on no notice?"

"The police."

"Of course. Quick and easy." She cast a glance across the console, did a double take. "You're not joking, are you?"

Evan pulled over beneath the green cross of a marijuana dispensary, fished out his RoamZone, and dialed 911.

The cruiser pulled up, and two venerable cops emerged, slamming the doors behind them. The driver hit the key fob, the car putting out a *chirp-chirp* as it locked.

Joey sat on the steps of the dispensary, holding Evan's phone and pretending to text. Her dark wavy hair fell across her face, blocking one eye, an artful dishevelment.

"What are you doing here?" the officer said. He had a dewlapped face, eyes gone weary from seeing too much shit for too many nights.

"My pops works here," Joey said.

The second cop, a tough-looking redhead with sun-beaten skin, stood over Joey. "We had an anonymous report of shots fired on this block."

"Oh, yeah?"

"You hear anything?"

"All the time."

An annoyance passed between the cops. "Care to elaborate?"

Joey sighed. Pocketed the phone. "C'mere." She brushed past the redhead, took the driver by the arm, walked him to the curb, and pointed across the street. "See that alley there? There's a auto-salvage yard at the end of it. That's where to go if you need a piece on the down-low. A shitty little .22, something like that. That's what everyone says around here. People test the goods before they pay up." She stood back, crossed her arms. "So yeah, I heard shots fired. Tonight and every night."

The redhead let out a sigh that smelled of coffee and cigarettes. "Let's go."

She and her partner headed across the street and disappeared up the alley.

Evan emerged from the darkness at the side of the store. Joey flipped him the keys she'd lifted from the driver's pocket.

Evan thumbed the fob, popped the trunk

to reveal a mounted gun-locker safe.

Also remote-controlled.

He thumbed another button on the key chain, and the gun locker opened with a brief metallic hum.

Inside, cartons of shells and a Benelli M3 combat shotgun.

His favorite.

He grabbed two cartons, took the shotgun, then closed the gun locker and the trunk. He pointed at a spot on the sidewalk. "Drop the keys there."

Joey did.

They walked over to the Subaru and drove off.

22
DEAD MAN'S POCKET

The headquarters were on Northeast Thirteenth at the very tip of Portland proper in a long-abandoned pest-control shop sandwiched between a trailer lot and a precast-concrete manufacturing plant. The drive over had been a descent into rough streets and heavy industry — truck parts, machining, welding. Gentlemen's clubs were in evidence every few blocks despite the absence of any actual gentlemen.

The small pest-control shop, no bigger than a shack, had been retrofitted as a command center. Evan recognized the make of steel door securing the front entrance — the kind filled with water, designed to spread out the heat from a battering ram's impact. A ram would buckle before it would blow through a door like that. That was incredibly effective.

When there wasn't a back door.

Which Evan watched now. At the edge of

the neighboring lot, he'd parked the Subaru between two used trailers adorned with cheery yellow-and-red sales flags. He had the driver's window rolled down, letting through a chilly stream of air that smelled of tar and skunked beer. Joey sat in the passenger seat, perfectly silent, perfectly still.

Two cartons of different shotgun shells were nestled in his crotch, the shotgun across his lap. He had not loaded it yet.

A few blocks over, a bad cover band wailed an Eagles tune through partially blown speakers: *Some-body's gunna hurt someone, a'fore the night is through.*

Evan thought, *You got that right.*

A Lincoln pulled up to the rear curb of the building. Evan sensed Joey tense beside him. A broad-shouldered man climbed out of the sedan. He knocked on the back door — shave and a haircut, two bits. Even at this distance, the seven-note riff reached the Subaru through the crisp air.

A speakeasy hatch squeaked open, a face filling the tiny metal square.

A murmured greeting followed, and then various dead bolts retracted, the door swung inward, and the broad-shouldered man disappeared inside.

Now Evan knew how he wanted to load the shotgun.

One nine-pellet buckshot load for the chamber, two more on its heels in the mag tube. He followed those with three shock-lock cartridges and had a pair of buckshot shells run anchor.

He popped in the triangular safety so it was smooth to the metal, the red band appearing on the other side. When he pumped the shotgun, he felt the *shuck-shuck* in the base of his spine.

"Stay here," he said. He reached for the door handle, then paused. "You may not like what you're about to see."

He got out, swung the door closed behind him.

He walked across the desolate street, bits of glass grinding beneath his tread. The midnight-black Benelli hung at his side.

He could feel Jack fall into step beside him, hear Jack's voice, a whisper in his ear. *It's too late for me.*

"I'm sorry I wasn't there," Evan said quietly.

I want to know that I'm forgiven.

"You are." Evan quickened his stride, bearing down on the door. He knocked out the brief melody and raised the shotgun, seating the butt on his good shoulder.

I love you, son.

The speakeasy hatch squeaked open, and

Evan pushed the muzzle into the surprised square of face and fired.

There was no longer a face.

He shoved the shotgun farther inside, the muzzle clearing the door, and unleashed two buckshot rounds, one to the left, one to the right.

The three shock-locks were up next, copper-powdered, heavy-compressed centered shots that provided a total energy dump on one spot with no scatterback or frag.

Hinge removers.

He shifted the action to manual so he could cycle the low-powered breaching rounds and give them more steam. Then he stepped back and fired top to bottom — *boom-boom-boom.* The last slug knocked the door clear off the frame, sending it skidding across the floor.

Cycling buckshot into the chamber and toggling the switch back to autoload, he stepped through the dust into the metallic tang of cordite, shotgun raised.

The blow-radius effect of the initial blasts in the contained shop was biblical. With no air movement, the powdered smoke had stratified, hovering like gray mist.

Five men, either dead or in various stages of critical injury, shuddered on knocked-over folding chairs, tilted against blood-stained walls, sprawled over a central table. No sign of the Orphan. The broad-shouldered man was the only one able to do more than bleed out.

He bellied across the floor, dragging himself away with his forearms, a combat crawl. His right leg was a mottled fusion of denim and flesh.

He kept on, making for a rack of rifles and shotguns beside the steel front door.

Evan walked toward him, stuck a toe in his ribs, flipped him over.

The man tried to look away. "Oh, God," he said. "You're — are you — Orphan X? Oh, God."

Evan seated a boot square on his barrel chest, hovered the hot muzzle over his throat. "You killed Jack Johns."

The man's fine hair, so blond it was almost gray, was shaved in a buzz cut. His scalp showed through, glistening with sweat. "No — not me. I didn't go up in the chopper, man. There was a special crew."

"But you were there. On the ground in Alabama. You were all there."

"Yes."

Evan swung the shotgun to the side and blew off his hand.

The howl was inhuman.

But so was making a man in his seventies jump out of a Black Hawk with his wrists cuffed together.

Evan rotated the Benelli back to the man's head. "Van Sciver?" he said. "Where?"

Somewhere behind them, a final sputtering wheeze extinguished.

"I don't know. I swear. Never even met him."

Evan moved the Benelli over the guy's other hand.

"*Wait!* Wait! I'll tell you — tell you everything. Just don't . . . don't take me apart like this."

"How many freelancers did he bring in? Not including the helo crew."

"Twenty-five. He hired twenty-five of us."

Evan surveyed the wreckage, added it to the train-station tally. "Fifteen now," he said.

"Sixteen." The man risked a look at his hand, failed to fight off a full-body shudder. "I make sixteen." And then, more desperately, "I . . . I still make sixteen."

"Who's running point here?"

The man looked over at the red-smeared linoleum where his hand once was and dry-heaved. His face was pale, awash in sweat. Evan put more pressure on his chest, cracking a rib, snapping him back to attention.

"Jordan Thornhill," the man said. "Or-

190

phan R. Nicest guy in the world. Until he kills you."

"What's he look like?"

"Black dude, all muscle. Could scale a cliff with his bare hands, he wanted to." The man started hyperventilating. "God, oh, God, I think I'm bleeding out."

"You've got enough for the next five minutes. Where is he?"

"Van Sciver called him home. I don't know where."

Evan twitched the barrel slightly.

"I DON'T KNOW WHERE! I don't know anything. I swear. They keep us in the dark about everything."

Evan let the weight of the hot barrel press into the hollow of the man's throat. The flesh sizzled. "Not improving your situation, hired man."

"Hang on! I overheard Thornhill saying something about a female Orphan. Candy something. Orphan V."

At this, Evan's face tightened.

"Please." Saliva sheeted between the man's lips. "That's all I know. I told you everything. Can I . . . will you let me live?"

"You were dead the minute Van Sciver told you my name." Evan pulled the trigger.

He heard a creak behind him and pivoted, dropping the empty shotgun and drawing his ARES.

He found himself aiming at Joey.

She stood in the doorway, surveying the wreckage. A flush had come up beneath her smooth brown cheeks. The shack smelled of blood iron and the insides of men. Through the lingering smoke, her emerald eyes glowed, unguarded, overwhelmed.

"I told you to stay in the car."

"I'm fine."

"Pull the car around. Hurry."

She stepped back and was gone.

He flung a corpse off the central table and rifled through the items beneath. Coffee cups, battery packs, a half-eaten sub. Useless. Beneath a pack of black gel pens, he found a red-covered notebook. Seizing it, he thumbed through the stiff pages. Nothing inside.

He tossed it, moved to the chipped counter em-dashing half of the east wall. Coffeepot, microwave, utility sink. The cabinet beneath held rusted pipes, water spots, a crusted bottle of Drano.

He turned in his crouch, giving the room a last, hurried scan.

Blood dripped from the edge of the table. A strip of duct tape shimmered beneath the lip.

A laptop, adhered to the table's underside.

He tore it free and turned for the door. As he stepped over what was left of the broad-shouldered man, something chimed. Evan paused to fish a familiar-looking Samsung Galaxy from the dead man's pocket.

He used the man's shirt to wipe a crimson smear off the screen. Location services were toggled off, GPS disabled.

Out front he heard the Subaru squeal to the curb.

Keeping the phone, he exited through the fortified steel door. As it swung open, he heard the faint slosh of water within.

It was a nice security measure, if you thought about it.

23
DAMAGED GOODS

As Joey sped away, Evan checked out the Samsung. It appeared to be wiped of data, holding only the operating system and a single app.

Signal.

The encrypted comms software showed several incoming contact attempts.

Sirens wailed, a squadron of cop cars rocketing past one block over on Lombard Street, blues and reds lasering through the night air.

Joey had gotten them quickly away from the pest-control shop. She darted nervous glances at the seemingly endless procession. The cruisers were visible only at intersections and alleys, strobing into view behind warehouses and buildings.

"We're fine," Evan said. "Get on the 5."

"And then?"

"Head north."

Signal only worked over Wi-Fi, but —

God bless Portland's waxed mustaches, artisanal beers, and municipal benefits — they remained under the umbrella of free city-wide service.

The sirens reached an earsplitting pitch and then faded quickly.

Joey blew out a breath, letting it puff her cheeks.

Evan kept his eyes on the Samsung, waiting for it to chime.

Joey said, "What are you —"

It chimed.

Two words appeared: EVENTFUL AZURE.

Joey glanced over at him. Her eyes held the frantic alertness of cornered prey. "That's him, isn't it?"

Evan tapped the screen.

Van Sciver's voice came through. "Code."

"You don't need to bother with that anymore," Evan said.

A long, static-free pause ensued. Van Sciver finally spoke again. "How did you hack this connection?"

"I didn't," Evan said. "I hacked your men instead."

He let Van Sciver digest that fact. Forty percent of his manpower, gone. Freelancers were replaceable, sure, but getting them vetted, up to operational standards, and read in on an Orphan mission took time. And time was a luxury Evan wasn't going to allow him. Van Sciver had lit the fuse the instant he'd put Jack in that Black Hawk.

Evan checked to see if the Wi-Fi connection had dropped, but they were still in range.

Van Sciver finally replied. "X."

"Y."

"I didn't figure you'd hang around the area. After you surface, you always go to ground."

"Things are different now."

"Ah, right. The old saw — 'This time it's personal.' I thought you were better than that."

Evan let the line hum.

"Jack jumped out of that helo himself," Van Sciver said. "You watched it with me. We didn't push him."

"But you were going to."

"Yes," Van Sciver said. "We were."

Evan pointed through the windshield, and Joey veered up the on-ramp, accelerating onto the 5.

"Can't blame me, can you?" Van Sciver said. "Hell, I learned it from you. To be ruthless."

"From me?"

"You had to be. You were never the best. Everyone loves a thoroughbred, sure. But they root for the underdog."

"Who's rooting, Charles?"

Van Sciver kept on. "Helluva move you pulled all those years ago back at the home. Beat me to the starting gate."

"That was long ago."

"It was the past, yes. And it's the present, too. You define me, Evan. Just like I define you."

Evan watched the headlights blur past on the freeway. He could sense Joey's gaze heavy on his face.

"The Mystery Man wanted me," Van Sciver said. "Not you."

"Yes," Evan said. "He did."

"We were so young. Remember when we thought he was important? Remember when he held all the power in the world?"

"I remember."

"Now he works for me. The Program's pared down, way down, but when I decided to recruit a little fresh blood . . . well, he's still the best. Though even *he* makes a mistake now and again. Like the girl. I'm sure she's told you all about it."

Joey's hands tightened on the wheel. Van Sciver's voice, deep and confident, was carrying from the receiver.

"A mistake," Evan echoed. "I asked her how to find you. She couldn't tell me anything. She's not even bait. She's useless."

Joey looked straight ahead, drove steady, but Evan could hear her breathing quicken.

"She's another stray mark we have to erase," Van Sciver said. "She knows my face."

"What's she gonna do? Hire a sketch artist? She doesn't have the skills. She's damaged goods. She's not even worth killing."

"Yeah, but Johns took her in, so I'm gonna kill her anyway. Because he took her in. Because that makes her important to you."

"Your call to make," Evan said. "If you think you can afford not to concentrate on me."

Van Sciver sounded amused. "You have no idea, do you? How high it goes?"

"What does that mean?"

He laughed. "You still think it's about me and you."

"That is all it's about," Evan said. "From the minute you took Jack."

The reception weakened and then came back, the Subaru skirting the edge of the Wi-Fi hot zone.

"For years I'd reconciled myself to living off the radar," Evan said. "I was content to hide in the shadows. To leave you alone. Not anymore."

Joey had inched above the speed limit, and Evan gestured for her to slow down.

"Evan," Van Sciver said. "That's what we're counting on."

The connection fizzled into static, then dropped.

Evan turned off the Samsung and pocketed it. He leaned to check the speedometer. "Keep it at sixty-five."

Joey's chest rose with each breath, her nostrils flaring. " 'Not worth killing?' " She shot his words back at him.

"Everything's strategic, Joey."

"Didn't seem that way to me."

"We don't have time for this," he said.

"What?"

He tore the dangling duct tape off the laptop and popped it open. "Your feelings."

They drove in silence.

24
A TEACHING MOMENT

Given the events at Portland Union Station, Evan decided to get Joey safely out of the state before parting ways. In the past he'd had a few near misses with Van Sciver around Los Angeles, so Van Sciver likely knew that Evan had a base there. Putting himself in Van Sciver's shoes, Evan figured he'd bulk up surveillance on routes leading south from Oregon. So rather than head for California, Evan and Joey rode the bell curve of the I-90, routing up through Washington and cutting across the chimney stack of Idaho.

They swapped seats at intervals, Evan driving the current leg. His attempts to access the laptop had been unsuccessful. The Dell Inspiron had proved to be heavily encrypted. Breaking in would require time, focus, and gear, none of which he could get until he had Joey off his hands.

Van Sciver's words returned, a whisper in

his ear: *You have no idea, do you? How high it goes? You still think it's about me and you.* No matter how many ways Evan turned the conversation over in his head, he couldn't make sense of it. Van Sciver was working off an agenda unknown to Evan.

That scared him.

It felt as though Van Sciver were sitting at the chessboard and Evan was a pawn.

It was ten hours and change to Helena, Montana, a destination chosen for its unlikeliness and because they had to cross three state lines to get there. His stomach started complaining in hour six. It had been nearly eighteen hours since he'd eaten.

Joey had finally dozed off, slumped against the passenger window, a spill of hair curled in the hollow of her neck. It was good to see her sleeping peacefully.

Evan pulled off at a diner, braking gently so as not to wake her. He parked behind the restaurant, out of sight from the road, and reached to shake her awake.

She jolted upright, shouting and swinging. "Get off me! Get *off* —"

Awareness came back into her eyes, and she froze, backed against the door, fists raised, legs pulled in, ready to kick.

Evan had leaned away, giving her as much space as possible. He'd taken the brunt of her fist off the top of his forehead. If he'd been a second slower, she would have re-broken his nose.

Her chest was still heaving. He waited for her to lower her shoulders, and then he relaxed his.

She unpacked from her protective curl, looked around. "Where are we?"

"I thought we'd get some food."

She straightened her clothes. "This isn't a thing, okay? Like some big window into me."

"Okay."

"You don't know anything about me. You don't know what happened to me. Or *didn't* happen to me."

"Okay."

"I just have a temper, is all."

Evan said, "I'd noticed."

They sat in a booth in the far back of the empty diner, Evan facing out. Despite the stuffing peeking through the cracked vinyl benches, the restaurant was clean and tidy and appealed to his sense of order. The aroma of strong coffee and fresh-baked pies thickened the air. A Wall-O-Matic jukebox perched at the end of their table, the Five Satins "shoo-doo 'n' shooby-doo"–ing in between hoping and praying. Salt and pepper shakers, syrup bottles, and sugar jars gathered around the shiny chrome speaker like children at story time.

From the old-school baseball pennants to the inevitable Marilyn poster, the manufactured nostalgia made the place seem like a location from a TV show, a faux diner set decorated to look like a real diner.

Evan ate egg whites scrambled with spinach and dosed heavily with Tabasco. Joey picked at a stack of pancakes, furrowing the pooled butter with the tines of her fork.

Conversation had been in short supply since the incident in the car.

Evan set down his fork, squaring it to the table's edges. A few drops of coffee formed a braille pattern next to his plate, remnants from the waitress's lazy pour. He resisted for a few seconds and then caved, wiping them clean with his napkin.

Joey remained fascinated with her pancakes. Her rucksack rested next to her, touching her thigh, the closely guarded life possessions of a street dweller.

Evan searched for something to say. He had no experience when it came to matters like this. His unconventional upbringing had turned him into something sleek and streamlined, but when he collided with the everyday, he felt blunt, unwieldy.

Then again, he supposed she wasn't very good at this either.

He watched her eviscerate her short stack.

"If you're fighting off an attacker — a *real* attacker — go for the throat or eyes," he finally said. "Up and under. If you swing for the head, he can just duck, protect his face, take the blow off the top of the forehead where the skull is thickest."

Her mouth gaped, but for once no words were forthcoming.

He sensed he had said something wrong.

"Are you seriously turning this into a *teaching* moment?" she said.

The best course of action, he decided, was to consider the question rhetorical.

But she pressed on. "Everything doesn't have to be some learning experience."

He thought of his upbringing in Jack's farmhouse, where every task and chore held the weight of one's character — making the bed, drying the dishes, lacing your boots.

How you do anything is how you do everything.

"Yes," Evan said. "It does."

"You've seen me fight," she said. "I know how to fight. That wasn't about fighting. It was just . . . a startle response."

"A startle response."

"Yes."

"You need a better startle response."

She shoved her plate away. "Look. I just got caught off guard."

"There is no 'off guard,' Joey. Not once you get on that bus in Helena. Not for a second. That's how it is. You know this."

She collected herself. Then nodded. "I do." She met his stare evenly. "Throat and eyes."

Though the sky still showed a uniform black, a few early-hours patrons filtered in — truckers with stiff hats, farmers with worn jeans and hands that rasped against their menus.

"You'll be okay," Evan said. "The farther you are from me, the safer you'll be."

"You heard him. He's not gonna let me go."

"He's gonna have his hands full."

"I think we're safer together."

"Like at your apartment? The train station? That pest-control shop in Central Eastside?"

She held up her hands. "We're here, aren't we? And they're not."

The sugary scent of the syrup roiled his stomach. "This isn't — can't be — good for you."

"I can handle it."

"You're sixteen."

"What were *you* doing at sixteen?" She glared at him. "Well? Was it good for you? Or is that different? Because, you know, I'm a girl."

"I don't care that you're a girl. I care that you're safe. And where I'm going? It's not gonna be safe."

A patter of footsteps announced the waitress's approach. "I just started my shift, and already I'm winded trudging all the way to you two back here." She grabbed her ample chest, made a show of catching her breath.

Evan managed a smile.

"Anything else I can get you or your daughter, sweetie?"

Evan touched her gently on the side, not low enough to be disrespectful. "Just the check, thanks."

"It's really nice, you know, to see. A road trip. I wish my daddy spent time with me like that."

As she dug in her apron pocket, Joey gave her a look that bordered on toxic.

The waitress pointed at her with the corner of the check. "Mark my words, you'll appreciate this one day."

She spun on her heel, a practiced flourish, and left them.

The bill had been deposited demurely

facedown. Evan laid two twenties across it, started to slide out.

Joey said, "I didn't do it."

He paused. "What?"

"The duffel bag. The guy. I didn't do it. I couldn't pull the trigger."

Evan let his weight tug him back into the seat. He folded his hands. Gave her room to talk. Or to not talk.

She took her time. Then she said, "I stood there with the gun aimed, Van Sciver at my back. And I couldn't."

"What did he do?"

"He took the gun out of my hand. And showed me . . ." Her lips trembled, and she pressed her knuckles against them, hard. "The mag was empty. It was just a test. And I failed. If I'd done it, if I'd passed the test, I could've been like —" She caught herself, broke off the thought.

"Could've been like what?"

"Like you."

Silence asserted itself around them. Kitchen sounds carried to their booth, pots clanking, grills sizzling. In a booming voice, the short-order cook was telling the staff that he hadn't had much luck with the rainbow trout but he had a new spinning lure that just might do the trick.

"Van Sciver unzipped the duffel, let the

guy out. He was acting all along. Probably some psyops instructor. Van Sciver said he was gonna walk him out, that I should wait there for him. But the thing is?" Her voice hushed. "I noticed something standing there, looking down at the duffel bag. It had a smudge of blood on the lining. And I knew that I hadn't just failed the test. I'd failed Van Sciver. And at some point it would be me in that duffel bag and another kid outside it. And when *that* happened? The gun wouldn't be empty."

She sat back, breaking the spell of the memory. "That raised office in the hangar, it had a window with a shitty lock. I kept a hairpin hidden in my hair. I thought it'd be wise to GTFO before he got back. So I did. I was on the run eleven months until Jack."

"How'd Jack find you?"

The distinctive ring sounded so out of place here among the retro candy-apple-red vinyl and Elvis clocks and display counter up front stocked with Dentine. It was a ring from another place, another life, another dimension.

It was the RoamZone.

Someone needed the Nowhere Man.

25
HONOR-BOUND

The RoamZone's caller ID generated a reverse directory, autolinking to a Google Earth map of Central L.A. Evan zoomed in on a single-story residence in the Pico-Union neighborhood.

The phone rang again. And again.

Evan's thumb hovered over the TALK button.

He could not answer this call. It was out of the question. He had a girl to unload. A laptop to hack into. A death to avenge.

Jack's murder had sent Evan's life careening sharply off course. His dying message had shattered any semblance Evan retained of order, routine, procedure. He should be home right now, concerned only with his vodka supply and his next workout. Instead he was in a diner outside Missoula, stacking his proverbial plate higher and higher until everything on it threatened to topple.

Why hadn't Jack made arrangements for

Joey? Why had he saddled Evan with her? Jack had known that Evan had his own honor-bound obligations as the Nowhere Man. Jack had known that being a lone wolf had been drummed into Evan's cells — hell, Jack had done the drumming himself. Jack had to have known that Joey would be an inconvenient aggravation at the very moment that Evan's universe would compress down in the service of a single goal — the annihilation of Charles Van Sciver.

An unsettling thought occurred. What if there was some design behind the plan? Jack's teachings always carried a hint of back-alley Zen to them.

If you don't know what you don't know, how can you know what to learn?

But why this? What could Evan possibly have to gain from this disruption?

Everything doesn't have to be a learning experience.

And Jack answered him, as clearly as if he'd been facing him across the breakfast table in that quiet farmhouse in the Virginia woods.

Yes. It does.

Evan banished the thought. There was no design. No artful master plan. Jack had found himself at the end of the road and had sent up a flare because he'd been desperate and needed Evan to clean up his mess.

It was nothing more.

Joey was staring at him. "You gonna answer that?"

Another ring.

He clenched his teeth, gave Joey a firm look. "Do not speak."

Her nod was rushed, almost eager.

He answered as he always did. "Do you need my help?"

"Yes. Please, yes."

The man's gravelly voice had a tightness to it not uncommon for people calling the number for the first time. Like he was forcing the words up and out. A heavy accent, Hispanic but not Mexican. It was just past four in the morning. Evan imagined the man pacing in his little house, clutched in the talons of late-night dread, working up the courage to dial.

Joey had gone bolt upright, her elbows ledging the table, darkly fascinated.

"What's your name?" Evan asked.

"Benito Orellana. They have my son, Xavier —"

"Where did you get this number?"

"A girl find me — her cousin is friend with my cousin's boy. She is called Anna Rezian. She is from good Armenian family."

Evan had never — not once — conducted a Nowhere Man call in the presence of someone else. Though he trusted Joey sufficiently to answer the phone in front of her, her presence felt intrusive. He wondered if this was what intimacy felt like. And if so, why anyone would want it.

Evan said, "Describe her."

"She have the thin face. Her hair, it have missing patches. She is sweet girl, but she is troubled."

"Who has your son?"

"I cannot speak the name." The deep voice fluttered with fear.

"They kidnapped him?" Evan asked.

"No," the man said. "He has joined them. And he cannot get out."

"A gang?"

A silence, broken only by labored breathing.

"If you don't talk to me, I can't help you."

"*Sí.* A gang. But you don't know this gang. Please, sir. My boy. They will turn him into a killer. And then he will be lost. I'm going to lose my boy. Please help me. You're all I have left."

"Sir, if your son joined a gang of his own volition, I can't help him. Or you."

Beneath the words Evan sensed the pulse of his own relief. He couldn't take this on as well. His focus was already maxed, the plate stacked too high. The Seventh Commandment — *One mission at a time* — blinked a red alert in his mind's eye.

Evan pulled the phone away from his face to hang up. His finger reached the button when he heard it.

The man, sobbing quietly.

Evan held the phone before him against the backdrop of his wiped-clean plate, the sounds of hoarse weeping barely audible.

He blinked a few times. Joey was like a statue, every muscle tightened, her body like an arrow pointed over the table at him. Breathless.

Evan drew in a deep inhalation. He brought the phone back to his cheek. Listened a moment longer, his eyes squeezed shut.

"Mr. Orellana?"

"*¿Sí?*"

"I see the location you're calling from. I'll be there tomorrow at noon."

"Thank God for you —"

Evan had already hung up. He slid out of the booth, Joey walking with him to the back door. She shot glances across at him, her face unreadable.

He pushed through the chiming door into the parking lot, the predawn cold hitting him at the hands and neck. He raised the set of keys he'd lifted from the waitress's apron and aimed at the scattered cars, clicking the auto-unlock button on the fob. Across the lot a Honda Civic with a rusting hood gave a woeful chirp.

The waitress's shift had just started, which gave them six hours of run time. Even so, he'd steal a license plate at the first truck stop they saw, from a vehicle boondocking in an overnight lot.

He and Joey got into the Civic, their doors shutting in unison.

She was still staring at him. He hesitated, his hand on the key.

He said, "This is what I do."

"Right, I get it," she said. "You help people you *don't* know."

26
How Can You Know You're Real?

Dawn finally crested, a crack in a night that seemed by now to have lasted for days. Evan pushed the headlights toward the golden seam at the horizon, closing in on Helena. In the passenger seat, Joey had retreated into a sullenness as thick and impenetrable as the blackness still crowding the cones of the headlights.

By the time he reached the Greyhound bus station, a flat, red-roofed building aproned with patches of xeriscaping, the morning air had taken on the grainy quality of a newspaper photo. Frilly clouds fringed a London-gray sky.

He drove twice around the block, scouting for anything unusual. It looked clear. The three-state drive had served them well.

He pulled into the parking lot and killed the engine.

They stared at the bus station ahead. It looked as though it had been a fast-food

215

restaurant in the not-too-distant past. A few buses slumbered in parallel, slotted into spots before a long, low bench. There was no one around.

Evan said, "They start leaving in twenty minutes. I'll pick one headed far away. When you get there, contact me as we discussed. I can send you money and IDs —"

"I don't want your money. I don't want your IDs."

"Think this through, Joey. We've got three Orphans and fifteen freelancers circling. How are you gonna make it?"

"Like I always have. On my own." She chewed her lower lip. "These last few months with Jack? They were a daydream, okay? Now it's back to life."

A band of his face gazed back from the rearview. The bruises beneath his eyes had faded but still gave him the slightly wild, insomniac look of someone who'd been down on his luck for too long.

"Listen," he said. "I have to honor Jack's last wish —"

"I don't give a shit. Honestly. I don't need you." She reached into the backseat and yanked her rucksack into her lap. "What? You think I thought you were my friend?" She gave a humorless laugh. "Let's just get this over with."

She got out, and Evan followed.

She headed for the bench outside while he went in and bought her a ticket, a routine they'd established at the train station in Portland. He tucked a thousand dollars into the ticket sleeve and stepped back outside.

She was sitting on the bench, hugging her rucksack. Her jeans were torn at the knees, ovals of brown skin showing through. He handed her the ticket.

"Where am I going?" she asked.

"Milwaukee."

She took the bulging ticket. "Thank you," she said. "For everything. I mean it."

Evan nodded. He shifted his body weight to walk away, but his legs didn't listen. He was still standing there.

She said, "What?"

Evan cleared his throat. "I never knew my mom," he said. "Or my dad. Jack was the first person who ever really *saw* me." He swallowed, which was harder than he would have expected. "If no one sees you, how can you know you're real?" He had Joey's complete attention. He would have preferred a little less of it. It took him a moment to get out the next words. "Van Sciver took that from me. I need to set it straight. Not just for Jack. But for me. And I can't have anything or anyone in my way."

She said, "I get it."

He nodded and left her on the bench.

He got back into the Civic and drove off.

One distraction down.

If he stopped only for gas, he'd make it home in seventeen hours. Then he could hack into the laptop belonging to Van Sciver's muscle and follow where it led. Tomorrow at noon he'd see about helping Benito Orellana. He still had plenty to do and an unforgiving timeline.

The Honda's worn tires thrummed along the road. The windows started to steam up from his body heat. He pictured Jack's writing scrawled there.

GET PACKAGE.

Jack's final words.

His dying wish.

Evan cranked on the defroster, watched the air chase the fog from the panes.

He said, "I'm sorry."

He's the best part of me.

Again he remembered waking up in that dormer bedroom his first morning in Jack's house, the crowns of oak trees unfurled beyond his window like some magical cloud cover. He remembered how trepidatious he'd been padding down the stairs, finding Jack in his armchair in his den. And Jack's gift to him on that first morning of his new life: *My wife's maiden name was Smoak. With an* a *in the middle and no* e *on the end. Want that one?*

Sure.

Evan screeched the car over onto the shoulder of the road. Gravel dust from the tires blew past the windshield. He looked for patterns in the swirling dust, saw only chaos.

He struck the steering wheel hard with the heels of his hands.

Then he made a U-turn.

He parked in the same spot, climbed out. A bus was pulling in, blocking the bench. For a moment he thought she was already gone.

But then he stepped around the bus, and there she was, sitting in precisely the same position he'd left her in, hugging the rucksack, her feet pressed to the concrete.

She sensed his approach, looked up.

"Let's go," he said.

She rose and followed him back to the car.

27

NEVER BEEN AND NEVER WAS
AND NEVER WILL BE

The man was ill. That much was easy to see. A tic seized his face every few seconds, making him shake his head as if clearing water from an ear.

He'd once been a paragon of excellence, one of the finest weapons in the government's arsenal. And now this.

He clutched a rat-chewed sleeping bag. Dirt crusted his earlobe. He wore sweatpants over jeans to ward off the cold.

He jittered from foot to foot, then halted abruptly and screwed the toe of his sneaker into the earth, back and forth, back and forth. He was mumbling to himself, spillage from a brain in tatters. Gray hair, gray stubble, gray skin, a face caving it on itself.

Jack had come to Alabama to find him.

But locating a homeless man was like trying to find a glass cup in a swimming pool. Hard to know where to start and easy to miss even when you're looking right at it.

Yet Van Sciver had resources that Jack didn't.

It had taken some time, but now here they were, in the shadow of the freeway overpass. Commuters whizzed by above them, an ordinary Birmingham morning in ordinary motion, but down here among the puddles and heaps of wind-blown trash, they might've been the last humans on earth. Nearby a fire guttered in a rusted trash can, the stench of burning plastic singeing the air.

The man convulsed again, one shoulder twisting up, plugging his ear. Van Sciver reached out and clamped the man's jaw, the hand so big it encircled the lower half of his face.

The man stilled. Van Sciver stared into his mossy brown eyes. Saw nothing but tiny candlelight flickers from the trash-can fire behind him.

Van Sciver said, "Orphan C."

The man did not reply.

Around the concrete bend, Van Sciver could hear Thornhill shooing away the last of the homeless from the makeshift encampment. They were skittish and tractable and had good reason to be. There'd been a rash of attacks against the community of late, a neo-Nazi group curb-stomping victims in

221

the night, lighting them on fire.

Van Sciver snapped his fingers in front of the man's nose. The man jerked away. The tic seized him once more, the skin of his cheeks shuddering beneath Van Sciver's hand. Van Sciver squeezed harder, firming the man's head.

"Do you remember Jack Johns?" Van Sciver asked.

"I'm dead Orphan dead man walking never knew never never knew."

"Back in 1978 Jack Johns conducted your psyops training. Nine sessions at Fort Bragg. Have you been in touch with him since?"

"The woman's head like an open bowl it was an open bowl and I did it used to kill people for a living you know used to kill them and poof I'd be gone and no one ever knew no one ever knew anything ever knew me I never knew me never did."

"Did Jack Johns ever mention Orphan X?"

The man's eyes widened. His tongue bulged his lower lip. "Don't know don't never he's a ghost he's never been and never was and never will be."

"Do you know anything about Orphan X?"

The man's eyes achieved a momentary clarity. "No one does."

Van Sciver released the man, and he staggered back. Van Sciver knew from Orphan C's file that he was fifty-seven years old. He could've passed for eighty.

The last medical tests before he'd retired and dropped out of sight had shown the beginnings of traumatic brain injury, likely from a rocket-propelled grenade that had nearly gotten him in Brussels. Since then he'd deteriorated further, PTSD accelerating what the physical trauma had begun, taking him apart piece by piece. It made him unsafe, a glitchy hard drive walking around unsecured.

"R!" Van Sciver called out.

Thornhill ducked back through a sagging chain-link fence and jogged over, sinew shifting beneath his T-shirt. He wasn't wearing his usual shoes today.

He was wearing steel-plated boots.

"I'm done here," Van Sciver said. "He's got nothing for us." He regarded the man again, felt something akin to sadness. "There's nothing left to get."

The man's face seized again, and he tweaked forward, facial muscles straining. "People taking and taking like bites little piranha bites until there's nothing left until they've nibbled you down to the bone and you're dead a skeleton held together by

223

tendons just tendons."

"I got this," Thornhill said, putting his arm around the man and walking him to the drain. "Come on, buddy. You're okay. You're good."

The man shuddered but went with him.

Van Sciver folded his arms across his broad chest and watched.

"I'm sorry you've had a rough time," Thornhill told the man. "It's not your fault. None of this is your fault. You can't help what you are. Hell — none of us can."

The man nodded solemnly, picked at the scruff sprouting from his jaundiced neck.

Thornhill removed a can of spray paint from his jacket pocket, gave it a few clanking shakes, and started to spray something on the concrete by the drain. The man watched him nervously.

"I knew a guy," Thornhill said, the sprayed lines coming together to form a giant swastika. "Loved dogs. Had a whole raft of them taking over his house, sleeping on his couches, everywhere. Well, one day he's out driving and sees a sign on the road. Someone's giving away baby wolves."

He pocketed the can of spray paint, set his hands on the man's shoulders, and turned him around. Then he knocked the back of the man's leg gently with his own kneecap and steered him down so he was kneeling before the drain.

"So he figures what the hell. He takes this baby wolf home, raises him just like a dog. Feeds it, shelters it, even lets it sleep on his bed. The wolf gets bigger, as wolves do, grows up. And one morning just like any morning, this guy, he's building a shed, fires a nail gun right through his shoe."

Thornhill tilted the man forward toward the raised strip of concrete running above the drain. "There you go. Just lie forward on your chest." He positioned the man. "So this guy comes limping through his backyard, scent of blood in the air. His dogs are all frantic, worried. Can sense his pain, right? They're worried for him. But that wolf? The wolf doesn't see a problem. He sees an *opportunity.*"

Thornhill reached down, opened the man's jaw, set his open mouth on the concrete ridge. "So he tears out his owner's throat." The man was trembling, his stubble glistening with trapped tears, but he did not resist. He made muffled noises against the concrete lip. Thornhill leaned over him, mouth to his ear. "Because that wolf was just biding his time. Waiting, you see, for his owner to show the tiniest vulnerability." Almost tenderly, he repositioned the man's head. "No matter how docile it seems, a wolf will always be a wolf."

Thornhill reared back to his full height, his shadow blanketing Orphan C. Thornhill firmed his body, raised one of his steel-plated boots over the back of C's head.

Van Sciver climbed into the passenger side of the Chevy Tahoe. Even with the armored door closed, he heard the wet smack.

That was okay. Yesterday had given them a pair of solid leads. C had been the least promising of the two.

On to the next.

Van Sciver opened his notebook and peered at the address he'd written inside. This one held his greatest hope.

Outside, Thornhill tugged off his boots and threw them into the trash-can fire.

Van Sciver removed his phone from the glove box and called Orphan V.

28
HER VERSION OF NORMAL

In a McMansion in the impressively named and decidedly unhilly gated community of Palm Hills, Candy McClure strode through the kitchen wearing two oven mitts patterned with cartoon drawings of the Eiffel Tower.

Classy.

Her fuck-me lips, which would be her best feature if there weren't so many to choose from, were clamped around a candy cane. Sucking. She'd plumped them out further with lip liner and tinted gloss, which made things entirely unfair for anyone with hot blood in his — or her — veins. This was by design.

She had more assets than the other Orphans, and she was unafraid to deploy them.

Contour-fitting Lululemon yoga pants and a muscle tank gripped her firm body, showing off everything she had to show off while hiding everything she needed to hide.

Such as the scar tissue that turned her back and shoulders into an angry, swirling design better suited to pahoehoe lava than to human skin.

She leaned forward and removed a fresh apple pie from the oven. It smelled wonderful. On the counter rested a bag of powdered sugar, a tub of shortening, and a flask of concentrated hydrofluoric acid, effective at dissolving flesh and bone.

She was a domestic goddess.

On the easy-care quartz-topped island, her phone chimed. She flung off the mitts, leaned beneath the hanging copper pots, and picked up.

Her boss's voice came through. "Code."

She glanced at the screen. " 'Iridescent motor,' " she said. "My nickname in high school."

"Are you still undercover?"

Steam rose lazily from the pie. A lawn mower started up somewhere outside. Curlicue writing on her apron read *"Kiss The Baker!"*

She said, "*Deep* cover."

"Target identified?"

She smiled, felt the peppermint seep between her teeth, cool and tingly. "Yeppers."

She pulled her red notebook over from its

place by the salt and pepper shakers, tapped it with a Pilot FriXion pen. The notebook held her extensive and detailed mission notes. And a new recipe for delicious shortbread cookies.

For nearly two weeks, she'd been living here in this steamy slice of Boca Raton paradise, drawing the attention of the men and the ire of their wives. She'd been tasked with identifying who in the upscale community was on the verge of bundling $51 million in a super PAC opposing Jonathan Bennett. Van Sciver had backtracked bank records and data comms and found that someone in Palm Hills had masterminded the operation from a rogue cell-phone tower. Given that the negative campaign threatening to hit the airwaves was the start of a push for post-election impeachment, it was no wonder the mastermind was doing his best to keep his machinations — quite literally — off the grid.

So Orphan V had moved into the neighborhood and was doing a suburban divorcée hot-as-fuck desperate-housewife routine, renting the house for a few weeks as her post-signing-of-the-papers "gift to herself." She mingled with the denizens and took plenty of night walks, surveilling who might be in their backyard or on the roof, erecting or disassembling a ghost GSM base station.

Last night she'd watched him through the slats of a no-shit white picket fence as he'd toiled red-faced over a tripod and a Yagi directional antenna.

"Neutralize now," Van Sciver said. "I need you on X."

Her expression changed. Orphan X always took priority.

"Something rang the cherries," Van Sciver continued. "It requires your feminine wiles. Finish now, get clear, contact me for mission orders."

She said, "Copy that."

The call disconnected.

Time to clean up.

She placed the notebook on the rotating glass turntable of the microwave and turned it on. Pocketing her flask of hydrofluoric acid, she cast a wistful gaze at the apple pie. She'd grown oddly fond of this house and her time here in Stepfordia, nestled into real life — or at least a simulation of it. Living among families, privy to their hidden resentments and petty squabbles. Yesterday at the country-club pool, she'd witnessed a disagreement over sunscreen application escalate into a battle worthy of the History Channel. She enjoyed her neighbors' small triumphs, too. Billy learning to ride a two-wheeler. A husband rushing out to the driveway to help his wife carry in her groceries. Teaching the new puppy to heel.

Candy had made a home here. A new wardrobe displayed on hangers in the walk-in. Essential oils by the bathtub to soothe her burns. Microfiber sheets on the bed, so soft against her aching skin. Satin sheets worked, too, of course, but they always seemed too porny.

The microwave dinged. She removed the notebook and, on her way out, dumped it into the trash atop a confetti heap of apple peelings.

She paused in the foyer, taking in the sweep of the staircase.

How odd to have grown fond of this place.

Was it a sign of weakness? Since Orphan X had inflicted the hydrofluoric-acid burn on her, Candy sometimes woke up late at night gasping for air, her back on fire. In those first breathless moments, she swore she could feel her deficiencies burrowing into her, seeping through her flawed, throbbing flesh, infecting her core. The sensation had worsened since last month. In an alley outside Sevastopol, one of Candy's colleagues had turned a beautiful young Crimean Tatar girl into collateral damage.

Candy didn't mind killing. She thrived on

it. But this one had been unnecessary and the girl so sweet and lost. She'd come up the alley and seen something she shouldn't have. Right up until she was stabbed in the neck with a pen, she'd been offering to help.

Her name had been Halya Bardakçi. She visited Candy in the late hours, her sweet, almond-shaped face a salve for the pain. She could have been fifteen or twenty — it was hard to tell with these too-attractive-for-their-age streetwalker types — but Candy had felt her death differently.

Like a part of herself had died in that alley, too.

A craven sentiment, unbefitting an Orphan.

She shuddered off the notion, turned her thoughts to stepping through her faux-Tuscan iron front door. She loved heading out into the community. She got so much attention here.

She stretched down and touched her toes, feeling the tight fabric cling to her, a second skin more beautiful than her own. Then she walked outside, putting on her best divorcée prance and twirling her tongue around the sharp point of the candy cane.

The entire street alerted to her presence. The snot-nosed fifteen-year-old across the street rode his hoverboard into a tree. Long-suffering Mr. Henley swung to chart Candy's course to the driveway, watering no longer the begonias but his wife's comfortable shoes.

Candy reached the RYNO one-wheel motorcycle she'd parked in the driveway. Before putting on the helmet, she took the candy cane's length down her throat and held it there. She was good like that.

She straddled the electronic bike and motored down to the club. It took a bit of balance, but not as much as you'd think. It moved at the pace of a stroll, ten miles per hour.

Whereas all the other Orphans strove to blend in, Candy preferred to stand out. When people looked at her, they weren't really seeing her. They were seeing their fantasy of her. At a moment's notice, she could bind her chest, change her hair, alter her dress, and transform into someone else. And all those gawkers would realize — they'd never really seen her at all.

Right now she was interested in creating an alibi. Which meant being noticed.

At that she excelled.

She parked the RYNO at the country club between a yellow Ferrari and the tennis pro's beleaguered Jetta. She unscrewed her head from the helmet and shook her honey locks free. The curve of the candy cane rested snug against her cheek. She produced the red-and-white-striped length from her throat and got back to sucking.

The towel boy did a double take, his jaw open in mid-chew, the dot of his gum glowing against perfect molars. An elderly foursome paused on the facing tennis court, the ball bouncing untouched between two of the partners. A trio of wattle-necked women sipping iced tea tsk-tsked to one another as Candy blew past.

Three seconds, eight eyewitness.

Not bad.

Candy entered the club, breezing by reception, and walked down a rubber-matted hall into the eucalyptus-scented women's locker room. She locked herself in the spacious handicapped toilet stall.

A toilet stall that happened to have a window overlooking the back of the golf course's little-used eighteenth hole.

She squirmed out the window, hit the grass silently. Moved twenty yards behind the building to a familiar white picket fence.

She hurdled it.

She walked up to the rear sliding door, her luscious lips making an O around the stalk of the candy cane.

Her target sat at a sun-drenched workstation off the kitchen. He was shirtless, horizontal parentheses of untanned skin delineating the paunch of his hairy belly.

She leaned toward the glass. "Knock-knock."

She didn't want to touch the pane and leave prints.

He caught sight of her and found his feet in a hurry, fumbling at the lock.

"Hi, hello, welcome," he said. "Wow."

She floated inside. "Wow yourself."

She glanced at his workstation, where two monitors ran stock-price tickers, an endless stream of industry. A financial titan like him would have so, so many enemies, which meant so, so many convenient investigative trails.

"You're renting the house on Black Mangrove Street," he told her.

She leaned close. "You've been keeping tabs on me?"

He was sweating. She had that effect on men.

"Why are you in my backyard? I mean — don't get me wrong — I'm delighted, but . . ." He lost the thread of the sentence.

She had that effect, too.

She slid the candy cane out of her mouth. "It's more *private,*" she said, shaping her lips around the word, making it something dirty.

He blinked several times rapidly. His own meaty lips twitched. He scratched at a shoulder. "Okay. Um. That's nice. Private's nice."

A billion-dollar hedge-funder reduced to a teenager at a school mixer.

She placed a hand on his cheek, which was sticky with sweat. A breath shuddered out of him. He closed his eyes. She moved her hand up to his hair, grabbed his thinning curls, and tugged back his head.

He gave a little groan of pleasure.

Then she rammed the sharpened candy cane into his jugular.

The first gush painted the monitors. Arterial spurts were always mesmerizing. He went down fast, hand clamped to his neck, legs cycling on the cool tile floor. Then they stopped cycling.

She stared down at him. Dead people looked so common.

She removed her flask, poured hydrofluoric acid into the wound, the familiar scent rising as it ate through flesh. That would take care of any DNA from her saliva. She crossed to the kitchen sink, dropped the candy cane down the disposal, and ran it, pouring in a dose of hydrofluoric acid for good measure.

She picked up the cordless phone, called 911, wiped the buttons clean with a wet dish rag, and set it on the counter. The coroner would reach a precise time of death eventually, but why not help him out?

She walked out the open back door, hopped the white picket fence, and jogged along the rear of the clubhouse, breathing in the fresh-cut grass of the golf course. She'd miss it, being here, being normal. Her vacation had come to an end, but she had another "gift to herself" in mind.

Catching Orphan X and making him feel every ounce of pain that she lived with day and night.

She crawled through the window back into the toilet stall, walked out of the bathroom, turned left into the crowded gym, and mounted the StairMaster.

Beneath her shirt her ruined skin itched and burned, but she blocked out the pain. She'd keep at it for two hours, time enough for the cops to arrive and find Mr. Super PAC back-floating in a pool of his own blood.

So many residents could say precisely where the fetching divorcée had been since the moment she stepped out of her rented house this morning.

The gym was mirrored from wall to wall, and in the countless reflections, she could see every eye on her.

After all, Candy could work a StairMaster.

29
END-STOPPED

As they barreled along the freeway, Joey reached into the backseat to retrieve the laptop that Evan had taken from the head-quarters in Portland. She fired it up, then flexed her fingers like a gymnast about to tackle the uneven bars.

Evan glanced over from the driver's seat. "Careful you don't trip an autoerase —"

"Yeah," she said. "I got it."

He drove for a while as she clicked around. The late-morning sun beat down on the windshield, cooking the cracked dashboard.

A pine-tree air freshener long past expiration spun in circles from the rearview. Above the speedometer a hula girl bobbed epileptically on a bent spring.

"Finding anything?"

Joey held up a wait-a-sec finger. "This is some heavy-ass encryption."

"Can you break it?"

"I don't know."

" 'I don't know' isn't an answer."

"Thanks, *Jack.*" Her fingers skittered across the keyboard. It was like watching someone play an instrument. "I'll tell you this, *you* certainly couldn't."

"Yes or no, Joey."

"There are maybe a handful of people in the world who could hack this," she finally said, " 'n' I'm one of them. But it'll take some time. And a fast Internet connection."

"Van Sciver knows you're with me. So we have to assume he knows you can get to whatever information's guarded in there. He trained you."

"Please. I was better than him to begin with. It's the only thing I had, growing up. We're talking sixteen, eighteen hours a day online, checking out 2600, using the dark-net and stuff. I put in lots of private IRC hacker chat-room time, too, like, browsing the chans, vulns, and sploit databases, fooling around with Scapy, Metasploit, all that. It was one of my selling points. Back when I was, you know, a wanted commodity. Before I was useless." She grinned and closed the lid. "He knows I'm good but has no idea *how* good."

"Once we hit L.A., I'll set you up in a safe house. I want what's in that laptop as quickly as possible."

"I'm gonna require a crate of Red Bull and a Costco tub of Twizzlers."

"You'll have what you need."

"And Zac Efron. I want Zac Efron."

"Who's Zac Efron?"

"God, you're old." She smiled, and it was like turning on a light, her face luminous. She observed him observing her. "What?"

"I haven't seen you smile."

She looked back at the road. "Don't get used to it."

As the Civic filled with gas, Evan scanned the parking lot and the freeway. Joey climbed out and stretched like a cat, slow and luxurious.

"Want any road food?" she asked.

"Road food?"

"Corn nuts, Slim Jims, Mountain Dew?"

"I'm good."

She brushed past him, heading inside. "Don't leave me here."

He looked at her. "Why would I leave you here?"

She shrugged, not breaking stride.

They were heading south on the I-15, Idaho ten exits away. Borders were always tricky — choke points, easy to surveil. So far it had been smooth sailing, but so far hadn't been long.

The gas pump clicked off, and Evan got back into the car to wait for Joey. Her rucksack tilted in the passenger-side foot well. Another greeting card had fallen out.

Evan leaned over and picked it up.

A cartoon of a nervous-looking turkey against a backdrop of orange and yellow leaves. Fresh concern pulled at Evan. He opened the card.

Sweet Girl,

I hope you have lots to be thankful for this Thanksgiving of your 16th year! Know that even though we're apart, I miss you and hold you in my heart.

Xoxo, M.

Again it seemed that Joey had read the card many times. Creases, wrinkled corners, a patch of ink worn off where she'd held it.

Thanksgiving. Your 16th year.

That was troubling.

He set the card on her seat and waited.

She approached, chewing gum, and opened the door. She spotted the card, hesitated, then picked it up and climbed in slowly. She stared straight through the windshield at the air pump. She smelled like Bubblicious.

"Why are you going through my stuff?"

"It fell out of your rucksack."

"Answer my question."

"There are more important questions. Like who is M and how did she have your address?"

"What do you mean 'my address'?"

"This is a Thanksgiving card. Thanksgiving was last Thursday. You were in the apartment Jack had set up for you. And Jack was in Alabama. No one should have known how to reach you."

"No one did know how to reach me."

"Joey, what if this is how they found your apartment?"

"Look, I promise you, it's okay."

"Who is M?"

Scowling, Joey grabbed her hair in a fist and pulled it high, showing the shaved side of her head.

"Joey, we have to have total trust. Or none of this works."

She took in a lungful of air, let it out slowly. "She's my maunt."

"Your maunt?"

"My aunt, but more like a mom. Get it?"

"Yes."

"She raised me until she couldn't, okay? Then I went into the system for a lotta years. Until Van Sciver's guy pulled me out."

"How did she know where to send you

this Thanksgiving card?"

Joey's eyes filled with tears. It was so sudden, so unexpected that Evan's breath tangled in his throat.

She said, slowly, "It's not a risk, okay? I promise you. If we have total trust, trust me on this."

"They can track anything, Joey."

She tilted her head back, blinked away the tears. Then she turned to him, fully composed. It was a different face, stone cold and rock steady, the face of an Orphan. "I am end-stopped there. Completely end-stopped."

He stared at her a moment longer, deciding whether or not he believed her. Then he fired up the engine and pulled away from the pump.

Evan's focus intensified as they neared the border. He kept it on rotation between the mirrors, the on-ramps, the cars ahead. He changed speeds and lanes.

Meanwhile Joey changed channels on the radio, responding with enthusiasm or disgust to various songs that Evan found indistinguishable from one another.

Despite everything, she was still sixteen.

A hunter-green 4Runner had been behind them for a while now. White male driver, wispy beard. Evan pulled to the right lane and slowed down, timing it so another car shielded them from view as the 4Runner drove past. The driver did not ease off the gas or adjust his mirror. Which meant he was either not interested or well trained.

Ensuring that passing drivers didn't get a clean look at them was no easy task on a seventeen-hour road trip. Van Sciver's people would be looking for a man traveling with a teenage girl — not an uncommon combination but not common either. The Honda's windows had been treated with an aftermarket tint, which helped decrease visibility. The sun was near its peak, turning the windshields into blinding sheets of gold, another momentary benefit.

A truck pulling a horse trailer sidled up alongside them. Evan tapped the brake, tucking into the blind spot.

"Hold on," Joey said, cranking up the volume. "Listen — this is my jam."

He listened.

It was not his jam.

The horse trailer exited. He watched it bank left and amble up into the hills.

At last the billboard flashed past: WEL-COME TO IDAHO! THE "GEM STATE."

While Joey bounced in the passenger seat, the Gem State flew by in a streak of brown.

Scrubby flats, a few twists carved through hills, more scrubby flats.

The gas needle had wound down to a quarter tank by the time he pulled off. The service plaza was at the top of a rise, a mini-golf bump in the terrain with good visibility in all directions.

A single strip of parking lined the front of the plaza, which made for easy scouting. Of the vehicles only a blue Volvo pinged Evan's mental registry, but when it had passed twenty miles back, he'd noted three children quarreling in the back.

After he'd filled the tank, he and Joey went into the plaza, splitting up as was their protocol. Joey drifted up the junk-food aisle while Evan dumped four bottled waters and a raft of energy bars before the register. As the woman rang him up, he caught sight of his reflection in the mirrored lenses of a pair of cheap sunglasses on the counter display.

The bruises beneath his eyes made him conspicuous. Memorable.

He snapped off the price tag, laid it on the counter, and put on the glasses. They'd be helpful for the moment, but he'd require something less obvious. He remembered Lorilee in the elevator, how she'd concealed the finger marks where her boyfriend had grabbed her.

"Just a second, please," he told the lady at the register.

One aisle over he found a cheap beige concealer.

Joey appeared, pressing a bag of Doritos to his chest. She took in his sunglasses with amusement. "Nice look," she said. "Did you misplace your fighter jet?"

"Don't worry. I'm getting this." He held up the concealer wand. "I'd ask to borrow yours, but I didn't figure you for the makeup type."

"I wouldn't exactly call our last few outings makeupworthy," she said. "But you couldn't use mine anyways. I'm browner than you. Thank God."

He headed back to the counter and laid the concealer and chips on top of the energy bars.

The woman gave a smile. "Picking up some makeup for the missus?"

"Yes, ma'am."

She handed him the plastic bag.

Joey was waiting outside, her arms crossed, staring through a patch of skinny trees down the long ramp to the freeway.

"What?" Evan asked.

She flicked her chin.

A hunter-green 4Runner exited the freeway and started up the slope toward the service plaza.

30
DO YOUR BUSINESS

Evan pulled Joey around the side of the building. They stood on the browning grass beneath the window of the men's room, peering around the corner at the travel plaza's entrance. A good vantage.

"That truck," she said. "Kept time with us for at least forty miles."

He thought of her bobbing in her seat, singing along to the radio. "I didn't think you were paying attention."

"That's my superpower."

"What?"

"Being underestimated."

The men's-room window above them was cracked open, emitting the pungent scent of urinal cakes. Through the gap they heard someone whistle, spit, and unzip. Evan set the shopping bag on the ground.

They waited.

The 4Runner finally came into view, cresting the rise.

It crept along the line of parked vehicles, slowing as it passed the Civic. The driver eased forward, closer to the pumps, and stopped with the grille pointed at the on-ramp below.

"Hmm," Joey said.

Evan leaned closer to the building's edge, Joey's hair brushing his neck. They were thirty or so yards away from the 4Runner.

Leaving the truck running, the driver climbed out, scratching at the scraggly blond tufts of his beard. Cowboy boots clicking on the asphalt, he walked back to the Civic, approaching it from behind. As he neared, he untucked his shirt. His hand reached back toward his kidney, sliding under the fabric. He hooked the grip of a handgun, slid it partway out of the waistband.

It looked like a big-bore semiauto, maybe a Desert Eagle.

Not a law-enforcement gun.

The man approached cautiously, peering through the windows, checking that the car was empty. Then he let his shirt fall back over the gun and entered the travel plaza.

"He didn't see us," Evan said. "Not directly, not from behind us on the freeway. At best he could tell that we were a man and a young woman. He's trying to confirm ID."

"So what do we do?"

"*You* don't do anything."

"I could handle that guy."

"He's bigger than you," Evan said. "Stronger, too."

In the bathroom a toilet flushed, the rush of water amplified in the cinder-block walls. A moment later they heard the creak of hinges and then the hiss of the hydraulic door opener. A sunburned man waddled into sight around the corner and headed off toward his car.

Joey snapped her gum. "I could handle him," she said again.

"We're not gonna find out," Evan said. "Stay here."

"You're going into the plaza?"

"Too many civilians. We'll let him come to us. He'll check the bathrooms next."

Sure enough, the driver emerged from the plaza and started their way. They pulled back from the corner.

Evan moved his hand toward his holster. "Don't want to use the gun," he whispered. "No suppressor. But if I have to —"

She completed the thought. "I'll have the car ready."

A crunch of footsteps sounded behind

them. Was there a second man? Evan put his shoulders to the cinder block, flattening Joey next to him, and switched his focus to the rear of the building.

A Pomeranian bobbed into view, straining a metal-link dog leash. It sniffed the grass, its rhinestone-studded collar winking.

Evan came off the wall.

The little dog pulled at its chain, producing an older woman clad in an aquamarine velour sweatsuit. She frowned down at the dog. "Do your business, Cinnamon!" She looked up and saw Evan. "Oh, thank God. Excuse me. Can you watch Cinnamon for me just for a second? I have to use the ladies' room."

Evan could hear the driver's boots now, tapping the front walkway behind him, growing louder. "I can't. Not now."

Creak of hinges. Hiss of hydraulic door opener.

The woman said, "Maybe your daughter, then?"

Evan turned around.

Joey was gone.

He tapped his holster through his shirt.

Empty.

He hissed, "Joey!" and leaned around the front corner.

He caught only a flicker of brown-black

hair disappearing through the men's-room door as the hydraulic opener eased it shut.

The woman was still talking. "Teenagers," she said.

Evan stood at the corner, torn. If he shouted Joey's name, he'd give her away. If he barreled in after her, he could alert the driver and get her killed. As it stood, she had Evan's gun and the element of surprise.

On point, he strained to listen, ready to charge.

The woman misread his agitation, her face settling into an expression of empathy. "I raised three of them," she went on, holding up three fingers for emphasis. "So believe me, I know. It's hard to learn to let them go."

The dog yapped and ran in circles.

"What with the driving and drinking," the woman said. "Making choices about their bodies."

Through the cinder-block walls, Evan heard a thud. A grunt. In the window just over the woman's shoulder, a spatter of blood painted the pane, and then the man's face mashed against the glass, wisps of beard smudging the blood.

The woman cocked her head. "Do you hear that?"

"I think they're cleaning the bathroom,"

Evan said.

Another pained masculine grunt and the snap of breaking bone.

"*Deep* cleaning," Evan said, as he shot around the corner.

He shouldered through the men's-room door.

The first thing he took in was Joey facing away, her tank top slightly twisted, arms raised, shoulders flexed. He couldn't see her hands, but his ARES pistol was tucked in the back of her pants.

The man was on his knees, his cheek split to the bone, his front teeth missing, his chest bibbed with blood. One arm dangled loosely at his side, broken. The other hand was raised palm out, fingers spread. Evan took a careful step forward, bringing Joey into full view. She was standing in a perfect Weaver stance, aiming the man's own Desert Eagle at his head, the long barrel made longer by a machined suppressor.

Joey's finger tightened on the trigger.

Evan held out a hand calmly, stilling the air. "Joey," he said.

The man ducked his head. Blood dripped from his cheek, tapped the floor. The acrid smell of his panic sweat hung heavy.

"Lower the gun," Evan said. "You don't want to cross this line."

"I do." Her eyes were wet. "I want to prove it."

"There's nothing to prove."

The barrel trembled slightly in her grasp. Evan watched the white seams of flesh at her knuckle.

"It's just one more ounce of trigger pressure," Evan said, "but it'll blow your whole world apart."

"What's the difference?" she said. "If I do it or you do it?"

"All the difference in the world."

She blinked and seemed to come back to herself. She inched the gun down. Evan stepped to her quickly and took it.

He faced the man. "A directive came from above to have me killed. I want to know *where* it came from."

The man sucked in a few wet breaths. He didn't answer.

Evan took a half step closer. "Who's Van Sciver taking orders from now?"

The man spit blood. "He keeps us in the dark, I swear."

Evan shot a glance at the bathroom door. Time was limited. "How'd he find you? Are you former military?"

The man tilted his face up to show a crooked smile, blood outlining his remaining teeth. "Now, that would give away too much, wouldn't it? But it's your lucky day, X. I can help you. I'll send a message to Van Sciver."

"Yes," Evan said. "You will."

He shot the man in the chest. The suppressor was beautifully made, reducing the gunshot to a muffled pop. The man jerked back against the tiles beneath the window and sat in a slump, chin on his chest, head rocked to one side.

Eleven down.

Fourteen to go.

Evan dropped the gun, took Joey's arm, and walked out. No one at the gas pumps had taken notice.

He flipped Joey the keys to the Honda. "Get your rucksack and the laptop."

She jogged off to the right, and he veered left.

When he stepped around the corner to check on the woman, she was bent over the dog, scolding it. "Do your business, Cinnamon. Do your business!"

She sniffed at him. "You know, there was a time when strangers helped each other."

"I'm sorry, ma'am," he said, picking up his shopping bag. "It's the teenager. Unpredictable."

Her face softened. She returned her focus to the Pomeranian.

Evan walked swiftly past the gas pumps to the 4Runner, which waited for them, motor still on, already angled downslope for a quick getaway. Joey met him there, climbing in as he did, tossing her rucksack ahead of her.

She was still winded from the fight and the adrenaline rush, her clavicles glistening with sweat.

He said, "You are a powerful young woman."

He pulled out onto the freeway and headed for home.

31
SPRINT THE MARATHON

By the time they arrived at Evan's Burbank safe house twelve hours and twenty-nine minutes later, they were driving a Prius with the license plates of a Kia. Bottlebrush and pepper trees shaded the street of single-story midcentury houses. Evan's sat apart at the end of the block behind a tall hedge of Blue Point juniper. When he'd bought it, one of a half dozen he kept at the ready, the neighborhood had been affordable, the houses charming if slightly ramshackle. But owing to Burbank's fine schools and proximity to the studios, the block's gentrification had reached a fever pitch; now remodels perennially clogged the quiet street. He'd been planning to unload the place and would do so as soon as he and Joey were done with each other. He maintained a labyrinthine and impenetrable network of shell corporations that allowed him to shuffle and discard assets without fear of being traced.

He parked in the garage next to a decade-old Buick Enclave that had served him loyally. The garage door shuddered down, and then he and Joey were cocooned in darkness, safe.

He started to get out when she said, angrily, "What does it matter?"

"What?"

"Whether I kill someone?"

He took a moment to consider. "It changes you in ways you can't understand. You'd never be able to have a normal life."

"A normal life? So I can . . . what? Hang out at the mall? Go to prom? Take a thousand fucking selfies?"

Her voice held an anger he did not understand.

"Yeah," she said. "I'd fit right in."

"It's about more than that," he said. "We've talked about the Tenth Commandment. 'Never let an innocent die.' But maybe there's another part to it: 'Never let an innocent kill.' "

"I'm not an innocent."

"No. But maybe we could get you back there."

She did not seem satisfied with that.

She made no move to get out of the car. Sitting in the Prius, they stared through the windshield at nothing.

"I'm weak," she said.

Her face cracked, contorting in grief, a flicker so fast that he'd have missed it if he'd blinked.

"Why do you think that?"

"I couldn't pull the trigger on the guy in the duffel bag. I couldn't do it at the rest stop either."

"That's not because you're weak," Evan said. "It's because you're stronger."

"Than who?"

He hadn't seen where the words were headed, not until now. He set his hands on the wheel, breathing the dark air.

"Than me," he said.

For Evan, maintaining the safe houses was a part-time job. Every few days he watered the landscaping, cleared flyers off the porch, took in the mail, programmed the lighting-control systems. Each location had what Jack called "loadouts" — mission-essential gear and weapons.

He entered the Burbank house, disarming the alarm system. The interior was dark, hemmed in by trees, the backyard shaded by a steeply sloped hillside. The house always smelled slightly damp, moisture wicking up through the foundation.

Joey walked from room to room, mouth gaping. She came back into the living room, let the rucksack drop on the thick brown carpet along with a bag of junk food he'd bought her at the last gas station. Twizzlers and Red Bull, as promised, as well as instant ramen packs, Snickers bars, and sandwiches in triangular plastic containers.

"You just have houses everywhere?"

"Not everywhere."

"Where do *you* live?"

"That's off-limits."

She held up her hands. "Whoa, cowboy. I got it. X's place — off-limits. But how do you have so much money?"

"When I was operating, they set me up with an excess of resources. They wanted me to have no reason ever to be heard from. It was a huge investment, but it paid well."

"Paid well?"

"How much is regime change worth?" Evan said.

Joey pursed her lips.

He said, "A well-placed bullet can change the direction of a nation. Tip the balance of power so a country's interests align with ours."

She shook her head as if shaking off the thoughts. "How has Van Sciver not tracked you down through your bank accounts?"

"He's tried."

"But you're too good."

"No. *Jack* was too good. He set everything up, taught me what I needed to know about keeping it untraceable."

"But things have changed since then."

"Right. I've refined the practices. After an unfortunate event last month, I diversified a little more. Bitcoin mining."

She smiled. "Because it's delinked from government regulation and oversight."

"That's right."

"So. That's why you can afford to have safe houses everywhere."

"Not everywhere."

She spun in a full circle, taking it all in. "And I can stay here?"

"Yes. And work." Evan fired up the Dell laptop, set it on a round wooden table that, along with a mustard-colored couch, passed for the living-room furniture. "I need what's in here. Getting Van Sciver? It's a marathon, not a sprint. But we want to sprint the marathon. Understand?"

She folded her arms. "Let me explain to you what we're looking at here. This Dell Inspiron is using a crazy strong encryption algorithm."

"So you can't brute-force the key?"

She gave a loud, graceless guffaw that was

almost charming. "We're talking a substitution-permutation cipher with a block size of sixty-four bits and key sizes up to two hundred and fifty-six bits. So no, we can't brute-force the key unless you've got like a hundred or so years."

"What's the best way to get the key?"

"With a hammer from someone who knows it."

"Joey."

She sigh-groaned, sat down, and pulled the laptop over to her. "What's your password to get online?"

He told her. Waited. Then asked, "What are you doing?"

Her fingers blurred. "Downloading the tools I need."

"Which are?"

"Look," she said, "going up against the algorithms could take weeks. We have to figure out the key. Which in all certainty will be composed — at least in part — of words or specific numeric sequences that are familiar to these guys in some way. So I need lists. I'm talking every name in the English language, European names, nicknames, street addresses, phone numbers, combinations of all of the above. Did you know there are only one and a half billion phone numbers in North and South America?"

"I did not."

But she was barely listening. "There's this newish thing from Amazon? Called an AMI — an Amazon Machine Image. Basically it runs a snapshot of an operating system. There are hundreds of them, loaded up and ready to run."

Evan said, "Um."

"Virtual machines," she explained, with a not-insubstantial trace of irritation.

"Okay."

"But the good thing with virtual machines? You hit a button and you have two of them. Or ten thousand. In data centers all over the world. Here — look — I'm replicating them now, requesting that they're geographically dispersed with guaranteed availability."

He looked but could not keep up with the speed at which things were happening on the screen. Despite his well-above-average hacking skills, he felt like a beginning skier atop a black-diamond run.

She was still talking. "We upload all the encrypted data from the laptop to the cloud first, right? Like you were explaining poorly and condescendingly to me back at the motel."

"In hindsight —"

"And we spread the job out among all of them. Get Hashkiller whaling away, throwing all these password combinations at it. Then who cares if we get locked out after three wrong password attempts? We just go to the next virtual machine. And the one after that."

"How do you have the hardware to handle all that?"

She finally paused, blowing a glossy curl out of her eyes. "That's what I'm telling you, X. You don't buy hardware anymore. You rent cycles in the cloud. And the second we're done, we kill the virtual machines and there's not a single trace of what we did." She lifted her hands like a low-rent spiritual guru. "It's all around and nowhere at the same time." A sly grin. "Like you."

"How long will this take?"

"Not sure. I have to oversee the control programs, check results, offer the occasional loving guidance. After all, they *are* just machines."

"Okay. I have to get back. Towels in the bathroom. The fridge is stocked with food."

"Wait — you're leaving me here?"

He crossed to a cupboard, pulled out a burner cell phone, and fired it up for the first time. "Only call me. You know the number?"

"Yeah, 1-855-2-NOWHERE. One digit too long."

"Yes."

"So that's it?" She looked around at the blank walls, the mustard-colored couch. "This is my life?"

"For now."

"Is there a TV?"

"Nope."

"What do I do?"

He picked up the keys to the Enclave from a dish on the kitchen counter. He'd left his Ford F-150 in a long-term parking lot at Burbank Airport; he'd do one last vehicle swap before going home. "Get into that laptop."

"Okay," she said. "And when I do?"

He headed for the garage. "Then I follow the trail."

"No — I mean, what happens to *me*?"

He spun the keys around a finger once and caught them in his fist. He started out. "Just crack it, Joey."

"So what? We'll just figure out me later?"

"This isn't about you, Joey. It's about Van Sciver. You understand what I need to do here. That's my only concern."

He held her eye contact. She gave a little nod.

And he left her.

32
CLEANING AGENT

Home.

Evan nudged the big Ford pickup into his spot between two concrete pillars, killed the engine, and released a sigh. Castle Heights' subterranean parking level was vast and gloomy and more pristine than any garage had a right to be. A pleasing whiff of oil and gasoline lingered beneath the aggressive lemon scent of environmentally friendly floor cleaner. The cleaning agent, part of the HOA's "go green" initiative, had passed by a narrow margin after a heated debate at the monthly meeting, a debate that Evan — as the resident industrial-cleaning-supply expert — had been roped into. His tie-breaking vote for the more expensive ecological product had drawn the ire of some of the older, fixed-income residents.

That was life in the big bad city.

At times he found the inner workings of Castle Heights — the rivalries, squabbles, and bureaucratic maneuverings — to be more exhausting than eluding teams of hit men.

He stayed in the truck. It was so quiet here in the garage.

He took a moment to inventory his body. His broken nose looked passable but still ached across the bridge. The cut in his gums from the exploded windshield had mostly healed, but it gave an angry throb when he ran his tongue across it. Lower back, still stiff from the collisions with police cruisers on the road outside Hillsboro. A sharp pain under his armpit, maybe a cracked rib. His hands, scuffed from swinging off the metal overhang on the train platform. His shoulder injury, exacerbated by the recoil of the Benelli shotgun. All of which he could cover up.

But his eyes were still sufficiently bruised to elicit inquiries.

Turning on the dome light, he took out the concealer wand and dabbed a bit of beige makeup on his lower eyelids. As he smudged it with his fingertip, he couldn't help but grin a bit.

He'd let down his guard and a sixteen-year-old had broken his nose. Joey had played him perfectly. Crouched against the wall to hide her combat knife, that wounded-bird glance over her shoulder. *Can you help me?*

He got out of the truck and climbed the steps to the lobby. As he passed the mail slots and headed to the elevators, he spotted Lorilee outside in the porte cochere, waiting for the valet to bring around her car. She was arguing with her boyfriend, a fit man with long hair who looked to be in his late forties. He grasped her biceps, making a point. Evan's focus narrowed to the fingers curled around Lorilee's arm. He didn't like the laying on of hands in a dispute.

But this was none of his business.

Joaquin sat cocked back in an Aeron at his security desk. He was pretending to monitor the bank of security screens, but his eyes were glazed and Evan saw that he had one earbud in, hidden beneath his cap.

Evan said, "Twenty-one, please, Joaquin."

The guard bounced forward in his chair, tapping the control to summon the elevator and specify its destination, an old-timey Castle Heights security convention. "Got you, Mr. Smoak. How was your business trip?"

"Another day, another airport lounge. But I got a lot done."

"That's good."

"What's the score?"

Joaquin colored slightly. "Twenty-six–fourteen. Golden State."

"Sorry."

" 'Member when the Lakers used to be good?"

Before Evan could respond, Joaquin pulled out his earbud and straightened up abruptly. Ida Rosenbaum, 6G, walked through the front door, shuffling along. She was bent forward, oversize purse pinned beneath one elbow as if it were at risk of fluttering away.

Evan turned to face the elevator, praying it would arrive before she made it across the lobby. In the dated brass doors, his reflection came clear.

Thanks to the unforgiving light of the lobby, he saw now that his nose was still out of alignment. Not much, but it was shifted a few millimeters to the left, noticeable enough for the sharp eyes of Ida Rosenbaum.

As she neared, presaged by the smell of old-lady violet perfume, he reached up and cracked his nose to center.

It stung enough to make his eyes water.

"You again," she said, sounding less than delighted.

He stayed facing forward, blinking back

the moisture; if he made his concealer run, that would provoke another conversation entirely. "Good morning, ma'am."

"Again with the 'ma'am,' " she said. "Call me Ida, already."

"Okay," Evan said.

The elevator arrived, and he got on, holding the door for Mrs. Rosenbaum. He felt heat building up in his sinuses and prayed his nose wouldn't start bleeding. The pain of the rebreak radiated out beneath his cheekbones.

"This weather," Ida said as the elevator started to rise. "It's playing games with my allergies. You wouldn't believe the aggravation. Feels like I'm snuffling through hay."

The blood was coming now — he could feel the warmth inside his nose. He didn't want to reach up and pinch it, so he tilted his head back slightly and gave a sharp inhale. The floor numbers ticked by in slow motion. His eyes no longer watered, but moisture still welled at his bottom lids, threatening to spill and wreak havoc with the concealer.

"And my hip. Don't even get me started." Ida waved a dismissive hand at him. "What would you know about it? My Herb, may he rest in peace, always said that no one in your generation learned how to handle pain.

Everyone's off to get a massage or smoke medical marijuana."

He tried to compress his nostrils. "Yes, ma'am."

The elevator at last reached the sixth floor, and she stepped out, casting a final look back at him. "Slow learning curve, too," she observed.

As the doors glided shut, the bumpers blocking out Mrs. Rosenbaum, Evan tilted his face into his hand just in time to catch the blood.

In Evan's freezer drawer, one bottle of vodka had remained untouched for several years.

Stoli Elit: Himalayan Edition.

Evan opened the walnut chest and beheld the Bohemian hand-blown glass bottle.

Made with the finest variety of winter wheat from the Tambov region and water tapped from reservoirs buried beneath the famed mountain range, the vodka underwent a sophisticated distillation process, after which it was frozen to minus-eighteen degrees Celsius to segregate any additives or impurities. It came accompanied by a gold-plated ice pick. Given the price of the bottle, the best use for the pick was presumably to defend oneself against would-be vodka bandits.

Evan cracked the seal and poured two fingers over a spherical ice cube.

He lifted the tumbler to admire the clarity of the liquid. It smelled of ice and nothing more. The mouth feel was velvety, and the aftertaste carried a surprising hint of fruit.

Vodka's original purpose was to cleanse the palate after eating fatty foods. But Evan loved it for its quiet ambition. At first glance it looks as plain as water. And yet it strives to be the purest version of what it is.

He set the tumbler on the poured-concrete surface of the kitchen island, leaned over it, and exhaled.

An image came to him unbidden, the wind tearing through the Black Hawk, fluttering Jack's shirt, his hair. He'd taken a wide stance, steady against the elements.

Always steady against the elements.

Evan lifted the glass halfway to his mouth, set it back down.

His cheeks were wet.

"Goddamn it, Jack," he said.

He closed his eyes and dropped into his body. Became aware of its shape from the inside. Felt the pressure of the floor against the soles of his boots. The coolness of the counter beneath his palms. He stayed with his breath, feeling it at his nostrils, in his windpipe, his chest. Drew it into his stomach, belly-breathing a count of ten.

Right now, in this moment, there was no Nowhere Man mission, no Van Sciver, no sixteen-year-old stashed in a safe house. There was no past or imagined future, no bone-deep ache of grief, no figuring out how to live in a world without Jack.

There was only the breath. Inhale, exhale. His body doing what it did twenty thousand times a day, except this time he was mindful of it.

And this time.

And this time.

The brief meditation and the vodka sent warmth through his veins. He felt decontaminated.

He opened his eyes and headed to the Vault.

33
A Lot of Variables

Benito Orellana.

That was the name of the man who had called the Nowhere Man for help, the man Evan was to meet tomorrow at noon.

At least that's what the caller had claimed his name was.

Evan approached each pro bono job with the same meticulous mission planning with which he'd once plotted the assassination of high-value targets. The First Commandment: *Assume nothing.*

Including that the client is who he says he is.

Or that he might not be planning to kill you.

Evan had parked himself behind his sheet-metal desk in the Vault, sipping vodka in the pale glow of the monitors neatly lined up before him. From here he could access hundreds of state and federal law-enforcement databases. This required only a single point of entry: a Panasonic Tough-book laptop hooked to the dashboard of any LAPD cruiser. Because officers rotated through a squad car with every shift change, the laptop passwords were generally straightforward, often simply the assigned unit number: LAPD_4012. Over the years Evan had broken into various cruisers from various stations and uploaded a piece of reverse-SSH code into their dashboard laptops. Firewalls face out to keep people from breaking in. They don't regulate out-going traffic. When Evan needed to access the databases remotely, he initiated his hidden code, prompting the police computer to reach out through its firewall to him. Then he could sail right through the open ports and browse wherever he liked.

He'd already learned much about Benito Orellana.

An undocumented worker from El Salvador, he'd received amnesty in 1986 under the Immigration Reform and Control Act. His tax records showed Benito holding down three jobs — a dishwasher at an Italian restaurant downtown, a valet parker, and an Uber driver. Over the years he had diligently reported cash tips. If the information Evan was collecting was real, it revealed an honest, hardworking man.

Benito's wife had died in February. Medicaid test results from last year showed black spots on a chest CT scan, and the L.A. County death certificate listed lung cancer as her cause of death. It had been fast. Benito had one son, Xavier, who had taken a few courses at East Los Angeles College and then dropped out around the time of his mother's diagnosis. No other information on Xavier was to be found. Benito's financials seemed to be clean until recently; he'd racked up debt in the form of credit-card charges to Good Samaritan Hospital. The house in Pico-Union was leveraged, a second mortgage with a predatory lending rate gaining momentum by the month.

Evan looked over at Vera II. "The guy seems legit."

Vera II said nothing.

Evan took the last expensive sip of vodka, fished out what was left of the ice cube, and rested it in her serrated spikes. An ice cube a week was all the watering the fist-size aloe vera plant required.

He removed the Samsung cell phone from his pocket — the one he'd stolen from Van Sciver's man in Portland — and turned it on. No messages. There was a single coded contact. Push the button and it would ring through to Van Sciver. That would prove

278

useful at some point. Evan turned the phone back off and charged it.

A Lot of Variables

He started to get up, but Vera II implored him.

"Okay, okay," he said.

He called up feeds from the hidden security cameras in the Burbank safe house.

He found Joey at the wooden table, chewing on a Twizzler, tapping at the keyboard. She had her own laptop set up next to the Dell now, connected with a cord. After a time she got up, fished in her rucksack for something, and retreated to the couch.

He couldn't see what she was staring at.

Finally she shifted, and he caught a vantage over her shoulder. She was reading the Thanksgiving card again, tracing her finger across the handwriting as if it were braille.

She looked forlorn there on the couch, leaning against the arm, her legs tucked beneath her.

Evan glanced at Vera II.

"Fine," he said.

He called Joey's burner phone. He watched her start, and then she crossed to the table and picked up.

"X?"

"How are you doing?"

She glanced at the laptops. "Making head-way."

She'd misunderstood what he was asking about. It seemed awkward to backtrack now.

He said, "Good."

She went into the kitchen and slid a pack of ramen noodles into a bowl.

"Do we have an ETA?" he asked.

"We're dealing with ten thousand virtual machines," she said, filling the bowl with water and shoving it into the microwave. "There are a lot of variables."

"We need to —"

"Sprint the marathon," she said. "Right. Consider me chained to the laptop. When I'm done with this, maybe I could stitch some wallets for you."

An unfamiliar ring sounded deep in the penthouse, and Evan stood up abruptly. It had been so long since he'd heard it that it took a moment for him to place what it was.

The home line.

When he'd moved in, he'd had it installed so he could have a number to list in the HOA directory. Aside from a telemarketer three months ago, no one had called it in years.

"I'll check in on you in the morning," he said to Joey, and hung up.

He raced out of the Vault, through his

bedroom, down the hall to the kitchen, and snatched up the cordless phone. "Hello?"

"Hi."

Hearing her voice caught him completely off guard.

34
THE JOB TO END ALL JOBS

"I know we decided not to be in touch," Mia said, her voice light and nervous over the phone. "But, I don't know, you seemed messed up when I saw you in the parking garage last week."

Evan cleared his throat.

"And . . ." she said. "I know you were gone for a while. I saw your truck back in your spot tonight and figured . . . I guess I figured maybe you could use a home-cooked meal."

In the background he could make out some Peter-related commotion. She muffled the receiver. "Put the lid back on that!" she shouted. Then she was back. "Anyway, it was just a thought."

He heard himself say, "I'd like that."

"Really?"

He was asking himself the same thing. He'd responded before thinking. What part of him had that answer teed up, ready to deploy?

"Yes," he said.

"Okay. Well, come down in twenty?"

"Okay." He was, he realized, pacing nervously. There was something else he was supposed to say here, something he'd heard people say on movies and TV shows. The words sounded clunky and robotic in his mouth, but he forced them out. "Can I bring anything?"

"Just yourself."

That was how the script went. He'd watched it dozens of times but now he was inside it, saying the lines.

There was some other rule, too. Her job was to say no, but his job was to bring something anyway. Except what did he have to bring? Cocktail olives? An energy bar? A Strider folding knife with a tanto tip for punching through Kevlar vests?

Ordinary life was stressful.

He said, "Okay," and hung up.

Jack had trained him for so many contingencies, had made him lethal and worldly and cultured.

But not domestic.

Checking the adjustment of his nose, he padded back to shower.

■ ■ ■ ■

Mia yanked open the door, a blast of too-loud TV cartoons hitting Evan in the face along with the smell of cooking garlic and onion. "Hi, welcome. Wow — vodka."

He stood nervously, holding a frost-clouded bottle of Nemiroff Lex, which was neither too expensive nor too cheap, not too showy nor too understated, not too spicy nor too citrusy.

There had been deliberations over the freezer drawer.

Feeling decidedly unmasculine, he'd also touched up his makeup on the bruises beneath his eyes. The discoloration was nearly gone; he hoped he could forgo the concealer come morning.

He hoisted the bottle. "It's Ukrainian," he said, sounding disconcertingly rehearsed. "Wheat-based and aged in wood for six —"

"Hi, Evan Smoak!" Peter blurred by, juggling oranges, which seemed mostly to involve dropping them.

Mia whipped around. "I am taking this house back! That's what I'm doing! So help me —"

A crunch punctuated a sudden pause in Peter's movement. He looked down at his feet. Remorse flickered across his face. "The remote got broken," he announced in his raspy voice, and then he bolted over the back of the couch and resumed his not-juggling.

Mia seemed to register the afterimpression of her son. " 'Got broken,' " she said. "That's what we call a strategically passive sentence construction."

She turned and hurried back into the kitchen, Evan following. With a pasta ladle, she scooped out a piece of linguine and tossed it against the cabinet. It stuck beside various strands that had previously dried and adhered to the wood. She caught Evan's expression and held up a hand, swollen by an oven mitt to inhuman proportions. "That means it's ready," she said, raising her voice over the blaring TV. As she dumped the pot's contents into a colander, rising steam flushed her cheeks.

The smoke alarm began bleating, and Mia snatched up a dish towel and fanned the air beneath it. "It's fine. It'll just . . ."

The rest of her statement was lost beneath an orchestral change in the intensity of Bugs Bunny's adventure.

In the midst of the chaos, Evan took a still moment. He set down the vodka bottle on the counter. Grabbing a steak knife from the block, he headed into the living room, sidestepping a toppled barstool. He found the remote on the carpet by the couch, the buttons jammed beneath the plastic casing, as he'd suspected.

He sat and worked the tiny screws with the tip of the steak knife. Three oranges tapped the couch cushion, light footsteps approached, and then Peter sat opposite Evan, cross-legged.

"What are you doing?" the boy asked.

Evan extracted the first screw, went to work on the second. "Unscrewing."

Peter said, "Why are you using a steak knife?"

"Because that's what I've got."

"But knives are for eating."

"Among other things." The screw popped up, and the top casing of the remote lifted, the rubber buttons jostling back into place beneath it. Evan fastened the faceplate back on, then touched the power button.

The TV mercifully silenced just as the smoke alarm stopped bleating. A moment of perfect, blissful quiet.

Mia said, "We are ready to plate."

While Peter disappeared to brush his teeth, Mia and Evan sat at the table, empty dishes between them. In the background, singing softly from an iPod speaker dock, Linda Ronstadt was wondering when she'd be loved.

Mia took a sip of vodka. "This *is* good. It tastes . . . aged in wood."

Evan said, "You're making fun of me."

"I'm making fun of you."

She held up her glass, and they clinked.

From the depths of his bathroom, Peter yelled, "Done!" and Mia shouted, "That wasn't two minutes!"

It was cold, and she had her sweater sleeves pulled over her hands. Her hair was a rich mess of waves and curls. The glow of the overhead light spilled through it, showing off all the colors, chestnut and gold and auburn.

Evan remembered that he was supposed to comment on the food. "That was delicious."

"Thank you." She leaned forward, cupped a hand by her mouth, gave a stage whisper. "I blend spinach in the marinara sauce. It's how I get him to eat vegetables."

Unexpectedly, Evan found himself thinking of Joey dining alone in the safe house, Twizzlers and ramen in the dead blue light of the laptop. A sensation worked in his chest, and he gave it some space, observed it, identified it.

Guilt.

That was interesting.

He looked across at the kitchen, where a new Post-it was stuck above the pass-through.

Remember that what you do not yet know is more important than what you already know.
— Jordan Peterson

Mia left quotations around for Peter, rules to live by. As she'd once remarked to Evan, it took a lot of work to raise a human.

"Peter's lucky to have you," Evan said.

"Thanks." She smiled and peered into her vodka, her fingers peeking out of the sweater cuff to grip the glass. "I'm lucky to have him, too. It's the predictable response, but it's true."

"*Really* done now!" Peter yelled. "Can I read?"

"Ten minutes!"

"Tell me when time's up!"

"Okay! I'll be in to tuck you in!"

Evan looked at the freshly folded laundry, still in the basket on the floor. The homework chart above the kitchen table, bedazzled with puffy stickers. "It's so much work," he said.

"Yes. And that's on a good week. Then there's the strep-throat week, the getting-bullied week, the cheating-on-the-simplifying-fractions-test week."

"Fair enough," he said. "Fractions."

She laughed. "Kids turn your life upside down. But maybe that's where anything matters. In the big fat mess of it all. Of course, I'd like to do more. Travel. Relax." She hoisted the glass. "Drink." Her grin faded. "Sometimes parenting, it feels like . . . an anchor." Her expression lightened. "But that's the good part, too. You have this anchor. And it holds you in the world."

Evan thought, *Like having Jack.*

"God," she said. "Sometimes I miss Roger so much. It's never the big stuff like you'd think. Candlelight dinners. The sex. Wedding veils and vacations. No. It's coming home when you're at the end of a brutal day and there's someone there. Consistency. You know?"

Evan said, "No."

She laughed. "Your bluntness, it's refreshing. It's always yes and no with you. Never 'I'm sorry' or 'I get it.' "

He thought, *That's because I don't get it.*

"This personal thing you're dealing with," she said. "What is it?" He took another sip, let the vodka heat his throat. "It is," he said, "the job to end all jobs."

"Truly?"

"I think so."

"If that's the case," she said. "Maybe a DA and a . . . whatever you are can be friends."

"Friends."

She rose from the table, and he followed her cue.

"Maybe we could do this," she said. "Just this. Maybe again Friday? Peter enjoys it. I enjoy it."

Evan thought of Jack, stepping silently into space, giving his life to protect Evan's. Joey, working furiously to get him back on Van Sciver's trail. Benito Orellana, besieged by debt, his wife dead, his son in danger. *Please help me. You're all I have left.*

Evan didn't deserve to have something this nice on a regular basis.

Mia was staring at him.

He said, "What?"

"This is where you say you enjoy it, too."

Evan said, "I enjoy it, too."

They were at the door. Mia was looking at his mouth, and he was looking at hers.

"Can I kiss you?" she asked.

He drew her in.

Her mouth was so, so soft.

They parted. She was breathless. He was, too. An odd sensation — odder even than guilt.

He said, "Thank you for dinner."

She laughed as she closed the door after him.

He had no idea why.

35
PATRON SAINT OF
DISPOSSESSED ORPHANS

It was a new look.

Chocolate-brown hair, cut in a power A-line bob with razorblade bangs. Cat-eye glasses. A B-cup bra tamping down her voluptuousness beneath a professional white blouse. A fitted wool skirt curving her lower assets, delivering the package neatly into rich-girl riding boots.

Candy made sure the back view was on full display, leaning into the trunk of her car, struggling with the spare tire.

Her just-past-warranty Audi A6 quattro had blown a tire, you see, conveniently right beside the rear parking lot of the New Chapter Residential Recovery Center.

Candy was going for young Georgetown junior associate at a white-shoe firm, successful but not yet arrived, dressing and living beyond her means in hopes that she was on the verge of that next promotion. Few things were less threatening to men than a woman trying slightly too hard to make up professional ground.

She kept pretending to wrestle the tire, making sure that her face was getting a nice damsel-in-distress flush. It was 6:58 A.M., New Chapter unlocked its doors at seven o'clock sharp, and her target — from the intel Van Sciver had given her — would be jonesing for his early-morning hit of nicotine.

Orphan L's smoking habit was the one thing he wasn't currently faking. And the one thing he couldn't suppress even if his life depended on it.

Which, of course, it did.

Find what they love. And make them pay for it.

She heard the clunk of the dead bolt unlocking, footsteps, the snick of a lighter.

She stayed buried in the trunk, let the view do the talking. The skirt, sexy-conservative as was befitting the town, strained a bit at the seams.

She made exasperated sounds.

Oh, dear me. If only there were a strapping man who could —

"Excuse me?"

She extricated herself from the trunk, blew out an overwhelmed breath, pressed a hand to her sweaty décolletage.

He was walking toward her already, salt-and-pepper stubble, tousled hair. He looked convincingly like shit — she'd give him that — but he would've been handsome were he not playing addict.

"Need a hand?"

In the Orphan Program's prime, Tim Draker had been one of the best. But he'd recently broken with Van Sciver, taken early retirement, and blipped off the radar. Then he'd found out there was no retiring from the Orphan Program.

Not with Van Sciver.

"God, yes. The tire went out, and I don't really know how to change it. I'm late for work — my boss is gonna *kill* me."

He drew nearer, flicking his cigarette aside with a practiced flourish. A broad smile, full of confidence. Too much confidence for a recovering heroin addict. It was too tantalizing — *she* was too tantalizing — for a trained Orphan to keep his tongue in his mouth, hold his distance, act his legend.

Her ass alone could do the work of a full team of Agency spooks.

Draker wore a T-shirt, a wise choice since it showed off the scabs and dark, wilted bruises at the crooks of his elbows. Terrific visuals, likely produced from a mixture of vitamin-C powder, Comet, and Visine shot just beneath the epidermis. Then you wolf down enough poppy seeds and Vicks cough syrup to ding the intake opiate-drug tests. After that it's just about theatrics. Rub your eyes with soap, slam Red Bull, Vicks, and Sudafed, and you have your basic amped, twitchy, rheumy-eyed, nauseated, sweating addict. Claims of suicidality buy you more time off the streets, out of the system, protected under that umbrella of total patient confidentiality offered by a drug-treatment facility.

A plan worthy of Jack Johns, Patron Saint of Dispossessed Orphans.

Van Sciver would never have known.

But for a single eyelash.

That had put him on the scent of anonymous treatment facilities. But what a bitch to search them. Had it been anyone but Van Sciver with his MegaBot data-mining lair, it never would've happened. Draker would've lain low, undergone another three-month fake treatment in another facility, and then skipped off into the wide world once the heat died down.

Draker sidled up, pretended not to eye her cleavage. "Let's take a look, shall we?"

"Oh, my God," Candy said, all breathy like. "Thank you so much."

Draker leaned into the trunk, reaching for

the tire, his T-shirt straining across his muscular back. Candy withdrew a syringe from the top of her riding boot, popped the sterile plastic cap, and sank the needle into his neck.

He went limp immediately.

She flipped his legs into the trunk after him.

That was a nice feature of the Audi A6.

Good trunk space.

She slammed the trunk shut, got in, and drove away. The snatch-and-grab had taken three seconds, maybe four.

Men were so easy.

They had a single lever. You just had to give it a tug.

Van Sciver and Thornhill pulled the armored Chevy Tahoe through the tall chain-link gate and parked alongside the humble single-story house. Weeds had overtaken the backyard, and a BBQ grill had tipped over, rusting into the earth.

Van Sciver got out, the sun shining through his fine copper hair, and rattled the gate shut on stubborn wheels, sealing them in. Thornhill opened the back door.

They started to unload the Tahoe.

Padlocks and plywood.

Nylon ropes and boards of various lengths.

A decline bench press and jugs of water.

Mattresses and drop cloths.

Rags and a turkey baster.

Duct tape and a folding metal chair.

Thornhill whistled a tune the entire time. Van Sciver wondered what it would take to wipe that permanent smile off the guy's face.

When they finished, Van Sciver's cheeks and throat had gone blotchy pink from exertion. His shirt clung to the yoke of his shoulders. He had an Eastern European peasant's build — arms that barely tapered at the wrists, thighs stretching his cargo pants, a neck too thick to encircle with both hands. In another life he would've been a 60 gunner, hauling the massive, belt-fed pig for a platoon, a one-man artillery unit.

But this life was better.

He grabbed the last of the supplies, closed up the Chevy, and came inside.

Thornhill was doing handstand push-ups in what passed for the kitchen, his palms pressed to the peeling linoleum. The forks of his triceps could have cracked walnuts.

Van Sciver's phone alerted. He juggled the items he was holding and picked up. "Code."

" 'Potluck chiaroscuro,' " Candy said. "They're getting arty on us."

297

"Is the package in hand?"

"What do you think?"

"V." He packed the syllable with impatience.

"Yes," she said. "It is."

He walked to the chipped counter. Set down a dog collar next to a galvanized bucket.

"Good," he said. "We're just getting ready."

36
FRESH AIR

Joey answered the front door of the Burbank safe house. She looked like hell —
swollen eyes, gray skin, her hair mussed.

Evan moved past her off the porch, swung
the door shut. "Did you check the security
screen before opening?"

"Nah. I figured I'd play door Russian
roulette. You know, maybe it's you, maybe
it's Van Sciver."

"It's increasingly hard to get a direct
answer out of you," Evan said.

"Yeah, well, sprinting the marathon means
not a lot of sleep."

He glanced immediately at the laptops,
code streaming across both screens, progress
bars filling in. "So nothing yet." He failed
to keep the impatience from his voice.

"I would've called."

He took in the bare-bones house, wondering if it felt similar to the hangar in which
Van Sciver had kept her. Or the apartment

Jack had hidden her in. That familiar feeling compressed his chest again. He thought about her reading that Thanksgiving card last night, her legs tucked beneath her on the couch.

"How are you doing?" he asked.

"How do you think I'm doing? I've been either running for my life or staring at a screen for longer than I can remember. What kind of bullshit existence is that?"

She went to the kitchen counter, cracked another Red Bull.

He had a few hours before his meeting with Benito Orellana in Pico-Union. "Let's go for a walk," he said.

"Great. A walk. Like I'm a dog. You're gonna take me around the block?" She stopped herself, rubbed her face, heaved an exhale through her fingers. "Fuck. I'm sorry. I'm being a bitch."

"You're not," Evan said. "Come on. Fresh air."

She gave a half smile, swept her hair to one side. "I remember fresh air."

She followed him out. The invigorating smell of Blue Point juniper reminded him of the parking lot in Portland. They'd had a lot of close calls already, a lot of hours together in the trenches.

They turned left and headed up the street,

Evan keeping alert, scanning cars, windows, rooftops. Wild parrots chattered overhead, moving from tree to tree. Their calls were loud and strident and somehow lovely, too. As Evan and Joey walked, they watched the birds clustering and bickering and flying free. Evan thought he detected some longing in Joey's face.

"You still haven't told me your full first name," Evan said.

"Right. Let me think. Oh, that would be . . . none of your business." She gave him a little shove on his shoulder, pushing him into the gutter.

"I'll tell you my full first name," he said. "I've never told anyone."

"It's not just Evan?"

"It's Evangelique."

"Really?"

"No."

She laughed a big, wide laugh, covering her mouth.

A pair of guys came around the corner ahead, one riding on a hoverboard, the other a longboard, the wheels skipping across the cracks in the sidewalk. They wore hoodies with skater logos and throwback checkered Vans.

The hoverboard hit a concrete bump pushed up by a tree root and the guy fell over, skinning his hands.

Evan was about to tell Joey to keep walking when she called out, "You okay?"

The guy picked himself up as they approached. "All good."

His friend, a burly kid, stepped on the tail of his longboard and flipped it up, catching it by the front truck. He looked to be in his late teens, maybe twenty. His hair was cropped short on the sides, the top gathered tightly in a man bun.

Evan didn't like him.

And he didn't like how he was looking at Joey.

"Hey, I'm Connor. You guys live around here?"

"No," Evan said. "Visiting a friend."

"Well," the guy said, directing his attention at Joey, "if you're around again, we hang at the old zoo most nights." He pointed up the street toward Griffith Park. "To chill. You should come."

Evan mentally graphed the angle of uppercut that would snap both hinges of his jaw.

"She's busy," he said.

"When?"

"Forever."

As they passed, Connor said in a low voice, "Dude. Your pops is intense."

Joey said, "You have no idea."

They left the guys behind, turning the corner for their street.

"Think he's a plant?" Joey asked.

"No. I think he's a useless reprobate. Loose body language. The stoner nod. He's not good."

"I thought he was kinda cute."

Evan said, "You're grounded."

"Like, locked-in-a-safe-house-and-forced-to-hack-an-encrypted-laptop grounded?"

Evan said, "Yes."

A smile seemed to catch her by surprise. She looked away to hide it.

He gave her a little nudge on the shoulder, tipping her into the gutter.

37
BLOOD IN, BLOOD OUT

Benito Orellana twisted his hands together, shifting his weight back and forth, anguish throttling through him. He wasn't crying, but Evan could see that it was taking most everything he had not to. His stained dishwasher's apron was slung over a chair back; before Evan's arrival he had changed into an ironed white T-shirt. No money, but proud.

"A parent, they are only as happy as their least happy child," Benito said. "*Mi mamá* used to tell me this. You understand?"

Not at all, Evan thought. He said, "Tell me what happened to Xavier."

In the square front room of the tiny house in Central L.A., Evan stood across from Benito, facing the picture window. The view looked out onto a massive empty lot razed by bulldozers and the top floors of a tall building being constructed beyond. Workers were visible clinging to the steel skeleton, steering in I-beams as if they were planes on the tarmac.

In Pico-Union any direction you went, you hit a thoroughfare — the 110 Freeway to the east, Normandie Avenue to the west, Olympic Boulevard up top, and the Santa Monica Freeway below.

A lot of getaway routes. Which meant a lot of crime.

Evan had safed the block, the surrounding blocks, and the blocks surrounding those. A three-hour undertaking, wholly necessary before the approach in case Benito was the bait in a trap.

On these initial forays, Evan used to bring a briefcase embedded with all sorts of operational trickery, including signal jamming if digital transmitters happened to be in play. But the briefcase had been unwieldy.

Also, he'd had to detonate it.

Now he used a simple portable RF jammer in his back pocket, no bigger than a pack of cigarettes.

Within minutes he believed that Benito was not an undercover agent for Van Sciver and that his plight was real.

Benito swallowed. "When my wife pass, I don't know how to cook, how to do anything."

"Mr. Orellana. I'm here about Xavier."

"She would have known how to talk to him. But I am working so hard. Even right now my friend, he cover for me at the restaurant. I have too much month at the end of the paycheck. I am working three jobs, trying to provide for Xavier. But I lose track of him. There just wasn't the time to earn and to also . . . also . . ."

He was at risk of breaking down.

"Mr. Orellana," Evan said. "What did Xavier do?"

Benito swayed on his feet, his eyes glazed, far away. "There is a gang where I come from. They kill anyone. Women, children. They are so bad that the government, they make a prison just for them in San Salvador. The police do not even go in. Instead they keep an army outside. The gang, they run this prison on their own. They are . . ." He searched for the right words. "They are the people you would least want to anger in the entire world."

"MS-13," Evan said. "Mara Salvatrucha."

Benito closed his eyes against the words, as if they held an evil spell.

"It is the most dangerous country in the world," Benito said. "For a young man, there is nothing but gangs and violence. A hand grenade, it sells for one dollar there. When Xavier was born, we came here for a better life." Now tears fell, cutting tracks down his textured cheeks. "But it turn out they came, too."

"And Xavier joined them?"

"He hasn't been initiated yet," Benito said. "I know this from my friend. His son, he is one of them. There is still hope."

"Initiated?"

"Blood in, blood out. You kill to get in. They kill you before they will ever let you leave." Benito wiped at his cheeks. "I am running out of time."

"Where is the gang's headquarters?"

"I don't know."

"Where do I find Xavier?"

"I don't know. We fought last week. He run away. I haven't seen him since. I lost my wife, and now I can't lose him. I promised her. When she was dying, I promised her I would take care of him. I did my best. I did my best."

"I don't understand," Evan said. "What do you want me to do?"

"Don't let them make my boy a killer."

"No one can make someone a killer." The words were out of Evan's mouth before he saw the irony in them.

"Yes," Benito said. "They can. They will."

The philosophical point was lost on Benito and not worth arguing.

"I promised I would meet with you," Evan said. "But there's nothing I can do here."

"Please," Benito said. "He is a good boy. Help him."

"I'm not a social worker."

"You can convince him."

"Convincing people isn't part of my skill set."

Benito walked over into the kitchen and pulled a photograph off the refrigerator, the magnet skittering across the floor. He returned to Evan, held up the picture in both hands.

Evan looked at it.

It had been taken at a backyard barbecue, Xavier in a wife-beater undershirt and too-big olive-green cargo shorts, a tilted beer raised nearly to his mouth. Raw-boned but handsome, clear brown eyes, carrying a trace of baby fat in his cheeks despite the fact that he was twenty-four. His smile made him look like a kid, and Evan wondered what it felt like for Benito to watch this human he raised transform into a confusion of opposing parts, menacing and sweet, tough and youthful.

Had Jack felt that way about Evan?

He's the best part of me.

"When he lose his mother," Benito said, his hands trembling, "he lose his way. Grief makes us do terrible things."

Evan saw himself in the pest-control shop in Portland, his foot pinning a man's chest, shotgun raised, the wreckage of a hand painting the floor red.

He gritted his teeth and took the photo.

38
STEEL BONES

The construction workers drifted away from the site, heading upslope where an old-fashioned roach coach competed with an upscale food truck featuring Korean tacos. Three vast parking lots had been torn up to make way for a low-rent retirement community, which was portrayed in idyllic watercolors on the massive signage. Pinning down the southern end of the six-acre drop of cleared land were the steel bones of a five-story building, the first to go vertical in the new development. It backed on the high wall of the 10 Freeway, making it an oddly private spot in the heart of the city.

Which made it useful for Evan's purposes now.

A yellow tower crane was parked haphazardly among piles of equipment and supplies. Cement mixers and steel pedestals, hydraulic torque wrenches and bolts the size of human arms.

Way up above, the workers reached the trucks, their laughter swept away by the wind. And then there was only stillness and the white-noise rush of unseen cars flying by on the other side of the freeway wall.

A wiry man with orange hair darted into sight, shoving a wheelbarrow before him, his muscular arms shiny with sweat. He reached a mound of copper plumbing pipes and started loading them into the wheelbarrow, shooting nervous glances at the workers upslope.

Evan stepped out from between two Porta-Potties and came up behind him.

"Excuse me," Evan said.

The man started and whirled around, a length of pipe gripped in one fist. He looked street-strong, his muscles twitching from uppers, which would make him stronger yet. He had a face like a pug's — underbite, bulging eyes — and his complexion was pale and sickly.

"The fuck you want?"

"A couple of answers."

They were in the shadow of the freeway wall, and not a soul was in view all the way up to the trucks above. No one could see them down here.

A fine place to steal copper.

"You're local," Evan told the man.

311

"Clearly you've cased the place, timed the workers. I have a few questions I need answered by someone who lives here."

"I'm gonna give you two seconds to walk away. Then I'm gonna cave in your fucking head."

The man inched forward. Evan did not move.

"Your first instinct is to escalate," Evan said. "That shows me you're a punk."

The man ran his tongue across jagged, rotting teeth. "Why's that?"

"Because you've spent your life around people it's feasible to escalate against."

"I'm not some West Coast pussy, okay? I'm from Lowell, Mass, bitch. I grew up street-fighting with boxers who —"

Evan daggered his hand, a basic *bil jee* finger jab, and poked him in the larynx.

The man's windpipe spasmed. His mouth gaped.

The man dropped the pipe, took a step back, sat down, an leaned over. Then he lay flat on his back. Then he sat back up. His mouth gaped some more. Then he managed to suck some oxygen in with a gasp. He coughed and then dry-heaved a little.

Evan waited, staring up the erector-set rise of the structure. From the fourth floor, you could see Benito Orellana's house. From the fifth you'd be able to see most of Pico-Union. For all the crime, this was a small neighborhood. Intimate. People who lived on these streets would know things.

The man finished hacking and drew in a few deep lungfuls of air. "Fuck, man," he said, his voice little more than a croak. "What'd you do that for?"

"To speed up the conversation."

The man still couldn't talk, but he waved his hand for Evan to continue.

"MS-13," Evan said. At this the man's eyes darted up to find Evan's. "I need to know where their headquarters are here."

"I can't tell you that, man."

Evan took a step forward, and the man scrambled back, crab-walking on hands and heels until his shoulders struck the top flange of an I-beam. Evan shadowed his movement.

"Wai-wai-wait. Okay. *Okay.* I'll tell you."

He cowered against the steel, Evan standing above him.

He kept one hand clamped over his throat, the other raised defensively. "Just lemme catch my breath first."

39
VISIONS OF THE OCCULT

A reinforced steel door gave the first indication that the abandoned church was not what it seemed. The half dozen men on guard outside, smoking and bickering, were a more obvious second. Their heads were shaved, their faces and skulls covered with tattoos. Devil horns on foreheads. The numbers *1* and *3* written in roman numerals rouging each cheek. Dots in a triangle at the corner of the eye, showing the three destinations for Mara Salvatrucha members after they're recruited — hospital, prison, or grave.

To a one, the men wore Nike Cortez sneakers, blue and white for the flag of their home country. One shirtless bruiser had the monkeys of lore inked across his torso — see no evil, hear no evil, speak no evil.

Evan walked past on the far side of the street, then cut around the block and took his bearings. The church was north of Pico along the 110 Freeway, surrounded by buildings in steep decline. A textile plant. A bodega with plywood replacing the glass of one front window. Graffiti everywhere, covering Dumpsters, parked cars, walls. On the corner a shrine of flower wreaths and sanctuary candles remembered a young boy who peered out of a framed school picture with bright, eager-to-please eyes.

A street vendor hawked knockoff Nikes on a ratty bedspread, the swooshes positioned suspiciously low. They, too, were blue-and-white Cortezes, fan paraphernalia for residents who wanted to be seen rooting for the home team.

Evan headed up an alley and scaled a fire-escape ladder to the roof of a crack house. He walked across the rotting shingles toward the spire rising from the neighboring building and crouched by the rusted rain gutter, peering through a shattered stained-glass window into the church below.

The pews had been shoved aside, gang members congregating in the nave. A pistol on every hip, submachine guns leaning in the corners, at the ready. They weren't a gang.

They were an army.

The men exchanged rolls of cash, sorted baggies of white powder, collected from street-worn hookers. Electronic scales topped table after table like sewing machines in a sweatshop. Pallets of boxed electronics lined the far wall, fronted with heaps of stolen designer clothes. A hive, buzzing with enterprise.

Evan searched the milling crowd for Xavier. The tattoos were overwhelming. Pentagrams and names of the dear departed. Crossbones, grenades, dice, daggers, machetes. And words — words in place of eyebrows, blue letters staining lips, nicknames rendered across throats in Old English letters. Other tattoos coded for crimes the men had committed — rape, murder, kidnapping.

Their rap sheets, inked right on their faces.

Xavier was nowhere to be seen.

A broad-chested man descended from the sanctuary, and the body language of the others changed. Everyone quieted down, their focus drawn. The man had MS in a Gothic font on his forehead, showing him to be a high-ranking member; it was an honor to display the gang's initials above the shoulders. But that wasn't what drew Evan's attention first.

It was his eyes.

They were solid black.

For the first time in a long time, leaning

over the eaves of the crack house, Evan felt a chill. It took a moment for him to recalibrate, to pull himself out of visions of the occult.

The man had tattooed the whites of his eyes.

He had a lean, lupine face, a crucifix running down the bridge of his nose, unfolding its wings across his cheeks. Twinned rows of metal studs decorated his cheeks, and his lower lip bore shark bites, double-hoop piercings on either side. Block letters spelling FREEWAY banded his chin like a drooled spill of blood.

Freeway hugged one of his lieutenants, a hand clasp to shoulder bump, and headed out. The army parted for him.

Benito's words came back to Evan — *They are the people you would least want to anger in the entire world* — and he shivered against the wind.

Walking along the edge of the roof, Evan watched Freeway clang out through the steel door. The guards quieted instantly and stepped aside. Evan mirrored Freeway's movement from above, walking along the rim of the roof as Freeway turned the corner.

A few men threw heavy-metal devil's-head signs at him from the alleys, their fingers forming an inverted *M* for the gang name. Freeway did not return the signs.

When passersby saw him coming, they averted their eyes and stepped off the sidewalk into the gutter to let him pass.

Still no sign of Xavier.

Freeway entered the bodega. Through the remaining window, Evan saw the store owner stiffen. He scurried over and turned the sign on the front door to CLOSED.

Freeway walked through the aisles, grabbing items off shelves, and disappeared into a back courtyard without paying. The owner waited a few moments, catching his breath, and then followed.

Evan's RoamZone rang, the piercing sound startling him. He hadn't noticed how tense he'd grown while watching the gang leader.

The burner cell's number registered in the RoamZone's caller ID.

Evan answered, "Go."

Joey said, "I cracked it."

Evan took in a breath of crisp rooftop air.

"You'd better get over here," she said. "It's worse than we thought."

40
ENHANCED INTERROGATION

Candy pulled the Audi through the side gate, released Tim Draker from the trunk, and marched him in through the rear door. She stayed five feet behind him, pistol aimed at the back of his head. She'd zip-tied his hands at the small of his back, but you couldn't be too cautious. Not with an Orphan.

Draker stepped into the living room, blinking as his eyes adjusted to the gloom. Mattresses covered the windows and walls, soundproofing the space. An array of implements were spread out on a drop cloth. Across the room stood Charles Van Sciver, his log-thick arms crossed.

Candy couldn't help but smirk a bit when she saw Draker sag at the sight of him, as if someone had put slack in the line.

Van Sciver stared over the ledge of his arms, one eye sharp and focused, the other dilated, a dark orb. "Let me tell you what we know," he said. "Jack Johns has long been aware of the directive from above to neutralize washouts, dissenters, Orphans who tested high-risk for defiance. But the shadow file? He knew of its existence before I did. And he knew it was only a matter of time before I got my hands on it. So he reached out to anyone he could and hid those people any way he knew how. He got to a few before we got to him. You were one of them. After you left the Program, he helped you hide. He also took care of the asset you'd recruited for me. David Smith. Twelve years old. Now thirteen."

Van Sciver paused, but Orphan L gave no reaction.

At the mention of the boy, Candy felt cool air across the back of her neck. An uncomfortable sensation, like when she thought about that alley outside Sevastopol, Halya Bardakçi with her baby-giraffe legs and that almond-shaped face. East Slavic through and through, beautiful and alluring, cheaply had and cheaply dispatched. After she'd been stabbed in the neck and dumped in the back of the car, she was still alive. Rattling against the hatch as she bled out.

Van Sciver took a step toward Draker. "We know Jack hid the boy here in Richmond. We know that you helped him before you went to ground. I want to know where the boy is."

Draker said, "Even if I did know anything about this, why would you want the boy? You think he can lead you to X?"

"No," Van Sciver said. "I think he can bring X to me."

Draker said, "I don't know anything about this."

"Is that so," Van Sciver said.

The men regarded each other solemnly.

Then Van Sciver took a step back and tapped on the wall lightly with his knuckles.

A moment later Thornhill entered from the next room. He was holding the turkey baster. He walked a casual arc in front of Van Sciver.

"Enhanced interrogation," Thornhill said, with that broad, easygoing grin. "It's such a well-considered term. Gotta hand it to the Agency. They do know their marketing." He gazed into the middle distance, tapping the baster in his palm. "You know another one I like? Rectal rehydration. It sounds so . . . therapeutic." His stare lowered. "When your intestines are all swollen up with fluid and you get a steel-toed boot in the gut, do you have any idea how much it hurts?"

Draker said, "I do."

"That's just the start," Van Sciver said.

"Have a look around."

Keeping her gun raised, Candy watched Draker take in the items arrayed on the floor.

There were padlocks and plywood.

Nylon ropes and boards of various lengths.

A decline bench and jugs of water.

Mattresses and drop cloths.

Duct tape and a folding metal chair.

A sheen of perspiration covered his face now, and it was no longer a fake-addict sweat. He lifted his head again. Set his jaw.

He said, "Let's get to it, then."

41
BORROWED TIME

Joey chewed her thumbnail, leaning over Evan's shoulder as he sat before the Dell laptop, staring at a list.

Five names.

One of them was Joey Morales.

Morales. All this time he didn't know her last name. He'd been unable even to get her full first name out of her.

The hillside crowded the back windows of the safe house, shadows making the interior dismal. That ever-present moisture had taken hold in the trapped air, turning the place dank. It smelled of microwaved food and girl's deodorant. Evan ran his eyes across the screen once again.

"So much encryption," Evan said, "for five names."

She paused from chewing her thumbnail. "Not just five names. It's a list of people in the Program who were associated with Jack in some way. Look." She shouldered him aside, taking over the keyboard. When she hovered the cursor above the top name, a hidden file appeared. She clicked it, and a host of images proliferated. "This guy? Jim Harville? He was Orphan J. One of the original guys. Jack was his handler way back when. It says it was Jack's first Program assignment."

Evan scanned the files. "How the hell did Van Sciver get his hands on this? This is intel that isn't supposed to *exist.*" He scrolled down the page. "And it's from channels *outside* the Orphan Program. Look here. See, this is NSA/CSS coding."

"What does that mean?"

"It means someone else in the government is watching Van Sciver and the Program — keeping tabs. Van Sciver didn't oversee this intel collection, and he doesn't control it."

"Well," Joey said, "till he *got* control of it."

Dread crept into Evan's stomach, digging in its nails. Van Sciver's cryptic comments looped through his head once again: *You have no idea, do you? How high it goes? You still think it's about me and you.*

Evan said, "What happened to Orphan J?"

"They caught up to him in Venice." She brought up a crime-scene photo of a man lying in a flooded piazza, the back of his head blown off. Another red spot bloomed below one of his shoulder blades. Blood ribboned the water around him. The picture had been taken moments after he was shot, a cell-phone snap.

Evan noted the time stamp on the photo. "Van Sciver's updating the initial files, building on the intel pieces he got his hands on. He's taken these five names and turned them into active hit missions."

"That's right. Like Orphan C." She brought up a picture of an older man, half in shadow, moving through the concourse of a shopping mall in Homewood, Alabama. He was dressed shabbily, toes showing through one of his sneakers. "Now look at this." She'd dug up an article about an unidentified homeless man murdered beneath a freeway ramp in Birmingham. A picture from a local shelter accompanied the article, showing the man at a soup kitchen.

Evan sank back in the chair. "That's why Jack was in Alabama. He knew this was coming, that this file could leak."

"And that's why he found me," Joey said. "Why he moved me to Oregon and hid me."

Evan stared at the name, bare on the screen: *Joey Morales.*

"It's beyond creepy." Joey slid the cursor

over her own name, and a surveillance grab from a 7-Eleven security camera popped up, showing her walking through the aisles, baseball hat pulled low. But the angle was sufficient to capture her face. It was dated nearly a year ago, an address listed in Albuquerque. Same faded NSA/CSS stamp at the bottom of the page.

"This is from a week after I took off from Van Sciver," Joey said. "But it was enough to get them on my trail. And lead them here."

She tapped another link, and zoom-lens surveillance photos of the Hillsboro apartment populated the screen. Joey through a rear window, brushing her teeth. Joey shadowboxing, no more than a silhouette in the unlit apartment. Joey in the open doorway, casting a wary eye as she paid for a take-out order. She minimized the windows, exposing a report beneath that listed sixty-three nodal points of facial recognition and the same Oregon address that Jack had scrawled on his truck window right before he'd been forced aboard that Black Hawk and lifted sixteen thousand feet in the air.

"You were right," Joey said. "They had someone sitting on me. Waiting for you."

Evan looked at the remaining two names.

"Tim Draker," he said. "Jack told me

about him. Orphan L. He was one of Van Sciver's guys until they fell out about a year ago. Is he dead, too?"

"Probably," she said.

Evan put his finger on the trackpad, targeted Draker's name. A streetlight camera had caught him exiting an anonymous drug-rehab center in Baltimore ten months ago. The imagery featured the NSA/CSS stamp.

A newer surveillance photo caught Draker smoking outside a facility in Bethesda, Maryland. It was dated November 28, two days ago, the time stamp showing 8:37 P.M. Minutes before Evan had blasted through the door of the pest-control shop, killed everyone inside, and taken the laptop. Van Sciver's update must have just come in. This second photo had no stamp or coding of any kind.

"The NSA intel put Van Sciver on the trail of drug-treatment places," Joey said. "From there it was only a matter of time."

Evan stared at the date on that surveillance photo and knew in his gut that Draker was lost.

"Which means that we're down to one little Indian," Joey said.

Evan stared at the last name: *David Smith.* Moved his fingertip a few inches. The ghost file opened.

A photo of a twelve-year-old boy. A birth certificate. A file painting a familiar story, various foster homes in various poverty-stricken counties. And then it showed a recruitment report from two years ago, listing Tim Draker as David's handler.

Evan looked for more information, but there wasn't any to be had. "That's it?"

"That's it."

"Won't Van Sciver have found him by now?"

"There are 33,637 people named David Smith in the country," Joey said. "And believe me, with how well Jack's been stashing people? The kid ain't using that name anymore." She jabbed a finger at the screen. "These people are hidden as well as it is possible to hide someone. Everything I know — hell, everything *you* know about being invisible? We learned from Jack. So I think Van Sciver's still searching for this kid. I think he's chasing him down now. And if we don't find him first, he's gonna kill the kid like he killed everyone else."

Evan stood up. Laced his hands at the back of his neck and breathed. "All this . . ."

Joey completed the thought. "All this is because of you."

He looked at her.

"Van Sciver's killing his way to you right now," she said. "All of us — these five names and however many more Van Sciver doesn't have yet? We're *all* on borrowed time."

"How do we help that kid?" Evan said.

"We find him."

"We can't compete with Van Sciver's resources. I have access to databases, but he's at a whole other level."

"You're right." Joey was chewing her thumb again, drifting behind the table, her eyes intense. "When it comes to David Smith we have an absence of data."

"Right," Evan said. "How do you look for an absence of data?"

"Deep-learning software," she said. "Believe me, that's what Van Sciver's using."

She looked over at Evan, saw that he wasn't following.

"It's machine learning using advanced mathematics," she said.

"That doesn't help."

She leaned over the table, peering at him from above the laptop screen. "It finds patterns you don't even know you're looking for." She took another turn around the table, passing behind Evan. "Between the name David Smith, potential fake names befitting a thirteen-year-old white kid, facial characteristics, his birth-certificate information, physical developmental changes, purchase patterns for foster kids fitting his analytics, past locations, receipts, meds, and thousands of other factors we're not aware of but can be extrapolated from on the basis of that thin file" — she jabbed a finger at the screen — "let's say that there are five billion combinations of data. Being conservative."

"Conservative."

"Yes. Without a machine learning system, it would be impossible to correlate all that data, let alone zero in on David Smith under his new name in his new hiding place."

"Okay," Evan said. "So what's the best way for us to do that?"

She paused long enough to flick a smile his way. "Someone who knows where he is —"

"— and a hammer," Evan said. He stood up. "Seriously, Joey. Can we break into somewhere that has these capabilities and run the data?"

"No. This kind of processing takes time. Days even."

"What equipment do we need?" he said.

"A pile of hardware," she said. Mutual exasperation had given the discussion the tenor of an argument. "And like, say, a shit-ton of common graphics-processing unit chips. The mathematics involved in machine learning take advantage of the massive parallelism of the thousands of cores in those things. We'd need giant-ass GPU arrays, computer towers stuffed full of graphics cards, linked together with a high-speed InfiniBand network, running at eighty gigabits and —." She stopped, looked at him. "More stuff I'd explain to you if I thought you could understand."

"So how do we do that? Right now?"

"Raid the computer-graphics lab building at Pixar." She studied his expression. "Joking."

Frustration mounting, he drifted over and leaned against the couch. The cushions and pillows had been rearranged for her to sleep there, a T-shirt balled up for a pillow.

He stared across at an old-school photograph of David Smith on the screen. He wore a dated bowl cut and a collared three-button shirt with a frayed shoulder. Lank blond hair with a cowlick parting his bangs, hazel eyes, pleasingly even features. His gaze was lifted from the camera, as if the photographer's last directive had caught him off guard. He looked lost. They always did.

"I'm not gonna let Van Sciver get to that kid," Evan said. "So give me an answer for how to find you what you need to figure this out."

"It's complex shit, X," she said. "It's not like we can just drive through a Best Buy. Your average person doesn't have —"

She stopped, mouth slightly ajar. She bowed her head, pinched her eyes at the bridge of her nose.

"Joey?"

"Don't talk."

"Joey —"

She held up a hand. He silenced. She stayed that way for thirty seconds. Thirty seconds is longer than it sounds.

And then, with her face still buried in her hand, she said, "Bitcoin mining."

"What?"

"You do bitcoin mining." She lowered her hand, and her face held something more than joy. It held triumph. "No government regulation, no oversight."

"Yes."

"Which means you have a 2U rackmount computer bay."

"Two of them."

Her eyes were shining. "I could kiss you. Figuratively. Each rack has sixteen graphics cards. At four chips per card and 2,048 cores per chip, that gives us 8,192 graphics cores per card. We have thirty-two cards, which makes" — she closed her eyes again, her lips twitching — "262,144 graphics cores." She looked up. "That's a lotta horsepower."

"So I can just use my bitcoin-mining setup?"

"No." Her irritation flared again. "Everything has to be reconfigured."

Evan looked at the Snickers wrapper on the kitchen counter, the T-shirt pillow on the couch. "Pack up your stuff," he said.

"What? Why?"

"I just came up with a new Commandment."

At this her eyebrows rose. "A new Commandment? What is it?"

" 'Don't fall in love with Plan A.' "

42
UNDONE BY TARGET

Joey stood in the great room of Evan's penthouse in Castle Heights, staring at the tall ceiling, her mouth gaping. After the places she'd lived, it probably seemed like the Serengeti to her.

Watching her, Evan felt discomfort beneath his skin, an awareness of his posture, how he was holding his arms. He could count on his fingers the number of people who had been inside 21A, and not one of them had known Evan's real identity.

"By bringing you here, I am giving you my absolute trust," he said. "Trust I have given no one before. Ever."

Joey was taking a pass through the kitchen, trickling a finger across the countertops, the island, the Sub-Zero, like a housewife at an open house. But at his words she paused and looked over at him. The weight of the moment was potent enough that it quieted the air between them.

"What if I don't deserve it?" she said.

"If you didn't deserve it, I wouldn't give it to you."

"This place," she said. "It's like something made up."

"What did you expect?"

"Judging by your taste in motels and your lovely safe-house decor, I thought you lived in . . . I don't know, a shoe."

"A shoe."

"Yeah. But this? This is like a Louboutin."

"What's that?"

"A fancy shoe they talk about on TV."

"Oh."

"Where do I stay?" She looked around. "I guess I could sleep on the dumbbell rack."

He hadn't thought about it. "There's a couch in the reading loft."

"The reading loft. Of course."

He pointed at the steel spiral staircase. "Full bathroom, too."

She gestured tentatively. "May I?"

"Yes."

She twisted up the stairs and disappeared.

Another human. Out of sight. Inside his place. Doing whatever humans did.

He looked over at the vertical garden. It looked back. He wondered if the plants were as uncomfortable as he was.

"This might be a very bad idea," he told them.

He thought again of David Smith in his frayed school shirt and swallowed his own discomfort.

After a moment Joey came back downstairs, running a hand along the curved handrail as if she wasn't sure it was real.

"Is it okay?" he asked.

"It is," she said, "more than okay."

"Let's get to work."

"Okay. Quick question: Where are the extra sheets? And pillows?"

He looked at her.

"Like for guests," she said.

"Guests," Evan repeated. He gave a nod. "We'll figure that out later."

Joey turned to the east-facing windows, gawking at downtown in the distance. The discreet armor sunshades were raised, the glass tinted. She took a step closer. The entire wall was transparent. At least in one direction.

She said, "You can see into so many apartments from here."

Evan said, "Yes."

She set her palms against the Lexan pane. He made a note to wipe off the smudges later.

"Did Jack teach you about the Mango-day?" she asked.

"Genghis Khan's cavalrymen."

"Yeah." She laughed, her breath clouding the glass. "He said they were the first elite special-operations force. They fought without fear, beyond the limits of the human body. Know how Khan trained those warriors?"

"Built a regimen based on starving wolves."

"Yeah," she said. "The hungrier a wolf is, the braver and more ferocious he gets."

"You're saying that's what we are."

"Yes. That's what we are. And this place? This place looks like the home of someone who's always hungry."

"For what?"

She looked back at him, her hair flicking over one shoulder. Her hands remained on the window. "For everything out *there.*"

Evan broke off her stare, heading down the hall to the master suite. "Let's get to work," he said again.

He could hear Joey jogging to catch up. He opened the door and stepped into his bedroom. She crossed the threshold and halted.

"Um," she said. "Your bed is floating."

"Yes."

"You have a bed," she said. "That floats."

"We've covered that."

"Why?"

Evan blinked at her. "Can we please just get to work?"

She looked around. "Where?"

When they stepped through the hidden door into the Vault, Joey actually gasped. She circled the cramped space, checking the equipment, noting the monitors. "Is this . . . ? Am I in . . . ? This is heaven."

She picked up Vera II in her glass bowl. "Cute."

"Put her down."

"Her?"

Before he could respond, Joey spotted the 2U rackmount computer bays and beelined over to them. "Good. Good. This is good." She checked the setup. "You already have an InfiniBand cable, so you're not entirely useless, but we have to pick up some basic Cat 6 cables."

"This is a state-of-the-art system. Why do we need Ethernet cables?"

"What we're building? It's basically a bunch of graphics cores tied together. We need to hook up the machines, and the best way to do that is using plain old GigEthernet." She studied his blank expression. "People today. You know how to work everything, but you don't know how anything works."

She breezed past him, heading out. "Come on. Let's go to Target."

"Target?"

"Yeah, we can grab the cables there. Plus, I need stuff."

"Like what?"

She faced him, filling the doorway. "There's no soap. Or shampoo. Or conditioner. Or sheets. Or pillows. And I need some other stuff."

"I can get it for you."

"Girl stuff."

Oh.

"Target it is," he said.

Red signs blared 50-percent-off discounts. A kid stutter-stepped past, trying on a pair of sneakers still connected by a plastic loop while his mom shouted, "How's the toe? Is your heel slipping?" A cluster of girls modeled sunglasses, checking themselves out using their iPhones as mirrors. A stern-looking father was saying, "Read the ingredients. There's no food in food anymore." A husband and wife were having a heated debate over detergent. "No, the *lavender* scent is the one that gives you the rash!"

Evan stood frozen in the wide aisle of the

second floor next to Joey.

She did a double take at his stunned expression. "You okay?"

A worker wheeled a pallet piled with jumbo diaper packs, nearly clipping Evan's knee.

He swallowed. "I'll wait outside," he said.

Evan stood in the parking structure just past Target's sliding glass doors, breathing the night air, catching his breath. Brimming shopping carts rattled past concrete security posts, shoved by flustered parents in sweatpants. Evan kept his hand near his hidden pistol and his eyes on the circuslike surroundings. Parking disputes proliferated. Car horns blared. Remote-controlled minivan doors wheeled open. By the shopping-cart rack, kids fought over coin-operated kiddie rides.

Exclamations crowded in on him.

"— not gonna buy you a toy every single time we go to the —"

"— I was already backing up! I saw the reverse lights before I was past the —"

"— not the kind your mom uses, thank God, or the powder room would smell like the potpourri Olympics —"

And then, mercifully, Joey was there. A few bags dangled from either arm. She was regarding his face with what seemed to be amusement.

"Let's go," Evan said.

"Aw. You're all uncomfortable like. That's so cute."

"Joey."

"Okay, okay."

"You got the cable."

She smacked her forehead with her palm. "Shoot. I knew I forgot something."

He felt himself blanch. "Really?"

"No." She smiled that luminous smile. "Of course I have it. Let's get you away from the big, scary discount retailer."

He gritted his teeth and turned for his truck.

That's when he saw Mia and Peter climbing out of Mia's Acura.

He stiffened. Turned back to Joey. Her face grew serious. "What's wrong?" she said.

"Nothing. Someone I can't see here. Now. With you. Go there. Pretend you're . . . I don't know, playing on the ride."

Joey took in the coin-operated kiddie rides. "The choo-choo train?"

"Yes."

"I'm sixteen."

"I don't care."

"You don't know much about kids, do you?"

He put a hand on her side, hustled her toward the front of the store.

"Lemme help you out," Joey said. "I'll just pretend I'm playing on my phone."

"Okay. Fine. Good."

From behind him he heard Peter's raspy voice: "Evan Smoak!"

He turned as Mia and Peter approached.

Mia said, *"Evan?"*

"Hi."

"Wait. I didn't think you knew where Target was. Lemme guess — there's a sale on vodka?"

"Just needed some . . . things."

"Is that girl with you?"

"Who?" Evan said. "No."

Joey remained immersed in her phone. For all their collective tradecraft, the ruse was paper thin.

"Yes," Evan said.

Joey looked up, gave a flat smile.

Mia's head cocked. Her gaze narrowed — the district-attorney gaze.

"She's sort of . . . my niece." Evan said. "Staying with me awhile. She needed some . . ." He winced. "Girl things."

"I thought you didn't have any family."

"She's the closest to it, I guess. Kind of a . . . a second cousin's kid. Through a marriage. But then her parents died. Sort of thing."

He took a deep breath, let it burn in his lungs. All his impeccable training, living his cover, becoming his legend. Never a skip, a stutter, a false move. And here he was.

Undone by Target.

"It's a weird situation," he conceded.

"Indeed." Mia's glare softened only when she looked over at Joey. "Hi, honey. I'm Mia."

Joey came over and shook her hand. "Joey."

"Super-cool girl name," Peter said.

Mia's ringtone sounded — the theme to *Jaws,* which signaled a call from her office. She said, "Gimme a sec," and stepped away to answer.

Peter blinked up at Joey and Evan. "I was in class today? And Zachary had an egg-salad sandwich? And he took it out right before lunch, and it totally smelled like someone farted, and it was on my side of the classroom, so everyone was looking at *me,* and what am I gonna say? Like, 'I didn't fart'? I mean, who believes that?"

Joey looked over at Evan. "Does it have an off button?"

Standing a few paces away, Mia paused from her call to glance across at Evan, her displeasure clear.

Was she mad at him for having a sort-of niece? For being at Target? For not introducing her to Joey right away?

Peter had cornered Joey against the choo-choo ride. "What's your favorite color?"

"Matte black," Joey said.

"What do you like to play?"

"I don't."

"What do you like to play *with*?"

"The entrails of children."

"What's an entrails?"

"Guts."

"Really?"

"Yes."

Peter processed this behind his charcoal eyes. "Really they're the guts, or really that's what you like to play with?"

Evan cleared his throat. "Time we get going."

Mia wrapped up her phone call and stepped back over, ruffling Peter's hair.

"Mom," Peter said, "Evan Smoak's niece person is *awesome.*"

"I'm sure she is," Mia said. "It was nice to meet you, sweetheart."

She shot Evan a look that seemed to code for murderous rage, put her arm around Peter's shoulders, and disappeared through the automated glass doors.

Evan exhaled a breath he hadn't known he was holding.

"Well played," Joey said. "Orphan X."

Evan started for his truck, not caring if she kept up.

43
GROWN-MAN PROBLEMS

Evan crouched gargoyle-still at the edge of the crack-house roof, peering through the shattered stained-glass window into the church next door.

Freeway sat on the carpeted steps leading to the altar, a king on his throne. A series of kids entered, each slinging a giant zippered bag at his feet. They looked no older than Evan had been when he was taken from the Pride House Group Home.

Indoctrination — best started early.

The boys entered the church with swagger, but all signs of confidence evaporated by the time they reached the altar. They kept their heads lowered, afraid to meet Freeway's stare.

It was a hard stare to meet.

He cast his solid black eyes over his spoils, giving a faint nod to dismiss each child in turn.

Evan scanned the other gang members

clustered in groups around the tipped-over pews, searching for Benito's son. But just like this morning, there was no sign of Xavier. Evan had left Joey in the Vault, hard at work reassembling his hardware. The thought of her in his sanctuary unattended, pulling cords and handling his possessions, caused a discomfort that was physical, insects running beneath his skin. He couldn't think about it right now and keep his focus.

And given that he was surveilling the deadliest gang in the world, he needed to keep his focus.

A commotion at the front door drew his attention. A group of women were corralled into the vestibule. Bright makeup, torn stockings, stiff hair. One was missing the heel on one of her red pumps.

Evan was surprised to see that the men who had brought them were not yet visibly tattooed. Lowly initiates, given the lowly task of gathering the street girls.

As the newcomers shuffled through the sporadic falls of light from the overheads, Evan caught a glimpse of a young man in the back. Xavier. He helped herd the women through the nave toward the altar. He wore a flannel shirt with the sleeves ripped off, the gym-toned muscles of his shoulders rippling.

The women rotated before Freeway, handing over wads of crumpled cash that he eyed and then handed to one of his lieutenants. None of the women met Freeway's eyes. Several seemed to hold their breath until they scurried away to gather by the bags of stolen goods.

The last woman in the group, the one with the broken heel, stepped forward and offered up a few tattered bills. Freeway examined them, clearly unimpressed, then let them fall to the floor.

He stood up.

The effect was momentous.

All the gang members went on point. The woman started trembling, shaking her head. Evan couldn't hear her beg, but he knew that she was.

Freeway gripped her chin, squeezing her cheeks. He flicked out a straight razor, which gleamed in the low lights from the altar.

She cowered, her back to Evan, blocking his view. Freeway towered over her. Evan saw his hand rise and move across her face, two strokes, each punctuated with an artistic flair of the wrist. Her shriek was clear, even above the wind rushing over the rooftop.

Evan moved his gaze away from Freeway and the woman, finding Xavier. Benito's son stood in the half shadows to the side of the altar. The other gang members looked on with reverence, but Xavier's arms were crossed uncomfortably. His face was pale, blood draining away, and his blink ratio had picked up — signs of an anxiety reaction.

Freeway flung the woman aside. She landed on her belly with her torso twisted, bringing her face into view, and Evan saw the damage inflicted on it.

Matching slashes across both cheekbones, red streaming like war paint.

Freeway hadn't just punished her. He'd marked her for life.

She sat on the floor, hands cupping her face, blood spilling through her fingers.

All the gang members were watching Freeway.

Except Xavier.

He watched the woman.

Noteworthy.

Freeway dismissed his men with a flick of his fingers and headed back to the sanctuary to attend to other business. They streamed out. Xavier got halfway to the door, then paused and looked back at the woman, on her knees before the altar.

His jaw shifted with discomfort. He looked torn.

One of the other initiates said something to him, and he snapped to, exiting the church.

Evan watched the woman unsteadily find her feet. The other women finally broke out of their paralyzed trance by the bags of stolen goods and rushed to her. The injured woman collapsed into their embrace.

They helped her out a side door.

Evan backed away from the edge of the roof.

He caught up to Xavier four blocks north as he said good-bye to two fellow initiates at a street corner. Xavier peeled off, heading up a dark block alone, ignoring the invitations of the street girls: "Hey, Big Time, wanna get warm?"

Evan shadowed him, keeping a half block back. After a quarter mile, Xavier cut up the stairs of a dilapidated house that had been diced into a fourplex. From across the street, Evan waited and watched. Most of the windows of the apartment building behind him were open, *banda* radio music and the smell of charred meat streaming out.

After a moment a light clicked on in a

window on the fourplex's second floor.

Evan waited as a low-rider scraped past and then he crossed the street. The front door's lock was a joke, the metal guard bent back from previous B&Es. Evan pulled out his fake driver's license, used the edge to slide the turtle head of the latch bolt level with the plate, and eased the door open.

He took the stairs up to a tiny entry between two facing doors. The floorboards, though battered, looked to be oak, probably the surviving section of a study from before the house had been carved up.

He rapped on the door to the left.

Footsteps. The peephole darkened.

"Who the hell are you?"

"Your father sent me."

"Go away. You're gonna get yourself hurt."

"Open the door."

"You threatening me, fool? Do you have any idea who the fuck I am?"

"Why don't you open the door and show me?"

The door ripped open. Xavier stood there holding a crappy .22 sideways, like a music-video gangsta. His head was drawn back, chin tilted up.

Evan stood there staring at him over the barrel.

Xavier cleared his throat, then cleared it

again. Apparently the gun was not having the effect he'd hoped.

"Your throat's dry," Evan said.

"What?"

"Because you're scared. Adrenaline's pumping. It acts like an antihistamine, lessens the production of saliva."

Xavier stuck the muzzle in Evan's face.

Evan regarded it, a few inches before his nose. "You're holding your weapon sideways."

"I *know* how to hold my *goddamn* —"

Evan's hands blurred. He cranked Xavier's arm to the side, snatched the .22 neatly from his grasp, and stripped the gun. Pieces rained down on the floor. Slide, barrel, operating spring, magazine, frame.

Xavier stared at his empty hand, the red streak on his forearm, his dissected gun littering the floor around his Nikes.

"Step inside," Evan said.

Xavier stepped inside.

Evan followed, sweeping the remains of the gun with his boot, and closed the door behind him.

It was a run-down place, sleeping bag on the floor, flat-screen TV tilted against the Sheetrock, floor strewn with dirty clothes. An add-on kitchenette counter bulged out one wall — hot plate, microwave, chipped sink. An exposed snarl of plumbing hung beneath the counter like a tangle of intestines.

"Life's not fair," Evan said. "Your mom died. You pulled a dumb move and joined a gang. The wrong gang. I think you're scared. I think you're in over your head and you don't know how to get out."

The sleeveless flannel bulged across Xavier's chest. Veins wiggled through his biceps. He was a big kid.

"You don't know nuthin' about me, *baboso.*"

"You sure you want me to work this hard to like you?"

"I didn't ask you to come here."

"No. Your father did."

"That old man don't know shit."

Evan cuffed him, an open-handed slap upside the head. The sound rang off the cracked drywall. When Xavier pulled his face back to center, his cheek bore the mark of Evan's palm.

"Make whatever choices you want to fuck up your life," Evan said. "But don't disrespect that man."

Xavier touched his fingertips to his cheek. Down near the elbow, his forearm had a tattoo so fresh it was still scabbed up. An elaborate *M* — the beginning of *Mara Sal-*

vatrucha.

He stared at Evan. And then he nodded. "Okay."

"We both know you're not a killer," Evan said. "But they're gonna make you one."

Xavier's face had softened, his cheeks full, his eyes as clear as in that photograph Benito had shown Evan. He looked much younger than twenty-four.

"I know," he said.

Evan recalled the tremble in Benito's voice when he discussed his son. This boy he'd taught to put on socks, ride a bike, throw a baseball. Countless hours of loving attention, late nights and early mornings, and then your son winds up here, with grown-man problems. And you — the father who once held the answers to the universe — you're helpless.

A memory flash penetrated Evan's thoughts: *Jack squinting into a handheld camera at sixteen thousand feet, wind whipping his hair.* Evan banished the image.

"I *am* out of time," Xavier said. "I swore the oath." He held up his arm, showed the tattooed *M* at his elbow. "It's written on my flesh. Know why they do that?"

"It's good business," Evan said. "Once you're marked, you can't ever join another gang. They own you. Which means they can treat you however they want and you can never leave."

Xavier looked confused at that. "It's to show allegiance. For *life,* get it?"

"Nothing is for life. We can remake ourselves in any image we want. One choice at a time."

"I'm out of choices."

"We're never out of choices."

"Know what their motto is? *'Mata, viola, controla.'*" Xavier snarled the words, suddenly the raw-boned gang member again. " 'Kill, rape, control.' "

"*Their* motto," Evan said.

"What?"

"You said, 'Their motto.' Not 'Our motto.' "

"I already robbed a store. I stole stuff from a truck. They make me collect from the *putas*. I brought one in today, and she . . . she got her face cut open." Xavier put his hand over his mouth, squeezed his lips. "I'm already one of them."

"Does anyone beyond this chapter know about you?"

"No. I'm just getting jumped in."

"No one back in El Salvador?"

Xavier's eyes shone with fear. "No."

"You've got one chance to get out."

Xavier paced a tight circle by the kitchenette, came back around to face Evan. "Why do you care?"

"I got into something when *I* was young," Evan said. "I'll never get out. Not clean. You still can."

"What about them?"

"I can handle them."

"You can't do that. No one can do that."

Evan just smiled.

Human engineering had been part of Evan's training, no less than savate and marksmanship and endurance. He had been trained to disappear into a crowd and fire three-inch clusters at a thousand yards. He had been trained to intimidate, to make grown men afraid. He could convey breathtaking menace when he had to.

So he just smiled, and that was enough.

"You decide what you want," Evan said. "And call if you need me: 1-855-2-NOWHERE. Say it back to me."

Xavier said it back.

Evan started for the door. He'd stepped over the stripped gun and set his hand on the doorknob when Xavier spoke.

"This girl today, her face . . ." Xavier lowered his head. "There's a point you cross where you can't get yourself back. Where you can't find, I don't know. Redemption."

"Every choice holds redemption."

Xavier lifted his eyes to meet Evan's. "You really believe that?"

Evan said, "I have to."

44
RUNNING THE SAME RACE

A half-drunk glass of milk rested on the kitchen island. Standing just inside his front door, keys still in hand, Evan stared across the open stretch of floor at it.

There was filmy white residue up one side where Joey had sipped.

He unlaced his boots and then crossed to the kitchen.

He picked up the glass. It had left a circle of milk on his counter. Beside it a pile of crumbs rested next to a torn-open box of water crackers. The inside bag was left open, the crackers exposed to the air, growing stale.

What kind of feral creature ate like this?

The rest of the world could be filthy and chaotic and lawless. But not in here. After scraping through the underside of society, Evan needed to return to order.

He washed the glass by hand, dried it, and put it away. There was another glass missing from the cupboard, an empty spot leaving the left row incomplete. It occurred to him that two glasses had never been out of the cupboard at the same time. He nudged the clean glass into place, the set of six still down one soldier.

Maybe she needed another glass upstairs.

Maybe that's how people did things.

Joey could have used more time with Jack. The Second Commandment: *How you do anything is how you do everything.*

Evan put away the box of crackers, swept the crumbs into his hand, dumped them into the garbage disposal. He waved his hand beneath the Kohler Sensate touchless kitchen faucet, turning on the clean blade of water so he could run the disposal. There were smudges on the polished chrome.

Who touched a touchless faucet?

He cleaned off the smudges and then got out a sheet of waxed paper and used it to wipe down the chrome. It prevented water spots. When he was done, he sprayed and paper-toweled the counter, washed his hands, got an ice cube for Vera II, and headed across the great room and down the brief hall.

The door to his bedroom was open.

He didn't like open doors.

The bedspread on his Maglev floating bed

was dimpled where someone had sat and not bothered to smooth it back into place.

The door to his bathroom was open.

One of Joey's sweatshirts was tossed on the floor by the bathmat. One corner of the bath mat was flipped back. With a toe he adjusted it.

The shower door was rolled open.

The hidden door to the Vault left wide.

He took five deep breaths before proceeding.

"Joey," he said, stepping into the Vault. "The milk glass —"

The sight inside the Vault left his mouth dry. An adrenaline antihistamine reaction.

Various monitors had been yanked off the wall and rearranged on the floor, data scrolling across them. The computer bays had been dissected, torn from their racks. Cables snaked between hardware, connecting everything by no evident design.

Joey lay on her back like a car mechanic, wearing a tank top, her sleek arm muscles glistening with sweat. She was checking a cable connection. She rolled over and popped to her feet.

"Check this shit out!"

"I am. Checking this shit. Out." Evan picked Vera II up off the floor, nestled an ice cube in her serrated spikes, and eyed her accusatorily: *I left you in charge.*

Joey breezed past him, using her bare foot to swivel a monitor on the floor so she could check the screen. The scent of girly soap tinged the air, lilac and vanilla, anomalous here among the weapon lockers and electronic hum.

She laced her fingers, inverted her hands, cracked the knuckles. "You are looking at a beautifully improvised machine learning system — 262,144 graphics cores devoted to a single cause. Tracking down David Smith."

Evan figured maybe he could forgive the milk. And the crumbs. And the smudges on the faucet.

He set Vera II back on the sheet-metal desk. She was now the only item in the Vault in the proper place.

He looked at the open door to the Vault and the rolled-back shower door beyond and bit his lip. Managed the words "Good job."

She held up a hand, and they high-fived. "At least now you and Van Sciver? You're running the same race."

45

A Bit More Incentive

Listening to all that gurgling and choking wore on a man.

Van Sciver set down the watercooler jug of Arrowhead and wiped his brow. Enhanced interrogation was hard work.

Orphan L was strapped onto a decline bench, a soaked towel suctioned onto his face. Van Sciver had been pouring a steady stream of fresh springwater through the towel and into L's sinuses, larynx, oropharynx, trachea, and bronchi. It didn't actually reach the lungs.

It just felt like it.

Van Sciver had been waterboarded as part of his training. All Orphans were.

The discomfort almost defied explanation.

He'd been drownproofed as well, and by comparison that was a breeze. Bound at the bottom of a swimming pool, breathing in water, the head going hazy as in a dream.

But this felt like having a water hose

opened up inside your skull. The more you gasped for air, the further you pulled the towel into your mouth, an octopus clutching your face, expelling an endless stream of fluid through your orifices.

Van Sciver nodded at Thornhill, who lifted the soaked towel from Orphan L's face. For a time Draker bobbed on the bench, blood-shot eyes bulging, mouth guppying. He didn't make a noise.

When the upper respiratory tract filled, water obstruction prevented the diaphragm from expanding and contracting to produce a suitable cough. You had to fight to earn your oxygen.

Five seconds passed as Draker contorted, clutching for air.

Thornhill gazed down at him with empathetic eyes. "I feel you, pal. I feel you."

Candy leaned against the mattress cushioning the far wall, examining her fingernails. They looked freshly painted. Aubergine.

Van Sciver looked back at Thornhill, nodded again. Thornhill undid the straps around L's chest and thighs, and L rolled off the bench onto his side. When he struck the floor, the impact loosed his lungs, his head seeming to explode with jets of water.

He coughed, heaved, coughed some more.

Thornhill slapped his back a few times, encouragingly. "There you go."

Draker whipped up in a violent sit-up, driving his forehead at Thornhill's nose. Thornhill wheeled back, nearly losing his footing. He looked down at his shirt, darkened by the spray from Draker's wet hair. Draker's head butt had missed him by inches.

"Whoa, cowboy," Thornhill said, seemingly pleased by the effort. "That was close."

Draker collapsed flat on the floor, spent.

Van Sciver squatted beside him, knees cracking, alert. "The boy," he said. "The address."

Draker gagged a few times. Van Sciver pressed two fingers into his solar plexus, and Draker vomited a water-clear stream so calmly and steadily that it was like opening up a tap. When he was done, he took a few seconds to catch his breath. Then he said, "What boy?"

"Right on," Candy said. "Gotta admire the grit."

She peeled herself from the wall and tested the plywood covering one of the rear windows. It was screwed in tight but not too tight. Which was perfect.

Van Sciver said to Thornhill, "Get the dog collar on him."

The next technique, walling, was a Guantánamo Bay special. There they slipped a rolled towel around the detainee's neck and used it to slam him into a semiflexible wall. The shoulder blades hit first, snapping the head. The collision gives off a sound like a thunderclap, like someone banging cymbals in the space between your ears.

Van Sciver preferred to use an actual collar. They were more durable, and his meaty hand never slipped. Plus, when he squeezed tight, he'd found, his knuckles shoved into the larynx, which added a bit more incentive.

Thornhill secured the collar around L's neck.

"I don't know about this, bud," Thornhill said, flashing that carefree smile. "I was you, I'd just talk to the man."

L lay there, curled on his side, panting. Van Sciver knew how it was. You had to enjoy the respites when you had them.

It was tough work from both sides.

"Get him on his feet," Van Sciver said.

Draker was limp, his muscles turned to rubber. Candy and Thornhill juggled him up, holding most of his weight. He'd gone boneless.

Van Sciver seized the collar and dragged L over to the plywood sheet.

"Where is David Smith?" he asked again.

Draker couldn't speak, not with the knuckles, but he managed to shake his head.

"Damn," Van Sciver said, setting his feet and firming his grip. "You must really love the kid."

46
Menu of Even More Specialized Services

At the edge of an industrial park in Northridge, through two security doors, past a warehouse humming with painters and restorers reviving valuable vintage movie posters, down a back hall tinged with the smell of petroleum and cleaning surfactants, Melinda Truong stood in a dark-walled photography room, fists on her slender hips, regarding Evan and Joey.

Melinda wore yoga pants and spotless robin's-egg-blue Pumas that looked to be limited-edition and pricier than most vehicles. Straight black hair fell to her waist, which was gripped by a construction worker's tool belt that required freshly awled holes so it could be cinched tighter in order to accommodate her tiny frame. The tool belt held an Olympos double-action airbrush, a 000 paintbrush, and various sizes of X-Acto blades, their grips padded with pink tape to discourage her workers from borrowing them.

She was the sole woman in the building. She was the owner of the operation. She was also the finest forger Evan had ever encountered.

One of her fists still gripped a retrofitted insecticide atomizer. Evan had interrupted her at the wet table over a *Frankenstein* one-sheet from 1931, cleaning a coffee spot off Boris Karloff's cheek. The restored movie poster would be worth hundreds of thousands of dollars. But that was far less than she made from her menu of even more specialized services, conducted here in the photography room with its windows blacked out, ostensibly to prevent reflections during shooting.

She ticked the muzzle of the atomizer at Evan now, a show of mock annoyance. "It's a good thing I have a secret crush on you," she said. "Or I'd never let you stomp in here with this child and interrupt my work."

"I'm not a child," Joey said.

Melinda did not look over at her, instead holding up a finger. "Seen but not heard."

Joey zippered her mouth.

Evan said, "Apologies."

Melinda swept back her hair, a gesture that was at once concise and sensuous, and tapped her cheek. Evan complied, moving forward to kiss it. At the last minute, she turned, catching his lips with hers.

She lingered a moment, then shoved him back. "Now. What do you want?"

Joey took this in speechlessly.

"I need full papers for her," Evan said. "Multiple IDs, Social, driver's, birth certificate, travel visas, a backstopped history. Make her eighteen."

"When?" Melinda asked.

"Now."

Melinda looked over at her cobbler's bench covered with etched metal plates, embossing tools, letterpress drawers holding passport stamps. She sighed.

Then she snapped her fingers at Joey, who stepped forward as if jabbed with a cattle prod. Melinda took her chin in hand and turned her face this way and that, assessing the face behind which she was going to build a new identity.

"Beneath all that scowling and the weird haircut, you are a very pretty girl," she finally conceded.

"Thank you."

"It's not a compliment. It's an observation."

The sounds of the workers in the warehouse carried up the hall — suction tables roaring, equipment racks wheeling from station to station, exclamations rising above the din.

Melinda released Joey's face, picked up a phone on the desk next to an AmScope binocular microscope, and punched a button. Then she said in her native tongue, *"Be quiet. I can't hear myself think in here, and when I can't think, I act on emotion."*

The entire building silenced immediately. She hung up the phone. When she turned back, Joey's mouth was slightly ajar.

Joey said, "You are one badass lady."

"Yes, honey," Melinda said. "I am sure."

47
THE LANGUAGE OF COMFORT

Before bed Evan showered, dressed, and then finished tidying up the Vault as best he could. He found himself trying to align the monitors on the floor and finally gave up.

Chaos was a small price to pay when a thirteen-year-old boy's life was at stake.

He stared at the various progress bars, all that software dredging the Web for signs of David Smith. "Work faster," he said.

As he turned to leave, a rapid-fire series of beeps chimed from the alarm system, indicating an intruder at the windows or balconies. His eyes darted around the Vault, searching the rejiggered monitors to find the one holding the appropriate security feed. He was two steps to the gun locker when he found it and relaxed.

On the screen he watched a dark shape hover outside his bedroom window, bumping the glass.

He sighed and stepped through the shower

and the bathroom. As he emerged into his bedroom, Joey entered from the hall. She was wearing pajama bottoms and a loose-fitting T-shirt.

She said, "What's that noise?"

Evan pointed to the window. An old-fashioned diamond kite flapped in the breeze, smacking against the pane.

Peter's bedroom was directly below Evan's, nine floors down.

"A kid's kite?" Joey said.

Evan opened the window and pulled in the yellow kite. Scotch-taped to the underside was a small freezer bag containing a folded piece of loose-leaf paper and a pencil. He removed the note.

Written in blue crayon: *"Yor neece person is cool. Does she like me to? Check Yes or No. Your friend, Peter."*

There were two boxes.

He handed the note to Joey.

She took it, her eyebrows lifted with surprise. As she read, a microexpression flickered across her face, gone as soon as it appeared. But he'd noticed. She was charmed.

When she looked up at Evan, she'd fixed her usual look of annoyance on her face. "Nice spelling," she said.

He handed her the pencil.

She sighed. "Seriously?"

"Seriously."

She held the paper, tapped the pencil against her full bottom lip, as if contemplating. Then she checked a box, not letting Evan see. She stuffed the note back into the little bag and tossed the kite out the window.

It nose-dived from view.

He knew which box she'd checked.

She said, "You going to bed?"

"After I meditate."

"Meditate?"

"Jack never taught you?"

"No. We didn't have time for that." She wet her lips, seemingly uncomfortable. "Why do you do it? Meditate?"

He contemplated. Jack had taught him this along with so much else. How to find peace. How to embody stillness. How to punch an eskrima dagger between the fourth and fifth ribs, angling up at the heart.

It struck Evan anew how Jack had embodied so many contradictions. Gruff but gentle, insistent but patient, firm but hands-off. He'd known how to raise Evan, how to push him further than he wanted to go.

Joey was watching him expectantly, slightly nervous, a flush rouging her smooth cheeks. Her question touched on the intimate, and that put her out over her skis.

He remembered telling her that Jack was the first person who ever really saw him. *If no one sees you, how can you know you're real?*

Evan tried to imagine how Jack might see Joey.

"Your Rubik's Cube," he said. "From the motel — the shape-shifter with all the different planes?"

She nodded.

"You told me that to bring it into alignment you solve one dimension at a time. Shape first, then color. You said you look for the wayward pieces, find the right patterns to make them fall into place. Right?"

"Right."

"That's what meditating is. Finding the wayward pieces of yourself, bringing them into alignment."

"But *how*?"

He went to the bed, sat crossed-legged, pointed to a spot opposite him. She climbed on the bed and mirrored his pose. Hands on thighs, straight spine, shoulders relaxed.

"What now?" she asked.

"Nothing."

"So I just breathe?"

"Yes."

"Just sit here and breathe?"

"If you want to."

Her eyes shone.

"Focus on your breath," he said. "And nothing else. See where it leads you."

He let his vision loosen until Joey blurred into the wall behind her. He tracked the cool air through his nose, down his windpipe, into his stomach. Beneath his skin he sensed a turmoil, blood rushing through his veins. His thoughts cascaded, cards in a shuffled deck. Jack in free fall, a cup of half-drunk milk, the frayed shoulder of David Smith's shirt —

Joey's words slashed in at him. "This is fucking stupid."

He opened his eyes fully. She'd come out of the pose, slumping forward, at once lax and agitated. He watched her twist one hand in the other.

"Okay," he said.

"We done?"

"Sure."

She didn't move. She was glaring at him. "It didn't do anything."

"Sure it did," Evan said. "It led you to anger."

"That's real useful. What am I supposed to do with that?"

"Ask yourself, what are you angry about?"

She got off the bed and stood facing the door. He watched her shoulders rise and fall with each breath.

"Do you want to talk about it?" he asked.

She wheeled on him. "Why would I tell you shit? You'll just leave anyways. Once you're done with me and we're done with this." She gestured to the bathroom and the Vault beyond. "Won't you."

"That doesn't sound like a question," Evan said. "It sounds like a dare."

"Don't turn it around on me," she said. "It's the only outcome."

"There's never only one outcome."

"Yeah? How do you see it working? You're gonna what? Drive me to school? Bake muffins for the PTA? Help me with my fucking calculus?"

"I think you'd probably help me with *my* calculus."

She didn't smile, barely even paused. "You're just using me, like everyone else. You don't get it. Why would you? You *chose* to leave the Program. You don't know what it's like to just be *discarded*. They threw me away 'cuz I was" — her lips pursed as she searched out the word — "deficient."

"You're not deficient."

"Yeah, I am. I'm broken."

"Then let's unbreak you."

"Oh, it's that easy."

"I'm not saying it's easy. I'm saying it's

376

worth doing. Pain is inevitable. Suffering is optional."

"Easy for you to say." She wiped her nose, pigging it up. She looked so young. " 'Suffering is optional.' "

"Yes. Let me know when you're ready to start giving it up."

"I'll fucking do that."

She walked out.

He listened to her feet tap up the brief hall and across the great room, the noise echoing off all those hard surfaces. Then her steps quickened up the spiral stairs to the loft.

Evan exhaled, rubbed his eyes. When he was younger, Jack had always known what to do. When to answer, when to leave a silence for Evan to fill.

Right now Evan felt adrift. He reached for the Commandments, but none were applicable. He'd gone down the path and arrived at a wall.

Another Jack-ism: *When you're at a wall, start climbing.*

There he was, still pushing Evan from beyond the grave. Maybe that's what this final mission was, placing Joey in his care, a living, breathing package. Maybe this was just another version of Evan walking behind Jack, filling his footsteps.

But this was a different trail. It required different rules. Evan thought of the Post-it note Mia had put up in her kitchen: *Remember that what you do not yet know is more important than what you already know.*

He tried to meditate again. Couldn't.

Then he was up on his feet. Moving silently along the hall. Keying off the alarm and slipping out the front door. Riding the elevator down, still pinching his eyes, shaking his head.

Walking up to 12B. Raising a fist to knock. Lowering it. Walking away. Coming back.

He tapped gently.

There. Now it was too late.

The door opened. Mia looked at him.

"I know you're angry with me," he said.

"You told me you didn't have any family," she said. "Either you lied before. Or you're lying now."

"It's complicated."

"Save it for Facebook."

She started to close the door.

"Wait," he said. "Joey is from . . . my job. I'm trying to help her. And I wanted to keep you and Peter clear of anything that's related to that world. So I tried to cover it up. I was dumb enough to think I was being helpful."

"That's even more alarming."

He held his arms at his sides, considered his blink ratio, resisted an urge to put his hands in his pockets. "I'm not sure what you would have preferred me to do. At Target."

"God," she said, more in wonderment than anger. "You really don't get it."

"No."

"How about 'Hey, Mia. I'm in an unusual situation and I'm not sure how to talk about it with you.' How 'bout that? Actually just being honest and trusting that we'll figure it out? Was that an option you considered?"

He said, "No."

She almost laughed, her hand covering her mouth. When she took her hand away, the smile was gone. "Okay. I'm angry. But I've also learned not to trust my first reaction. To *anything.* So. Let me figure out my second reaction before we talk about this anymore."

She started to close the door again.

"I need advice," he said, the words rushed. It had taken a lot to get them out.

"Advice?" she said. "You're asking me. Advice."

"Yes."

She pulled her head back on her neck. Blew out a breath. Let the door swing open.

Evan entered, and they sat on her couch.

She didn't offer him wine. The door to Peter's bedroom, bedecked with Batman stickers, a pirate-themed KEEP OUT! sign, and a Steph Curry poster, was open a crack. The heat was running, the condo toasty, a few candles casting gentle light. They were grapefruit-scented — no, blood orange. A burnt-red chenille throw draped one arm of the couch. So many things he would never have thought of, the things that turn a house into a home. They were words from a different language, the language of comfort, of knowing how to belong.

Evan kept his voice low. "How do you talk to a teenage girl?"

"Very carefully," Mia said.

"That much I've figured out."

"She seems like a great kid. But she's had it tough."

"How do you know that?"

"I'm a DA." Mia set her hands on her thighs, tilted her head to the ceiling, took a breath. "Don't push. Just be there. Be steady."

He thought of Jack's even pace through the woods, not too fast, not too slow, his boots stamping the mud, showing Evan where to step.

Mia pointed at Evan. "When it comes to kids, honesty matters. And consistency.

That's why I thought, you know, you coming for dinner once a week. It's important to Peter. Stuff like that's a clock they set their hearts to."

He nodded.

"At the end of the day, all they *really* want to hear?" Mia ticked the points off on her fingers. "You're okay. You're gonna be fine. You're worth it."

He nodded again.

She studied him. "What?"

"*Are* they worth it?"

"Yes." She rose to see him out. "But if you're ever gonna say it, you better believe it first." She shot him a loaded look. "Because she'll know if you're lying."

Evan paused halfway up the spiral stairs to the loft. A clacking sound carried down to him, and it took a moment for him to place it: Joey working a Rubik's Cube. Lifted halfway between floor and ceiling, he had a glorious view of downtown. The shimmering blocks, a confusion of lights shivering in the night air. Overhead, the cube clacked and clacked. He heard Joey cough.

It felt so odd to have another moving body in the penthouse.

He continued up to the reading loft. Joey sat in a nest of sheets on the plush couch.

Her head stayed down, that rich chocolate hair framing her face, which was furrowed with concentration. The cube, smaller than the previous one he'd seen, was a neon blur in her hands.

She'd turned off the overheads and pulled the floor lamp close. It was on the lowest setting, casting her in a dim light. The cube alone was bright, glow-in-the-dark colors radiating in the semi-dark. Chewing-gum green and fluorescent yellow. Safety-cone orange and recycling-can blue.

At the second-to-top step, he halted.

"Can I come in?" he asked.

"It's your place."

"But it's not my room."

Her deft fingers flicked at the cube, transforming it by the second. "Yeah it is."

He noticed that she wasn't trying to solve the cube; she was alternating patterns on it, the colors morphing from stripes into checkers and back to stripes.

He said, "Not right now."

Her eyes ticked up. But her hands still flew, the cube obeying her will. It changed into four walls of solid color, and she let it dribble from her hands into her lap.

"Yeah," she said. "You can come in."

He stepped up into the loft and sat on the floor across from her, his back to one of the bookshelves. By her knee was the worn shoe box from her rucksack. The lid was off and one of the greeting cards pulled out. She'd been reading it. He remembered what Mia had told him and said nothing.

Joey picked up the cube. Put it down again.

"It's such a big world," she said. "And I don't want it to just be this."

"What?"

"My life. My whole life. Kept here, kept there, always hiding. There's so much out there. So much I'm missing out on."

Evan thought of the burnt-red chenille throw draping the arm of Mia's couch.

"Yeah," he said. "There is."

Joey put the card into its envelope, slipped it into her shoe box, and set the lid back in place.

"Sorry I'm such an asshole sometimes," she said. "My maunt used to say, *'Tiene dos trabajos. Enojarse y contentarse.'* It doesn't really translate right."

Evan said, " 'You have two jobs. Getting angry. And getting not angry again.' "

"Something like that, yeah."

He said, "You were close to her."

Joey finally looked up and met his stare. "She was *everything.*"

It was, Evan realized, the longest they had

ever held eye contact.

Joey finally slid off the couch. "I have to brush my teeth," she said.

She lifted the shoe box from the sheets. As she passed, she let it drop to the floor beside him.

A show of trust.

She entered the bathroom, closed the door. He heard water running.

He waited a moment and then lifted the lid. A row of greeting cards filled the shoe box from end to end. He ran his thumb across the tops of the cards. The front two-thirds had been opened. The rear third had not.

And then he understood.

He felt his chest swell, slight pressure beneath his cheeks, emotion coming to roost in his body.

He used his knuckles to push back the stack so he could lift out the first card. Flocked gold lettering read:

It's your ninth birthday
A most happy day
A time to sing
And a time to play . . .

He opened the card, ignoring the rest of the printed greeting. An iris was pressed inside, already gone to pieces. Familiar feminine handwriting filled the blank page.

My sweet, sweet girl,
The first one without me will be the hardest. I'm sorry I'm not there with you. I'm sorry I got sick. I'm sorry I wasn't strong enough to beat it. Let my love for you be like a sun that warms you from above.

Forever and always, M.

Evan put the card back. He flicked through the ones behind it.

New Year's. Valentine's. Easter. Birthday. First day of school. Halloween. Thanksgiving. Christmas.

He took a wet breath. Let the next set of cards tick past his thumb.

New Year's. Valentine's. Easter. Birthday. First day of school. Halloween. Thanksgiving. Christmas.

The last opened card was Thanksgiving, the one that had fallen out of her rucksack in the foot well of the stolen car yesterday.

He pulled out the one behind it, sealed in an envelope that said *"Christmas."*

He scrolled ahead, the labels jumping out at him. *"Easter."*

"Halloween."

"Your 18th Bday."

And then they stopped.

In the bathroom the sink water turned off.

He closed the shoe box, set it back on the couch, and returned to where he'd been sitting.

Joey emerged, wiping her face on a towel. She slung it over the couch back and sat again on the cushions and sheets. She noted the shoe box's return and then stared at her lap.

Finally she said, "That's when I went into the system."

"I'm sorry."

"The cards, they're gonna run out when I turn eighteen," Joey said. "Then what'll I have?"

He showed her the respect of not offering an answer.

"After I ran away from Van Sciver, that's where Jack found me. Visiting her grave." She looked down, gave a soft smile. Her thick mane was swept across, the shaved side exposed, two halves of a beautiful whole. "He was smart like that. He knew how my heart worked."

Evan nodded, not trusting his voice. *Yes, he was. Yes, he did.*

After a time Joey slid down into the sheets and curled up, her head on the pillow. "I never fall asleep with anyone in the room," she said.

"Should I leave?"

"If you want to stay, it's fine."

Evan said, "I do."

He sat and watched the curve of her shoulder, the tousled hair on her cheek. Her blinks grew languorous. And then her eyes closed. Her breathing grew regular, took on a rasp.

He rose silently and eased from the room.

48
SOMETHING AKIN TO PRIDE

After checking the deep-learning software in the Vault before sunrise the next morning, Evan meditated, showered, and then walked down the hall to the kitchen.

Joey was up early as well, digging in the freezer, an ice pack in one hand, the bottle of Stoli Elit: Himalayan Edition in the other.

She heard him coming and looked over her shoulder. "Don't you have any frozen burritos or whatever?"

"Careful with that," Evan said, nodding at the Stoli. "It's three thousand dollars a bottle."

Joey appraised it. "Is it worth it?"

"No vodka is worth three thousand dollars."

"Then why do you have it?"

"What else am I gonna spend it on?"

She stared into the pristine white void of his freezer. "I don't know. Food."

He came around the island.

"Out of my way," he said.

Two eggs dropped in the frying pan with a this-is-your-brain-on-drugs sizzle. Joey sat on a stool, leaning over the island counter, chin resting on her laced fingers. Fascinated.

"You know how to cook?" she asked.

"I'd hardly call this cooking."

"How'd you learn?"

"Jack."

"You fit it in between drownproofing and close-quarters combat?"

"Yes."

"Mr. Humor."

The toaster dinged, and Evan flicked two pieces of sourdough onto a plate. "Butter?"

"Duh."

He buttered the toast and slid the eggs atop the two slices. "Go snap some parsley off the living wall."

"Living wall?"

"The vertical garden. There."

She walked over. "Which one's the parsley?"

"Upper left quadrant near the edge. No. No. Yes."

She tore off a piece, brought it over as he twisted pepper from the mill onto the sunny-side-ups.

He halved the sprig, laid a piece on each

yolk. Then he set the plate before her, nudging it so it was precisely between knife and fork.

She stared down at the plate, not moving.

"What?" he said.

"Just appreciating it," she said.

"Eat."

She looked up at him, cleared her throat. "Thank you."

Before he could reply, a chime sounded over the wireless speaker system. His head snapped up.

"What's that?" she asked.

He was already heading back. "Software just hit on David Smith."

They stood side by side within the damp concrete walls of the Vault, staring at the monitors. The interconnected web of metadata on display was fascinating.

From the scant information on David Smith and a few photos, the software had made height and weight projections, assessed facial-structure changes, checked hospital intakes, flight and bus records, school registrations, and foster-home placements in targeted regions on the East Coast. These criteria correlating space, time, visuals, database entries, and events had been dynamically created so the machine would heuristically improve itself, learning as it went, ever evolving. Strange algorithms tracked online purchase orders, grouping vehicular-themed *Star Wars* Lego sets costing $9.95 or less, industrial-strength drain cleaner, bulk-ordered Little Hug Fruit Barrel drinks, Lavex Janitorial brown paper towel rolls, and dozens more items, narrowing the scope even further. These results were paired with Instagram photos and other social-media posts clustered around specific neighborhoods.

A YouTube video of a schoolyard fight at Hopewell High in Richmond, Virginia, posted in September of the previous year had caught a wink of a passing car in the background. Despite the midday glare off the passenger window, a freeze-frame had captured the ear of the boy in the passenger seat, which had been picked apart using precise distances and ratios, measuring the upper margin of the ear canal's opening to the tip of the lower lobe and the flap of the tragus. It gave an 85-percent probability that the ear belonged to their David Smith.

Two days previous a girl had been adopted out of McClair Children's Mental Health Center in Richmond's Church Hill neighborhood, opening a spot in what had previously been a steady forty-bed population.

No new child showed to have been committed at the center since, the population seemingly remaining at thirty-nine. However, a
bill from a local health clinic the following
week showed a new patient-intake exam,
and the number of flu shots administered
the next month remained a steady forty.

A child taken into the center under a false
claim of domestic violence would have been
kept off the books.

The deep-learning software gave a
99.9743-percent likelihood that the mystery
patient was the boy previously known as
David Smith.

Joey jotted down the address, biting her
lower lip, frowning with concentration. The
light of the monitors played off her smooth
cheeks. Evan watched her, feeling something
akin to pride.

She caught him looking. "What?"

He said, "Nothing."

All you could hear was the man's panting.

Blood flecked the floor, the plywood over
the windows, the mattresses on the walls. A
molar rested on the plastic tarp. The room
stank of vomit, body odor, and worse.

Two of the three Arrowhead watercooler
jugs were empty. That was ten gallons of
fluid forced through Orphan L's face holes.

Draker lay on the floor curled up in a ball. His head was duct-taped, a slit left open for the nostrils.

Van Sciver squatted, waiting.

Thornhill was balanced on his hands again, doing inverted push-ups.

The guy was the friggin' Energizer Bunny.

Candy had left to organize the freelancers Van Sciver had called up from Alabama. Things were about to get busy.

Van Sciver finally rose with a groan. He was feeling it in his back.

"Thornhill," he said.

Thornhill's boots hit the ground with a thump. He started unwinding the duct tape from L's head. As he did, a faint tinny music became audible, growing louder with each loop of tape unstripped. At last he got to the final layer, which he tore free, ripping out clumps of L's hair and splotching his flesh with broken capillaries. The Beats headphones adhered to Draker's head were now laid bare, Josh Groban blaring "You Raise Me Up" at top volume.

Thornhill turned off the music, tugged off the headphones. He stroked Draker's hair, pushing the sweat-pasted bangs out of his eyes.

"You did good," Thornhill said. "Better than Jack could have asked. But this will

393

continue forever."

Draker managed a single hoarse syllable. "No."

"You know it's gotta go this way," Van Sciver said. "It is what it is and that's all that it is."

Draker squeezed his eyes shut and panted some more. He'd developed a tic at the top of his left cheek, the skin spasming, tugging the eyelid into a droop.

"Okay," Van Sciver said. "Get him back on the bench."

Thornhill started for the Arrowhead jug.

Draker began to sob.

Van Sciver held up a hand, freezing Thornhill.

This was the glorious moment right before they broke. He let Draker weep. The sound was gut-wrenching, dredged up from the depths.

Thornhill petted his hair. "It's okay," he said. "You did good. You did so good."

Draker keened and keened. Finally he quieted. Van Sciver waited for his breathing to slow. After all L had been through, he deserved a few moments of rest before the end.

Draker looked up through bloodshot eyes. "I'll tell you," he said. I'll tell you where he is."

49
GOOD ISN'T ENOUGH

"You missed him by an hour, Mr. Man," the charge nurse said.

A broad woman packed into navy-blue polyester pants and a billowing white nurse coat, she conveyed warmth and authority in equal measure. A sunshine logo on her coat accompanied equally cheery canary-yellow lettering, which read MCCLAIR CHILDREN'S MENTAL HEALTH CENTER.

Evan put away his forged Child Protective Services credential, flapping closed the worn brown billfold. The wallet, in addition to his frayed Dockers and Timex watch, were props that screamed Ordinary Guy on State-Employee Salary.

Tapping his clipboard against his thigh, he hurried to accompany the nurse as she ambled down the hall.

"Missed him?" Evan said. "What do you mean missed him? His caseworker visitation is overdue."

"Baby doll, the only things here that *ain't* overdue are the late notices on the bills. We are bailing out a rowboat with a Dixie Cup."

In one of the rooms, a kid was thrashing against the wall and bellowing. Two orderlies restrained him, one for each arm.

The nurse stopped in the doorway. "C'mon now, Daryl," she said. "Act like you got some sense in you."

The boy calmed, and she kept on.

A few perfunctory posters were gummed to the bare walls, tattered and ripped. Lichtenstein apple. Picasso face. A faded *Starry Night*. Stacked on a service cart were dining trays filled with half-eaten meals. Watery green beans. Cube of corn bread. Hard-crusted grilled-cheese sandwiches. The place smelled of industrial detergent, bleach, and kids of a certain age kept in close proximity.

Evan knew this place, knew it in his bones.

He cleared his throat as if nervously, adjusted his fake glasses. "You said I missed Jesse Watson?"

Joey's additional online machinations had confirmed that this was the name David Smith had been living under at the Richmond facility. Joey was outside now in the rented minivan, a block away in an overwatch position near the intersection.

396

The nurse paused and heaved a sigh that smelled of peppermint. "He ran away."

"Ran away? When?"

"Like I said, he was gone before seven-o'clock bed check. So call it a hour, maybe a hour and a half. Musta slipped out the back door during the commotion." Her mouth tweaked left, a show of sympathy. "Girl in six had a grand mal at mealtime."

Evan shoved his glasses up his nose, a cover for the actual dread he felt rising from his stomach into his throat.

She registered his concern. "We already filed the police report. I'm sorry, but it's in their hands now."

"Okay. I'll just do a living-conditions check and be on my way."

"We do the best we can do here with the state funds shrinking all the time."

"I understand."

"Do you?"

"I do."

She stopped and took his measure, the raised freckles bunching high on her copper-colored cheeks. Then she blew out a breath, deflating. "Look at us, acting like we on different sides. I'm sorry, Mr. . . . ?"

"Wayne."

"Mr. Wayne. I know you're just trying to do the best you can, too. I guess it's . . ."

Her not-insignificant bosom heaved. "I guess I'm embarrassed we can't do better by them. I use my own salary for Christmas and birthday gifts. The director, too. He's a good man. But good isn't enough sometimes."

"No," Evan said. "Sometimes it's not. Which room was he in?"

"Fourteen," she said. "We group the kids with less severe conditions in the C Hall. We're talking ADHD, dyslexia, visual-motor stuff."

"And Jesse's condition was . . . ?" Evan flipped through the pages.

"Conduct disorder."

"Of course."

She waved a hand adorned with hammered metal rings. "C'mon, I'll walk you."

The walk took longer than Evan would have liked, but he held her pace. They passed a girl sitting on the floor picking at the hem of her shirt. Her fingernails were bitten to the quick, leaving spots of blood on the fabric.

"Hi, baby doll, be back for you in a second, okay?" the nurse said.

The girl turned vacant eyes up toward them as they passed. She had beautiful thick hair like Joey's, a similarity Evan chose not to linger on.

The nurse finally arrived at Room 14, knocked on the door once briskly, and opened it. The three boys inside, all around the age of thirteen like David Smith, lounged on bunk beds, tapping on cheap phones.

In another time, in another place, Evan had lived in this room.

"This is Mr. Wayne," the nurse said.

The oldest-looking kid shot a quick glance at Evan and said, "Lucky-ass us. Another social worker."

"Respect, Jorell, or I'll notch you down to red on the board again."

Evan asked, "Did any of you see Jesse Watson run away?"

They all shook their heads.

"He didn't talk about it before? No planning? Nothing?"

"Nah," Jorell said. "That fool was *bent.* For a skinny white boy? He was nails. Could fight like a mofo. He had things his *own* way."

"Jorell," the nurse said wearily.

It wasn't the first time she'd said his name like that. Or the hundredth.

"Where were you guys before bed check?" Evan said.

"Still in the caf," another kid said. "Mindin' our bidness. Jesse come back to the room early, do push-ups and shit. He say he gonna be a marine."

Evan stepped inside, pointed. "This his bunk?"

"The very one," Jorell said.

Jorell was a smart kid. Smart kids in places like this tended to have worse outcomes. A nice dumb boy could toe the line, graduate with C's, get a steady job at a fast-food joint, live to see thirty.

On the radiator by the empty lower left bunk rested a Lego version of a *Star Wars* rebel commanding a Snowspeeder. Evan recognized it from one of Peter's comic books. He picked it up. "This was Jesse's?"

"Yeah. Ain't that some white-boy shit?"

All three kids laughed, even the Caucasian one.

The charge nurse said, "You just dying for me to level you down tonight, ain't that so, Jorell?"

He silenced.

Holding the Snowspeeder, Evan stepped back to her, said quietly, "I'm guessing this was one of the gifts that came out of your salary."

She nodded.

Evan said, "It's probably the only thing in the world he has that's actually his."

Her mocha eyes held the weight of all

forty lives she'd been charged with. "That's probably right."

"I doubt he'd run away and leave it behind."

"What are you saying, Mr. Wayne? The boy broke out. Happens all the time."

Evan set the Lego rebel back on the radiator and stepped toward the sash window. It rattled up arthritically. He leaned out, noted the fresh gouge marks in the paint on the sill.

"They usually break out from the outside?" he said.

The charge nurse came over and looked at the window, and her hand pressed against her neck. Seeing her expression, he regretted his phrasing.

"I'll call the police again," she said quietly.

The boys had silenced; even Jorell had sobered up.

Evan started for the door. "Like you said, it's in their hands now."

As he hustled out, he passed that girl in the hall, forgotten, picking at the hem of her shirt with bloody fingernails. In his mind's eye, he pictured Joey sitting in her place.

He blinked away the image, banishing it from his thoughts, and kept on.

50
THE BEST HAT TRICK

Evan sat in the passenger seat of the mini-van, the Virginia sun pounding the wind-shield. Joey had taken the news of David Smith's kidnapping stoically, though he'd noticed her fists whiten on the steering wheel as he'd filled her in.

"One hour," she finally said. "One hour earlier and we could've saved him."

"We don't know that he's dead," Evan said.

"Orphan J. Orphan C. Orphan L. All the other names on that file are dead. Except me. If Van Sciver kidnapped David Smith, he already killed him."

They stared up the block at the crumbling façade of the McClair Children's Mental Health Center. It radiated a kind of despair that resonated in Evan's cells. He thought of the boys he'd grown up with in Pride House. Andre and Danny and Tyrell and Ramón. Every so often Evan checked in on them from the safe remove of the Vault, searching them out in the databases. Danny was serving a dime for armed robbery at the Chesapeake Detention Facility, his third stint. Ramón had overdosed in a by-the-hour motel in Cherry Hill. Tyrell had finally managed to join the army, KIA outside Mosul on his first deployment.

Any one of their fates should have been shared by Evan. He was them and they were him.

Until Jack.

Searching for hope here on this block was hard, but Evan tried. David Smith was owed that much.

"If Van Sciver wanted him dead, why didn't they just shoot him in the room?" Evan said.

"Because that would be a big public thing," Joey said. "A runaway's just another story."

"When a kid gets killed in a neighborhood like this, it's not a big public thing. It's two lines of print below the fold. Everyone would think it was gang retribution. Remember, no one in the world knows who David Smith is."

"Except Van Sciver," Joey said. "And us."

Evan felt it then, the first ray of hope, straw-thin and pale, not enough to warm him but enough to lead the way. "The smart move isn't to kill him. The smart move is to use him for bait."

"So what do we do?" Joey asked.

"Swallow the hook. Let them reel."

"And if he's already dead?"

Evan stared at the sign above the security gate of the facility's front door. A number of the letters were smashed or broken.

He said, "It's a chance I have to take."

"That sounds less than strategic."

"The Tenth Commandment."

" 'Never let an innocent die,' " she quoted. "So where do we start?"

Evan took out the Samsung Galaxy cell phone he'd lifted off the dead man in Portland. He called up Signal, the encrypted comms software that led directly to Van Sciver. He was about to press the icon to call when he realized that his emotions around this place and these foster kids were infecting him, making him reckless.

He thumbed the phone back off.

"We need to gather more intel before I make contact," he said. "There's an ATM at the gas station two blocks that way, facing the street. Maybe we can get the security footage, see what we see."

Joey made a sound in her throat. Unimpressed.

"What?"

"*If* they drove that route," she said. "*If* we know who we're looking for." She was leaning forward, straining the seat belt, seemingly peering up at the telephone wires overhead.

"You have a better suggestion?" Evan asked.

"As a matter of fact, I do." She pointed through the windshield. "See those streetlights?"

"Yes."

"They're not just streetlights." She reached into the backseat, retrieving her laptop. "Those are Sensity Systems lights. We're talking thermal, sound, shock, video — they continuously gather information and suck everything into the cloud." She ran her fingers through her hair, flipped it over so the shaved strip showed above her right ear. " 'Member how Van Sciver got onto Orphan L?"

"A surveillance photo of him smoking."

"Taken from a streetlight," she said. "We're gonna use Van Sciver's game against him."

Evan stared at the streetlights, but they looked ordinary to him. "You sure those are the kind you're talking about?"

She gave him a look, then booted up her

computer.

He said, "How can they afford something like that in a broke neighborhood like this?"

Her fingers were already working the keys in a fury. "Federal funding. It's part of the Safe Cities initiative. Detroit got a hundred mil off the government, and if Detroit can get it . . ." She glanced over. "You don't keep up on this stuff, do you?"

"No."

"The streetlights are all LED. The whole system gets paid for by the money cities save from the reduction in electricity costs. How 'bout that? A government plan that *isn't* a total cluster. Not that it started with the government. The software was developed to track foot traffic at shopping malls, see what stores people go into, what they look at, how they respond to sales announcements, coupons, all that."

"Can you hack it?"

She kept her head lowered, her fingers moving. "I'm gonna pretend you didn't ask me that."

He cast an eye toward the facility's front door. "The cops are gonna be here soon."

"Well," she said, "then it's a good thing I'm fast."

"Turn left up there. No, the *next* intersection. Good. Now run it straight for a half mile."

Evan was driving the minivan, Joey in the passenger seat, directing him through traffic and simultaneously hammering away at the laptop. He felt increasingly like her chauffeur, an observation that, he was chagrinned to note, Mia had once made in regard to Peter.

Evan was becoming just another suburban dad.

Joey had what looked like a dozen windows open on the screen. He risked a glance over. On one of them she seemed to be reviewing footage angled on the eastern flank of the McClair Children's Mental Health Center.

"Anything?" he asked.

"Patience, young Padawan." The laptop was humming. "Wait. You were supposed to turn left back there. Hang on." She popped another window to the fore, this one featuring a GPS map. "Go left, left, right."

He obeyed. Focusing on the road and the rearview mirrors rather than on Joey's active laptop screen took some discipline.

"Okay. Just — pull over here. We're in range."

He looked around. A fenced park. A courthouse. A McDonald's.

"In range of what?" he said.

She ignored the question. "Let's get you up to speed." She punched a button, swiveled the laptop on the minivan's roomy center console. Evan watched the exterior of C Hall, the image so steady that save for a few leaves blowing past and the sound of out-of-frame traffic it might have been a photograph.

At last a pair of shadows darkened the bottom of the screen. Two men approached the window of Room 14. One held a crowbar, the other a pistol lengthened by a suppressor. The guy holding the pistol moved aggressively, sweat glistening on his bald head. The men flattened to either side of the window.

Evan told his heartbeat to stay slow and steady, and it obeyed.

He didn't recognize either man; Van Sciver had sent more freelance muscle. The gunman raised a black-gloved hand, his ridged, shiny skull gleaming as he did a three-finger countdown. The other guy jammed the crowbar beneath the sash window and slid it up. The bald man spun into the open frame, pistol raised, his mouth moving.

Issuing orders.

The streetlight sensor was too far away to capture the words, but a moment later David Smith appeared at the sill, holding his hands before him, showing his palms. He looked more shocked than scared. The bald man grabbed the boy's shirt and ripped him through the window. As he manhandled the kid away from the building, another figure emerged at the edge of the screen, her back to the camera.

Her face wasn't visible, but Evan recognized her form.

Orphan V.

Candy McClure pointed at the gunman, clearly issuing an admonition, and he lightened his grip on the boy. The freelancers kept David between them, hustling him away. An instant later the frame was as empty and serene as before.

The snatch-and-go had taken six seconds.

Evan looked at Joey across the console. "Seems like they want to keep him."

"Or kill him off site."

"No," Evan said. "You saw the way Orphan V spoke to that guy. Van Sciver wants the kid unharmed."

"Or *she* does. She might have to duke it out with Van Sciver."

"She can be convincing," Evan said.

Joey read something in his face and let the point drop. She leaned over, bringing up a freeze-frame of the men standing on both sides of the window before the break-in. Reference points littered their heads, a digital overlay.

"I go with Panasonic FacePro Facial Recognition," she said. "It's the best. Two for two."

"Two for two?"

"Fast *and* accurate. They use it at SFO."

"When do we get the results?"

"We have them."

Another window, another revelation. The two men, identified as Paul Delmonico and Shane Shea. Delmonico was the one who'd jimmied the window and Shea the gunman. Shea had a bony build, his forehead promi-nent, the grooves of his cranial bones pronounced on his shiny bald skull. Their records had recently been classified top secret, which put their backgrounds and training out of reach for the time being. Evan figured they were dishonorably dis-charged recon marines, Van Sciver's favorite source of renewable muscle. For now Evan and Joey had faces and names, and that was all they needed.

Next Joey pulled up a United Airlines itinerary she had unearthed. "They came in on a flight this morning from Alabama."

"Where Van Sciver killed Orphan C." And where Jack had plowed into the dirt from sixteen thousand feet.

"Right. And they rented this at the airport." *Click.* "A black Suburban. I know, inventive, right? License plate VBK-5976."

She paused to check if he was impressed. He was.

"The same credit card was used to get another matching Suburban, license plate TLY-9443. So I'm thinking four men."

"Looks like it," Evan said.

"You know what ALPR is?" she asked.

"Automated license-plate recognition," Evan said, relieved to be back on familiar turf. "Police cruisers have sensors embedded in the light bars that scan the plates of all surrounding vehicles. They can swallow numbers eight lanes across on cars going in either direction up to eighty miles per hour. They process the plates for outstanding warrants in real time and store them for posterity."

"Gold star for the old guy," Joey said. "I already input the licenses into the ALPR system and coded the system to send me and only me an alert when one of the light-bar sensors picks up either Suburban. We're gonna use Virginia's Finest to track down these guys for us." Her grin took on a devious cast. "In more ways than one."

Evan followed her gaze up the street to

the courthouse. It was a beautiful Colonial Revival building — weathered brick, white columns, hipped roof. A trickle of men and women scurried across the front lawn, some black, some white, some in suits, others in overalls, each of them moving with a sense of purpose. A sign in front read CRIMINAL GENERAL DISTRICT COURT.

"Oh," Evan said. *"Oh."*

Already Joey was pulling up the courthouse's private Wi-Fi network reserved for judges, DAs, and clerks. Hashkiller's 131-billion-password dictionary required only twenty-seven seconds to get her on. The Records Management System took two and a half minutes. And then there it was before them on the screen, glowing like a holy relic.

A bench warrant.

Evan and Joey smiled at each other.

"First move," Joey said. "Get the bad guys off the street. Or at least the two we have names for."

"You're kind of a genius."

"I agree with everything but the 'kind of.' " She wiggled her fingers in glee and then typed in a phony case record.

If the cops brought in the men, red-tape confusion would tangle them up for days.

"What should we have them arrested for?" Joey asked. "Homegrown terrorism is always good, gets the local constabulary all hot and bothered."

"Terrorism?" Evan said. *"Delmonico* and *Shea?"*

"You have a point."

"Let's make them pedophiles," Evan said.

She typed, her smile growing broader as she warmed to the idea. "And prison escapees."

"Who are also wanted for killing a police officer."

"That is *so* the best hat trick," she said. "It's like making a list for Santa."

She finished filling out the arrest warrant, issued a statewide BOLO, and fed the forms into the legal and law-enforcement machinery of greater Richmond.

Then she held up her palm.

He slapped it.

51
PUSH A LITTLE MORE

Candy's back was on fire, but she granted her skin no concessions when on a mission. She refused to scratch it, even resisted tugging at her shirt so the fabric would rub against the ruinous flesh and soothe the burn. Candy had pulled Van Sciver into the hall of the safe house to talk to him privately.

Van Sciver was as unyielding a man as she'd ever encountered, but he was still a man, which meant she had a shot at getting what she wanted from him. He'd pulled his pistol out of his underarm tension holster.

An FNX-45 with a threaded barrel and holographic red-dot sights.

A lot of firepower for the skull of a thirteen-year-old.

"The hard part's over," Van Sciver said. "We have him now. X knows it or will soon enough. The kid's served his purpose."

Van Sciver's eyes twitched across the threshold to where David Smith sat on the decline bench, a pillowcase cinched over his head, hands pressed between his knees. He hadn't made a noise since Delmonico and Shea had delivered him. The two men stood by the rear door, guarding it with M4s in case the skinny thirteen-year-old kid went Dwayne "The Rock" Johnson on them. The other pair patrolled the front of the house as if working perimeter duty at a presidential inauguration.

L's corpse had been removed, the spillage from his body more or less cleaned up, though the smell of vomit lingered.

Over in the kitchen, Thornhill stirred something in a pot, humming to himself. It smelled delicious and spicy, and Candy wondered where Thornhill was from, how he'd learned to cook and who for. It brought back a memory from high-altitude SERE training in her seventeenth year. She'd summited a tree-blanketed rise in the Rockies, nearly stumbling onto a family of four picnicking out of the back of their Range Rover. The mom had laid down a blanket, and there were sliced apples in bowls and cold fried chicken and thermoses of hot cider. The daughter was around Candy's age. Candy had hidden behind the tree line, staring down at the exotic sight before her, scarcely breathing lest she spook them.

She'd remained long after they'd driven off, her boots embedded in a film of snow, trying to loose the tangle of emotions that had knotted up her throat.

Thornhill lifted the wooden spoon for a taste, smacked his lips at a job well done. In a holster snugged to his hip, he had an FNX-45 that matched Van Sciver's. He was so disarming that it was easy to forget how lethal he was. With Thornhill it was a pleasant conversation right up until the minute the bullet entered your brain.

Candy refocused on Van Sciver, keeping her voice low. "I'm saying let's not have a failure of imagination here."

"Which means what, precisely?"

"L took the kid out of circulation. And Jack kept him off the books after that. David Smith has got no real record — no files, no fingerprints, nothing. Aside from a few kids in a loony ward, no one knows his face." She paused for dramatic effect. Pursed her distractingly plump lips. "Which means he's a blank check."

Van Sciver's fair-complected face was mottled from the exertion of the past twenty-four hours, splotches of red creeping up from his shirt collar. That blown pupil was like a void. Candy felt that if she stared long enough, she might fall into it and keep tumbling.

She thought of the beautiful young woman locked in a car trunk in an alley outside Sevastopol. The rattle of her fists against the metal as she bled out. The scraping of her nails.

Candy shuddered off the thought, looked away from Van Sciver's lopsided gaze so he couldn't read anything in her face. The pillowcase fluttered in the spot where the boy's mouth was, the fabric pulsing like a heartbeat, surprisingly steady.

"L acquired him for you initially," she said. "Now you have your asset back."

"What if Jack Johns turned him?"

"Jack Johns only had him a few months before dumping him at that facility. Not enough to fully indoctrinate him. But the kid did get the benefit of Johns's training. Johns is good at that. Maybe the best."

Van Sciver gritted his teeth, neither confirming nor denying. "What are you suggesting?"

"After we get X, we pick up with the kid where L and Jack left off."

"I don't have the time or interest to train some boy myself."

"I'll do it. Assuming he's the right material."

The dilated pupil pegged her where she

stood, that weird, hazy starfish floating in the depths. She wasn't sure where to look.

Van Sciver said, "This have to do with Sevastopol? Dead girl in the alley?"

"Of course not." She hoped she hadn't rushed the words. "We need more arrows in our quill." She pointed into the living room. "And that could be one of them."

Van Sciver's jaw shifted to the side and back. He holstered his .45.

Candy did not let him see her exhale.

He tugged a red-covered notebook from one of his wide cargo pockets and flipped it open. Inside were various intel scribblings and the list of five names.

Orphan J. Orphan C. Orphan L.

All crossed out.

Then Joey Morales, circled twice.

And David Smith.

Van Sciver removed a Pilot FriXion pen from the fold and erased the boy's name. He lifted that bottomless stare to Candy. Then he tossed the notebook onto a side table and walked into the living room. The former marines stood at attention the way former marines did.

Thornhill pulled the pot off the stove to cool, came around to confer with Candy and Van Sciver.

Van Sciver said, "You got the propofol?"

Thornhill flashed that million-dollar grin. "*Now* it's a party."

He went to a black medical kit and came up with a syringe filled with a cloudy white liquid. They didn't call it "milk of amnesia" for nothing. The medication provided a quick knockout and a rapid, clear recovery. Push a little, it was an anesthetic. Push a little more and you had a lethal injection.

In all matters Van Sciver strove to have a full range of choices.

How the boy responded in the next few minutes would determine how much pressure Thornhill's thumb applied to the plunger.

Candy found herself biting the inside of her cheek.

Van Sciver walked over to the boy and tugged off the pillowcase.

David Smith blew his lank bangs off his forehead and took in the plywood-covered windows, the empty jugs of water, the fresh plastic tarp on the floor. Then he squinted up at Van Sciver.

"Is this a test?" he asked.

52
CHESS-MATCHING

Evan didn't want to risk checking in to a motel, not when he and Joey were this close to Van Sciver. Not when Van Sciver knew he was coming.

Instead he used a false Airbnb profile to book a room for forty-nine dollars a night. The owner, who listed several dozen apartments in seedy sections of greater Virginia, seemed to be a digital slumlord who oversaw his holdings from afar. The key waited inside a Realtor lockbox hooked around the front doorknob. The neighbors would be accustomed to high turnover, lots of renters coming and going. Which was good, since Evan's profile represented him as Suzi Orton, a robust middle-aged blonde with a forceful smile.

The L-shaped complex had seen better days. Paint flaked on the fence around the pool out front, which had algaed itself to a Gatorade shade of green. A cluster of shirtless young men wearing calf-length charcoal denim shorts smoked blunts on strappy lawn chairs. Several of the doors remained open, women — and one fine-boned young man — lingering at the thresholds in off-the-shoulder tops, offering more than just a view. The thrumming bass of a remix rattled a window on the second floor. Pumping music, paired with the scattered regulars at the fringes, gave the place the woeful feel of a sparse dance floor at a club that couldn't get up steam.

It was dusk by the time Evan had completed his second drive-by and parked the minivan several blocks away. He and Joey moved unnoticed up the sidewalk and then the corridor. Evan punched in the code to free the keys. He handed one to Joey, turning the other in the lock, and they stepped into a surprisingly clean small room with two freshly made twin beds.

He tossed his stuff onto the mattress closer to the door as Joey plugged in her laptop and then checked her phone for the fiftieth time for updates. She grabbed a change of clothes from her bag and went to shower as Evan worked out — push-ups, sit-ups, dips with his heels on the windowsill and his hands ledging the seat of the solitary chair. Joey came out, sweeping her hair up into a towel, and he turnstiled past her in the tight space.

When he finished showering and emerged from the bathroom, she was at the laptop again, chewing her lip. He checked his RoamZone to see if Xavier had called. He hadn't. Evan used the wall to stretch out the tendons of his right shoulder. Almost back to full range of motion.

It occurred to him that neither he nor Joey had uttered a word in the preceding forty-five minutes and yet the silence had been comfortable. Pleasant, even.

It reminded him of when he was a kid, walking around the farmhouse with Jack, wiping the counters, taking turns on the pull-up bar by the side of the house, filling Strider's water bowl. At times Jack and he cooked, ate, and cleared an entire meal without a word passing between them.

They were so in sync that they didn't need to speak.

Joey looked over from the bluish screen, saw Evan watching her. That dimple floated in her wide cheek.

She said, "What are you thinking about?"

"Nothing," he said.

They blinked at each other for a moment.

"What are you doing over there?" he asked.

"Catching up on the latest and greatest. There's a disposable, disappearing chat room for black-hat hackers."

"I won't ask if it's secure."

"No," she agreed. "That would be condescending."

"Do you want to try meditating again?"

She gave a one-shouldered shrug. "I seem to suck at it."

"Meditating?"

"Being out here." She made a halfhearted gesture at the laptop. "Easier to be online. I feel real in there."

"But it's not," he said. "Real."

"What is?"

"Trauma."

Her lips tensed until they went pale. "What's that supposed to mean?"

"I don't ever have to know what happened to you in those foster homes," he said. "But you've got it inside you. It's holding on in your body."

"Why do you say that?"

"Because it's waiting when you close your eyes and get quiet."

"Bullshit. I just don't like sitting still."

He went over to his bed and sat with his back to the headboard. He stayed very still.

"Fine," she said. "Fine."

She logged out, bounced from chair to

bed. Crossed her legs.

"Get relaxed but not too relaxed," he said. "Become aware of any tightness or tingling. Rest your tongue on the roof of your mouth, your hands on your knees. Focus on the breath moving through you. Follow it and see where it takes you."

He straightened his spine, pulled his shoulders back into alignment, made a two-millimeter adjustment to the column of his neck. Slowly the laughter and music from outside faded. He became acutely aware of the pressure of the mattress beneath him, a twinge in his right shoulder, the scent of laundry detergent. He started to constrict his focus, the outside world irising shut. But he sensed an unease inside the room.

Joey, rocking from side to side. She rolled her neck.

"Try not to squirm," he said.

"I'm not squirming."

"Just keep coming back to your breath. And to sitting still."

She remained motionless, but her agitation grew, a physical force clouding the air between them.

She exhaled sharply and flopped back. She stared at the ceiling. When she blinked, tears streamed down her temples. She was breathing hard.

Then she got up violently, the mattress springs whining, her bare feet hitting the floor with a thud. She rushed out, slamming the door behind her.

Evan stared at the door. She'd caught him off guard, perhaps even more than when she'd broken his nose.

He uncrossed his legs, stood up, hesitated.

She wanted to be alone. Should he respect that? In *this* neighborhood?

He reminded himself that she could take care of herself just fine.

Somewhere outside, a car horn blared.

He noted the concern swelling in his chest with each breath. An odd sensation. She was fine.

But he wasn't.

Already he was walking to the door and then moving swiftly through the outside corridor. The other apartment doors were closed now, the denizens busy inside from the sound of it. He swept around the other arm of the complex — no sign of Joey. He circled back around the pool, the same young men telling the same stories, smoking different blunts, not noticing him or anything else. His chest tightened even more as he cut between the cars in the parking lot.

Still no Joey.

He jogged up the block. A pimped-out Camaro drove past, windows down, rap booming from the radio. Eminem was cleaning out his closet and doing a damn fine job of it.

She wasn't at the minivan.

She wasn't visible from the next intersection or the one after that.

He checked the RoamZone. She hadn't called. Nor had Xavier. His worry compounded when he considered what he'd do if Xavier decided to contact him now. *Sorry about your gang situation, but I'm busy running around Virginia trying to prevent a boy's execution, chess-matching with the world's most lethal assassins, and my sidekick just went missing.*

Sidekick.

The word had tumbled naturally into his thoughts.

He cut over one block, walked back across cracked sidewalks, pit bulls gnashing at him from behind fences. Activity swirled inside an abandoned house, unsavory customers visible through the missing windows and front door. Evan strode across the gone-to-seed front lawn and through the rectangular hole where the front door used to reside. His boot crushed the shards of a dropped crack pipe. Half the back wall was missing, bodies milling ten deep in the packed living room. A couple was having sex on a couch shoved against one wall, their pale skin nearly glowing in the darkness.

Evan shoved through toward the backyard.

"Hey, fucker, you'd best watch where you're —"

Palm — jaw — floor. The guy dropped as if brought down with a lasso, and Evan broke through the remaining fringe of bodies. More faces, more hands clutching crinkled brown paper bags, more glass pipes. A fire leapt inside an enormous clay pot, casting irregular light across bare midriffs, shaved skulls, a guy with glasses missing one lens.

No Joey.

Evan cut up the side yard, jogged back to the apartment complex, his stress quickening. The guys remained on the lawn chairs, the smell of weed contact-high thick in the corridor.

The door to the rented room was open.

Evan jogged forward, hand resting on the grip of the skinny ARES shoved into his waistband. He came around the doorway, stepping inside, ready to draw.

Joey stood in the middle of the room, shoulders hunched, her face in her hands. Her back shuddered.

He heeled the door shut behind him. "Joey?"

She wheeled on him. "Where were you?" She came at him, striking blindly. "Why'd you leave me here? I got back, and you . . . you weren't here. Why weren't you here?"

He retreated, but she launched at him again, pounded with her fists, not like a trained operator but like an angry sixteen-year-old. "You left me. I thought . . . I thought . . ."

He tried to gather her in, but she shoved him away. She slammed the closet door off its tracks, kicked the chair across the room, threw the lamp against the wall, knocking a divot through the paint.

He moved to get out of her way, sat on the floor, and put his back to the door.

She ripped the hanger pole off its mounts in the closet, kicked the bed hard enough that the metal feet gouged marks in the carpet, drove her hand through the drywall.

Finally she finished.

She was facing away from him, her body coiled, her hands in loose fists at her sides. Blood dripped from a split knuckle.

She walked over. She sat across from him, facing away from his bed. Her huge eyes were wet, her shoulders still heaving.

"Where were you?" she said.

"I went to look for you."

"You weren't here."

He swallowed. *"Tiene dos trabajos. Enojarse y contentarse."*

She pressed both hands over her mouth. Tears ran over her knuckles, but she did not make a sound.

They sat on the floor together for a very long time.

53
MY BREATH ON YOUR NECK

The next morning Evan and Joey sat on their respective beds spooning gas-station-bought oatmeal into their mouths from Styrofoam cups. He'd told Joey to put the room back together, and she'd done her best, but still the closet door was knocked off its tracks, the lamp shattered, the walls battered. The wreckage of the chair was neatly stacked in the corner, a pyre of kindling. It was a foregone conclusion that Suzi Orton, cheery Airbnb patron, was going to have to retire her profile after they cleared out.

"Look," Joey said. "Sorry I kinda freaked out last night. It's just . . . I was —"

Her phone gave a three-note alert, a bugle announcing the king.

She thumped her Styrofoam cup down on the nightstand, oatmeal sludge slopping over the brim, and swung off the bed into a kneeling position before her laptop at the desk.

"A police cruiser hit on the plate," she said, her voice tight with excitement.

He leaned over her shoulder, saw a screen grab of the black Suburban captured by the light bar of a passing cop car. The SUV was parked in a crowded Food Lion grocery-store lot, the GPS specifics spelled out below.

"Damn it." Joey nibbled the edge of her thumbnail. "By the time we get there, they'll be gone."

"No," he said. "This is good. No one drives across town to get groceries."

She caught his meaning, nodded, and snapped her laptop shut. They threw their stuff together in less than a minute.

Before heading out, Evan left ten crisp hundred-dollar bills on the floor beneath a fist-size hole punched through the drywall.

He started at Food Lion and drove in an expanding spiral, creeping through increasingly rough neighborhoods. A few miles along their winding path, he pulled abruptly to the curb.

Joey said, "What?"

He pointed at a ramshackle single-story house a half block up that looked like most every other house they'd passed. A chunk of missing stucco on the front corner, planters filled with dirt, overstuffed trash cans at the curb. A tall rolling side gate had been turned impenetrable by green plastic strapping interwoven with the chain-link. One of the gutters had come loose and dangled from the fringe of the house like a coal chute.

"I don't get it," Joey said.

"The trash cans," he said. "See those green plastic strips poking up?"

She leaned toward the dash, squinting through the windshield. "They match the fence filler."

"Right. Someone cut and installed that privacy screen on the gate this week." He unholstered his ARES and opened the door. "Wait here."

He crossed the street, darted through front yards, hurdling hedges. He slowed as he came up on the house, keeping his arms firm but not too firm, the pistol pointed at a spot on the ground a few feet ahead of the tips of his boots.

The gate was lifted two inches off the concrete to accommodate the wheels. Easing onto the edge of the driveway, Evan dropped to his stomach and peered through the gap.

The driveway continued past the gate to where the yard ended at a rotting wooden fence. Parked halfway there at an angle was a black Suburban. Weeds pushed up from cracks in the concrete, brushing the vehicle's flanks. But they weren't dense enough to cover the license plate.

VBK-5976.

Next to it on the baked dirt of the yard were the second rented Suburban and a Chevy Tahoe.

Evan withdrew.

Jogging back up the street, he flicked a finger for Joey to get out. She climbed from her perch in the driver's seat, locking the vehicle behind her.

"It's there?" she asked.

"It's there."

As they circled the block, he could hear Joey's breathing quicken.

They cut through a side yard next to a partially burned house. The frame of an Eldorado rested on blocks in a carport that sagged dangerously on heat-buckled steel beams. They stepped carefully, moving into the backyard. A rear patio had served as a firebreak, preserving a yard filled with dead, waist-high foxtails. Evan and Joey waded into the weeds, their shoes crunching as they headed for the rotting wood of the rear fence. Though the fire looked to be a few days old, ash still scented the air, the smell just shy of pleasing.

The warped fence had plenty of cracks and crevices that provided a ready vantage across the target house's backyard. On what was left of the lawn, an old-fashioned round barbecue grill melted into a puddle of rust. The reddish tinge on the earth brought a host of associations to Evan, which he pushed aside, focusing instead on the house beyond.

Plywood covered two of the living room's three windows. One sheet had been removed and set to the side, presumably to let in light. The high kitchen window over the sink had been left exposed, and the rear door was laid open.

Paul Delmonico and Shane Shea, Van Sciver's freelancers, stood at semi-attention, focused on someone in one of the blind spots. Evan assumed the other two freelancers were holding down the front of the house. In the kitchen window, Thornhill's head was visible. A moment later a woman stepped beside him, facing mostly away from Evan.

Midlength hair, confident posture, athletic shoulders that tapered to a slender but not-too-slender waist — Evan would recognize her bearing anywhere.

Orphan V turned around.

In the shaft of light falling through the kitchen window, she looked quite striking. As she murmured something to Thornhill, she reached over her shoulder and scratched at a spot on her back. Evan thought of the burned flesh beneath her shirt and felt a jagged edge twist inside him.

Palms pressed to the splintering fence, he breathed the rot of the wood and watched the freelancers watching whoever was in that blind spot, two attack dogs waiting for a command. Beside him Joey shifted her weight uncomfortably, rolling one sneaker onto its outer edge. She was humming with nervousness.

The person in the blind spot stepped out of the blind spot and into view.

That broad form, the thin copper hair, the muscular forearms and blocky wrists. But it wasn't just Van Sciver who made Joey's breath hitch audibly in her throat; it was what he was carrying.

David Smith's frail form draped across his arms.

Van Sciver dumped the body onto a tarp on the floor. His arms were swollen with exertion, bowed at his sides. The lines on the right side of his face caught the shadows differently — perhaps scarring, perhaps a trick of the light. Evan hadn't laid eyes on him, not directly, since they'd shared a tense drink in Oslo nearly a decade ago.

Seeing him now in the stark light of day, Evan felt emotions shifting along old fault lines. They'd spent so many years circling each other from the shadows that some small piece of Evan wondered from time to time if he'd conjured Charles Van Sciver entirely.

But there he was, in the flesh.

And the body of the boy who used to be David Smith.

"He's dead," Joey said. Despite the cool December air, sweat sparkled across her temple, emotion flushing her cheeks.

Staring at the motionless, slender form on the tarp, Evan felt heat pulse in his windpipe, fired by a red-hot coal lodged in his chest.

He pushed away from the fence, looked down at the tips of his boots. He pictured the crowded bunks of Room 14 at McClair Children's Mental Health Center. A Lego rebel riding a Snowspeeder across a rusting radiator. Jorell, too smart for his own good. In another life Jorell would be a lawyer, a philosophy professor, a stand-up comedian. In another life David Smith would be sitting down to dinner with a real family. In another life Jack was still alive and he and Evan had plans on the books to share a meal in a two-story farmhouse in Arlington.

"Wait," Joey said. "Evan — he's breathing."

Evan's head snapped back up. He watched as the boy stirred and rolled onto his side.

Evan's jaw had tightened. That red-hot coal singed the inside of his throat, fanned with each breath. "We have to get him."

"There are three Orphans and four muscleheads in that house," Joey said. "Armed to the teeth. And we're out here in the weeds with your girly gun."

"Yes."

"So how do you plan on getting to him?"

Evan fished the Samsung Galaxy from his pocket. "By telling Van Sciver where we are."

He thumbed the Signal application.

A moment later a xylophone chime of a ringtone carried to them on the breeze. Evan put his eye to a knothole and peered into the house.

Van Sciver lifted the phone from his pocket and looked down at the screen. Candy and Thornhill alerted to his expression and went to him, the three of them standing in a loose huddle by the kid's body.

They were in close enough proximity that

a tight grouping of nine-millimeter rounds could take them down.

If they weren't Orphans, Evan might consider hurdling the fence and rushing the house to get within range. But he knew he wouldn't get three steps past the rusting barbecue before they alerted to him.

Van Sciver's thumb pulsed over the screen, and he lifted the phone to his face. Evan watched his lips move, the familiar voice coming across the line on a half-second delay; there was a lot of encryption to squeeze the single syllable through. "X."

"Now you're catching on."

"I suppose you're calling about the boy."

From the remove of one backyard and a disintegrating fence, Evan watched Van Sciver turn. Through the phone he heard the rustle of the big man's boots on the tarp. Candy had one hip cocked, directing the two freelancers to keep eyes up. Thornhill's muscles coiled, thrumming with energy, ready to go kinetic. He walked to the front of the house to alert the others.

Van Sciver said, "You took one of mine . . ."

Joey must've heard the words from the receiver, because she stiffened at the mention of herself.

". . . so I took one of Jack's," Van Sciver

continued. "But he doesn't have Joey's weaknesses. He's like you and me. Tabula rasa. Jack found him and tucked him away somewhere safe. Now we have him. Like a gun without a serial number."

"Disposable," Evan said. "You'll train him up, spend him when you need to."

"That's what we're for, Evan, remember?"

"Orphan J. Orphan C. Orphan L. Jack. Joey. And now this boy. All to get to me."

"That's right."

Candy was close at hand, hanging on Van Sciver's words, her lips pursed into a shape evocative of a kiss. But the eyes told a different story, of dark appetites unsatiated.

Van Sciver's stare picked across the backyard and snagged on the rear fence. His eyes looked lopsided even from this distance, and it took Evan a moment to realize that it was because the right pupil was larger. Evan could have sworn Van Sciver was looking through the knothole right at him. It was impossible, of course, and yet Evan still pulled back a few inches from the wood.

He knew that look, the same one Van Sciver used to issue when they gathered on the cracked asphalt of the basketball courts across from Pride House, a group of punkass kids with nothing to do and nowhere to go.

A look like he was trying to see inside you.

Evan took a breath, eased it out. "How 'bout you get around to telling me what makes me so special?"

Again he watched Van Sciver's lips move, the dubbing off from the voice coming through the line. "You really haven't put it together?"

Evan didn't reply.

Van Sciver laughed. "You don't really think this is *just* personal?"

Evan didn't indulge him. Their earlier conversation played back in his head. *You have no idea, do you? How high it goes?*

"It's amazing," Van Sciver said. "You don't even know how valuable you are."

He pivoted slightly, meeting Candy's loaded gaze. She was clearly read in on whatever reason had escalated the hunt for Evan.

Van Sciver's shoulders rose, his neck corded with muscle, his blocky hand firming around the phone. "They sent me to the Sandpit a few times, needed to pick another name off that deck of playing cards. I caught up to him in Tikrit. Shitty little compound in Qadisiyah, jungle-gym bars and rusty Russian munitions. We'd already rained down with aerial munitions, but Habeeb's still strolling around his little

440

fenced-in yard, lord of his domain. I was set up with my .300 Win Mag on a rooftop at twelve hundred meters, ready to shoot the dick off a mosquito. And Habeeb comes around the yard into sight. I have the head shot, clear as day. But at the last minute, I move the crosshairs from his face to his arm, take it off at the shoulder." His breath came as a rush of static across the receiver. "He'll bleed out, right? But I wanted it to be slow. Guess why."

Evan said, "To draw out the other targets."

"No," Van Sciver said, his voice simmering with latent rage. "Because I wanted him to *know.*"

Evan let the silence lengthen.

Van Sciver said, "When I catch up to you, Evan, you're gonna have time also. To know. All your questions? I'll fill you in at the very end. When you're bleeding out on the ground at my feet."

His whole body had tensed, but Evan watched him try to relax his muscles now, a snake uncoiling.

"I am hot on your trail," Van Sciver said.

"And I'm hot on yours," Evan said, the Samsung pressed to his cheek. "Can you feel my breath on your neck?"

Van Sciver's expression turned uneasy. He walked into the kitchen, peered out the window into the backyard once more. "Is that so?"

"Yeah," Evan said. "We've got a lock on the kid."

Next to him Joey bristled. Her hands flared wide — *What are you doing?* — but he held focus on the house.

Van Sciver muffled the phone against his shoulder and snapped his fingers. The free-lancers readied M4s and spread around the interior, taking up guard positions. Thornhill drew an FNX-45 from his hip holster and ambled out of sight.

Van Sciver kept his pistol in his underarm tension holster. He moved the phone back to his mouth. "If you want him," he said, "come and get him."

Evan said, "Okay," and hung up.

"What the hell?" Joey hissed. "Now they're on high alert. If they come back here —"

Evan pulled out his RoamZone, pressed three buttons, held up a finger to Joey while it rang.

A feminine voice came over the line. "911."

"Yeah, hi," Evan said. "I work at the Mc-Clair Children's Mental Health Center in Church Hill. A man and a teenage girl have been lingering around the building all morning. One of our nurses said she saw that the man had a gun. Can you please get someone here right away? Hang on — *Shit.* I think they're approaching."

He hung up.

Joey gestured for him furiously, pointing through the gap. Crouching, he peered again through the knothole.

Candy swung through the kitchen, heading for the rear of the house. He couldn't see her body until it filled the doorway to the backyard.

She held an M4.

She moved swiftly across the porch and strode out to recon the yard.

Joey backpedaled, her sneaker tamping down the foxtails loudly. She cringed at the noise, wobbled to avoid landing her other foot. Evan shot out a hand and grabbed her arm. She was frozen with one leg above the dead weeds. The brittle foxtails stretched all around them, an early-warning system that would broadcast to Candy any move they made.

Firming his grip on Joey's biceps, Evan swung his head back to the fence. He peered through the knothole, now a foot away. The perspective had the effect of lensing in on the yard.

Candy, twenty yards away and closing.

With his free hand, Evan reached down

and tugged his ARES 1911 from the holster. He kept his eyes locked on the knothole.

Candy passed the rusted barbecue, the bore of the M4 facing them, a full circle of black.

She swept toward the fence.

Evan lifted the pistol and aimed through the silver-dollar-size hole.

54

ILLEGAL IN POLICE DEPARTMENTS FROM COAST TO COAST

Evan's torso twisted, pulled in two directions, Joey's weight tugging him one way, his drawn ARES aimed the other. He felt a pleasing burn across his chest, ribs unstacking, intercostals stretching.

If he pulled the trigger, he'd drop Candy but the sound would alert Van Sciver and his men. Then he'd be in retreat with a sixteen-year-old and eight in the mag, pursued by six trained men armed with long guns.

Not ideal.

But he'd handled not-ideal before.

Candy neared the rear fence. He sighted on the hollow of her throat. Her critical mass filled the knothole, blocking out everything else.

His finger tightened on the trigger.

"V!"

Van Sciver's voice from the house halted her in her tracks. She pivoted, M4 swinging low at her side.

She was no more than four feet from the fence line.

The gun was steady in Evan's hand, aimed at the fabric of her shirt fluttering across her back. He'd punch the round through her marred flesh, two inches right of her spine beneath the blade of her shoulder.

Despite Evan's grip, Joey wobbled on her planted foot, her other arm whipping high as she rebalanced herself. In Evan's peripheral vision, he sensed her raised boot brush the tips of the foxtails.

"We just picked up a 911 call!" Van Sciver shouted across the yard. "Armed man and a teenage girl at McClair Children's Mental Health Center."

"They're one step behind," Candy said.

"Let's meet them there."

Candy jogged back toward the house, her figure shrinking in the telescope lens of the knothole. As she receded, Evan released Joey's arm. Joey eased her other foot down to the ground, the weeds crackling softly. She came to Evan's side to watch through the fence.

At the house Van Sciver swung out of the rear door, keys in hand. Thornhill and Candy flanked him across the yard, Delmonico and Shea in their wake.

446

The two other freelancers had been drawn onto the back porch by the commotion.

"Hangebrauck — wipe the notebook," Van Sciver called out to the bigger of the two, a hefty guy with an armoring of muscle layered over some extra girth.

"Yes, sir."

"Bower, eyes on the front."

Bower, a lanky man with sunken eyes, scratched at his neck. "Yes, sir."

Across the yard Delmonico slid back the gate, the rusty wheels screeching. Van Sciver and Candy hopped into the Tahoe, Shea and Thornhill into the nearest Suburban, and they backed the SUVs out. The Suburban idled in the driveway, waiting on Delmonico as he closed the gate, wiping himself from view.

There was a moment of stillness, Hangebrauck's head tilted back as he sniffed the ash-tinged air. And then he went into the house again.

Bower met him in the kitchen with a red notebook.

It looked just like the notebook Evan had found in the Portland headquarters.

Hangebrauck carried it into the kitchen. Then he placed it in the microwave. The lit carousel spun, rotating the notebook.

Joey looked over at Evan, her brow furled.

447

Bizarre.

As Bower disappeared once again to the front of the house, Hangebrauck walked into the living room and stared down at David Smith. The boy lay quietly, half off the tarp, his cheek smashed to the floorboards, his thin shoulders rising and falling.

Hangebrauck slung his M4 and sat on the high end of the decline bench, a bored expression on his face. He dug something out from beneath a thumbnail.

Joey leaned toward Evan, her sneakers crackling in the weeds. "There are still two of them," she whispered.

Evan smiled.

Evan didn't have a suppressor. A gunshot would alert the neighbors. He would have to use his hands.

He moved silently along the side of the house and came up on the open back door. Hangebrauck remained on the decline bench, gazing blankly through the sole uncovered rear window into the yard. A dark hall led to the front of the house and to Bower.

Evan waited.

After a time Hangebrauck stood and stretched his back, his shirt tugging up and showing off a pale bulge of flesh at the waistband. He gave a little groan. Resting his hand on the butt of the carbine, he walked to the window.

Over his shoulder Evan's reflection ghosted into sight in the pane.

Evan's right elbow was raised, pointing at the nape of Hangebrauck's neck.

The big man's eyes barely had time to widen before Evan reached over his crown, grabbed his forehead, and yanked his head back into his elbow.

The bony tip of Evan's ulna served as the point of impact, crushing into the base of Hangebrauck's skull, turning the medulla oblongata into gray jelly.

A reinforced horizontal elbow smash.

The man didn't fall so much as crumple.

Evan stripped the M4 cleanly from Hangebrauck as he dropped out of the sling.

The thump made a touch more noise than Evan would have liked.

He tilted the M4 against the wall and moved quickly down the hall. He got to the entryway just as Bower pivoted into sight, rifle raised.

Evan jacked Bower's gun to the side, the man's grip faltering. He spun Bower into the momentum of the first blow and seized him from behind, using a triangular choke hold made illegal in police departments from coast to coast. Evan bent Bower's head forward into the crook of his arm, pinching off the carotid arteries on either side. Bower made a soft gurgling sound and sagged, heavy in Evan's grip.

Evan lowered him to the floor.

Thirteen down.

Twelve to go.

Evan walked back to David Smith. Crouching, he found a strong pulse on the boy's neck. He noticed a slit on the forearm, recently sutured, but otherwise the kid looked fine. He'd probably gotten sliced during the snatch and Van Sciver had patched him up.

The room looked to have been recently cleaned, but despite that a bad odor lingered. Sporadic water spots darkened the walls, the plaster turning to cottage cheese. Scrub marks textured the floorboards. The bristles had left behind a thin frothed wake of bleach, the white edged with something else not quite the shade of coffee.

Evan knew that color.

He stepped into the kitchen. The glass plate was still spinning inside the microwave. He stopped the timer, grabbed the red notebook from inside, and shoved it into his waistband.

He went back to David Smith, slung him

over his shoulder, and walked out the front door into broad daylight.

Joey had the minivan on the move already, easing to the front curb, the side door rolled back. Evan set the boy down gently inside, climbed in, and they drove off.

55
VANISHED IN PLAIN SIGHT

They were halfway across Richmond when the kid woke up.

Puffy lids parted, revealing glazed eyes. David Smith lifted his head groggily, groaned, and lowered it back to the bench seat of the minivan.

Joey peered down from the passenger seat, concerned. "He's up. Pull over."

Evan parked across from a high school that stretched to encompass the entire block. He killed the engine and checked out the surroundings. On the near side of the street, magnolias fanned up from a verdant park, their crooked branches bare and haunting. A man-made river drifted beneath the low-swooping boughs, white water rushing across river stones to feed an elaborate fountain at the center. There were speed walkers and young couples and dogs chasing Frisbees — a good amount of activity to get lost in.

Evan leaned around the driver's seat to peer back at the boy.

"You're okay, David," he said. "You're safe now."

The boy blinked heavily. "That's not my name."

"We know it is. We know you were trained by Tim Draker, that you had to go on the run, that Jack Johns hid you in that mental-health center until you were kidnapped yesterday."

"Is this another mind game?" the boy asked.

"What?"

"You know, like SERE stuff. You take me, mess with my head, see what I'll give up."

Evan said, "Not even close."

A bell warbled, and kids started streaming from the school, pouring down the front steps, zombie-mobbing the minivan on their way to the park. The added movement was good, even easier to blend into.

Joey pointed to the sutured slice on the back of David's left forearm. "What happened there?"

The boy regarded the cut and his arm as if he'd never seen them before. "I don't . . . I don't remember."

He tried to sit up, wobbled, finally made it. His face was pale, his lips bloodless. He shook his head. "I don't feel so good."

"Let's get him some fresh air," Evan said, already stepping out into the sea of high-schoolers.

He slid back the side door, and Joey helped David out.

"Off the street," he said, and she nodded.

They joined the current of kids flowing through the magnolias and across the park. Kids clustered to take phone pics and compare the results. Braying laughter, deafening chatter, a cacophony of ringtones. Evan led Joey and David, cutting between cliques. They stopped at the fountain. Students rimmed the encircling concrete. The air smelled of chlorine, hair spray, the skunky tinge of pot. A family of black ducks paddled across the still water at the fountain's edge. Buried treasure glimmered beneath, copper wishes waiting to be fulfilled.

No one took note of the three of them; they'd vanished in plain sight.

Color crept back into David's cheeks, his lips pinking up. He sat on the rim of the fountain, poked at the sutures.

"Looks like you were drugged," Joey said.

His head bobbled unevenly. "But why? I woulda done whatever."

To one side a crew of girls crowded

around a ringleader with gel nails and green-and-white Stan Smiths. "Loren's totally gonna uninvite her from her sweet sixteen, because — get this — she posted a pic of herself with Dylan in his backseat. They were just sitting there, but still. Hashtag: tr*ashy*."

This doubled the girls over. Leaning on each other, weak with laughter, retainers gleaming. Their sneakers matched. Their haircuts matched. Their backpacks were mounded at their heels, different shades of the same Herschel model.

Joey regarded them as one might a herd of exotic animals.

"Where's that guy?" David asked. "The big guy?"

Joey refocused. "We got you from him."

"But he was gonna put me in that program. The one Tim was training me for." David's gaze sharpened. "Wait — where's Tim? What happened to him?"

Evan said, "They killed him."

David's mouth opened, but no noise came out.

Evan crouched and set his hands on David's knees. "We're gonna make sure you're taken care of."

"Evan," Joey said. *"Evan."*

She'd clocked something at the park's

perimeter. He picked up her gaze, spotting a black Suburban flickering into view behind clusters of students and the skeletal branches of the magnolias. It turned at the corner, creeping along the front of the high school.

Shea at the wheel, Delmonico in the passenger seat, Jordan Thornhill in the back, bouncing his head as if to music.

Joey somehow had one of the Herschel backpacks at her feet, unzipped. She'd already taken out an iPhone hugged by a rubber Panda case. She tapped in 911. When she put the phone to her ear, her hand was trembling.

They watched the Suburban prowl.

Evan popped the bottom two magnetic buttons of his shirt, creating an unobstructed lane to his hip holster. The breeze riffled the fabric, tightened his skin. Thornhill and the two freelancers would try to flush Evan, Joey, and David from the park. Presumably Candy and Van Sciver were in the surrounding blocks somewhere, lying in wait.

There were at least two hundred kids on scene — a lot of flesh to catch stray bullets.

"I just spotted two fugitives," Joey said into the phone. "Paul Delmonico and Shane Shea."

As she named the high school and the park, paranoia bubbled up in Evan. He looked down at the slit on David's arm.

Dried blood at the seam. Fresh sutures. Good placement.

David blinked up through bleary red eyes. "What? What is it?"

"Come," Evan said. *"Now."*

As the Suburban drifted around the block, Evan circled to the far side of the fountain, keeping the spouting water between them and their pursuers.

Joey brought the stolen backpack, still talking into the phone. "There's kids all over here, and those guys are armed, and they're gonna start shooting people."

The Panda phone case undercut the gravity of her tone, lending a surreal touch to the situation.

Youthful movement churned all around. Two skinny kids sat cross-legged at the base of a tree, testing each other with math equations on flash cards. An older kid in an artfully torn flannel snickered with his compatriots. "Dude, I am *so* gonna hit that this weekend." One of the girls on the far side of the fountain had produced a selfie stick, and she and her friends were leaning together, making pouty lips, adjusting wisps of bangs. A half block away, three assassins glided down the street.

Joey hung up, pocketed the ridiculous Panda phone. "Let's see how long it takes PD to respond to prison-escapee pedophile cop killers in a park full of children."

David said, *"What?"*

She shushed him.

Through a jetting arc of water, they watched the Suburban ease into a parking spot a half block behind their minivan. Evan did a full 360. Nothing but kids on the grassy expanse, the weaving faux river, more trees. Van Sciver and Candy weren't showing themselves.

They didn't have to.

All around the park's periphery, parents were picking up their kids, the Suburban just another SUV. Its doors opened, and the three men got out. They stood at the curb, scanning the park.

Joey said, "How?"

"His forearm," Evan said.

She looked down at the four-inch seam sliced through David's flesh.

"Wait," David said. "What do you mean?"

"They chipped you."

Thornhill's stare moved to the fountain.

And locked onto them.

He rocked back on his heels, a small display of delight, and said something to

Delmonico and Shea. All three sets of eyes pegged them now.

They were about a quarter mile away. The spray beneath the bent spurt of fountain caught the fading sunlight, suspending a rainbow in its web of drops. Evan glared through the gauzy veil of color. The men glared back. Except Thornhill.

Thornhill was grinning.

They stepped forward in unison, cutting through groups of students. Delmonico and Shea wore trench coats. With each step the barrels of their M4s nosed forward into view beside their knees. Thornhill angled away from them behind one of the gnarled tree trunks, opening up a second front.

Evan slid his hand through the gap of his shirt, clenched the grip of the ARES, and readied to draw.

56
CRIMSON FIREWORK

As Delmonico and Shea started for the fountain, Thornhill sidled farther to the side, dividing Evan's attention. Even from this distance, Evan could see that his lips were pursed. Was he whistling?

Evan tightened his hand around the pistol. David bristled at his side. Though the men were still way across the park, Joey had instinctively slid one foot back into a fighting stance.

There were countless students before them. And countless behind them.

Evan would have to thread the needle.

Three times.

He unholstered the ARES, held it low by his thigh, let a breath out, tried to relax his clenched jaw.

All at once scores of cop cars erupted onto the block.

There was nothing gradual about it; one moment they were absent, the next a half-dozen units had morphed into existence on the street behind Delmonico and Shea, sirens screaming, lights strobing. Officers sheltered behind car doors and spread across the sidewalk, aiming shotguns and Berettas at the two freelancers — 180 degrees of firepower.

The kids bucked and surged, going up on tiptoes, straining their necks, the murmur of their voices heating to a low boil.

A captain had a radio mike snugged beneath his gray mustache, barking orders over the loudspeaker.

Delmonico and Shea halted and raised their arms. Their trench coats gaped wide, revealing the slung M4 carbines.

A few of the kids screamed, those close to the action going skittish. Anxious excitement rippled across the park as a vanguard of cops pressed forward and took the freelancers down.

Evan barely watched them. He kept tabs on Thornhill, lingering by the perimeter of the cop cars, watching him right back.

Evan gave him a *What can ya do?* shrug.

Thornhill smiled good-naturedly and threw his hands up, like a magician tossing cards. The legion of officers faced the park, Thornhill mere feet behind them, unnoticed. He heeled backward across the street, which had been conveniently cleared for him, then turned and strolled up the wide steps of the school.

He started jogging as he reached the top stairs, building steam. Then he leapt from a planter onto a doorframe, pinballed his way up a crevice between a concrete pillar and a wall, and flipped himself onto the roof. His jacket flared like a cape, his powerful wrestler's build momentarily silhouetted against the sky.

"Holy shit," David said. "Did you see that? The guy's friggin' *Spider-Man.*"

Instead of fleeing, Thornhill took a seat at the lip of the roof above the school's entrance, legs crossed. He curled over his lap like weeping Buddha, the muscles of his shoulders undulating.

Across the park the cops hauled Delmonico and Shea onto their feet and steered them at a diagonal away from the high school. They angled across the grass to where a police van waited on the neighboring street, clear of the traffic jam of responding cruisers. The freelancers shuffled along compliantly, hands cuffed behind them. Though a good number of students had scattered, others remained, rubbernecking from what they considered a safe distance. Many of the parents were out of their cars, rushing to their kids, pulling them away.

Up on the roof of the high school, Thornhill straightened up, and Evan saw what he'd been doing.

Screwing a suppressor onto the threaded barrel of his FNX-45.

"How far away are we?" Joey said.

Evan squinted, assessing. "Just under five hundred yards."

"It's impossible for him to hit us."

"He's not aiming at us."

It took a beat for Joey to catch his meaning. "Jesus," she said. "Really?"

Thornhill popped onto his feet at the roof's edge, a single deft movement.

Evan said, "Van Sciver can't afford for them to be in custody."

David started to step up onto the fountain's basin so he could see, but Evan set a hand on his shoulder, firming him to the ground.

This the boy could skip.

The cops steered Shea and Delmonico farther into the park and away from the school, but Thornhill appeared unhurried. He took a supported position against an A/C unit, his off hand braced against the housing.

"He can't make that shot," Joey said. "Not through the trees. Not at that distance."

A black bulge rode the top of the gun — holographic red-dot sights. The suppressor stretched the barrel into something lean and menacing. Most common loadings for a .45 ACP kept the gun subsonic, so Thornhill could squeeze off both shots without making a sound signature loud enough for the cops to source.

Delmonico and Shea disappeared from view, temporarily lost in a cocoon of officers. They were at least two hundred yards from Thornhill. Maybe two-fifty. A few cops moved ahead, clearing the rest of the way to the police van.

Evan swept his view back across the park, the street, and up the stairs to the roof of the school. Shouldered into the A/C unit, Thornhill was so still he might have been part of the building.

Two hundred seventy-five yards, at least.

The clump of blue uniforms reached the intersecting street. Two transport officers emerged from the paddy wagon, laying open the rear doors.

The arresting cops jerked Delmonico and Shea to a rough halt and stepped forward to confer with the transfer officers. The other cops milled around, spreading out into the street.

Creating gaps.

On the roof, the .45 twitched in Thorn-hill's grip.

Delmonico fell, a crimson firework paint-ing the side of the van.

Confused, the cops crouched and ran for cover.

Having his hands cuffed at the small of his back put Shea on a half-step delay. His head was cocked with confusion, the cloud-muffled sun gleaming off his bald dome. For an instant he stood wide open there in the street, twisted around, looking in the wrong direction. The cuffs yanked his shoulders back, nicely exposing the expanse of his chest.

A dark flower bloomed on his shirt. He staggered backward, his spine striking the side of the police van. His knees were bent, tilting him into the vehicle, physics momen-tarily holding him on his feet.

Then his heels slipped and he fell, landing with his legs splayed before him.

Evan turned to look again at Thornhill way across on the roof and was not sur-prised to see Thornhill looking back.

Fifteen dead.

Ten left.

Evan gave a respectful nod.

Thornhill placed one hand on his chest and flourished the other as if to accompany a bow, accepting the compliment. He holstered the pistol and stepped back from sight.

Gone.

Pandemonium swept across the park. The cops spread out, weapons drawn, eyes whipping across rooftops and vehicles in every direction. The remaining students stampeded out of the park, trampling abandoned backpacks. Pages of dropped textbooks fluttered in the breeze. One girl stood frozen, sobbing amid the chaos, fists pressed to her ears. Parents hauled their children away, one father sprinting with his son flopped over his arm like a stack of dry-cleaned shirts. Horns blared. Brakes screeched. Fenders crumpled. A girl had tripped near the fountain and was curled up, holding a bloody knee.

David yanked on Evan's arm. "What happened? What's going on?"

"We gotta move," Joey said. "Ride the chaos out of the park."

Evan took David's arm in his hands, turned it to show the slice. "This first."

He sat David on the wall of the fountain and moved his thumbs along the sides of the forearm scar, pressing gently. David winced. Behind him in the fountain, the black ducks glided by, unperturbed by the commotion.

Cops moved swiftly through the park, corralling stray students. Joey vibrated with impatience, her head swiveling from the approaching officers to the surrounding streets. "We don't have time for this."

Evan felt nothing unusual around the scar. He ran his fingers across the unmarred flesh up toward the boy's elbow.

Something hard beneath the flesh pressed into the pad of his thumb.

A thin disk, about the size of a watch battery.

"What is it?" David asked.

"A digital transmitter."

"Up there?" Joey said. "How are we supposed to get it out?"

The tiny bulge was about six inches up from the incision; it had been slid up toward the elbow to conceal it. Seventy-eight percent of Orphans were left-handed. Van Sciver had inserted the transmitter on the left side, Evan assumed, so that if David noticed it and tried to cut it out, he'd be forced to use his nondominant hand to do so.

Evan said, "We need a magnet. A strong magnet."

Two of the cops had closed to within a hundred yards of the fountain. Joey ducked behind its low wall. "We have to figure this out later."

"As long as this is in him, Van Sciver has our location."

Joey's wild eyes found Evan.

His hands went to his shirt buttons, but the magnets wouldn't be strong enough; they were designed to give way readily. He said, *"Think."*

Joey snapped her fingers. "Hang on." She reached for the purloined Herschel backpack and whipped a silver laptop out of the padded sleeve in the back. She smashed it on the lip of the fountain, dug around in its entrails, and tore out the hard drive. Gripping the drive in both hands, she hammered it against the concrete until it split open. She yanked out the spindle, revealing a shiny top disk, and then dug out a metal nugget to the side. With some effort she pried apart its two halves, which Evan was surprised to see weren't screwed together.

"Wa-la," she said. "Magnets."

Evan checked on the cops. The nearest pair were now thirty yards away, temporarily hung up with a sobbing mother. He reached into his front pocket for his Strider, raking it out so the shark-fin hook riding the blade snared the pocket's hem and snapped the knife open. He spun the blade around his hand, caught it with the tanto tip angled down.

David said, "Is this gonna —"

Evan slipped the knife beneath the sutures. With an artful flick of his wrist, he laid the four-inch cut open. David gaped down at it.

Evan held out his hand. "Magnet."

Joey slapped it onto his palm with a surgical nurse's panache.

Evan laid the magnet over the bulge in David's elbow and tracked down to the incision.

Joey's head flicked up. "Cops're almost here."

The transmitter followed the magnet down the forearm, tugging the skin up, and popped out through the wound, snicking neatly onto the magnet.

David expelled a clump of air.

One of the black ducks hopped up onto the concrete ledge, bobbing its head, its pebble eyes locked on a stray rind of bread by Evan's shoe.

From the far side of the fountain, a young cop shouted, "Stand up! Lemme see your hands!"

Evan peered across the fountain at the cop and his partner. The park was dense with officers. Two SWAT units rolled up in front of the high school, new cruisers screeching to block the intersections in every direction.

"Too late," Joey said under her breath.

Evan rose slowly, hands held wide, and stared into two drawn Berettas.

57
WHAT HE THOUGHT
HE KNEW

David stood on shaky legs between Evan and Joey. Across the dancing water, both cops aimed at Evan's head.

The entire block was now locked down by backup officers and SWAT.

Evan gauged his next move. The young cop stood in front of his partner, taking lead. He seemed capable, more confident than nervous.

Evan could work with that, play to the cop's ego. He let a worried breath rattle out of him. "Thank God. Is it clear, Officer? I was picking up my daughter, and . . . my son, he got knocked over. His arm's cut open, and —"

"Calm down. Sir? Calm down."

David cupped his hand over the wound, red showing in the seams between his fingers.

The officer's elbows stayed locked, but he swung the gun down and to the side. "Does he require medical attention?"

"I can take him to urgent care," Evan said. He put his arm around Joey's shoulders, gathered her in. "I just want to get my kids out of here. I wasn't sure it was safe to come out yet."

The cop's partner, a tough-looking woman, said, "Where's your car?"

Evan pointed. "Minivan over there."

"Come with us."

The cops gave them an armed escort across the park, passing by dozens of officers, none of whom took notice.

They reached the curb, and the young cop gestured at the SWAT trucks to allow the minivan to pull out.

Evan rushed the kids into the van. "Thank you so much, Officer."

The cop nodded, and he and his partner jogged off to resume the search.

Evan pulled out of the spot, driving past the rows of police cruisers with flashing lights. Two units at the intersection, parked nose to nose, reversed like a parting gate to let the minivan through.

At the next street, Evan signaled responsibly and then turned. The flashing blue and red lights slid out of his rearview mirror.

Joey tilted her head back and shot a breath at the roof.

Evan waited until they'd cleared city limits to pit-stop. He parked behind a liquor store and wrapped David's forearm using gauze pads and an Ace bandage he'd pulled from the first-aid kit lodged beside the spare tire.

The alley behind them gave off the sickly-sweet odor of spilled beer. Flies swayed above an open Dumpster. Broken glass littered the asphalt around it; somebody had practiced empty-bottle free throws with a twelve-pack, showing all the accuracy one would expect from somebody who'd drunk a twelve-pack.

The hatch was raised, David sitting at the edge of the cargo space, his legs dangling past the rear bumper. Crouched before him, Evan smoothed down the bandage and snared the fabric with the metal clips to secure it.

Joey came around to check on their progress. "All good?"

David turned his arm this way and that. "Yeah. Can this be stitched once we get there?"

"Get where?" Evan asked.

"To the Program HQ or wherever."

Past the boy, Evan sensed Joey pull her

head back slightly.

"We're not going to any HQ," Evan said. "You're not joining any Program."

David's tone hardened. "What are you talking about?"

"That's no longer an option," Evan said.

"No way. That big guy said I could be part of it."

"That big guy will dispose of you if you don't make the grade," Joey said.

David spun to face her. "I'll make the grade," he said. "It's all I ever wanted." He glared up at them. "I want a way out. I finally got it. And you want to take it from me?"

"These guys killed Tim," Evan said.

"Then Tim wasn't good enough."

"Watch your fucking mouth." Joey stepped forward, shouldering Evan aside, her intensity catching him off guard. "He died for you."

David's mouth pulsed as he fought down a swallow. But his eyes stayed fierce.

Joey leaned over him. "You don't even know what the Program is."

"I don't care what," David said. "I don't care. I want to go back with the guy who took me. I want something better than a shitty life in some shitty facility."

"Did Jack teach you anything?" Joey said.

"Yeah. To be better. I deserve better than this."

Joey said, "None of us *deserves* anything."

"Maybe so," David said, hopping to his feet and finger-stabbing at Joey. "But that's *my* choice. I'm not going with you if you're not part of the Program. You take me back to those guys, or the first chance I get, I'll tell that you kidnapped me."

His features were set with a bulldog stubbornness that seemed well beyond his thirteen years. Given the life he'd led up to now, that made sense. Hard years counted double.

Evan had been a year younger than David was now when he'd stepped off the truck-stop curb into Jack's car and never looked back. He thought about who he was then and what he thought he knew.

Evan said, "Is there anything we can say to dissuade you?"

David's face had turned ruddy. "No."

"Can we give you more information to —"

"No." The boy was on tilt, his nose angled up at Evan, shoulders forward, fists clenched by his hips.

Evan looked at the boy calmly until he settled onto his heels. David shook his head, eyes welling. "I don't want to be a nobody."

Evan said, "You go down this road, that's

all you'll ever be."

At that, Joey touched her hand to her mouth as if trying to stop something from escaping.

"Maybe so," David said. "But it's *my* road."

Evan watched him for ten seconds and then ten seconds more. Not a thing changed in his expression.

Evan said, "Stay here."

He walked over toward the Dumpster, Joey trailing him. They huddled up, facing the minivan to keep an eye on David.

Joey looked rattled. "We have to change his mind."

"It's not gonna happen," Evan said.

"So we just what? Leave him for Van Sciver to pick up again?" She took a few agitated breaths. "He'll kill him, you know. Sooner or later, directly or indirectly."

Evan said, "Unless."

"Unless what?"

Evan cleared his throat, an uncharacteristic show of emotion.

"Unless what?" Joey repeated.

"We take him public."

She gawked at him.

"He doesn't know anything yet," Evan said. "Not one proper noun in his head."

"He knew Tim Draker. And Jack."

"Both of whom are dead. Anything he has to say about them will sound like a foster-kid fantasy."

The words were so true that saying them out loud felt like a betrayal.

"There's safety in exposure," he said. "No one wants a spoiled asset."

"Then why didn't Jack just do it months ago?"

"Tim Draker was alive. I'm sure he wanted to get David back once it was safe."

Joey flipped her hair over, revealing the shaved band. She lowered her head, crushed shards of glass with the toe of her sneaker. "I don't know. It's a risk."

"Everything's a risk. We're juggling hand grenades."

She didn't respond.

Evan said, "With everything else going on, with us still out here, you really think Van Sciver's gonna burn resources and risk visibility for a screwed-up thirteen-year-old kid?"

She fussed with her hair some more. Then she pinched the bridge of her nose, exhaled. "Okay," she said. "Fuck. Okay."

When she looked up, all emotion was gone, her features blank.

She walked back over to David, her hand digging in her pocket. She came out with the phone in the stupid Panda case, held it four feet from David's face. The shutter-click sound effect was more pronounced than necessary.

She bent her head, a sweep of hair hiding her eyes, and clicked furiously with a thumb.

"What the hell?" David said. "What are you doing?"

She kept on with her thumb.

David grew more uncomfortable. "I said, what are you doing with my picture?"

" 'My cousin's best friend was kidnapped by the U.S. government,' " Joey read slowly. " 'Jesse Watson. Please retweet. Exclamation point.' " Now her eyes rose, and Evan was startled by how little they seemed to hold. "Twitter. Facebook. Instagram."

A few chirps came from the phone, notifications pinging in.

Joey frowned down at the screen. "Looks like BritneyCheer28's a popular girl. Lotta 'friends.' "

She held up the phone. David's face duplicated with each new post, a Warholian effect on the endlessly refreshing screen. The chirps quickened, reaching video-game intensity.

"You bitch." David's voice was so raw it came out as little more than a rasp.

"I don't expect you to understand," Joey

478

said. "Maybe you'll get it when you're older."

"You just took away any shot of me being anything."

"No, you stupid little shit," Joey said. "We *saved* you. We just gave you a normal *life*. Where you don't have to spend all your time running away from . . . running away from yourself." Her voice cracked, and beneath the vehemence there was something wistful, something like longing. She swallowed hard and turned away to stare at the rear of the liquor store.

"Go back to the McClair Center," Evan said to David. "There's a charge nurse who'll be happy to see you."

"Fuck McClair." Tears streaked David's red cheeks. "Fuck the charge nurse."

"I'm going to give you my phone number in case you ever need my help."

"I'm never gonna call you. I'm never gonna ask for your help. I never want to see you again."

Evan took the first-aid kit out of the trunk and dropped it at David's feet. Then he walked to the driver's seat and got in.

Joey stayed in the alley, gazing at the cracked stucco wall, her arms folded. It took her a moment to start moving, but she did.

She climbed in, slammed the door louder

than she needed to.

Evan said, "Look up the number of the McClair Children's Mental Health Center and tell them you spotted him here. I already called. It should be a different voice."

Joey said, "Gimme a moment."

David didn't move as Evan backed out. The side mirror passed within a foot of his shoulder. Evan hit a three-point in the cramped space and spun the steering wheel toward the open road.

They left him in the alley, staring at nothing.

58
AN AD FOR DOMESTICITY

A few minutes past eight o'clock, the GPS dot finally stopped moving. In the passenger seat, Van Sciver pointed up a suburban street and said, "There."

Thornhill steered the Chevy Tahoe into a hard left. Van Sciver held his phone up and watched the blipping dot, finally at fucking rest. Candy hunched forward from the backseat, bringing a faint hint of perfume.

"Two houses up?" she said.

The muscles of Van Sciver's right eye ached from all the focus. He nodded. "Backyard."

They slowed as they passed a white Colonial house that had recently undergone a Restoration Hardware facelift. A family of four ate at a long wooden farm table, displayed in the picture window like an ad for domesticity.

Thornhill threw the gear stick into park.

Three doors opened. Three Orphans

climbed out.

Van Sciver and Candy parted at the curb, each heading to a different side of the house. Thornhill leapt from trash can to fence top to a second-floor windowsill, vaulting onto the roof. Inside, the family dined on, oblivious.

The Orphans converged on the backyard at the same time, Van Sciver and Candy crowding in with drawn pistols as Thornhill dropped down from the decidedly un-Colonial veranda, landing panther-soft on the patio.

The backyard was empty.

A family of black ducks bobbed in the swimming pool.

Van Sciver stared at them, his jaw shifting.

Then he sighted with the holographic red dot and pulled the trigger. The suppressor pipped once, a pile of feathers settling over the water. The ducks winged off vocally into the night. Van Sciver held the unit in one meaty hand and watched the blinking beacon fly away.

Candy said, "I told you GPS was sloppy."

Van Sciver's phone chimed, an alert muscling in on the GPS screen. He thumbed it to the fore and read the brief report. The visuals were distressing — David Smith's face propagating out through the Information Age.

Candy's phone had gone off, too, and she drifted over, reading the same update on her screen.

Thornhill gave them their space.

"Let's head back to McClair," Van Sciver said. "Put the kid down."

"Sure," Candy said. "That's strategic. A kid whose picture just went viral, let's turn him into a media event."

"He's a loose end."

As Van Sciver started back through the side gate, Candy stayed at his elbow. "Does he know your name?" she said.

"No."

"Does he know anything about the Program?"

"No."

"Then let him rot in a kid's mental ward, spin his delusions in group therapy with the rest of them." She shook her phone. "Taking him out after this is gonna bring press. Why add fuel for the conspiracy theorists?"

Van Sciver halted in the cramped space at the side of the house. *"So X doesn't get what he wants."*

His eruption caught Candy by surprise. It seemed to have caught him by surprise, too.

He turned and continued on. As they neared the front yard, the door to the kitchen opened, the father leaning out in front of them, hands on hips. He was wearing a red-and-green Christmas sweater, seemingly without irony.

"Ex*cuse* me," the man said.

Van Sciver kept moving, eyes forward. But he lifted the .45 and aimed it at the man's nose. "Back inside. Call the cops and I'll come back and rape your wife."

Candy smiled. "Me, too."

The man jerked back as if yanked by puppet strings, the door closing with enough force to tangle the cutesy country curtains.

As Van Sciver and Candy stepped out into the driveway, he felt his nostrils flaring, and he tried to contain the rage in his chest. Thornhill dropped from the garage and sauntered up beside them.

Candy kept her focus on Van Sciver. "You're playing X's game. Don't let him trick you —"

He wheeled on her, grabbing her shirt with both hands. "*Don't* try to manipulate me."

Leaning over her, his face in hers, he was struck by just how much more powerful than her he was. If he slipped his hands up from the fabric, he could catch her chin in one palm, the back of her skull in the other, and twist her head halfway off.

Her expression remained impressively placid.

"I *am* trying to manipulate you," Candy said. "But I'm also right."

He observed the ledge of her chin, the thinness of her neck.

Then he released her and stormed for the Tahoe, his breath clouding in the night.

"I know," he said.

59
All Fucked Up

Evan kept one hand on the wheel of the stolen rig, a Toyota pickup with a leaf blower rattling around in the bed. Joey looked out the window at the passing night. Evan hoped that Van Sciver and what remained of his crew were still on their wild-duck chase, pursuing the partially digested digital transmitter Evan had smashed into the bread rind by the fountain.

He wasn't going to risk going out of any of the airports in neighboring states. Dulles International was too obvious, Charlotte and Nashville clear second choices. St. Louis, however, was just under twelve hours away and featured one-stop service to Ontario, California, an unlikely airport forty miles east of Los Angeles. Just before boarding time tomorrow morning at the airport, he'd purchase two tickets under their fake names for the first leg only. He'd buy the second set of tickets during the layover in

Phoenix.

Joey finally broke the two-hour silence. "What do we do now?"

"Go home. Regroup."

"How?"

"I haven't figured that part out yet."

The highway this time of night was virtually empty. Dark macadam rolled beneath them like a treadmill belt. The headlights were as weak and pale as an old man's eyes.

Joey said, "You think that kid has a shot?"

"Everyone does."

"He was so stubborn. Refusing to go with us, refusing our help. It's like he's locking himself in his own prison."

Evan thought of the gunmetal grays and hard surfaces of his penthouse, such a contrast with Mia's throw blankets and candles.

He said, "A lot of people do."

Joey muffled a noise in her throat.

Evan said, "What did you want?"

"I don't know." Anger laced her voice. "To help him. More."

"You can't help people more than they want to help themselves."

He looked at her. Her eyes were wet.

She turned back to the window, shook her head.

"Stupid fucking kid," she said.

■ ■ ■

He and Joey sat in their parallel twin beds,
Joey with her laptop across her knees, Evan
sipping vodka poured over cubes from the
motel ice maker. The front desk sold miniature bottles of Absolut Kurant, which Evan
didn't buy because he wasn't a fucking
savage. A twenty-four-hour liquor store five
blocks away had a bottle of Glass, a silky
vodka distilled from chardonnay and sauvi-
gnon blanc grapes. It had a tangy finish,
unvarnished by added sugars or acids, and
if he swirled it around his tongue enough,
he could catch a trace of honeysuckle.

It wasn't Stoli Elit, but at four in the
morning in a less-than-tony neighborhood
adjacent to St. Louis International, he'd
take what he could get.

He flipped through the red notebook he'd
recovered from the microwave in the Richmond house. The pages were blank.

Baffling.

Joey looked over at his glass. "Can I have
some?"

"No."

"Oh, I can help steal a shotgun from a
cop car, fly on a fake ID, kidnap a kid from

a safe house, but God forbid I drink alcohol."

Evan considered this a moment. He handed her his glass. The room was small enough that he barely had to lean to reach her.

She took a sip.

The taste hit, and she screwed up her face. "This is *awful.* You actually like this?"

"I tried to warn you."

She shoved the glass back at him.

"It always reminds me of my foster home," she said. "The smell of alcohol. And hair spray. Menthol cigarettes."

Evan set down his glass. He thought about how Jack used to leave silences for Evan to fill, room for him to figure out if he wanted to talk and what he would say if he did. He remembered Mia's advice: *At the end of the day, all they* really *want to hear? You're okay. You're gonna be fine. You're worth it.*

"She always smoked them," Joey said after a pause. "The 'foster mom.' " The words came with teeth in them. "We all called her Nemma. I don't know if that was her real name, but that's what everyone called her."

Evan cast his mind back to Papa Z sunk in his armchair, as snug as a hermit crab in a shell, one fist clamped around a Coors, the other commanding a remote with lightsaber efficiency as the boys swirled around him, fighting and shoving and laughing. Van Sciver always reigned supreme, the king of the jungle, while Evan slunk mouselike around the periphery, trying to get by unseen. It was a lifetime ago, and yet he felt as if he were standing in that living room now.

Joey kept her gaze on her laptop screen. "She was a beast of a woman. Housedresses. Caked-on blush. And her favorite phrase."

Evan said, "Which was?"

"This is gonna hurt you more than it hurts me." She laughed, but there was no music in it. "God, was she awful. Breath like an ashtray. Big floppy breasts. She had a lot of girls under her roof. She always had boyfriends rotating through. That's how she kept them."

She paused, wet her lips, worked the lower one between her teeth.

Evan remained very still.

"I don't remember much about them," she said. "Just the faces." The glow of the screen turned her eyes flat, reflective. "There were a lot of faces."

For a moment she looked lost in it, her shoulders raised in an instinctive hunch against the memories. Then she came out of it, snapped the laptop shut. "I don't want to talk about it."

Evan said, "Okay."

She wouldn't look over at him.

He got up with his glass and the bottle with its elegant clear stopper. He dumped his drink in the bathroom sink and poured out the rest, the vodka *glug-glugging* down the drain. He dropped the empty bottle in the trash can, came back to his bed, and returned to leafing through the red notebook.

He sensed her stare on the side of his face.

"That's why I'm all fucked up," she said.

"You're not any more fucked up than everyone else."

"I'm angry," she whispered. "All the time."

He risked a glance over at her, and she didn't look away.

"Those are the skills you learned to survive," he said. "They're what got you through."

She didn't reply. The thin sheets were bunched up beneath her knees, the folds like spread butter.

He said, "But you also have a choice."

She swallowed. "Which is?"

"To ask yourself, do they still serve you? You can keep them and be angry. Or let them go and have a real life."

"*You* can't," she said. "Let go and have a

real life."

"Not so far," he agreed.

"I feel like I'm stuck," she said. "I hate the Program, and I hate that I wasn't good enough for it. And then I wonder — is that the only reason I hate it? Because I wasn't good enough?"

"You were good enough to get out," he said. "You know how many people have done that and are alive?"

She shook her head.

"For all we know, we're the only two."

She blinked a few times.

"You did that," he said. "On your own."

"Yeah, well, you never know what kind of strength you have until you have to have it." She reached over, clicked off her light, and slid down onto her pillow.

"Good night," Evan said.

He turned his light off as well. The blackout curtains left the room as dark as a crypt. He heard her shifting, burrowing into the sheets. And then a silence so pure that it hummed.

"Good night," she said.

Evan's RoamZone vibrated in his pocket. He drew it out and stared at caller ID, which sourced to a mobile with an area code in downtown L.A. He stood and took a few steps away from the final passengers waiting to get on the connecting flight in Phoenix. The flight attendant had just announced the last boarding group, so Evan waved for Joey to go ahead. He'd catch up in a second.

He clicked to answer. "Do you need my help?"

Breath fuzzed the connection.

"Yes," Xavier Orellana said. "I want out. I want out of the gang."

Evan said, "I'm coming."

He hung up and got on the plane.

60
NOT GOOD

"Know any good your-mama jokes?" Peter peered up at Evan and Joey as the elevator doors clanked shut.

His charcoal eyes were dead earnest, as if he were asking for a physician referral.

Evan and Joey had pulled in to Castle Heights right behind Mia in her Acura, returning from picking up Peter at school. Peter had practically run circles around the two of them across the lobby and onto the elevator.

Standing beside his mom, Peter yanked the straps of his oversize backpack. It looked like it was loaded with bricks. How many textbooks could a nine-year-old possibly require?

Joey said, "What are you talking about?"

"Like: Your mama's so fat she jumped in the Red Sea and said, 'Take that, Moses.' "

Mia said, "Your public-education tax dollars at work."

Peter kept on, undeterred. "Your mama's so ugly she made a blind kid cry."

Mia said, "I like that one because it's offensive in two distinct ways."

"Your mama's so fat she can't even fit in the chat room."

Joey looked away to hide her grin.

They reached the twelfth floor, and Peter shot out, holding the elevator open with one skinny arm.

"See you for dinner tonight, right, Evan Smoak?"

Evan's face failed to conceal the fact that he'd forgotten.

Contacting Xavier upon touching down in Ontario, Evan had laid out a plan that required him to be in Pico-Union by ten o'clock. Dinner at seven put him clear by eight-thirty, which gave him time to get across town. As he ran this quick calculation, he felt the heat of Mia's gaze. The elevator door bumped impatiently against Peter's arm, retracting with an angry clank.

"Yes," Evan said.

Peter smiled and let the door go.

Evan pounded the heavy bag, the blows echoing off the floor-to-ceiling glass. He reached his count and stopped, drenched with sweat, breath heaving through him.

He'd just started back to the shower when he heard Joey call his name with urgency.

He jogged across the empty expanse and up the winding staircase to the loft.

She was sitting on the couch, the open laptop discarded on the cushion beside her. She peered at him over the red notebook he had pulled from the microwave in Richmond.

"Pilot FriXion pens," she said.

He waited.

"Know how erasable ink works?" she asked.

"You use the eraser."

"Funny," she said, sans smile. "The ink they use is made of different chemical compounds. When you use the eraser, you create friction, friction creates heat, heat makes one compound activate an acid compound, which neutralizes the dye."

"The microwave."

"Right. They figured out how to use heat to make the ink disappear without friction. You can wipe out all your mission notes with a quick zap in the microwave."

"But that would leave behind —"

"Impressions," she said. "Unfortunately, it looks like the notebook pages are treated to, like, replump with heat to prevent that."

"Is 'replump' a word?"

She ignored him. "Know how they feel a little stiffer, like higher stock?"

By way of display, she rubbed a page between thumb and forefinger.

"So everything's wiped out?" he said.

"Almost. One page in the middle didn't quite get there. Like, you know the cold spot in the center of a frozen burrito?"

"No."

"Never mind. C'mere." She fanned the pages at him, and he could see that she'd shaded every single one with a pencil all the way to the margins. They were uniform charcoal except for one of the innermost pages, on which a snippet of writing had been brought into negative relief.

"6-1414 Dark Road 32."

It reminded him of Jack's last message, the one he'd written invisibly on the driver's window of his truck.

"A partial address?" Evan asked.

"Would you believe there isn't a single address that includes '6-1414 Dark Road 32' in America?"

"How about not in America?"

"There isn't one in any English-speaking country. I checked translations, too. No, it's gotta be a code. Which got me thinking about what kinds of codes Van Sciver might be using with his men. Remember how Del-

monico and Shea's files had top-secret clas-
sification?"

" 'Had'? Past tense?"

"Check it out." She tapped her laptop
screen, and Evan was surprised and not
surprised to be looking at several documents emblazoned with the highest classified designation. "They were former marines, all right. That's why you got that read
on them. But after they left the Corps? They
became Secret Service agents."

Staring at the eagle-and-flag security
stamp, Evan felt a weightless rise in his gut,
the moment before a roller-coaster plummet. Van Sciver's taunt over the phone came
back to him once more: *You have no idea,
do you? How high it goes?*

Evan had once found himself hugging a
cliff edge in the Hindu Kush in the dead of
night, waiting for an enemy convoy to pass
on the narrow road above. One of his boots
had slipped from a thumb-size lip in the
sheer face, sending a cascade of stones
tumbling. He'd managed to cling to the wall
and, looking down, he'd watched the stones
vanish into darkness. It was a rare windless
night, the mountain air chilled into silence,
and yet he'd never heard them hit bottom.

He had the same sense now — holding on

for his life with no sense of the greater terrain.

"What does that mean?" Joey asked. "That they used to be Secret Service, too?"

"I don't know for certain," Evan said. "But it's not good."

61
Unacceptable

Charles Van Sciver stood on his Alabama porch as the remaining freelancers loaded out of the plantation house behind him, hauling Hardigg Storm Cases filled with gear and ammo. Their work on this coast was done. It was time to reposition the pawns on the chessboard and stake out key positions so they'd be fast-strike-ready the instant Orphan X reared his head.

Van Sciver had his phone out, the number cued up, but was reluctant to press the button.

He gathered his will.

And he pressed.

Jonathan Bennett had a number of remarkable skills as you would expect from a man of the Office. The most valuable one the public saw almost every day without even noticing.

Impeccable body control.

He'd once slogged through a Louisiana heat wave for a four-day swing — twenty-seven stops from stump speeches to union rallies in humidity so high it felt like wading through a swamp. He'd flipped the state as promised, and never once had he broken a sweat. Not beneath the hot light of the campaign trail, not during the nine debates, not in the situation room contemplating an aerial bombardment to unfuck the rugged north of Iraq.

That's what had killed Nixon. The sweating.

But Bennett was different.

He was the un-Nixon.

Before law school in his early days as a special agent for the Department of Defense, he'd learned to exert control over functions of his body he'd previously thought uncontrollable. This skill had served him well, then and now. He'd never been photographed with a sheen across his forehead or sweat stains darkening a dress shirt. He didn't stammer or make quick, darting movements with his eyes.

Most telling, his hands never shook.

The American people required that in this day and age. A leader with a steady hand. A leader who knew how to sell image, his and theirs. They never noticed the minutiae that projected this competence, at least not consciously, but they registered it somewhere deep in their lizard brains.

That's what you appealed to. What you targeted. What you ruled.

The lizard brains.

Instinct. Survival. Fear.

He studied his staff through the wireframe eyeglasses he'd selected to convey authority and a certain remoteness. Right now his people were at odds over a housing bill that was threatening to blow up in the Senate and, more importantly, on CNN. For the last five minutes, he'd listened with predatory repose, but now it was time to strike.

He cleared his throat pointedly.

The debate ceased.

Before he could render his judgment, one of three heavy black phones rang on his desk. When he noted which one, he rose from the couch, crossed the rug featuring his seal in monochromatic sculpting, and picked up the receiver with his notably steady hand.

He put his back to the room, a signal, and the murmured discussion resumed behind him.

"Is it done?" he asked.

Orphan Y replied, "No."

Bennett waited two seconds before replying. Two seconds was a long time in the life of a conversation, particularly when one half of that conversation was emanating from the Oval Office.

Bennett was out of earshot of the others, but he lowered his voice anyway. "This cannot get to NSA, CIA, or State. That's why I assigned you my own personally vetted men. It gets out of your hands, it could get out of mine. And that is unacceptable."

Van Sciver said, "I completely —"

Bennett took off his eyeglasses and set them on the blotter. "When I ran the DoD, we had a saying. 'It takes wet work to do a clean job.' I need this to be watertight. I cannot have him out there. He may not know why, but he's the only remaining connective tissue. Someone can connect the dots, and those dots lead through X. Without him they're just dots." Bennett allowed another two-second pause. "Clean out the connective tissue or I'll consider you part of it."

"Yes, Mr. President."

Bennett set the receiver down gently on the cradle that sat on the weighty Resolute desk. A quick internal inventory showed his pulse to be normal, his breathing as calm as ever.

He turned around to face his staff. "Now, where were we?"

62
NOT EASY

Still cool from the shower, Evan stood before his dresser in his boxer briefs. He opened the top drawer. Identical dark Levi's 501s on one side and on the other, tactical-discreet cargo pants. They were sharply folded, stacked so neatly they looked machine-cut. He pulled on a pair of cargo pants and snugged the Kydex high-guard holster on the waistband, relieved to be wearing a normal-size pistol again. Then he slid two backup magazines into the streamlined inner pockets. They gave no bulge.

The next drawer down housed ten unworn gray V-neck T-shirts. He put one on, tucked it behind his hip holster. In the closet he grabbed the top shoe box from a tiered tower in the corner. He changed out his Original S.W.A.T. boots regularly, ensuring that he couldn't be tracked by microfibers or soil residue trapped in the tread. Nine Woolrich shirts hung in parallel, magnetic buttons clamped. They were straight from the shipping package, though he'd cut off the price tags and ironed out the wrinkles before hanging them. As he donned the nearest shirt and snapped the buttons shut, he thought about what he was planning to do just a few hours from now.

He was going to walk into the den of the world's most dangerous gang.

Innumerable variables, a risk level too high to assess. That was why he needed every other facet to be locked down, predictable, second-nature. He knew each contour, thread, and operation spec of his gear. Every magazine had been painstakingly validated on a desert range, tested to ensure that it dropped from the well without the slightest hitch.

A passel of fresh Victorinox watch fobs waited in a hinged wooden box. He'd just clipped one to the first belt loop on the left side when it occurred to him that he'd dressed for the mission and not for the preceding dinner at Mia's. He was due downstairs in twenty-three minutes.

Showing up to a DA's condo with illegally concealed firearms didn't strike him as the most prudent idea.

He went back into the bedroom, took off the hip holster, and then removed the magazines from his hidden pockets. The Victorinox fob seemed vaguely militaristic, so he unclipped it and set it aside. The cargo pants and S.W.A.T. boots were low-profile enough, but a wary eye might find them aggressive. He kicked them off, stood there in his boxer briefs and Woolrich button-up.

Now he was questioning the shirt. Tactical magnetic buttons — Mia couldn't possibly notice those. Could she?

He took the shirt off. Then the one under that.

Down to boxer briefs.

This wasn't going well.

There was a knock on his door. Joey called through, "Wanna try that meditating stuff before you go?"

Evan said, "Yes, please."

Evan and Joey sat facing each other in the loft. After Operation Getting Dressed for Dinner, he figured he needed to meditate more than she did. He'd thrown his clothes back on hastily and headed up to meet her in the loft.

She assumed an erect yogi's posture. "Back in Richmond you told David Smith, 'You can't help people more than they want to help themselves.'"

Evan said, "Yes."

He could see that it was taking everything she had to get the words out.

"I want to help myself," she said. "I want to wind up better."

"Okay."

"Clearly I suck at meditation."

"That's not clear. It might be doing exactly what it should be doing."

"Walk me through how to do it again?"

Jack had taught Evan proper procedures for everything from fieldstripping a pistol to readying for meditation. He started to haul out the directives now when he caught himself and thought of the new Commandment he'd invented for himself — and for Joey.

Don't fall in love with Plan A.

She was waiting on him, puzzled by his delay.

"You know what?" he said. "Maybe we've been approaching this wrong."

"What do you mean?"

"Sit however's comfortable. However makes you feel safe."

She gave a nervous laugh. "I don't know."

"Then figure it out."

She looked around. Then she rolled her shoulders. Cracked her jaw. She crossed her legs and uncrossed them. "Can I go to my couch?"

"You can do anything you want."

She got up on the couch, hugged her pillow, pulled her knees in to her chest. She took a cushion and pressed it against her shins. She put another against her exposed side, building a burrow. "Is this weird?"

"There's no such thing as weird."

"Okay," she said. "Okay."

"Does that feel all right?"

She nodded, two quick jerks of her head.

"Just focus on your breath now, and let your body talk to you."

He closed his eyes. As the first minute passed, he acquainted himself with the silence. He barely had time to narrow his focus when she broke. The first shuddering breath and then the storm.

She stayed hugging her knees, curled into herself, sobbing. He waited for her to get up and stomp out like before. She didn't. She rocked herself and cried until the pillow was dark with tears, until her hair stuck to her face, until he thought she'd never stop.

He sat still, being with her without being with her. After a time it occurred to him that might not be enough.

He said, "May I sit by you?"

She shoved tears off her cheeks with the heels of her hands, gave a nod.

He took a seat on the couch at a respect-ful distance, but she nudged the cushion aside and leaned into him.

He was surprised, caught off guard, unsure of what was expected of him.

At first his arms floated above her stiffly. She was shuddering, hands curled beneath her chin. He thought about what Jack might do and then realized that Jack might never have found himself in a situation like this.

So instead Evan asked himself what *he* might do.

He lowered his arms to comfort her.

He wasn't sure if his touch would elicit anger or flight, but she stayed there, her face buried in his chest.

She felt like an anchor to him, not drag-ging him down but mooring him to this spot, to this moment, locking his location for once on the grid. For the first time in his life, he felt the tug as something not unpleasant but precious.

Her legs flexed, jogging her back and forth ever so slightly. He held her, rocking her, as she wept. He brushed her hair from his mouth. Cleared his throat.

"You're okay," he said.

"You're gonna be fine," he said.

"You're worth it," he said.

■ ■ ■ ■

Downstairs in his bedroom, he called Mia. When she answered, he took a deep breath.

"Hi, Mia. It's Evan. I know I was supposed to be there twenty minutes ago. But I can't come over for dinner with you and Peter. I'm sorry."

Joey had finally pried herself off the couch to wash her face, and Evan had told her he'd be right back up. He had to head to Pico-Union in an hour and change, and he wasn't willing to leave her alone until he had to. The imperative was as much for him as for her, the protective impulse spilling over into something more intimate, paternal.

It felt threatening and out of control, and he could afford neither at the moment. But he knew that if he left that sixteen-year-old girl alone after what she'd just gone through, he wouldn't forgive himself for it.

There was a brief, surprised silence. And then Mia said, "Okay. Can I ask why?"

He was torn between what he owed Mia and what he owed Joey. "Something personal came up."

"And you couldn't call to let us know? I mean, before?"

"I really couldn't. I'm sorry."

"Peter made place cards and set the table an hour ago. Wait — scratch that." Her breaths came across the receiver. "Sorry. I don't mean to guilt-trip you. And I don't mind that he learns to handle disappointment. That's part of life. But I guess I'm not sure how to handle stuff about you with him when *I* don't even have any answers. And that seems to come up more and more. No answers, I mean. Which I'm not sure is gonna work, Evan. I thought it might. But I don't think it will."

Something inside him crumbled away, brittle and dead. He thought about the dishes stacked on her counter, the smell of laundry, the instructive Post-its, and how they'd always seemed to be from some other life better than he deserved. Nine floors separated Evan from Mia and Peter, and yet they were out of reach. They always had been. But for a brief time, it had been lovely to pretend otherwise.

He said, "I understand."

"You understand." She made an unamused sound of amusement. "You know, I've never seen you upset. Never seen you get mad, flustered, lose it. At first I thought it was a kind of strength. But then I realized it's just a kind of . . . nothing."

Her words weren't just true. They were

profoundly true. They landed on him with the tonnage of decades.

"Look," she said. "Even if this is our last conversation, I don't want to do this. I don't want to play the role of the one who cares. And you get to play the role of the wanted asset. We can't figure it out, whatever 'it' is. That's fine. We're both adults with complicated lives. But I wish you at least had the spine to say that you cared, too."

It exploded out from the core of him, a blinding heat, escaping before he could trap it. "You think I'm *pretending,* Mia? That this is some game to me? You think I don't want to just cook linguine and chat over dinner and be with you? I don't have the same choices you do. I lost someone very close to me, and I need to set that right, whether I'm stuck with some kid I don't know what to do with, whether I have other jobs I have to see through, whether you want me to come to dinner. It's what I have to do."

His head hummed. His vision felt loose, as if he'd had a drink. He wondered if he'd actually said the words out loud. It seemed improbable that he had.

"Okay," Mia said. "That's a start. Thank you."

There was not a trace of sarcasm in her

voice. He was as stupefied by her reaction as he was by his outburst. He had no slot for any of this, no bearings to guide him into familiar shore.

Across the penthouse he heard the slam of his front door.

His pistol was already drawn, aimed at the open bedroom door, a familiar calm descending over him like a drape. He welcomed it.

"I have to go," he said, and cut the call.

He moved out into the hall, noted a crumpled piece of paper halfway to the great room. He eased past and emerged onto the concrete plain, swinging wide for the best vantage on the closed front door. The elaborate internal locks were unbolted.

Which meant it had been opened from inside.

He holstered the pistol, stuck his head out into the corridor. The elevator had already reached the lobby. He reversed and hustled across to the spiral staircase and up, confirming that, yes, the loft was empty. Joey's rucksack was still there, her treasured shoe box out on the sofa.

That was good. She'd have to come back for those.

With increasing chagrin he padded downstairs, walked to the end of the hall, and stared at the ball of paper ten yards from his open bedroom door. From this position his words to Mia would have been clear and crisp: *I'm stuck with some kid I don't know what to do with.*

He moved forward on numb legs. Crouching over the paper, he uncrumpled it. Fragile pieces of blue and yellow fell out — the remains of a pressed iris from Joey's maunt.

Joey had written a note of her own on the paper.

Thanks for being there for me. I know I'm not easy.

L, J.

63
DEVIL HORNS

The night breeze cut straight through Evan's shirt. Outside the abandoned church, Mara Salvatrucha members clustered loosely in front of the reinforced steel door, their shaved heads making them look sleek and feral. Here on the street, they kept their weapons hidden, but their shirts bulged in predictable places.

When they noted Evan's approach, their skulls pivoted in unison. It was hard to distinguish their eyes from the ink spotting their faces. They flicked their cigarettes aside, shoved off the pillars fronting the church entrance, and presented a unified front that called to mind an NFL defensive line.

As Evan drew within reach, they tugged up their shirts to expose gleaming handguns.

A man with devil-horn tattoos rolled his head back, regarded Evan down the length of his nose. "I think you in the wrong neighborhood."

Evan said, "I want to talk to Freeway."

The men laughed. "A lotta folks want to talk to Freeway."

Evan let the breeze blow.

"Do you have *any idea* who we are, *gringo culero?* We are Mara Salvatrucha. I translate it for you. *Mara* means 'gang.' *Trucha* means 'fear us.'"

Evan stepped forward. The men drew their pistols but did not aim them. "Your tattoos are designed to elicit fear. You're probably used to scaring people when you walk down the street, into a store, a restaurant. Because you've written right on your face how little you care about how you're perceived. And that signals that you're capable of anything. I'm sure you're used to that working. So look at me. Look at me very closely. And ask yourself: Do I look scared?"

For a moment there was nothing but the white-noise hum of traffic in the distance. Devil Horns sniffed, rolled his lower lip between his teeth.

Evan said again, "Tell Freeway I'm here to see him."

The men cast nervous looks between them. Then Devil Horns said, "You packing?"

517

"Yes. One pistol. And I'm not giving it up. Ask your leader if he's afraid to meet me inside his own headquarters with fifty armed men."

"Be careful what you wish for, *cabrón.*" He turned to his compatriots. "Watch this *hijo de puta.*"

The steel door creaked open and shut heavily behind him.

Evan waited, keeping a level stare on the remaining men. They returned it, shifting on their blue-and-white Nikes.

At last the door opened again, and Devil Horns emerged. He held the door ajar for Evan. When Evan walked inside, he caught a whiff of incense and body odor.

Dozens of men waited in the nave, holding pistols and submachine guns. They folded behind Evan, encircling him. Freeway sat on the broad carpeted steps beneath the altar like a demon god, his hands clasped.

Tables rimmed the room, covered with baggies and electronic scales. Most of the pallets of boxed TVs had been moved out, but plenty of shoplifted iPhones, Xboxes, and Armani jackets remained. The smaller goods spilled out of booster bags — duffels lined with aluminum foil to thwart stores' electronic security detectors.

From the corner of his eye, Evan noted Xavier in the shadowed phalanx, but he made sure not to look at him directly. Evan walked up the aisle between the shoved-aside pews and stopped ten yards shy of Freeway. The man did not rise. Now that Evan was closer, he could discern the features beneath the ink. A pit-bull face — broad cheeks, near-invisible eyebrows, a snub nose that smeared the nostrils into ovals. He had a round head, a bowling ball set on the ledge of his powerful torso. The *MS* tattoo banded his forehead, an honor and a distinction.

Freeway spread his hands, clasped them again. An unspoken question. Ambient light glimmered off the steel studs embedded in his cheeks and lips.

"I have business with one of your men," Evan said. "I want to buy him out."

Freeway's eyes flickered in a blink. It was hard to tell, the tattooed lids blending with the tattooed sclera. "Which man?"

"That's between me and him. Once you agree."

"And if I lie to find out?"

Evan said, "I trust you're a man of your word."

Looking into those black eyes was like looking into death itself.

"Nobody takes what's mine," Freeway said. "I own these men. As much as I own the *putas* I run in the streets. Drugs and guns are good, *sí*. But with those? Everything is a onetime sale. A woman? I can sell ten, fifteen times a day. A man I can use a hundred different ways in the same week." He rose, and the stairs creaked beneath his weight. "There will be no sale. My men are my most valuable possessions."

"I understand. That's why I'm offering to pay you for him."

"If you move on one of my men," Freeway said, "I will kill him, his entire family, and you."

A wet breeze blew through the shattered stained-glass window above. Evan glanced through it at the rooftop where he'd perched just two nights before. He realized he was tired. Tired of the miles he'd put on the tread and tired for the road ahead.

"I don't want a war with you," Evan said. "But I'm not afraid of one."

Freeway showed his teeth. "You. A war. With us."

"I'll give you twenty-four hours to decide. I'll come back. I'll ask again. And either you'll let him leave. Or you will all die."

Some of the men laughed, but Freeway just stared at Evan.

"What are you planning to do?" he asked.

"I'll figure something out."

A rumbling stirred in the ranks.

"Kill this bitch now, Freeway!" a man called from behind Evan.

Freeway reached to the small of his back, came out with a straight razor. "What stops me from gutting you right here?"

"Nothing," Evan said. "But I assume you don't take orders from your underlings."

Freeway pulled the razor open a few inches, let it snick shut. "Why don't we handle this now?"

"It's inconvenient for me," Evan said.

"Inconvenient."

"Yes. I have other business to handle."

"You are an interesting man."

"Twenty-four hours. I'll come back. You give me your decision then." Evan stepped forward, and he heard movement behind him, guns clearing leather, slides being jacked.

Freeway held up a hand, and the gang members silenced.

Evan said, "Assuming you're not afraid to face me again."

The black orbs, sunk in Freeway's face, fixed on Evan.

"I like this game," Freeway said. "Twenty-four hours. I will look forward to this."

When Evan turned, he sensed Xavier somewhere in the back of the crowd. As Evan walked out, the men spread to let him through and then filled the space behind him, moving like a single living organism.

64
STEADY AS A METRONOME

Joey had left the Uber car back at the vintage merry-go-round and asked directions to the old zoo from a group of high-school kids decked out in varsity jackets. She felt like she was inside a CW show. Everything outside was beautiful and night-lit. But inside she was a jumble of raw emotion.

Connor, the skateboarder she and Evan had bumped into outside the safe house, had said that he hung here most nights with friends. She wasn't sure why she'd thought to come here. She just wanted to be out.

To feel like she was normal.

She made her way up the hill, leaving the lights of Griffith Park behind. The farther she got upslope, the sketchier the surroundings. Homeless men rustled in bushes, and tweakers swapped crumpled bills for tinfoil squares. At last she reached the brink of the abandoned zoo.

An empty bear exhibit shoved up from the ground, a rise of Disneyesque stone slabs covered with spray-painted gang tags and fronted by a handful of splintering picnic benches. It looked haunted. She wound her way into the heart of the place, passing rows of cages, the bars vined with ivy. Stone steps led to fenced-off dead ends. A grounds-keeper's shack had been turned into a squat house, laughter echoing off the walls, a campfire stretching dancing figures up the walls. She peeked inside but saw only drug-gies. She kept on, peering through the dark-ness. Syringes and used condoms littered the narrow path between the cages.

And then she heard the drawl of his voice.

He was inside one of the cages with his friend, the one who'd fallen off the long-board. A few skinny girls around their age were in there, too, their eyes glazed.

Connor looked up through the bars and saw Joey. "Hey."

Her smile felt forced. "Hey."

"Hold this, Scotty." Connor handed off the water bong to his friend and pointed to the back of the enclosure. "Go around. There's a hatch back here."

She circled in the darkness and ducked to squeeze through the narrow opening. As she entered the enclosure, Connor and Scotty held out their fists, and she bumped them.

"This is Alicia," Connor said. "Tammy and Priya."

Joey held up her fist, but the first girl just stared at it. Her lipstick was smeared. "Who's the little girl?" she drawled.

Her friends didn't laugh, but they shook their shoulders as if they were, the effect creepy and detached.

"Forget Alicia," Connor said. "She's fucking wasted." He gestured at Scotty. "Give her the bong. She needs a hit."

"I'm good," Joey said.

Connor smiled, his man bun nodding at the back of his head. Though he was clearly several years older than her, his handsome face was still padded with baby fat. His cheeks looked smooth and white, like he barely needed to shave. The smell of bud and Axe body spray wafted off his untucked shirt. "Okay. Give her a beer."

Scotty passed Joey a beer, and she cracked it and took a sip. It tasted skunky, but she didn't make a face.

"S'good," she said.

"Then tell your face," Alicia said.

Joey wondered what was wrong with her expression. She was too aware of it now, wearing it like a mask. The bottle suddenly felt large and silly in her hand, a prop. The girls seemed so much older, their frail frames and drugged high lending them an otherworldly aura, as if their feet were floating an inch above the dirt. Joey felt clumsy and common by comparison, a flightless bird.

Scotty enabled the light on his iPhone and rested it on a concrete ledge by a pile of rusted beer cans. Graffiti covered the walls and ceiling, the bubble letters and vulgar sketches made menacing in the severe light.

"Alicia," Connor said, "that was the last beer. Wanna grab the other sixer from the cooler?"

Alicia's lips peeled back in a smile. She ran her hand up her throat as if feeling her skin for the first time. "Sure, Connor."

She held up a pale fist to Joey. "I was just kidding earlier," she said. "C'mon, gimme knucks."

Joey lifted her hand, but Alicia lowered her fist and turned away, the other girls snickering in a matching low key. Alicia slid an anorexic shoulder along the wall to the hatch, the other girls trailing her, so pale and insubstantial they looked like shades. They slipped through the cramped space without slowing.

As soon as they vanished, Scotty stepped over, blocking the way out. Joey sensed

Connor sidle up behind her.

Blocking her in.

All of a sudden, Joey felt her awkwardness lift. She was aware of the scuff of Connor's shoe in the dirt, the distance to the concrete walls around her, the latent power of her muscles. Her heartbeat ticked in the side of her neck, as steady as a metronome.

This part wasn't scary or intimidating, not like drinking beer or bumping fists or figuring out how to smile the right way.

This part felt like home.

As she started to turn, Connor grabbed her belt in the front and pulled her close. She let him. He was big enough to bow her lower back, her face uptilted to his. His breath smelled like tea leaves.

His hand curled over her belt, knuckles pressed into her lower stomach.

"You know why you came," he said.

Joey said, "Let go of me."

He kissed her.

She kept her mouth closed, felt his stubble grate her lips. Behind her she heard Scotty laugh. Connor pulled his face back but kept the front of her jeans clamped in his fist.

She said, "Let go of me."

Connor loomed over her. "I don't think I want to just yet."

She stepped away, but he tugged her

527

buckle, snapping her back against his chest.

"Oh," she said sympathetically. "You think you're in charge."

Calmly, she chambered her leg high and pistoned her heel through his ankle.

The snap sounded like a heavy branch giving way.

Connor stared down at his caved shin in disbelief. His foot nodded to the side, ninety degrees offset from the ankle.

Joey said, "Three . . . two . . ."

He screamed.

Scotty yelled, "Crazy bitch!" and charged her, lowering his shoulder for a football tackle. Sidestepping, she took his momentum and redirected him into the wall. His face smacked the concrete. It left a wet splotch. He toppled over, his legs cycling against the pain, heels shoving grooves in the dirt.

Joey placed her hand on Connor's barrel chest and shoved. He fell hard, landing next to Scotty. He was still making noises.

She squeezed through the narrow hatch, emerging from the cage. As she stepped out, she sensed the world opening up all around her. Starting back down the hill to civilization, she felt a part of her flutter free from the trap inside her chest and take flight against the canopy of stars.

65
NOT AN INNOCENT

Joey stepped through the unlocked door of 21A and stared at the cavernous great room. All the lights were off, but the city shone through the giant windows, making the contours of the penthouse glimmer darkly.

A silhouette rose from one of the bar chairs at the kitchen island.

Evan.

He said, "I made up your bed."

Joey stepped inside and shut the door behind her. "Thanks."

"I'm not very good at it," he said.

"What?"

He gestured from her to him. "This."

"You're better than you think."

"I didn't mean what I said on the phone. What you overheard."

"I know."

She came forward, and they stared at each other.

"I went to see that guy with the stupid

hair," she said. "From outside the safe house?"

Evan nodded.

"He's a useless reprobate," she said. "You were right."

Evan said, "I don't want to be right."

She leaned into him stiffly, her forehead thunking against his chest, her arms at her sides. He hesitated a moment and then hugged her, one hand holding the back of her head, her thick, thick hair.

He said, "Rough night all around, huh?"

"Yeah." Her voice rose an octave and cracked. "I think I'm done pretending."

"Pretending what?"

"Acting like I didn't need anything from anyone. I started after my maunt died, because . . . you know, I wasn't gonna get it anyways." She straightened up. "But I was lying. Now and then I still think about what mighta been. Someone to tuck me in, maybe. You know, 'How was your day?' Cute boy in homeroom. A soccer team. All that normal shit. Instead. Instead." Her lips wobbled. "Do you think I ever could?"

"Yes."

"It's not too late?"

"No. Once we get Van Sciver, we'll find what comes next for you. It doesn't have to be this."

She blinked, and a tear glided down her flawless brown cheek. "How 'bout you?"

"It's not an option anymore for me. It's different."

She looked up at him. "Is it?"

He nodded.

"Even after you get Van Sciver?"

"There will always be Van Scivers."

"But what about Mia? And the kid?"

"There will always be Van Scivers," he said again.

She pursed her lips and studied him in the semidarkness. "I remember I was fourteen, bleeding from my ear. Van Sciver put me with a demolition breacher who let me get too close to a door charge. I thought it was a punctured eardrum. He took me back to town and dropped me at a park, you know, for pickup. Anyways, I was worse than anyone thought. I was stumbling along off the trail. And I came up behind a guy on a bench, rocking himself and murmuring. At first I thought he was injured, too. Or crazy. But then I saw he had a baby. His baby. And he was holding it so gently. I snuck up behind him in the bushes. And he was saying . . . he was saying, 'You are safe. You are loved.' " Her eyes glimmered. "Can you imagine?"

Walking behind Jack in the woods, placing

his feet in Jack's footprints.

"Yes," Evan said.

"Maybe that's all anyone needs," Joey said. "One person who feels that way about you. To keep you human."

"It's a gift," Evan said. "It's also a weakness."

"Why?"

"Because it's a vulnerability they can exploit. Jack protecting me. Me protecting you. Us protecting David Smith. But we're gonna stop all that now. Instead of letting them use it against us, we're gonna start using it against them. The Ninth Commandment."

" 'Always play offense,' " she said. "But how?"

"We have what they want."

She stared at him, puzzled.

He said, "Us."

Her eyes gleamed. "Use me as bait."

Evan nodded. "And we know where to drop the line."

They left at five in the morning, switched out Evan's truck for a black Nissan Altima he kept at a safe house beneath an LAX flight path. Seven hours and four minutes later, they reached Phoenix. They did a few hours of recon and planning before pulling over in the shade of a coral gum tree. The car windows were cracked open, and the arid breeze tasted of dust.

The downtown skyline, such as it was, rose a few blocks away. They were on the fringe of suburbia here, two blocks north of the 10 Freeway, a handful more to the 17. A tall-wall ad on the side of a circular parking structure proclaimed ARIZONA'S URBAN HEART and featured a cubist rendering of a heart composed of high-rises.

Evan and Joey had worked out a dozen contingencies and then a dozen more, charting escape routes, meet points, emergency scenarios. Because they'd driven from Los Angeles and didn't have to concern themselves with airport security, he'd brought a trunkful of gear and weaponry, a mission-essential loadout that left him prepared for virtually anything. But at the end of the day, when you went fishing, you never knew precisely what you'd get on the line.

As if reading his thoughts, Joey said, "Okay. So if they go to grab me. What do you do?"

"Grab them."

She shifted the bouquet of irises in her lap. "And then what?"

"Make them talk."

"How?"

Evan just looked at her.

"Right," she said. "And if we're not so lucky as to have *that* work out?"

"Don't fall in love with Plan A."

The sunlight shifted, and at the peak of the hill above, the arched sign over the wrought-iron gate came visible.

SHADY VALE CEMETERY.

This was where Jack had found Joey, visiting her maunt's grave. As she'd said, he knew how her heart worked.

Van Sciver knew, too, though not from the inside out. He understood people from a scientific remove, learning where the soft spots were, which buttons to push, where to tap to elicit a reflex.

He had kept Joey for eleven months, had trained, analyzed, and assessed her. Evan was counting on the fact that Van Sciver was strategically sharp enough to surveil a location that held this kind of emotional importance to her. Whether that surveillance took the form of hidden cameras or freelancers on site, he wasn't sure.

For Van Sciver vulnerability was little more than a precipitating factor in a chain reaction. Joey's maunt would lead to Joey. Joey would lead to Evan.

Evan thought about the GPS unit Van Sciver had planted in David Smith's arm and wondered how they'd plan to tag Joey if they caught her here.

He recalled the Secret Service background of at least two of the freelancers Van Sciver had hired. Van Sciver had never drawn operators from the Service before, and it was unlikely a random choice for him to do so now. Evan's train of thought carried him into unpleasant terrain, where the possibilities congealed into something dark and toxic.

Joey screwed in her earpiece and started to get out of the black car. Evan put his hand on her forearm to halt her. A memory flash hit him — the image of himself at nineteen years old climbing out of Jack's truck at Dulles International, ready to board a plane for his first mission. Jack had grabbed Evan's arm the same way.

It was the first time Evan had ever seen him worried.

Evan reminded himself that he wasn't worried now. Then he reminded himself again. Joey was looking at him in a way that indicated that his face wasn't buying what he was telling himself.

"What?" she said.

"The Tenth Commandment," Evan said. " 'Never let an innocent die.' " He paused. "This is a risk."

"I'm not an innocent," Joey said.

He nodded. For this mission she wasn't.

"Plus, they need me to get to you," Joey added. "Like you said, they want to snatch me, direct the action."

"That's our play, but it's still a guess. With former Secret Service in the mix, we don't know how far this reaches. But we know what they're willing to do."

"I'm fast," she said. "I'll stay in public, keep my head on a swivel."

"If we do this . . ."

"What, Evan?"

"Don't fuck up."

"What does *that* mean?"

"After what happened to Jack, nothing will stop me from getting to Van Sciver. Nothing. And no one." His throat was dry, whether from the dry desert air or the air-conditioning, he didn't know. "Don't put me in a position to make that choice."

She read his meaning, gave a solemn nod, and climbed out of the car.

66
FRICTION HEAT

Lyle Green handed off the binoculars to his partner, Enzo Pellegrini, who raised them to his face and blew out a breath that reeked of stale coffee. They were sitting in a parked truck, focused on a particular headstone on a rolling swell of grass. It was a shade of green you only got from well-fertilized soil, which meant corpses or gardeners, and Shady Vale had an excess of both.

Enzo said, "Eyes up, south entrance."

Lyle said, "Right, like your 'eyes up' on the pregnant broad or the guy with the prosthetic leg."

"It was a limp."

"Because that's what you do when you have a prosthetic leg."

"Girl, midteens."

Lyle pulled the detached rifle scope from the console and lifted it to his face. The girl cut behind a stand of bushes and stepped into view. "Holy shit. That's her."

"Raise Van Sciver. Now."

Lyle grabbed his Samsung, dialed through Signal.

A moment later Van Sciver's voice came through. "Code."

Lyle checked the screen. " 'Merrily dogwood.' "

"Go."

"It's her. It's the girl."

She drifted close enough that Lyle no longer required the scope. She set a bunch of flowers before the grave and paused, her face downturned, murmuring something to the earth.

"Do not approach," Van Sciver said. "Repeat: Do not approach. Track her at a distance in case X is watching. Pick your moment and get her tagged. Let her lead us to him."

Enzo dropped open the glove box. Inside were a variety of GPS tracking devices — microdots, magnetic transmitters for vehicle wheel wells, a vial of digestible silicon micro-chips.

The girl headed off, and Lyle tapped the gas and drifted around the cemetery's perimeter, keeping her in sight. "Copy that."

Twenty minutes later Lyle sat in a crowded taqueria, sipping over-cinnamoned horchata and peering across the plaza to where the target sat at a café patio table. Lyle had a Nikon secured around his neck with camera straps sporting the Arizona State University logo. Smudges of zinc-intensive sunscreen and a proud-alumnus polo shirt completed the in-town-for-a-game look.

He pretended to fuss with the camera, zeroing in with the zoom lens on the girl. Scanning across the patio, he picked up on Pellegrini inside the café, leaning against the bar and swirling a straw in his Arnold Palmer. A few orders slid across the counter, awaiting pickup. Pellegrini removed a vial of microchips, dumped them in a water glass, and used his straw to stir them in.

He'd just resumed his loose-limbed slump against the bar when the waitress swung past and grabbed the tray. As she carried the salad and spiked water glass over to Joey's table and set them down, Pellegrini exited the café from the opposite side and walked to the bordering street where they'd parked the truck.

Lyle kept the Nikon pinned on the water glass resting near Joey's elbow. From this distance the liquid looked perfectly clear, the tiny black microchips invisible. Once ingested, they would mass in the stomach, where they'd be stimulated by digestive juices and emit a GPS signal every time the host ate or drank. The technology had recently been improved, no longer requiring a skin patch to transmit the signal, which made for easier stealth deployment. But with this upgrade came a trade-off; the signal's duration was shorter, remaining active for only ten minutes after mealtime. The microchips broke down and passed from the system in just forty-eight hours.

Van Sciver was banking on the fact that at some point within two days she'd be in proximity to Orphan X.

The girl poked at her salad, then rested her hand on the water glass. Lyle willed her to pick it up and drink, but something on her phone had captured her attention. She removed her hand, and he grimaced.

He had to put the camera down to avoid suspicion, so he took another chug of sugary horchata while he watched her thumb at her phone and not drink water.

His Samsung vibrated, and he answered.

"Code," Van Sciver said.

Lyle checked the screen. " 'Teakettle lovingly.' "

"Update."

"The table's set. We're just waiting on her to do her part."

"Mechanism?"

"Water glass."

"I'll hold on the line," Van Sciver said.

Lyle swallowed to moisten his throat. "Okay."

The silence was uncomfortable.

Enough time had passed that Lyle could fiddle with his Nikon again without drawing attention. He lifted it up, watched Joey chewing and gazing absentmindedly into the middle distance. The sun was directly overhead, warming the patio. They were in fucking Arizona. Why wouldn't she just take a sip of water?

At last she wiped her mouth. She reached for the glass. She lifted it from the table.

A figure loomed behind her, blurry in the zoom-lens close-up. A hand lifted the water glass out of the girl's hand.

Lyle adjusted the focus, found himself staring at Orphan X.

How the hell did X know the water had been spiked?

Abruptly, Lyle was perspiring. The ASU polo stuck to the small of his back. X was saying something to the girl.

Lyle's breathing must have changed, because Van Sciver said, "What? What is it?"

Lyle started at the voice; he had forgotten about the phone pressed to his cheek. His mind whirled, assessing the best phrasing of the update. He opened his mouth, but dread prevented any words from exiting.

The girl rose to leave.

Orphan X paused by her chair, water glass still in hand.

Then he drank it down.

As X followed the girl out of the plaza, Lyle felt his mouth drop open a bit wider. A chime announced the GPS beacon going live on his Samsung.

Van Sciver said, "What happened?"

It took Lyle two tries to get the words out. "We just hit the jackpot."

Samsung in hand, Lyle ran across the plaza to where Pellegrini waited in the idling truck. Lyle jumped in, eyeing the GPS grid, gesturing madly for Pellegrini to turn right.

"There, there, there! We only have seven minutes left."

Pellegrini looked confused by Lyle's urgency. "We got the girl?"

Lyle said, "We got Orphan X."

Pellegrini's expression went flat with shock. The tires chirped as he pulled out. Lyle directed him around the block, following the blinking dot on his screen.

"Do we do this ourselves?" Pellegrini said. "Or wait for backup?"

Lyle held up the screen. As former Secret

Service, they had a clear operational sweet spot, and that encompassed surveillance, prevention, and protection. When they had to be, they were proficient assaulters as well, but that wasn't where the critical mass of their training had been spent. That had been made all too apparent by the death count of their fellow recruitees.

"We have Orphan X tagged," Lyle said. "We can get the drop on him if we move right now."

Pellegrini nosed the truck around the corner, and they saw it up ahead, a black Nissan Altima with a spoiler, Orphan X in view behind the wheel, the girl in the passenger seat. Lyle texted the vehicle description and license plate to Van Sciver.

Van Sciver had access to satellites, and once they locked the car in from above, there was nowhere on God's green earth it could go that it wouldn't be found.

Van Sciver's text confirmed: BIRDS ONLINE NOW.

ARE YOU EN ROUTE?

ALMOST AT THE AIRPORT.

The Nissan wheeled around the corner. As it turned, Orphan X's face rotated slightly toward them.

"Shit," Pellegrini said. "Did he see us?"

"I don't know," Lyle said. "I don't think so."

"Tell Van Sciver."

Lyle texted: MIGHT HAVE BEEN MADE. UNSURE.

Van Sciver's reply: PROCEED. BE CAUTIOUS.

The Nissan kept driving, neither quicker nor slower. They stayed on its tail.

"Holy shit," Lyle said. "We're gonna be the ones. We're gonna be the ones."

"Calm down," Pellegrini said.

Up ahead the Nissan pulled into a six-story parking structure.

Lyle texted Van Sciver: ENTERED PARKING GARAGE.

The reply: BIRDS ARE UP. WE'LL PICK HIM UP WHEN HE EXITS. FLUSH HIM OUT BUT DO NOT PURSUE.

Lyle brought up the GPS screen, watched the dot rise and rise. "He's heading to an upper floor."

Pellegrini turned into the parking structure. As he slowed to snatch a ticket from the dispenser, Lyle pointed ahead. The black car, now empty, was parked next to the handicapped spots by the elevators.

The truck pulled through, and Lyle hopped out and circled the car, confirming it was empty. As he ran back to the truck, he was already keying in his next text to Van Sciver: CAR EMPTY, PARKED BY ELEVATORS ON GROUND FLOOR.

The last reception bar flickered, but the text sent just before the Samsung lost service. Lyle climbed into the truck. "Go, go, go. He went upstairs."

Pellegrini said, "Why?"

"If he's switching cars on another level, we have to get there to ID the new vehicle for the satellites. We've only got a few minutes before we lose GPS."

A circular ramp looped around a hollow core at the center of the parking structure. Pellegrini accelerated into the turn, centrifugal force shoving Lyle against the door as they rode up the spiral to the second level.

He watched the dot. It was way above them on six.

Pellegrini made a noise, and Lyle glanced up from the screen.

A black rope was now dangling down the center column of the parking structure.

Lyle's brain couldn't process the rope's sudden appearance. He looked back at the screen. The dot was no longer way above them. It was on the fifth level. Now the fourth.

Pellegrini was slowing the truck, reaching for his handgun.

Lyle looked back at the thick nylon cord dangling ten feet away from them.

A *rappelling* rope.

As they curved around onto the third floor, Orphan X zippered down the rope, a pistol steady in his gloved hand.

The driver's window blew out as he shot Pellegrini through the temple.

Even after the spatter hit Lyle, he hadn't caught up to what was happening. Orphan X rappelled down as the unmanned truck banged up the ramp to the third level, their fall and rise coordinated like the two sides of a pulley.

There was a suspended moment as the two men drew eye level, Lyle catching a perfect view of X's face over the top of the aligned sights.

He saw the muzzle flare and nothing else.

Evan hit the ground floor, coming off the fast rope and crouching to break his fall. He threw his gloves off with a flick of his wrists and they dangled from clips connecting them to his sleeves, the full-grain leather steaming with friction heat.

Seventeen men down.

Eight left.

Joey stepped out from the stairwell and ran across to meet Evan at the Nissan Altima. As he tore off the detachable spoiler and ran it over to a Dumpster, she stripped carbon-fiber wrap from the Altima, revealing the car's original white coat. Evan unscrewed the Arizona license plates, exposing the California plates beneath.

A few puzzled pedestrians gawked up the ramp at the rappelling rope. Near the third level by the smashed truck, horns blared. There was enough confusion that Evan and Joey went largely unnoticed. They stuffed the Arizona plates and fiber wrap in the trash container near the elevator, climbed into the now-white Nissan, and pulled out into the flow of traffic.

67
THE PRETTY ONE

As Orphan X, Evan had left behind a spaghetti snarl of associations, connections, and misery. Every high-value target he neutralized anywhere on the globe was a stress point in a vast web. The Secret Service's involvement meant that somewhere in his dark past a silken thread trembled, leading back to the heart of the District.

As he neared the freeway exit, Joey said, "Hang on."

Pulled from his thoughts, he glanced over the console at her. "We've gotta get back to L.A."

"There's something I want to do first."

The set of her face made him nod.

He followed her directions, winding into an increasingly shabby part of east Phoenix. Joey studied the passing scenery with an expression that Evan knew all too well.

"They call this area the Rock Block," she

said. "Can't walk down the sidewalk without tripping over a baggie of crack."

Evan kept on until she gestured ahead. "Up here," she said.

He got out and stood by the driver's door, unsure in which direction she wanted to go. She came around the car and brushed against him, crossing the street. He followed.

Behind a junkyard of a front lawn sat a house that used to be yellow. Most of the cheap vinyl cladding had peeled up, curling at the edges like dried paint. An obese woman filled a reinforced swing on one corner of the front porch.

Joey stepped through a hinge-challenged knee-high front gate, and Evan kept pace with her through the yard. They passed an armless doll, a rusting baby stroller, a sodden mattress. Joey stepped up onto the porch, the old planks complaining.

Despite the cool breeze, sweat beaded the woman's skin. She wore a Navajo-print dress. Beneath the hem Evan could see that half of one foot had been amputated, the nub swaying above the porch. The other leg looked swollen, marbled with broken blood vessels. Evan could smell the sweet, turbid smell of infection. A tube snaked up from an oxygen tank to the woman's nose. The swing creaked and creaked.

The woman didn't bother to look at them, though they were standing right before her.

Joey said, " 'Member me, Nemma?"

Fanning herself with a *TV Guide,* the woman moved her gaze lazily over to take Joey in.

"Maybe I do," the woman said. "You were the pretty one. Little bit dykey."

Joey said, "I wonder why."

Air rattled through the woman's throat, an elongated process that sounded thick and wet. "There's nuthin' you can do to me the diabetes ain't done already. And that's just the start. They cut out the upper left lobe of my lung. Five, six times a day, I get the coughs where I can't even clear my own throat. I have to double over, give myself the Heimlich just so's to breathe. Bastards took away my foster-care license and every-thing."

Joey eased apart from Evan, putting a decaying wicker coffee table between them. She said, "You want me to feel sorry for you?"

The woman made a sound like a laugh. "I don't want anything anymore."

Evan noticed that his hip holster felt light. Joey stood with her body bladed to him so he couldn't see her left side. The woman's gaze had fixed on something in Joey's hand. Evan recalled how Joey had brushed against him by the Altima after he'd parked. He didn't have to move his hand to the holster to know it was empty.

Joey had positioned herself nicely. The angle over the coffee table was tricky. He wouldn't get to her in time, not given her reflexes and training.

The woman gave a resigned nod. "You came to hurt me?"

Evan sidled back a step, but Joey eased forward, keeping the mass of the table between them. Her eyes never left the woman's face.

He stopped, and Joey stopped, too. He still couldn't see her hand, but her shoulder was tense, her muscles ready.

The only sound was the sonorous rasp of the woman's breathing.

Joey exhaled slowly, the tension leaking from her body. "Nah," she said. "I'd rather let life take you apart piece by piece. Like you did to all us girls. The difference is, I can put myself back together."

The woman didn't move. Evan didn't either.

Joey stepped forward and leaned over her. "You don't get to live in me anymore. You get to live in yourself."

She turned and walked off the porch. As she passed Evan, she handed his pistol back to him.

They left the woman swaying on the porch.

68
LOCKED-ROOM MYSTERY

Candy stepped up to the police cordon at the Phoenix parking structure. The cops had loosened up the crime scene by degrees, CSI coming and going.

An officer stopped her. "Are you parked inside, ma'am?"

"Yeah, I work at the PT office across the plaza, and — Oh my God, what happened?"

"We can't disclose that, ma'am. Please claim your vehicle and exit immediately."

She nodded nervously and stepped inside, scanning the cars on the ground level. Van Sciver had kept satellite monitoring on the garage all day, and there'd been no sign of a black Nissan Altima exiting.

The ramp was still blocked off, cops dispersed through the parking structure. Candy strode toward the elevators, taking in the remaining cars. No black Altima.

The car hadn't left the building. And it wasn't in the parking spot where Lyle

Green's last text indicated.

Which made for the kind of locked-room mystery she wasn't in the mood for.

Her gaze pulled to the trash can beside the handicapped spaces. It was stuffed with what looked like black tarp. She drew closer.

She said, "Fuck."

She twisted the lid off the concrete trash container and looked down at the heap of stripped-off carbon-fiber wrap. Digging through the detritus, she pulled out the pieces, checking each one for distinguishing marks. Midway through the stack, she found a tiny copyright logo at the edge of a band of stiff carbon fiber: ©FULL AUTO WRAPAT-TACK.

She took a picture with her cell phone and texted the image to Van Sciver. As she shoved the material back into the trash, she noted the ditched license plates in the bottom of the container.

She exited the structure through a side door, slipped past a break in the cordon, walked across the plaza, and got into the backseat of one of two Chevy Tahoes waiting at metered spots. They were heavily armored, just like the one in Richmond.

Van Sciver and Thornhill occupied the seats in front of her.

Thornhill held up his phone with a location pin-dropped on Google Maps. "Full Auto WrapAttack," he said, "At 1019B South Figueroa. Los Angeles. One shop, they custom-make their own materials on site. What do you think?"

Van Sciver weighed this a moment. "It's not a sure thing," he said. "But it's the best bet. Let's move headquarters."

Thornhill said, "Good thing we're mobile."

Candy turned to look into the Tahoe parked one spot behind them. Through the tinted rear window, she could barely make out the outlines of the eight freelancers crammed into the bench seats. "Which one's the pilot?" she asked.

"Guy in the passenger seat," Van Sciver said. "I have a Black Hawk on standby. We'll set up downtown, striking distance to most points in the city. The minute X eats or drinks something, we'll have ten minutes to scramble to his location and put him and the girl down."

"You think the girl's worth killing?" Candy said.

"Why take the chance?" Thornhill said.

Candy said, "You pay him extra to answer for you?"

Van Sciver met Candy's stare in the rearview.

She knew she had overstepped her bounds, and she had no idea what might happen next.

Van Sciver said, "Step out of the car, Thornhill."

Thornhill obeyed.

Candy could feel the pulse beating in the side of her neck. "Let's skip the part where you beat your chest and I back down," she said. "Consider me backed down. Why don't we think about this. And by 'we' I mean you and I — the ones with brains. Thornhill's a blank space. A good body and a nice set of teeth. There's nothing there."

She pictured Van Sciver wheeling around in the driver's seat, his hand clamping her larynx, squeezing the air passage shut. But no, he remained where he was, a large immovable force, his eyes drilling her in the mirror.

"He's an extension of me," Van Sciver said. "He's a scope."

"And scopes have their use," she said. "But we're talking strategy. It's a surgical operation. We want clean margins. What is unnecessary brings with it unnecessary complications. We X out Evan, we leave no trace. We kill a sixteen-year-old girl, that makes a bigger ripple in the pond. Which means unforeseen ramifications. Then who do we have to kill to take care of those?"

That blown pupil in the rearview seemed to pull her in. She found herself leaning back to avoid tumbling down the rabbit hole.

"I don't care," Van Sciver said.

"But the man in charge might."

For the first time, Van Sciver looked away. His trapezius muscles tensed, flanking the neck. She was certain he was going to explode, but instead he gave a little nod. Then he gestured at Thornhill, who was waiting patiently at the curb. Thornhill climbed back in, started up the nav on his phone, and both Tahoes pulled out in unison.

The two-SUV convoy headed for Los Angeles.

69
A Drool Not of Saliva

By the time they returned to Castle Heights, Evan and Joey were ragged from the drive and the detour to switch vehicles. Evan pulled his trusty Ford pickup into his spot on the subterranean parking level, and they climbed out. He took a moment to stretch his lower back before heading in.

They heard the voice before they stepped through the door to the lobby.

"— just saying you should go easy on the carbs at your age. I mean, have you *seen* you? You could stand to tighten up."

As Evan and Joey came around the corner, Lorilee and her boyfriend came into view standing before the bank of mail slots. Her head was lowered, her cat eyes swollen. The boyfriend swept his long hair off his face with a practiced flick of his head and continued flipping through the stack of mail in his hands.

"And where's my new credit card?" he

continued. "I thought you said you ordered it already."

As Evan came up on them, Lorilee wouldn't meet his gaze. Evan thought about what Joey had just confronted on that porch in Phoenix and how an argument like this would sound to her ears. He felt bone-tired and angry.

Lorilee's reply was soft, the voice of a little girl. "I did."

"Yeah, well, then is it magic that it's still not —"

Evan's elbow moved before he told it to, knocking the boyfriend's arm and dumping the sheaf of mail onto the floor.

"Oops," Evan said. "Didn't see you."

He crouched down to gather the envelopes, reading the boyfriend's shadowy reflection on the polished tiles.

"No worries, man," the boyfriend said, leaning to help.

Evan rose abruptly, shattering the guy's nose with the back of his head.

The boyfriend reeled back, leaning against the mail slots, hand to his face. Bright red blood streamed down his forearm.

"Oh, jeez," Evan said, "I'm so sorry."

Behind him Joey coughed into a fist. He saw something in Lorilee's eyes, something like a smile.

Evan gave an apologetic nod, patted the guy on the back, and started for the elevator. "Keep pressure on that and send me the bill."

Inside the Vault, Evan fed Vera II an ice cube. He hadn't watered her in a while, and the tips of her spikes were browning. Then he crossed to the gun locker, unclipped his holstered ARES from his waistband, and put it away.

Sitting on the sheet-metal desk, Joey watched him disarm. "This is so stupid. It's *way* too dangerous."

He removed the spare magazines from the hidden pockets of his cargo pants and set them aside as well. "Yes."

"You're just gonna walk in there? Confront the entire gang?"

"Yes."

They'd been having this argument for hours, and it was showing no sign of abating.

"You cannot go into that church unarmed," Joey said.

"I told them I was coming back to kill them all," Evan said. "There's no way they let me in with a weapon. Not this time."

He smoothed down his shirt, checked his Victorinox watch fob. It was almost time.

"If *every single thing* doesn't go exactly right —"

"Joey," he said. "I know."

"Why don't you wait until we figure out a better plan?"

"I told Freeway twenty-four hours. A guy like him will get restless if I don't show, start asking questions, exerting pressure. If he finds out Xavier's behind it, he'll kill him."

"You're really gonna do this? For some guy you barely even know?"

"Yes."

Unarmed, he started out.

She slid off the desk, put her palm on his chest. Her yellow-flecked green eyes were fierce. *"Why?"*

"Because he needs help. And I'm the only one who can give him this kind of help."

She implored him with her eyes.

"Joey," he said. "This is what I do. It's what I've always done. Nothing's changed."

"I guess . . . I guess *I* have."

"What do you mean?"

"Once you realize you want a life," she said, "it's a lot harder to risk it."

He thought of Jack stepping out of that Black Hawk, riding the slipstream, spinning through darkness.

He moved her hand off his chest and walked out.

■ ■ ■ ■

The Mara Salvatrucha contingent outside the church had been beefed up, no doubt in anticipation of Evan's return. At 9:59 P.M. he emerged from the shadows and walked up to the crew of waiting men.

The handguns came out quickly, ten barrels aimed at Evan's face. He halted a few steps from the doors.

Devil Horns said, "Spread your arms. We need to make sure you ain't jacketed up like some Mohammed motherfucker."

Evan obeyed.

Two younger MS-13 members came forward and patted him down roughly from his ankles to his neck. Puzzled, they looked back at the others and shrugged. "He's clean."

Devil Horns smiled, shaking his head as he reached for the reinforced door. "You play one crazy-ass fool."

The hinges squealed as the door swung open. It seemed the rest of the gang was waiting inside, scattered among the overturned pews. Only a dim altar lamp illuminated the interior, falling across Freeway's shoulders, backlighting him.

Dozens of tattooed faces swiveled to chart

Evan's progress through the nave. He didn't bother to look for Xavier; he'd contacted him earlier and told him to make sure he wasn't on site.

Xavier would not survive what was about to happen.

Evan reached the center of the church and paused. Freeway pressed one fist into the other palm, the knuckles popping one at a time.

"Twenty-four hours," Freeway said.

"That's right."

Freeway curled his lower lip, the piercings clinking on his teeth. "And now you've come to kill us all."

"That's right."

A few of the men laughed.

"How you gonna do that?" Freeway asked.

"With this." Evan reached for his cargo pocket. In the shadows countless submachine guns rose and countless slides clanked.

Freeway held up his arms for his men to calm down. Then he nodded at Evan to proceed.

The Velcro patch on Evan's pocket flap gave way with a tearing noise that sounded unreasonably loud in the quiet church. Evan stuck his hand in the pocket and came out with a Snickers bar.

There was a disbelieving silence.

Evan peeled the wrapper and took a bite. He chewed, swallowed. He couldn't remember the last time he'd eaten a candy bar.

He'd taken it from Joey's rucksack.

One of the men cracked up, a deep rumble, and then the laughter spread.

No amusement showed on Freeway's face. He skewered Evan with his black stare. "This *pendejo* is fucking *loco.*"

"We should skin him," someone called out from the darkness.

Freeway flicked open his straight razor. "Not you. Me." He started down the carpeted stairs, those tattooed eyes never leaving Evan. "Big dog's gotta eat."

Evan took another bite. "I'm not done yet," he said through a full mouth.

"You want to finish your candy bar?" Freeway said.

Evan nodded.

Freeway kept the razor open, but he crossed his arms, the blade rising next to the grooved ball of his biceps. "Okay," he said. "Your last meal."

Evan chewed some more, then popped the last bite into his mouth. He crumpled up the wrapper, let it fall from his hand onto the floor.

Freeway started forward, but Evan held

up a finger as he cleared the caramel from his molars with his tongue. He strained his ears but heard nothing. A spark of concern flared to life in his stomach. He was out of time.

And then he sensed it.

The air vibrating with a distant thrumming.

It grew louder.

Freeway took a half step back toward the altar, his eyes pulling up to the ceiling. The other men looked spooked, regarding the church walls around them. The thumping grew louder. A few shards of stained glass fell from the high frame.

From beyond the front door came the unmistakable sound of sniper rounds lasering through the air. Then the thud of falling bodies.

Evan said to Freeway, "You might want to go see about that."

The steel front door blew open, Devil Horns sailing back through the vestibule, the top of his head blown off. A Black Hawk whoomped down at the entrance, gusting wind through the nave. Operators in balaclavas spilled out with military precision, subguns raised, firing through the doorway, dropping the first ranks of gang members.

The inadvertent cavalry, right on time.

As the gang members scrambled to return fire, Evan walked to the side of the church where the stolen goods were stored. Ducking behind a head-high pallet, he dumped out a booster bag, emptying a load of RFID-tagged Versace shirts onto the floor. Then he climbed into the roomy duffel and zipped himself in. The inside, lined with thick space-blanket foil, crinkled around him.

His own miniature Faraday cage.

It would mute the GPS signal emanating from his stomach.

The sounds from the church nave were apocalyptic. Cracking rounds, panicked shrieks, crashing bodies, wet bellowing, splintering wood — a full-fledged urban firefight.

Two birds, one stone.

At last the frequency of gunfire slowed. A prayer in Spanish was cut off with a last report.

The smell of cordite reached Evan even here, hidden in the bag. He heard heavy boots moving through the nave, and then Thornhill said, "*Clear.* Jesus F. Christ. Who knew we were wading into Fallujah?"

Van Sciver's deep voice carried to Evan. "What a shitshow. How many did we lose?"

Candy's voice said, "Three. I count three."

In the darkness of the booster bag, Evan thought, *Twenty dead. Five to go.*

Van Sciver's voice came again. "Where's X?"

Thornhill again. "I don't know. The GPS signal, it vanished."

"Vanished? We had at least four more minutes by my count."

"I don't know what to tell you."

"How 'bout the blood trail there at the back of the altar?"

"One of the gang members. I saw him stumble out. It wasn't X."

"Get me optics on thermal signatures in the building. *Now.*"

Shuffling boots. Then Thornhill said, "There's nothing on premises except the dead bodies, and we've looked under them." A beat. "I think homeboy played us."

A few seconds of silence. Then Van Sciver swore loudly, the sharp syllable booming off the walls.

Evan had not heard him lose his cool, not since their Pride House days. In his booster bag tucked behind the pallet, he stayed perfectly still.

Van Sciver said, "Get our bodies out of here. We need to lay down a cover story. Gang violence, cartel involvement, whatever. We were never here."

Thornhill issued orders over a radio, and then more boots thumped in. The sounds of corpses being dragged.

The floorboards groaned as someone drew near. They groaned again, nearer yet. Evan felt faint tremors through the foundation.

Then Van Sciver's voice came, no more than ten feet away. "No," he said.

And then, "No."

And once again, with an undercurrent of worry, "No."

A phone call.

Van Sciver had stepped to the side of the church for privacy.

"Okay," he said. "We won't. Not a trace." A beat, and then, "I understand the Black Hawk is high-profile. We won't use it again. This was our best shot —" Another pause. "Not very well."

Van Sciver took another step, so close now that Evan could hear him breathing.

"I understand he's the only connective tissue. But 1997 is a long ways back."

Evan could hear the voice on the other end of the line now, not the words but the tone. Firm and confident, with a hidden seam of rage.

Van Sciver replied, "Yes, Mr. President."

The phone call terminated with a click.

Van Sciver exhaled through what sounded

like clenched teeth. He shifted his weight, the floorboards answering.

Then his steps headed out.

A moment later Evan heard the Black Hawk rotors spin up and the helo lift off. The sound faded. There came an instant of peace.

And then sirens wailed faintly somewhere in the night.

Evan unzipped himself, releasing the humidity of the booster bag. He climbed out. The air tasted of smoke and blood.

Bodies covered the nave, folded over pews, sprawled on the floor, heaped against the walls.

No sign of Freeway.

The sirens were louder now.

Bullets riddled the old wooden altarpiece. Blood painted the Virgin Mary's forehead, an Ash Wednesday smudge. The arc of the cast-off spatter pointed to the right side.

Evan followed, mounting the carpeted steps.

A brief hall behind the altar led to a rear door.

He stepped out into the crisp night. Drops of blood left a fairytale trail out of the back alley. Evan followed them.

He came to the street and crossed it as a swarm of cop cars screeched up to the front of the church. A crowd had gathered, and he melted into its embrace.

More crimson drops on the sidewalk. The transfer pattern of a handprint on a street-lamp. A red dab stained a flyer by the bodega with the plywood-covered window.

The bodega sign was turned to CLOSED.

Evan slipped inside. The owner stood behind the cash register, trembling.

Evan said, *"Lárgate."*

The owner scrambled out through the front door.

The blood drops were thicker now on the floor tiles. Evan followed them up the aisle and into the back courtyard.

Freeway was leaning against a metal post, clutching a gunshot wound in his side. His other hand held the straight razor. He firmed his posture and held the blade to the side.

Those black eyes picked across Evan. "You're stupid to come here with no weapon."

"Maybe so," Evan said. "But I have one advantage."

Freeway bared his teeth. "What's that?"

"I don't have metal in my face."

He hit Freeway with a haymaker cross. The studs moored the skin. There was a great tearing and a drool not of saliva. The straight razor clattered to the concrete as Freeway hit his knees, the wreckage of his face pouring through his fingers.

Evan picked up the razor from the ground, looked down at Freeway.

"Look what I found," he said. "A weapon."

Sitting at his kitchen island, Evan fanned through Van Sciver's red notebook again. He stared at the scrawl standing out in relief from the pencil-blackened page in the middle.

"6-1414 Dark Road 32."

He'd returned to Castle Heights to make a few arrangements, laying the groundwork for the battle to come. In light of the conversation he'd overheard in the church, he needed to check the notebook again. Staring at the words now, he sensed the puzzle piece slide into place.

He walked past the living wall, catching a whiff of mint, and stepped through one of the south-facing sliding doors onto the balcony. He crouched before a square planter at the edge that held a variety of succulents and slid clear an inset panel. It hid a camouflage backpack, which he removed and carried inside.

He returned to the island, the notebook page looking up at him, the scrawl rendered clear in the negative space.

Joey came down from the loft, ready to go. She paused and took him in sitting over the notebook.

"You know what it means now," she said.

He nodded absentmindedly.

"You gonna share?"

Evan shut the notebook as if that could somehow contain the problem within. "Yeah. (202) 456-1414 is the main switchboard for the West Wing," he said.

She processed this. "And 'Dark Road'?"

"A code word. Presumably to kick the caller to a security command post in the White House."

"And the 32," she said. "That's an extension."

He nodded again.

"That goes to who?" she asked.

He looked at her.

"Holy hell," she said.

"Indeed."

"Why?" she said. "Why would he be involved?"

Evan rubbed his face. Again he pictured Jack dropping him off at departures at Dulles back when Evan was a nineteen-year-old kid. Jack's hand on his forearm, not wanting to let him go.

Evan said, "When I was in that booster bag, I heard Van Sciver reference 1997."

"And?"

"That was the year of my first mission."

"What was it?"

"I can't tell you that," he said. "But in 1997 President Bennett was the undersecretary of defense for policy at the DoD."

"And the Orphan Program existed under the Department of Defense's umbrella," Joey said slowly, putting it together.

All at once the rationale for the shift of the Program's aim under Van Sciver's leadership came clearer. So did the sudden push to exterminate Orphans — Evan most of all.

He didn't just know where the bodies were buried. He'd buried most of them himself.

Joey said, "So Bennett greenlit your first mission."

"Yes. And as the leader of the free world now, he wants to clean up any trace of his involvement in nonsanctioned activities. Any trace of me."

Joey set her elbows on the island and leaned over, her eyes wide. "Do you get what this means? You've got dirt on the president of the United States."

Evan spun back in time to his twelfth year, riding in Jack's truck, Jack describing the Program to him for the first time in that tengrit voice: *You'll be a cutout man. Fully expendable. You'll know only your silo. Nothing damaging. If you're caught, you're on your own. They will torture you to pieces, and you can give up all the information you have, because none of it is useful.*

"I know the who," Evan said. "But not the what."

"What do you mean?"

"I know what I did in '97. But I don't know anything else. Or how it connects to Bennett." He looked down at the red notebook as if it could tell him something. "But someday when this is all over, I'm gonna find out."

"When *what's* all over?"

"Come and I'll show you." He shouldered the camo pack, grabbed the keys, and started for the door.

The Vegas Strip rose from the flat desert earth like a parade, a brassy roar of faux daylight. Evan kept on the I-15, let the bombastic display fly by on the right-hand side, Joey's head swiveling to watch it pass. For a few minutes, it was impossible to tell that it was nearly four in the morning, but as the glow faded in the rearview and the stars reasserted themselves overhead, it became clear that they were driving through deepest night.

Joey worked her speed cube without looking. Whenever Evan glanced over, he saw that she was once again spinning it into patterns from memory. The clacking of the cube carried them across the dark miles.

Once the grand boulevard was far behind them, Evan pulled over and wound his way through back roads. The pickup rumbled onto a dirt road that narrowed into a sagebrush-crowded trail. At last he pulled over at a makeshift range. Tattered targets fluttered on bales of hay beneath the moonlight, Monet gone bellicose. When they stepped out of the truck, shell casings jingled underfoot.

"What are we doing here?" Joey asked.

"Planning."

"For what?"

"For the next time I eat something and light up the GPS in my stomach."

"Now Van Sciver'll know it's a trap," she said.

"Right."

"So he'll spring a trap on our trap."

"And we'll spring a trap on the trap he's springing on our trap."

She squinted at him through the darkness. He felt a flash of affection for this girl, this mission that had blown through his life like an F5 tornado. He thought of his words to Jack in their final conversation — *I wouldn't trade knowing you for anything* — but he couldn't make them come out of his mouth now, in this context. They stopped somewhere in his throat, locked down behind his expressionless stare.

Far below, a solitary set of headlights blazed through the night. Evan and Joey watched them climb the dune, disappearing at intervals on the switchbacks. Then a dually truck shuddered up beside Evan's F-150, rocking to a halt.

The door kicked open, and Tommy Stojack slid out of the driver's seat and landed unevenly. His ankles were shot from too many parachute jumps, as were his knees and hips. The damage gave him a loose-limbed walk that called to mind a movie cowboy.

"Shit, brother, I was way out at the ranch prepping for Shot Show when you called. Just had time to wash pits and parts and haul ass out, but here I is."

He and Evan clasped hands in greeting, and then Tommy looked over at Joey, his biker mustache shifting as he assessed her.

"This the one you told me about?"

"It is."

Tommy gave an approving nod. "She looks lined out."

Joey said, "Thanks."

"For a sixteen-year-old broad, I mean."

Joey smiled flatly. "Thanks."

Tommy stroked his mustache, cocked his head at Evan. "Last we broke bread, I said if you needed me, give a holler. You hit a wall, and you figured what the fuck."

"I figured exactly that," Evan said.

"Well, I can't scoot like I used to, but I can still loot and shoot. I know you well enough to know if you're calling in air support, you're up against it."

"Yes," Evan said.

"Well, with what you're asking, I'm gonna need you to make more words come out your mouth hole."

"They're trying to kill me. And they're trying to kill her."

A long pause ensued as Tommy chewed on this. "*You* I understand," he said finally, his mustache arranging itself into a smirk. "But still, I suppose it'd be unsat for me to sit back and let a good piece of gear like you hit a meat grinder. So. What services of mine are required?"

Evan said, "Your research for DARPA . . ."

Tommy's eyes gleamed. "Before we get to puttin' metal on meat, I'd best know what we're looking at so I can see if it falls within my moral purview. So if you want me to put on the big boy pants and the Houdini hat, let's go back to the shop, I'll drink a hot cuppa shut-the-fuck-up, and you read me in on what's read-in-able."

"Wait a minute," Joey said. "DARPA?" She looked from Evan to Tommy. "What are you guys talking about?"

"What're we talking about?" Tommy smiled, showing off the gap in his front teeth. "We're talking about some Harry Potter shit."

71
BRING THE THUNDER

A cup of yerba maté tea and a plate of fresh-sliced mango, both lovingly served, both untouched, sat before Evan on the low coffee table of the front room. Benito and Xavier Orellana occupied the lopsided couch opposite him.

Benito said, "My son and I, we don't know how to express our —"

Evan said, "No need."

Xavier folded his hands. The forearm tattoo he had recently started, that elaborate *M* for *Mara Salvatrucha,* had taken a new direction. Rather than spelling out the gang's name, it now said *Madre.* The last four letters looked brand-new, hours old. They were interwoven with vines and flowers.

Xavier saw Evan looking and shifted self-consciously. "You said we can remake ourselves however we want. So I figured why not start here."

Benito's eyes welled up, and Evan was worried the old man might start to cry. Evan didn't have time for that.

He looked over their shoulders and out the front window to the brim of the valley of the vast razed lot. Sounds of construction carried up the slope. At the edge of the lot, way down by the 10 Freeway, the fifth story of the emergent building thrust into view. It had been roughly framed out now, workers scrambling in the cross section of the visible top floors. Their union shifts would end in two hours, and then the lot would be deserted for the night.

"How can we repay you for what you've done?" Benito asked.

"There is one thing," Evan said.

"Whatever you ask," Xavier said, "I'll do."

Beside him his father tensed at the edge of the couch cushion.

"Find someone who needs me," Evan said. "Like you did. It doesn't matter how long it takes. Find someone who's desperate, who's got no way out, and give them my number: 1-855-2-NOWHERE."

Both men nodded.

"You tell them about me. Tell them I'll be there on the other end of the phone."

Benito said, "The Nowhere Man."

"That's right."

As Evan rose, Xavier found his feet quickly. "Sir," he said, the word sounding ridiculous and old-fashioned in his mouth, "why do you do this?"

Evan looked at the floor. An image came to him, Joey standing in front of that house in the Phoenix heat, gun in hand, staring down a woman on a porch swing. And then handing the pistol back to him, unfired.

The words were surprisingly hard to say, but he fought them out: "Because everyone deserves a second chance."

Xavier extended his hand, that *Madre* tattoo bleeding and raw and beautiful. "I'll do it. I'll find someone else."

Evan shook his hand.

The front door banged in, Tommy shouldering through, gripping a Hardigg case in each hand.

Xavier and Benito looked at the stranger with alarm.

"Also," Tommy said, "we're gonna need to borrow your roof."

At the base of the sloped lot, Evan and Joey stood between a tower crane and a hydraulic torque wrench, staring up at the five-story development. Beyond the tall concrete wall to their side, afternoon rush-hour traffic hummed by.

The workers had retired for the night. The six-acre blind spot provided an unlikely patch of privacy in the heart of Los Angeles. Upslope, the lot ended at a street, but the houses beyond, including Benito Orellana's, were not visible.

The construction platform's lift, an orange cage half the size of a shipping container, had been lowered for the work day's end. Joey stepped forward, rocked it with her foot. It didn't give. Then she leaned back and appraised the steel bones of the building-to-be.

"Which route?" Evan asked.

Joey squinted. Then she raised an arm, pointing. "There to there to there. See that I-beam? Third floor? Then across. Up that rise. There, there, and then up."

Evan visualized the path. "How do you know?"

"Geometry."

"Okay," he said. "Now you're done. Let's get you somewhere safe."

"You're kidding, right?"

"No," he said. "You're out. Me and Tommy will handle it from here."

"You and Tommy are gonna have your hands full. You need me. Any way you cut it, it's a three-man plan."

He knew she was right. Evan could handle

five freelancers, skilled as they were. But not three Orphans on top of that.

He leaned against the blocky 1980 Lincoln Town Car they'd driven down the slope. Beside it the lowered claw of a backhoe nodded downward, a crane sipping from a lake.

Joey looked up to the top of the building, the breeze lifting her hair, a wisp catching in the corner of her mouth. "You laid it out yourself. Van Sciver won't deploy drones on U.S. soil. The president ordered him not to use choppers anymore. We can control some of the variables."

"This is different," Evan said.

"I'm not leaving you to this alone. And you only got a few more hours before those GPS chips break down in your stomach. You'd better eat something and throw a signal while you still can." She reached into her jacket pocket, pulled out a Snickers bar, and wiggled it back and forth.

He didn't smile, but that didn't seem to faze her.

"I'm not going anywhere," she said. "So quit wasting time."

"Joey. It's too dangerous."

"You're right. Anywhere I go, he'll find me. You know that. You know it in your gut. I will never be safe until he's dead. And you know you need me to make this plan work."

Evan studied her stubborn face. Then he came off the car and pointed at her, trying to keep the exasperation from his voice. "After this you're out."

"I'm out. Some other life." Her smile held equal parts trepidation and excitement. "Ponytails and white picket fences."

"The minute this operation goes live —"

"I'll just sail out of here," she said. "*I'll* be fine." She paused. "But you? I don't see you getting out of this."

He listened to the wind whistle through the I-beams overhead. Jack, paraphrasing the German field marshal and the Scottish poet, used to say, *Even the best-laid plan can't survive the first fired bullet.* Evan had taken his measurements, charted his course, laid his plans. He had escape routes planned and off-the-books emergency medical support on standby. Despite all that he knew Joey was right, that this man-made valley could well prove to be his grave.

"Maybe not." He placed a wire-thin saber radio in her hand; the bone phone would pick up her voice and allow her to listen directly through her jaw.

She said, "We could still get into that ugly-ass Town Car and just drive away."

A wistful smile tugged at his lips. He

shook his head.

The breeze blew across her face, and she swept her hair back. "He's gonna come with everything he has. And he's gonna kill you like he has everyone else. You think Jack would want this?"

"It's not just about Jack anymore. It's about everyone else who Van Sciver's got in his sights." His throat was dry. "It's about you, Joey."

He'd said it louder than he'd intended and with anger, though where the anger came from, he wasn't sure.

Her eyes moistened. She looked away sharply.

For a time there was only the breeze.

Then she said, "Josephine."

"I'm sorry?"

"My name. You wanted to know my full name." Her eyes darted to his face and then away again. "There it is."

Beyond the concrete rise, vehicles whipped by on the freeway, oblivious people leading ordinary lives, some charmed, some not. On this side of the wall, there was only Evan and a sixteen-year-old girl, trying their best to say good-bye.

Joey lifted the forgotten Snickers bar from her side and tossed it to him. She took a deep breath.

"Okay," she said. "Let's bring the thun-
der."

72

THIN THE HERD

The freelancers came in first, and they came by foot. The five men wound their way toward the valley in a tightening spiral, a snake coiling.

Former Secret Service agents, they brought the tools of the trade designed to protect the most important human on earth. Electronic noses for hazardous chemicals and biologicals, bomb-detection devices, thermal-imaging handhelds. Though it wasn't yet dusk, they had infrared goggles around their necks, ready for nightfall. After safing the surrounding blocks, they meticulously combed through every square foot of the valley, communicating with radio earpieces, ensuring that anything within view of the construction site below was clear.

Each man wore a Raytheon Boomerang Warrior on his shoulder, an electronic sniper-detection system. Developed for Iraq, it could pinpoint the position of any enemy shooter within sight lines up to three thousand feet away.

Two of the freelancers rolled out, hiking back up the slope, giving a final check, and disappearing from view.

Ten minutes passed.

And then two Chevy Tahoes with tinted windows, steel-plate-reinforced doors, and laminated bullet-resistant glass coasted down the slope. They parked at the base of the construction building in front of the porta-potties.

Van Sciver got out, swollen with body armor, and stood behind the shield of the door. Candy and Thornhill strayed a bit farther, the freelancers holding a loose perimeter around them, facing outward. The operators now held FN SCAR 17S spec-ops rifles, scopes riding the hard-chromed bores. Menacing guns, they looked like they had an appetite of their own.

Van Sciver cast his gaze around. "Well," he said. "We're here."

Thornhill scanned the rim of the valley. "Think he'll show?"

Van Sciver's damaged right eye watered in the faint breeze. He wristed a tear off the edge of his lid. "He called the meet."

"Then where is he?" one of the freelancers asked.

"The GPS signal from the microchips is long gone," Thornhill said. "It's up to our own selves."

The faint noise of a car engine rose above the muted hum of freeway traffic behind the concrete wall. The freelancers oriented to the street above.

The noise of the motor grew louder.

The men raised their weapons.

A white Lincoln Town Car plowed over the brim of the valley, plummeting down the slope at them. Already the men were firing, riddling the windshield and hood with bullets.

The Town Car bumped over the irregular terrain, slowing but still pulled by gravity. The men shot out the tires, aerated the engine block.

The car slowed, slowed, glancing off a backhoe and nodding to a stop twenty yards away.

Two of the freelancers raced forward, lasering rounds through the shattered maw of the windshield.

The first checked the car's interior cautiously over the top of his weapon. "Clear. No bodies."

The other wanded down the vehicle. "No explosives either. It's a test."

Twenty yards back, still protected by their

respective armor-plated doors, Van Sciver and Candy had already spun around to assess less predictable angles of attack that the diversion had been designed to open up.

Van Sciver's gaze snagged on the side of the under-construction building, the platform lift waiting by the top floor. "He's there," he said.

"We would've picked up thermal, sir," the freelancer said.

Van Sciver pointed at the mounted platform's lift control. Thornhill jogged over to the base of the building, keeping his eyes above, and clicked to lower the lift.

Nothing happened.

The bottom control mechanism had been sabotaged.

All five freelancers raised their SCARs in concert, covering the building's fifth floor.

Van Sciver said, "Get me sat imagery."

Keeping his rifle pointed up, one of the freelancers shuffled over and passed a handheld to Van Sciver, who remained wedged behind the armored door of the Tahoe. Van Sciver zoomed in on the bird's-eye footage of the building, waiting for the clarity to resolve.

Stiff, canvaslike fabric was heaped a few feet from the open edge of the fifth floor.

"He's hiding beneath a Faraday-cage cloak," Van Sciver said. "The metallized fabric blocked your thermal imaging. It's not distinct enough to red-flag on the satellite footage unless you know to look for it."

"He's holding high ground," Candy observed. "And we've got no good vantage point."

Van Sciver stared at the concrete wall framing the 10 Freeway. Posting up on the fifth floor was a smart move on X's part. The open top level was in full view of the freeway and the buildings across from it. They couldn't come at him with force or numbers without inviting four hundred eyewitnesses every second to the party.

"What's he waiting for?" one of the freelancers asked through clenched teeth.

"For me to step clear of the armored vehicle and give him an angle," Van Sciver said. "But I'm not gonna do that."

With a gloved hand, the freelancer swiped sweat from his brow. "So what are *we* gonna do? We can't get up there."

Van Sciver's lopsided stare locked on Thornhill. An understanding passed between them. Thornhill's smile lit up his face.

Van Sciver said, "Fetch."

Thornhill snugged his radio earpiece firmly into place. Then he sprinted forward, leaping from a wheelbarrow onto the roof of a porta-potty. Then he hurtled through the air, clamping onto the exposed ledge of the second floor. The freelancers watched in awe as he scurried up the face of the building, frog-leaping from an exposed window frame to a four-by-four to a concrete ledge. He used a stubbed-out piece of rebar on the third floor as a gymnast high bar, rotating to fly onto a vertical I-beam holding up the fourth story.

Mere feet from the edge of the fifth floor, he paused on his new perch, shoulder muscles bunched, legs bent, braced for a lunge. He turned to take in the others below, giving them a moment to drink in the glory of what he'd just done.

Then he refocused. His body pulsed as he slide-jumped up the I-beam's length. He gripped the cap plate with both hands and readied for the final leap that would bring him across the lip to the top of the building.

But the cap plate moved with him.

It jerked free of the I-beam and hammered back against his chest, striking the muscle with a thud.

One of the high-strength carriage bolts designed to secure the cap plate to the I-beam's flange sailed past his cheek.

The other three bolts rattled in their bore-holes, unsecured.

He clasped the cap plate to his chest, a weightless instant.

His eyes were level with the poured slab of the fifth floor, and he saw the puddle of the Faraday cloak there almost within reach.

The cloak's edge was lipped up, a face peering out from the makeshift burrow.

Not X's.

But the girl's.

She raised a hand, wiggled the fingers in a little wave.

"It's the girl," Thornhill said. His voice, hushed with disbelief, carried through his radio earpiece.

He floated there an instant, clutching the cap plate.

And then he fell with it.

Five stories whipped by, a whirligig view of construction gear, Matchbox cars drift-ing through fourteen lanes of traffic beyond the concrete wall, his compatriots staring up with horrified expressions.

He went through the roof of the porta-potty. As he vanished, one sturdy fiberglass wall sheared off his left leg at the hip, paint-ing the dirt with arterial spray.

A moment of stunned silence.

Van Sciver tried to swallow, but his throat

clutched up. One of his finest tools, a weaponized extension of himself as the director of the Orphan Program, had just been splattered all over an outdoor shitter.

Candy moved first, diving into the Tahoe. Van Sciver's muscle memory snapped him back into focus. Raising his FNX-45, he set his elbows in the fork of the armored door and aimed upslope. He said, "It's another decoy."

The freelancers spread out, aiming in various directions — up the partially constructed building, across the valley, at the freeway wall.

The lead man squeezed off a few shots, nicking the edge of the fifth floor to hold Joey at bay.

The wind reached a howl in the bare beams of the structure.

"Fuck," Van Sciver said. "Where is . . . ?"

Twenty yards away the trunk of the white Lincoln Town Car popped open and Evan burst up in a kneeling stance, a Faraday cloak sloughing off his shoulders.

He shot two freelancers through the heads before they could orient to the movement. The third managed to and took a round through the mouth.

The remaining pair of freelancers wheeled on Evan, their rifles biting coaster-size chunks of metal from the Town Car's grille. Evan spilled onto the dirt behind the Town Car and flattened to the ground. The big-block engine of the old Lincoln protected him, at least as well as it had on the car's descent into the valley, but time was not on his side.

The reports were deafening.

He clicked his bone phone on. "Joey, jump now and get gone."

She'd played bait one last time. Her only job now was to vanish.

Evan had set her up with the camouflage backpack he kept hidden in the planter on his balcony. The pack was stuffed with a base-jumping parachute. A running leap off the backside of the fifth-floor platform would allow her to steer across the immense freeway, land in the confusion of alleys and buildings across from it, and disappear.

Evan risked a peek around the rear fender. He spotted Candy rolling out of the Tahoe's backseat with a shotgun an instant before one of Van Sciver's bullets shattered out the brake light inches from his face. He whipped back, felt the Town Car shuddering, absorbing round after round as the freelancers advanced.

He spoke again into the bone phone. "Tommy, you're up."

Flattening against the car, he rested the back of his head to the metal, pinned down to a space the width of a rear bumper.

Tommy emerged from the umbra beside Benito Orellana's chimney and bellied to the edge of the roof where his two Hardigg cases waited, lids raised. The first held optical-sighting technology, and a half-dozen eightball cameras nestled in the foam lining.

He had no direct sight line onto the valley or the construction site below.

He plucked free the first eightball and hurled it across the street. It bounced once, disappearing over the lip and rolling down-slope, its 360-degree panorama replicated on the laptop screen. The round camera landed behind a backhoe, providing him a view of the dirt slope beyond, the clear blue sky, and nothing else.

He threw the second and third eightball cameras in rapid succession. The second landed in a ditch, but the third stopped three-fourths of the way down the slope, providing a lovely perspective on the mayhem unfolding at the construction site below. Two freelancers stood in the open, but Van Sciver and Candy were wisely tucked away, using the armored SUVs for cover.

That was okay. Tommy could still thin the herd for Evan.

In front of the second Hardigg case, an assembled Barrett M107 awaited him. He'd chosen the self-loader for rapidity — once this shit went down, the boys below would be scrambling every which way, all asses and elbows.

Firming the .50-cal into position, he lay at the roof's edge. He would have preferred a spotter, but given the sensitive nature of the mission and Evan's wishes, no one else could be in the loop. It would be a helluva challenge to crank off two shots in rapid succession, especially since he had to steer the first one in. Microelectronics distorted the shape of the round after it left the barrel, changing its line of flight. As good as Tommy was and as state-of-the-art the technology, there was only so much guidance you could lay on a projo hurtling along at 2,850 feet a second. He checked the optics screen, using the eightball's feed to index locations for landmarks.

Then he set his eye to the scope and prepared to bend a bullet in midair.

Evan read the freelancers' shadows. That

was all he could do. Braced against the rear bumper of the Town Car, he watched them stretch alongside him, upraised rifles clearly silhouetted. If he rolled to either side, he presented himself not just to them but to Van Sciver and Candy, who were posted up in the SUVs twenty yards beyond.

"We got you pinned behind the car and the little girl stuck up on the roof!" Van Sciver shouted. "Even if she has a rifle, she can't cover you, not from there. I've seen her shoot."

Tommy still hadn't announced himself. The technology was fledgling; Evan had always known that any help would be a literal and figurative long shot.

Cast forward, the shadows on the earth inched past his position crammed behind the Town Car. They advanced in unison. Any second now Evan would have to make the choice to move one way or the other.

He decided to expose his right side. He could shoot with either hand but was stronger with his left, so if an arm went down, better the right one.

If he was lucky enough to merely take a round to the limb.

He sucked in a breath, tensed his legs, counted down.

Three . . . two . . .

The whine of a projectile was followed by a snap on the wind. The shadow to Evan's right crumpled, a body falling just out of sight by the side of the Town Car. A bright spill oozed into view by Evan's boots, staining the dirt.

Twenty-four down.

One left.

The last freelancer pulled back. "Holy shit. How the fuck . . . ?"

Evan popped up to drop him, but Candy was waiting by the other Tahoe. She unleashed the shotgun, and Evan dropped an instant before the scattershot hit the trunk. The trunk slammed down, nearly sawing off his chin, and banged back up. The edge clipped his shooting hand, the ARES flying out of reach, landing ten yards in the open.

Slumped low at the rear fender, he panted in the dirt.

The bullet holes in the raised trunk cut circles of light in the shadow thrown on the ground behind Evan. He rose to reach for a backup pistol in the trunk, but Candy fired again, the slugs tearing through the metal, whistling past his torso. The trunk slammed down, banging his forearm. Evan hit the ground again, dust puffing into his mouth.

The freelancer was crawling away; Evan could see him for an instant beneath the carriage of the Town Car. Another of Tommy's rounds whined in and bit a divot from the dirt four inches from the freelancer's pinkie finger.

The man bellowed and rolled away, grabbing at the screen of the Boomerang Warrior unit mounted on his shoulder. A third round clipped the butt of the man's slung rifle, kicking it into a hula-hoop spin around his shoulder.

He dove behind a heap of gravel next to the tower crane, shouting, "How the hell does he see me? I'm showing nothing in our line of sight!"

Van Sciver's calm, deep voice rode the breeze. "Check for cameras."

A moment later, "The Boomerang Warrior's picking up a remote-surveillance unit in the valley with an angle on us."

Evan debated going again for the backup ARES in the ravaged trunk of the Town Car, but there were enough holes now that the raised metal no longer offered protection; it would be like standing behind a screen door. He got off a glance around the punctured rear tire, catching Van Sciver's thick arm reaching past the Tahoe's door to haul in a fallen FN SCAR 17S.

Even without an earpiece, Evan heard Van Sciver say, "Send me the coordinates."

The simple directive landed on Evan like something physical, the weight of impending defeat.

Twenty seconds passed, an eternity in a battle.

Then the rifle cracked, and Evan saw metal shards jump up from the earth upslope, glinting in the dying sunlight.

Van Sciver's voice carried, ghostly across the dusty expanse. "We are clear. Candy, haul ass up there and find who's behind that camera."

At the Town Car's rear bumper, Evan heard Tommy's voice come through the bone phone. "I'm blind."

"Fall back to the rally point," Evan said quietly. "Immediately. Do not engage any further."

Tommy was a world-class sniper, but past his prime. If he went head-to-head with Candy, an Orphan at the top of her game, she would kill him.

Evan heard one of the Tahoes screech away. It barreled upslope, giving Evan's position wide berth. He caught a glimpse of Candy's hair in a side mirror as the SUV bounced across the razed lot.

Through the radio Tommy's voice sounded scratchier than usual. "What about you?"

Evan stared at his ARES 1911 where it had landed in the dirt ten yards away. His backup was out of reach in the trunk behind him. Tommy neutralized. Van Sciver beaded up on the Town Car with his rifle.

"I got you covered," Van Sciver called to his freelancer. "Make the move."

A crunch of footsteps signaled the man's emergence from behind the gravel pile.

Evan realized what Van Sciver's counter-move was, the genius of it turning his insides ice-water cold.

He heard the clang of footsteps on metal rungs. Then the door to the elevated operator's cabin of the crane hinged open and slammed shut.

Evan was finished.

He still owed Tommy an answer. He set a finger on the bone phone, said, "I'll be fine."

"You're clear?" Tommy asked.

Evan swallowed. "I'm clear."

"Falling back," Tommy said. "Call me for extraction?"

The Tahoe creaked as Van Sciver posted up and slotted a fresh twenty-round mag into the big rifle.

"Sure thing," Evan said. His mouth was dry. "And, Tommy?"

"What, pal?"

"Thanks for everything."

73
THE BLACK HEREAFTER

Joey stood at the edge of the fifth floor, the poured-concrete slab solid underfoot, the base-jumping pack snug to her back, fist gripping the rip cord. The sound of gunfire carried up, pops muffled by the concrete wall and the roar of traffic beyond. She picked her spot across the fourteen lanes of traffic, a parking lot glistening with shattered glass. The city had started to granulate with dusk. Night wasn't far off, and blackness would aid in her escape.

From her perch she'd watched most of the action unfold. Tommy had rolled off the roof of the Orellana house and disappeared well before Candy McClure had forged upslope in the Jeep. Her pursuit would be in vain; Tommy had too much of a jump on her.

That left Evan pinned down without a weapon, facing off against Van Sciver and a freelancer. Last Joey had peeked, they'd taken up strategic positions at a ninety-degree spread, vectoring in at him from two angles he couldn't cover even if he had a gun.

But he was Orphan X, and Orphan X always found a way.

And so she'd donned the backpack and retreated to the far edge as promised.

Now she was here, freedom a single leap away.

A mural decorated the far wall of the freeway, visible to the eastbound passing cars. Cesar Chavez and Gandhi, Martin Luther King and Nelson Mandela. A cacophony of quotations and languages painted the drab concrete, but one sentence in particular stood out.

"If you've got nothing worth dying for, you've got nothing worth living for."

She read it twice, felt it pull at something deep inside her.

Pushing away the sensation, she took a few backward steps to allow herself a running start.

Then she heard another sound.

A large piece of machinery rumbling to life.

At the dead center of the uppermost slab, she hesitated.

Run.

Or turn.

She closed her eyes, took a deep breath, heard a voice that was part Jack's, part Evan's, part her own.

The Sixth Commandment, it said. *Question orders.*

She turned.

Easing to her former position, she had a perfect vantage on the scene below.

Van Sciver in the embrace of the armored Tahoe, rifle raised. Evan hidden behind the increasingly frayed Town Car, his 1911 well out of reach on the ground.

The slewing unit of the colossal crane below squealed, the horizontal jib lurching into motion. The freelancer had climbed up into the operator's cab and swiveled it into position directly below the orange cage of the raised platform lift.

Directly below her.

The freelancer worked the controls, getting the hang of the massive unit. The jib rotated unevenly and then halted, aligned with the Town Car. The massive steel lifting hook lowered, scooping up the carry cables of an I-beam.

The I-beam rose.

But only a few feet off the ground.

The trolley engaged, running the load out from the crane's center. The I-beam traveled a few yards, nosing the Town Car like a rhino checking out a Jeep full of safari-goers. The Town Car tilted up onto the tires of its left side, not quite high enough to expose Evan. Then it settled back down.

The load hadn't acquired sufficient momentum.

The crane screeched, the trolley pulling the I-beam away from the car toward the mast. It drew back and back, like the windup of a massive battering ram. The Town Car stood directly in its path, an empty can awaiting a mallet.

If you've got nothing worth dying for, you've got nothing worth living for.

Joey let the camo backpack slip from her shoulders. She stepped onto the platform lift and clicked the big red button to lower herself.

Evan knew what was coming, and this was not an instance where that was a good thing.

The crane hummed, its motor a low-grade earthquake that rumbled the ground. He stretched his neck, watched the I-beam reach the end of the track and pause, swaying mightily, preparing its journey back along the jib and into the side of the Town Car.

Once it went, the car would be swept

away, laying Evan bare.

The I-beam stilled, readying to reverse course.

Evan calculated five possible moves, but they all ended the same way — with Van Sciver putting a tight grouping through his torso. When the time came, Evan would choose one of them. His instinct and training demanded as much.

But this time he already knew the outcome.

Riding the platform lift, Joey watched the I-beam dangling way below the jib. It had reached the terminus of its backswing. Her thumb jammed the down button so hard her knuckle ached. She willed the orange cage to descend faster, but it kept its infuriatingly steady pace.

The freelancer was partially visible inside the operator's cab — a downward slice of forehead and one cheek. The noise of her descent was lost beneath the roar of the motor driving the slewing unit.

The platform lift inched lower, the operator's cab coming up below. The freelancer's hands were locked around two joystick-like controllers.

He threw his right fist forward.

The I-beam rocketed toward the Town

Car an instant before Joey's orange cage struck the top of the cab.

It was too late.

Evan couldn't see anything, but he felt the rush of a forced breeze, the air shuddering as the I-beam swept for the Town Car.

Five seconds to impact, now four.

He had to go for the backup 1911 in the trunk even if it meant getting shot by Van Sciver.

He sprang up, painfully aware of the full presentation of his critical mass, and grabbed the ARES where it lay against the carpeted cargo space. Through the holes in the raised trunk, he could see Van Sciver twenty yards away, shielded by the armored door of the Tahoe.

He expected to be staring at the full-circle scope of the rifle, the last sight he'd ever see.

But miraculously, Van Sciver wasn't looking at him. He was aiming up at the lowering platform lift, firing round after round.

His shots sparked off the edge of the lift as it crushed into the top of the operator's cab. The freelancer leapt out of the cabin an instant before it crumpled and gave way. As the lift continued its descent, he began monkeying down the caged rungs, staying ahead of it.

Was that *Joey* riding the orange cage down?

Before Evan could react, the I-beam swept in, a massive blur in his peripheral vision.

He snatched the backup gun from the trunk and whipped down out of sight.

One instant the Town Car was at his back, solid as a bulwark.

The next it was gone, Evan alone on the open stretch of dirt.

The mass of metal had hurtled close enough to him that its wake spun him around onto one knee.

He achieved a single instant of clarity.

The freelancer at the base of the tower, jumping free of the rungs, a second or two away from being able to aim his rifle.

Van Sciver twenty yards away, his SCAR rotating back to lock on Evan.

In an instant Evan would have two targets on his head from two angles, a 7–10 bowling split.

Evan got off the X, throwing himself to the side, hitting a roll, elbows locked, ARES extended before him. He had nine shots to spend — eight in the mag, one in the spout.

Upside down, Evan aimed at the space beneath the Tahoe's door. One of Van Sciver's rounds flew past his ear, trailing heat across his cheek.

Evan kept rolling, lining the sights, the target spinning like a vinyl record. He fired one, two, three, four shots before a round clipped the back of Van Sciver's boot, tearing free a chunk of durable nylon and Achilles tendon.

Van Sciver grunted but kept his feet, cranking off another round that buried itself in the dirt two inches from Evan's nose, blowing grit in his eyes.

Evan shot at the armored door. The impact drove the door back into the frame, hammering Van Sciver with it. The blow disoriented him, the rifle joggling in his hands.

Evan used the pause to flip himself into a kneeling position.

The freelancer now stood in a sniper's standing pose, feet slightly spread, right elbow tucked tight to the ribs to support the rifle, butt held high on his shoulder to bring the scope into alignment.

Evan fired through the scope atop the rifle and blew out the back of the man's head.

He quick-pivoted to Van Sciver, who was hauling his weapon into position again, still protected by the armored door.

Evan advanced and shot the door again, slamming Van Sciver backward into the truck. The rifle spun free. Evan pressed his advantage, firing again into the door. Van Sciver banged into the Tahoe once more, this time spilling partially out from his position of cover.

Van Sciver's head was protected by the armored door, but his body, made bulkier by a Kevlar vest, sprawled in full view. Night was coming on, but Evan was close enough that visibility was not a problem.

He had one shot left.

He lined the sights on the gap in the body armor where the arms usually hung. Van Sciver's tumble had twisted the vest around his torso, the vulnerable strip pulled toward his belly.

Evan fired his last round.

The fabric frayed as the bullet entered Van Sciver's abdomen.

A clod of air left him.

Blood poured from the hole.

Evan kept the pistol raised, images spinning through his mind.

Jack leaning back in his armchair and closing his eyes, letting the opera music move right through him. Young Evan at his feet, soaking it in by osmosis, these strange and beautiful sounds from another life that was now somehow his as well.

Van Sciver fought himself up to a sitting

position against the Tahoe.

Evan cast his empty gun aside and advanced on him. The fallen rifle lay between them. He could pick it up, stave in Van Sciver's skull with the butt.

Firelight playing across Jack's face in the study as he read Greek mythology out loud to Evan, his excitement contagious, the stories coming to life, winged horses and impossible labors, Gorgons and demigods, underworlds and Elysian fields.

Van Sciver pressed his hands to his stomach. He'd been gut-shot, the bullet entering the mid-abdominal area north of the belly button and beneath the zyphoid, where the ribs came together. Judging from the rush of bright red seeping through Van Sciver's hands, the bullet had severed the superior mesenteric artery. He was held together by the Kevlar vest and little else. The vest just might prove sufficient to hold him together long enough to get to a surgical suite.

Which was why Evan would beat him to death with his bare hands.

Jack stepping off into the black hereafter, not a trace of fear in his eyes. What could have filled him with such peace as he'd spun to his impact?

Van Sciver's permanently dilated pupil stared out, glossy with hidden depths, a bull's-eye waiting for a round. Evan pictured his thumb sinking through it, scrambling the frontal lobe.

Evan closed to within ten yards of him when something stopped him in his tracks.

Van Sciver was smiling.

With some effort he raised his arm and pointed behind Evan.

As Evan turned, Joey stumbled off the lowered platform lift onto the dirt, both hands locked around her thigh just above the knee.

She wobbled on her feet.

Bleeding out.

74
BRIGHTNESS OFF HER SKIN

Evan froze between Van Sciver and Joey, his body tugged in opposite directions. A few strides ahead was the man who had killed Jack. And fifteen yards behind, Joey stood doubled over, the life draining from her body.

A feeling overtook Evan, that of freefalling through the night sky just as Jack had. There were no bearings, just a spin of sensation and the pinpoint light of distant stars.

He stared at the butt of the fallen rifle ahead, the dilated pupil beckoning his thumb.

Van Sciver was breathing hard. "Looks like I clipped her superficial femoral artery."

Evan glanced back at Joey. She gasped, her legs nearly buckling.

Evan tore his gaze away, took another step for Van Sciver.

"She's gonna die," Van Sciver said. "You

wanna be with her when she does."

Evan halted again, teeth locked in a grimace.

He thought about Jack plummeting through a void, his willingness to step off a helicopter to protect Evan.

The best part of me.

Evan took an uneven step backward. And then another. Then he spun and ran to Joey.

Behind him he heard Van Sciver's laugh, the rasp of sandpaper. "That's the difference between me and you."

Evan reached Joey as her legs gave out, catching her as she collapsed.

He flicked out his Strider knife and sheared her jeans to the thigh, exposing the bullet hole. There was blood, so much blood.

The femoral artery, just as Van Sciver had said.

Evan initiated the bone phone. "Tommy, get here. Now. Get here now."

He did not recognize his own voice.

He clamped his hand over Joey's thigh.

"Copy that," Tommy said. "En route."

"*Now.* We have to get her to medical."

Across the stretch of dirt, Evan watched Van Sciver wriggle his shoulders up the side of the Tahoe, shoving himself to a standing position. He fell into the driver's seat.

The SUV drove off, its momentum kicking the door shut.

"You let Van Sciver . . . go," Joey said weakly.

Evan pictured again the serene expression on Jack's face as he'd stepped from the Black Hawk, and he understood at last what had filled him with such peace.

Joey blinked languidly. "Why'd . . . come back for me?"

Evan drew in a breath that felt like broken glass. He said, "That's what my father taught me."

He bent over Joey, his hand still sealed on her leg. The sound of the Tahoe faded, leaving the valley desolate, overtaken by late-twilight gloom. They were a stone's throw from the busiest freeway intersection in the world and yet not another human was in sight.

She looked up at him, her emerald eyes glazed.

"You were supposed to jump," he said. "Across the freeway. Away from all this." His eyes were wet. "Goddamn it. What did I teach you?"

She said, "Everything."

Her dark hair was thrown back, exposing the bristle of that shaved strip, the faraway city lights turning a few strands golden, and he realized that at some point over their days and nights he'd come to know the scent of her, a citrus brightness off her skin.

"You're okay," he said.

"You're gonna be fine," he said.

"You're worth it," he said.

Her lips pressed together. A weak smile.

He tightened his clamp on her leg.

Headlights swept the valley, a vehicle approaching. It parked, the glare making him squint.

The door slammed shut. A figure stepped forward, cut from the brilliance of the headlights.

Not Tommy.

Candy.

Evan's last ray of hope left him.

Candy approached, appraising them.

"Find what they love," she said. "And make them pay for it."

Evan would have to let go of Joey's leg to reach for his knife on the ground.

He did not.

He stayed where he was, his palm covering her wound.

He closed his eyes, saw his tiny feet filling Jack's footsteps in the woods. This was the path he was born to follow. A path into life, no matter the cost.

When he opened his eyes, Candy was

standing right over him, the barrel of her pistol inches from his forehead. In his arms he could feel Joey's breaths, each more fragile than the last.

Evan stared up the barrel at Candy. "After you kill me, clamp this artery."

Candy said nothing.

He said, "Please."

The end of Candy's pistol trembled ever so slightly. Her face contorted.

Evan looked back down at Joey. After a moment he sensed the pistol lower. Candy eased back from view. He barely registered the sound of the SUV driving away.

Joey jerked in a few shallow breaths. She raised a hand to his cheek, left a smudge of blood under his eye. He sensed it there, a weighted shadow.

"I see you," she said. "You're still real."

As he heard Tommy's truck shudder to a stop behind him, her eyes rolled up and closed, and her head nodded back in his arms.

75
THE BLACKNESS TO COME

Evan's hands rested in his lap, covered with blood.

Crimson gloves.

Tommy drove through darkest night. Los Angeles was well behind them, Las Vegas well ahead.

They had handled what they'd needed to handle.

"I know you're emotional," Tommy said, "but we gotta think straight."

Evan said, "I'm not emotional." His voice shook.

"This is next-level shit," Tommy said. "We gotta go to ground. A few weeks, minimum. See what shakes out. I got a ranch in Victorville, completely off the grid."

Evan stared out the window. The blackness sweeping by looked like the blackness before and the blackness to come.

Tommy kept talking, but Evan didn't hear

him.

Candy McClure sat on the carpet of her empty safe house, knees drawn to her chest. Past the tips of her bare feet, her phone rested on the floor. It was after midnight, and yet she'd felt no need to turn on the lights.

She had no idea how long she'd been sitting like this. Her hamstrings and calves ached. Even her Achilles tendons throbbed.

She was having what more poetic types might call a crisis of conscience.

The Samsung might ring.

Or it might never ring again.

If it did, she had no idea what she'd do.

It was one of those wait-and-see things, and she wasn't really a wait-and-see girl. Or at least she didn't used to be.

What was she now?

The phone vibrated against the carpet, uplighting her face with a bluish glow. The Signal application, presenting her with a two-word code.

It was Van Sciver.

Somehow alive.

She found herself not answering.

An unanswered phone seems to ring forever.

At last it stopped rattling against the floor-boards.

She picked it up.

She keyed in a different phone number.

1-855-2-NOWHERE.

She stared at the phone, the empty house seeming to curl around her like the rib cage of some long-dead beast.

She hung up before the call could ring through.

She pressed the Samsung to her lips and thought for a time. Then she set it on the floor, rose, and walked out.

She took nothing. She didn't bother to lock the door behind her.

She wouldn't be coming back.

76
SOMETHING FLAT
AND UNCHANGING

Van Sciver reclined on his bed in the ICU, his face washed of color. A gray sweat layered his flesh as he dozed, his eyelids flickering. A urinary catheter threaded between his legs. A monitor read his heart rate, oxygen saturation, respiratory rate, blood pressure, and half a dozen other vitals. A central line on the left side of his chest fed in nutrition and vitamins from a bright yellow bag of TPN.

It was a private room, the curtains pulled around to shield his bed from the glass walls and door.

In one hand he clutched his Samsung.

It chimed, awakening him.

The Signal application. Was it Candy, finally back in contact?

Weakly, he raised the phone to his unshaven cheek. "Code," he said.

Orphan X's voice said, "Behind you."

The words came at Van Sciver in stereo.

Through the phone, yes. But also from inside the room.

Evan stepped into view, let the Samsung slide from his hand onto the sheets. Van Sciver stared at him, mouth open, jaw slightly askew.

Evan lifted Van Sciver's personal Samsung from his frail clutch.

Finding him hadn't been easy. But it hadn't been hard either.

Without immediate surgical intervention and repair, an injury to the superior mesenteric artery compromised blood flow, which in turn meant that the patient usually lost most of the small bowel to necrosis.

Small-bowel transplants were rare and donors rarer yet, but given Van Sciver's resources, he'd know how to get himself to the top of the list. Due to the severity of the injury, he would not have been able to travel far. The UCLA Medical Center was the only adult small-bowel transplant center in the Greater Los Angeles Area.

Without Joey around to help, it had taken some doing for Evan to hack into UCLA's Epic medical-records system, but when he had, he'd found an anonymous patient admitted on December 4, two weeks back, who showed no health-care history.

Evan eased forward so Van Sciver could

see him without straining.

"I did go back for Joey," Evan said. "And that does make us different. You know what else makes us different? You're in that bed now. And I'm standing." He held up an empty syringe. "With this."

Van Sciver peered up helplessly. His hand fished in the rumpled sheets and emerged with the call button. His thumb clicked it a few times.

"I disconnected it," Evan told him. "Then I watched you sleep for a while."

Through gaps in the curtain, they could see doctors and nurses passing by, their faces lowered to charts. Evan knew that Van Sciver wouldn't cry out for help. Help would come too late, and he had too much pride for that anyway.

Van Sciver's features grew lax, defeated. A milky starburst showed in that blown pupil, floating like a distant galaxy.

Evan reached over and crimped the tube feeding the central line, stopping the flow of fluorescent yellow nutrition into Van Sciver's chest.

"You killed Jack to get to me," Evan said. "Congratulations. You got your wish."

He slid the needle into the tube above the crimp, closer to Van Sciver's body.

Together they watched the air bubble

creep along the line, nearing Van Sciver's chest. It would ride his central vein into his heart, causing an embolism. The dot of air inched along, ever closer.

Van Sciver's face settled with resignation. He said, "It is what it is and that's all that it is."

"No," Evan said, "it's more than that."

The air bubble slipped through the line into Van Sciver's chest.

A moment later he shuddered.

His left eye dilated, at last matching the right.

The symphony of beeps and hums from the monitor changed their melody into something flat and unchanging.

When doctors and nurses crashed into the room, they found the motionless body and no one else.

77
ORIGINAL S.W.A.T.

She remembered two rough men minding her in the darkness, one scented of soap and sweat, the other moving through a haze of cigarette smoke and wintergreen tobacco. And there was a hospital room that was not in a hospital and a doctor or two drifting through the miasma of her drugged thoughts.

Now she looked out her dorm window onto the stunning view beyond — Lake Lugano and the snowcapped Alps. It was an English-speaking school filled with affluent kids, a demographic to which she supposed she now belonged. Seven hundred ninety-three students from sixty-two countries speaking forty different languages.

A good pot to melt into and disappear.

Her passport and papers had her at eighteen years old, a legal adult, so she could oversee her own affairs. Her cover was thorough and backstopped. She'd been recently orphaned, set up with a trust fund that released like a widening faucet, a little more money every year. She was repeating coursework here after some understandable emotional difficulties given the fresh loss of her parents. She'd pick up courses at the second semester, which began in a few weeks.

The campus was spectacular, the resources seemingly unlimited. There was a downhill-ski team and horseback riding and kickboxing, though she'd have to be careful if she chose to indulge in the last.

She was due to matriculate today, a simple ceremony. Her roommate, an unreasonably lovely Dutch teenager, was coming to fetch her at any minute.

She set her foot on her bed and leaned over it, stretching the scar tissue. The last thing she'd remembered before going out was looking up at Evan, his hand over her leg, holding her blood in her veins.

Holding her tight enough to keep her alive.

They could never see each other again. Given who he was, it was too risky, and he was unwilling to put her in harm's way.

But he had given her this.

He had given her the world.

She pulled open the window and breathed in the air, fresher than any she'd ever tasted.

There was a knock at her door.

She opened it, expecting Sara, but instead it was the school porter, a kindly man with chapped cheeks. He handed her a rectangular box wrapped in plain brown paper and said, in gently accented English, "This came for you, Ms. Vera."

"Thank you, Calvin."

She took it over to the bed and sat. The package bore no return address. Postage imprints indicated that it had traveled through various mail-forwarding services.

She tore back the brown wrapping and saw that it was a wide shoe box. Lettered on the lid: ORIGINAL S.W.A.T. BOOTS.

Her heart changed its movement inside her chest.

She opened the shoe box's lid.

Inside, dozens and dozens of sealed envelopes formed razor-neat rows.

With a trembling hand, she lifted the first one.

On the front, written in precise block lettering: OPEN NOW.

She ran a finger beneath the envelope flap and slid out an undecorated card. She opened it.

Inside, the same block lettering.

IT'S YOUR FIRST DAY. TRY NOT TO SCREW IT

UP TOO BAD.

X

Her hand had moved to her mouth. She stared at the words and then over at the box of envelopes. The next one up said CHRIST-MAS.

As she slipped the card back into the envelope, she noticed some lettering on the back.

Y.A.S.

Y.A.L.

It took a moment for the meaning to drop. These were the words she'd overheard that young father speak to his newborn in the park the day she'd wandered by, bleeding from one ear.

You are safe.

You are loved.

Another knock sounded, and she wiped at her eyes.

Sara's gentle voice carried through the door. "Are you ready?"

Joey slid the shoe box beneath her bed and rose.

"Yeah," she said. "I am."

78
WORTH THE TRYING

As Evan crossed the lobby of Castle Heights, Lorilee looked up from her mail slot and caught his eye. She was alone. She smiled at him, and the smile held deeper meaning.

He nodded, accepting her thanks.

He neared the security desk across from the elevator. "Twenty-one, please, Joaquin."

Joaquin looked up, his security hat tilted. "Hey, Mr. Smoak. Haven't seen you in a while."

Evan grimaced. "Sales conferences."

"Livin' for the weekend."

"You got that right."

A voice floated from behind Evan. "Twelfth floor, too, Joaquin."

"Sure thing, Mrs. Hall."

Evan held the elevator doors, and Mia slipped past him, her curly hair brushing his cheek.

The doors closed, and they regarded each other.

He tried not to notice the birthmark at her temple. The line of her neck. Her bottom lip.

"Sales conferences." She smirked. "Ever wonder which identity is the real one?"

He said, "Lately."

And now that full grin broke across her face, the one he felt in his spinal cord. "How are you, Evan? Really, how are you?"

"Good. I'm good."

And he was.

At long last Charles Van Sciver was wiped off the books. All that remained of him was the Samsung in the right front pocket of Evan's cargo pants, pressing against his thigh.

Other matters had been put to rest as well.

Benito Orellana's next credit-card bill would show a balance of zero, the medical debts from his wife's illness settled in full. He would still have his primary mortgage, but the second lender who had nailed him with a predatory rate had been paid off. An unfortunate glitch in the same lender's system had led to the disappearance of a six-figure chunk from the escrow account.

This morning the McClair Children's Mental Health Center in Richmond had received an anonymous donation that happened to match the six-figure chunk that had gone missing from the escrow account. The money had been earmarked for improving living conditions, quality of care, and the security system.

It could also pay for a lot of Lego Snowspeeders.

The package of letters that Evan had sent would have arrived today, helping kick off a new life for a sixteen-year-old girl an ocean away.

Jack had always taught Evan that the hard part wasn't being a killer. The hard part was staying human. He was superb at the former. And growing proficient at the latter.

It was worth the trying.

"I'm sad it didn't work out between us like we hoped," Mia said.

"Me, too."

"Peter misses you. I miss you, too."

Evan thought about a different life in which he could have been another man for them. For himself.

"I have to look out for him," Mia said. "No matter what I might want for myself, I have to protect him at all costs."

Evan said, "I get it."

She tilted her head, seemingly moved. "Do you?"

"Yes," he said. "I do."

The doors opened at the twelfth floor, and Mia got out. She turned and faced him, as if she wanted to say something else, though there was nothing else to say.

He knew the feeling.

The doors slid shut between them.

He rode to his floor, entered the penthouse. He went immediately to the freezer and removed the walnut chest. Opening the hand-blown glass bottle, he poured himself two fingers of Stoli Elit: Himalayan Edition, at about a hundred bucks a finger.

He'd earned it.

The penthouse felt vast and empty. A ring remained on the counter from Joey's OJ glass. He'd have to scrub it in the morning. He thought about the mess of gear awaiting him in the Vault, a mirror for the exquisite complexities inside Joey's head. The equipment would take days to untangle.

He paused at the base of the spiral staircase. Her absence flowed down from the loft, a stillness in the air. He found himself listening for the clack of her speed cube. Or the bump of a kite against his bedroom window.

But now there would only be quiet.

Drifting to the floor-to-ceiling windows, he let the first sip burn its way down his throat, exquisite and cleansing. He looked out at all those apartments on vertical display. Families were beginning to light up their Christmas trees.

He heard Jack's voice in his ear: *I love you, son.*

Evan raised his glass in a toast. "Copy that," he said.

Only once he'd finished the two fingers of vodka, only once he'd washed and dried the glass and set it back in its place in the cupboard did he remove Van Sciver's Samsung from his pocket.

He read the last texted exchange from December 4 yet again.

VS: AFTER I GET X, CAN THE GIRL LIVE?

And the reply: NO ONE LIVES.

The sender of the response was coded as *DR.*

Dark Road.

It was amazing that someone so high up would risk so much because of a mission Evan had carried out nineteen years ago. He didn't know where the tendrils of that job culminated, but he intended to follow them. They led, no doubt, to the farthest reaches of power. That's where the darkness was. And the gold.

He'd raised the question himself, to Joey: *How much is regime change worth? A well-*

placed bullet can change the direction of a nation. Tip the balance of power so a country's interests align with ours.

He had fired a number of such bullets in his lifetime. Maybe the round he'd let fly in 1997 had been one of them.

Clearly he'd been a link in a chain, and he would devote himself now to discerning the contours of that chain, to seeing just how far up it stretched.

He stared at that text once again: NO ONE LIVES.

He had something else to devote himself to as well.

He crossed to the kitchen island where the red notebook waited. He flipped it open, that scrawl standing out in relief where Joey had shaded the page.

"6-1414 Dark Road 32."

A switchboard. A code word. An extension.

He took out his RoamZone.

And he dialed.

On the Resolute desk, the middle of the three black phones rang.

President Bennett was not sitting there waiting.

He remained on the couch alone, holding a glass of Premier Cru Bordeaux in his famously steady hand.

No sweat sparkling at his graying temples. His breath slow and steady. The past few weeks would have reduced a lesser man to a stressed-out wreck, but he was Jonathan Bennett and his body obeyed his will.

He crossed the Oval Office and lifted the receiver.

He said nothing.

A voice said, "You should have left 1997 in the past."

Bennett gave his allotted two-second pause and then said, "If you look into it, I will crush you."

Orphan X saw Bennett's two seconds and raised him a few more. Then he said, "I think you misunderstand the purpose of this call, Mr. President. Looking into it is not good enough for me."

"What does that mean?" Bennett said, only now realizing he'd rushed his response.

The disembodied voice said, "You greenlit Jack Johns's death. And the girl's death. And so many others."

Bennett reseated his eyeglasses on the bridge of his nose, which felt suddenly moist. "I'm listening."

Orphan X said, "This is me greenlighting yours."

The phone clicked, the line severed.

Bennett breathed and breathed again. He placed the phone receiver back in its cradle. He circled the Resolute desk, sat down, and set his hands on the blotter.

They were shaking.

ACKNOWLEDGMENTS

Despite his propensity for operating alone, Evan Smoak gets a lot of air support. I owe a slew of thanks to my team and to my advisers.

I am privileged to have an exceptional crew at Minotaur Books. Thanks to Keith Kahla, Andrew Martin, Hannah Braaten, Hector DeJean, Jennifer Enderlin, Paul Hochman, Kelley Ragland, Sally Richardson, and Martin Quinn.

And to Rowland White and his team at Michael Joseph/Penguin Group UK, as well as my other foreign publishers who have deployed Evan around the world.

And to my representatives — Lisa Erbach Vance and Aaron Priest of the Aaron Priest Agency; Caspian Dennis of the Abner Stein Agency; Trevor Astbury, Rob Kenneally, Peter Micelli, and Michelle Weiner of Creative Artists Agency; Marc H. Glick of Glick & Weintraub; and Stephen F. Breimer of

Bloom, Hergott, Diemer et al.

And to my subject-matter experts — Geoff Baehr (hacking), Philip Eisner (early-warning system), Dana Kaye (propaganda), Dr. Bret Nelson and Dr. Melissa Hurwitz (medical), Billy S_____ (_____), Maureen Sugden (IQ), Jake Wetzel (cubing), and Rollie White (geography).

And my family. In the words of the Beach Boys, patron saints of the sun-kissed and the charmed: God only knows what I'd be without you.

ABOUT THE AUTHOR

Gregg Hurwitz is the *New York Times* bestselling author of more than fifteen novels, including *The Nowhere Man*. His novels have been shortlisted for numerous literary awards, graced top ten lists, and have been published in 30 languages. He is also a *New York Times* bestselling comic book writer, having penned stories for Marvel (Wolverine, Punisher) and DC (Batman, Penguin). Additionally, he's written screenplays for or sold spec scripts to many of the major studios (*The Book of Henry*), and written, developed, and produced television for various networks. Gregg resides in Los Angeles.

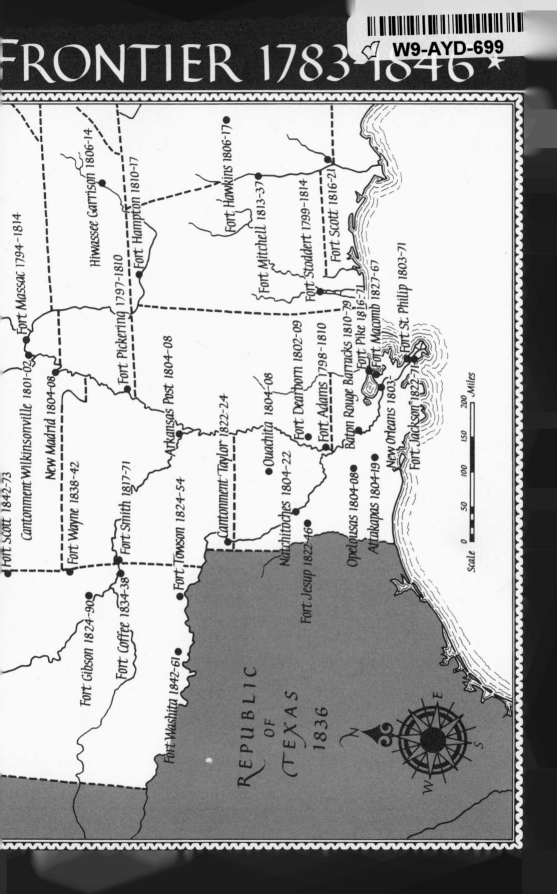

FRONTIER 1783–1846 ★

W9-AYD-699

Fort Hawkins 1806-17

Hiwassee Garrison 1806-14

Fort Hampton 1810-17

Fort Mitchell 1813-37

Fort Stoddert 1799-1814

Fort Scott 1816-21

Fort Massac 1794-1814

Fort Pickering 1797-1810

Fort St. Philip 1803-71

Fort Pike 1816-71

Fort Macomb 1827-67

Fort Jackson 1822-71

Cantonment Wilkinsonville 1801-02

New Madrid 1804-08

Arkansas Post 1804-08

Fort Dearborn 1802-09

Fort Adams 1798-1810

Baton Rouge Barracks 1810-79

New Orleans 1803-

Fort Scott 1842-73

Fort Wayne 1836-42

Fort Smith 1817-71

Cantonment Taylor 1822-24

Ouachita 1804-08

Natchitoches 1804-22

Opelousas 1804-08

Attakapas 1804-19

Fort Gibson 1824-90

Fort Coffee 1834-38

Fort Towson 1824-54

Fort Jesup 1822-46

Fort Washita 1842-61

REPUBLIC OF TEXAS 1836

Scale 0 50 100 150 200 Miles

N E S W

The Sword of the Republic

THE WARS OF THE UNITED STATES

Louis Morton, *General Editor*
DARTMOUTH COLLEGE

VOLUMES PUBLISHED

HISTORY OF THE UNITED STATES ARMY
Russell F. Weigley
TEMPLE UNIVERSITY

FRONTIERSMEN IN BLUE
The United States Army and the Indian, 1848–1865
Robert M. Utley
NATIONAL PARK SERVICE

PRESIDENT WILSON FIGHTS HIS WAR
World War I and the American Intervention
Harvey A. DeWeerd
THE RAND CORPORATION

THE SWORD OF THE REPUBLIC
The United States Army on the Frontier, 1783–1846
Francis Paul Prucha
MARQUETTE UNIVERSITY

VOLUMES IN PREPARATION

THE COLONIAL WARS
Douglas E. Leach
VANDERBILT UNIVERSITY

THE AMERICAN REVOLUTION
Don Higginbotham
LOUISIANA STATE UNIVERSITY

THE WAR OF 1812
R. A. Preston
ROYAL MILITARY COLLEGE OF CANADA
S. F. Wise
QUEENS UNIVERSITY (CANADA)

THE INDIAN WARS 1865–1890
Robert M. Utley
NATIONAL PARK SERVICE

THE MEXICAN WAR
Richard W. Van Alstyne
HENRY E. HUNTINGTON LIBRARY AND ART GALLERY

THE CIVIL WAR
Jay Luvaas
ALLEGHENY COLLEGE

BLOOD ON THE BORDER
The United States Army and the Mexican Irregulars
Clarence C. Clendenen
HOOVER INSTITUTION ON WAR, REVOLUTION, AND PEACE

WORLD WAR II (Pacific)
Louis Morton
DARTMOUTH COLLEGE

HISTORY OF AMERICAN MILITARY DOCTRINE
Fred Greene
WILLIAMS COLLEGE

HISTORY OF THE UNITED STATES AIR FORCE
James C. Olson
UNIVERSITY OF NEBRASKA

AMERICAN MILITARY INTERVENTIONS
Annette Baker Fox
INSTITUTE OF WAR AND PEACE STUDIES, COLUMBIA UNIVERSITY

HISTORY OF THE UNITED STATES NAVY
Raymond G. O'Connor
TEMPLE UNIVERSITY

THE SPANISH-AMERICAN WAR
J. A. S. Grenville
UNIVERSITY OF LEEDS
David Trask
STATE UNIVERSITY OF NEW YORK (STONY BROOK)

WORLD WAR II (Europe and Africa)
Hugh M. Cole
RESEARCH ANALYSIS CORPORATION

THE KOREAN WAR
Martin Blumenson

HISTORY OF THE UNITED STATES MARINES
Henry I. Shaw, Jr.
DEPARTMENT OF DEFENSE

THE
Sword of the Republic

THE UNITED STATES ARMY
ON THE FRONTIER
1783-1846

☆　　　☆

☆

by Francis Paul Prucha

The Macmillan Company

Collier-Macmillan Ltd., London

/ 3 / 2 7
9 3 7

FOR THE MEMBERS OF

John LaFarge House

☆ CONTENTS ☆

List of Maps

List of Illustrations

(following page 206)

Preface

THE years from 1783 to 1846 form a difficult period for historians of the United States Army because there wasn't much of an army and only occasionally was there any military action. The tendency in military histories is to jump from the Revolutionary War to the War of 1812 to the Mexican War, with perhaps a quick glance at the Black Hawk War and at the Seminole difficulties in Florida. The years between 1783 and 1812 are treated briefly as a time of beginnings only. The period from 1815 to 1846 is dismissed as "the thirty years' peace," or discussed in terms of the "professionalization" of the army, as West Point began to produce a corps of professional officers. To many it seems only a time of waiting and of preparation for some significant event.

Yet it was in these very years, 1783–1846, that the United States made good its claim to the region between the Appalachians and the Mississippi and then to the vast Louisiana Purchase. Through treaties of peace and purchase the United States had legally acquired the territory, but paper title had to be followed by physical occupation, and it was in this process that the regular army played a most significant role. The surge of expansionism and accompanying nationalism that marked these dramatic years owed a great deal to the small United States Army. The early challenge to American dominion in the Old Northwest made by the Indian nations, supported as they were by the British in their claim that the Ohio River must be the boundary between white settlement and Indian country, was met ultimately by military force at Fallen Timbers, Tippecanoe, and the Thames. American control of the fur trade and the subordination of the Indians to American, rather than British, jurisdiction depended upon the line of military posts at strategic points on the Great Lakes and the western rivers, forts that awed the Indians by their very existence and whose garrisons gave force to the pronouncements of the Indian agents, protected the factors and their stores, and enforced the Indian intercourse laws drawn up "to preserve peace on the frontiers." There can be no doubt that the sovereignty of the United States in the region northwest of the Ohio depended upon the presence of regular army troops.

South of the Ohio, as well, where Spanish claims extended north through the lands of the Cherokees, Creeks, Choctaws, and Chickasaws to the Tennessee or the Cumberland and where French dreams of a vast Mississippi valley empire had a strange way of recurring, the American troops secured the land by moving into the posts on the Mississippi and the Tombigbee finally evacuated by the Spanish. In the Louisiana Purchase, occupation and exploration (itself a prelude to firm possession) were the work of military men. The crumbling edges of the territory, where the influence of Spanish and British officials or traders weakened effective American power, were shored up by army endeavor.

The army men were not acting for themselves to set up the sort of military despotism that was so deeply feared, but as the instruments of the Congress and the President in vindicating American rights, in meeting or preventing challenges to American authority by Indian tribes or foreign powers, and in blunting the sharp edges of conflict as two races with diverse cultures met on the frontier. In the period of transition from wilderness to substantial settlement, the pioneer citizens could not always act effectively and often would not act justly. To maintain the honor of the nation, reliance had to be had on the regular army, not as the tool of one faction or another but (in the words of the first Secretary of War) as the "sword of the Republic," which alone was adequate to "guard a due administration of justice, and the preservation of the peace."

It was in bringing about these political effects that the United States Army was indispensably necessary. In a previous book, I argued that the important work of the army in the decades after the War of 1812 was its pioneering—its economic and social effects in the West, where by its own exertions it replaced the wilderness with the multifarious activities of a complex society and thus opened the way for orderly white settlement. I see now that this was too limited a view. The army men were policemen, farmers, roadbuilders, scientists, and lumbermen, true enough, but first of all they were agents of empire, who made possible the development of the American republic throughout the lands it now enjoys.

The United States almost failed to provide a usable military arm, for there were great qualms about a regular army, and everyone gave lip service to the principle that the defense of the nation rested on the militia. The history recounted in the following pages shows how far it was necessary to depart from these fine pronouncements and how fortunate the nation was that doctrinaire republican principles did not prevent the building of a regular army and its use on the frontier.

I have relied heavily on the pioneering work of others, as the footnotes and bibliography will make clear, but I have also used the innumerable sources, both private and official, which have been printed in great profusion. I am indebted, of course, to many for aid in researching and writing the book, but I wish to thank especially the staffs of the Harvard Library, the State Historical Society of Wisconsin, the Milwaukee Public Library, the Library of Congress, the National Archives, and the Marquette University Library. The book was completed while I held a Fellowship from the John Simon Guggenheim Memorial Foundation. A special word of appreciation is due, finally, to Louis Morton, the editor of the series in which this volume appears.

Marquette University   Francis Paul Prucha
January, 1968

☆ ONE ☆

Beginnings

THE regular army of the United States owed its existence to the American frontier. The American Revolution, it is true, had been fought and won in large part by the Continental troops, a kind of regular army, to whom were added a generous portion of militia.[1] But the republican principles dominant at the end of the war ruled against a standing army. It was only the exigencies of the Indian frontier that convinced the members of Congress to authorize a handful of regular troops, and in the decades that followed the Revolution it was the tiny regular army, augmented occasionally by additions of regular soldiers and enlarged now and then in times of crisis by state militia, that secured and maintained American sovereignty in the West in the face of Indian intransigence and the schemes of the British and the Spanish to limit the expansion of the new nation.[2]

The United States at the end of the Revolution inherited frontier problems whose magnitude Congress did not at first fully realize. The English colonists, coming to the New World in the seventeenth cen-

[1] The total number of soldiers furnished the Continental Army during the Revolution was 231,771; in addition there were an estimated 164,087 militia. Emory Upton, *The Military Policy of the United States* (Washington, 1917), p. 58.

[2] James R. Jacobs, *The Beginning of the U. S. Army, 1783–1812* (Princeton, 1947), pp. 3–39, gives a good account of the initial formation of the regular army. For an accurate and complete factual account of the legislation dealing with the army in the period of the Confederation, see Edgar B. Wesley, "The Military Policy of the Critical Period," *Coast Artillery Journal*, LXVIII (April, 1928), 281–290. Upton, *Military Policy*, gives data on the various changes in the "peace establishment" in the early period. Harry M. Ward, *The Department of War, 1781–1789* (Pittsburgh, 1962), is a thoroughly documented study of the early War Department and the work of its first secretaries.

tury, found scattered Indian tribes on the lands which the king had granted to them. These aborigines initially welcomed the white strangers and in the case of the Pilgrims gave them vital aid in establishing their settlement. It was not long, however, before conflicts arose between the two races, as the English settled upon the lands claimed by the Indians and as liquor and fraud entered into trading relations. The European powers claimed ultimate sovereignty over the New World by right of discovery, and although a possessory right of occupancy or right to the soil was generally conceded to the Indians (and frequently enough purchased from them), the Indians were pushed off the lands that the rapidly growing English population needed.

When international rivalries developed in North America among the British, French, and Spanish, the Indians often became pawns in the wars and diplomatic maneuvers of these European powers. Trade monopolies with the Indians were sought in order to bind the tribes in allegiance, so that in time of war their aid would be assured against the enemy. Political allegiance of the tribes, in turn, helped to guarantee that the furs from their regions would flow into the proper depots. Politically astute tribes, such as the Iroquois and the Creeks, balanced one European power against another for their own advantage, but in the long run the Indians, often weakened by internal factions and dissensions, were no match for the Europeans.

The British, successful in their struggle to drive the French from North America, faced a growing resentment from the Indians in the West, who feared encroachment on their lands. Pontiac's Conspiracy of 1763 convinced the British government that some sort of line between white settlement and Indian country had to be established, and by the Proclamation Line of 1763 it sought to delimit the westward advance of the colonists. The principle of an inviolate Indian country, which could not be reduced by private purchase but only by formal treaty between Indian nation and white nation and which could be entered only by persons licensed to do so, became the foundation on which the United States built its own relations with the tribes.

During the Revolution the antagonism of the Indians against white advance into their lands was transferred from the British to the Americans. Skillful British agents were easily able to convince the Indians that the king was their friend and protector and that it was the patriot colonists who threatened their lands and defrauded them in trade. With a few exceptions, the Indian nations sided with the British in the war. The military activity involving the Indians was largely limited to frontier skirmishes.

The Treaty of Paris, 1783, confirmed the American victory over Great Britain and set the Great Lakes, the Mississippi, and the thirty-first parallel as the boundaries of the American nation. It brought peace with Great Britain, but it did nothing about the Indian allies of the British. It was up to the Congress under the Articles of Confederation to make peace with the Indians as best it could. The United States thus found itself in possession of a huge western territory, claimed and occupied by Indian nations whose friendship and allegiance had yet to be established and into which fingers of white settlement were already probing. It discovered, furthermore, that the British in Canada were unwilling to give up their fur trade dominance in the Northwest, that they were holding on to their military posts within United States boundaries on Lake Champlain, and at Oswego, Niagara, Detroit, and Mackinac, and that through trade they continued to hold the allegiance of many Indians, whom they supported in a desire to make the Northwest a permanent Indian buffer state.

At the end of the Revolution, too, the Floridas were returned to Spain, thus cutting off the Trans-Appalachian region from the Gulf of Mexico and furnishing sites from which the southern Indians could be stirred up by anti-American agitation. New Orleans and the lands beyond the Mississippi were controlled by the same foreign power.

Not fully aware of the threats to American sovereignty in the West posed by these circumstances, or ignoring them, the victorious Americans set about to disband completely their regular military forces. On April 11, 1783, the Continental Congress approved a proclamation declaring the cessation of hostilities on land and sea.[3] Then began the discussion to decide what should be done with the soldiers still in uniform. Washington, knowing the eagerness of the troops to go home, hesitated at first to publish the proclamation, but he wisely decided to do so and ordered the proclamation read on April 19. His general orders pointed out to the soldiers, however, the distinction between the cessation of hostilities and a definitive declaration of peace, and he urged them to be faithful to the end. "Nothing now remains," he exhorted them in far from military rhetoric, "but for the actors of this mighty Scene to preserve a perfect, unvarying, consistency of character through the very last act; to close the Drama with applause; and to retire from the Military Theatre with the same approbation of Angells and men which have crowned all their former vertuous Actions." And he ordered an "extra ration of liquor to be issued to *every* man tomorrow,

[3] *Journals of the Continental Congress* (34 vols., Washington, 1904–1937), XXIV, 238–241.

to drink Perpetual Peace, Independence and Happiness to the United States of America."[4] In more worried tones he wrote to Congress asking for directions about the discharge of men who had been *"engaged for the War."*[5]

Washington's letter was referred to a special committee, and following its recommendations Congress resolved that the men's service expire only with the ratification of the definitive treaty of peace, but that the Commander in Chief at his own discretion could grant furloughs or discharges—a compromise, according to Madison, "between those who wished to get rid of the expence of keeping the men in the field, and those who thought it impolitic to disband the army whilst the British remained in the United States."[6] Washington was concerned about the frontier posts held by the British and to be evacuated by them according to the terms of the treaty. "The Posts should certainly be occupied by United States Troops, the Moment they are evacuated by the British," he wrote to Congress. "Should this be neglected, I have my fears, that they might be burned or destroyed by the Indians, or some other evil minded persons, whose disaffection to the Government of the United States may lead them to such Enormities."[7] Congress gave him authority to occupy the posts with troops enlisted for a three-year term whose service had not yet expired, but this was viewed as a temporary expedient until further determinations could be made.[8] There was little thought of keeping any sizable portion of the Continental Army in service as a regular peacetime army, and on October 18, 1783, all the federal troops who had enlisted to serve during the war and who had been furloughed at various times were absolutely discharged.[9] Only the men who had enlisted for a definite period of time remained.

With the slate wiped nearly clean of British and Revolutionary War military markings, Congress discussed patterns for the "Peace Establishment" of the new nation. There was a strong feeling, as Elbridge Gerry expressed it, that "standing armies in time of peace, are incon-

[4] General Orders, April 18, 1783, *The Writings of George Washington from the Original Manuscript Sources, 1745–1799*, ed. John C. Fitzpatrick (39 vols., Washington, 1931–1944), XXVI, 334–337.

[5] Washington to the President of Congress, April 18, 1783, *ibid.*, pp. 330–334.

[6] Resolution of April 23, 1783, *Journals of the Continental Congress*, XXIV, 269–270; Madison's notes for April 23 and May 20, 1783, *ibid.*, XXV, 963, 965–966.

[7] Washington to the President of Congress, May 3, 1783, *Writings of George Washington*, XXVI, 398–400.

[8] Resolution of May 12, 1783, *Journals of the Continental Congress*, XXIV, 337–338.

[9] Proclamation of October 18, 1783, *ibid.*, XXV, 703.

sistent with the principles of republican Governments, dangerous to the liberties of a free people, and generally converted into destructive engines for establishing despotism." An armed citizenry, to be called to service when crises arose, was to be the defense of the republic.[10]

To be sure, there were some voices that called for a regular army establishment in peacetime. Foremost among these was George Washington, who in response to a request from a committee of the Continental Congress of which Hamilton was chairman, drew up and sent to Congress on May 2, 1783, a detailed memoir which he called "Sentiments on a Peace Establishment."[11] Realizing the popular feeling against a regular army and in favor of the militia, Washington cautiously suggested no more than he thought feasible under the circumstances. He asked first of all for a regular force to garrison West Point and such other posts on the frontiers as were necessary "to awe the Indians, protect our Trade, prevent the encroachment of our Neighbours of Canada and the Florida's, and guard us at least from surprizes." He willingly admitted, good patriot that he was, that "a *large* standing Army in time of Peace hath ever been considered dangerous to the liberties of a Country," but a few, he insisted, were not only safe but indispensable. He asked for a modest total force of 1,908 infantry and 723 artillery. To justify such a number he pointed to the power of the British in Canada, the great extent of the frontiers, and the "numerous, soured and jealous" Indian tribes, to whom it would be wise to appear respectable as the nation began to treat with them. He was thinking, of course, in terms of an immediate transfer of British posts on American soil to United States garrisons, and he drew up a list of sites to be garrisoned from the Great Lakes in the northwest to the frontiers of the Carolinas and Georgia on the south. He was especially concerned about the adequate garrisoning of West Point, which he considered the "key of America." The soldiers he enumerated were to be Continental troops, who looked to Congress, not to the states, for their orders and their support. He hoped to construct the army to begin with out of the three-year men still in service, and in a burst of optimism repeatedly belied by subsequent events he predicted, "When the Soldiers for the War have frolicked a while among their friends, and find they must have recourse to hard labour for a livelyhood, I am persuaded numbers of them will reinlist upon almost any Terms."

[10] *Ibid.*, XXVII, 518–519.
[11] The document is printed in *Writings of George Washington*, XXVI, 374–398.

In the second place, Washington asked for a well-organized militia that would be uniform throughout the nation, premised on the principle that every citizen who enjoys the protection of a free government owes his personal service to defend it. He outlined a detailed proposal for enrolling, training, and organizing the militia.[12] As additional parts of his peace establishment, Washington recommended arsenals for military stores and academies for instruction in military arts (especially engineering and artillery).

Washington conferred with the committee and submitted remarks on matters of pay and the organization of the troops, and on October 23 and 24, 1783, Hamilton's report was considered in Congress.[13] The report was substantially the same as Washington's, although it called for four regiments of infantry with a total strength of 2,404 and a corps of engineers (artillery) of 630, plus a corps of artificers.

Congress took no action to carry out these intelligent plans. The discharging of the men from the army had continued steadily; on January 3, 1784, Major General Henry Knox, who had succeeded Washington as Commander in Chief, reported to Congress that only about 620 men remained in service.[14] Even these were soon disposed of, for on June 2, 1784, succumbing to fears of the dangers of a standing army, Congress ordered the discharge of the fragment of soldiers still left in service, except for twenty-five men at Fort Pitt and fifty-five at West Point to guard the military stores. No officers above the rank of captain were to remain in service.[15]

☆

From this nadir, however, Congress immediately began to build up a new military force under federal direction, for the realities of national

[12] Russell F. Weigley, *Towards an American Army: Military Thought from Washington to Marshall* (New York, 1962), pp. 11–14, points out that what Washington had in mind for the militia force was a far cry from the untrained, undisciplined, and poorly led troops that actually were resorted to in recurring times of crisis. He discusses the ideas behind the formation of a regular army on pages 1–29.

[13] *Journals of the Continental Congress*, XXV, 549–551, 722–745. Hamilton's report is reprinted in *The Papers of Alexander Hamilton*, ed. Harold C. Syrett and Jacob E. Cooke (11 vols. to date. New York, 1961–), III, 378–397. These editors date the report June 18, 1783, at which time they believe it was initially submitted to Congress; see note, p. 378.

[14] Knox to the President of Congress, January 3, 1784, Papers of George Washington, Library of Congress.

[15] *Journals of the Continental Congress*, XXVII, 513–524.

existence called for order and protection in the West, which even the republican-minded delegates could not ignore. Still believing that the British posts would soon be evacuated, Congress on June 3, 1784, asked the states for 700 men to garrison these posts, to protect the northwestern frontier, and to guard the public stores. Of these troops, 165 were to come from Connecticut, a like number from New York, 110 from New Jersey, and 260 from Pennsylvania. They were to be taken from the militia of those states and were to serve for one year unless sooner discharged. These semifederal troops were organized into one regiment, comprising eight companies of infantry and two companies of artillery.[16] The command of this "First American Regiment" fell to Lieutenant Colonel Josiah Harmar of Pennsylvania, since his state furnished the largest contingent of troops. Other states, in fact, produced very few men. The New Jersey corps was recruited and sent to assist the commissioners who were treating with the Indians at Fort Stanwix in New York. But Connecticut's quota was raised too late to help with the Indian conferences in 1784 and was discharged early in April, 1785; New York did not recruit a single man.[17]

The incipient army stood guard at West Point and at Fort Pitt and furnished protection for the commissioners who went to Fort McIntosh in January, 1785, to treat with the Wyandots, Delawares, Chippewas, and Ottawas for a cession of land.[18] The post, built in the autumn of 1778 thirty miles down the Ohio from Pittsburgh, had been abandoned at the end of the Revolution, and now Harmar sent troops to reestablish it. They found the post dilapidated, and Harmar reported that emigrants to Kentucky had "destroyed the gates, drawn all the nails from the roofs, taken off all the boards, and plundered it of every article."[19]

The Treaty of Fort McIntosh, signed on January 21, 1785, was an indication of the hope of the Continental Congress to resolve the Indian difficulties by postwar treaties with the tribes. Working on the premise that the Indians had forfeited their rights to their lands because they had supported the British in the Revolution, the United States called the

16 Resolution of June 3, 1784, *ibid.*, pp. 530–540.
17 John K. Mahon, "Pennsylvania and the Beginnings of the Regular Army," *Pennsylvania History*, XXI (January, 1954), 33–44, is a good article about the formation of the first regiment.
18 The treaty was signed January 21, 1785. Charles J. Kappler, ed., *Indian Affairs: Laws and Treaties* (2 vols., Washington, 1904), II, *Treaties*, 6–8.
19 Harmar to John Dickinson, December 5, 1784, and February 8, 1785, in Consul W. Butterfield, ed., *Journal of Capt. Jonathan Heart . . .* [and] *Dickinson-Harmar Correspondence of 1784-5* (Albany, 1885), pp. 47, 58. A history of the post is given in Louis E. Graham, "Fort McIntosh," *Western Pennsylvania Historical Magazine*, XV (May, 1932), 93–119.

nations to sign treaties by which the United States "gave" the Indians peace and allowed them to keep large tracts of land they still claimed as theirs. The language of the report of a committee on Indian affairs of October 15, 1783, indicated a naïveté toward the Indians that was soon to be dispelled by the harsh facts of frontier warfare. The Indians were to be informed that because they "could not be restrained from acts of hostility and wanton devastation, but were determined to join their arms to those of Great Britain and to share their fortunes," they now might well be "compelled to retire beyond the lakes." The American people in their generosity were willing, however, to "draw a veil over what is passed" and to establish a boundary line that would allow the Indians to keep their lands west of the Great Miami River.[20] The Treaty of Fort McIntosh set a boundary line through the middle of Ohio and "allotted" the lands to the Indians beyond the line, promising at the same time to withdraw protection from any American citizens attempting to settle on them.

From Fort McIntosh the colonel sent out detachments to disperse settlers who had settled illegally on the northern side of the Ohio, but he could hardly keep pace with the influx. "The number of settlers farther down the river is very considerable," he wrote to the President of Congress on May 1, 1785, "and, from all accounts, daily increasing." He could sweep the area for a distance of 120 to 150 miles from Fort McIntosh, but no farther, and he sought authority to establish a post at a more suitable spot down the Ohio. When Congress authorized a post between the Muskingum and the Great Miami, Harmar in October, 1785, sent Captain John Doughty with a company of artillery and Captain Jonathan Heart's company of infantry to build a new fort at the mouth of the Muskingum, about 140 miles below Fort McIntosh. He expected that the new post, called Fort Harmar, would be in a good position to exclude intruders on the public lands, protect the surveyors of the Seven Ranges, and convince the Indians that Congress meant to protect legal settlers on the lands that had been ceded by treaty.[21]

Harmar was now dealing with Henry Knox, for on March 8, 1785, Congress elected the general as Secretary of War, at an annual salary of $2,400, with authorization for three clerks and a messenger. On him, with the meager support of his office staff and a tiny army of ill-trained

[20] Report of October 15, 1783, *Journals of the Continental Congress*, XXV, 684–686.
[21] Harmar to President of Congress, May 1, 1785, and Harmar to Knox, October 22, 1785, Butterfield, *Journal of Capt. Jonathan Heart*, pp. 65–66, 92–94.

troops furnished by the states, rested the burden of garrisoning the West, of protecting settlers, and above all in his mind, of maintaining the honor of the United States by just and humane dealings with the Indian tribes.[22]

In the midst of Harmar's activity in the West, the terms of the one-year men called for in June, 1784, began to expire, but conditions on the frontier, where treaties with the Indians were being negotiated, would not permit another complete disbandment. Congress, accordingly, in the first two weeks of April, 1785, authorized the raising of 700 troops, this time for a three-year term, "for the protection of the northwestern frontiers, to defend the settlers on the land belonging to the United States, from the depredations of the Indians, and to prevent unwarrantable intrusions thereon, and for guarding the public stores." The allotments to the various states were the same as in the previous year's legislation, but the three-year term of service and the crossing out of the original resolution of the words "from their militia" signaled the real beginning of a regular army, small as it was.[23]

Harmar had hoped, and no doubt this was the mind of Congress, too, that many of the one-year men could be persuaded to reenlist, so that the whole army would not have to be recruited anew. In this he was disappointed. Despite all his exertions, he could not retain men in service who lacked "confidence in the public respecting their pay" and who were eager to return to their homes in the East. Of the four companies of Pennsylvania troops only seventy effective men were reengaged.[24] This company, just barely scraped together in time, was dispatched with Captain Walter Finney in late September, 1785, to the mouth of the Miami River, where a temporary post was built (Fort Finney) and a treaty signed with the Shawnees on January 31, 1786, which was written in much the same language as that drawn up at Fort McIntosh.[25] Soon thereafter troops under Captain John F. Hamtramck were sent to protect

[22] The work of Knox as Secretary of War is discussed in Ward, *The Department of War.* For a full biography of Knox, see North Callahan, *Henry Knox: General Washington's General* (New York, 1958). An older biography, useful for documents it contains, is Noah Brooks, *Henry Knox: A Soldier of the Revolution* (New York, 1900). During the period of the Confederation Knox's official title was Secretary at War.

[23] Resolutions of April 1, 7, and 12, 1785, *Journals of the Continental Congress,* XXVIII, 223–224, 239–241, 247–248.

[24] Harmar to Dickinson, September 1, 1785, Butterfield, *Journal of Capt. Jonathan Heart,* p. 85; "Military Journal of Major Ebenezer Denny," *Memoirs of the Historical Society of Pennsylvania,* VII (1860), 260.

[25] Harmar to Knox, October 22, 1785, Butterfield, *Journal of Capt. Jonathan Heart,* p. 92; Kappler, *Treaties,* pp. 16–17.

the surveyors, and during the winter they built Fort Steuben on the right bank of the Ohio about forty-five miles below Fort McIntosh. The small western army, recruited with difficulty and short of pay and clothing, played a game of leapfrog with the forts it established down the Ohio, trying to keep up with the settlers who floated down the river. Captain Finney evacuated his fort at the mouth of the Miami River on August 12, 1786, and moved his troops down the river a few miles below Louisville, where on August 23 the men began to build a new Fort Finney on the north bank of the Ohio about three-quarters of a mile above the rapids.[26]

Then special problems on the Wabash called for the extension of federal troops into that valley. The French settlers at Vincennes were endangered by Indian raids, and expeditions of Kentucky militia moving across the Ohio to tangle with the Indians only added to the problems, for the troops were unruly and little likely to pacify the Indians. An unauthorized expedition of 1,200 Kentucky militia under George Rogers Clark moved up the Wabash in 1786, but some of the troops mutinied and provisions ran out, forcing Clark to establish a post at Vincennes and make a shaky truce with the Indians. Alarmed by the dangers inherent in such a situation, the Virginia Council reprimanded Clark for raising recruits, establishing a garrison, and impressing supplies without express authority and ordered him back to Virginia to explain his actions.[27]

The intrusion of such parties into the area north of the Ohio presented a grave challenge to the authority of the United States, which Secretary of War Knox was quick to realize. Such usurpation, he reported to Congress, more than any other factor was likely to prevent "the great national advantages resulting from a wise administration of the western territory." He insisted that unless such seizures were nipped in the bud, future attempts to remove intruders would be impossible. Only Colonel Harmar's federal troops on the Ohio would be able to correct the evils, and Knox asked for authority to employ the army for that purpose. Congress concurred on April 24, 1787, and a movement of troops to Vincennes got under way.[28]

[26] "Diary of Major Erkuries Beatty, Paymaster of the Western Army, May 15, 1786, to June 5, 1787," *Magazine of American History*, I (April, 1877), 239, 241, (June, 1877), 382.

[27] Gayle Thornbrough, ed., *Outpost on the Wabash, 1787–1791* (*Indiana Historical Society Publications*, No. 19, Indianapolis, 1957), pp. 14–16; Leonard C. Helderman, "The Northwest Expedition of George Rogers Clark, 1786–1787," *Mississippi Valley Historical Review*, XXV (December, 1938), 317–334.

[28] Report of Knox, April 19, 1787, *Journals of the Continental Congress*, XXXII, 222; Resolution of April 24, 1787, *ibid.*, 231.

In arranging his troops on the upper Ohio, Harmar withdrew the soldiers from Fort Pitt, sent a company under Captain Heart up the Allegheny to Venango, and left sixteen men at Fort McIntosh, sixty men at Wheeling to protect the surveyors, and parts of two companies at Fort Harmar. Fort Steuben was abandoned altogether. The rest of his men (only 329) he concentrated at the rapids of the Ohio.[29] From there Harmar moved on to Vincennes, where at the end of July he established a post called Fort Knox. Leaving the new post in command of Major Hamtramck with ninety-five men, he returned to Fort Harmar.[30]

☆

Congress could not ignore the news of Indian difficulties on the frontier. A special committee considering the reports from the war office declared that if speedy measures were not taken to counteract the movements of the Indians, the war would become general, and the committee urged the necessity of immediately augmenting the regular army —"not only for the protection and support of the frontiers of the states, bordering on the western territory and the valuable settlements on and near the margin of the Mississippi, but to establish the possession and facilitate the surveying and selling of those intermediate lands which have been so much relied upon for the reduction of the debts of the United States." On the recommendation of the committee, Congress authorized the raising of 1,340 noncommissioned officers and privates to be added to the 700 already provided for. These new troops were to serve for three years and were apportioned among the states as follows: infantry and artillery from Massachusetts 660, from New Hampshire 260, from Connecticut 180, from Rhode Island 120; cavalry from Maryland and Virginia, 60 each. Congress resolved unanimously that these states "use their utmost exertions, to raise the quotas of troops respectively assigned them, with all possible expedition."[31]

Knox and Congress no doubt also had in mind the disturbances in

[29] Harmar to Knox, June 7, 1787, William Henry Smith, *The St. Clair Papers: The Life and Public Services of Arthur St. Clair* (2 vols., Cincinnati, 1882), II, 22–23.

[30] Harmar to Knox, November 24, 1787, Thornbrough, *Outpost on the Wabash*, pp. 46–57. This book, which reprints correspondence from the Harmar Papers, gives a good picture of life at Fort Knox. See also Milo M. Quaife, ed., "Fort Knox Orderly Book, 1793–97," *Indiana Magazine of History*, XXXII (June, 1936), 137–169. A brief biography of Hamtramck is F. Clever Bald, "Colonel John Francis Hamtramck," *ibid.*, XLIV (December, 1948), 335–354.

[31] *Journals of the Continental Congress*, XXXI, 891–893.

Massachusetts known as Shays's Rebellion. Writing to Washington on October 23, 1786, after he had returned from a quick trip to Boston and Springfield, Knox said in speaking about the new authorization for troops: "This measure is important, and will tend to strengthen the principles of government, if necessary, as well as to defend the frontiers. I mention the idea of strengthening government as confidential. But the State of Massachusetts requires the greatest assistance, and Congress are fully impressed with the importance of supporting her with great exertion."[32]

Such was the state of affairs under the Articles of Confederation, however, that of the new authorization only two companies of artillery from Massachusetts saw extended service, for on April 9, 1787, Congress assigned these troops to guard the military stores at Springfield and ordered all others discharged and further enlistments stopped. The Massachusetts troops, unhappy that they alone were required to serve, deserted in large numbers.[33]

In the summer of 1787 Knox reported about 500 men in service, considerably short of the number authorized and too few for the demands made upon them to cover the surveyors, prevent intrusions on the public lands, and protect the frontier inhabitants. Knox requested at least 1,500 men for these purposes. For want of such a force, he told Congress, "the public designs and interests languish—the Subjects of Spain have been plundered—And the whole western territory is liable to be wrested out of the hands of the Union, by lawless adventurers, or by the savages whose imperfect perceptions render them unable to distinguish between the aforesaid description of persons, and the regular authority of the United States." The troops Knox would distribute in a chain of posts along the frontier, hoping thereby to overawe the savages and thus keep them at peace, for in the "embarrassed state of public affairs and entire deficiency of funds" an Indian war would be disastrous.[34]

Congress paid no attention to his request, and as the year drew toward a close, Knox began to worry about what would happen to the small army he then had when the term of service of the three-year enlistees of 1785 ran out. These troops had been disciplined to some

[32] Brooks, *Henry Knox*, p. 196. See also the discussion in Wesley, *Coast Artillery Journal*, LXVIII, 287–288.

[33] Resolution of April 9, 1787, *Journals of the Continental Congress*, XXXII, 158–159; Knox to the President of Congress, September 26, 1787, *ibid.*, XXXIII, 544–545.

[34] Knox to Congress, July 10, 1787, Clarence E. Carter, ed., *The Territorial Papers of the United States* (26 vols., Washington, 1934–1962), II, 31–34.

extent and had acquired knowledge of the western country, and Knox persuaded Congress to renew the authorization on October 3, 1787. The 700 men, together with the two companies of artillery raised under the resolution of October 20, 1786, were organized into one infantry regiment of eight companies and one artillery battalion of four companies. Knox and Congress hoped by reenlisting many of the old troops to save the expense of transporting new companies to the distant frontier.[35]

☆

The weakness of the United States under the Articles of Confederation—what Knox referred to as the "imbecillity of government"—was soon to be corrected by the Constitution, drawn up and debated in Philadelphia while Harmar was trying to spread his thin line of troops in some effective sort of pattern in the West. The new instrument of government clearly gave Congress the power to raise and to support an army without begging the states for troops, but it reopened a vigorous debate about standing armies in a republic in times of peace. Against those who opposed ratification of the Constitution because it did not expressly prohibit standing armies, Alexander Hamilton in *The Federalist* offered extensive arguments. He went to great lengths to show that there was no danger to liberty, and he pointed to the necessity of at least a few professional soldiers. He cast aside the idea that militia alone could be the bulwark of the nation. "The steady operations of war against a regular and disciplined army," he argued, pointing for confirmation to the recent experience of the Revolution, "can only be successfully conducted by a force of the same kind." And he added, "War, like most other things, is a science to be acquired and perfected by diligence, by perseverance, by time, and by practice."[36] But aside from these professional considerations on the art of war, what Hamilton noted about the needs of the West were well borne out in the subsequent history of the nation. In *The Federalist* No. 24 Hamilton wrote:

> Previous to the revolution, and even since the peace, there has been a constant necessity for keeping small garrisons on our western frontier. No person can doubt that these will continue to be indis-

[35] *Journals of the Continental Congress*, XXXIII, 544–545, 596–597, 602–604.
[36] The Federalist No. 25, in Jacob E. Cooke, ed., *The Federalist* (Middletown, Conn., 1961), p. 162.

pensible, if it should only be against the ravages and depredations of the Indians. These garrisons must either be furnished by occasional detachments from the militia, or by permanent corps in the pay of the government. The first is impracticable; and if practicable, would be pernicious. The militia would not long, if at all, submit to be dragged from their occupations and families to perform that most disagreeable duty in times of profound peace. And if they could be prevailed upon, or compelled to do it, the increased expence of a frequent rotation of service and the loss of labor, and disconcertion of the industrious pursuits of individuals, would form conclusive objections to the scheme. It would be as burthensome and injurious to the public, as ruinous to private citizens. The latter resource of permanent corps in the pay of government amounts to a standing army in time of peace; a small one indeed, but not the less real for being small. Here is a simple view of the subject that shows us at once the impropriety of a constitutional interdiction of such establishments, and the necessity of leaving the matter to the discretion and prudence of the legislature.[37]

He argued, furthermore, that the frontier posts had to be manned with an eye to the British and Spanish on our borders and that if the United States did not want "to be exposed in a naked and defenseless condition to their insults or encroachments," it would find it expedient to increase the frontier garrisons in proportion to the ability of the foreign nations to annoy them. The western posts, too, were keys to the Indian trade. "Can any man think it would be wise," he asked, "to leave such posts in a situation to be at any instant seized by one or the other of two neighbouring and formidable powers? To act this part would be to desert all the usual maxims of prudence and policy."

Although the compelling arguments of Hamilton and his friends carried the day, an adequate army for the needs of the West was by no means immediately forthcoming. In the summer of 1788 a committee of the Continental Congress presented a detailed report on the military establishment.[38] It found 174 men whose enlistments ran until 1789, 171 more reenlisted at the several posts when their terms expired, and 250 new recruits ready to be marched to the frontiers from Pennsylvania, New Jersey, and Connecticut—a grand total of 595

---

[37] *Ibid.*, pp. 156–157.
[38] The report was originally submitted on July 21, 1788, but it was resubmitted and approved on October 2. *Journals of the Continental Congress*, XXXIV, 345–348, 578–594.

noncommissioned officers and privates. In addition to these were the two Massachusetts artillery companies enlisted in 1786, reduced now to only 71 men and split between Springfield and West Point, plus another small detachment of 13 men at West Point. The frontier stations began at the north with Fort Franklin, near Venango, which was intended to defend the frontiers of Pennsylvania from Indian incursions. "The excellent construction and execution of this work," the committee said, "reflects honor on the abilities and industry of Captain Hart [Jonathan Heart] who garrisons it with his Company and who was his own engineer." Fort Pitt had only one officer and a few men to receive and forward supplies. Fort McIntosh was expected to be replaced by a blockhouse a few miles up Big Beaver Creek to "cover the Country." The headquarters was at Fort Harmar, "a well constructed fort with five bastions and three cannon mounted," which had four companies intended to reinforce posts either up or down the river. At the rapids of the Ohio (the post was called Fort Steuben now rather than Fort Finney) were two companies to protect that region and the communications to the post on the Wabash. This latter, Fort Knox, had two companies and four small brass cannon. A year later, on August 8, 1789, Knox reported that of the 840 men authorized, 168 were still needed to complete the establishment.[39]

The new government under the Constitution, on September 29, 1789, took over this small and rudimentary defense force, and on April 30, 1790, Congress added four more companies of infantry, bringing the total authorized strength of noncommissioned officers and privates to 1,216 men.[40] But Henry Knox, who was appointed to head the newly created War Department, was soon faced with problems both north and south of the Ohio River for which this puny "sword of the Republic" was hardly sufficient.

[39] *American State Papers: Military Affairs* (7 vols., Washington, 1832–1861), I, 5–6.
[40] *U. S. Statutes at Large*, I, 95–96, 119–121.

TWO

The Army in the Old Northwest

THE military strength of the new nation was severely tested in the Northwest Territory. Here was a crucible in which to try the glorious republican principles of the Founding Fathers, which decreed that a standing army was a threat to freedom and not to be tolerated, much less encouraged, in a nation so newly dedicated to the goddess Liberty. Filibustering Kentuckians, eager for scalps, and Ohio Indians, their patience drawn as taut as their bow strings, were not easily overawed by Knox's scraggly troops, haphazardly trained and scantily clothed and equipped.[1]

A crisis in the Northwest rapidly approached as waves of white settlers appeared along the Ohio. New Englanders of the Ohio Company, led by General Rufus Putnam, floated down the Ohio on a barge christened "Mayflower" and established Marietta at the mouth of the Muskingum in April, 1788; it was the first permanent settlement in

---

[1] The Indian wars of the 1790's in the Northwest Territory, despite their rather limited scope, have been the subject of innumerable historical studies. A detailed account that includes much material on army life is in James R. Jacobs, *The Beginning of the U. S. Army, 1783–1812* (Princeton, 1947), pp. 40–188. The narrative in Theodore Roosevelt, *The Winning of the West* (4 vols., New York, 1889–1896), III, 277–310, and IV, 1–100, though old is still good and written with dramatic effect. An excellent study that emphasizes the Indian side of the conflict and the peace maneuvers is Randolph C. Downes, *Frontier Ohio, 1788–1803* (*Ohio Historical Collections*, III, Columbus, Ohio, 1935). See also Downes, *Council Fires on the Upper Ohio: A Narrative of Indian Affairs in the Upper Ohio Valley until 1795* (Pittsburgh, 1940), pp. 310–338. Printed government documents dealing with the campaigns and peace efforts are in *American State Papers: Indian Affairs* (2 vols., Washington, 1832–1834), I, and *American State Papers: Military Affairs* (7 vols., Washington, 1832–1861), I. The supply of the campaigns is discussed in Erna Risch, *Quartermaster Support of the Army: A History of the Corps, 1775–1939* (Washington, 1962), pp. 84–110.

the Northwest Territory and soon the seat of government for Arthur St. Clair, the territorial governor. Others came to the grant of John Cleves Symmes between the Little Miami and Great Miami rivers and established the nascent city of Cincinnati. Once the gates were opened the flow was steady, and thousands of immigrants on flatboats and barges entered the new land. Major Doughty at Fort Harmar wrote to Knox that between April 6 and May 16, 1788, a total of "181 boats, 406 souls, 1,588 horses, 314 horned cattle, 223 sheep and 92 wagons" had passed his post. "It will give you some idea," he added, "of the amazing increase flowing into the western world from the old Atlantic states."[2]

The Indians refused to accept this invasion. The treaties of Fort McIntosh and Fort Finney were not acknowledged because they had not been approved by the confederacy of the northwest Indians. The lands north of the Ohio had never been won from the Indians by conquest—no matter what the Continental Congress and its committees might say—and they had never been given up in a binding treaty. The Ohio River was to be the boundary the Americans were not to cross; supported by the British, the Indians maintained this position until forced to abandon it in the Treaty of Greenville in 1795.

To uphold this position, the Indians were willing to treat again with the United States. But from a council in Detroit they sent a message to Congress, insisting that all treaties should be concluded with the confederacy as a whole. All land cessions must be "by the united voice of the confederacy"; all partial treaties were to be considered null and void. Protesting a sincere desire for friendship and peace, the assembled Indians begged the United States to "prevent your surveyors and other people from coming upon our side [of] the Ohio river."[3]

The issue was joined. The Americans were intent upon settlement north of the Ohio and were making good their intentions. The Indians were equally resolved that the Ohio was to be a permanent and irrevocable boundary between the white settlers and themselves. A council at Fort Harmar in January, 1789, faced these irreconcilable positions. Rifts, however, had appeared among the Indians, and the

2 Quoted in North Callahan, *Henry Knox: General Washington's General* (New York, 1958), p. 317.
3 Speech of the United Indian Nations, November 28 and December 18, 1786, *American State Papers: Indian Affairs*, I, 8–9.

treaties signed at Fort Harmar were for them another defeat. The Indian dissensions made it easy for the American commissioner, Governor St. Clair, to dictate the terms of the two treaties signed on January 9 with the Six Nations and with the northwest tribes. The United States, perceiving the folly of insisting upon the rights of conquest arising from the Revolution, now agreed to compensate the Indians for the land cessions, but the territorial provisions were much the same as in the previous treaties. On paper the Americans were again triumphant and the Indians humiliated.[4] St. Clair, ending the council on a pious note, told the Indians: "I fervently pray to the Great God that the peace we have Established may be perpetual."[5] But his words were soon echoing in mockery through the forests of the Northwest Territory.

The military force of the United States in the West had already shown that it was insufficient to maintain the peace. The sporadic raids of individuals or small groups of Indians might have died out had the United States been able to restrain the frontiersmen. But the westernmost post, Fort Knox, was weak and ill-provisioned and could not prevent Indian raids along the Ohio. The Kentuckians in turn, angered by the failures of the federal troops, repeatedly retaliated on their own with expeditions into the valley of the Wabash. In August, 1788, a group of sixty Kentuckians, defying the restraining orders of Hamtramck, attacked friendly Piankashaws near Fort Knox and killed nine Indians. The senseless attack, so typical of frontiersmen's lack of discrimination among groups of Indians, aroused the tribes, and the tempo of their raids was stepped up. As Kentuckians renewed their expeditions, the peace was severely shaken. The Treaty of Fort Harmar did little to help, and demands for aggressive action on the part of the federal government became more insistent.

The War Department, however, was not to be pushed precipitously into war. Henry Knox, in a long memoir relative to the Indians northwest of the Ohio sent to the President on June 15, 1789, weighed carefully the two alternatives of overwhelming the Indians by military force or of treating with them in justice for their lands. He concluded that to crush the Indians in the Northwest would require an army of 2,500 men and $200,000, "a sum far exceeding the ability of the

---

[4] Charles J. Kappler, ed., *Indian Affairs: Laws and Treaties* (2 vols., Washington, 1904), II, *Treaties*, 18–25.
[5] Quoted in Downes, *Frontier Ohio*, p. 16.

United States to advance, consistently with a due regard to other indispensable objects." To treat with the Indians by a "conciliatory system" would cost much less—Knox estimated $15,000 a year—and would absolve the United States from "blood and injustice which would stain the character of the nation . . . beyond all pecuniary calculation."[6]

☆

The pressures for war became too strong for Knox to resist, as reports of Indian incursions and atrocities poured in from the West.[7] General Harmar in the fall of 1789 had transferred the seat of his command to Fort Washington, a new post built at the mouth of the Little Miami. Now the Secretary of War directed him to "extirpate, utterly, if possible," the banditti who were wreaking havoc on the frontier.[8] On September 30, 1790, Harmar launched a punitive attack against the Miami towns. He led out a force of 1,453 men, of whom only 320 were regulars, the rest militia from Kentucky and Pennsylvania. They moved north slowly, averaging about eight miles a day, and when they arrived in the Miami country, they found the towns deserted. On October 18, 19, and 20, the army destroyed the Indian towns on the Maumee by fire and on the next day headed back toward Fort Washington. The expedition sought to destroy Indians as well as villages, but the encounters of Harmar's troops with the Indians during the campaign ended in disaster.[9]

On October 18, 300 militia and regulars had been sent out to search for the Indian warriors while the rest of the command attended to

---

[6] *American State Papers: Indian Affairs*, I, 12–14.

[7] See the reports of Indian disturbances, *ibid.*, pp. 84–96.

[8] Knox to Harmar, June 7, 1790, *ibid.*, pp. 97–98.

[9] On Josiah Harmar and his campaign, see Jacobs, *Beginning of the U. S. Army*, pp. 40–65; Randolph G. Adams, "The Harmar Expedition of 1790," *Ohio State Archaeological and Historical Quarterly*, L (January–March, 1941), 60–62; Howard H. Peckham, "Josiah Harmar and His Indian Expedition," *ibid.*, LV (July–September, 1946), 227–241. Gayle Thornbrough, ed., *Outpost on the Wabash, 1787–1791* (*Indiana Historical Society Publications*, No. 19, Indianapolis, 1957) gives correspondence between Harmar and Major John Francis Hamtramck, commander at Fort Knox. Published first-hand accounts of Harmar's campaign include: "Military Journal of Major Ebenezer Denny," *Memoirs of the Historical Society of Pennsylvania*, VII (1860), 237–409, and Basil Meek, "General Harmar's Expedition," *Ohio Archaeological and Historical Quarterly*, XX (January, 1911), 74–108. Documents on the campaign appear in *American State Papers: Indian Affairs*, I, 104–106.

the destruction of the villages, but the men returned the same day with nothing to report beyond the meeting and killing of two Indians. On the next day Colonel John Hardin of the Kentucky militia, irked at the poor showing of the day before, determined to accomplish the task himself. With 180 militia and 30 regulars he set forth, losing on the way perhaps a third of his men who sneaked back to camp. Despite warning shots, Hardin moved carelessly on until met by a sudden Indian attack from all sides. Most of the militia panicked and fled. The regulars and the few militia who stood their ground were cut to pieces. Hardin gathered together the survivors and retreated to Harmar's column, now on its way back to Fort Washington.

On the 21st came a second defeat. After the return toward Fort Washington had begun, Harmar sent back to the villages a detachment of about 300 militia and 60 regulars, in the hope of surprising the returning Indians. The Indians were indeed caught by surprise, but the unruly militia in pursuing them left the regulars unsupported, and the Indians cut them down and killed their commander, Major John P. Wyllys. Harmar returned as quickly as he could to Fort Washington, the militia completely demoralized and out of control. He discharged the militia and put on a victory dinner for his officers, but no one could hide the obvious failure. Having set out gallantly with 1,400 men to punish the Indians and strike fear into their hearts, he had instead inflicted a few casualties upon the Indians at a tremendous cost to himself. Of the 320 regulars, 75 were killed and 3 wounded; of the militia, 108 were dead and 28 wounded. Equipment had been lost or destroyed, a third of the packhorses killed or stolen. What boded still worse for the future—the Indians, instead of being cowed, had been infuriated by the attack and tremendously encouraged by their success.

A coordinate expedition from Fort Knox achieved no more, although it suffered no casualties. Hamtramck on September 30 marched north with 330 troops. He lacked supplies, and those he expected did not arrive. Unwilling to force his command to continue on half rations, he retraced his steps to Fort Knox.

General Harmar made a weak attempt to report his expedition a success—"our loss was heavy, but the headquarters of iniquity were broken up." He was rebuked, nevertheless, by Secretary of War Knox and asked to request a court of inquiry. The general was entirely exonerated; the blame was placed not on his leadership but on the undisciplined and unequipped militia who made up the bulk of his command.[10]

☆

The effects of Harmar's defeat were at once evident on the frontier. Rufus Putnam at Marietta summed up the situation: "Our prospects are much changed. in stead of peace and friendship with our Indian neighbours a hored Savage war Stairs us in the face. the Indians in stead of being humbled by the Destruction of the Shawone Towns & brought to beg for peace, appear ditermined on a general War, in which our Settlements are already involved." The Indians, Putnam reported, "were much elated with there success & threatened there should not remain a Smoak on the ohio by the time the Leaves put out."[11]

The Americans for their part were determined to strike again. Congress on March 3, 1791, provided an additional regiment of infantry (of 912 men not counting officers) and authorized the President to call out 2,000 militia cavalry. To pay for all this Congress appropriated $312,686.20.[12]

Governor Arthur St. Clair himself was given command, with a commission as major general. He was a man of parts, with a substantial, if not distinguished military career. He had been an ensign in the British army, but he had joined the patriot cause and served with Washington at Trenton and Princeton. He was president of the Continental Congress in 1787, and when the Northwest Territory was created, he was appointed territorial governor.

St. Clair was convinced of the need of a successful punitive expedition against the hostile tribes. After the failure of 1790 it was now his turn to try, and he began with much greater chances of success than did the hapless Harmar. His instructions were explicit and detailed. He was to send out emissaries of peace, but if they were not successful, he was to strike the tribes on the Wabash and Maumee, and he was instructed to establish a strong military post in the heart of the Indian country linked by a chain of supporting posts to Fort

[10] The report of the court of inquiry is in *American State Papers: Military Affairs*, I, 20–36.

[11] *The Memoirs of Rufus Putnam and Certain Official Papers and Correspondence*, ed. Rowena Buell (Boston, 1903), pp. 113, 247.

[12] *U. S. Statutes at Large*, I, 222–224.

The Military Frontier, 1785–1800

Washington.[13] The peace overtures failed, and two preliminary raids by Kentucky militia were set on foot against the towns of the upper Wabash, one led by Brigadier General Charles Scott and the other by Lieutenant Colonel James Wilkinson. Scott captured a few Indians and Wilkinson burned an Indian village and destroyed some corn, and the expeditions were hailed as great successes, but they did little to weaken Indian power and much to anger the tribes.[14]

Meanwhile St. Clair was assembling men and supplies at Fort Washington for the major expedition. Both were difficult to obtain. There were few regular troops at Fort Washington when St. Clair arrived in May, and the general drew on the garrisons of Forts Harmar, Steuben, and Knox to fill out his regiment. Recruiting for new soldiers was slow, and many of the new troops did not arrive until the end of the summer, and even then the number fell short of what St. Clair expected. Supplies of clothing were equally short, and some of the soldiers lacked essential equipment.[15]

Although the campaign had been set originally for July 10, it was not until August 7 that St. Clair moved out of Fort Washington and then only to a temporary camp six miles away. Here Winthrop Sargent, St. Clair's adjutant general, worked diligently to tighten the organization of the little army, but his personal coldness won little cooperation. Finally on September 17 the army began to creep northward toward its objective, cutting roads through the wilderness without good axes or expert woodsmen. On the banks of the Miami River, some twenty-five miles north of Fort Washington, St. Clair's army constructed the first of the chain of forts as a depot and link in the line of communi-

[13] Knox to St. Clair, March 21, 1791, *American State Papers: Indian Affairs*, I, 171–174.

[14] Scott's report of June 28, 1791, *ibid.*, pp. 131–133; Wilkinson's report of August 24, 1791, *ibid.*, pp. 133–135.

[15] On St. Clair and his campaign, in addition to specific references given below, see Jacobs, *Beginning of the U. S. Army*, pp. 66–123. See also William Henry Smith, *The St. Clair Papers: The Life and Public Services of Arthur St. Clair* (2 vols., Cincinnati, 1882), and Frazer E. Wilson, "St. Clair's Defeat," *Ohio Archaeological and Historical Quarterly*, XI (July, 1902), 30–43. Published first-hand accounts touching on the campaign include: *Journal of Capt. Daniel Bradley: An Epic of the Ohio Frontier*, ed. Frazer E. Wilson (Greenville, Ohio, 1935); *A Journal of the Adventures of Matthew Bunn* (Providence, 1796; facsimile ed., Chicago, 1962); and "Military Journal of Major Ebenezer Denny," *Memoirs of the Historical Society of Pennsylvania*, VII (1860), 237–409. Supply problems are seen in "Memoirs of Benjamin Van Cleve," ed. Beverley W. Bond, Jr., *Quarterly Publication of the Historical and Philosophical Society of Ohio*, XVII (January–June, 1922), 1–71. Official documents are printed in *American State Papers: Indian Affairs*, I, 136–202.

cation. To build the fort, called Fort Hamilton, took two weeks of valuable time, but on October 4 the main army started forward again, making painfully slow progress through the woods and swamps. Desertions were heavy; although new detachments of recruits arrived, their condition and training made them of little use. The adjutant general fulminated against the recruits as "too generally wanting the essential stamina of Soldiers." He described them as "the offscourings of large Towns and Cities;—enervated by Idleness, Debaucheries and every species of Vice," declared that "it was impossible they could have been made competent to the arduous duties of Indian Warfare," and found them "badly cloathed, badly paid and badly fed."[16] The regular army troops and the militia and levies made a poor mixture, and the numerous camp followers who were allowed put an added strain on the never-sufficient supplies.[17]

At a point reached on October 13, forty-five miles north of Fort Hamilton, St. Clair built a second fort, called Fort Jefferson, smaller than the first and only ten days in the building; but the delay brought a winter campaign that much closer. The forward march began again on October 24 toward Indian villages thirty miles distant. The weather was miserable with rain, hail, and snow, St. Clair himself so ill that he was carried by his men in a litter, and expected rations always late in arriving. By November 3 the army was encamped nearly one hundred miles from Fort Washington, near the east bank of the upper Wabash at what is now the western border of Ohio. Only a limited defense was prepared even though signs of Indians were numerous, and when patrols brought in word of Indians drawing close, the messages never were passed on to St. Clair. On the morning of November 4 the Indians attacked the ill-prepared camp. The militia, without training or discipline, fled headlong, and the regulars could not withstand the onslaught. St. Clair, overcoming his gout, ordered a series of charges, but each time the men fell back and the Indians drew closer.

[16] *Diary of Col. Winthrop Sargent, Adjutant General of the United States' Army, During the Campaign of MDCCXCI* (Wormsloe, Ga., 1851), pp. 9–10. The diary has been reprinted as "Winthrop Sargent's Diary While with General Arthur St. Clair's Expedition against the Indians," *Ohio Archaeological and Historical Quarterly*, XXXIII (July, 1924), 237–273.

[17] Nearly 200 women and children accompanied the army on its march, many of whom were killed or captured. Some of the problems they caused in matters of discipline and supply are vividly portrayed in "A Picture of the First United States Army: The Journal of Captain Samuel Newman," ed. Milo M. Quaife, *Wisconsin Magazine of History*, II (September, 1918), 40–73.

The panic was general and St. Clair ordered retreat. Sargent outlined his diary entry for the day in black as he declared: "the fortunes of this day have been as the cruellest tempest to the interests of the Country and this Army, and will blacken a full page in the future annals of America."[18]

The troops retraced their way to Fort Jefferson and Fort Hamilton, until on November 8 the decimated army reached Fort Washington. Here some evaluation could be made of the extent of the disaster. Sargent reported 35 officers and 588 noncommissioned officers and privates killed and 29 officers and 229 men wounded, plus 14 artificers and 10 packhorse men killed and 13 wounded; other estimates were comparable.[19]

It was now St. Clair's turn to face an inquiry. He resigned his commission on April 7, 1792, and a committee of the House of Representatives investigated the campaign. The group exonerated St. Clair, declaring that the failure of the campaign could "in no respect, be imputed to his conduct, either at any time before or during the action," and that "as his conduct in all the preparatory arrangements was marked with peculiar ability and zeal, so his conduct during the action furnished strong testimonies of his coolness and intrepidity." Blame was placed on the delay in passing the act providing for St. Clair's army since it did not allow time to organize and discipline the troops in time for a summer campaign, on "gross and various mismanagements and neglects" in the quartermaster's and contractor's departments, and on the "want of discipline and experience in the troops."[20]

Without doubt the troops of St. Clair's army were not of high quality. John Cleves Symmes, the entrepreneur of a large land grant at Cincinnati and one of the three judges of the Northwest Territory, wrote to a friend in Philadelphia after the debacle: "Too great a proportion of the privates appeared to be totally debilitated and rendered

[18] *Diary of Col. Winthrop Sargent*, p. 25. St. Clair's report—his "meloncholy tale," as he phrased it—is in *American State Papers: Indian Affairs*, I, 137–138.

[19] *Diary of Col. Winthrop Sargent*, p. 36. See Jacobs, *Beginning of the U. S. Army*, p. 115, for sources of other estimates.

[20] Report of May 8, 1792, *American State Papers: Military Affairs*, I, 36–39. Secretary of War Knox and the quartermaster, Samuel Hodgdon, considering the report harmful to their reputations, submitted communications to the committee, which on February 15, 1793, made a supplementary report. *Ibid.*, pp. 41–44. St. Clair's later vindication of his action appears in *A Narrative of the Manner in Which the Campaign Against the Indians in the Year One Thousand Seven Hundred and Ninety-one Was Conducted, Under the Command of Major General St. Clair* (Philadelphia, 1812).

incapable of this service, either from their youth (mere boys) or by their excessive intemperance and abandoned habits. These men who are to be purchased from the prisons[,] wheelbarrows and brothels of the nation at two dollars per month, will never answer our purpose for fighting of Indians."[21]

☆

A makeshift force was not enough. St. Clair's defeat had been a national disaster, and plans were immediately proposed to strengthen the army. Knox on December 26, 1791, at the conclusion of a long statement relative to the northwestern frontier, declared: ". . .principles of justice as well as policy, and, it may be added, the principles of economy, all combine to dictate, that an adequate military force should be raised as soon as possible, placed *upon* the frontiers, *and disciplined according to the nature of the service*" in order to meet any possible combination of the enemy. He drew up a plan for an army of 5,168 noncommissioned officers and privates, to be enlisted for three years; in addition the President should be authorized to employ militia, expert woodsmen as patrols or scouts, and friendly Indians.[22]

Knox was decidedly cool toward further reliance on militia. He acknowledged the effectiveness of mounted militia "for sudden enterprises, of short duration," but he judged militia in general "utterly unsuitable to carry on and terminate the war in which we are engaged, with honor and success." He argued, furthermore, that to keep militia away from home for extended periods would upset their farming operations, and he concluded with an old general's view of a regular army:

> Good troops, enlisted for a considerable period, armed and well disciplined in a suitable manner, for the nature of the service, will be equal, individually, to the best militia; but, when it is considered to these qualities are added, the obedience, the patience, the promptness, the economy of discipline, and the inestimable value of good officers, possessing a proper pride of reputation, the comparison no

[21] Symmes to Elias Boudinot, January 12, 1792, "John Cleves Symmes to Elias Boudinot," *Quarterly Publication of the Historical and Philosophical Society of Ohio*, V (July–September, 1910), 95–96.

[22] "Statement Relative to the Frontiers Northwest of the Ohio," December 26, 1791, *American State Papers: Indian Affairs*, I, 197–202.

longer holds, and disciplined troops attain in the mind, and in actual execution, that ascendancy over the militia, which is the result of a just comparative view of their relative force, and the experience of all nations and ages.[23]

Congress soon took action. After extensive debate in which opponents of the bill argued against the necessity of raising additional troops and against the cost, it passed, on March 5, 1792, an "Act for making farther and more effectual Provision for the Protection of the Frontiers of the United States." The act ordered the battalion of artillery and the two regiments of infantry then in service to be completed to their full strength and authorized the raising of three additional regiments consisting of 960 men each. They were to be enlisted for a term not exceeding three years, with the proviso that they be discharged "as soon as the United States shall be at peace with the Indian tribes." The act in addition authorized the President to call into service such militia cavalry as he judged necessary for the protection of the frontiers and to employ such Indians as he deemed expedient.[24]

Washington exercised great care in choosing a successor to St. Clair as major general in command of the army. He drew up a list of all the general officers then living who were not useless because of age or health (he found sixteen) and set down under their names his candid evaluations of their ability and promise, noting as well who might be unwilling to serve under whom. Some, like Benjamin Lincoln—"Sober, honest, brave and sensible, but infirm; past the vigor of life"—were passed over because they no longer had the youthful aggressiveness and stamina needed for an Indian campaign. Others, like George Weedon—"rather addicted to ease and pleasure; and no enemy it is said to the bottle"—were not tight enough disciplinarians to whip an army into shape. Men like Rufus Putnam—"there is nothing conspicuous in his character. . . . he is but little known out of his own State, and a narrow circle"—would not get wide, enthusiastic support. Of Anthony Wayne, the President observed:

More active and enterprising than Judicious and cautious. No oeconomist it is feared. Open to flattery; vain; easily imposed upon; and liable to be drawn into scrapes. Too indulgent (the effect per-

---

[23] *Ibid.*, p. 199.
[24] *U. S. Statutes at Large*, I, 241–243. For debate on the bill in the House, see *Annals of Congress*, 2 Congress, col. 337–355.

haps of some of the causes just mentioned) to his Officers and men. Whether sober, or a little addicted to the bottle, I know not.

The memorandum was considered at the cabinet meeting of March 9, at which Hamilton, Jefferson, and Knox were present.[25]

☆

Perhaps action and enterprise were just what were needed to create an army and to carry a campaign against the Indians to a victorious conclusion, and the choice fell upon Wayne.[26] On April 12 a commission was sent to him, appointing him "Major General and of course commanding Officer of the troops in the service of the United States." Wayne accepted the following day.[27]

[25] Opinion of the General Officers, [March 9, 1792], *The Writings of George Washington from the Original Manuscript Sources, 1745–1799*, ed. John C. Fitzpatrick (39 vols., Washington, 1931–1944), XXXI, 509–515.

[26] General Anthony Wayne has received extensive treatment from historians and historical editors. A scholarly biography based largely on manuscript sources is Harry Emerson Wildes, *Anthony Wayne, Trouble Shooter of the American Revolution* (New York, 1941); a popular life is Thomas Boyd, *Mad Anthony Wayne* (New York, 1929). A straightforward, well-documented account of the campaign and subsequent peace is Dwight L. Smith, "Wayne's Peace with the Indians of the Old Northwest, 1795," *Ohio State Archaeological and Historical Quarterly*, LIX (July, 1950), 239–255. See also Samuel F. Hunt, "General Anthony Wayne and the Battle of 'Fallen Timbers,'" *ibid.*, IX (October, 1900), 214–237, and Clarence M. Burton, "Anthony Wayne and the Battle of Fallen Timbers," *Michigan Pioneer and Historical Collections*, XXXI (1901), 472–489.

Extensive correspondence between Wayne and the Secretaries of War is printed in Richard C. Knopf, ed., *Anthony Wayne, A Name in Arms: The Wayne-Knox-Pickering-McHenry Correspondence* (Pittsburgh, 1960). Official documents are in *American State Papers: Indian Affairs*, I, 487–495, 524–529. Wayne's orders are in Clarence M. Burton, ed., "General Wayne's Orderly Book," *Michigan Pioneer and Historical Collections*, XXXIV (1904), 341–733.

Published journals and other first-hand accounts, in addition to those cited specifically below, include: [John Boyer], "Daily Journal of Wayne's Campaign, From July 28th to November 2d, 1784, Including an Account of the Memorable Battle of 20th August," *The American Pioneer*, I (September, 1842), 315–322, (October, 1842), 351–357, reprinted as *A Journal of Wayne's Campaign* (Cincinnati, 1866); *Journal of Capt. Daniel Bradley*; Richard C. Knopf, ed., "A Precise Journal of General Wayne's Last Campaign," *Proceedings of the American Antiquarian Society*, LXIV (1954), 273–362; *A Surgeon's Mate at Fort Defiance: The Journal of Joseph Gardner Andrews for the Year 1795*, ed. Richard C. Knopf (Columbus, Ohio, 1957); Knopf, ed., "Two Journals of the Kentucky Volunteers, 1793 and 1794," *Filson Club History Quarterly*, XXVII (July, 1953), 247–281; *Journal, Thomas Taylor Underwood, March 26, 1792 to March 18, 1800, an Old Soldier in Wayne's Army*, ed. Lee Shepard (Cincinnati, 1945).

[27] Knox to Wayne, April 12, 1792, and Wayne to Knox, April 13, 1792, Knopf, *Anthony Wayne*, pp. 15–17.

As Wayne set about to organize and discipline his troops for war, a new peace offensive was begun. The chances for success did not look auspicious, for the victory over St. Clair had greatly heightened the Indians' spirit and reunited the tribes in their determination to defend their lands and their civilization against the whites. "The Indians began to believe them Selves invinsible, and they truly had great cause of triumph," as General Putnam observed.[28] In these views the Indians got full support from the British until they developed an exaggerated opinion of the aid they could count on in the struggle with the Americans.

The Indians adopted an adamant stand that rejected all compromise. The United States, for its part, was now willing to withdraw its insistence on the Fort Harmar Treaty line, and its commissioners were sent deep into the Indian country to treat with the Indians. In July, 1793, the commissioners arrived at Detroit, but their meeting with the Indians did not ensure peace. The arrogant chiefs on August 16 insisted that the Americans withdraw from all the lands north of the Ohio. The ultimatum was unacceptable to the commissioners, and they returned empty-handed.[29]

The general had not been idle while the peace commissioners were sailing back and forth across Lake Erie to Detroit. The army law of March, 1792, had given the President the power to organize the troops in any manner he saw fit, and at the beginning of the summer Washington provided a dramatic reorganization into what was grandiloquently called the Legion of the United States. In command was a major general or "Legionary General," with appropriate staff. The Legion itself was divided into four Sub-Legions, each consisting of a troop of dragoons, a company of artillery, four companies of riflemen, and eight companies of infantry. This made an aggregate of 1,280 men exclusive of officers in each Sub-Legion—a grand total of 5,120 men in the Legion.[30]

Wayne, making Pittsburgh his headquarters, started in the summer

[28] *Memoirs of Rufus Putnam*, p. 116.

[29] Downes, *Council Fires on the Upper Ohio*, pp. 320–324.

[30] "Organization of the Army in 1792," December 27, 1792, *American State Papers: Military Affairs*, I, 40–41, gives the makeup of the Legion, which was determined much earlier than the date of this report. Knox, after repeated promises for a month, on July 13, 1792, sent to Wayne the assignment of officers and troops for each Sub-Legion. Knopf, *Anthony Wayne*, p. 32. For a fanciful comparison of Wayne's Legion with the ancient Roman army directed against the barbarians, see Fletcher Pratt, "Anthony Wayne, The Last of the Romans," in *Eleven Generals: Studies in American Command* (New York, 1949), pp. 37–58.

of 1792 to assemble the raw material from which the fighting Legion would be made. He insisted from the very first upon the strictest discipline and kept the troops busy "between Manoeuvring & fatigue," as they slowly appeared at the post from the various recruiting centers. The recruits never came in full numbers, for the recruiting officers could not offer inducements enough to attract men to fill up the Legion, and many soldiers deserted between the rendezvous and Pittsburgh. In one instance a sixth of two detachments marching from Carlisle to Pittsburgh disappeared.[31]

Wayne resorted to extreme measures to maintain the sort of military discipline he thought necessary. In August, when hostile Indians were reported in the vicinity, the general ordered his men to the redoubts. "But such was the defect of the human heart," he reported, "that from excess of Cowardice, One third part of the *sentries* deserted from their stations, so as to leave the most accessible places unguarded." He sent a detachment of dragoons to recover the fugitives with orders "to put them to instantanious Death," if any resisted, and he planned to brand the word *coward* on the foreheads of a couple of the greatest offenders and force them to perform the most menial duties around the camp. In September Wayne reported to the Secretary of War the results of a general court-martial in which four soldiers had been condemned to death and one to be shaved, branded, and whipped. One man was pardoned; three were shot to death on a Sunday morning. But in the same letter he reported that no desertions had occurred for two weeks and noted with pride that the troops were improving rapidly in firing at marks and in field maneuvers.[32]

Punishments in general were harsh and immediate. Wayne's guide was the set of Articles of War that had been approved by the Continental Congress on September 20, 1776,[33] and he was not sparing in his execution of punishment. In a fourteen-month period in 1792–1793 courts-martial in his army tried 190 cases. Of these, 84 were concerned with desertion (almost 44 percent), and in 16 more the soldiers were charged with "intention to desert." Another 49 cases were for "bad conduct," a general category in which about half the cases were related to drunkenness. Other offenses punished were sleeping on guard duty or leaving one's post, stealing, and fraudulent enlistment.

[31] Wayne to Knox, July 20, 1792, and Wayne to Knox, July 27, 1792, Knopf, *Anthony Wayne*, pp. 44, 49.
[32] Wayne to Knox, August 10 and September 7, 1792; Knox to Wayne, September 14, 1792, *ibid.*, pp. 64–65, 89, 96.
[33] *Journals of the Continental Congress*, V, 788–807.

The most frequent punishment was flogging—one hundred lashes was standard—but in 10 percent of the cases the sentence was death by hanging or before a firing squad. Reprimands, pay stoppage, extra duty, shaving of one's head, drumming out of camp appear in other sentences.[34] This was severe justice tempered with little mercy, and Wayne was not known as a martinet for nothing. "Another conflict with the savages with raw recruits is to be avoided by all means," Knox had warned him, and "Mad Anthony" had taken the charge seriously.[35]

Wayne hoped to move his troops away from Pittsburgh, but the extraordinarily low water in the Ohio made navigation impossible. He continued to train the recruits there, encouraged frequently by Washington and Knox not to let up on his disciplining of the troops. "Everything depends upon that pivot," Knox reminded him in September. "The public interest, the national character and your personal reputation—Aware of the consequences, no doubt can be entertained that you will continue unremittingly to pursue in every proper way, the accomplishment of so indispensible a qualification of your troops." Wayne put his hopes for peace on the frontier in well-trained regulars sent out on patrol, and he spoke in the most sarcastic terms of the demands made by the frontiersmen for militia "supported at publick charge & detailed, *as Usual* two or three to each house, to Assist the farmer in harvesting seeding &c."[36]

At the end of November, 1792, Wayne moved his force twenty-two miles down river from Pittsburgh, to escape the blandishments the city offered his men, and he set up a camp of huts, which he christened Legionville.[37] Here he continued to form the men into a fighting force.

The indecision of the Congress and the nation between negotiations for peace and preparations for war irritated Wayne, for as long as hopes for peace were held out, recruiting for the army languished. In October, 1792, Wayne wrote to Knox, "I hope that by this time every Idea of peace is done away—& that more efficient measures will be adopted to Complete the Legion," for he was convinced that "by the sword we must procure peace."[38]

[34] Richard C. Knopf, "Crime and Punishment in the Legion, 1792–1793," *Bulletin of the Historical and Philosophical Society of Ohio*, XIV (July, 1956), 232–238.
[35] Knox to Wayne, August 7, 1792, Knopf, *Anthony Wayne*, p. 61.
[36] Wayne to Knox, August 31, 1792; Knox to Wayne, September 14, 1792; Wayne to Knox, September 28, 1792, *ibid.*, pp. 80, 96, 107–108.
[37] Wayne to Knox, November 29, 1792, *ibid.*, p. 142.
[38] Wayne to Knox, October 19 and 26, 1792, *ibid.*, pp. 120–121, 122.

But the political leaders could not rush the people as headlong to war as the military commander might have wished. Knox, an old military man, was perhaps as uncomfortable as Wayne, but as civilian Secretary of War he was more keenly alert to the political necessities of the republic, only recently freed from a long war and hankering for continuing peace. He tried to explain to Wayne at the beginning of 1793 that all avenues for peace must be explored before the signal for war could be sounded. "We shall always possess the power of rejecting all unreasonable propositions," he wrote. "But the sentiments of the great mass of the Citizens of the United States are adverse in the extreme to an Indian War and although these sentiments would not be considered as sufficient cause for the Government to conclude an infamous peace, yet they are of such a nature as to render it adviseable to embrace every expedient which may honorably terminate the conflict." Knox cited the President's hope that fair and humane motives exhibited by the United States would themselves pacify the tribes and his fear that with war "the extirpation and destruction of the Indian tribes" was inevitable. Nor could the young nation afford to ignore world opinion. "The favorable opinion and pity of the world is easily excited in favor of the oppressed," Knox noted. "The indians are considered in a great degree of this description—If our modes of population and War destroy the tribes the disinterested part of mankind and posterity will be apt to class the effects of our Conduct and that of the Spaniards in Mexico and Peru together—." Nevertheless, if every measure for peace was found unavailing without a "sacrifice of national character," Knox "presumed" the citizens would unite to prosecute the war with vigor.[39]

Part of Knox's concern was certainly economic. The new government was not yet on firm financial ground, and the costs of an Indian war could have been overwhelming. An interesting indication of the drive for economy was Knox's continuing insistence that Wayne's army experiment with using beef cattle as beasts of burden. He wanted the cattle that were driven in to supply beef for the troops to carry on their backs the flour and other commodities that completed the rations. Wayne and his quartermaster sensibly would have none of it.[40]

Knox's arguments for peace could not have been very encouraging to Wayne, who was further upset by the attempts of a group in Congress to disband the very Legion that was being gathered together

[39] Knox to Wayne, January 5, 1793, *ibid.*, pp. 165–166.
[40] See the correspondence, *ibid.*, pp. 126–127, 131, 136, 186, 240.

with so much effort and by the effects this had on his officers, many of whom were resigning. He continued strong in his resolve, however, for as he replied to Knox, "I can not bring my mind to believe that the United States of America will sacrifice National honor Character & Interest—to British intrigue & influence with the savages or the more dangerous—opposition of a restless Juncto—."[41]

While Wayne disciplined the main part of the Legion at Pittsburgh and Legionville, a second part of the army, under James Wilkinson, was operating out of Fort Washington. Wilkinson, of questionable character but with a brilliant record as a young officer in the Revolution and a man of vigor and considerable affability, had been commissioned a lieutenant colonel in the regular army in October, 1791. He had been directed by Knox to find out what he could about the Indians in the region and to assure them of the peaceful intentions of the government, but at the same time to strengthen the line of forts running north from Fort Washington and to lay in supplies at them in preparation for a possible future campaign. On March 5, 1792, Wilkinson was appointed brigadier general, and although subordinate to Wayne, worked largely independently of him and frequently corresponded directly with the Secretary of War. Then in April, 1793, Wayne was given permission by the War Department to move down the Ohio, and he took personal command in the West. His relations with Wilkinson were strained, for the subordinate commander was hostile to him, fearing perhaps that his own reputation would be overshadowed. Though no open break occurred between the two officers, Wilkinson in private excoriated the major general, and he was a focus of opposition to Wayne within the Legion.[42]

On May 5 Wayne encamped a mile below Fort Washington near the river. It was the best spot he could find for the Legion, in fact the

[41] On December 20, 1792, Representative John Steele of North Carolina introduced a resolution to reduce the military establishment. The resolution was debated on December 28 and considered by the House in Committee of the Whole on January 2 and subsequent days. The resolution was finally defeated. See *Annals of Congress*, 2 Congress, col. 750, 762–768, 773–802. The debate exposed the arguments pro and con for a regular army as opposed to militia for defending the nation. For Wayne's views, see Wayne to Knox, January 15, 1793, Knopf, *Anthony Wayne*, pp. 170–172.

[42] James R. Jacobs, *Tarnished Warrior, Major-General James Wilkinson* (New York, 1938), pp. 130–157, contains details on this relationship. The following journals show indications of an anti-Wayne spirit: "William Clark's Journal of General Wayne's Campaign," ed. R. C. McGrane, *Mississippi Valley Historical Review*, I (December, 1914), 418–444, and Dwight L. Smith, ed., "From Green Ville to Fallen Timbers: A Journal of the Wayne Campaign, July 28–September 14, 1794," *Indiana Historical Society Publications*, XVI (1952), 239–333.

only spot, and he called the camp Hobson's Choice. Here he continued the training of his army, and while awaiting the final outcome of all the peace maneuvers he made preparations for the campaign to the north that he was sure would come.[43]

One of his tasks was to make arrangements for the auxiliary force of militia or volunteers contemplated by the act of 1792. Knox warned him that simple militia were likely to be unsatisfactory, for the Kentuckians on whom Wayne was to depend disliked to serve as mere militia and would send hired substitutes instead. It was otherwise with mounted volunteers, whose greater effectiveness would make up for their greater expense. The whole idea of non-regular troops, however, exasperated Wayne, and in a confidential letter to Knox he spoke contemptuously of them as making a triumphant return from expeditions that skirted wide of any enemy forces, leaving the Legion to stand up to the real dangers from the Indians. But with the continued failure of the recruiting service to replace men whose terms had expired and to fill up the Legion, reliance had to be placed on citizen soldiers, and in the end the good work of the Kentucky volunteers caused Wayne momentarily to revise his estimate of them.[44]

What Knox called the "procrastinated and fruitless, but absolutely necessary negociations with the hostile Indians" consumed the summer of 1793.[45] When Wayne received news on September 11 that the peace commissioners had failed and that he could expect renewed hostility from the Indians, it was too late to mount a major campaign that season. But in October the Legion cautiously headed north from Hobson's Choice. Six miles north of Fort Jefferson Wayne encamped for the winter, building a fort which he called Fort Greenville. His perseverance through the winter at this advanced spot would give the Indians pause, and a well-constructed stockade would enable him to repel attacks and to service his troops on later marches into the Indian lands. In December his troops built a still more advanced post, Fort Recovery, on the site of St. Clair's defeat.

Wayne was directed, also, to refortify Fort Massac, an abandoned French fort on the north bank of the Ohio about ten miles below present-day Paducah, Kentucky, and detachments under Major Thomas Doyle of the First Sub-Legion left Cincinnati for that purpose on

[43] Wayne to Knox, May 9, 1793, Knopf, *Anthony Wayne*, p. 234.
[44] Knox to Wayne, May 17, 1793; Wayne to Knox, June 20, 1793, and October 17, 1794, *ibid.*, pp. 239, 244–245, 360.
[45] Knox to Wayne, November 25, 1793, *ibid.*, p. 285.

May 24, 1794. The post was intended to check incursions of the Wabash Indians on the settlements across the Ohio, but the immediate order for the post came from the threat of Citizen Genet's activities in the West. The intention of "some restless people of the frontier settlements, to make hostile inroads into the dominions of Spain" made the fortification of the site indispensable in the mind of the Secretary of War, and he directed the use of military force to prevent such parties moving down the Ohio if they could not be dissuaded by peaceful means.[46]

In the face of the advances by the American forces the Indians, encouraged by the British, remained arrogant. They assembled in the early summer, some 2,000 strong, but Wayne's troops were safely ensconced at Fort Greenville and Fort Recovery. The Indians' only hope was to attack the supplies and paralyze Wayne's army, but they were too confident and too impetuous to be satisfied with such undramatic tactics. Instead, on June 30 and July 1, they boldly threw their forces against Fort Recovery, but the assaults on the fort were without avail, and the humiliated Indians retreated down the Maumee.[47]

It was Wayne's turn to advance. On July 26, 1,500 mounted volunteers under Major General Charles Scott arrived at Greenville; on the 28th Wayne's army marched out, 3,500 men strong, into the Indian stronghold. By August 8, Wayne had reached the confluence of the Maumee and the Auglaize, where he built Fort Defiance to protect his rear as he advanced upon the Indians. On the 15th he continued his march down the Maumee and by the 18th had reached a point about ten miles from the British Fort Miami. Signs of Indians increased, and Wayne expected to meet heavy resistance to his advance. He threw up a rough barricade to protect his equipment and stores and, leaving 200 men as a guard, started forward again on the morning of August 20.

The line of march followed the northern bank of the Maumee; Wilkinson commanded the right wing, Hamtramck the left. Facing Wayne were perhaps no more than 500 Indians, for many of the red men, having gone without food all night awaiting an attack, had left their positions. Those who were left to meet the Legion occupied a position

[46] Extract of letter from the Secretary of War to Wayne, March 31, 1794, *American State Papers: Foreign Relations* (6 vols., Washington, 1832–1859), I, 458–459. On the founding and history of the fort, see Norman W. Caldwell, "Fort Massac: The American Frontier Post, 1778–1805," *Journal of the Illinois State Historical Society,* XLIII (Winter, 1950), 265–281.

[47] Wayne's report of July 7, 1794, *American State Papers: Indian Affairs*, I, 487–488. A British account appears in [John Chew], "The Diary of an Officer in the Indian Country in 1794," *American Historical Magazine*, III (November, 1908), 639–643; IV (January, 1909), 69–71.

amidst fallen and uprooted trees, left by a tornado that had passed through the area years before. Wayne believed that the full force of Indians was awaiting his attack, and he ordered a charge, with his second line moving up to reinforce the first. As the soldiers closed in on the Indians with bayonets fixed, they carried all before them. The Indians were driven from their protection and fled headlong, and within forty-five minutes the Battle of Fallen Timbers was over.[48]

The British at Fort Miami, not willing to risk an open conflict with United States troops, closed their gates in the face of the retreating Indians, and with this action collapsed the Indians' final hope of succor from those who had encouraged their defiance of the Americans.[49]

Wayne was exultant as he reported to Knox: "It's with infinite pleasure that I now announce to you the brilliant success of the Federal army under my Command."[50] And he at once set about to consolidate his victory. As he moved back up the Maumee, he strengthened Fort Defiance and then moved on to the headwaters of the Wabash, where by the end of October his troops had built Fort Wayne. By November 2 he was back at his headquarters at Greenville. Only Wilkinson was unimpressed.[51]

For a year Wayne remained and watched the army he had built slip away as enlistments ended and recruiting lagged. He insisted that Congress take measures to raise troops for the western posts and not rely on "the mistaken policy & bad economy of substituting Mounted Volunteers in place of Regular troops," lest his army had "fought bled & conquered in vain." He got little encouragement from the Secretary of War, who reported that the "general prosperity of the Country and the

[48] There is a detailed description of the battle, with references to primary sources, in Jacobs, *Beginning of the U. S. Army*, pp. 173–176.

[49] The notes passed between Wayne and Major William Campbell, the commander at Fort Miami, are printed in *American State Papers: Indian Affairs*, I, 493–494. The part played by the British in encouraging the Indians to resist Wayne is shown in Reginald Horsman, "The British Indian Department and the Resistance to General Anthony Wayne, 1793–1795," *Mississippi Valley Historical Review*, XLIX (September, 1962), 269–290.

[50] Wayne to Knox, August 28, 1794, Knopf, *Anthony Wayne*, p. 351.

[51] On November 10 Wilkinson wrote to Harry Innes: "The whole operation presents us a tissue of improvidence, disarray, precipitancy, Error & Ignorance, of thoughtless temerity, unseasonable Cautions, and shameful omissions, which I may safely pronounce, was never before presented to the view of mankind; yet under the favor of fortune, and the paucity & injudicious Conduct of the enemy, we have prospered beyond calculation, and the wreath is prepared for the brow of the Blockhead." Quoted in Jacobs, *Tarnished Warrior*, p. 143. Wilkinson's own report of the campaign appears in "General James Wilkinson's Narrative of the Fallen Timbers Campaign," ed. Milo M. Quaife, *Mississippi Valley Historical Review*, XVI (June, 1921), 81–90.

high price of labour of all sorts precludes the expectation of any considerable augmentation of the legion." Wayne negotiated with the Indians, who were stunned by their defeat and the failure of the British to support them, and he was determined to conclude a treaty even if he had to treat at a place chosen by the Indians, for he asserted, "I am as sick and tired of this kind of war as any man in America, the meekest Quaker not excepted."[52]

In the summer the Indians began to assemble at Greenville. Their hope of maintaining the Ohio boundary was now gone, and on August 3 they agreed to Wayne's terms, giving up once and for all the two-thirds of Ohio and sliver of Indiana marked by the Treaty of Greenville line.[53]

"Mad Anthony's" work was done. He bade farewell to his loyal Legion on December 14, 1795, turned his command over to Wilkinson for the time being, and returned to the East. The next year, on an inspection tour of the western posts, he made new dispositions of the troops and then headed back again toward Philadelphia. He got no farther than Presque Isle on Lake Erie, where he died on December 15, 1796, and was buried as he had requested at the foot of the flagpole.[54]

☆

While Wayne's regular troops and militia were subduing the Indians in the Northwest, American diplomatic endeavors were bearing fruit in London. Jay's Treaty, signed with Great Britain on November 19, 1794, whatever its political ramifications within the United States might have been, made a signal contribution to American control of the Northwest. The British agreed to withdraw all troops and garrisons within the boundaries assigned to the United States in 1783; June 1, 1796, was set as the date for the final evacuation. The provision in the treaty that permitted Indian traders from Canada to operate unrestricted within American territory was a continuing threat to American sov-

[52] Wayne to Knox, October 17, 1794; Knox to Wayne, December 5, 1794; Wayne to Knox, January 24, 1795, Knopf, *Anthony Wayne*, pp. 360–361, 366–367, 381.
[53] Kappler, *Treaties*, pp. 39–45. The cession is shown in Charles C. Royce, *Indian Land Cessions in the United States (Eighteenth Annual Report of the Bureau of American Ethnology*, Part II, Washington, 1899), Plates 19 and 49, Cession 11. For a careful analysis of the terms of the treaty and their origin, see Dwight L. Smith, "Wayne and the Treaty of Greene Ville," *Ohio State Archaeological and Historical Quarterly*, LXIII (January, 1954), 1–7.
[54] Jacobs, *Beginning of the U. S. Army*, pp. 182–188.

ereignty because of the inimical influence of the traders upon the Indians, yet the transfer of Fort Mackinac and Detroit (as well as the other posts) was a significant recognition of American authority that was not lost upon the Indians.[55]

The delay in the actual transfer of the posts is an interesting commentary on the state of the American military force, for when the time arrived for the American occupation, the United States was not ready. Secretary of War James McHenry sent a Captain Lewis of the First Sub-Legion to Quebec to make arrangements with Lord Dorchester, the Commander in Chief of Canada. Lewis asked for a delay in the British evacuation of the posts until the United States could gather troops to garrison them, and Dorchester agreed. On June 1 and 2 orders were issued to the commanders at Forts Ontario, Niagara, Miami, Detroit, and Mackinac to evacuate their posts, but they were directed to retain small detachments at the posts to guard the works and public property until the American forces actually arrived.[56]

Colonel John Hamtramck was directed toward Detroit, and with 500 troops he moved from Fort Wayne to within a half-mile of Fort Miami. When he received orders to take over Detroit, he dispatched Captain Moses Porter by boat with sixty-five men. They arrived at Detroit on July 10, and on the following day at noon the American flag was raised and the British troops marched out for the new post at Malden across the river. On the same day Hamtramck occupied Fort Miami and then moved on to Detroit, where he took command.[57] The British delivered Fort Ontario at Oswego on July 14, and on

[55]Hunter Miller, ed., *Treaties and Other International Acts of the United States of America* (8 vols., Washington, 1931–1948), II, 245–274. For discussion of Jay's Treaty and its provision for transfer of British posts on United States soil, see Samuel Flagg Bemis, *Jay's Treaty: A Study in Commerce and Diplomacy* (rev. ed., New Haven, 1962); Howard L. Osgood, "The British Evacuation of the United States," *Rochester Historical Society Publication Fund Series*, VI (1927), 55–63; and A. L. Burt, *The United States, Great Britain, and British North America from the Revolution to the Establishment of Peace after the War of 1812* (New Haven, 1940), pp. 141–165.

[56] McHenry to Lord Dorchester, May 10, 1796; Dorchester to Duke of Portland, May 28 and June 11, 1796; Orders for evacuating the posts, June 1 and 2, 1796; Adjutant General George Beckwith to McHenry, June 3, 1796. "Copies of Papers on File in the Dominion Archives at Ottawa, Canada, Pertaining to the Relations of the British Government with the United States During the Period of the War of 1812," *Michigan Pioneer and Historical Collections*, XXV (1894), 117–124. These documents also appear in William R. Manning, ed., *Diplomatic Correspondence of the United States: Canadian Relations, 1784–1860* (3 vols., Washington, 1940–1943), I, 472–474.

[57] Hamtramck to Wilkinson, July 11 and 17, 1796, "Letters of Col. John Francis Hamtramck," *Michigan Pioneer and Historical Collections*, XXXIV (1904), 739–740.

August 11 the American flag went up at Niagara. But not until September 11, 1796, did American troops under Major Henry Burbeck take over Fort Mackinac. The British retreated to St. Joseph Island at the mouth of the St. Mary's River, where they built a new post.

The exchange of forts had gone remarkably smoothly. Timothy Pickering wrote to Rufus King, "The *Posts* have been delivered up in a manner perfectly acceptable; and at present we have peace on all our borders, accompanied with internal tranquility."[58]

☆

The tranquility did not last forever. Advancing white settlement pushed against the Treaty of Greenville line and revived the temporarily quieted antagonisms of the Indians. The chain of posts established between the Ohio and the Maumee during the Indian campaigns had been abandoned after the Treaty of Greenville, leaving Fort Washington (itself given up in 1804), Fort Wayne, Fort Knox, and Fort Massac to stand guard in the Indian country. In 1802, when the Indians along the Mississippi in southern Illinois were disturbing the scattered settlements there, a company of troops took station at Kaskaskia. The next year Secretary of War Dearborn sent a company to occupy the mouth of the Chicago River at the southern tip of Lake Michigan. The troops, marching overland from Detroit, arrived at the site on August 17, 1803, where they began at once to build the fort that bore Dearborn's name, dragging timbers themselves to the spot because of the shortage of draft animals.[59]

There soon appeared on the scene the celebrated Shawnee chief, Tecumseh, and his brother, the Prophet. Tecumseh by all acounts was a great man, noted for his humanity and uprightness of character. While the Prophet practiced mystical rites and preached a return to primitive ways, he himself became a political leader, determined to stop the westward advance of the whites. Arguing that no sale of Indian land could be valid unless agreed to by all the tribes, he set about to form a confederacy that would unite the Indians to block white aggrandizement. For aid in this great project Tecumseh depended upon

[58] Manning, *Diplomatic Correspondence: Canadian Relations*, I, 100.
[59] For the story of the founding of the fort, see Milo M. Quaife, *Chicago and the Old Northwest, 1673–1835: A Study of the Evolution of the Northwest Frontier, Together with a History of Fort Dearborn* (Chicago, 1913), pp. 127–152.

the British and from them drew arms and ammunition. With the increased tension between Great Britain and the United States that grew out of the "Chesapeake" affair in 1807, the British in Canada were quite willing to renew the active allegiance of the Indians. The vision of Tecumseh thus reopened problems that the Americans thought had been resolved at Fallen Timbers and Greenville. American sovereignty north of the Ohio had not yet been secured in the face of rising Indian apprehensions, and from 1807 to the War of 1812 Indian relations in Indiana and Illinois territories steadily worsened.[60]

Tecumseh and his brother won many supporters among the northwest Indians, and in 1808 the Prophet and his followers moved to the upper Wabash at the mouth of Tippecanoe Creek. This concentration of warriors on the Wabash alarmed William Henry Harrison, Governor of Indiana Territory, and he was convinced that serious trouble was brewing. Yet in the face of growing Indian intransigence, Harrison concluded a new treaty at Fort Wayne on September 30, 1809, with the Miamis, Weas, and Delawares, by which he purchased a large tract of land in Indiana.[61] The treaty greatly agitated Tecumseh even though no Shawnee lands were involved, and in 1810 he visited Harrison at Vincennes, where he threatened the governor with hostile gestures and announced that he would never submit to the Fort Wayne Treaty. A truce was arranged, but no ultimate compromise seemed possible. The following summer Tecumseh appeared again with a large retinue. He told Harrison that he was on his way south to bring the southern nations into his confederacy.[62]

Harrison made use of the opportune absence of the Shawnee leader to advance against the Prophet's town. With regular troops of the Fourth Infantry under Colonel John P. Boyd, who had been dispatched to the Wabash by Secretary of War Abraham Eustis, and with militia and volunteers—some 1,000 troops in all—he moved north from Vincennes on September 19. On October 1 he reached the site of modern

[60] Numerous extracts from letters written by officials in the West describing the hostile movements of the Indians are printed in *American State Papers: Indian Affairs*, I, 797–804.

[61] Kappler, *Treaties*, pp. 101–102.

[62] The troubles between Harrison and Tecumseh and the Prophet are discussed in Dorothy Burne Goebel, *William Henry Harrison: A Political Biography* (Indianapolis, 1926), pp. 109–127; Freeman Cleaves, *Old Tippecanoe: William Henry Harrison and His Time* (New York, 1939), pp. 51–111; and Glenn Tucker, *Tecumseh: Vision of Glory* (Indianapolis, 1956), pp. 134–231. These accounts rely heavily on *Messages and Letters of William Henry Harrison*, ed. Logan Esarey (2 vols., Indianapolis, 1922). See also *American State Papers: Indian Affairs*, I, 776–780, 797–811.

Terre Haute and three miles north of the spot began to erect a fort, called Fort Harrison. By the end of October the blockhouse was finished, and leaving the sick and a small guard at the new post, Harrison moved on toward Tippecanoe. He reached the area early in November and sought a parley with the Indians, which failed to materialize. On November 7 the Indians attacked Harrison's army and were repulsed only after severe fighting in which Harrison's losses were heavy. The Battle of Tippecanoe was described by Harrison as "a complete and decisive victory," but in the end the battle settled nothing. The Prophet's town was burned and his followers were scattered, but the enmity against the whites only increased, and another step had been taken toward all-out war to see who would control the Old Northwest.[63]

[63] Reports of Harrison to the Secretary of War, November 8 and 18, 1811, in *Messages and Letters of Harrison*, I, 614–615, 618–630. See also Alfred Pirtle, *The Battle of Tippecanoe* (Louisville, 1900). General accounts of the drift toward war are in Jacobs, *Beginning of the U. S. Army*, pp. 356–363, and Louise Phelps Kellogg, *The British Regime in Wisconsin and the Northwest* (Madison, Wis., 1935), pp. 265–282. See also Christopher B. Coleman, "The Ohio Valley in the Preliminaries of the War of 1812," *Mississippi Valley Historical Review*, VII (June, 1920), 39–50.

☆ THREE ☆

Military Frontiers in the South

I N the region south of the Ohio River, for more than a decade after the Revolution, American sovereignty was maintained as precariously as in the Old Northwest. The territory north of the 31st parallel and east of the Mississippi, to be sure, had been given to the United States by Great Britain at the Treaty of Paris in 1783, but in actual fact much of the present state of Tennessee and most of Alabama and Mississippi was held by the Choctaws, Chickasaws, Creeks, and Cherokees. Spain, in possession of the Floridas and Louisiana, claimed jurisdiction as far north as the Tennessee River. She sought by controlling the trade of the southern tribes and by entering into alliances with them to use the Indians as a barrier against the American settlers, who were already pushing hard against the Creeks and the Cherokees. It is clear that the Baron de Carondelet, who became governor of Louisiana at the end of 1791, would have welcomed an American-Indian war in the Southwest, if he did not indeed encourage such a conflict.[1]

[1] An excellent recent survey of conditions in the Old Southwest is Thomas P. Abernethy, *The South in the New Nation, 1789–1819* (Baton Rouge, 1961). An older but still valuable study is Arthur P. Whitaker, *The Spanish-American Frontier, 1783–1795* (Boston, 1927). For a clear understanding of the Indian problems in the South, see the following articles, in addition to those cited specifically below: Jane M. Berry, "The Indian Policy of Spain in the Southwest, 1783–1795," *Mississippi Valley Historical Review*, III (March, 1917), 462–477; Kenneth Coleman, "Federal Indian Relations in the South, 1781–1789," *Chronicles of Oklahoma*, XXXV (Winter, 1957–1958), 435–458; Randolph C. Downes, "Cherokee-American Relations in the Upper Tennessee Valley, 1776–1791," *East Tennessee Historical Society's Publications*, VIII (1936), 35–53; Downes, "Indian Affairs in the Southwest Territory, 1790–1796," *Tennessee Historical Magazine*, Second Series, III (January, 1937), 240–268; Albert V. Goodpasture, "Indian Wars and Warriors of the Old Southwest, 1730–1807," *ibid.*, IV (March, 1918), 3–49, (June, 1918), 106–145, (September, 1918),

Despite serious provocation and the clamor for military support from Georgia and the Southwest Territory, the federal government refused to declare war in the South. It had committed its meager regular army to resolving the question of effective American sovereignty in the Northwest Territory, and it had no resources to be directed in another direction. Nor could the United States afford to antagonize or irritate Spain while delicate negotiations were under way about the southern boundary and navigation of the Mississippi. The Indian problem was merged with the boundary dispute, and one could not be negotiated or solved without the other.

The southern tribes, like most of those in the north, had supported the British during the Revolution, and in addition to the border raids that were common on the whole frontier, the patriots had mounted a successful campaign against the Cherokees. At the end of the war the Indians, deserted by the British, had to come to terms with the United States. The difficulties in reaching agreement were great, however, for the Indians held tenaciously to their lands and state officials seriously interfered with the federal government's handling of Indian affairs. The committee of the Continental Congress charged with Indian affairs in the South placed emphasis on precise determination of a boundary line between the Indian country and the whites, and after troubles with North Carolina and Georgia, which objected to the composition of the board of commissioners, treaties were negotiated at Hopewell, South Carolina, with the Cherokees, Choctaws, and Chickasaws in late 1785 and early 1786. The treaties defined the boundaries for the Indian

---

161–210, (December, 1918), 252–289; Philip M. Hamer, ed., "The British in Canada and the Southern Indians, 1790–1794," *East Tennessee Historical Society's Publications*, II (1930), 107–134; Arthur P. Whitaker, "Alexander McGillivray, 1783–1798," *North Carolina Historical Review*, V (April, 1928), 181–203; Whitaker, "Alexander McGillivray, 1789–1793," *ibid.*, V (July, 1928), 289–309; and Whitaker, "Spain and the Cherokee Indians, 1783–1798," *ibid.*, IV (July, 1927), 252–269. See also Walter H. Mohr, *Federal Indian Relations, 1774–1788* (Philadelphia, 1933), and R. S. Cotterill, "Federal Indian Management in the South, 1789–1825," *Mississippi Valley Historical Review*, XX (December, 1933), 333–352.

Voluminous documentation on southern Indian-military problems appears in *American State Papers: Indian Affairs*, I, and *American State Papers: Military Affairs*, I. See also "The Correspondence of General James Robertson," *American Historical Magazine*, II–V, *passim;* and John W. Caughey, *McGillivray of the Creeks* (Norman, Okla., 1938), which prints McGillivray's correspondence and related papers. "The Letter Book of General James Jackson, 1788–1796," *Georgia Historical Quarterly*, XXXVII (September, 1953), 220–249, (December, 1953), 299–329, and John Twiggs, "The Creek Troubles of 1793," ed. E. Merton Coulter, *ibid.*, XI (September, 1927), 274–280, give information on militia operations in Georgia.

country and withdrew United States protection from squatters on the Indian lands who would not leave within six months.[2]

Although the United States thus agreed that American citizens could not settle on the Indian lands and were to be subject to Indian punishment if they did, it was not as simple as that. Encroachments of the whites continued, and in July, 1788, Secretary of War Knox reported to Congress on outrages committed by the white frontiersmen of North Carolina against the Cherokees in direct violation of the Treaty of Hopewell—outrages of such an extent "as to amount to an actual although informal war of the said white inhabitants against the said Cherokees." He urged Congress to uphold the treaty provisions and thus the reputation of the United States.[3] The flood of settlers, however, could no longer be contained, and the government found it impossible to remove the whites who had moved in south of the French Broad River in violation of the treaty. The only alternative to forcible removal of the whites was a new treaty of cession. This was arranged with the Cherokees in 1791, and at the Treaty of Holston a new boundary line was determined.[4]

The treaties and pledges were not sufficient to bring peace to the Southwest. In 1790, after North Carolina's western lands were finally ceded to the United States, the Territory South of the River Ohio (or Southwest Territory) was organized in the region that became the state of Tennessee. On William Blount, who was appointed governor of the Territory, fell much of the responsibility for maintaining order. Continually hoping for federal troops to restrain the Indians and the frontiersmen, he was told instead to rely on militia, and then reprimanded for calling out too many at federal expense.[5]

The War Department did not mean to turn its back completely on the Southwest. In March, 1791, Knox wrote to St. Clair that a military post on the Tennessee below the Muscles Shoals was being considered to prevent white usurpation on Indian lands and also a post at some proper place on the Mississippi. But he hastened to add that St. Clair's projected campaign would prevent the establishment of either post until

[2] Charles J. Kappler, ed., *Indian Affairs: Laws and Treaties* (2 vols., Washington, 1904), II, *Treaties*, 8–16; Mohr, *Federal Indian Relations*, pp. 139–172.

[3] *Journals of the Continental Congress* (34 vols., Washington, 1904–1937), XXXIV, 342–344.

[4] Kappler, *Treaties*, pp. 29–33.

[5] For Blount's activities, see William H. Masterson, *William Blount* (Baton Rouge, 1954), pp. 180–285. The history of the Territory can be followed in the documents printed in Clarence E. Carter, ed., *The Territorial Papers of the United States* (26 vols., Washington, 1934–1962), IV.

the northern war had been won.[6] Blount himself looked for federal succor, and he was moderately encouraged by the Secretary of War, who wrote him in August: "The expence of military posts is very considerable, and that of an army much more so. The exertions making to punish the Indians north west of the Ohio has prevented the Company being sent to your government, that was intended—But I should hope that immediately after the expedition that [sic] one or two could be spared. . . ." The governor was told in the meantime to call up as many militia, by voluntary engagement or otherwise, as he deemed indispensable for the defensive protection of the frontier.[7] Then St. Clair's disastrous defeat in November destroyed all hopes for a sizable federal army on the Tennessee and the Cumberland.

With the northwestern Indians emboldened by victory and the dangers of a general conflagration in the West increased, Knox hastened to conciliate the southern nations, lest they be drawn into the war against the United States. At least to keep them neutral was his aim, at best to include them to join the American forces against the tribes of the Northwest. To this end early in 1792 Knox sent Leonard Shaw, a young Princeton graduate, as a special emissary to the Cherokees, bearing medals for the chiefs and presents for the nation and a speech of friendship from President Washington. He entrusted to Shaw similar gifts and messages for delivery to the Choctaws and Chickasaws. The annuities due the Cherokees were quietly increased by 50 percent.[8]

Indian attacks and white retaliation continued. A group of Cherokee banditti, the Chickamaugas, who had broken away from the parent nation, were forced to seek new hunting lands along the Cumberland and incessantly pressed upon the growing white settlement there. They were joined by Creeks, whose predilections of hostility against the Americans were aggravated by the activities of the Spanish and by English adventurers in their midst.

In the face of impending war, Governor Blount called up the militia, until in the fall of 1792 he had fourteen companies of infantry and a troop of cavalry in service, and he fully expected an offensive move by the federal government against the hostile tribes.[9] Instead he got a

---

[6] Knox to St. Clair, March 21, 1791, *American State Papers: Indian Affairs*, I, 173.

[7] Secretary of War to Blount, August 18, 1791, Carter, *Territorial Papers*, IV, 76. See also Blount to James Robertson, September 21, 1791, *ibid.*, p. 82.

[8] *American State Papers: Indian Affairs*, I, 203–206, 247–248, 265–266; Kappler, *Treaties*, 32–33.

[9] Blount to the Secretary of War, September 27, 1792, Carter, *Territorial Papers*, IV, 175.

warning and then a stinging rebuke from the Secretary of War. In August, before the worst of the storm, Knox had told him that war in the territory would be considered "by the general government as a very great, and by the mass of the citizens of the middle and eastern States as an insupportable evil," and Blount was urged to remove every just pretence of grievances on the part of the Indians. This was not very encouraging, and though Blount described in detail the disturbances with which he was faced, Knox's reply was extremely critical. In the first place, the President did not feel authorized to direct offensive operations against the hostile Indians. Declaring war was a power reserved to Congress, which hesitated to act since "the extension of the Northern Indian War to the Southern Tribes would be a measure into which the Country would enter with extreme reluctance." Second, Knox strongly suggested that it was the whites, not the Indian banditti, who were responsible for the frontier encounters. The United States, he told Blount, "never will enter into a War to justify any sort of encroachment of the Whites." He then criticized Blount for calling out more militia and keeping them in service for a longer time than was necessary. The only encouraging note in the letter was information that a company of regulars being recruited in North Carolina under Captain Joseph Kerr, was being sent to Knoxville, to be subject to the disposal of the governor. This was the first distribution of regular troops to the Territory and the total complement of ninety-five noncommissioned officers and privates was only a little more than half filled when Knox wrote.[10]

Blount continued to hope for offensive war against the Indians, but the failure of the peace negotiations with the northern Indians in the summer of 1793 and the extreme measures taken by the whites destroyed the chances that the federal government would come in aggressively on the side of the frontiersmen. On June 12, in one instance, John Beard, a territorial militia captain, and his company murdered a number of peaceful Cherokees. Knox directed that those responsible be brought to immediate trial and punished, and he ended hopes for federal action against the Indians. "[I]f the United States are constrained to enter into a war with any tribes," he wrote, "it ought to be under the auspices of Justice as it is not supposed for a moment that they will support the expences of a war brought on the frontiers

[10] Secretary of War to Blount, August 15, 1792, and November 26, 1792, *ibid.*, pp. 163–164, 220–226; Blount to the Secretary of War, November 8, 1792, and January 14, 1793, *ibid.*, pp. 208–216, 226–234.

by the wanton blood thirsty disposition of our own people, or any other unjustifiable conduct." Blount and the Tennesseans had to carry on alone, hoping for more enlightenment from the next Congress, and they did it with energy, mounting an invasion into the Cherokee and Creek country more extensive than any since the Revolution. Mounted militia under General John Sevier penetrated into the Indian country, defeated the Indian warriors, and laid waste their towns.[11]

The territorial legislature petitioned Congress for a chain of permanent garrisons on the frontier, and forts were provided for in a House bill, only to be rejected by the Senate. Blount was told to raise militia troops again for the defense of the Tennessee country. "Had there been any regular troops who could have been spared for this service, they would have been ordered to have performed it," Knox wrote, "but this not being the case recourse must be had to the Militia." The failure to get adequate federal support maddened the frontiersmen, and when news of the victory at Fallen Timbers was received, an offensive force was sent to destroy the Chickamauga towns. Before Blount could stop these illegal movements, the deed was done by Major James Ore and the territorial militia.[12]

The chastisement of the Chickamaugas and the triumph of Anthony Wayne (which left the military forces of the United States free to deal with the southern Indians if need be) brought peace to the Cherokee frontier. The body of the Cherokees had already been appeased by the increase in their annuities.[13] And in the summer of 1794 blockhouses with regular army troops were established at Southwest Point (near present-day Kingston, Tennessee), at Fort Granger (near Lenoir City), and Tellico Blockhouse (near Loudon). The Creeks remained a problem, and Blount again looked for federal aid. With the northwestern Indians no longer tying down the regular troops, he wrote to James Robertson on December 4, 1794, "I cannot suffer myself to doubt but the present Session of Congress will order an Army in the Course of the next Spring or Summer, sufficient to humble if not destroy the Creek Nation and thereby give Peace to the Southwestern frontier, from the Mouth of the St. Mary's to the banks of the Cumberland."[14]

Blount moved ahead on his own to stir up the Cherokees and Chicka-

[11] Secretary of War to Blount, August 26, 1793, *ibid.*, pp. 299–300; *American State Papers: Indian Affairs*, I, 468–470.

[12] Knox to Blount, April 14, 1794, Carter, *Territorial Papers*, IV, 339. See the account of Ore's campaign in Downes, *Tennessee Historical Magazine*, Second Series, III, 260–261.

[13] Kappler, *Treaties*, pp. 33–34.

[14] "The Correspondence of General James Robertson," *American Historical Magazine*, III (October, 1898), 375–376.

saws against the Creeks, but Congress turned down his request for a Creek campaign. Timothy Pickering, who had replaced Knox as Secretary of War, sent a report to Blount that finally destroyed his expectations. "All ideas of offensive operations," he told Blount, "are therefore to be laid aside and all possible harmony cultivated with the Indian Tribes." The governor's intrigue in intertribal conflicts was condemned. "It is plain that the United States are determined, if possible, to avoid a direct or indirect war with the Creeks," Pickering continued. "Congress alone are competent to decide upon an offensive war, and congress have not thought fit to authorize it." The President, however, would authorize a regular army post on the Tennessee in the Chickasaw country, provided the full and free permission of that nation were obtained, but the troops were to come from the regular garrisons already in the territory, which might be reduced now that hostilities in some areas had subsided.[15]

☆

While the Southwest Territory and its governor were contending with the Cherokees and Creeks, another border contest was being fought in Georgia, where a conflict between state and national jurisdiction over Indian affairs further complicated matters. White settlement in Georgia had long been limited to the eastern sections of the state. Probably no more than one-eighth of the present state was occupied by the time of the Revolution; the rest was still under Indian title. The Georgians pushed vigorously for a diminution of Indian holdings, and ignoring the established principle that only the federal government could negotiate with the Indian nations for cessions of land, they signed three treaties with a minority of Creek chiefs that provided for white expansion. These illegal treaties of Augusta (1783), Galphinton (1785), and Shoulderbone (1786) were strongly opposed by the majority of the Creeks under the half-breed chief Alexander McGillivray, and border hostilities increased. Attempts at conciliation were made, but neither the Georgians nor the Creek leaders would yield their positions.[16]

[15] Pickering to Blount, March 23, 1795, Carter, *Territorial Papers*, IV, 386–393. The post on the Tennessee was not established.

[16] On the Georgia-Creek treaties and the general Creek situation, see Randolph C. Downes, "Creek-American Relations, 1782–1790," *Georgia Historical Quarterly*, XXI (June, 1937), 142–184, and Ulrich B. Phillips, *Georgia and States Rights (Annual Report of the American Historical Association for the Year 1901*, II, Washington, 1902), pp. 39–48.

As long as the problems in the Northwest had not been resolved, Congress was determined to keep the peace in Georgia at any cost, and federal commissioners were at length able in 1790 to conclude an agreement with McGillivray and the Creeks at New York. This treaty validated some of Georgia's agreements with the Creeks, but the chiefs refused to sanction any land cessions south or southwest of the Altamaha River. The desperation of the United States, which feared a general war in the South, was reflected in the treaty, some of whose articles, it has been suggested, "bore the earmarks of being provisions for paying tribute to the Creek." McGillivray was made a brigadier general in the American army and a United States agent to the Creeks and received a secret pension of $1,200 a year.[17]

Since Georgia had not been consulted in the Treaty of New York and since she refused to back down on her claims to Indian lands, the explosive border situation was no more than dampened. In March, 1793, trouble flared up anew. A party of Creeks on the extreme southern frontier raided the white settlements, and all of Georgia was alarmed as marauding Creeks seemed to threaten the whole border. At the end of April Governor Edward Telfair of Georgia informed the Secretary of War that there was "little expectation of avoiding a general war with the Creeks and the Cherokees," and that he had directed fourteen blockhouses to be erected between the St. Mary's River and the Tugaloo, to be garrisoned with militia troops. "I shall follow this plan of operation," he reported, "until measures be taken by the President for the better protection of the unfortunate settlers on this exposed frontier." Ten days later he wrote in great excitement: "Such is the havoc and carnage making by the savages, in every direction on our frontier, that retaliation by open war becomes the only resort." In June General John Twiggs with 700 Georgia militia invaded the Creek country as far as the Ocmulgee River, but they turned back when provisions ran out. The governor convened a council of his general officers and determined to reduce the enemy towns of the Creeks.[18]

[17] Randolph C. Downes, "Creek-American Relations, 1790–1795," *Journal of Southern History*, VIII (August, 1942), 353–354. The treaty is in Kappler, *Treaties*, pp. 25–28; the secret provisions are printed in Hunter Miller, ed., *Treaties and Other International Acts of the United States of America* (8 vols., Washington, 1931–1948), II, 344.

[18] Telfair to the Secretary of War, April 29, May 8, June 12, June 18, and August 13, 1793, *American State Papers: Indian Affairs*, I, 368–370. See also John K. Mahon, "Military Relations Between Georgia and the United States, 1789–1794," *Georgia Historical Quarterly*, XLIII (June, 1959), 138–155.

The rambunctious Georgians were put in their place by the President and the Secretary of War. As Telfair sent flaming reports from Augusta, Washington and Knox replied with cold water from Philadelphia. When the urgent requests for action against the Creeks first came in, Knox replied that negotiations with Spain and the pending treaty with the northern Indians (the great hope of the summer of 1793) made it "advisable to avoid, for the present, offensive expeditions into the Creek country." He authorized calling up militia (to be paid for by the federal government) for defensive purposes only, but he informed the governor that all the regular troops were needed in the Northwest and that none could be sent to Georgia. As Telfair's ardor showed no signs of cooling, Knox reminded him of the President's opinion that an open war with the Creeks would be "a complicated evil of great magnitude," and when reports of the aggressive plans by the Georgia militia reached Philadelphia, Knox fired off to Augusta an unequivocal statement of utter disapproval: "The President of the United States . . . deems the intended expedition against the Creeks as unauthorized by law, as contrary to the present state of affairs, and as contrary to the instructions heretofore given; and he has directed me to express to your Excellency his expectations that it will not be undertaken." The right of Congress alone to declare war against the Creeks was insisted upon, and until Congress acted Georgia would have to be reined in. Knox suggested on the basis of reports from the agent among the Creeks, furthermore, that the great majority of the nation were peacefully disposed. Moreover, a war against the Creeks, connected as they were with the Spaniards, would seriously hazard the delicate negotiations being carried on in Madrid.[19]

In the light of such remonstrances, little aid could be expected from the federal government, and overtures by peaceful Creeks removed the immediate fears of war. Georgia, however, did not give up hope of gaining the Creek lands between the Oconee and the Ocmulgee, and in December, 1794, the state requested the federal government to treat with the Creeks for such a cession. In June, 1796, the federal commissioners appointed by Washington met with the Creeks at Coleraine in southern Georgia. It was to no avail. The Creeks refused to cede their lands, and the treaty drawn up did no more than ratify the Treaty of New York and reassert peace between the nation and the United States. The treaty, however, provided for a military or trading post on

[19] Knox to Telfair, May 30, June 10, September 5, 1793, *American State Papers: Indian Affairs*, I, 264–265.

the south side of the Altamaha and at other spots on the Indian lands adjoining the Oconee, if the President so decided.[20] In 1797 Fort Wilkinson was built on the site of present-day Milledgeville, and it became the principal fortification on the Georgia frontier.

☆

When Henry Knox left office and retired to private life at the end of 1794, he left for President Washington a forthright statement of his final conclusions about defense of the western frontiers, both north and south.[21] He reasserted his policy of peace through justice, and this meant calming Indian fears for their lands by control of the avaricious frontier whites, who desired to seize them by force or by fraud. Until the Indians could be quieted on this point and rely upon the United States government to protect their country, he argued, "no well grounded hope of tranquillity can be entertained." He sought to contain the war in the Northwest and prevent its spreading to the south, where the Indians were in greater strength and where an open war could lead to serious diplomatic repercussions. In ending his public career he sounded the same high note of moral righteousness that had always marked his hope for peaceful relations with the Indians. "As we are more powerful, and more enlightened than they are," he wrote, "there is a responsibility of national character, that we should treat them with kindness, and even liberality." He noted the "melancholy reflection" that the United States in its dealings with the aborigines had been more destructive than the conquerors of Mexico and Peru, and he feared that future historians might mark the causes of this destruction in "sable colors."

In practical terms, Knox proposed a line of military posts garrisoned by regular army troops along the frontier within the Indian country. He wanted 1,500 men at posts on the southwestern frontier stretching from the St. Mary's River on the border of Georgia to the Ohio. North of the Ohio, in addition to the posts on American soil soon to be surrendered by the British, he advocated one at the Miami village on the Wabash and connecting posts south on the Wabash toward the Ohio

[20] Kappler, *Treaties*, pp. 46–49. Georgia commissioners remonstrated against the provision for posts unless the state approved, and the Senate in ratifying the treaty accepted, Georgia's qualifications.

[21] Knox to Washington, December 29, 1794, *American State Papers: Indian Affairs*, I, 543–544. The quotations following are from this document.

and northeast on the Maumee toward Lake Erie, plus a post at Presque Isle. Knox outlined here a cordon of military posts strung along the border of contact between the red men and the white, which became a staple of American frontier defense policy. Regular army garrisons, at the crucial meeting points of the two cultures, were to restrain the whites and overawe the savages and protect the two races from each other. The expense would be no more than the federal support of state militia. Knox suggested that Indian criminals—those committing murders or thefts in the white communities—be turned over to a military post for court-martial and that white banditti invading the Indian lands be likewise subject to martial law.

"If to these vigorous measures," Knox concluded, "should be combined the arrangements for trade, recommended to Congress, and the establishment of agents to reside in the principal Indian towns, . . . it would seem that the Government would then have made the fairest experiments of a system of justice and humanity, which, it is presumed, could not possibly fail of being blessed with its proper effects—an honorable tranquillity of the frontiers."

☆

Knox's wise plans called for adequate regular troops to man the cordon of posts, troops whose very presence on the frontier would uphold American authority without war. With the cessation of hostilities in the Northwest, however, Congress turned to consider whether the military establishment called into being to pacify the Indians should be continued. Both Timothy Pickering, who followed Knox as Secretary of War, and his successor James McHenry submitted observations and recommendations to guide the lawmakers. As an added argument Pickering sent along a statement from William Blount: "Peace now *actually* exists between the United States and the Indian tribes, and, in my opinion, may be preserved by the establishment of strong military posts of regular troops upon the frontiers, at proper places, with cavalry of the same description, to patrol between them." Blount's experience told him that peace between frontier people and the Indians could not be maintained without the presence of the government. Pickering accepted this reasoning and asked for the retention of the present military establishment "to preserve peace with the Indians, and to protect theirs, and the public lands," and he outlined in detail a chain of military stations from Lake Champlain in the north to the St. Mary's River in the south. Both he and McHenry had their eyes also on the British and Spanish frontiers and viewed the army, as McHenry put it, as a means to preserve "a model and school for an army, and experienced officers to form it, in case of war." Both men recommended keeping the existing establishment and making no change at least until future developments could be seen and evaluated.[22]

Congress did not listen. The committee on the military establishment, viewing the end of hostilities against the Indians, decided that "the force to be provided for the defensive protection of the frontiers, need not be so great as what had been contemplated for carrying on the war against the different tribes of hostile Indians, and which is the basis of the present military establishment," and Congress on May 30, 1796, reduced the army from the 5,120 men authorized for the Legion to a corps of artillerists and engineers, two companies of light dragoons, and but four regiments of infantry of eight companies each. The act was to go into effect on October 31, 1796, and the President was authorized to reassign the troops from the old legionary organization to the new establishment.[23]

☆

The newly organized and reduced army, besides stretching to garrison the posts along the northern border turned over by the British after Jay's Treaty, had also to step into the area from which the Spanish withdrew in accordance with the Treaty of San Lorenzo, signed with Spain on October 27, 1795.[24] Although the United States claimed the territory south to the 31st parallel on the basis of the cession from Great Britain at the end of the Revolution, it had taken no action to dislodge the Spanish posts that were still garrisoned in the region, supporting Spanish claims to the area and reinforcing Spain's sphere of influence over the southern Indian tribes. Such Spanish garrisons in 1795 were located at Chickasaw Bluffs (Memphis), Walnut Hills (Vicks-

---

[22] William Blount to the Secretary of War, November 2, 1795; Pickering to Committee on the Military Establishment, February 3, 1796; McHenry to Committee, March 14, 1796, *American State Papers: Military Affairs*, I, 112–114.
[23] *Ibid.*, p. 112; *U. S. Statutes at Large*, I, 483–486.
[24] Miller, *Treaties and Other International Acts*, II, 318–345. For a discussion of the treaty see Samuel Flagg Bemis, *Pinckney's Treaty: A Study of America's Advantage from Europe's Distress, 1783–1800* (Baltimore, 1926), pp. 280–355, and Arthur P. Whitaker, *The Mississippi Question, 1795–1803: A Study in Trade, Politics, and Diplomacy* (New York, 1934), pp. 51–78.

burg), and Natchez on the east bank of the Mississippi, and at Fort Confederation and Fort St. Stephens on the Tombigbee above Mobile. With the signing of the treaty (also known as Pinckney's Treaty), which provided that any troops or garrisons were to be withdrawn within six months after ratification, Spain began to evacuate the posts. In the spring of 1797 Chickasaw Bluffs and Fort Confederation were razed and the garrisons moved to St. Louis and to Fort St. Stephens, respectively. Conflicts between the two nations about violations of the treaty delayed further withdrawals for some time, but in 1798 the remaining posts along the Mississippi were given up, and the joint survey of the boundary specified by the treaty was begun.

American troops replaced the Spanish both on the east bank of the Mississippi and above Mobile. On May 26, 1797, Captain Isaac Guion of the Third Infantry, a detachment of two companies of his regiment, and a few artillerymen left Fort Washington at Cincinnati to take over on the lower Mississippi from the departing Spaniards. Chickasaw Bluffs was occupied on July 20, but the process of fort building was slow in the hot summer, and it was not until October 22 that the gates were finished, the flagpole raised, and the fort, with the firing of a salute, christened Fort Adams—a name that was soon dropped in favor of Fort Pickering. The new fort was left in the hands of a lieutenant and thirty soldiers, to be reinforced by two companies of the Third Infantry on February 9, 1798. Meanwhile the rest of Guion's command on November 9 moved down the river to Natchez, which they reached on December 6. Here the determination of the Spanish not to withdraw created tension between the two forces. Captain Guion encamped about a thousand yards from the Spanish fort, but with a change in Spanish policy, the Spanish forces slipped down the river during the night of March 29, and on the 30th American troops marched in.[25]

General Wilkinson, who had been ordered to descend the river with reinforcements from Pittsburgh, reached Natchez on September 27, 1798, but he soon moved down the river to Loftus Heights, where he established a new post, called Fort Adams in honor of the President. This site, which Wilkinson considered "the most southerly tenable position within our limits,"[26] was about six miles above the Spanish border as defined in Pinckney's Treaty and was of strategic importance in

[25] The story of the occupation of the posts is told in the documents in "Military Journal of Captain Isaac Guion, 1797–1799," *Seventh Annual Report of the Director of the Department of Archives and History of the State of Mississippi* (Nashville, Tenn., 1909), pp. 25–113.
[26] James Wilkinson, *Memoirs of My Own Times* (3 vols., Philadelphia, 1816), I, 434.

American occupation of the Trans-Appalachian West. It was a watch-tower to keep an eye on the Spanish in West Florida and in Louisiana, and it could stop any large-scale movement up or down the Mississippi. The Spanish post at Walnut Hills had been evacuated on March 23, 1798, and occupied by the Americans, who called it Fort McHenry, but the post was not regularly garrisoned.[27]

Captain Guion served in multiple capacities as he proceeded down the Mississippi, the agent of the United States in exerting its control at last over the land it had claimed since 1783. He was directed to sail with the American flag prominently displayed, to notify the Spanish posts of his arrival and to exchange salutes, but not to be deflected from his purpose. He carried presents for the Indians in an effort to conciliate the Chickasaws, and his distribution of presents to them with a certain largess had the desired effect. From Natchez he did what he could to win the support of the Choctaws. Through the difficult days before the withdrawal of the Spanish troops and on until August 8, 1798, when Winthrop Sargent, governor of the newly established Mississippi Territory, arrived, he was in control of affairs.

The Spanish were still slower to give up Fort St. Stephens on the Tombigbee, some ninety miles above Mobile, which was not handed over to an American commander until February 5, 1799. Instead of occupying this site, however, the American forces in July established Fort Stoddert four miles below the juncture of the Alabama and Tombigbee rivers, almost on the Spanish-American boundary line.[28]

☆

The peaceful transfer of Spanish-held territory into American hands was still in process when a new threat to the Mississippi valley arose from the French. There is no doubt that France wanted to regain her

[27] James Wilkinson wrote to Governor Claiborne, May 10, 1803: "I do not consider the Walnut Hills a protecting point for our Northern frontier, and it has been the grave of too many men & officers, to be reoccupied if we can avoid it—situated on the extremity of our Western flanks, without a single Settlement in rear of it, it has nothing to cover and will not serve as a convenient rallying point. . . ." Carter, *Territorial Papers*, V, 216–217.

[28] The date of the evacuation of Fort St. Stephens is given in Memorial to Congress by the Territorial Legislature, December 14, 1804, and repeated in William Lattimore to the President of the United States, March 9, 1807, Carter, *Territorial Papers*, V, 363, 524. Fort Stoddert was established in July, 1799, and was named for Benjamin Stoddert, the first Secretary of the Navy and at the time acting Secretary of War. Dunbar Rowland, ed., *The Mississippi Territorial*

power in the region. She tried to get Spain to retrocede Louisiana, and with this as a base she hoped by intrigue with the Indians and the western frontiersmen to gain the Alleghenies as an eastern boundary.[29] From Jay's Treaty at the end of 1794 to 1800, the United States and France were close to the brink of war; toward the end of that period there was actual war, although undeclared, on the high seas. Rumors and fears of war were rampant. In the summer of 1798 Captain Guion at Natchez felt constrained to investigate rumors (which proved groundless) that the French had landed in force at Pensacola and Mobile. At the same time Pickering, then Secretary of State, was writing to the newly appointed governor of Mississippi Territory: "I consider war between France & the U. States to be inevitable. Nothing but the surrender of our independence—the overturning of our government & unlimited tribute will satisfy French ambition and rapacity." Pickering rejoiced that the new federal appointees to Mississippi—Governor Sargent and the three judges—were "all military men, who have seen real and dangerous service."[30]

The Federalists, no lovers of France, took steps to meet any threatened invasion. To protect the seacoast a new regiment of artillerists and engineers was added to the regular establishment, but it would help little in a massive land invasion, and Congress on May 28 authorized the President, in case of declaration of war against the United States, invasion, or imminent danger of invasion, to enlist and call into service a "provisional army" of 10,000 men for a period not to exceed three years. To command this army the President could appoint a lieutenant general and other necessary officers and could organize the troops into corps of artillery, cavalry, and infantry as he thought best. Less than three weeks later, Congress increased the size of each regiment of the regular army by nine officers and 204 enlisted men. It authorized the President, furthermore, to raise twelve new regiments of infantry and

---

Archives, 1798–1803 (Nashville, Tenn., 1905), p. 472n. A little of the early history of the fort can be found in "Fort Stoddart [sic] in 1799: Seven Letters of Captain Bartholomew Schaumburgh," ed. Jack D. L. Holmes, *Alabama Historical Quarterly*, XXVI (Fall–Winter, 1964), 231–252.

[29] Frederick Jackson Turner, "The Policy of France toward the Mississippi Valley in the Period of Washington and Adams," *American Historical Review*, X (January, 1905), 249–279; Whitaker, *Mississippi Question*, pp. 101–129; Mildred Stahl Fletcher, "Louisiana as a Factor in French Diplomacy from 1763 to 1800," *Mississippi Valley Historical Review*, XVII (December, 1930), 367–376.

[30] Guion to the Secretary of War, June 13, 1798, "Military Journal of Captain Isaac Guion," p. 91; Pickering to Sargent, May 10 and June 15, 1798, Carter, *Territorial Papers*, V, 33, 38.

six troops of light dragoons "to be enlisted for and during the con-
tinuance of the existing differences between the United States and the
French Republic." Before the Fifth Congress adjourned in March it
added authorization for still more troops in case of war or imminent
danger of invasion, including twenty-four regiments of infantry, a regiment and a battalion of riflemen, a batallion of artillerists and engineers,
and three regiments of cavalry.[31]

To lead this new army, when and if it should be raised, Adams appointed the retired George Washington lieutenant general; Alexander
Hamilton and Charles C. Pinckney were appointed major generals. Since
Washington accepted with reluctance and chose to remain at Mount
Vernon until some actual military crisis might necessitate his taking
the field, the army planning and organization fell to Hamilton, who
was given rank above Pinckney and who acted as commander in chief
in the status of inspector general. Hamilton, who had assumed charge
of the western sections of the army while Pinckney commanded the
eastern, called James Wilkinson to New York for consultation.

Wilkinson arrived in New York on August 1 and, after personal con-
versations, addressed to Hamilton on September 4, 1799, a long memoir
concerning military posts and troops for the frontiers on the Great
Lakes and the Mississippi. He wanted to eliminate interior posts like
those at Oswego and Pittsburgh, as well as Fort Wayne, Fort Washington, and Fort Knox, "for by such fritterings, we destroy the usefulness of both officer and soldier, and expose ourselves always to be beaten
in detail." Instead, he wanted to concentrate troops at the passageways
between the Great Lakes, by which channels the British might invade
from the north. On the Mississippi he would place a small detachment
at Fort Pickering "to preserve our exclusive intercourse with the Chickasaw Indians" and a strong garrison at Fort Adams to command the
river. Along the 31st parallel he recommended "a chain of small posts,
to prevent foreign intrigues with our Indians, and to arrest any desultory
movements which might be attempted by our left, and towards our
rear." Washington approved Wilkinson's plan for the disposition of

---

[31] *U. S. Statutes at Large*, I, 552–553, 558–561, 604–605, 725–727. A brief
account of the Provisional Army with a roster of all the officers commissioned
for it appears in Carlos E. Godfrey, "Organization of the Provisional Army of
the United States in the Anticipated War with France, 1798–1800," *Pennsylvania Magazine of History and Biography*, XXXVIII (April, 1914), 129–182.
There are good details on recruiting for the Provisional Army in William H.
Gaines, Jr., "The Forgotten Army: Recruiting for a National Emergency (1799–
1800)," *Virginia Magazine of History and Biography*, LVI (July, 1948), 267–
279.

troops on the northern and southwestern frontiers, but the execution of them was arrested by the sudden peace with France and the consequent reduction of the strength of the army.[32]

Hamilton's interests in the West have received much attention. His scheme to attack Spanish holdings if war came with France has been read as a broad imperialist dream of glory.[33] But Hamilton did not want war with France, and his energies as inspector general were devoted rather to reorganizing the army and attempting to recruit the regiments to full strength than to intrigues against Spanish America.[34]

The overthrow of the Directory in November, 1799, in any case, eased the tension between France and the United States, and the increases in the military establishment that had been begun were halted. Recruiting for the twelve new regiments of infantry was stopped, and those that had been enlisted (numbering only 3,399) were ordered discharged. The six troops of light dragoons had not been recruited at all. At the beginning of 1800, Secretary of War James McHenry reported on the distribution of the existing establishment of two companies of cavalry (116 men), two regiments of artillerists and engineers (1,501 men), and the four old regiments of infantry (1,812 men). One regiment of infantry and the two companies of cavalry were on the frontiers of Tennessee and Georgia. The other three regiments of infantry with a battalion of artillerists and engineers were spread along the lakes from Niagara to Michilimackinac, on the Miami and Ohio rivers, on the Mississippi, and on the Tombigbee. "This entire force," the Secretary lamented, "is manifestly inadequate to the purposes it is intended to answer on our Northern, Western, and Southern frontiers."[35]

Adequate or not, these men would have to do, for the new administration of Thomas Jefferson, with its republican fears of a standing army and its opposition to federal expenditures, set about to reduce the author-

[32] Hamilton to Wilkinson, February 12, 1799, and Wilkinson to Hamilton, September 4, 1799, Wilkinson, Memoirs, I, 435–436, 440–458. Hamilton and Wilkinson did not seem to be in agreement about where the troops should be concentrated on the Mississippi, whether on the lower river or closer to the Ohio. See the discussion in Norman W. Caldwell, "Cantonment Wilkinsonville," Mid-America, XXXI (January, 1949), 9–11.

[33] Whitaker, Mississippi Question, pp. 116–129; Nathan Schachner, Alexander Hamilton (New York, 1946), pp. 360–388; John C. Miller, Alexander Hamilton: Portrait in Paradox (New York, 1959), pp. 466–508.

[34] See the reasonable account of this episode in Hamilton's career in Broadus Mitchell, Alexander Hamilton: The National Adventure, 1788–1804 (New York, 1962), pp. 423–453.

[35] Report of Secretary of War, January 5, 1800, American State Papers: Military Affairs, I, 137–139.

ized military force. Henry Dearborn, the new President's Secretary of War, at the end of 1801 submitted an "Estimate of all the Posts and Stations where garrisons will be expedient, and of the number of men requisite for each garrison." From Michilimackinac to Fort Adams and Fort Stoddert along the western frontier and from Maine to Georgia along the Atlantic coast, he would scatter twenty companies of infantry and a like number of artillery, seventy-six enlisted men per company—a grand total of a few more than 3,000 regular army troops to guard the republic.[36] Such modest estimates Congress could approve, and on March 16, 1802, a new law to be effective June 1 reduced the "standing army" to two regiments of infantry, of ten companies each, one regiment of artillery (five battalions of four companies each), and a rudimentary corps of engineers.[37]

With so few troops it was necessary to deploy them with care. A post, named Cantonment Wilkinsonville, was established on the right bank of the Ohio almost at its confluence with the Mississippi in January, 1801, with the idea that it could stand guard on both rivers.[38] The post proved unhealthy and Dearborn soon directed that a more suitable site be found on the Mississippi near the mouth of the Ohio at a situation "well calculated for a settlement and ultimately for a place of Business, where the military may have the command of the Mississippi and the Ohio Both." Then as rumors reached Washington of the uneasy status of the Trans-Mississippi region in European diplomacy, fears for the navigation on the Mississippi led Dearborn to direct a new concentration of troops in the spring of 1803. He ordered a company of artillery under Amos Stoddard from Pittsburgh down the Ohio and up the Mississippi to the mouth of the Illinois. Troops at Chickasaw Bluffs were to move down to Fort Adams and the companies at Southwest Point in eastern Tennessee were to be held in readiness to move down to the lower Mississsippi.[39]

The Louisiana Purchase soon changed the whole complexion of Mississippi valley defense, for the withdrawal of the Spanish from New

[36] "Numerical Force of the Army," December 23, 1801, ibid., pp. 154–156.
[37] U. S. Statutes at Large, II, 132–137. The distribution of this force in 1803 and 1804 is given in American State Papers: Military Affairs, I, 174–177.
[38] Caldwell, Mid-America, XXXI, 3–28. The author links the post with Hamilton-Wilkinson schemes for the West, but the post was not built until after Hamilton gave up command of the army, and few references to the post have survived so it is difficult to determine the reasons for its establishment.
[39] Dearborn to Bissell, July 6, 1802; Dearborn to Wilkinson, March 7, 1803; and Dearborn to Thomas Cushing, March 9, 1803, National Archives, Records of the Secretary of War, Letters Sent, vol. 1, pp. 235–237, 380–382, 385–387.

Orleans and the acquisition of the right bank of the Mississippi from its source to its mouth removed the obstacles to western commerce that had long irritated the frontiersmen. Spain, however, was still present in the Floridas, which cut off the South from the Gulf, and the southern Indians maintained their hold on vast stretches of territory. The Creeks, instigated by British traders and the Spanish, remained a special problem, but little military movement occurred in the Southwest. Fort Hampton was established near the great bend of the Tennessee River in 1810 to prevent illegal settling of whites on Indian lands, and in the same year troops were sent to the West Florida border to apprehend any Negroes who might be stirred to insurrection by the troubled political state in that province.[40] Otherwise there was relative quiet until the approach of the War of 1812.

[40] Secretary of War to Wade Hampton, May 4, June 14, 1810, and David Holmes to Thomas Cushing, September 26 and 28, 1810, Carter, *Territorial Papers*, VI, 63–64, 70–71, 120–122.

Military Occupation
of the Louisiana Purchase

THE sale of Louisiana to the United States by Napoleon on April 30, 1803, brought new duties and responsibilities to the officers and men of the regular army of the United States. At the stroke of the pen, the young nation doubled its territorial size. It acquired a new empire of undreamed-of extent and almost totally unknown character. In taking possession of this acquisition and in occupying and establishing American sovereignty over the land and the people, the army played a primary and indispensable role.

This work of bringing the authority of the United States government to the empire beyond the Mississippi shows in a striking way that the regular army on the frontier was not exclusively an Indian-fighting army. When the army commanders in the West were alerted to the imminent transfer of Louisiana, they did not ready themselves for sudden Indian assaults nor prepare to launch attacks upon hostile tribes. American settlement had not yet to any degree reached the new area; there was no frontier line between Indians and whites to be maintained or advanced, as was the case to the east. The immediate task instead was to establish American dominion over a vast territory that had paid allegiance to the French and then to the Spanish. The concentrations of population were French and Spanish, not American, and the Indians had become accustomed to acknowledge the dominion of the Spanish officials and traders—although infiltration of British traders from Canada had already begun. How would the inhabitants of Spanish Louisiana, who had had no part in the decision, react to the sudden change of masters? What precautions should the United States take as it prepared to receive Louisiana? To whom should the responsibility be given to carry out this delicate political maneuver?

It was assumed almost as a matter of course that the occupation would be accomplished largely by the army, acting in a civil as well as military capacity. Only when the transfer had been firmly accomplished would the Indian problems that plagued the nation in the Old Northwest and the South rise to prominence in the Trans-Mississippi West.

The treaty of purchase provided that immediately upon ratification all military posts at New Orleans and in other parts of the ceded territory would be turned over to commissioners of the United States. The French and Spanish troops would then cease to occupy them and would embark as soon as possible within three months of the ratification.[1] This would necessitate a movement of United States troops into Louisiana to fill the vacuum left by the departing troops of Spain (for France never really occupied the territory after it received it from Spain by the Treaty of San Ildefonso in 1800), and the troops would be essential to make sure that the transfer to the United States was not obstructed by the inhabitants of Louisiana. The purchase, furthermore, changed the whole picture of western defense and necessitated a reorganization of the military forces in the Mississippi valley.

Official word of the treaty was received in Washington on July 14, 1803, and appeared in summary form in the public press on July 18, and although the treaty was not ratified and proclaimed until October 21, the President and the War Department started the wheels turning.[2] On July 17 Jefferson wrote to Governor William C. C. Claiborne of Mississippi Territory asking him to procure for Congress "all the information necessary to enable them to take understandingly the best measures for incorporating that country with the Union, & for it's happy government." Jefferson could not restrain his joy over the purchase. "I consider the acquisition of this country," he told Claiborne, "as one of the most fortunate events which have taken place since the establishment of our independence. . . . [I]t secures to an incalculable distance of time the tranquility, security & prosperity of all the Western country."[3] On the following day Jefferson asked Claiborne to act as the United

---

[1] The treaty and accompanying conventions are in Hunter Miller, ed., *Treaties and Other International Acts of the United States of America* (8 vols., Washington, 1931–1948), II, 498–528.

[2] See the notes, *ibid.*, p. 507, and in Clarence E. Carter, ed., *The Territorial Papers of the United States* (26 vols., Washington, 1934–1962), IX, 4.

[3] Jefferson to Claiborne, July 17, 1803, Carter, *Territorial Papers*, IX, 3.

States commissioner in receiving the territory from the French, an office Claiborne accepted with alacrity. Jefferson suggested sending three companies from Fort Adams to man the fortifications at New Orleans, to which Claiborne agreed.[4] Immediately, with the changed circumstances in the West, the Secretary of War wrote to the commanding officers at Fort Adams and at the post being established at Washington, the capital of Mississippi Territory, telling them to halt any extensive construction since the posts would lose their significance with the cession of Louisiana.[5]

As the weeks passed and more information floated in, rumors and fears multiplied and greater emphasis came to be placed on the military aspects of the occupation. Claiborne, at the end of September, suggested three or four companies of regular troops to take care of the fortifications at New Orleans and between that city and the mouth of the Mississippi, but he wanted in addition four or five thousand stands of arms and a suitable amount of ammunition to arm the whites in case the Negroes and mulattoes might make the change of government an occasion for insurrection. On October 5 the Secretary of War thought it necessary to write to General Wilkinson, to alert him to possible dangers should Spain oppose United States possession of Louisiana. Wilkinson was directed to work in concert with Claiborne to prepare for eventualities, not only by providing for the regular troops that would be sent but secretly providing also for militia who might be raised as necessary. Orders were to be sent also to the commanders at Fort Massac and Fort Pickering to have their companies ready to move down the river at short notice.[6]

When the treaty of cession was ratified on October 21, arrangements were begun for the transfer. Ten days after the ratification Congress authorized the President to take possession of and occupy the new territory and to appoint temporary officials for governing the region. The President was authorized to employ any part of the army, navy, or militia that he considered necessary. On the same day a joint commission was issued to Governor Claiborne and General Wilkinson, giving them full power to take possession of the territory ceded by France, and a

[4] Jefferson to Claiborne, July 18, 1803, and Claiborne to Jefferson, August 12, 1803, ibid., pp. 5, 11.

[5] Secretary of War to the Commanding Officer at Fort Adams, July 18, 1803, National Archives, Records of the Secretary of War, Letters Sent, vol. 2, p. 28.

[6] Claiborne to Jefferson, September 29, 1803, and Secretary of War to Wilkinson, October 5, 1803, Carter, Territorial Papers, IX, 59, 71.

separate commission was issued to Claiborne empowering him to govern the territory until further provisions were made by Congress.[7]

In addition the Secretary of State and the Secretary of War sent long letters of instruction to Claiborne and Wilkinson, respectively, advising them of their responsibilities. Madison informed Claiborne that if peaceful transfer was obstructed by the Spanish, military force should be used to effect it, and he and Wilkinson were to decide what that force would need to be. The force should consist of the regular troops near at hand, as many militia as could be drawn from Mississippi, 500 mounted militia from Tennessee, and "as many volunteers from any quarter as can be picked up." Claiborne was given authority to act before the full reinforcements arrived if he considered an immediate stroke necessary. "In order to add the effect of terror to the force of arms," Madison added, "it may be given out that measures are in train, which is a truth, for sending on from Kentucky and elsewhere a very great force, such as may be sufficient to overwhelm all possible resistance."[8]

Dearborn's instructions to Wilkinson were of like tenor, with somewhat more detail about the military action to be taken if force became necessary. The officials in Washington hoped for a peaceful transfer, however, and the Secretary of War urged the general to be solicitous of the feelings of the inhabitants and to treat them all "with the most polite and soothing attentions." Only when it was clear beyond all doubt

[7] U. S. Statutes at Large, II, 245; commissions dated October 31, 1803, Carter, Territorial Papers, IX, 94.

The military occupation of the Louisiana Purchase is described in James R. Jacobs, The Beginning of the U. S. Army, 1783–1812 (Princeton, 1947), pp. 309–334. Histories of Louisiana contain sections on the transfer and occupation of Lower Louisiana, but most of them are understandably more concerned with political than military matters. See François-Xavier Martin, The History of Louisiana from the Earliest Period (2 vols., New Orleans, 1827–1829), a sort of annals written by a man who had come to Orleans Territory as a territorial judge in 1810; Charles Gayarré, History of Louisiana (4 vols., 3d edition, New Orleans, 1885); and Alcée Fortier, A History of Louisiana (4 vols., New York, 1904). James K. Hosmer's The History of the Louisiana Purchase (New York, 1902) is a popular account written at the time of the centennial celebration. A detailed scholarly account of certain aspects of the occupation is Isaac J. Cox, "The Louisiana-Texas Frontier: Part II, The American Occupation of the Louisiana-Texas Frontier," Southwestern Historical Quarterly, XVII (July, 1913), 1–42; (October, 1913), 140–187. The legislative history of the act establishing territorial government for the Louisiana Purchase is told in Everett S. Brown, The Constitutional History of the Louisiana Purchase, 1803–1812 (Berkeley, Calif., 1920). The printed sources are relatively rich. Most valuable are the Official Letter Books of W. C. C. Claiborne, 1801–1816, ed. Dunbar Rowland (6 vols., Jackson, Miss., 1917). Carter, Territorial Papers, IX, is an exceptionally able selection of documents, both political and military, dealing with Lower Louisiana.

[8] Madison to Claiborne, October 31, 1803, Carter, Territorial Papers, IX, 91–94.

that there would be forceful opposition was he to use his troops. Dearborn on the same day wrote to Governor John Sevier of Tennessee, directing him to assemble with the least possible delay 500 mounted and armed militia, to be formed into a regiment of eight companies and marched to Natchez, where they would be subject to Wilkinson's orders. From Governor Gerard of Kentucky and Governor Tiffin of Ohio he requested similar forces, to be held in readiness to move at short notice if necessary.[9]

These measures of caution—if not panic—fortunately proved unnecessary. The Spanish inhabitants, although unhappy about the change of masters, made no attempt to hinder the official transfers. On November 30 Louisiana, which had continued under Spanish control despite the retrocession to France in 1800, was formally and ceremoniously transferred to France in the person of Pierre Clement Laussat, the French commissioner, who held possession for only twenty days.

Claiborne and Wilkinson on December 4 met at Fort Adams, where the troops were assembling—about 200 Mississippi volunteers plus the regulars, making a total of 450–500 men. The Tennessee militia were not yet in sight, but the peaceful transfer to France and Laussat's solicitude for the imminent arrival of the American commissioners had restored an air of tranquility to the operation. On about December 10 the American force dropped down the river, landing at a point two miles from New Orleans on the 15th. Here the troops encamped while they awaited the formal transfer set for the 20th.

The transfer itself was a ceremonious affair. The Spanish militia were drawn up on the public square in front of the City Hall. At noon the American troops entered the city to a salute of twenty-one guns, and they took their position on the opposite side of the square, facing the militia. In the City Hall Wilkinson and Claiborne presented their credentials to Laussat, which were publicly read along with the powers of the French commissioner and the treaty of cession. Laussat delivered the province to the United States, presented the keys of the city to Claiborne, and absolved the inhabitants of their allegiance to the French Republic. Then Claiborne rose to address the crowd assembled in the grand salon of the Hall. He congratulated them and received them as brothers of the American people, and he promised them security in their liberty, property, and religion under the American government.

[9] Dearborn to Wilkinson, October 31, 1803, *ibid.*, pp. 96–98; Dearborn to Sevier, October 31, 1803, National Archives, Records of the Secretary of War, Letters Sent, vol. 2, pp. 97–99.

As the three commissioners moved out onto one of the balconies of the City Hall, the French flag at the top of the pole in the middle of the square came down and the American flag was raised amidst a firing of the land batteries. The Spanish militia were delivered to the command of the Americans, and American occupation began with a formal proclamation of the new governor.[10]

Wilkinson reported the affair hastily to the Secretary of War. The quiet did not quite satisfy him, however, and he added: "I conjure you sir, as you value the continuation of this tranquillity, dispose of a Garrison of 500 Regulars for the place as soon as possible, for indeed I apprehend difficulties from various causes—The formidable aspect of the armed Blacks & Malattoes, officered & organized, is painful & perplexing, and the People have no Idea but of Iron domination at this moment."[11]

There was to be a little delay in the surrender of the outlying posts, and Wilkinson's troop returns for the end of the year show 276 officers and men at New Orleans and 42 at the fortification below the city at Plaquemines (Fort St. Philip). Only a handful of regulars manned the older posts in the Mississippi valley—117 at Kaskaskia, 78 at Fort Massac, 39 at Fort Pickering, and 54 at Fort Adams.[12]

The Spanish officials and troops were slow to move from New Orleans, and Wilkinson was perturbed because they did not make room for his own men. For a while the American soldiers occupied the ground floor of the barracks while the Spanish troops retained occupancy of the upper story, an arrangement not at all to the general's liking. On January 3 Wilkinson discharged the militia, although he did not want the War Department to think that this move indicated satisfaction with the size of the regular force at New Orleans. The militia were discharged "because of their importunity, their impatience, the irregularities into which they were run[n]ing & the expence they occasioned." The fear of a black uprising still haunted Wilkinson. "The People of Colour are all armed," he wrote, "and it is my Opinion a single envious artful bold incendiary, by rousing their fears & exciting their Hopes,

[10] James R. Jacobs, *Tarnished Warrior, Major-General James Wilkinson* (New York, 1938), pp. 202–203. There are descriptions of the ceremony in Martin, *History of Louisiana*, II, 198–200, and Gayarré, *History of Louisiana*, III, 619–620. Claiborne's address and proclamation are in his *Official Letter Books*, I, 307–310.

[11] Wilkinson to Secretary of War, December 21, 1803, Carter, *Territorial Papers*, IX, 139.

[12] *American State Papers: Military Affairs* (7 vols., Washington, 1832–1861), I, 175.

might produce those Horrible Scenes of Bloodshed & rapine, which have been so frequently noticed in St Domingo." The Secretary of War ordered three companies from the Atlantic posts to sail for New Orleans, alarmed by the "extremely unpleasant" state of affairs in the city described by Wilkinson.[13]

Meanwhile the outlying posts were gradually passing into the hands of the Americans as orders were issued by Laussat for their delivery. Early in January Ferdinand L. Claiborne, an ex-army officer and brother of the governor, was sent to receive Concordia, the post opposite Natchez, and detachments under Lieutenant Henry Hopkins of the First Infantry moved out to occupy Attakapas and Opelousas. Governor Claiborne appointed Hopkins civil commandant in the district and was much impressed with the young officer's knowledge and prudence. Lieutenant James B. Many of the artillery was sent on March 23 to Fort San Esteban de Arkansas (Arkansas Post), and on April 15 Lieutenant Joseph Bowmar received the post and district of Ouachita (Fort Miro). Bowmar found a population of about 150 families settled along the river, but he was forced to build cabins for his command because there were no public buildings available for his use. There was no disturbance or opposition in these transfers, and the officers in their combined military and civil capacities were well received by the inhabitants.[14]

More crucial was the Spanish post at Natchitoches on the Red River. This was the westernmost outpost in Lower Louisiana and the contact point with Texas. Although Wilkinson had intended to send troops to occupy the post when the other outlying stations were transferred, long delays occurred, ostensibly because of the need to keep troops in New Orleans until the Spanish forces had withdrawn. Finally at noon on April 26 Captain Edward D. Turner of the First Infantry with a detachment of about sixty soldiers raised the American flag at Natchitoches, just an hour after the French flag had superseded the Spanish.[15] The Spanish garrison withdrew beyond the Sabine to Nacogdoches. The two posts faced each other across the Sabine, focal points of military

[13] Wilkinson to Secretary of War, January 11, 1804, Carter, *Territorial Papers*, IX, 159–160; Secretary of War to Wilkinson, Cushing, and Freeman, February, 1804, National Archives, Records of the Secretary of War, Letters Sent, vol. 2, pp. 163ff. The militia requested from Kentucky, Tennessee, and Ohio were not needed because of the peaceful occupation, and on January 16, 1804, the Secretary of War canceled the request made on October 31.

[14] Commission to Hopkins, January 20, 1804; Claiborne to Madison, January 24 and August 9, 1804, *Official Letter Books*, I, 336–338, 347, II, 298–299; Bowmar to Claiborne, April 15, 1804, Carter, *Territorial Papers*, IX, 223–224.

[15] Jacobs, *Beginning of the U. S. Army*, p. 314; Turner to Claiborne, May 1, 1804, Carter, *Territorial Papers*, IX, 238–239.

force and national pride, which on occasion were on the brink of open conflict.

General Wilkinson, his initial military occupation completed peacefully, left New Orleans on April 25, 1804, for Washington, not to return to the Mississippi valley until he entered St. Louis late in June, 1805, as Governor of Louisiana Territory. His place in New Orleans was taken by Colonel Constant Freeman, who was warmly welcomed by Claiborne since his knowledge of French and his Catholic religion made him particularly acceptable to the people of Louisiana. Claiborne furnished the colonel with a public building for his quarters, hoping that with house rent saved the officer might be able to live on his meager pay in the expensive city.[16]

☆

Although Claiborne and Wilkinson theoretically received all of Louisiana from Laussat at the transfer ceremonies in New Orleans on December 20, in practice only Lower Louisiana and adjacent outposts changed their allegiance. The transfer of Upper Louisiana was a separate affair.[17] The key American figure there was Captain Amos Stoddard of the artillery, to whom was entrusted a multiple role.

On July 19, 1803, Dearborn wrote to Stoddard informing him of the cession of Louisiana and alerting him to the necessity, in a few months, of establishing an American military post on the west side of the Mississippi in Upper Louisiana. He was directed to move his company to Kaskaskia and from there to deal with the Spanish authorities at St. Louis. He was to gather as much information as he could about the state of affairs in Upper Louisiana and determine the most suitable site for a military post, which would among other things command the mouth of the Missouri River. Soon after the ratification of the treaty, definite instructions were sent to Stoddard. He was to wait until he got word from Claiborne or Wilkinson that the Spanish posts would be delivered up on American application, and then to make the neces-

---

[16] Claiborne to Dearborn, June 9, 1804, *Official Letter Books*, II, 199.

[17] There is a detailed account of the transfer of Upper Louisiana, with many documents included, in Louis Houck, *A History of Missouri, from the Earliest Explorations and Settlements until the Admission of the State into the Union* (3 vols., Chicago, 1908), II, 355–418. A very valuable collection of documents from Captain Amos Stoddard's papers is in "Transfer of Upper Louisiana," *Glimpses of the Past*, II (May–September, 1935), 78–122.

sary arrangements with the Spanish officers. Stoddard was authorized to act as commandant of Upper Louisiana (that is, as civil governor) until other arrangements for the government of the province were made. At the same time Captain Daniel Bissell was instructed to take over the Spanish posts at New Madrid and at Little Prairie and to post a lieutenant and twenty-five to thirty men at the two locations. Similarly Captain George W. Carmichael, the commanding officer at Chickasaw Bluffs, was instructed to reduce his garrison there to twenty or twenty-five men and use the rest of his command to take over the Spanish posts in his vicinity.[18]

Stoddard soon received his orders from New Orleans. He was first of all appointed commissioner and agent of France to receive Upper Louisiana from Spain, an arrangement proposed by Laussat in order to save France the expense and trouble of sending its own agents to such remote posts for what was after all a mere formality. At the same time he received commission as agent of the United States to receive the territory from France. Until Congress made some permanent provision for the governing of Upper Louisiana, all military and civil authority was to rest with Stoddard and the officials under him whom he sent to the separate posts. Whereas under Spanish rule, however, the two authorities had been "confounded & blended together," Stoddard was admonished to keep his civil and military functions "carefully separated & distinct." To this end he received one commission from Claiborne constituting him civil commandant and a second from Wilkinson instructing him on military matters.[19]

When Stoddard received the communications from New Orleans, he immediately opened negotiations with Lieutenant Governor Charles DeHault DeLassus for the formal transfer, and in a few days he dispatched his troops from Kaskaskia up river toward St. Louis. The exchange of formalities between the two officers was somewhat impeded because, as DeLassus wrote through his interpreter to Stoddard, "you do not Speack more the Spanish and French tongues than I do the English," but everything was carried out smoothly.[20]

The American troops landed at Cahokia opposite St. Louis on Febru-

[18] Secretary of War to Stoddard, July 19, and November 7, 1803; Secretary of War to Bissell, November 7, 1803; Secretary of War to Carmichael, November 7, 1803, Carter, *Territorial Papers*, XIII, 3–4, 8–10.

[19] Wilkinson and Claiborne to Stoddard, January 16, 1804, *Glimpses of the Past*, II, 80–81.

[20] Exchange of letters between Stoddard and DeLassus, February 18–25, 1804, *ibid.*, pp. 83–86.

ary 25, where they encamped until all the preliminary negotiations were completed. Ice on the river and the illness of the Spanish governor caused some delay, but on March 9 Stoddard received Upper Louisiana in the name of France, as DeLassus released the inhabitants from their allegiance to His Catholic Majesty. On the following day Stoddard assumed control of the territory in the name of the United States. His troops, ferried across the river under the immediate command of Lieutenant Stephen Worrell, marched to the garrison, where the American flag was raised and a salute fired. Stoddard published a circular address to the inhabitants, welcoming them as citizens, not subjects, into the "embraces of a wise and magnanimous nation." There was no opposition to the change of government on the part of the people, and Stoddard carried out his duties with firmness and grace. He reappointed the Spanish commandants of the several districts as civil, but not as military, commandants, and he began to organize the militia. He interfered as little as possible with the administrative machinery and largely confined himself to preserving public order until Congress made some more permanent arrangements for the government of the territory. Stoddard served as commandant until he was replaced on July 1 by a superior officer in the artillery, Major James Bruff.[21]

Upper Louisiana was still a primitive frontier except for St. Louis and one or two other villages, and the army continued to play a large part in the administration of the area. In the minds of some there was considerable doubt whether the region should get an organized government at all or be simply left as an Indian reserve. In the debate on the bill to erect a government in Louisiana, Senator James Jackson of Georgia pleaded with his colleagues not to organize Upper Louisiana:

I have high authority for saying it is the intention of our government to take effectual measures to induce all the Indians on this side of the Mississippi to exchange their lands for land in upper Louisiana. I think it a prudent and practicable measure—and that is one reason why I wish to prevent the establishment of a civil government in that territory. In the name of God have we not land enough for a settlement without this! I would buy up the title of those who have already gone there. The Indians would have gone there before this had not the Spaniards . . . prevented them. The Indian wars have cost us millions of dollars—and much blood. They are bad dangerous neighbors. There are already many Indians there

[21] See documents, *ibid.*, pp. 86–97.

—if you establish a civil government—if you permit settlers—you will find the expense of that government immense—it will render the purchase a curse.[22]

These arguments were not heeded, but when Congress on March 26, 1804, provided for the government of the Louisiana Purchase, Upper Louisiana was cut off from Lower at the 33d parallel. The lower section was erected into Orleans Territory with provisions comparable to other territorial governments, but the upper part was designated the "District of Louisiana." The District for administrative purposes was attached to Indiana Territory. It was to be subdivided into districts, over each of which a commanding officer was to be appointed, who was charged with "the employment of the military and militia of his district, in case of sudden invasion or insurrection . . . and at all times with the duty of ordering a military patrol, aided by militia if necessary, to arrest unauthorized settlers in any part of his district." The act was to take effect on October 1, 1804, and on that date by proclamation of Governor William Henry Harrison five districts were established, following closely the former Spanish divisions—St. Louis, St. Charles, St. Genevieve, Cape Girardeau, and New Madrid. Samuel Hammond, Representative in Congress from Georgia, accepted commission as brevet colonel and commandant of the St. Louis District, the most important post.[23]

Regular military garrisons were maintained only at St. Louis and at New Madrid, and the returns of the commanding general at the end of 1804 showed the following distribution of troops in the Mississippi valley: Fort Massac 61, Kaskaskia 80, St. Louis 57, New Madrid 16, Arkansas Post 16, Ouachita 19, Attakapas 14, Opelousas 47, Natchitoches 75, New Orleans 375, Fort St. Philip 67, Fort Adams 4, Fort Pickering 16.[24]

The political expedient of the "District" of Louisiana attached to Indiana Territory soon proved unsatisfactory, for the inhabitants objected to the idea that they were not significant enough to warrant their own territorial status, and on March 3, 1805, Congress acceded to

[22] Everett S. Brown, ed., "The Senate Debate on the Breckinridge Bill for the Government of Louisiana, 1804," *American Historical Review*, XXII (January, 1917), 359.
[23] *U. S. Statutes at Large*, II, 287; Proclamation of Harrison, October 1, 1804, and Commission to Hammond, Carter, *Territorial Papers*, XIII, 51–53. For further information on the appointment of the commandants, see Carter, *Territorial Papers*, XIII, *passim*, and Houck, *History of Missouri*, II, 382.
[24] *American State Papers: Military Affairs*, I, 176–177.

their wishes by creating the Territory of Louisiana. To serve as first governor of the new territory President Jefferson appointed General James Wilkinson, who thus combined in his one person both the civil and military authority in the region.[25] Jefferson, it is true, acknowledged a "qualm of principle" about uniting the two functions, but he satisfied himself that Wilkinson's office in Louisiana was considered "not as a civil government, but merely a military station," and that the civil and military powers had already been combined in the office of the commandants. To seek some semblance of separation, however, Wilkinson received instructions on his civil duties from the Secretary of State, while the Secretary of War directed his duties on military and Indian matters.[26]

The War Department charged Wilkinson in the vaguest of terms to "conciliate the friendship & esteem, of the Indians generally of that extensive Country, & to produce peace & harmony, as well among the several nations and tribes, as between them & the white inhabitants," but it at the same time demanded of him strict adherence to "the most riged economy" and forbade him to establish any permanent military posts.[27] Wilkinson was thus from the first hamstrung by principles of economy from carrying out the measures he deemed necessary for firmly establishing American sovereignty in the vast reaches of Upper Louisiana.

Although Wilkinson's fame has been tarnished by his association with Aaron Burr and his machinations with Spanish officials in the West, there is no doubt that he had a fundamental grasp of the problems facing the United States in its new empire in regard to the British in the north and the Spanish in the south and the influence of these powers through their traders upon the Indians. His experience in the Ohio valley had given his mind a distinctly anti-British set and what he learned at his post in St. Louis did little to change it. Even as he passed down the Ohio to assume his new duties, he made plans to exclude the British from the trade in Louisiana. "I truly beleive," he wrote to the Secretary of War from Fort Massac on June 15, 1805,

---

[25] *U. S. Statutes at Large*, II, 331–332; Commission, March 11, 1805, and Wilkinson to Secretary of State, April 7, 1805, Carter, *Territorial Papers*, XIII, 98–99, 114–115. Wilkinson's commission was effective July 3, although the Act of Congress establishing the Territory was not effective until July 4.

[26] Jefferson to Samuel Smith, May 4, 1806, *The Writings of Thomas Jefferson*, ed. Andrew A. Lipscomb (20 vols., Washington, 1903–1904), XI, 112; Secretary of War to Wilkinson, April 19, 1805, Carter, *Territorial Papers*, XII, 116–117.

[27] Secretary of War to Wilkinson, April 19, 1805, *ibid.*, pp. 116–117.

"I shall be able to rouse a sufficient spirit of enterprize in New orleans, to meet every exigency of Indian Commerce on the waters which pass by that City, within the period of two years from the present, and therefore I think the British Minister, should be authorized to warn the Merchants of Canada, that they will not, nor their goods & merchantdize, be permitted to pass the Mississippi, after the next autumn —the interdiction would operate as a bounty to our own adventurers, and therefore it should (in my judgement) have publicity." And he added, "irrelatively to any effect on our revenue or Industry, the poisonous policy of the British traders should exclude them our Indian Territories."[28]

The diplomatic consequences of Indian relations were clear in Wilkinson's mind and in his first letter to the Secretary of War after he arrived in St. Louis he spoke on "the Subject of Indian affairs in this New world," and noted that "to extend the name and influence of the United States to the remote Nations, will require considerable disbursements: and our relations to Spain & Britian on our Southern, Western & Northern *unexplored* frontiers Suggest the expediency of attaching to us, all the Nations who drink of the waters which fall into the Gulph of Mexico."[29]

Of immediate concern was the danger from the British traders. Wilkinson knew that he could not suddenly cut off the British merchandise which furnished the regular supplies of the Indians, but he urged the Secretary of State, as he had already urged the Secretary of War, to warn the British that the trade would be stopped and to make the warning public. To enforce the interdiction Wilkinson recommended the immediate establishment of a military post at the mouth of the Wisconsin River and another at the Mandan villages or at the falls of the Missouri, with customs officers to seize contraband goods. "These arrangements being once accomplished," he predicted, "in a very few years the trade of the Mississippi and Missouri, would take its ancient and natural course to New Orleans."[30]

While Wilkinson was calling for military posts on the upper Mississippi and upper Missouri to block the British traders, the War Department was quietly carrying out its own more modest plans by the establishment of a government trading post or factory with a military garrison to protect it near the confluence of the Missouri and the Missis-

28 Wilkinson to Secretary of War, June 15, 1805, *ibid.*, p. 135.
29 Wilkinson to Secretary of War, July 27, 1805, *ibid.*, p. 169.
30 Wilkinson to Secretary of State, July 28, 1805, *ibid.*, pp. 173–174.

sippi. In the treaty made with the Sacs and Foxes at St. Louis by William Henry Harrison on November 3, 1804, the United States had promised to establish such a trading house for the benefit of the tribes; even before Wilkinson had departed for St. Louis as governor the Secretary of War had directed him to locate the factory where it would be convenient for the Osages and other Missouri River tribes. Troops sent from Mackinac encamped at Portage des Sioux late in June, 1805, and a month later they were busily engaged in constructing the fort and the factory on a site on the Missouri River bottom selected by Wilkinson. It was located on the right bank of the river about four miles from the mouth, near a beautiful spring, which gave the post its name, Fort Belle Fontaine. For two decades the fort was a key post in the West.[31]

Wilkinson was not satisfied. In August, 1805, he drew up a more detailed plan for military deployment in Louisiana Territory. "Taking it for granted, that we shall not be able to controul the Indians, before we get possession of the interior of their Country," he proposed establishing small posts at the mouth of the Platte River, at the Pawnee villages on the Platte, at the mouth of the Wisconsin, and at the mouth of the Minnesota. Then, after taking counsel with the officials of Louisiana Territory, he issued a proclamation on August 26, 1805, prohibiting any citizen or subject of a foreign power from trading on the Missouri River, forbidding licensed traders from carrying into the country flags or medals or other ornaments "bearing the devices or emblems of any prince, Potentate, or foreign power whatsoever," and directing that only American goods or goods properly imported could be used in the trade. The proclamation had a serious effect on the British traders and no doubt increased their hostility to the Americans.[32]

Wilkinson continually harped on the same subject in his correspondence with Washington, and in early September he told the Secretary of War, "It is in my Judgement so necessary for us to take Post up the

[31] For the history of Fort Belle Fontaine, see Kate L. Gregg, "Building of the First American Fort West of the Mississippi," *Missouri Historical Review*, XXX (July, 1936), 345–364; W. T. Norton, "Old Fort Belle Fontaine," *Journal of the Illinois State Historical Society*, IV (October, 1911), 334–339. The factory was closed in 1808, and after floods in 1810 the fort was moved to a better site on the bluff, where it continued until replaced by Jefferson Barracks in 1826. For details on the government factory system, see pp. 205–207 below.

[32] Wilkinson to Secretary of War, August 10, 1805, Carter, *Territorial Papers*, XIII, 182–183; Proclamation and related documents, *ibid.*, pp. 200–203, and in Donald Jackson, ed., *Letters of the Lewis and Clark Expedition with Related Documents, 1783–1854* (Urbana, Ill., 1962), pp. 256–257.

Mississippi, that I should not hesitate, (did I feel my self fully authorised and could command Provisions) to send off Russell Bissell's comp^y from Kaskaskias, where it is perfectly useless, to Prairie des Chiens without a moments delay." And he spoke of plans for a post at the mouth of the Des Moines River.[33] All this was part of an overriding concern that the United States' push into the new territories would in fact be accomplished by some effective display of American authority and not by mere paper title. He poured out his concern to the Secretary of War:

> When I estimate the number and force of the Indian nations, who inhabit the Country watered by the Missouri and the Mississippi, and who if not made our friends will become our enemies—when I survey the Jealousies and the rivalry which exist on the side of Canada,—When I anticipate the fears, alarms and counteractions, which must necessarily be exerted on the side of New-Mexico,— When I cast my eyes over the expanse of Territory to be occupied or controuled, and glance at futurity, I hope you will pardon me Sir for observing, with all due deference and respect to my superiors, that we are not in sufficient strength, of men or means, to meet the occasion and profit by the favourable circumstances of the moment—[34]

The governor's earnest pleas fell on unsympathetic ears in Washington, where the needs of the frontier were less well understood than the needs of economy. He was admonished in October that it was better to consolidate his troops rather than disperse them in scattered posts on the upper Mississippi and Missouri, and although it was admitted that his proposed posts, especially on the upper Mississippi, might be "proper and highly useful," no movements were to be made until the matter had been considered more fully. The Secretary of War reinforced the directive two weeks later by the order that no detachments were to be made to establish posts and no arrangements were to be made for new and distant posts without the express prior approval of the President. Dearborn added as a sort of afterthought: "I hope you have not made any detachments or taken steps, which may not accord with the foregoing observations."[35]

[33] Wilkinson to Secretary of War, September 8, 1805, Carter, *Territorial Papers*, XIII, 199–200.
[34] Wilkinson to Secretary of War, September 22, 1805, *ibid.*, p. 230.
[35] Secretary of War to Wilkinson, October 16 and November 2, 1805, *ibid.*, pp. 239–240, 251–252.

The warnings came too late. On October 20 Wilkinson had sent out an expedition of twenty-five men under his son, Lieutenant James B. Wilkinson, to establish a fort at the mouth of the Platte River. The party, however, was stopped by the Indians some distance below the mouth of the Kansas River, and rather than risk hostilities, the expedition turned around and returned to Fort Belle Fontaine. The general was reprimanded for his precipitous action: when the Secretary of War got word of the expedition to the Platte, he sent Wilkinson a blistering note to recall the detachment and in the future to consider the establishment of distant posts as under the immediate direction of the President.[36]

The reprimand did not disturb Wilkinson, who argued that it was some times necessary to move first and get permission later, and he continued to describe the situation on the frontier to his superiors as he saw it. Drawing on his experience on the Ohio frontier a decade earlier, he proposed an apt analogy for the Secretary of War:

> The relative position of the Spaniards in New Mexico, of the United States on the Mississippi, & the intermediate hordes of Savages, may be compared to the former relations of the British Posts on the Lakes, our settlements on the Ohio, & the intervening tribes of savages, who so long Jeopardized our frontiers & defied our Force; and the Policy is so obvious, we ought not to doubt, that the Spaniards (however blind) will exert themselves to Erect a strong Barrier of hostile Savages, to oppose us in time of War, & to harrass our frontiers in time of Peace.—The Anology of circumstances fails indeed, in several important essentials unfavourable to us,—The Theatre before us is much more extensive—we are here feeble & far removed from substantial succour—The Savages are as ten to one—They are known to the Spaniards & unknown to us—and their Habits of Life, put it out of our Power to destress or destroy them.[37]

Wilkinson's words were lost among the noise of other disturbances, and instead of sending reinforcements for Upper Louisiana, the Secretary of War pulled troops away. Threatening dangers from the Spanish across the Sabine led the War Department to direct Wilkinson in March, 1806, to send all his regular soldiers to Fort Adams, except for one artillery company to be kept at Fort Belle Fontaine to guard the

[36] Wilkinson to Secretary of War, October 22 and December 10, 1805, and Secretary of War to Wilkinson, November 21, 1805, *ibid.*, pp. 244, 290, 297–298.

[37] Wilkinson to Secretary of War, December 30, 1805, *ibid.*, pp. 357–358.

factory. The governor was soon ordered to follow them, for on May 6 he was sent to take command of all the regular troops in that quarter as well as militia and volunteers to be called up to "repel any invasion, of the Territory of the United States, East of the river Sabine; or North, or West, of the bounds of what has been called West Florida." His career as governor, besides, had for some time been under severe attack, and opposition to him had built up at St. Louis among both his military and civilian subordinates. On August 16, after a delay that greatly irritated the Secretary of War, Wilkinson finally left St. Louis.[38]

[38] Secretary of War to Wilkinson, March 14 and May 6, 1806, *ibid.*, pp. 453, 505–507. For an account of Wilkinson's opposition in St. Louis, see Jacobs, *Tarnished Warrior*, pp. 226–229.

☆ FIVE ☆

Exploring and Protecting the Empire Beyond the Mississippi

THE cautious action in Louisiana that the War Department had enjoined upon Wilkinson, much to his irritation, did not hamper the farseeing projects of President Jefferson. The dream of empire, which fired him and which found reflection in some distorted way in James Wilkinson, demanded knowledge of the West. How could one *possess* the new land if he did not *know* it? The means were expeditions of discovery, and the agent of the United States in these important undertakings was the regular army.

The most daring and dramatic of the episodes in the unlocking of the continent was the expedition of Meriwether Lewis and William Clark to the Pacific and back in 1804–1806. There is no clearer indication of the enterprise of army officers and men than the triumphant passage of these two captains and their company through the tribes of the Trans-Mississippi West.[1]

[1] One can follow the expedition of Lewis and Clark fully in the printed journals. The most complete edition is Reuben Gold Thwaites, ed., *Original Journals of the Lewis and Clark Expedition, 1804–1806* (8 vols., New York, 1904–1905), but this must be supplemented by Milo M. Quaife, ed., *The Journals of Captain Meriwether Lewis and Sergeant John Ordway Kept on the Expedition of Western Exploration, 1803–1806* (Madison, Wis., 1916), and *The Field Notes of Captain William Clark, 1803–1805*, ed. Ernest S. Osgood (New Haven, 1964). Nicholas Biddle's rewriting of the journals appeared as *History of the Expedition Under the Command of Captains Lewis and Clark, to the Sources of the Missouri, Thence Across the Rocky Mountains and Down the River Columbia to the Pacific Ocean, Performed During the Years 1804–5–6* (2 vols., Philadelphia, 1814). Biddle's narrative forms the basis for Elliott Coues, ed., *History of the Expedition Under the Command of Lewis and Clark* (4 vols., New York, 1893), which is especially valuable for the extensive notes supplied by Coues. Essential for a full understanding of the expedition are the

The idea of course was Jefferson's. Even before the Louisiana Purchase had by good fortune passed to the United States, the President was planning an exploration west of the Mississippi, to probe for a passageway to the western ocean and the Orient that lay beyond. To lead the expedition he picked Meriwether Lewis, a young army officer whom two years earlier he had appointed his private secretary because of his "knolege of the Western country, of the army and of all it's interests & relations."[2] Lewis, commissioned a captain in the First Infantry, picked as his assistant—indeed co-commander—for the expedition William Clark, who was appointed second lieutenant in the artillery (although he used the title "captain" throughout the expedition). Lewis was authorized to call upon the services of such noncommissioned officers and privates from the army as he needed as well as civilian personnel. When the party left St. Louis to begin its historic journey, Lewis and Clark had a group of four sergeants, twenty-two privates, plus interpreters and hunters and Clark's Negro slave. The expedition, although an extraordinary one, was throughout an army operation, and military discipline was firmly enforced.

Lewis, in asking Clark to join him, outlined the purposes of the journey. With the expectation that the territory would soon become the property of the United States, he emphasized to Clark "the importance to the U. States of an early friendly and intimate acquaintance with the tribes that inhabit that country, that they should be early impressed with a just idea of the rising importance of the U. States and of her friendly dispositions towards them, as also her desire to become usefull to them by furnishing them through her citizens with such articles by way of barter as may be desired by them or usefull to them —the other objects of this mission are scientific, and of course not less interesting to the U. States than to the world generally."[3] To assert the "rising importance of the U. States" among the remote tribes and to tie them to the United States by trade, no doubt, were as important to Jefferson as the gathering of scientific data, concern with which takes up such a large part of the official instructions sent to Lewis at the beginning of the expedition.

---

documents printed in Donald Jackson, ed., *Letters of the Lewis and Clark Expedition with Related Documents, 1783–1854* (Urbana, Ill., 1962). See also John Bakeless, *Lewis & Clark, Partners in Discovery* (New York, 1947), and Richard Dillon, *Meriwether Lewis, A Biography* (New York, 1965).

[2] Jefferson to Lewis, February 23, 1801, Jackson, *Letters of the Lewis and Clark Expedition*, p. 2.

[3] Lewis to Clark, June 19, 1803, *ibid.*, p. 59.

The party began its ascent of the Missouri on May 14, 1804, after Captain Lewis on March 9 and 10 had served as principal witness in the transfer of Upper Louisiana to the United States. The scientific gathering of data went on from the very first, but it was not until August 3, 1804, that an official council with western Indians was held. Meeting with the Otos and Missouris at Council Bluffs, a few miles above present-day Omaha, Lewis presented the formal speech that became a staple in the future conferences with the natives. He told the Indians that the French and Spanish had withdrawn from the waters of the Missouri and the Mississippi and that the "great Chief of the Seventeen great nations of America" was now the one to whom they must turn: "[H]e is the only friend to whom you can now look for protection, or from whom you can ask favours, or receive good council, and he will take care that you shall have no just cause to regret this change; he will serve you, & not deceive you." Lewis described the power and great number of the Americans, and he promised to arrange for trade. With considerable ceremony the chiefs were given silver medals with Jefferson's image on one side and symbols of peace and friendship on the other, American flags, chiefs' coats, and other presents, with the admonition from the President: "He has further commanded us to tell you that when you accept his flag and medal, you accept therewith his hand of friendship, which will never be withdrawn from your nation as long as you continue to follow the council which he may command his chiefs to give you, and shut your ears to the councils of Bad birds." The chiefs were told to turn in their French, Spanish, and British flags and medals, for it was no longer proper for them to keep these emblems of attachment to any great father than the American one.[4]

Thus presenting medals, flags, certificates, and other evidences of allegiance to the United States, the captains passed up the Missouri, holding councils with the various tribes, until finally they reached the Mandan villages near present-day Bismarck on October 26, where a camp was set up for the winter. The captain took pains while in contact here with agents of the British North West Company to warn both the Indians and the traders that the presentation or acceptance of British flags and medals within the new lands of the United States would be totally unacceptable.[5]

Early in April, after sending a small party back to St. Louis with reports and natural history specimens, Lewis and Clark moved ahead

[4] Lewis and Clark to the Oto Indians, August 4, 1804, *ibid.*, pp. 203–208.
[5] Thwaites, *Journals of the Lewis and Clark Expedition*, I, 228.

with six small canoes and two pirogues into an unknown wilderness. The thrill of the moment did not escape the romantic Lewis: "This little fleet altho' not quite so rispectable as those of Columbus or Capt. Cook," he wrote the night before their departure from Fort Mandan, "were still viewed by us with as much pleasure as those deservedly famed adventurers ever beheld theirs; and I dare say with quite as much anxiety for their safety and preservation. [W]e were now about to penetrate a country at least two thousand miles in width, on which the foot of civilized man had never trodden; the good or evil it had in store for us was for experiment yet to determine, and these little vessells contained every article by which we were to expect to subsist or defend ourselves."[6] Toiling to the headwaters of the Missouri, crossing the rugged Bitterroot Mountains, and descending the Columbia to the Pacific, the party reached the western ocean on November 7. They found no trading vessels to succor them and after a miserable winter in a rude fort near the coast, they retraced their journey overland to St. Louis, where they arrived on September 23, 1806. It was a memorable and most successful journey, which not only opened a geographical expanse hitherto unknown but inaugurated military, political, and economic penetration of the Louisiana Purchase that was immediately seconded by the fur traders of St. Louis and supported (although in erratic fashion) by subsequent army endeavors.

Lewis and Clark were keenly alert to the defense needs of the upper Missouri and related upper Mississippi country. The intrigues and rumors of intrigue that came to their attention as they ascended the Missouri and during their wintering at Fort Mandan made it unmistakeably clear that American authority would not be established by fiat in the face of Indian and British opposition. Military force would be needed to pacify hostile Indians and to thwart the operations of foreign traders, and Clark early began to sketch plans for the distribution of such a force. While at Fort Mandan he drew up a rough chart in which he set forth the "Number of Officers & Men for to protect the Indian trade and keep the Savages in peace with the U S. and each oth[er]." From an anchor post at St. Louis, he suggested a chain of forts, manned by a company or two, at "elegable Situations" in the Missouri country and the upper Mississippi region. For the first he listed sites at the Osage River (or the Arkansas), at the mouth of the Kansas River, at Council Bluffs, at the mouth of the Cheyenne River, at the mouth of the Yellowstone, at the falls of the Missouri, and at the head of the Kansas or Arkansas. The places picked for the Mississippi were

6 *Ibid.*, pp. 284–285.

Prairie du Chien, the mouth of the Minnesota or the Falls of St. Anthony, Sand Lake, and somewhere on the Minnesota River.[7] The astuteness of the young lieutenant is demonstrated by the fact that later posts were established at two-thirds of these sites or their close vicinity.

Lewis's thinking on the problems of protecting the region and its fur trade was expressed at considerable length in a document written after his return, called "Observations and Reflections on Upper Louisiana." He pointed to the dangers of allowing the British traders a free hand on the upper Missouri, thus allowing the Indians to fall under the traders' influence and permitting them "to be formed into a rod of iron, with which, for Great Britain, to scourge our frontier at pleasure." He proposed restricting British traders, opening the trade under fair competition to American merchants, and prohibiting Americans themselves from unrestricted hunting and trapping in the Indian country. It was his hope, he wrote, to combine "philanthropic views toward those wretched people of America," with means "to secure to the citizens of the United States, all those advantages, which ought of right exclusively to accrue to them, from the possession of Upper Louisiana." This would take a delicate balance, Lewis knew, and in his rough outline of points to be considered he included this shrewd observation: "The first principle of governing the Indians is to govern the whites—the impossibility of doing this without establishments, and some guards at those posts."[8]

☆

Jefferson's plans for exploring the Louisiana Purchase went beyond his plans for Lewis and Clark. While these stalwart men were busy on what the President considered a mission "of major importance," which was not to be "delayed or hazarded by any episodes whatever," he was toying with other plans if he could get Congress to furnish the money. One party might go up the Red River to its headwaters, then cross over to the Arkansas and descend that river. A second was suggested for the Platte and Des Moines rivers and a third for the Kansas and Minnesota.[9]

[7] *Field Notes of Captain William Clark*, p. 188.

[8] Thwaites, *Journals of the Lewis and Clark Expedition*, VII, 378, 387–388.

[9] Jefferson to Lewis, November 16, 1803, *The Writings of Thomas Jefferson*, ed. Andrew A. Lipscomb (20 vols., Washington, 1903–1904), X, 434; Isaac J. Cox, "The Exploration of the Louisiana Frontier, 1803–1806," *Annual Report of the American Historical Association for the Year 1904* (Washington, 1905), p. 153n.

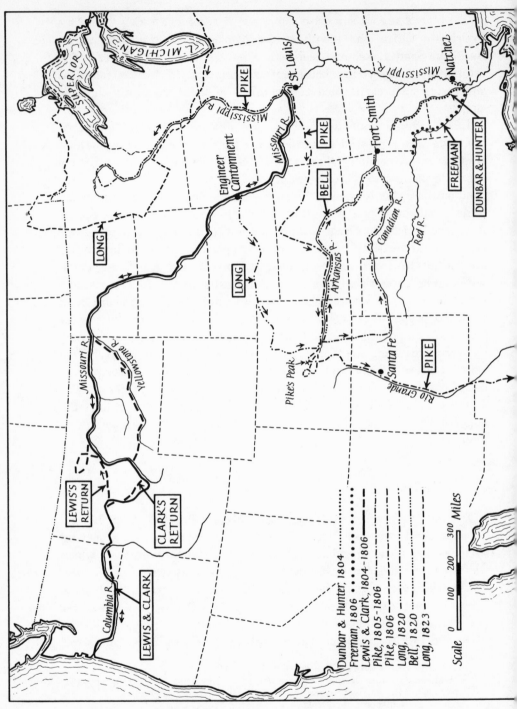

Western Exploration, 1804–1823

What was actually accomplished was considerably less than this, although two expeditions up the Red River were attempted. They were directly planned by the President and entrusted to the direction of civilians, but each was dependent upon a detachment of troops for protection and for transportation.

The first expedition was led by William Dunbar, a Scottish-born scientist living near Natchez, and Dr. George Hunter of Philadelphia. General Wilkinson was directed by the Secretary of War to furnish these gentlemen with an escort of "one Sober discreet active Serjeant & ten faithful sober Soldiers," preferably some who would volunteer for the duty, and the sergeant and an even dozen privates were eventually supplied by the commandant at New Orleans.[10] Originally scheduled to perform the full exploration of the Red and Arkansas rivers that Jefferson wanted, the party was forced to curtail its plans because of hostility among the Osage Indians and fear of Spanish interference, and it proceeded instead up the Ouachita River (always spelled "Washita" in the documents), which was protected from the Osages and remote from the Spanish frontier. The small party left St. Catherine's Landing near Natchez on October 16, 1804, went up the Ouachita as far as the hot springs (in present-day Arkansas), and in four months returned, bringing back no exciting tales and little scientific or geographical information that was not already known.[11]

In 1805 Congress appropriated $5,000 to continue these southwestern explorations, and a second party was organized, this one under Thomas Freeman, a civilian surveyor, and composed of Dr. Peter Custis, a botanist, Captain Richard Sparks of the Second Infantry, Lieutenant Enoch Humphreys of the artillery, two noncommissioned officers, seventeen privates, and a Negro servant. The exploring party did not leave Fort Adams on the Mississippi until April 19, 1806. At Natchitoches

[10] Secretary of War to Wilkinson, March 31, 1804, Clarence E. Carter, ed., *The Territorial Papers of the United States* (26 vols., Washington, 1934–1962), IX, 217.

[11] Cox, *Annual Report of the American Historical Association for 1904*, pp. 151–159. Dunbar's journal is printed in *Documents Relating to the Purchase and Exploration of Louisiana* (Boston, 1904); a summary of it appears in *Annals of Congress*, 9 Congress, 2 session, col. 1106–1146. See also Mrs. Dunbar Rowland, *Life, Letters and Papers of William Dunbar, of Elgin, Morayshire, Scotland, and Natchez, Mississippi: Pioneer Scientist of the United States* (Jackson, Mississippi, 1930), in which the journal appears on pages 216–320. Brief sketches of Dunbar are Arthur H. DeRosier, Jr., "William Dunbar, Explorer," *Journal of Mississippi History*, XXV (July, 1963), 165–185, and James R. Dungan, " 'Sir' William Dunbar of Natchez, Planter, Explorer, and Scientist, 1792–1810," *ibid.*, XXIII (October, 1961), 211–228.

they were reinforced by another army officer and twenty soldiers, for there were reports of Spanish plans to intercept the expedition. At a point 635 miles above the mouth of the Red River the explorers on July 29 ran into a large body of Spanish troops, commanded by Don Francisco Viana, who insisted that the party turn back. Freeman and Sparks, realizing that they had met an overwhelmingly superior force and following Jefferson's instructions to avoid hostilities, wisely acceded. They had been hardly more successful than Dunbar and Hunter.[12]

☆

Considerably more striking were two explorations initiated by Wilkinson himself. While Lewis and Clark were still working their way across the Great Divide, and shortly after his arrival in St. Louis, General Wilkinson set on foot an exploration of the upper Mississippi, the unknown northeastern boundary of the Louisiana Purchase. Following what he knew were Jefferson's wishes, although acting on his own authority as commanding general, Wilkinson detailed a young lieutenant of the First Infantry, Zebulon Montgomery Pike, to lead a party of soldiers in search of the source of the Mississippi.[13]

On July 30, 1805, Pike received his instructions. He was to note carefully the sort of geographical and scientific information that was essential for the development of the country—rivers, creeks, highlands, prairies, islands, rapids, shoals, mines, quarries, timber, water, soil, Indian villages and settlements, and the winds and weather—and to bring back specimens of whatever he might find "curious in the mineral, vegetable, and animal Kingdom." On a military level he was to ascertain

---

[12] Cox, *Annual Report of the American Historical Association for 1904*, pp. 160–174. A summary of the expedition is in Edwin James, *Account of an Expedition from Pittsburgh to the Rocky Mountains Performed in the Years 1819, 1820* (3 vols., London, 1823), reprinted in Reuben Gold Thwaites, ed., *Early Western Travels, 1748–1846* (32 vols., Cleveland, 1904–1907), XVII, 66–76.

[13] For journals and other documents on Pike's two explorations, see Donald Jackson, ed., *The Journals of Zebulon Montgomery Pike with Letters and Related Documents* (2 vols., Norman, Okla., 1966). An older edition with extensive notes is Elliott Coues, ed., *The Expeditions of Zebulon Montgomery Pike* (3 vols., New York, 1895). A biography is W. Eugene Hollon, *The Lost Pathfinder, Zebulon Montgomery Pike* (Norman, Okla., 1949). Secretary of War Dearborn discusses the authority for the expedition in his letter to Pike, February 24, 1808, *American State Papers: Miscellaneous* (2 vols., Washington, 1834), I, 944.

proper points for military posts between St. Louis and Prairie du Chien and on the Wisconsin River, as well as for forts and trading houses at the mouth of the Minnesota and the Falls of St. Anthony, and to arrange with the Indians for the land required. Finally, he was told he was "to spare no pains to conciliate the Indians and to attach them to the United States," and to invite chiefs who had never been to St. Louis to come down to pay Wilkinson a visit.[14] These written orders say nothing about counteracting the influence of the British traders in the Northwest, but it is clear from the attention given to the matter that Pike had strong directives from Wilkinson to this effect. The general's strong anti-British feelings, expressed with vigor in his correspondence with his superiors, could hardly have allowed him to do otherwise.[15]

Pike left St. Louis with a party of twenty soldiers and an interpreter on August 9, 1805, and at every opportunity the zealous officer made known to the Indians that their allegiance now was due to the United States and that symbols of British authority which they had long displayed on American soil were to be turned in and replaced by those of the United States.

On September 23 Pike met with the Sioux at the mouth of the Minnesota River. He explained to them how the English had withdrawn from the region of the lakes and the Mississippi and the Spanish from Louisiana, and he signed an agreement with them for parcels of land for military and trading purposes at the mouth of the St. Croix River and the mouth of the Minnesota. "They gave me the Land required," Pike wrote in his journal. The treaty left blank the amount of compensation to be given the Sioux, and the Senate in ratifying the treaty in 1808 allotted the Sioux $2,000 for the estimated 155,520 acres of the cession.[16]

The most notable example of Pike's zeal came early in February, 1806, when a small detachment from the winter camp at the mouth of the Swan River (near present-day Little Falls) penetrated to the North West Company trading post on Leech Lake. Here Pike met Hugh McGillis, the director of the Fond du Lac department of the company, to whom he sent a forceful letter asserting American rights in no uncertain terms:

[14] Wilkinson to Pike, July 30, 1805, Jackson, *Pike*, I, 3–4.
[15] See also Pike's clear statement of his purpose in his letter to Hugh McGillis, February 6, 1805, *ibid.*, pp. 256–259.
[16] Journal entry for September 23, 1805; council proceedings and treaty, September 23, 1805, *ibid.*, pp. 37, 242–246, 246n.

I have found, sir, your commerce and establishments, extending beyond our most exaggerated ideas, and in addition to the injury done our revenue, by the evasion of the duties, other acts which are more particularly injurious to the *honor* and *dignity* of our government. The transactions alluded to, are the presenting *medals* of his Britannic majesty, and *flags* of the said government, to the chiefs and warriors resident in the territory of the United States. If political subjects are strictly prohibited to our traders, what would be the ideas of the executive to see foreigners making chiefs, and distributing flags, the standard of an European power.[17]

Pike objected to "so many furnished posts" that might become arsenals to arm the savages against American citizens if a rupture should ever occur between Great Britain and the United States, and he requested McGillis to direct his agents to enter their trade goods through the custom house at Michilimackinac, under no pretence to hoist a British flag over American territory, and never to present flags or medals to the Indians or to hold political councils with them.

Not satisfied to depend on this remonstrance and the polite concession on all his points made by McGillis in a letter of February 15, Pike called the Chippewas into council so that he could let them know directly the political situation. After urging them to smoke the peace pipe he had brought from the Sioux (one of the purposes of his expedition into the Chippewa country), he directed the chiefs to turn in their flags and medals and invited them to accompany him back to St. Louis to get American ones in their stead. "Traders have no authority to make chiefs," he informed them; "and in doing this they have done what is not right. It is only great chiefs, appointed by your fathers, who have that authority."[18] The Indians agreed to follow his advice. The chiefs turned in their medals and flags or promised to do so, and some followed him to St. Louis to meet with Wilkinson.

Ostensibly the whole expedition had been a success. Pike had mistaken Leech Lake as the source of the Mississippi, to be sure, but he had penetrated with his American troops into a region long dominated by the British and had asserted American authority. He had acquired sites for military posts at the mouth of the St. Croix and at the confluence of the Minnesota and the Mississippi. And at Prairie du Chien

---

[17] Pike to McGillis, February 6, 1806, *ibid.*, pp. 257–258.
[18] Speech to Chippewas, February 16, 1806, *ibid.*, pp. 263–264.

on his way back to St. Louis he complained to the Indians about murders committed by the tribesmen and demanded that the guilty persons be turned over for punishment.[19]

Unfortunately, neither Pike nor Wilkinson was able to replace the medals and flags surrendered by the chiefs. Mere promises to do so were hardly sufficient with the Indians, who were influenced so strongly by these symbols of authority, and Pike was afraid that the government had compromised its faith with the Indians.[20] Nor was the single expedition to the upper Mississippi enough to undo the influence of the British traders over the Indians. McGillis's polite acquiescence to Pike's demands meant little when the army officer had disappeared down river. The power of the British trader Robert Dickson over the Indians when the War of 1812 broke out is positive proof that Pike was not enough.

☆

Lieutenant Pike had barely returned to St. Louis when General Wilkinson sent him out again, this time in the opposite direction into the Spanish sphere of influence in the Southwest. On June 24, 1806, while Lewis and Clark were still attempting to make their way out of the snowbound Rockies on their way home, Wilkinson gave Pike explicit instructions for his new duty. He was to travel first to the towns of the Osages, return to them Osage captives ransomed from the Potawatomis, and attempt to bring about a permanent peace between the Kansas and Osage Indians. Then he was to proceed to the Pawnee villages, as a step toward making contact with the Comanches. A main object was to make peace between the Comanches and the other tribes, especially the Osages; to further that purpose Pike was to induce some of the chiefs to make a visit to Washington, where their friendship could be cultivated and they could be impressed with the power and authority of the United States. Contact with the Comanches would lead the expedition to the headwaters of the Arkansas and Red rivers and into dangerous proximity to New Mexico, and Pike was warned to "move with great circumspection." As before, he was to bring back as many scientific data and natural history specimens as possible. While Pike was

[19] Council with Winnebagos, April 21, 1806, *ibid.*, pp. 271–272.
[20] Statement of Pike, *ibid.*, p. 276.

to come back down the Red River and wait at the post at Natchitoches for further orders, he was directed, if circumstances permitted, to detach a small party at the Arkansas to descend that river.[21]

Pike and his detachment of one lieutenant (James B. Wilkinson, the general's son), nineteen men, an interpreter, and a volunteer surgeon left Fort Belle Fontaine on July 15. When they reached the Osage villages they already ran into evidences of Spanish influence, for many Spanish medals and some commissions were shown to Pike, which he told the Indians to deliver to St. Louis. In the Pawnee country Pike barely escaped direct confrontation with Spanish troops, who had recently visited the nation, having moved into the country, as Pike believed, in explicit counteraction to his own expedition. With presents of medals, flags, and mules for the chiefs, the Spanish, Pike reported, were hoping to "renew the chains of ancient amity, which was said to have existed between their father, his most Catholic majesty, and his children the red people."[22]

Pike was again ill-prepared to match the medals and flags of the foreign rivals. He demanded that the Pawnees give up their Spanish medals and flags, but he had none to present in their place and left the tribe with only promises—pledges which were not redeemed until the factor from Fort Osage, George C. Sibley, visited the Pawnees in the summer of 1811 with an ample stock of American medals and flags.[23]

When he left the Pawnee villages, Pike moved south toward the Great Bend of the Arkansas River. Here, following his instructions, he detached Lieutenant Wilkinson with a sergeant and four privates to descend the Arkansas, while the main party turned west. Pike was searching for the headwaters of the Red River and for the Comanches, but he found neither. He made his way into present-day Colorado, where he passed an uneasy winter suffering from cold and hunger. When the New Mexico authorities heard of his presence, they sent out troops to arrest him, and Pike and his men were taken to Santa Fe and then to Chihuahua. Although his notes and papers were confiscated, Pike was treated with kindness and after several weeks in Mexico was escorted across Texas to the United States boundary. He reached Natchitoches on July 1, 1807.

[21] Wilkinson to Pike, June 24, 1806, ibid., pp. 285–287.
[22] Pike to Wilkinson, August 28, 1806, ibid., II, 144. Pike's account of the Spanish expedition is incorporated into his journal entry for September 25, 1806, in Coues's and Jackson's editions of the journal, although it was obviously written after Pike's return to the United States. Ibid., I, 323–325.
[23] Sibley journal extracts, June, 1811, ibid., II, 375–376.

How much Pike accomplished it is difficult to say. Many of his scientific notes were lost, and his descriptions of the area he traversed were hardly complimentary. "These vast plains of the western hemisphere," he wrote in one notable passage, "may become in time equally celebrated as the sandy deserts of Africa; for I saw in my route, in various places, tracts of many leagues, where the wind had thrown up the sand, in all the fanciful forms of the ocean's rolling wave, and on which not a speck of vegetable matter existed." And he went on to point out an advantage in all this. "Our citizens being so prone to rambling and extending themselves, on the frontiers," he wrote, "will, through necessity, be constrained to limit their extent on the west, to the borders of the Missouri and Mississippi, while they leave the prairies incapable of cultivation to the wandering and uncivilized aborigines of the country."[24] But he certainly proved that the Americans were eager and able to investigate all parts of their new domain and to establish there some evidence—or at least a remembrance—of American sovereignty. "Pike's expedition to the West ranks second in significance to that of Lewis and Clark [a statement he would have contested strongly]," concludes Donald Jackson of Pike's exploits, "but neither Pike nor his men rank second to anyone in courage and endurance. As the first explorers to journey from the settled eastern areas to the region now containing the states of Kansas, Colorado, and New Mexico, under conditions of hunger and cold which Pike's clumsy prose could but poorly describe, they deserved better from their government."[25]

What part Wilkinson's schemes had in sending out Pike's second expedition is difficult to determine. Wilkinson certainly had in mind an invasion of New Mexico or other Mexican provinces if a rupture should come between the United States and Spain, and as commanding general it was no doubt his responsibility to prepare for such an eventuality. In a letter to Secretary of War Dearborn on September 8, 1805, he estimated favorably "the Practicability of carrying an expedition from this point [St. Louis] into New Mexico," and he spoke of using the Arkansas River. "It therefore becomes extremely desireable it should be reconnoitred," he wrote, "and this cannot be done, with any prospect of safety, or Success, before we have brought the numerous Erratic nation of Y,a,tans, or Commanches to a conference, be-

24 *Ibid.*, pp. 27–28. Because of these passages Pike gets credit from many historians for beginning the myth of the Great American Desert.
25 *Ibid.*, I, x.

cause they reign the uncontrouled Masters of that Country. This I understand may be best accomplished through the Panis [Pawnees], and I am taking measures preparatory to the end, but without one Ct. of expense."[26] Wilkinson's instructions to Pike, it will be noted, closely paralleled these observations.

The expeditions of Lewis and Clark, of Dunbar, Hunter, and Freeman, and of Pike were not merely explorations seeking knowledge of the new lands. It is true that they were sent out in large part to gather as much information as they could that would prove useful economically, politically, or militarily, but they were also sent to display and to assert American authority. Their very presence in the land signified a present or future claim to possession of the land and sovereignty over it, and in contacts with the Indians and foreign agents or traders the commanders of the expeditions explicitly demanded acknowledgment of the economic and political rights of the United States.

☆

While Pike was carrying out his charge from Wilkinson, the general himself was engaged in delicate operations on the Louisiana-Texas border, where danger of war was serious and at a time when the Burr conspiracy was coming to a head. Wilkinson was called to take command of the troops in the South because of conflicting claims of the United States and Spain over Orleans Territory's western boundary. The United States claimed the territory as far west as the Sabine River, and pending final settlement of the dispute through diplomatic channels it was intent upon opposing any Spanish incursion east of that river. The Secretary of War in November, 1805, had directed the commanding officer at Natchitoches to send patrols through the country east of the Sabine, which he was "to consider as in our actual possession," and to repel any invaders.[27] On one occasion Spanish forces that had crossed the river were induced to withdraw, but the Spanish refused to acquiesce in the pretensions of the Americans.

Governor Claiborne of Orleans Territory was clearly dismayed by the lack of military force in his territory and made the usual cry to Washington for more troops. "A respectable Force in this quarter is,

[26] Wilkinson to Dearborn, September 8, 1805, *ibid.*, II, 100–110.
[27] Secretary of War to Commanding Officer at Natchitoches, November 20, 1805, Carter, *Territorial Papers*, IX, 534–535.

at the present Crisis, highly necessary.—The regular Troops here are few in number, and not prepared to take the Field to advantage. . . . I am *no friend* to a Standing Army;—my whole conduct in public life proves *the Fact;* but at the present period our best interests require, that there should be at least Twelve Hundred troops in this Territory! The presence of such a Force would not only deter the Spanish Agents in our vicinity from venturing on acts which are calculated to irritate; but what is infinitely of more consequence—it will give our new fellow Citizens a confidence in the American Government—which, I am sorry to say, many of them at this time, do not possess." For the militia Claiborne had little good word. He tried to inspire some martial spirit and "to keep up a degree of military ardor," but he was met by general apathy. The Secretary of War told Claiborne that six companies would be ordered from St. Louis to Fort Adams and that 200 recruits were on their way to New Orleans, and he attempted to reassure him that the Spanish government had no intention of beginning any hostilities.[28]

The governor's spirit was not cheered when early in August he heard that a considerable Spanish force (estimated as high as 1,500 men) had crossed the Sabine with the apparent determination to establish a garrison at Bayou Pierre, some fifty-five or sixty miles from Natchitoches. Claiborne, who sought without success to meet Wilkinson at Fort Adams or at Natchez, hastened alone to Natchitoches to rouse the militia, who would be needed if serious trouble arose. The governor regretted the absence of Wilkinson, who was still dawdling in St. Louis, but he felt no delay was possible and on August 24 was at Natchitoches. Irritated because the commanding officer of the post would not act without orders from Wilkinson, Claiborne satisfied himself by calling up the militia and by sending a sharp letter of remonstrance to Simon de Herrera, the commander of the Spanish troops. The Spanish, after advancing with patrols to within seven miles of Natchitoches, fell back to Bayou Pierre.[29]

Wilkinson reached Natchez on September 7 and on September 19 was writing to Claiborne from Rapides on the Red River for information about the probable strength of the Spanish forces and the number of troops necessary to force them out. The general was ready, he said, to insist on United States jurisdiction westward to the Sabine even

[28] Claiborne to Secretary of State, March 27, 1806, and Secretary of War to Claiborne, April 26, 1807, *ibid.*, pp. 617, 627–628.
[29] Correspondence in *Official Letter Books of W. C. C. Claiborne, 1801–1816,* ed. Dunbar Rowland (6 vols., Jackson, Miss., 1917), III, 377–399; IV, 1–23.

though hostilities ensued, and he spoke of resorting to force *"for the protection of our Western Frontier, and the vindication of our national Rights and Honor."* He expected to rely on 350 regular infantry, 250 militia from Mississippi Territory, and whatever added forces Claiborne could supply. On September 22, in his leisurely fashion, Wilkinson arrived at Natchitoches, where on October 3 the more than 500 militia ordered by Claiborne were to rendezvous. A sizable American army was concentrating at Natchitoches, and 100 regulars were soon to be sent forward from New Orleans.[30]

Wilkinson opened communications with Governor Antonio Cordero at Nacogdoches in a long letter of September 24, strongly reasserted American claims up to the Sabine, and demanded the withdrawal of Spanish troops. Cordero replied that he must await orders from his superior, Nimesio Salcedo, but before any further exchange between Wilkinson and the Spanish commanders was possible, Herrera on his own authority retreated on September 27 and on the 30th crossed to the west side of the Sabine with his troops.[31] A month later an American force marched to the east bank of the Sabine. Negotiations with Herrera across the river led to an agreement on November 5, by which the Spanish agreed not to cross the Sabine and the Americans not to cross the Arroyo Honda, leaving the intervening territory as a sort of neutral ground.[32]

With hostilities thus forestalled on the southwestern frontier, Wilkinson hastened to New Orleans, where the Burr conspiracy, in which he was so much implicated, was about to come to crisis.[33]

☆

In the summer of 1807, as a result of the "Chesapeake" affair, the United States was again in serious danger of war with Great Britain.

[30] Wilkinson to Claiborne, September 19, 1806, and Claiborne to Dearborn, October 8, 1806, *ibid.*, IV, 8–9, 25.

[31] Correspondence in *American State Papers: Foreign Relations* (6 vols., Washington, 1832–1859), II, 801–804; Wilkinson to Secretary of War, October 4, 1806, *Annals of Congress*, 10 Congress, 1 session, Appendix, col. 570–571.

[32] James Wilkinson, *Memoirs of My Own Times* (3 vols., Philadelphia, 1816), I, 413. There is an account of the crisis on the Louisiana-Texas frontier in Isaac J. Cox, "The Louisiana-Texas Frontier During the Burr Conspiracy," *Mississippi Valley Historical Review*, X (December, 1923), 274–284.

[33] The Burr Conspiracy, although blackening Wilkinson's reputation, had little effect upon military plans or army activity in the West. For a detailed account of the conspiracy, see Thomas P. Abernethy, *The Burr Conspiracy* (New York, 1954). A severely anti-Wilkinson account is the older study by

To bring that nation to terms Jefferson relied upon the economic sanction of the embargo, not military force, and in 1807 the authorized strength of the army stood at only 3,358 officers and men. With the increased threat of war, however, Congress on April 12, 1808, authorized a temporary additional force of eight regiments (five of infantry and one each of riflemen, light artillery, and light dragoons).[34]

Many of these new troops were soon being dispatched to New Orleans, for as the fear of a rupture with Great Britain continued, rumors reached the President that the British forces at Halifax were to be sent to take New Orleans in case the forces of the United States concentrated in the north. To counteract such a move the Secretary of War ordered the concentration at New Orleans and vicinity of as many of the regular troops as circumstances would permit. The Third, Fifth, and Seventh Infantry and four companies of the Sixth were to be ordered to the mouth of the Mississippi, as well as all of the newly authorized companies of light dragoons, riflemen, and light artillery raised in the states and territories south of New Jersey. The eastern troops were to be gathered at Atlantic posts and transported by sea, while the western forces were directed to descend the Ohio and the Mississippi. To command this assembly of troops, some seasoned but many raw, Dearborn appointed General Wilkinson and ordered him to New Orleans as soon as practicable to prepare the men to meet any invading force.[35]

General Wilkinson arrived in New Orleans on April 19, 1809, by way of Norfolk, Charleston, Havana, and Pensacola. He found some 2,000 troops in disarray in the city. Newly appointed officers, ignorant and often indifferent, did little to discipline the troops, for whom the temptations to dissipation were soon overpowering. The disregard for sanitation and the overindulgence of the troops soon sent many to the hospitals; by the time Wilkinson arrived, almost one-third of the com-

---

Walter F. McCaleb, *The Aaron Burr Conspiracy* (New York, 1903; expanded ed., 1936). The biography of Wilkinson by James R. Jacobs, *Tarnished Warrior, Major-General James Wilkinson* (New York, 1938), is critical of Wilkinson's character and some of his actions. Thomas R. Hay and M. R. Werner, *The Admirable Trumpeter: A Biography of General James Wilkinson* (Garden City, New York, 1941), is somewhat more favorable to Wilkinson. See also Thomas R. Hay, "Some Reflections on the Career of General James Wilkinson," *Mississippi Valley Historical Review*, XXI (March, 1935), 471–494. Francis S. Philbrick, *The Rise of the West, 1754–1830* (New York, 1965), almost completely exonerates Wilkinson of any wrongdoing.

[34] "Military Force in 1807," *American State Papers: Military Affairs*, I, 222–223; *U. S. Statutes at Large*, II, 481–483.

[35] Dearborn to Wilkinson, December 2, 1808, *American State Papers: Military Affairs*, I, 272.

mand was sick.[36] On April 30 Secretary of War William Eustis directed Wilkinson to move the troops out of New Orleans to healthier spots on the high ground behind Fort Adams or behind Natchez, but instead of following these directions (which he declared he did not get until the middle of May), the general set up his camp at Terre aux Boeufs, on the left bank of the Mississippi below New Orleans at the so-called English Turn.[37]

The miserable site proved to be the undoing of Wilkinson's assembled army. The tents leaked, the bread was wormy and the pork rancid, and filth littered the camp. Rain turned the area into a sea of mud, and swarms of mosquitoes added to the misery. The sick lists lengthened, and on June 22, 1809, the Secretary of War ordered Wilkinson to embark with all his troops immediately for Fort Adams or Natchez.[38] But the large-scale movement of men made matters worse. On overcrowded boats or struggling overland through the hot summer wilderness, the troops died in unbelievable numbers. More than 1,000 noncommissioned officers and men out of a total of 2,036 were lost between February, 1809, and January, 1810. Of these 166 deserted; the rest had died.[39] Wilkinson had himself been ill, and soon after he rejoined his remnant army at Natchez in November he turned over command to Brigadier General Wade Hampton and departed for the East, where two investigations of his conduct were pending in the House of Representatives.

☆

After Wilkinson left St. Louis in 1806, management of affairs in Upper Louisiana passed into the hands of Lewis and Clark, whose remarkable exploits no doubt had marked them for important offices. Meriwether Lewis was appointed governor of Louisiana Territory to succeed Wilkinson, and at the same time William Clark was appointed

[36] Jacobs, *Tarnished Warrior*, pp. 251–252, gives a graphic account of the evils.

[37] Eustis to Wilkinson, April 30, 1809, and Wilkinson to Eustis, May 29 and June 19, 1809, *American State Papers: Military Affairs*, I, 273–274.

[38] Eustis to Wilkinson, June 22, 1809, *ibid.*, 274.

[39] See Jacobs, *Tarnished Warrior*, pp. 252–260, for gruesome details on the episode. The high mortality was investigated by a special committee of the House of Representatives, which presented its report on April 27, 1810; the documents are collected in *American State Papers: Military Affairs*, I, 268–295.

Indian agent for Louisiana Territory.[40] It was Clark who was most conscious of the Indian war clouds gathering over the upper Mississippi and the Missouri. He had no sooner taken office, in fact, than he began to plead with the Secretary of War for troops in the Indian country to watch the emissaries of Spain and Great Britain, whose intrigue with the Indians he feared, and to enforce the Indian trade and intercourse laws. The Indians on the upper Mississippi, he noted in late 1807, "Shew Some hostile Simtoms," which he attributed again to British action, and he feared that the British traders had already made inroads on the upper Missouri.[41]

The War Department could not be entirely quiet in the face of the continued remonstrances from responsible men of good judgment on the frontier. Its first answer was to push the government trading factory system into the region, protected as necessary by military garrisons. Early in 1808 the decision was made to establish a trading house among the Osages and another on the upper Mississippi near the mouth of the Des Moines River, and the army commander at Belle Fontaine was directed to establish military posts to guard these factories. Each post was to consist of thirty men, "to be commanded by discreet careful Officers," and a stockade and blockhouse with barracks for the troops were to be erected as soon as possible. The directions sent to the factors appointed to the new establishments indicate the motives behind the move: "The principal object of the Government in these establishments . . . [is] to secure the Friendship of the Indians in our country in a way the most beneficial to them and the most effectual & economical to the United States." Although the factors were instructed to be on their guard against fraud and deception, each was told, "You will nevertheless be conciliatory in all your intercourse with the Indians & so demean yourself toward them generally and toward their chiefs in particular, as to obtain and preserve their Friendship & to secure their attachment to the United States—." This clearly reflected the policy of Jefferson, who warned Governor Lewis that "nothing ought more to be avoided than the embarking ourselves in a system of military coercion on the Indians. . . . [C]ommerce is the

[40] Lewis was appointed on March 3, 1807, but he did not arrive in the Territory to act as governor until March 8, 1808; the Secretary of the Territory, first Joseph Browne and then Frederick Bates, served as acting governor until Lewis returned from the East. Clark's commission was dated March 7, 1807. Carter, *Territorial Papers*, XIV, 107–109.

[41] Clark to Secretary of War, June 1, September 12, and December 3, 1807, *ibid.*, pp. 126–127, 146–147, 153–154.

great engine by which we are to coerce them, & not war." Jefferson meant to hold the Indians in line by cutting off their supplies if they misbehaved, but this plan rested on a premise of American monopoly of trade with the Indians, a condition far from actuality.[42]

Colonel Thomas Hunt was to be in charge of the expedition going up the Mississippi, but he suddenly became ill and died, and command fell upon Lieutenant Alpha Kingsley. His convoy of keelboats with the troops and factory stores reached the mouth of the Des Moines River about September 11, 1808. It was here that the War Department orders specifically directed that the factory be located, but Kingsley feared the land there was subject to flooding, so he proceeded up the river, passed the rapids in the river, and stopped ten miles above the rapids at a site that pleased him. "This situation is high," he wrote to the Secretary of War, "commands an extensive view of the river and the adjacent country—also an excellent spring of water—and I believe there is no place on the river which will prove more healthy, and more advantageous to the Indian trade." He called the post Fort Belle-vue, but soon the name was changed to Fort Madison, to honor the new President. The lieutenant's judgment in locating the post was faulty, as later military men viewing the site of the fort were quick to point out. Behind the fort was a ridge from which an enemy could fire down upon the fort.[43]

The new fort and factory on the upper Mississippi could hardly maintain a toehold in the threatening Indian country, which had long been dominated by British traders. In April, 1809, Clark reported that the fort was in "a bad state of defence, the pickets being so low that the Indians could with great ease *jump* over them, and no Blockhouses for Defence," and regular troops with new ordnance were dispatched by water and two companies of militia sent overland to strengthen the place in the face of Indian insolence.[44] This seemed to solve the problem for the moment, but the respite was only temporary, and as the tension between the Indians and the Americans increased, the little post, standing isolated on the west bank of the upper Missis-sippi, was no match for the new waves of anti-American sentiment.

[42] Secretary of War to Thomas Hunt, May 17, 1808; John Mason to John Johnson, May 20, 1808; Jefferson to Lewis, August 21, 1808, Carter, *Territorial Papers*, XIV, 184, 185–187, 219–220.

[43] Donald Jackson, "Old Fort Madison—1808–1813," *Palimpsest*, XXXIX (January, 1958), 1–64.

[44] Clark to Secretary of War, April 5 and April 29, 1809, Carter, *Territorial Papers*, XIV, 260, 265–266.

The Secretary of War had directed that the second factory and military post be established on the Osage River, but Governor Lewis informed the Secretary that the river with "its fluctuating and uncertain navigation" made an unsuitable location, and he recommended instead a position on the Missouri about 300 miles from its mouth. To this site up the river the army commander at Belle Fontaine dispatched a company of soldiers under Captain Eli Clemson, and the governor ordered twenty cavalrymen and sixty mounted riflemen of the militia under William Clark (who was major general of the militia) to go overland to aid Clemson in setting up the station. Twenty thousand dollars worth of factory goods from Belle Fontaine was sent with George C. Sibley, the factor at the new post, along with Clemson's command. Clark picked out the exact site for the fort—"this Situation I had examined in the year 1804," he wrote, "and was delighted with it and am equally so now."[45]

The new posts did not prevent the drift toward open war. Word from Fort Madison was disheartening, and Clark was convinced that the Winnebagos were determined for war and were attempting to get support from other tribes for an attack on Fort Madison, Fort Dearborn, and the frontier settlements. Governor Benjamin Howard of Missouri Territory requested authorization to call upon the commander at Belle Fontaine for regular troops to use as he saw fit and recommended a spring campaign against the hostile Indians on the Illinois River. There was insistence from the Indian agent at Prairie du Chien that a strong garrison there would keep the Indians in awe of the United States and "impress them with that respect they ought to possess towards this government," and Clark at one point suggested taking possession of the mouth of the Fox River as a means of cutting the channels of British traders into the Mississippi valley.[46]

But the answer of Congress was not as forthright as this. Less concerned with the assertion of American sovereignty by military pos-

[45] Kate L. Gregg, "The History of Fort Osage," *Missouri Historical Review*, XXXIV (July, 1940), 439–442. See also Lewis to Secretary of War, July 1, 1808, and Clark to Secretary of War, August 18 and September 23, 1808, Carter, *Territorial Papers*, XIV, 196–203, 207–210, 224–228.

[46] Nicholas Boilvin to Secretary of War, February 11, 1811; Howard to Secretary of War, January 13, 1812; Clark to Secretary of War, February 13, 1812, *ibid.*, pp. 440–441, 505, 518–520. For discussion of the approach of war, see Robert L. Fisher, "The Western Prologue to the War of 1812," *Missouri Historical Review*, XXX (April, 1936), 267–281, and Louise Phelps Kellogg, *The British Regime in Wisconsin and the Northwest* (Madison, Wis., 1935), pp. 265–282.

session of the lands in the Northwest gained at the Treaty of Paris in 1783 and confirmed by Jay's Treaty in 1794 than with immediate protection of frontier settlements from Indian raids, it authorized on January 2, 1812, the raising of six companies of rangers for the protection of the settlers from Indian incursions. Two were being raised in Ohio, one each in Kentucky, Indiana, Illinois, and Louisiana Territory. These troops were enlisted for twelve months and were to equip and provide for themselves and their horses at an allowance of $1.00 a day. The rangers brought some feeling of security to the frontier settlements but did little to assert American rights.[47]

The only new post was a small blockhouse called Fort Mason, erected on the Mississippi not far from the site of present-day Hannibal, Missouri. In February, 1812, on the request of Governor Howard, Colonel Daniel Bissell sent a detachment of two officers and thirty men from Belle Fontaine to the settlement at the site, where an Indian raid had occurred. The Secretary of War authorized the establishment of a post at Peoria on the Illinois River and promised a post, too, at Prairie du Chien "whenever a sufficient number of Recruits shall be raised in Kentuckey," but these forts had to wait until the long-feared war with England had actually begun.[48]

While Congress was making the final decision on war or peace, the line of defense in the West ran from Mackinac to Detroit, to Chicago, to Fort Madison and Fort Mason on the Mississippi, to Fort Belle Fontaine and Fort Osage on the Missouri. The line fell far short of the boundaries to which American jurisdiction extended, and the forts in the cordon were woefully weak. One by one the posts fell to the British and their Indian allies, and the Indian conflict merged into the Anglo-American conflict that we call the War of 1812.

[47] *U. S. Statutes at Large*, II, 670; Secretary of War to Howard, March 17 and March 28, 1812, Carter, *Territorial Papers*, XIV, 529, 541.
[48] Daniel Bissell to Secretary of War, February 19 and May 28, 1812; Secretary of War to Howard, April 13, 1812, *ibid.*, pp. 520–523, 543–544, 551.

☆ SIX ☆

The Indian Frontier in the War of 1812

WHEN the United States declared war on Great Britain on June 18, 1812, American military history entered a new phase. The republic, after long debate and with mixed motives, was once again at war with a European power, in what some historians have called the "second war for American independence." It was a test to see how the new nation would fare, without a military tradition, without a competent standing army, and without adequate preparation even when war was decided upon. The antagonism to things professionally military and reliance on citizen soldiery which made it so difficult even to control the primitive Indian nations and the scattered settlers spearheading the frontier were hardly touched as the enthusiastic nationalists talked glibly of seizing Canada and humiliating His Majesty's forces. That the United States did not suffer a disastrous defeat and could claim a victory out of a stalemate was due less to American prowess than to the circumstance of British involvement in a European war.[1]

[1] For the general course of the war I have relied largely on the recent history by Harry L. Coles, *The War of 1812* (Chicago, 1965), and on Alec R. Gilpin, *The War of 1812 in the Old Northwest* (East Lansing, Mich., 1958) All histories of the War of 1812, of course, give considerable attention to the campaigns on the northwest and southwest Indian frontiers. Henry Adams covers the war in *History of the United States During the Administrations of Jefferson and Madison* (9 vols. New York, 1889–1891), VI; the appropriate chapters have been reprinted in *The War of 1812*, ed. H. A. DeWeerd (Washington, 1944). More popular accounts are Francis F. Beirne, *The War of 1812* (New York, 1949), and Glenn Tucker, *Poltroons and Patriots: A Popular Account of the War of 1812* (2 vols., Indianapolis, 1954). For a contemporary account of the war, see Robert B. McAfee, *History of the Late War in the Western Country* (Lexington, Ky., 1816; reprinted, Bowling Green, Ohio, 1919).

Documents for the northwestern campaigns of the war appear in John Brannan, .d., *Official Letters of the Military and Naval Officers of the United States, Dur-*

If one looks at Hull's surrender of Detroit, the failure of the campaigns mounted along the northern frontier, the retreat of the President from the seat of government, and the burning of the capital, there is little national progress to be seen in the war. But in the West there were strong threads from the past and emerging patterns for the future which determined in large measure the picture of postwar America.

However much historians may argue about the causes of the war, frontier elements cannot be discounted. The continual agitation in the Northwest and in the Southwest caused by Indian disquiet had diplomatic undertones, for the encouragement of the Indians by the British in the north and by the Spanish in the south was without question. To rid the nation of such insecurity and such disruptions to tranquil national advance was a clear goal of many who promoted the war, and this goal was not forgotten in the strategy of the struggle.

The complete military history of the War of 1812 is beyond the scope of this volume, but the Indian elements were a continuation of the prewar conflict and set the stage for the military history of the American frontier in the decades after 1815. The Indians, by and large, maintained or renewed their allegiance to the British and the armies that the Americans met on the northwestern frontier were composed of more Indian troops than white. To a large degree the War of 1812 was a renewal of the struggle for control of large sections of the Old Northwest, which had ended its first act with Fallen Timbers and for which Tippecanoe was a kind of entr'acte. Tecumseh's dream of an Indian confederation, maintaining a united front against American territorial advance, seemed possible of fulfillment when the British were once again openly fighting the Americans.[2]

---

ing the War with Great Britain in the Years 1812, 13, 14, & 15 (Washington, 1823); E. A. Cruikshank, ed., Documents Relating to the Invasion of Canada and the Surrender of Detroit, 1812 (Ottawa, 1913); Messages and Letters of William Henry Harrison, ed. Logan Esarey (2 vols., Indianapolis, 1922); "Copies of Papers on File in the Dominion Archives at Ottawa, Canada, Pertaining to the Relations of the British Government with the United States During the Period of the War of 1812," Michigan Pioneer and Historical Collections, XV (1889); and Richard C. Knopf, ed., Document Transcriptions of the War of 1812 in the Northwest (6 vols., Columbus, Ohio, 1957–1959).

[2] For British Indian policy before the war and the part played by the Indians during the war, see Reginald Horsman, "British Indian Policy in the Northwest, 1807–1812," Mississippi Valley Historical Review, XLV (June, 1958), 51–66; Horsman, "The Role of the Indian in the War," in Philip P. Mason, ed., After Tippecanoe: Some Aspects of the War of 1812 (East Lansing, Mich., 1963), pp. 60–77; and George F. G. Stanley, "The Indians in the War of 1812," Canadian Historical Review, XXXI (June, 1950), 145–165.

In the territory stretching west of Lake Michigan the British and their Indian allies almost immediately reasserted control. When Captain Charles Roberts, the commander at St. Joseph, the British island forty miles northeast of Michilimackinac, got news of the declaration of war on July 8, he at once began preparations to assault Fort Mackinac, which the Americans had recovered in 1796 as a result of Jay's Treaty. With a force of between 700 and 800 men, put together from his small regular garrison, local residents, employees of the North West Company, and Indians, he invaded Mackinac Island. The red men made up more than half his force and included more than 100 Sioux, Winnebagos, and Menominees brought in by the trader Robert Dickson from the upper Mississippi and close to 300 Chippewas and Ottawas raised by John Askin, Jr., the British storekeeper at St. Joseph. The Americans on Mackinac Island were outnumbered ten to one and when the attacking force placed a six-pounder on the heights which commanded the fort and had its troops in position to storm the post, the American commander, Lieutenant Porter Hanks of the artillery, surrendered without a shot.[3]

The loss of the fort was the first great blow to the American cause in the Northwest, for it made possible the British hold on the area west of Lake Michigan, a hold Great Britain did not relinquish until the Treaty of Ghent. The Indians now came to Mackinac in great numbers, enthusiastic in their friendship for the British and eager to share in the captured goods. The fall of Mackinac was a severe loss of American prestige among the Indians, which further defeats coming one upon another only compounded.

Another link in the western cordon of posts was Fort Dearborn, which had been established at the mouth of the Chicago River at the foot of Lake Michigan in 1803. The post was uneasy in the face of Indian unrest, and General William Hull in July had sent orders to Captain Nathan Heald, commanding the post, to evacuate his command and move to Detroit or Fort Wayne. The orders reached Fort Dearborn early in August, and Heald, since his supply line through the Straits of Mackinac was cut off by the British, could do nothing but comply. In an attempt to assure a safe departure through the gather-

[3] Louise Phelps Kellogg, "The Capture of Mackinac in 1812," *Proceedings of the State Historical Society of Wisconsin* (1912), pp. 124–145. Dickson's role in the Northwest can be traced in Louis Arthur Tohill, "Robert Dickson, British Fur Trader on the Upper Mississippi," *North Dakota Historical Quarterly*, III (October, 1928), 5–49, (January, 1929), 83–128, (April, 1929), 182–203.

ing Indians, Heald distributed the public property of the fort and the factory to the Indians (except for the extra arms, ammunition, and liquor which were dumped into a well or into the canal). But before the Americans could depart, news of American reverses and a war belt from Tecumseh had reached the Potawatomis, and they and some members of other tribes planned to attack. As the 96 persons in the fort marched out on the morning of August 15, they were overwhelmed by a force of 400 Indians. Twenty-six regulars, twelve militiamen, two women, and twelve children of the post were massacred, the rest taken prisoner.[4] While this minor tragedy was being enacted in the far wilderness, a major disaster of the war—the fall of Detroit—was about to occur, sealing the fate of the northwestern frontier.

Plans to strengthen the Detroit area had been on foot for some months before the declaration of war. On January 11, 1812, Congress had increased the authorized strength of the regular army to 35,000, and on April 10 had authorized the President to enroll as many as 100,000 militia in the federal service.[5] By the spring of 1812 plans had been formulated for a three-pronged attack on Canada should war materialize—at Detroit, Niagara, and Lake Champlain. William Hull, Governor of Michigan Territory, reluctantly accepting commission as a brigadier general in early April, assumed command of the army being assembled for the Northwest. Hull was to assemble recruits for the Fourth Infantry and Ohio militia at Dayton or Staunton, Ohio, and then proceed to Detroit. He was to safeguard Michigan, counteract British influence with the Indians, and be prepared for war if it should come. Hull requested more men (he wanted at least 3,000 reinforcements), a naval force built on the Lakes, and additional provisions, but his requests were refused.

The formation of this Northwestern Army was beset with the usual difficulties. Recruits for the regulars appeared in less than required numbers, and although Governor Return J. Meigs of Ohio moved quickly to supply the 1,200 militia men called for, problems of supply and organization were not easily overcome. By June 1, however, the

---

[4] Gilpin, *War of 1812 in the Old Northwest*, pp. 126–128; Milo M. Quaife, *Chicago and the Old Northwest, 1673–1835: A Study of the Evolution of the Northwestern Frontier, Together with a History of Fort Dearborn* (Chicago, 1913), pp. 211–231, 378–436; Mentor L. Williams, "John Kinzie's Narrative of the Fort Dearborn Massacre," *Journal of the Illinois State Historical Society*, XLVI (Winter, 1953), 343–362.

[5] *U. S. Statutes at Large*, II, 671–674, 705–707.

army was on its way, uniting with the troops of the Fourth Infantry from Vincennes at Urbana, Ohio, then picking its way through difficult wilderness and Indian country toward Detroit. Not until early on July 2, when encamped a few miles below the River Raisin, did Hull and his army learn of the declaration of war two weeks earlier. The British had already known for four days.

Hull reached Detroit on July 5, and a week later American troops crossed into Canada and occupied Sandwich without opposition. Hull fortified the position and made preparations for an attack on Malden, writing optimistically to the Secretary of War that the Canadian militia were deserting. The American cause seemed to be in the ascendency, but the tide quickly turned. Instead of pushing his initial advantage Hull delayed, and with each day lost the will and strength of the enemy increased. On August 3 news of the fall of Fort Mackinac arrived—a serious blow to morale with its threat of an Indian avalanche from the north. Hull's supply line was tenuous, but to keep up the spirit of his men he ordered an attack on Malden on August 6, only to cancel it on the 7th when he heard of regulars being sent to reinforce the post. Leaving a small garrison at Sandwich, Hull took the bulk of his command back to Detroit. A relief expedition sent to open the supply lines to the south was engaged by the British and Indians below Detroit, and Hull timidly pulled back the garrison from Sandwich.

While Hull's army was deteriorating through the officers' loss of confidence in the general, the British forces under General Isaac Brock were strengthening their advantage. Brock augmented his forces, met with Tecumseh and his warriors, and shrewdly capitalized on the low morale of the Americans, which he knew about from captured letters. "Hull," says one recent historian of the war, "went into mental and moral paralysis."[6] When Brock was preparing for an immediate attack upon Detroit on August 16, Hull, fearing the massacre of the women and children by the Indian allies of the British should Detroit be taken by force, surrendered the city and his army. The blow to the American cause was incalculable, and the news was greeted at first with disbelief. When the truth was grasped, Hull became the target of anger and vituperation. He was branded a traitor and the court-martial he faced sentenced him to death for cowardice in the face of the enemy.

[6] Coles, *War of 1812*, p. 53.

Only the remission of his sentence by President Madison saved him from the ignominious death.[7]

☆

The surrender of Hull's Northwestern Army left consternation and confusion on the frontier, for the Indians were emboldened by the American disaster. In Ohio, where settlement was heavy and concentrated, little was to be feared, but in thinly settled Indiana and Illinois fears of Indian raids were well-founded. The governors of the two territories, William Henry Harrison and Ninian Edwards, ordered out mounted militia to patrol the frontier, and Colonel William Russell established a camp in southern Illinois for militia and for the United States rangers, the mounted troops authorized for protection against the Indians in 1812. Harrison sought militia from Kentucky to reinforce Vincennes, which had been weakened by the withdrawal of the Fourth Infantry to join Hull's army.

But clearly a new Northwestern Army would have to be organized to repair, if possible, the damage done by Hull's defeat. Reinforcements were already being assembled under Brigadier General James Winchester. Recruits for a new regiment, the Seventeenth Infantry, were being enlisted, and to them Winchester was authorized to add a thousand Kentucky militia and march toward Detroit. Governor Harrison was also gathering an army. Appointed a major general in the Kentucky militia, he took command of the militia and volunteers and moved toward Fort Wayne, which was under serious Indian threats. Then the young Harrison, more popular in the West than the aristocratic Winchester, on September 17 was appointed commander in chief of the Northwestern Army, which was to comprise regulars, rangers, volunteers and militia from Kentucky, Ohio, Indiana, Pennsylvania, and Virginia—a force that was expected to total 10,000 men. With an army four times as strong as Hull's had been, Harrison was directed to defend the frontier, retake Detroit, and invade Canada.[8]

[7] Historians have treated Hull almost as harshly as did his contemporaries. For two evaluations that are more balanced, see Milo M. Quaife, "General William Hull and His Critics," *Ohio State Archaeological and Historical Quarterly*, XLVII (April, 1938), 168–182, and Gilpin, *War of 1812 in the Old Northwest*, pp. 120–124.

[8] A favorable account of Harrison's part in the war is Beverley W. Bond, Jr., "William Henry Harrison in the War of 1812," *Mississippi Valley Historical Review*, XIII (March, 1927), 499–516. See also the extensive accounts in Dorothy

The Detroit Theater in the War of 1812

A winter campaign seemed out of the question, but Winchester, hearing that the Americans at Frenchtown on the River Raisin were subject to a garrison of only fifty Canadian militia and about one hundred Indians, determined on a relief expedition from his camp on the Maumee. On January 18 the American forces carried the town, but Winchester's army had overextended itself, and the British commander, Colonel Henry Proctor, took advantage of their weakness. With a large force he crossed the Detroit River on January 21 and moved his artillery into position against the town. The British and their Indian allies quickly overwhelmed the Americans, and Winchester, taken prisoner, surrendered his troops. The prisoners were marched into Canada; the wounded who were left behind were savagely murdered by the Indians. This River Raisin Massacre steeled the Americans in their determination to avenge the British victories.

With the loss of Winchester's men, Harrison could no longer think of an attack upon the British, and the offensive passed to the enemy while Harrison again worked to build up his army. For most of 1813 the Northwestern Army could do nothing but drive back Proctor's attacks on Fort Meigs and Lower Sandusky.

Admiral Perry's victory on Lake Erie on September 10, 1813, changed the entire complexion of the war in the Northwest. American control of the supply lines on the Lakes made possible Harrison's advance, and he began at once. Since the regulars did not bring the army up to strength, Harrison called upon Kentucky for more volunteers. His old friend Governor Isaac Shelby himself raised 3,000 troops and marched at their head to Harrison's camp. A regiment of 1,000 mounted volunteers under Colonel Richard M. Johnson augmented the force. The mounted men were sent by road to Detroit, while the rest were transported by boat. These landed on September 27 three miles below Malden, which they found deserted by Proctor. Two days later Harrison's army reached Sandwich, and 700 regulars under General Duncan McArthur were sent to occupy Detroit. On the next day Colonel Johnson's mounted regiment arrived, and plans were quickly drawn up to follow the retreating Proctor up the Thames River.

Harrison, leaving nearly 1,500 men at Detroit and Sandwich, began the pursuit on October 2 with a total force of over 3,000. The retiring army destroyed the bridges across the streams that flowed into the

Burne Goebel, *William Henry Harrison: A Political Biography* (Indianapolis, 1926), pp. 128–203, and Freeman Cleaves, *Old Tippecanoe: William Henry Harrison and His Time* (New York, 1939), pp. 112–228.

Thames, but the bridges were quickly rebuilt, and the scattered fire from Proctor's Indian allies that greeted the Americans was silenced. Proctor's force finally took a stand on October 5 two miles below Moravian Town. The British general had allowed his ammunition boats to be captured, and the British and Indians were outnumbered by the Americans at least two to one. Harrison used his cavalry to charge the open ranks of the British, which quickly collapsed, and then he turned against the Indian forces on his left flank. The Indians, ably led by Tecumseh, offered stiff resistance, but Tecumseh was soon killed, and the Indians followed the British in flight. The Americans took Moravian Town without trouble, but Proctor and his army escaped, leaving behind much valuable equipment. Although some of the Indians joined the British forces to the east, most of them were now willing to unite with the Indians at Detroit in suing for peace. The Americans had made a giant step toward redeeming the Northwest.

Harrison immediately planned to follow up the victory at the Battle of the Thames with an expedition against Mackinac, but a storm on October 10–12 drove off his provision boats, and then the whole operation was canceled because of the lateness of the season. Leaving Brigadier General Lewis Cass in command at Detroit, Harrison with most of the troops embarked for Buffalo. Harrison soon became convinced that his military usefulness was at an end. He had been ignored by Secretary of War John Armstrong and assigned to an inactive area, and on May 11 he submitted his resignation. Armstrong, in the absence of the President, quickly accepted it. Cass, who had been appointed Governor of Michigan Territory on October 29, 1813, resigned his military commission effective May 1, and the command at Detroit passed to Lieutenant Colonel George Croghan, the hero of the repulse of Proctor at Lower Sandusky, and he began to extend American occupation. Early in May he sent Captain Charles Gratiot to establish a post (Fort Gratiot) at the outlet of Lake Huron, and in July he commanded an expedition against Fort Mackinac, only to be repulsed on August 4 and forced to retire with severe losses. American attempts to gain control of the upper Mississippi, meanwhile, were meeting a like rebuff.

With the fall of Fort Mackinac, Fort Dearborn, and Detroit in the summer of 1812, the only American fort left west of Lake Michigan had been Fort Madison. It too was attacked by the Indians, and though it successfully withstood the attack, the post was considered indefensible and its troops burned the buildings and withdrew in November, 1813. The villages of Green Bay and Prairie du Chien were inhabited by British sympathizers, and the British domination of the fur trade in the whole region guaranteed the allegiance of the tribes to the British cause.[9]

The Americans, however, were not content to let the control of the upper Mississippi valley go uncontested. Prairie du Chien, especially, was an important center of the fur trade, and Governor Edwards of Illinois Territory and General Benjamin Howard, in command at St. Louis, requested permission to establish a post at the site. Secretary of War Armstrong agreed on July 29, 1813, but it was then too late to undertake the campaign in that year. Instead a fort was determined upon for Peoria, to protect the settlements in Illinois. Three detachments of troops converged on the area in late September, driving the Indians northward, and Fort Clark, garrisoned by a company of regulars, was built at the head of Lake Peoria.

In May, 1814, an expedition was undertaken to Prairie du Chien. Sixty men of the Seventh Infantry and 200 militia, traveling up the Mississippi in gunboats which had been ordered for the defense of the river by Governor William Clark of Missouri Territory, arrived at Prairie du Chien without mishap on June 2. The men constructed a fort there, which they named Fort Shelby. It was a short-lived occupation. Lieutenant Colonel Robert McDouall, the British commandant at Fort Mackinac, soon sent out a party to take the fort. At its head he appointed Major William McKay, who by the time he advanced on Prairie du Chien had accumulated a force of 120 whites and 530 Indians. Outnumbered more than ten to one, the Americans put up a brief resistance before surrendering the fort on July 20. The upper Mississippi remained in British hands, and the assertion of United States authority there would have to await the postwar era.

☆

While the war was thus being waged in the North, a parallel story unfolded in the South.[10] The hostile Creeks with their Spanish ties

[9] Affairs in the upper Mississippi valley during the war are recounted in Louise Phelps Kellogg, *The British Regime in Wisconsin and the Northwest* (Madison, Wis., 1935), pp. 283–329, and in Julius W. Pratt, "Fur Trade Strategy and the American Left Flank in the War of 1812," *American Historical Review*, XL (January, 1935), 246–273. See also Reginald Horsman, "Wisconsin and the War of 1812," *Wisconsin Magazine of History*, XLVI (Autumn, 1962), 3–15.

[10] The Creek War can be followed in John Spencer Bassett, *The Life of Andrew Jackson* (2 vols., Garden City, N. Y., 1911), I, 73–125, and Marquis James, *Andrew Jackson, The Border Captain* (New York, 1933), pp. 149–201. Parts of

were the counterpart to Tecumseh's confederacy, and the Battle of Horseshoe Bend destroyed the Indians' hopes as did the Battle of the Thames and the death of Tecumseh. The destruction of the Creeks was important for the history of the southern frontier, but it was crucial for the course of the war as well. Harry L. Coles, a recent historian of the War of 1812, asserts: "The conquest of the Creeks was as necessary as it was savage. Had the United States failed to clear out this pocket of resistance in the heart of the Southwest, the British could have landed anywhere on the Gulf, marched inland with the aid of their Spanish and Indian allies, and descended upon New Orleans from the north. If this had happened, no American commander, not even Jackson, could have saved New Orleans or any part of the Mississippi Valley the British might have chosen to appropriate."[11]

The first move in the South, however, was an abortive one. President Madison, hoping for authority to seize East Florida in order to thwart a British occupation, called upon the governor of Tennessee for 1,500 volunteers and told the commander of the Southern Department, Major General Thomas Pinckney, that a force was to be raised in preparation for offensive operations against East Florida. This was a popular move with the Americans in the Southwest, for hostile Indian operations were attributed to encouragement given by the Spanish in Florida. Andrew Jackson, major general of the Tennessee militia, had little difficulty in raising troops, therefore, and on December 10, 1812, he assembled 2,000 volunteers at Nashville. By the middle of February he had his army at Natchez. But between the time the call had gone out for the troops in October and Jackson's arrival at Natchez the situation of the war had materially altered. As the offensive movements against Canada failed, Congress withheld authority for the occupation

---

the story are told in Mrs. Dunbar Rowland, *Andrew Jackson's Campaign Against the British, or the Mississippi Territory in the War of 1812: Concerning the Military Operations of the Americans, Creek Indians, British, and Spanish* (New York, 1926), and in H. S. Halbert and T. E. Ball, *The Creek War of 1813 and 1814* (Chicago, 1895), but neither work is quite satisfactory. A summary of the Creek troubles appears in Arthur H. Hall, "The Red Stick War: Creek Indian Affairs During the War of 1812," *Chronicles of Oklahoma*, XII (September, 1934), 264–293. Numerous pertinent documents are in *Correspondence of Andrew Jackson*, ed. John Spencer Bassett (6 vols., Washington, 1926–1935), I. "Journal of James A. Tait for the Year 1813," ed. Peter A. Brannon, *Georgia Historical Quarterly*, VIII (September, 1924), 229–239, tells of the campaign under General John Floyd. Other information is supplied in "Letters of General John Coffee to His Wife, 1813–1815," ed. John H. DeWitt, *Tennessee Historical Magazine*, II (December, 1916), 264–295.

[11] Coles, *War of 1812*, p. 188.

of East Florida. Pinckney and Jackson were informed by the Secretary of War that the contemplated invasion was off and that the troops should be, dismissed. "You will accept for yourself and the Corps the thanks of the President of the United States," the Secretary of War wrote to Jackson.[12] Without pay, provisions, or transportation from the federal government, Jackson marched his army home on his own means and responsibility. It was left to General Wilkinson, commanding at New Orleans, to occupy Mobile and the Spanish territory west of the Perdido River—all that Congress was willing to allow.[13]

The Creeks still had to be dealt with. Whereas the Chickasaws and Choctaws took little part in the war and some of the Cherokees joined the United States forces, the Creeks developed a hostile faction, which posed a serious threat. Certain of the young Creeks were influenced by Tecumseh, who visited the nation in 1811 and again in 1812, soliciting southern Indian support for his confederacy. Although older chiefs warned against Tecumseh, the great Shawnee came with a bagful of magic tricks and on his second visit brought encouraging news of American defeats. With promises that Spanish and British aid would support the Indians he won over the young warriors, or Red Sticks, among them William Weatherford (Red Eagle), a nephew of the famous Creek leader Alexander McGillivray. A party of thirty Creeks went all the way to Canada in late 1812, where they participated in the River Raisin massacre, and on their way home they murdered some whites near the mouth of the Ohio. The Chickasaws, who feared they would be held responsible for the murders, demanded that the Creeks themselves punish the murderers. When this was done, the Upper and Lower Creeks broke out into civil war, and the war party against the United States was strengthened. To aggravate further the tense situation, a party of Red Sticks, led by the half-breed chief Peter McQueen, who were returning from a trip to Pensacola (where the Spanish governor had supplied them with ammunition), were attacked by white frontiersmen at a place called Burnt Corn, some eighty miles north of Pensacola. Although most of the Indians escaped, they lost their ammunition and pack animals.

The leaders of the attack upon the Creeks sought safety at Fort Mims, a stockade forty miles north of Mobile. There were 550 persons at the fort including 175 militia and men and women and children of

<hr />

[12] John Armstrong to Andrew Jackson, February 5, 1813, *Correspondence of Andrew Jackson*, I, 276.

[13] See Isaac J. Cox, *The West Florida Controversy, 1798–1813: A Study in American Diplomacy* (Baltimore, 1918), pp. 609–619.

all ages. On August 30, 1813, McQueen and Weatherford led an Indian attack upon Fort Mims. The fort was poorly defended and the attack overwhelmed the inhabitants. Except for a few Negroes who were spared to be slaves and seventeen whites who escaped, everyone was massacred. The nation was electrified, and campaigns to crush the hostile Red Sticks were immediately prepared.

These came from three directions. An expedition from Georgia under Brigadier General John Floyd was to move in from the east. Another army, made up of 1,000 Mississippi volunteers and regulars of the Third Infantry, was to come from the west under Brigadier General F. L. Claiborne. Tennessee called for 2,500 volunteers, to move south into the Creek country from Nashville and from the eastern section of the state.

The Creeks were not numerous—perhaps 4,000 warriors altogether, no more than 1,000 of whom were ever assembled for a given battle— but the remoteness of their lands and the difficulty of supplying the columns converging on their stronghold, the Hickory Ground, gave them great advantage. The American commanders, too, were plagued by the short-term enlistments of their volunteer troops, which frequently prevented action at a crucial point in a campaign. General Floyd with 1,000 Georgia militia attacked the Creek village of Autosee, twenty miles from the Hickory Ground, on November 29. He claimed to have killed 200 Indians, but then he was forced to retire to the Chattahoochee River for lack of supplies. The campaign of General Claiborne met a similar fate. Advancing from the south, his troops captured Weatherford's village and killed a few warriors, but then their provisions ran out. And Claiborne was forced to retreat because the terms of his volunteers were about to expire. The penetration of the Creek stronghold was left to Andrew Jackson.

When news of the Fort Mims massacre reached Jackson, he immediately issued orders for volunteers to assemble at Fayetteville, Tennessee, on October 4. With the cavalry under the command of John Coffee, Jackson marched rapidly through Huntsville to the Tennessee River, where he established a supply depot called Fort Deposit. He then continued south to the Coosa River, where he built Fort Strother, which was to serve as his base of operations. On November 3 at Tullushatchee General Coffee drew a party of warriors into a semicircle of his troops, closed the ring around the Indians, and killed over 180. Six days later at Talladega Jackson tried the same tactics, killing 300 of the 700 Red Sticks before his lines gave way. After such a promising beginning, it was Jackson's turn to be halted by low supplies

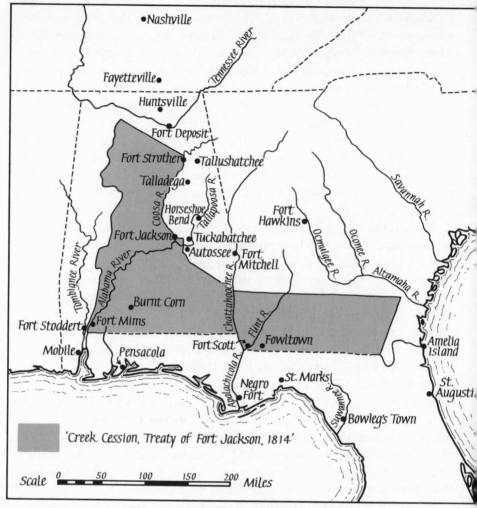

The Southern Frontier, 1813–1818

and dissatisfied enlistees. Low water on the Tennessee prevented the transport of the supplies he expected, and the one-year volunteers of December 10, 1812, after a respite at home before returning to active duty, were ready to depart on the anniversary of their original enlistment. Jackson threatened to shoot any of the men who departed and the troops stayed on. To Governor William Blount of Tennessee the campaign for the moment looked hopeless, and he suggested a withdrawal.

Jackson refused to consider such advice, and shortly his situation markedly improved as new enlistees arrived from Tennessee and the regulars of the Thirty-ninth Infantry came in to strengthen the army's resolve. By February Jackson's force totaled 5,000. He prepared to strike at a concentration of warriors holding a fortified position on the Tallapoosa River in the heart of the Creek country. The Indians occupied a peninsula of land formed by a sharp bend in the river. Across the neck they had constructed a stockade of logs, with portholes for delivering a crossfire against approaching forces. Along the river were gathered canoes for escape if the peninsula became untenable. On March 27, 1814, Jackson sent Coffee with the cavalry and about 200 Cherokee allies to close off the line of retreat, while he with the bulk of his men would attack the breastworks. In the morning the Cherokees crossed the river and made off with the canoes, which were used to attack the Creeks on the river side. When cannon bombardment of the breastworks made no opening, Jackson at noon ordered the infantry to storm the palisades. Stubborn resistance continued through the day, for the Creeks refused Jackson's offer of clemency to those who surrendered. When the battle ended, there were 550 Indians dead within the bend of the river, and many others had been killed outside. Jackson lost about 50 killed and 150 wounded.[14]

Jackson did not intend to lose his advantage. He moved down the river and built Fort Jackson where the Coosa and Tallapoosa rivers join to form the Alabama. From this headquarters his troops scoured the country for hostile Indians. Not many were found, for most of the Red Sticks fled into Spanish Florida and some, including William Weatherford, turned themselves in at Fort Jackson. Jackson now forsook his militia status and on Harrison's resignation accepted a commission as brigadier general in the regular army. He was almost immediately promoted to major general and given command of the Seventh Military District, which included Tennessee, Louisiana, and Mississippi Territory.

In this position he concluded a treaty with the Creeks at Fort Jackson on August 9. It was the friendly Creeks who attended the council, for the hostiles had been killed or had fled, and the chiefs protested the terms of the treaty. Jackson insisted, however, on large land cessions west of the Coosa and along the Florida border, as buffers

---

[14] Coles, *War of 1812*, pp. 201–202.

between the Creeks and Chickasaws and Choctaws on the west and the Spanish on the south.[15]

On August 27 Jackson was at Mobile where he strengthened defenses constructed by Wilkinson a year earlier, and enabled the garrison to drive back an attack of the British aided by Jean Lafitte and his pirates. In early November, after receiving a new increment of mounted volunteers, Jackson seized Pensacola, driving out the British who had been using it as a port and military depot. These southern escapades confirmed the action at Horseshoe Bend. The hostile Creeks might now well despair of active assistance from the British or the Spanish in the South. Jackson was ready to protect New Orleans if any British general should be so foolhardy as to make a direct attack by sea.

☆

The treaty of peace signed at Ghent on December 24, 1814, provided for a return to the *status quo ante bellum* and left unmentioned the basic maritime problems that had done so much to bring on the war, and it is easy to assert that the war accomplished nothing. This was clearly not the case on the frontier in the Northwest and the Southwest. The crushing defeats of the Indians at the Thames and at Horseshoe Bend and the failure of the British (or the Spanish) to substantiate Indian claims against the Americans put a new complexion on the military problems in the West. In one dramatic step the Indian-military frontier moved to the Mississippi and beyond. Tecumseh's confederacy and the Creek menace could be relegated as bad dreams to the past, which only occasionally broke forth into the nation's consciousness again. And danger that the British would dominate the fur trade moved from the Old Northwest to vaguely defined areas on the headwaters of the Missouri.

[15] Charles J. Kappler, ed., *Indian Affairs: Laws and Treaties* (2 vols., Washington, 1904), II, *Treaties*, pp. 107–110. The cession is shown in Charles C. Royce, *Indian Land Cessions in the United States* (*Eighteenth Annual Report of the Bureau of American Ethnology*, Part II, Washington, 1899), Plates 1 and 15, Cession 75.

SEVEN

The Surge of American Nationalism

THE War of 1812 awakened a new feeling of nationalism, which permeated all phases of American life. The exuberant self-consciousness that came to the nation with the realization that for the second time within a generation it had victoriously emerged from a military contest with a great European power was especially to be observed in the rapid flow of population into the Trans-Appalachian West. With the Indian dangers gone and foreign influence dissipated, the rich agricultural regions beckoned, and the tide of emigrants, dammed up for a decade, poured out over the land. Within five years after the War of 1812 five new western states entered the Union.

The army, too, basked temporarily in the warmth of the new nationalism. The end of the war brought the immediate question of reducing the army from its wartime status, and the old debates about a standing army in time of peace were rolled out on the floor of Congress, but the principle of a regular army of moderate strength won out without much trouble.[1] Secretary of War Monroe, worried about the large number of troops kept by the British in North America and about the unsettled state of Spain, recommended an army of 20,000.[2] Opponents of a standing army, on the other hand, bringing up their well-worn arguments, hoped to limit the force to a maximum of 6,000 men, but when the final vote was taken on March 3, 1815, an army of 10,000

---

[1] The debates are in *Annals of Congress*, 13 Congress, 3 session, col. 1196–1253. A detailed summary of the debates is in Edgar B. Wesley, *Guarding the Frontier: A Study of Frontier Defense from 1815 to 1825* (Minneapolis, 1935), pp. 66–72.

[2] *The Writings of James Monroe*, ed. Stanislaus M. Hamilton (7 vols., New York, 1898–1903), V, 321–327.

was authorized.[3] The law was interpreted as setting the limit for the military force exclusive of officers, so that the authorized strength under the act was actually about 12,000 men, although as usual the full strength was never reached. This peacetime army was to spearhead the expansion of American authority to the west, once the Indian tribes had been brought formally to a state of peace after the hostilities of the war.

The Indians, against whom so much of the American force in the War of 1812 had pressed, had not been made a party to the Treaty of Ghent. The ninth article of the treaty, however, provided that the United States would undertake to put an end to all hostilities with Indian tribes with whom it might still be at war at the time of ratification of the treaty and to restore to those tribes "all the possessions, rights, and privileges" that they had enjoyed previous to the war.[4] Accordingly President Madison on March 11, 1815, appointed three commissioners to treat with the Indians who had fought against the United States. These men were well selected to achieve the end in view: Governor William Clark of Missouri Territory and Superintendent of Indian Affairs west of the Mississippi, Governor Ninian Edwards of Illinois Territory and Superintendent of Indian Affairs in that political jurisdiction, and Auguste Chouteau, veteran fur trader of St. Louis.[5] Secretary of War Monroe directed the commissioners to notify all the tribes on the Mississippi and its tributaries who were at war with the United States that peace had been concluded with Great Britain and to invite them to a council to sign a treaty of peace and amity. Peace was to be the only purpose of the treaties; other ·matters could be attended to at a later time. The Indians were to be informed that the government intended to establish strong posts high up the Mississippi and between the Mississippi and Lake Michigan, and to open trading houses at these posts or at other suitable places for their accommodation.[6] Twenty thousand dollars worth of presents was placed at the disposal of the commissioners—"blankets, strouds, cloths, calicoes, handkerchiefs, cotton stuffs, ribands, gartering, frock

[3] *U. S. Statutes at Large*, III, 224–225.

[4] Hunter Miller, ed., *Treaties and Other International Acts of the United States of America* (8 vols., Washington, 1931–1948), II, 581.

[5] For an excellent account of the treaty negotiations carried on by these men, see Robert L. Fisher, "The Treaties of Portage des Sioux," *Mississippi Valley Historical Review*, XIX (March, 1933), 495–508. Copies of the treaties and related documents about the negotiations are in *American State Papers: Indian Affairs* (2 vols., Washington, 1832–1834), II, 1–12.

[6] Monroe to Commissioners, March 11, 1815, *ibid.*, p. 6.

coats, flags, silver ornaments, paints, wampum, looking-glasses, knives, fire-steels, rifles, fusils, flints, powder, tobacco, pipes, needles, &c.," according to the enumeration of the Secretary of War, who specified that the goods should equal in quality those that the Indians were accustomed to get from the British.[7]

On May 11 the commissioners met at St. Louis and prepared talks to be sent out to the Indian chiefs. News of continuing hostility among the tribes made it difficult to find messengers to carry the tidings into the Indian nations, but eventually thirty-seven talks were dispatched by means of army officers, Indian agents, Frenchmen (who it was thought would be better received by the Indians), or Indians themselves (who promised to deliver the messages to more remote tribes with whom they were in contact).

The site selected for the meeting was Portage des Sioux, a convenient spot on the west bank of the Mississippi above the mouth of the Missouri and a few miles below the mouth of the Illinois. Here the Indians began to gather as early as July 1. An impressive military guard of nearly 300 men was provided by the army commander at Fort Belle Fontaine, who reduced his garrison to a few guards and sent the regulars of his command under Colonel John Miller of the Third Infantry in two large gunboats to the treaty site. Miller's soldiers constructed an arbor or council house and established a camp for themselves, setting up about a hundred tents in orderly rows. Along the river bank were the temporary encampments of the Indian tribes. The Reverend Timothy Flint, who had arrived at St. Louis a few days earlier, was struck by the distinctions between the various tribes that had assembled:

> I remarked their different modes of constructing their water-craft. Those from the lakes, and the high points of the Mississippi, had beautiful canoes, or rather large skiffs, of white birch bark. Those from the lower Mississippi, and from the Missouri, had pirogues, or canoes hollowed out of a large tree. Some tribes covered their tents with bear-skins. Those from far up the Mississippi, had beautiful cone-shaped tents, made very neatly with rush matting. Those from the upper regions of the Missouri had their tents of tanned buffalo robes, marked in the inside with scarlet lines, and they were of an elliptical form. In some instances, we saw marks of savage progress in refinement and taste, in covering the earth under their

[7] Monroe to John Mason, March 27, 1815, *ibid.*, p. 7.

tents with rush or skin carpeting. They were generally dirty, rude, and disposed to intoxication.[8]

Most of the Indians seemed to be in a mood to listen to the peace talks, and on July 18 treaties were signed with the Potawatomis of the Illinois River and the Piankashaws. By the 20th treaties had been signed with four tribes of the Sioux and with the Omahas. During the first week of September negotiations were successfully completed with the Kickapoos, Osages, Missouri River Sacs and Foxes, and the Iowas; and on September 18 the council at Portage des Sioux came to an end. A thirteenth treaty, with the Kansas Indians, was signed by the commissioners at St. Louis on October 28. These were all merely peace pacts—providing that "every injury or act of hostility by one or either of the contracting parties against the other shall be mutually forgiven and forgot," promising "perpetual peace and friendship" between the Americans and the Indians, agreeing to the exchange of prisoners, and confirming previous treaties.

The Sacs and Foxes of the Mississippi were the most cantankerous. They refused to end their hostility to the United States and did not send representative chiefs to the council. Not until the spring of 1816 did these Indians consent to sign a treaty. Later in the same year additional treaties of peace were made with Sioux bands that had not been at the Portage des Sioux council and with the Winnebagos and the Ottawas. In 1817 and 1818 the Menominees, Otos, Poncas, and Pawnees completed treaties of peace and friendship.[9]

Meanwhile negotiations were carried on by General William Henry Harrison, General Duncan McArthur, and John Graham with the Indians of Ohio, Indiana, and Michigan. These Indians had technically been at peace with the United States at the time of the ratification of the Treaty of Ghent, and the provisions of that treaty did not apply, but "hostile excitement" among the Indians induced the Secretary of War to appoint a commission to conciliate the Indians and explain to them the provisions of the treaty.[10] "The object of these explanations will be to counteract any suppositions that the treaty of peace has placed Great Britain in a new and more advantageous relation to the

[8] Timothy Flint, *Recollections of the Last Ten Years, Passed in Occasional Residences and Journeyings in the Valley of the Mississippi* (Boston, 1826), pp. 142–143.

[9] Charles J. Kappler, ed., *Indian Affairs: Laws and Treaties* (2 vols., Washington, 1904), II, *Treaties*, pp. 126–133, 138–140, 156–159.

[10] Documents dealing with these negotiations are printed in *American State Papers: Indian Affairs*, II, 12–25.

Northwest Indians," Acting Secretary of War A. J. Dallas wrote to the commissioners on June 9, 1815; "to supersede the idea that the Indians have acquired by the treaty a more independent political character than they possessed before; and to beget a just confidence in the power as well as the resolution of our Government to maintain its rights against every opposition." Dallas considered the introduction of military posts and factories into the Indian country of increasing importance, and he directed the commissioners to inform the Indians that "in order to aid and protect them, and also to guard against encroachment upon the property and people of the United States" the President intended to establish a chain of posts from Chicago to St. Louis.[11]

A treaty was signed with the Wyandot, Delaware, Seneca, Shawnee, Miami, Chippewa, Ottawa, and Potawatomi Indians on September 8 at Spring Wells near Detroit, in which peace was reaffirmed and the Indians who had continued hostilities after 1811 were pardoned.[12]

☆

These treaties of friendship would be no more than paper documents unless the United States carried out its resolve to establish military posts on the Great Lakes and in the upper Mississippi valley.[13] Such action was indeed imperative if the United States did not want to forfeit for a second time its control over the Indian tribes of the Northwest. Americans in the West pleaded with the War Department for military establishments that would check the Indians, weaken or destroy their adherence to the British, and protect and extend the American fur trade in the region. Thus the Acting Governor of Michigan Territory, William Woodbridge, noting "a spirit of proud defiance & of unabated hostility," wrote from Detroit to the War Department on May 10, 1815:

I know of nothing that will check this murderous temper among the Indians, unless it be an active, extirminating war on our part—or

[11] Dallas to Harrison, McArthur, and Graham, June 9, 1815, *ibid.*, pp. 13–14.
[12] Kappler, *Treaties*, pp. 117–119.
[13] For general histories of the military expansion into the Northwest after the War of 1812, see Henry P. Beers, *The Western Military Frontier, 1815–1846* (Philadelphia, 1935); Wesley, *Guarding the Frontier;* and Francis Paul Prucha, *Broadax and Bayonet: The Role of the United States Army in the Development of the Northwest, 1815–1860* (Madison, Wis., 1953).

the location of a large military force—at this place—at Michilimackinac—at Green Bay & at Chicago—When they see a large force
strongly posted in their country, their fears may keep them quiet.—
They are in the habit of considering the Americans as their natural
enemies—Our settlements advancing upon [them], are cause of bitter
jealousy—Of the British they think very differently—Those who during this winter have come in praying for peace—now that they learn
the British are coming back in great force & with many hundred
Indians to Malden, have most openly expressed their pleasure at the
news—they have exchanged their meek submission towards us for
a haughty boldness not to be mistaken—Proximate motives have
strong influence with them—An imposing military force properly
located may probably save the sacrifice of many lives.[14]

But even before the letter reached Washington the movement was
under way. Dallas on May 22 announced his plans to Major General
Jacob Brown, commanding the Division of the North, and to Major
General Andrew Jackson, commanding the Division of the South. The
preservation of peace with the Indians and with the traders and government of Canada, he said, depended upon the positions which the
United States was now preparing to occupy in the Indian country. The
object was to establish posts "along the course of the British traders,
from Michilimackinac, by Green Bay, the Fox River, and the Ouiscon-
sin river, to Prairie du Chien, and thence up the Mississippi to St.
Anthony's Falls." He suggested posts, too, on a lower route from Chicago along the Illinois River to St. Louis.[15]

The army regiments, however, were only one agent of the War
Department in its combined policy of preserving the peace, improving
the country, and civilizing the Indians. This is clearly seen in the proposal for Green Bay that Dallas sent to President Madison on June 19,
1815. In order to restore harmony, preserve peace, and defeat "the arts
employed by intrusive traders to generate Indian hostilities," he proposed the establishment of an Indian agency on the Fox River near
Green Bay. The agent was to select a site with the approval of General
Brown; the establishment was to be a military station for two companies of troops or such other force as the general deemed competent;

[14] Woodbridge to A. J. Dallas, May 10, 1815, Clarence E. Carter, ed., *The
Territorial Papers of the United States* (26 vols., Washington, 1934–1962), X,
536–537.
[15] Dallas to Jackson, May 22, 1815, *Correspondence of Andrew Jackson*, ed.
John Spencer Bassett (6 vols., Washington, 1926–1933), II, 206; Dallas to
Brown, May 22, 1815, National Archives, Records of the Secretary of War,
Letters Sent, vol. 8, pp. 106–107.

and a government trading factory was to be connected with the post, providing a supply of suitable merchandise for the Indians.[16] Madison approved the plan the next day, and at once the troops began to move, not only for Green Bay but for the reestablishment of the post and factory at Chicago and for the extension of American military authority and government trading posts up the Mississippi valley.

If Dallas had any doubts about the propriety of his plans, he must have been set at rest by a long letter he soon received from Lewis Cass, the knowledgeable Governor of Michigan Territory. Cass pointed to the problem of the British traders among the northwestern tribes, to whose influence he traced most of the difficulties with the Indians, and he asserted that the British were about to renew their activities with increased energy. He noted the arrival of large supplies of trade goods at Malden and the influx of agents and subordinate officers. "These unerring indications," he announced, "give us timely warning that the same measures are to be adopted, the same lying system continued (pardon the epathet, could all the facts be presented to you, you would say that no milder term could be used) and the same plan of filling our Indian Country with their Agents and Interpreters, and traders, which have at all former periods kept the North Western frontiers in a state of feverish alarm." Cass admitted that broad reasons of state might necessitate some agreement with Great Britain which would admit British traders into the Northwest, but even then some effective check on their operations would be essential. To this end he proposed blocking off by military posts the three great channels of communication by which the British traders and their goods infiltrated into the American West. A post at Green Bay and another at Prairie du Chien would cut off the most important of the lines, the Fox-Wisconsin waterway. A fort at Chicago would block the second, that by way of Chicago and the Illinois River. The only alternative route, from Lake Superior to the headwaters of the Mississippi, could be checked if necessary by a post near the Grand Portage. If these military establishments were set up, the British (even if admitted under regulations) could be controlled and duties collected from them, and the Indians would be properly awed by the display of American military power in their midst.[17]

The occupation of Green Bay and Chicago had been entrusted to General Brown, and he began the concentration of soldiers at Detroit. He left Sackets Harbor on July 20, 1815, and on August 9 reached

---

[16] Dallas to Madison, June 19, 1815, *Wisconsin Historical Collections*, XIX (1910), 380–381.

[17] Cass to Dallas, July 20, 1815, Carter, *Territorial Papers*, X, 573–575.

Detroit, where headquarters for the Third and the Fifth Infantry were established. Although detachments were sent at once to Fort Mackinac, the season was too late for the move to Green Bay and Chicago, which had to be postponed until the following summer.

Meanwhile American soldiers began to move into the upper Mississippi valley from St. Louis. In the autumn of 1815 a detachment of the Eighth Infantry under Colonel Robert C. Nicholas ascended the Mississippi in keelboats, intending to establish a fort at or near Rock Island, to control the Sacs and Foxes and to open and protect the river communication to Prairie du Chien. The troops were stopped by ice at the mouth of the Des Moines River in November and built huts for winter quarters on the east bank of the Mississippi, calling their camp Cantonment Davis, which the next year became Fort Edwards.[18]

Early in 1816 Brevet Brigadier General Thomas A. Smith, who had taken command at St. Louis the previous September, energetically pushed the army up the river. In April he arrived at Cantonment Davis with his rifle regiment, took command of the entire expedition, and proceeded to Rock Island. In May a fort was begun on the southern tip of the island, named Fort Armstrong in honor of the former Secretary of War. General Smith supervised the construction of temporary fortifications at Rock Island, then leaving the Eighth Infantry troops there under command of Colonel William Lawrence to complete the construction of the fort, he advanced with his regiment to Prairie du Chien.[19]

On June 20 they arrived at the Prairie, where the site of Fort Shelby was reoccupied and a new installation begun, which was named Fort Crawford. For many years this was to be a key fort in the defense of the West. Located on the left bank of the Mississippi just above the mouth of the Wisconsin, it dominated the sleepy little French community of Prairie du Chien. It was at one of the great crossroads of the frontier, a convenient stopping place for travelers on the Mississippi and those passing up the Wisconsin River to the Great Lakes, and its troops wielded great influence over the Winnebagos, the Sacs and Foxes, the Chippewas, and the Sioux.[20]

---

[18] Daniel W. Flagler, *A History of the Rock Island Arsenal from Its Establishment in 1863 to December, 1876; and of the Island of Rock Island, the Site of the Arsenal, from 1804 to 1863* (Washington, 1877), pp. 14–15.

[19] *Ibid.*, pp. 15–16.

[20] For the history of Fort Crawford, see Bruce E. Mahan, *Old Fort Crawford and the Frontier* (Iowa City, 1926), and Peter L. Scanlan, *Prairie du Chien: French, British, American* (Menasha, Wis., 1937).

As the army was thus reasserting United States authority on the upper Mississippi, General Brown was fulfilling his responsibility in regard to the new lake posts. On March 27, 1816, he wrote to Major General Macomb, commanding the Fifth Department at Detroit, to make the necessary arrangements to occupy and fortify a position on the Fox River near the head of Green Bay and to reoccupy Fort Dearborn as soon as the weather permitted. He recommended a detachment of troops in each of these locations, "of strength to completely awe the Indians in the vicinity."[21] Difficulties in obtaining transports delayed the expeditions, but by June 8 Macomb could announce the sailing on the morrow of two companies of the Third Infantry to Chicago and one company to Mackinac, and the promise of an expedition to Green Bay in the near future.[22] By June 20 the disposition of the troops had been made as follows: at Mackinac, one company of artillery and three companies of the Third Infantry; at Chicago, two companies of the Third Infantry; at Green Bay, two companies of the Third Infantry and two companies of riflemen; and at Detroit and its dependencies, one company of artillery and the whole of the Fifth Infantry.[23]

One hundred and twelve men under Captain Hezekiah Bradley arrived at Chicago on July 4. The public buildings of old Fort Dearborn were all in ruins except for the magazine, which was badly damaged, and the soldiers, with aid of workmen brought from Detroit, erected a new installation. The Indian agency and the government trading post were reestablished as well. Small parties of Indians visited the garrison, but there were no manifestations of hostility.[24]

More important than Fort Dearborn, which was no longer an isolated outpost, was Fort Howard at Green Bay.[25] Colonel John Miller of the Third Infantry arrived on July 14, 1816, at Fort Mackinac, which was to be the headquarters for his regiment; on the 26th, he departed for Green Bay. Rumors that the Indians were opposed to the establishment of a military post on the Fox River had reached Mackinac and Detroit,

[21] Jacob Brown Official Letter Books, vol. 2, Library of Congress.
[22] Macomb to Brown, June 8, 1816, *ibid.*
[23] Macomb to Secretary of War, June 20, 1816, Carter, *Territorial Papers*, X, 652–653.
[24] Milo M. Quaife, *Chicago and the Old Northwest, 1673–1835: A Study of the Evolution of the Northwestern Frontier, Together with a History of Fort Dearborn* (Chicago, 1913), pp. 262–284. The same story is told in somewhat simpler form in Quaife, *Checagou: From Indian Wigwam to Modern City, 1673–1835* (Chicago, 1933), pp. 156–174.
[25] For the history of Fort Howard, see Louise Phelps Kellogg, "Old Fort Howard," *Wisconsin Magazine of History*, XVIII (December, 1934), 125–140.

and Miller exercised every precaution. He took with him all the troops he could spare from Fort Mackinac—four companies of infantry, two companies of riflemen, and a detachment of artillery—but on arrival he encountered an ostensibly friendly reception, which he attributed to the appearance of the strong force with him. Miller and Major Charles Gratiot of the engineers examined the country on both sides of the Fox as far as the first rapids and found no site as suitable as that near the mouth of the river on which the old French fort had stood. Miller soon returned to Mackinac, leaving Lieutenant Colonel Talbot Chambers in command with about 300 men, who proceeded to get houses and barracks ready for occupation.[26] For a quarter century Fort Howard figured prominently in any detailed plan for defense of the western frontier, since it occupied a key position on the strategic passageway between the Great Lakes and the Mississippi.

Plans for the northwestern military frontier did not stop at Prairie du Chien and Green Bay. President Madison authorized a board of officers to examine the coastal fortifications and the inland defenses of the nation.[27] Very likely as part of this activity an exploring party was sent up the Mississippi in the summer of 1817. A small group of soldiers and interpreters under the command of Major Stephen H. Long left Prairie du Chien on July 9 to survey the river and locate suitable sites for military posts. Long recommended a spot just below Lake Pepin, spoke favorably of the mouth of the St. Croix, and noted that on the bluff overlooking the confluence of the Minnesota and Mississippi rivers "a military work of considerable magnitude might be constructed," provided care were taken to secure the commanding height behind the fort. On his return down the river to Fort Belle Fontaine (which he reached on August 15), he stopped to examine Fort Crawford, Fort Armstrong, and Fort Edwards. He drew up detailed descriptions of the posts and commented on their possibilities for defense and on necessary improvements.[28] Long's report no doubt helped to determine plans for the move into the upper Mississippi valley that was soon to come.

[26] John Miller, "The Military Occupation of Green Bay," *Mississippi Valley Historical Review*, XIII (March, 1927), 549–553.

[27] Monroe to Jackson, December 14, 1816, *Correspondence of Andrew Jackson*, II, 269–270: Report of Calhoun, December 22, 1817, *American State Papers: Military Affairs* (7 vols., Washington, 1832–1861), I, 669.

[28] Long's report is in "Voyage in a Six-oared Skiff to the Falls of Saint Anthony in 1817," *Minnesota Historical Collections*, II (1860), 6–83. His descriptions of the forts give an excellent idea of the construction of these early posts. For a

In the South all Indian difficulties were presumed to have ended with the Treaty of Fort Jackson, which the triumphant Andrew Jackson had forced upon the Creeks on August 9, 1814. The Creeks, who had been crushed by Jackson's Tennessee volunteers and their friendly Indian allies, ceded large sections of their lands in Alabama and Georgia, which the United States demanded as "an equivalent for all expenses incurred in prosecuting the war to its termination." They promised, moreover, to abandon all communication or intercourse with any British or Spanish posts and to permit the establishment of American forts and roads in the territory they still retained. It was a harsh peace imposed, as the preamble to the treaty stated, because of the "unprovoked, inhuman, and sanguinary war" waged by the Creeks against the United States.[29]

The Indians felt differently about it. Many, unwilling to accept defeat, joined the Seminoles in Florida, where they continued to be a lively threat to the white settlers moving onto their vacated lands. Here they were encouraged by British adventurers like Colonel Edward Nicholls in their belief that the lands taken away from them at Fort Jackson would be returned now that the War of 1812 had ended. The Treaty of Ghent had indeed provided that the United States would restore to Indian tribes with whom it was still at war at the time of ratification the possessions, rights, and privileges which they may have enjoyed in 1811, but the American government did not consider that the Treaty of Ghent in any way negated the treaty made with the Creeks at Fort Jackson. The Indians, instigated and organized by Nicholls, waited for the Americans to evacuate the ceded lands.[30]

To maintain peace on this perilous frontier was the task of General Edmund P. Gaines, one of the two southern brigadiers appointed in the reduced and reorganized army at the end of the War of 1812. By June, 1815, Gaines had a force of 1,000 men on the frontier and had called for more in an attempt to overawe the warlike Indians on both

---

recent biography of Long as an engineer, see Richard G. Wood, *Stephen Harriman Long, 1784–1864: Army Engineer, Explorer, Inventor* (Glendale, Calif., 1966).

[29] Kappler, *Treaties*, pp. 107–109.

[30] For a scholarly account of the southern frontier from 1815 to 1821, see James W. Silver, *Edmund Pendleton Gaines, Frontier General* (Baton Rouge, 1949), pp. 54–88. The story is told in more detail in James Parton, *Life of Andrew Jackson* (3 vols., New York, 1860), II, 391–556. See also Marquis James, *Andrew Jackson, The Border Captain* (New York, 1933), pp. 308–326, and A. H. Phinney, "The Second Spanish-American War," *Florida Historical Society Quarterly*, V (October, 1926), 103–111.

sides of the Florida line. He ordered the Fourth Infantry to Augusta, Georgia, and in September wrote to the Secretary of War of the need for 6,000 men if the surveying of the boundary line of the Creek cessions was to be completed without Indian disturbance. The running of the boundary line could be carried on only with heavy army protection, and Gaines was convinced that nothing but a military defeat would quiet the Indians.[31]

A focal point of disturbance on the frontier was a fort on the Apalachicola River south of the American boundary, which had been well supplied with ammunition by Colonel Nicholls after the Battle of New Orleans. When Nicholls departed for England in the summer of 1815, he left the fort in the hands of the Indians he had befriended. They soon were dispossessed, however, by a band of Negro banditti, who terrified both the Americans and the Spaniards and whose fort served as an inviting refuge for runaway slaves. The post came to be known as the Negro Fort.

To keep watch on the Negro Fort as well as to protect surveyors— and in general maintain the peace in the area—Gaines in 1816 ordered the construction of Fort Scott at the confluence of the Flint and Chattahoochee rivers, almost on the Florida border. Supplies for the fort were to be brought from New Orleans and convoyed past the Negro Fort up the Apalachicola. Colonel Duncan Clinch of the Fourth Infantry, whose men had built Fort Scott, was dispatched down the river to aid the fleet bringing up supplies. When men from the convoy searching for fresh water were killed by the Negroes of the fort, the order was given to take the stronghold. As the gunboats moved up the Apalachicola, Clinch (aided by a group of friendly Seminoles) moved down from the north. After several days of intermittent firing, a red-hot ball from one of the ships' guns struck the main magazine on July 27, 1816, and the resultant explosion demolished the fort and its defenders. Of the 330 inhabitants of the fort, 270 were instantly killed by the blast and many others died soon after. The Negro commander of the fort, who escaped the destruction, was turned over to the Seminoles and put to death.[32]

This fortuitous demolition of the Negro Fort eased temporarily the dangers on the Florida frontier. The great arsenal of the dissident

[31] Silver, *Gaines*, pp. 57–58.
[32] Gaines to D. L. Clinch, May 23, 1816, *American State Papers: Foreign Relations* (6 vols., Washington, 1832–1859), IV, 558; J. Loomis to Daniel T. Patterson, August 13, 1816, *ibid.*, pp. 559–560.

Indians and Negroes was gone and the incendiary leaders dead. Yet there was an undercurrent of tension, and the lawless white frontiersmen committed acts of aggression that inevitably brought Indian retaliation.

In January, 1817, Gaines was ordered to establish his headquarters at Fort Montgomery in Alabama, and from there he strove to prevent the precarious peace from dissolving into border warfare. He refused to protect white squatters on the Indian lands and sought to persuade the Seminoles to surrender men accused of murdering whites. This the Seminoles refused to do and complained in turn about white incursions. The chief of Fowltown, an Indian village fourteen miles east of Fort Scott, threatened the Americans: "I warn you not to cross, nor cut a stick of wood on the east side of the Flint. That land is mine. I am directed by the powers above and below to protect and defend it. I shall do so."[33] Such obstinacy about lands that were within the Fort Jackson treaty cession could not be brooked, and Gaines started in the fall of 1817 to concentrate troops at Fort Scott. When the general himself arrived at Fort Scott, he sent for the chief of Fowltown, but that warrior refused to come, and on November 20, 1817, Gaines directed Major David E. Twiggs to remove the Indians of the village from American soil and to treat them as enemies if they resisted. The Indians fled and shortly Gaines ordered the town and its provisions destroyed.[34]

Gaines defended his action as necessary to give security to American citizens living on the frontier, but the destruction of Fowltown did not bring peace.[35] Instead the Indians struck back savagely in revenge. Within ten days a boatload of United States troops under Lieutenant Richard W. Scott with a number of soldiers' wives and children was ambushed on the Apalachicola not far from Fort Scott. Forty-five persons were killed or made prisoner, and the Indians, swinging the children by their heels, dashed out their brains against the side of the boat. The war had begun. Gaines hastened his concentration of troops on the border, warned the friendly Indians to stay in their villages, and waited orders from the War Department. He himself was sure that the Americans must strike hard. He foresaw no security or tranquility "until the towns south and east of this place shall receive a signal proof of our ability and willingness to retaliate for every outrage."[36]

[33] Parton, *Jackson*, II, 428–429.
[34] *Correspondence of Andrew Jackson*, II, 334n.
[35] See Gaines's long apologia in his letter to Calhoun, October 17, 1819, *American State Papers: Military Affairs*, II, 125–130.
[36] Parton, *Jackson*, II, 432.

Before Gaines could strike, he had been ordered to Amelia Island, a haven of smugglers and filibusters off the northeast coast of Florida, which complicated American relations with Spain. Gaines was ordered to take possession of the island for the United States. The War Department, when it finally got word of the outrages on the Apalachicola, directed General Andrew Jackson himself to take charge at Fort Scott. The entry of Jackson on the scene brought a new dimension to the war. Without waiting for the action of the governor of Tennessee, Jackson enrolled a corps of volunteers and hastened as fast as he could over the dismal roads of the rainy season to the scene of conflict. If Spain could not maintain order in Florida, Jackson would see to it himself.

Gaines, meanwhile, having seized Amelia Island without trouble, was hastening back across Georgia, hoping that from Fort Scott he could strike a decisive blow to end the war. To this end he enrolled a large army of Creek warriors (more than 1,600 in number), whom he organized in American army fashion with the Creek half-breed William McIntosh as a brigadier general in command. Jackson and Gaines met at Hartford, Georgia, and as news of the dire straits of Fort Scott from lack of provisions reached them, they hurried on. Jackson went overland and reached Fort Scott on March 9. The fort had no provisions for his men, so he pushed on down the Apalachicola until he met a boat of supplies ascending the river, and on the site of the old Negro Fort he built a new fortification, called Fort Gadsden. Here he awaited Gaines, who had struggled through the wilderness near starvation and clad only in his pantaloons after he had been shipwrecked coming by boat down the Flint.

The two American generals now moved against the Indian towns in Florida, aided by General McIntosh and his Creeks. The towns were easily taken as the Indians fled, and everywhere was evidence of American scalps and American property. Convinced that the Spanish were encouraging the Indians, Jackson invaded the town of St. Marks. Here he captured and executed two Indian chiefs and took into custody the British trader Alexander Arbuthnot. Still on the offensive, Jackson drove on to Bowlegs' Town on the Suwanee River over one hundred miles beyond St. Marks. Here, too, the Indians had dispersed, but Jackson captured two Englishmen, Robert C. Ambrister and Peter Cook, who stumbled by chance into his camp. Back at St. Marks Jackson convened a court-martial, with Gaines as president, which quickly tried Arbuthnot and Ambrister for aiding the enemy, and found them guilty. Arbuthnot was forthwith hanged and Ambrister shot.

Unmindful of the storm of controversy that would soon arise because of his execution of the two British subjects, Jackson moved next against Pensacola. On May 25 he invested the Spanish post and three days later he accepted its surrender. His proclamation of May 29 announced the appointment of one of his army officers as civil and military governor of Pensacola and the establishment of the revenue laws of the United States. His justification was explicit:

> The Seminole Indians inhabiting the territories of Spain have for more than two years past, visited our Frontier settlements with all the horrors of savage massacre—helpless women have been butchered and the cradle stained with the blood of innocence. . . .
>
> The immutable laws of self defense, therefore compelled the American Government to take possession of such parts of the Floridas in which the Spanish authority could not be maintained.[37]

Jackson moved north to Fort Montgomery, where on June 2, 1818, he sent off long letters to Monroe and to Secretary of War Calhoun, reporting what he had done and insisting upon the necessity of holding the posts in Florida he had taken. "The possession of St Marks, Ft Gadsden, and Frt don Carlos de Barancas [Pensacola]," he told the President, "puts an end to all Indian wars." To the Secretary of War he wrote: "The Seminole War may now be considered at a close. Tranquility [is] again restored to the Southern Frontier of the United States, and as long as a cordon of military posts is maintained along the gulf of Mexico America has nothing to apprehend from either foreign or Indian hostilities."[38]

Jackson returned to Nashville in triumph, while the diplomats were left to pick up the pieces. The Spanish minister, Don Luis de Onis, demanded the prompt restitution of St. Marks, Pensacola, and all other places wrested from the Crown of Spain by Jackson's forces, as well as an indemnity for all losses and the punishment of the general.[39]

---

[37] Correspondence of Andrew Jackson, II, 374–375.

[38] Jackson to Monroe, June 2, 1818, and Jackson to Calhoun, June 2, 1818, ibid., pp. 377, 380.

[39] Don Luis de Onis to the Secretary of State, July 8, 1818, American State Papers: Foreign Affairs, IV, 496–497. Because of the diplomatic posts in Florida and his execution of the British subjects, Arbuthnot and Ambrister, the whole operation became a cause célèbre, and reams of correspondence and reports found their way into print. Congressional debates on the Seminole War appear in Annals of Congress, 15 Congress, 2 session, col. 515–530, 583–1138, and in a 591-page book, Debate in the House of Representatives of the United States, on the Seminole War, in January and February, 1819 (Washington, 1819). The following items contain exhaustive documentation on the Seminole campaign and

The posts were returned, but the general was not punished, and resolutions in Congress condemning his action were voted down.

General Gaines meanwhile kept watch on the southern frontier, where the problems were not as completely solved as Jackson had asserted. The Indians had not been decisively beaten in combat, and until Florida finally passed into American possession in 1821 there was a continual threat of Spanish intrigue with the Indians. St. Augustine was a point of special concern, and Gaines was all for moving against it. His hands were tied, however, against aggressive action, lest the delicate negotiations with Spain for the purchase of Florida be still more entangled.[40]

☆

While Gaines and Jackson were thus aggressively upholding—and indeed stretching—American authority along the Florida border, the War Department was concerned to make more pervasive the nation's presence in the Northwest. A beginning had been made in 1816, but in a sense it had been a hesitant and negative endeavor. By the end of that year the losses sustained in the War of 1812 had been repaired, it is true. Detroit and Mackinac were restored to American control and Fort Dearborn rebuilt. The short-lived Fort Shelby at Prairie du Chien had been replaced by a more permanent military post, Fort Crawford, and Fort Howard at Green Bay had been firmly established. But these were conceived as limited and defensive moves designed to check and restrain the initiative of the British traders by cutting off their communications and thus to weaken or destroy their enterprise and with it their influence over the Indians.

Perhaps this was all that could be expected of the War Department, nearly foundering as it was after the war. By the fall of 1817 the unsettled accounts of the Department amounted to more than $45 million, an immense sum in the early nineteenth century. No over-all frontier policy had been developed and there were loud complaints

---

the diplomatic crisis resulting: *American State Papers: Military Affairs*, I, 680–769, 774–778, II, 99–132; *American State Papers: Indian Affairs*, II, 154–162; *American State Papers: Foreign Relations*, IV, 422–626; *Senate Documents* Nos. 35, 68, 100, 102, 15 Congress, 2 session; *House Documents* Nos. 65, 82, 86, 15 Congress, 2 session. See also *Correspondence between Gen. Andrew Jackson and John C. Calhoun, on . . . the Seminole War* (Washington, 1831), and *Correspondence of Andrew Jackson*, II.

[40] Silver, *Gaines*, pp. 81–88.

from both traders and settlers. The army supply system was in the hands of private contractors, whose avidity for profits could not easily be controlled. There was no unity of administration and no uniform system of discipline.[41]

It was no wonder, then, that President Monroe had difficulty in persuading someone to accept the cabinet post of Secretary of War. He offered the post to Clay and sounded out Jackson, but neither would accept the job. Isaac Shelby declined because of his age, and William H. Lowndes also refused. Finally, on October 10, 1817, the position was offered to John C. Calhoun, only thirty-five and without military experience, but already well known for his strong nationalism, his keen mind, and his political acumen. The unfavorable circumstances in the War Department did not discourage him. He entered the post on December 8 with a determination to learn, an astounding energy, and a vision that soon transformed the Department and made him one of the remarkable cabinet members of his age. On his tenth day in office he set forth his philosophy in a letter to General Brown: "In accepting the office which I now fill, I was actuated by a strong desire to contribute as much as possible, to the public prosperity, by giving our military establishment the greatest possible utility and perfection. For, however prosperous the country may be in other respects, if its means of defence are inadequate, or the military science unknown, those who are best qualified to judge, will readily see that its prosperity is uncertain and insecure. To attain this desired perfection, must be the work of time, accompanied with much labor and reflection. We have indeed much to do."[42]

Part of this task was the formulation of a defense policy for the western frontier. While the army officers were thinking in terms of a slow, limited advance of the frontier, Calhoun was thinking in terms of continental grandeur, and he set in motion a grand scheme of western defense that was breathtaking in its scope. Whereas General Brown declared himself satisfied with the permanent occupation of four positions—the outlet of Lake Huron (Detroit), the outlet of Lake Superior (Sault Ste. Marie), the outlet of the Fox River (Fort Howard), and the post at Chicago (Fort Dearborn)—with which he felt relieved "from any considerable apprehension of Indian invasion under any

[41] Wesley, *Guarding the Frontier*, pp. 76–77; Charles M. Wiltse, *John C. Calhoun, Nationalist, 1782–1828* (Indianapolis, 1944), pp. 149–151.
[42] Calhoun to Brown, December 18, 1817, National Archives, Records of the Secretary of War, Letters Sent, vol. 9.

circumstances whatever,"[43] the new Secretary of War was plotting a military line from Sault Ste. Marie to the mouth of the Minnesota River to the Mandan villages, 1,600 miles up the Missouri from St. Louis. The purpose of this grand scheme Calhoun set forth in brilliant fashion.[44]

With the disasters of the recent war etched deeply in his memory, he presented his arguments. The Indians in the Northwest, composed of warlike and powerful tribes, were unacquainted with American power and at the same time were "open to the influence of a foreign Power," and with the expansion of American settlements were becoming close neighbors. A new thrust of American force into the Northwest was thus necessary to overawe the tribes and to cut off once and for all the intercourse between the Indians and the British trader posts. "This intercourse," Calhoun said, "is the great source of danger to our peace; and until that is stopped our frontiers cannot be safe." The Treaty of Ghent did not continue the British right to trade with the Indians, and an Act of Congress in 1816 prohibited foreigners from trading with the Indians in our limits, but Calhoun admitted that "the act and instructions to Indian agents can have but little efficacy to remedy the evil." He would have preferred that through diplomatic means the British could be persuaded to put an end to the trade and to the generous distribution of presents to the Indians, but until the British acted, new military posts would "put in our hand the power to correct the evil."

The Lake posts could check all foreign trade in that quarter and effectively restrain the Indians from passing over the border into Canada. The sites at St. Peter's (the mouth of the Minnesota) and at the Mandan villages were selected for the same purpose. The convention of 1818 had extended the boundary west along the 49th parallel, and Calhoun believed that trading posts of the Hudson's Bay Company and the North West Company could be found south of that line. By means of the new posts the United States would finally have the power to exclude foreigners from trade and intercourse with the Indian tribes residing within the United States along the line. The advantages of the Mandan villages as a military site he especially

---

[43] Brown to Secretary of War, February 5, 1818, Jacob Brown Letter Books, vol. 2.

[44] The best statement of Calhoun's plan is found in his letter to Alexander Smyth, Chairman of the House Committee on Military Affairs, December 29, 1819, *American State Papers: Military Affairs*, II, 33–34. Except where otherwise indicated, the quotations following are from this source.

enumerated. They were at the point on the Missouri that was nearest to the establishment of the Hudson's Bay Company on the Red River of the North. It was a position that could protect points to the south from any enemy approaching from the north and was well situated, furthermore, to protect American fur traders operating towards the headwaters of the Missouri.

The restraining and overawing of the Indians and the destroying of their contacts with the British traders and posts were primarily military matters. "Trade and presents, accompanied by talks calculated for the purpose," Calhoun noted, "are among the most powerful means to control the action of savages; and so long as they are wielded by a foreign hand our frontiers must ever be exposed to the calamity of Indian warfare." Of two great objects in view, he said, "the permanent security of our frontier is considered by far of the greatest importance."[45] But the second object was also much in his mind—the enlargement and protection of the American fur trade. Military posts at Sault Ste. Marie, at St. Peter's, and at the Mandan villages, by enforcing the prohibition on foreign traders, would permit unrestricted access to the trade to the American traders. When the posts were all established and occupied, asserted Calhoun with a certain tone of exultation, "the most valuable fur trade in the world will be thrown into our hands." He noted, too, that the ease of communication with the new posts on the Mississippi and Missouri would be so much greater than that of the British to the same area "that our ascendency over the Indians of those rivers both as to trade and power ought, with judicious measures on our part, to be complete."

Calhoun wanted the establishment of the new posts and the movement of the troops up the Missouri and up the Mississippi to constitute a single system, and he expected all the elements in the system to work together. He was to be disappointed, for his grand vision was never fully realized.

[45] This statement of priority is in Calhoun's letter to Colonel Henry Atkinson, March 27, 1819, *Correspondence of John C. Calhoun*, ed. J. Franklin Jameson (*Annual Report of the American Historical Association for the Year 1899*, II, Washington, 1900), p. 159.

EIGHT

American Dominion on the Missouri and the Mississippi

THE extension of American military power up the Missouri, which Calhoun considered but one part of his master plan for western defense, seemed to have a separate existence in the mind of Congress and of the public. It was generally known as the Yellowstone Expedition, for Calhoun's original plan called for an advanced post at the mouth of the Yellowstone River.[1] Writing to General Thomas A. Smith, commanding the Ninth Military Department at St. Louis, on March 16, 1818, Calhoun declared his intention to build a permanent post at that remote spot. He directed Smith to take immediate steps to establish the post after consulting with Governor William Clark about the country and the force and disposition of the Indians. Two hundred recruits from Pennsylvania and Ohio were directed to St. Louis to be attached to Smith's rifle regiment. Calhoun conveyed to Smith his worries about the reaction of the British to this move. He wanted the officer detailed to command the movement to impress the Indians with our friendly intentions and to be alert for British traders attempting to create a contrary impression. "They have great advantages in controuling the savages thro' their commanding station

---

[1] The Yellowstone Expedition—or Missouri Expedition, as some historians prefer to call it—is discussed in Hiram Martin Chittenden, *The American Fur Trade of the Far West* (3 vols., New York, 1902), II, 562–587. Chittenden takes a very critical view of the enterprise and calls the results disappointing, "an unqualified failure if not a huge fiasco." "The arrangement for the transportation of the troops," he says, "disclosed a degree of folly, if nothing worse, which is a disgrace to the military history of the government." A sounder view, which places the Missouri River expedition in a wider context, is Cardinal L. Goodwin, "A Larger View of the Yellowstone Expedition, 1819–1820," *Mississippi Valley Historical Review*, IV (December, 1917), 299–313. Much the same approach is taken

on Red river; and as our contemplated establishment at Yellow Stone, will greatly curtail their trade towards the head of the Missouri, we must expect every opposition from them. No pains must be spared to counteract such efforts." Authority was granted to purchase $3,000 worth of presents for the Indians to augment the protestations of friendship.[2]

If such a troop movement could not be accomplished all the way to the Yellowstone in the first summer, Calhoun was willing to accept some intermediate post as a beginning. He suggested the Mandan villages to Smith and came more and more to speak in terms of this location rather than the more distant post at the Yellowstone.[3] The Secretary of War, in thus getting the movement started, was carried away by his ardent nationalism. The remoteness of the post on the Missouri, he admitted, would in some ways make it unpleasant for the soldiers,

> . . . but I am persuaded that the American soldier, actuated by the spirit of enterprize, will meet the privations which may be necessary with cheerfulness. Combined with the importance of the service, the glory of planting the American flag at a point so distant, on so noble a river, will not be unfelt. The world will behold in it the mighty growth of our republic, which but a few years since, was limited by the Alleghany; but now is ready to push its civilization and laws to the western confines of the continent.[4]

Such dreams of national grandeur were easily associated with the Yellowstone Expedition. "The establishment of this post," said the *St. Louis Enquirer*, "will be an era in the history of the West. It will

---

in Edgar B. Wesley, "A Still Larger View of the So-Called Yellowstone Expedition," *North Dakota Historical Quarterly*, V (July, 1931), 219–238, which is reprinted as Chapter X in Wesley, *Guarding the Frontier: A Study of Frontier Defense from 1815 to 1825* (Minneapolis, 1935), pp. 144–165. A recent, thoroughly researched account of the expedition from the standpoint of its commander is Roger L. Nichols, *General Henry Atkinson: A Western Military Career* (Norman, Okla., 1965), pp. 47–68. Supply aspects of the expedition are treated in Erna Risch, *Quartermaster Support of the Army: A History of the Corps, 1775–1939* (Washington, 1962), pp. 188–193.

[2] Calhoun to Smith, March 16, 1818, *Correspondence of John C. Calhoun*, ed. J. Franklin Jameson (*Annual Report of the American Historical Association for the Year 1899*, II, Washington, 1900), pp. 134–136.

[3] See Calhoun to Jackson, August 22, 1818, and March 6, 1819, *ibid.*, pp. 138, 153; Calhoun report of December 29, 1819, *American State Papers: Military Affairs*, II, 33–34.

[4] Calhoun to Thomas A. Smith, March 16, 1818, *Correspondence of John C. Calhoun*, p. 136.

go to the source and root of the fatal British influence which has for so many years armed the Indian nations against our Western frontier. It carries the arms and power of the United States to the ground which has hitherto been exclusively occupied by the British Northwest and Hudson's Bay Companies, and which has been the true seat of British power over the Indian mind. Now the American arms and American policy will be displayed upon the same theater."[5] The enthusiasm for what was possible led to romantic exaggerations. One westerner at Fort Osage, when he heard that steamboats would be used for the movement up the Missouri, declared that the expedition would open "a safe and easy communication to China, which would give such a spur to commercial enterprise that ten years shall not pass away before we shall have the rich productions of that country transported from Canton to the Columbia, up that river to the mountains, over the mountains, and down the Missouri and Mississippi, all the way (mountains and all) by the potent power of Steam."[6]

Everywhere the undertaking was a popular one, and President Monroe himself espoused it with enthusiasm. "The people of the whole Western country take a deep interest in the success of the contemplated establishment at the mouth of the Yellow Stone river," he wrote to Calhoun. "They look upon it as a measure better calculated to preserve the peace of the frontier, to secure to us the fur trade, and to break up the intercourse between the British traders and the Indians, than any other which has been taken by the government. I take myself very great interest in the success of the expedition, and am willing to take great responsibility to ensure it."[7]

A preliminary movement got under way in the fall of 1818. On August 30 Lieutenant Colonel Talbot Chambers left Fort Belle Fontaine with about 350 men of the rifle companies, accompanied by six keelboats. At Cow Island, a short distance above present-day Leavenworth, Kansas, and about eighty miles above Fort Osage, the expedition halted. Ice was forming on the river and provisions were low. A fort was built (called Cantonment Martin after the officer left in command by Chambers, who returned to Belle Fontaine), and the troops supplied themselves with game to keep from starving until relieved the next summer.[8]

[5] Quoted in Chittenden, *American Fur Trade of the Far West*, II, 564–565.
[6] *Ibid.*, p. 565.
[7] Monroe to Calhoun, July 5, 1819, *American State Papers: Military Affairs*, II, 69.
[8] Wesley, *Guarding the Frontier*, pp. 148–149.

Meanwhile during the winter and spring preparations for the main expedition went forward. Calhoun was much concerned that a proper officer should be given the command because of the prudence required in dealing with the Indians and the British traders, and he asked General Jackson to select the ablest and most experienced officer of the rifle regiment to lead the expedition.[9] Colonel Henry Atkinson was selected for the command, for he seemed to have the necessary qualities, but Calhoun, believing that the success of the enterprise would depend upon the character of the commander, again asked Jackson to "inculcate on him the necessity of the greatest caution and vigilance."[10] On March 27 Calhoun himself sent special instructions to Atkinson, urging him to conciliate the Indians and not to take any measures against illegal British traders until the posts were firmly established.[11] It was Calhoun's plan in the spring of 1819 to establish a fort at the Mandan villages that summer if possible, but if not, to install the troops firmly at Council Bluffs or at the Great Bend of the Missouri, positions that would have to be maintained as intermediate posts anyway.

The contracts for furnishing supplies and transportation were made with James Johnson of Kentucky, through the influence of his brother Richard M. Johnson, who was then serving in the House of Representatives. One contract called for transporting clothing, ordnance, and medical stores from Pittsburgh to St. Louis, a second for furnishing supplies, and a third for supplying transportation for the expedition.[12] By the third contract Johnson was obligated to furnish steamboats for carrying the troops and supplies up the Missouri, an untried endeavor enthusiastically backed at first by Atkinson and promised optimistically by Johnson. No doubt an enterprise of such magnitude and promise deserved the latest mode of river transportation. Johnson procured five steamboats, which arrived at St. Louis in the middle of May.

Trouble plagued the expedition from the very start. Weeks passed as the main body of troops waited to be transported up the Missouri. Johnson had legal battles with the Bank of Missouri, which prevented him from landing the supplies in Missouri for inspection by the quarter-

[9] Calhoun to Jackson, December 28, 1818, and January 5, 1819, *Correspondence of John C. Calhoun*, pp. 150–152.
[10] Calhoun to Jackson, March 6, 1819, *ibid.*, p. 153.
[11] Calhoun to Atkinson, March 27, 1819, *ibid.*, pp. 159–160.
[12] Documents pertaining to Johnson's contracts can be found in *American State Papers: Military Affairs*, II, 68–69, 324–325; *House Document* No. 110, 16 Congress, 2 session, serial 55.

master, but the basic cause of the delay was the inability of the steamboats to perform satisfactorily. Two of them apparently never even started up the Missouri.

Fortunately, the expedition did not have to rely solely on the steamboats. On June 14 Colonel Chambers left Fort Belle Fontaine with about 270 riflemen in five armored keelboats, reaching Franklin, Missouri, on July 2 and Fort Osage on July 20. There they waited for the main force under Colonel Atkinson. These troops, composed of the Sixth Infantry, left Belle Fontaine on July 4 and 5, four companies in keelboats and four on the three steamboats, the "Expedition," the "Johnson," and the "Jefferson." Progress was slow and uncertain in the steamboats, which proved unequal to their task. The "Expedition" reached Franklin on July 22 and Fort Osage on August 16. On the 23d it departed for Cantonment Martin, but it could not go beyond that point because of low water, and its cargo was transferred to keelboats. The "Johnson" reached Fort Osage about September 7, but near the mouth of the Kansas River it broke down and its load was transferred to keelboats. The "Jefferson" failed even to reach Franklin, and keelboats again were pressed into service. Little by little these boats made their way to Council Bluffs. The rifle regiment and five and one-half companies of the Sixth Infantry arrived on September 29 and construction of Camp Missouri was immediately begun on the river bottom, to house the 1,120 men of the two regiments.[13]

Camp Missouri was no sooner established than the whole expedition was called into question in Congress. Beginning in December, 1819, the House began to inquire into the objects and the expenses of the expedition, and great agitation arose over the Johnson contracts. The House insisted on cutting the appropriations of the quartermaster's department so that the expedition could not move beyond its station at Council Bluffs. Numerous criticisms were leveled at the whole enterprise, and despite the Senate's attempt to restore the cut in the appropriation, the opponents had their way.[14]

Calhoun's great dream of the American flag planted half way to the Pacific was shattered. He wrote to Atkinson on April 10, 1820, reporting the congressional action and conveying the President's decision that the troops were not to move beyond Council Bluffs. Atkinson was directed to make the defense of this most advanced post ample and of

[13] The history of this cantonment is told in Sally A. Johnson, "Cantonment Missouri, 1819–1820," *Nebraska History*, XXXVII (June, 1956), 121–133.
[14] See the documents cited in note 12 above.

a permanent nature.[15] An imposing cantonment was constructed along the river, but the flooding Missouri in June, 1820, and the heavy mortality among the troops forced the soldiers to abandon their position and seek refuge on the bluffs. Here they built a new fort, named Fort Atkinson in 1821, for many years the largest garrison in the nation and, until its abandonment in 1827, the most advanced outpost of America in the West.[16]

The troops were not idle at the post. A survey for a road from Council Bluffs to Chariton, Missouri, was made by Lieutenant Gabriel Field in November, 1819, and the next year the 330-mile road was constructed by the soldiers. And in July, 1820, an exploratory crossing was made between Council Bluffs and the St. Peter's. A party under Captain Matthew I. Magee made the survey, but the group found the country lacking timber and water and judged that "the high & precipitous Mountains & hills" they crossed made the country unsuitable for a road.[17]

Calhoun's plans for close cooperation between the posts on the Mississippi and the Missouri came to nothing.

☆

Associated with the movement of the Yellowstone Expedition was a scientific party under the direction of Major Stephen H. Long.[18] Cal-

[15] Calhoun to Atkinson, April 10, 1820, quoted in Johnson, *Nebraska History*, XXXVII, 128.

[16] For the history of Fort Atkinson and the activities of the soldiers there, see Sally A. Johnson, "Fort Atkinson at Council Bluffs," *Nebraska History*, XXXVIII (September, 1957), 229–236; Johnson, "The Sixth's Elysian Fields—Fort Atkinson on the Council Bluffs," *ibid.*, XL (March, 1959), 1–38; Edgar B. Wesley, "Life at Fort Atkinson," *ibid.*, XXX (December, 1949), 348–358; Wesley, "Life at a Frontier Post: Fort Atkinson, 1823–1826," *Journal of the American Military Institute*, III (Winter, 1939), 203–209; "Diary of James Kennerly, 1823–1826," ed. E. B. Wesley, *Missouri Historical Society Collections*, VI (October, 1928), 41–97.

[17] "Journal of Stephen Watts Kearny: Part I, The Council Bluff-St. Peter's Exploration (1820)," ed. Valentine Mott Porter, *Missouri Historical Society Collections*, III (January, 1908), 8–29, (April, 1908), 99–131. The map accompanying Edwin James's narrative of the Long expedition in Reuben Gold Thwaites, ed., *Early Western Travels, 1748–1846* (32 vols., Cleveland, 1904–1907), XIV, shows both Field's and Magee's routes, but the map does not agree with Kearny's journal, which makes it clear that Magee's party did not touch the St. Peter's River until they arrived at the fort at its mouth.

[18] For an account of the expedition and its personnel, see Richard G. Wood, *Stephen Harriman Long, 1784–1864: Army Engineer, Explorer, Inventor* (Glendale, Calif., 1966), pp. 59–119. A briefer account appears in William H. Goetzmann, *Army Exploration in the American West, 1803–1863* (New Haven, 1959),

houn had written to Jackson on March 6, 1819, that Long, "accompanied by several citizens eminent for scientific acquirements," would ascend the Missouri in a light steamboat at the same time as the main body of troops, in order to explore the West and acquire better knowledge of the territory between the Mississippi and the mountains. Long's party traveled in the "Western Engineer," a weird stern-wheel steamboat of light draught, launched in Pittsburgh in March, 1819. The boat was described as 75 feet long, 13 feet wide, and drawing 19 inches of water. It was so constructed that the steam escaped through the mouth of a large figurehead designed as a serpent. The boat made a striking impression: "The bow of this vessel exhibits the form of a huge serpent, black scaly, rising out of the water from under the boat, his head as high as the deck, darted forward, his mouth open, vomiting smoke, and apparently carrying the boat on his back. From under the boat at its stern issues a stream of foaming water, dashing violently along."[19] But despite its unusual construction, the "Western Engineer" made it all the way to Council Bluffs. It left St. Louis on June 21 and proceeded by slow stages up the river. From Cantonment Martin it was accompanied by a detail of soldiers in a keelboat. The party arrived at Fort Lisa, a Missouri Fur Company post five miles below Council Bluffs on September 17 and selected a site a half mile above for its encampment, which was christened Engineer Cantonment.

---

pp. 39–45. Extensive reports by members of the expedition are Edwin James, *Account of an Expedition from Pittsburgh to the Rocky Mountains Performed in the Years 1819 and '20* (2 vols. and atlas, Philadelphia, 1822–1823); the three-volume edition of James's work published in London in 1823, reprinted in Thwaites, *Early Western Travels*, XIV–XVII; and *The Journal of Captain John R. Bell, Official Journalist for the Stephen H. Long Expedition to the Rocky Mountains, 1820*, ed. Harlin M. Fuller and LeRoy R. Hafen (Glendale, Calif., 1957).

[19] Quoted from a letter of June 19, 1819, in Chittenden, *American Fur Trade of the Far West*, II, 571. A more modest description was given by Titian Ramsay Peale, the assistant naturalist of the expedition, at the beginning of the journal he kept: "Our boat is built in the most convenient manner for the purpose. She draws about two feet and a half of water, the wheels placed in the stern in order to avoid trees, snags and sawyers, etc. On the quarter deck there is a bullet proof house for the steersmen. On the right hand wheel is *James Monroe* in capitals, and on the left, *J. C. Calhoun*, they being the two propelling powers of the Expedition. She has a mast to ship and unship at pleasure, which carries a square and topsail, on the bow is carved the figure of a large serpent, through the gapping mouth of which the waste steam issues. It will give, no doubt, to the Indians an idea that the boat is pulled along by this monster." Quoted in Jessie Poesch, *Titian Ramsay Peale, 1799–1885, and His Journals of the Wilkes Expedition* (Philadelphia, 1961), p. 25.

Long left the party here for the winter while he himself returned to the East, and the scientists busied themselves collecting data about the geology, natural history, and Indians of the area. By spring the future of the exploration was in question, for the congressional decision to halt the Yellowstone Expedition also affected Long's part, and the extensive plans to explore the country between the Mississippi and the Rocky Mountains—the Missouri and its principal branches, then the Red River, the Arkansas River, and the Mississippi—were cut short.

Long instead set out directly west across the plains to seek the headwaters of the Platte, Arkansas, and Red rivers. The party followed the Platte to the foot of the Rockies and proceeded southward to the Arkansas. At the end of July they split their forces; Captain John R. Bell descended the Arkansas, while Long's group followed what he thought to be the Red, but which turned out to be the Canadian River. The results of the expedition were meager, in part no doubt because the revised plans had sapped much of the initial enthusiasm. The party discovered little that was new, and the published report made much of the barren nature of the country through which the expedition passed. The map that Long produced for the Secretary of War showed GREAT DESERT in the region directly east of the Rocky Mountains, and this map and the printed versions that accompanied the published report became the progenitors of several decades of maps of the West on which the Great American Desert was a prominent feature.[20]

Edwin James, who recorded the exploits of Long's party, explained the limited nature of the undertaking by the fact that the state of the national finances had called for a retrenchment in expenditures. This statement caught the eye of Edward Everett, who reviewed the report in the *North American Review;* he devoted two pages to a sarcastic diatribe against such shortsighted economy. "Detestable parsimony!" he wrote. "The only country but one in the world, that has not been reduced to an avowed or virtual bankruptcy; the country, which has

[20] On Long's part in the development of the Great American Desert myth, see Ralph C. Morris, "The Notion of a Great American Desert East of the Rockies," *Mississippi Valley Historical Review*, XIII (September, 1926), 190–200; Francis Paul Prucha, "Indian Removal and the Great American Desert," *Indiana Magazine of History*, LIX (December, 1963), 299–322; and Richard H. Dillon, "Stephen Long's Great American Desert," *Proceedings of the American Philosophical Society*, CXI (April, 1967), 93–108. On Long's map, see Carl I. Wheat, *Mapping the Transmississippi West* (5 vols., San Francisco, 1957–1963), II, 77–81. A portion of Long's route is traced in detail in John M. Tucker, "Major Long's Route from the Arkansas to the Canadian River, 1820," *New Mexico Historical Review*, XXXVIII (July, 1963), 185–219.

grown and is growing in wealth and prosperity beyond any other and beyond all other nations, too poor to pay a few gentlemen and soldiers for exploring its mighty rivers, and taking possession of the empires, which Providence has called it to govern!"[21] Everett, if not Congress, appreciated the role of the army in exploring and possessing the West.

☆

The second part of Calhoun's plan called for the establishment of a strong post on the upper Mississippi at the mouth of the St. Peter's (Minnesota) River. Calhoun in August, 1818, wrote to General Jackson informing him that with the extension of Michigan Territory to the Mississippi the Northern Division received a similar extension and that the upper Mississippi posts would fall under General Brown's jurisdiction rather than that of his own Southern Division, which was already heavily burdened with the advance up the Missouri. Calhoun considered it very important to establish a strong post at the St. Peter's, a great thoroughfare of British traders, and he proposed to increase the proportion of troops stationed in the upper Mississippi valley.[22] In his subsequent directions to General Brown, Calhoun repeated his insistence that the "force sent in the first instance ought to be as imposing as it can be rendered," and he advised stationing an entire regiment on the upper Mississippi from Rock Island to the St. Peter's, with the majority at the latter point. Once that post was firmly established, he proposed a fort at the head of navigation on the St. Peter's, as a link with the projected Mandan village post, and another at the head of navigation on the St. Croix River. Calhoun was concerned especially about Lord Selkirk's settlement on the Red River, which he apparently considered a threat to American interests in the Northwest, and about the powerful nations of the Sioux.[23]

By orders of February 10, 1819, Brown directed the Fifth Infantry to concentrate at Detroit in preparation for its movement to the Mississippi by way of the Fox-Wisconsin waterway. Part of the troops were to garrison Fort Crawford and Fort Armstrong, and the rest were to proceed to the mouth of the St. Peter's and there establish a post that

[21] Thwaites, *Early Western Travels*, XIV, 38; *North American Review*, XVI (January, 1823), 267–269.

[22] Calhoun to Jackson, August 22, 1818, *Correspondence of John C. Calhoun*, p. 138.

[23] Calhoun to Brown, October 17, 1818, *ibid.*, pp. 147–149.

would become the headquarters of the regiment. The main body of the Fifth, comprising about 300 men under Colonel Henry Leavenworth, left Detroit on May 14 and reached Prairie du Chien on June 30. More than a month's delay was caused by James Johnson's failure to send supplies on time, but the arrival of the stores finally enabled the expedition to proceed on August 8. The regiment was depleted by detachments left behind for Fort Crawford and Fort Armstrong, and only 98 men made the initial journey to the mouth of the St. Peter's which they reached on August 24. But soon more recruits arrived and the December returns showed 235 men for the fort. The camp was established on the right bank of the St. Peter's and optimistically called Cantonment New Hope, a name singularly ill-chosen, for in the first winter an epidemic of scurvy broke out and large numbers of the soldiers died.

In the following spring Colonel Leavenworth moved his command to the imposing bluff on the west bank of the Mississippi at the confluence of the two rivers. Here the men began the construction of a permanent garrison, called at first Fort St. Anthony after the magnificent waterfalls seven miles up the river, but renamed Fort Snelling in 1825, in honor of Colonel Josiah Snelling, who succeeded Leavenworth in command in 1820 and who was responsible for the excellent construction of the fort. The post must have pleased Calhoun, for it became an imposing structure and figured in all schemes for western defense.[24]

The third advanced outpost in Calhoun's original scheme was to be built at Sault Ste. Marie. General Brown considered the spot one of his four key locations in February, 1818, and General Macomb also recommended it for a military work before Calhoun incorporated the site into his grand proposal for advancing the military frontier. When General Brown returned from a tour of the lakes in the summer of 1819, he again strongly advised fortification of the straits as a means of cutting off intercourse between Indians in the United States and the British in Canada.[25] Yet, although the site was the least difficult to

[24] Marcus L. Hansen, *Old Fort Snelling, 1819–1858* (Iowa City, 1918), gives a detailed history of the post. The book was reprinted, Minneapolis, 1958, with numerous illustrations of the fort. The Indian agent who accompanied Leavenworth on the initial movement to establish Fort Snelling left an account: Thomas Forsyth, "Journal of a Voyage from St. Louis to the Falls of St. Anthony, in 1819," *Wisconsin Historical Collections*, VI (1872), 188–219.

[25] See Henry P. Beers, *The Western Military Frontier, 1815–1846* (Philadelphia, 1935), pp. 46–47, and Wesley, *Guarding the Frontier*, pp. 124–126. Brown's inspection trip is described by Roger Jones in "Gen. Brown's Inspection Tour Up the Lakes in 1819," *Publications of the Buffalo Historical Society*, XXIV (1920),

reach and the establishment of the fort occasioned no special controversy, the post here was the last of the cordon to be built.

☆

Before the site was fortified the importance of the region was emphasized by a special expedition made by Governor Lewis Cass in 1820
along the southern shore of Lake Superior and to the headwaters of
the Mississippi. Cass in November, 1819, had proposed to Calhoun
a trip to the Lake Superior region and the water communications between that lake and the Mississippi. The purpose in the first place was
to be scientific—"to examine the productions of its animal, vegetable,
and mineral kingdoms, to explore its facilities for water communication,
to delineate its natural objects, and to ascertain its present and future
probable value." Of special interest were the copper deposits in the
vicinity of Lake Superior. But as Governor of Michigan Territory and
ex officio responsible for its Indian affairs, Cass had other purposes in
mind that accorded well with Calhoun's general program for counteracting British influence in the Northwest. He wanted to explain to
the Indians the views of the government "respecting their intercourse
with the British authorities at Malden, and distinctly to announce to
them that their visits must be discontinued." He expected, furthermore,
to ascertain the state of the British fur trade within American territory.
He would be able to deal with the Indians about extinguishing their title
to lands at Green Bay, Prairie du Chien, and Sault Ste. Marie, and he
felt that it was important for the American flag to be carried into that
region by someone of his own official stature. Cass noted how little
the cost would be for the whole expedition and recommended that a
detachment of soldiers be sent along to give emphasis to his talks with
the Indians.[26]

With Calhoun's approval, Cass's party left Detroit on May 14, 1820.[27]

295–323. The Indians made frequent visits to Drummond's Island, where the
British built a post in 1815 after leaving Mackinac. The boundary commissioners in 1822 decided that Drummond's Island was in the United States, but
the British did not withdraw for another half-dozen years.

[26] Cass to Calhoun, November 18, 1819, *American State Papers: Indian Affairs*,
II, 318–319.

[27] For the history of Cass's expedition in 1820, see Henry R. Schoolcraft,
*Narrative Journal of Travels through the Northwestern Regions of the United
States . . .* (New York, 1821), which was reissued with certain changes in the
first half of his *Summary Narrative of an Exploratory Expedition to the Sources*

At Fort Gratiot a captain and twenty-two soldiers were provided as escort, and the expedition proceeded in its canoes to Fort Mackinac. Here more soldiers joined them, and in four canoes the party traveled on to the straits. A conclave was held with the Chippewas, which got off to a bad start. The Indians were opposed to the establishment of an American post on the site, but Cass strongly insisted that the United States intended to build one there under any circumstances. The council broke up without gaining the Indians' approval of a grant of land for the post, and the last chief to speak defiantly struck his war lance in the ground and kicked aside the proffered presents. On returning to their encampment, the Indians hoisted the British flag. When Cass heard this, he ordered his expedition under arms and accompanied only by an interpreter strode boldly into the Indian camp. He entered the lodge of the chief who had raised the flag, told him it was considered an indignity that would not be permitted on American soil, and took down the flag and carried it back to the American camp. The Indians struck their camp and both sides expected an attack by the other.

Cass's act of bravery impressed the Indians most favorably, and an overture made by some of the older chiefs brought a peaceful settlement. A treaty was signed on June 16 by which the Indians ceded to the United States a tract of land four miles square at the Sault, for which they were paid on the spot a variety of blankets, knives, broadcloths, and other trade goods.[28]

The soldiers from Mackinac returned to their station, while Cass's party continued on its way. The explorers examined the copper deposits on the Ontonagon River, reached the western tip of Lake Superior on July 5, and on July 13 reached Sandy Lake. Cass went up the Missis-

---

of the Mississippi River, in 1820 . . . (Philadelphia, 1855); James Duane Doty, "Official Journal, 1820, Expedition with Cass and Schoolcraft," Wisconsin Historical Collections, XIII (1895), 163–219; Charles C. Trowbridge, "With Cass in the Northwest in 1820," ed. Ralph H. Brown, Minnesota History, XXIII (June, 1942), 126–148; (September, 1942), 233–252; (December, 1942), 328–348. Mentor L. Williams has brought all these together in his edition of Henry R. Schoolcraft, Narrative Journal of Travels Through the Northwestern Regions of the United States Extending from Detroit through the Great Chain of American Lakes to the Sources of the Mississippi River in the Year 1820 (East Lansing, Mich., 1953). William L. G. Smith, The Life and Times of Lewis Cass (New York, 1856), pp. 117–140, prints pertinent letters and reports. A brief account of the expedition is Milo M. Quaife, "From Detroit to the Mississippi in 1820," Burton Historical Collection Leaflet, VIII (March, 1930), 49–64.

28 Charles J. Kappler, ed., Indian Affairs: Laws and Treaties (2 vols., Washington, 1904), II, Treaties, pp. 187–188.

sippi as far as Red Cedar Lake, and then the party moved down river to the new fort at the mouth of the St. Peter's. They continued down to Fort Crawford and up the Wisconsin-Fox passage to Green Bay, where the party divided, some going directly to Mackinac, others traveling with Cass to Chicago. On September 23 the reassembled party arrived at Detroit, having successfully completed a journey of more than 4,000 miles.

Cass's expedition reconfirmed the wisdom and necessity of a military post at Sault Ste. Marie, and an expedition of 250 men of the Second Infantry under Colonel Hugh Brady was ordered from Sackets Harbor in June, 1822. The troops arrived on July 6 and began the erection of the post, which was ultimately named Fort Brady.[29] Thus was this important link in Calhoun's chain of northwest defense finally forged. But the fulfillment of these plans did little to sweeten the defeat that Calhoun met in Congress on his proposals for a new, expansible organization for the regular army.

☆

The pressures to reduce the regular army had by no means subsided with the debate over the army bill of 1815, and as the war receded into the background, new attempts appeared in Congress to cut back the military force—and little by little the movement gathered strength. Calhoun resisted the trend, and he argued that because of the growth in the nation the army authorized in 1815 was no stronger proportionately than that of 1802.[30] A good many members of Congress, however, were determined to reduce the standing army to 6,000 men, and on May 11, 1820, the House of Representatives asked Calhoun to prepare plans for reducing the army to that number.[31]

Calhoun submitted his report on December 12, 1820, in one of the ablest state papers on military policy in American history.[32] Assuming that the proponents of a 6,000-man army would have their way in Congress, Calhoun set about to formulate a mode of reduction that would

[29] Wesley, *Guarding the Frontier*, p. 128.

[30] Calhoun's letter of December 11, 1818, to the House of Representatives, giving his reasons why no reduction should be made, is in *American State Papers: Military Affairs*, I, 779–782. Attached documents in support of his arguments follow on pages 782–810.

[31] *Annals of Congress*, 16 Congress, 1 session, col. 2233–2234.

[32] Report of Calhoun, December 12, 1820, *American State Papers: Military Affairs*, II, 188–198.

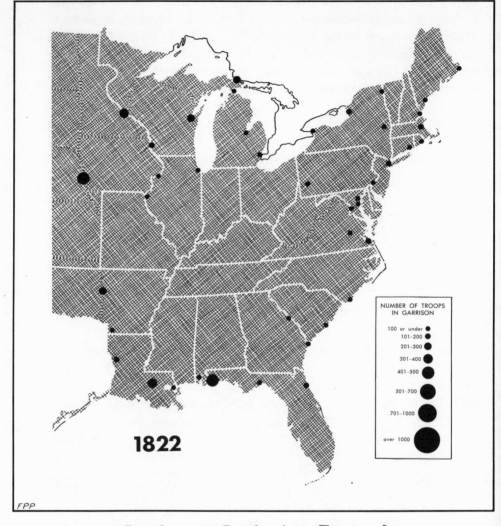

Distribution of Regular Army Troops, 1822

provide a skeleton army of trained officers and men which could be rapidly expanded if a war came. His basic principle was that "at the commencement of hostilities, there should be nothing either to new model or to create," and this meant reliance on the regular army, not militia troops called up for each crisis. To attain his end he developed plans for reducing the army that cut the number of privates in each unit without touching the number of regiments or companies with their officer complements. Thus would military skill and experience be perpetuated, army organization preserved, and a professional army safeguarded. When war came, the skeleton would be filled out to appropriate size, but no new units would be needed. The recruits entering the established regiments would be directed by trained officers and would quickly absorb the spirit and discipline of the old regulars.

Brilliant as was his conception and logical as were his arguments, Congress demurred. On March 2, 1821, the authorized strength of the army was reduced to 6,183, without incorporating in the act Calhoun's plans for an expansible army. Instead Congress consolidated and eliminated regiments and cut the number of officers.[33] With this truncated force of regular troops the military operations in the West were performed and on it the plans for military defense of the frontier had to rest.

☆

The failure to fulfill Calhoun's plans of 1819 for advancing high up the Missouri emboldened the Indians of the region and lessened the chances of attaching them to the American government. The red men were alert to what they considered American failures, and their arrogance seemed to grow whenever American force or resolution weakened. After being informed by Calhoun that no advance beyond Council Bluffs was immediately possible, Colonel Atkinson did not cease to plan for some action that would overawe the tribes. In November, 1820, he proposed to the Secretary of War a policy of annual summer troop movements up the Missouri, as a show of force and a warning to the Indians. He argued that the Indians had been expecting the army to appear on the upper reaches of the river for two years and if it did not move into the area to protect American fur traders, the Indians would be "so far drawn away by British influence that it may be impossible to recall them." The matter of expense did not disturb Atkinson. It would cost no more, he said, to send the troops out on the river than to keep them in the garrison, and he suggested sending a detachment of 400 men up the river each year until it was convenient to establish a permanent post. In addition to impressing the Indians and extending

[33] *U. S. Statutes at Large*, III, 615.

American influence, the expeditions would be "excursions of pleasure to the soldiery" who could enjoy the comforts of Fort Atkinson in the winter after spending the summer on the river.[34]

No heed was given to Atkinson's suggestions, and the conditions on the upper river worsened, as he had feared. The influx of American traders and trappers into the headwaters of the Missouri aroused hostility among the tribes, which soon manifested itself in death and destruction. In May, 1823, a party of the Missouri Fur Company suffered a serious defeat by the Blackfeet on Pryor's Fork of the Yellowstone. The two leaders and many of their men were killed. At the same time the Blackfeet attacked a party of Andrew Henry's men at the mouth of Smith's River, killing four of the eleven members of the group, and other Indians had run off with horses of the traders. The most striking of such disasters, however, was the attack on William Ashley by the Arikaras in June, an act of hostility that led to American military retaliation.[35]

Ashley, after a successful trading expedition in 1822, organized a second for the following year. With his band of recruits and two keelboats he left St. Louis on March 10 and on May 30 arrived at a point a little below the Arikara villages, which were located about six or seven miles above the mouth of the Grand River. Ashley was warned on the way up of hostile intentions on the part of the Arikaras, and he proceeded with due caution. Although he was greeted with a show of friendship by the Indians and began to trade with them for horses, early on the morning of June 2 the Indians began a general attack on his party. Thirteen of Ashley's men were killed and ten or eleven wounded, and he was forced to fall back down the river to a

[34] Atkinson to Calhoun, November 24, 1820, printed in Dale L. Morgan, *The West of William H. Ashley: The International Struggle for the Fur Trade of the Missouri, the Rocky Mountains, and the Columbia, with Explorations Beyond the Continental Divide, Recorded in the Diaries and Letters of William H. Ashley and His Contemporaries, 1822–1838* (Denver, 1964), p. liii.

[35] Accounts of the causes and conduct of the Arikara campaign can be found in Chittenden, *American Fur Trade of the Far West*, II, 588–607; Harrison C. Dale, *The Ashley-Smith Explorations and the Discovery of a Central Route to the Pacific, 1822–1829* (rev. ed., Glendale, Calif., 1941), pp. 74–82; Morgan, *The West of William H. Ashley*, pp. 52–58. Documents pertaining to the campaign are in *Senate Document* No. 1, 18 Congress, 1 session, serial 89, pp. 55–108. See also Leavenworth's final report and other documents in Doane Robinson, ed., "Official Correspondence Pertaining to the Leavenworth Expedition of 1823 into South Dakota for the Conquest of the Ree Indians," *South Dakota Historical Collections*, I (1902), 179–256. Newspaper items about the affair are printed in Donald McKay Frost, *Notes on General Ashley, the Overland Trail, and South Pass* (Worcester, Mass., 1945), Appendix B, pp. 68–154.

site at the mouth of the Cheyenne River. Ashley sent a keelboat with some of the wounded down the river to Fort Atkinson, to tell Colonel Leavenworth of the disaster and to request military aid in forcing a passage through the Arikara villages. He sent word also to Henry to notify him of the battle and to urge him to send aid.

Colonel Leavenworth received the word on June 18 and took upon himself the responsibility of sending aid to Ashley without waiting for approval from his superior, General Atkinson, at St. Louis. Accordingly, on the 22d he moved up the river with 220 men, comprising six companies of the Sixth Infantry. Three keelboats carried subsistence for the troops, ammunition, and two six-pounders. The river was high and the movement up river both by boat and on land was slow and arduous.

Leavenworth's regulars were soon augmented by other forces. Joshua Pilcher, a partner in the Missouri Fur Company, equipped two boats and took on board a five-and-one-half-inch howitzer at Fort Atkinson; he overtook Leavenworth on the 27th with a party of about forty men. Ashley's force meanwhile had been augmented by auxiliaries sent down the Missouri by Henry when he heard the news and numbered altogether about eighty men. Both these groups were organized into companies and accepted by Leavenworth, who reorganized his own men into five companies. He accepted also the proffered aid of Yankton and Teton Sioux, who were anxious to join the campaign against their enemies, the Arikaras. The whole force of regulars, mountaineers, voyageurs, and Indians numbered about 800 fighting men. Leavenworth called it the "Missouri Legion."

With the reorganization completed the march was continued, and the army arrived at the Arikara villages on August 9, having taken forty-eight days to cover the 640 miles from Council Bluffs. Here they were joined by 350 more Indian warriors, making a total attacking force of over 1,100 men against the 600–800 warriors in the two Arikara villages, who had not expected such a formidable attack and had made no special preparations to meet it.

After a sharp encounter between the Sioux and the Arikaras, in which two of the former were killed and thirteen of the latter left dead on the battleground, the attack was not aggressively pursued. The artillery was not successful in driving the Indians from the villages, and plans for an assault were laid aside. The Sioux, apparently discouraged by the inactivity of the whites and disappointed in their hopes for plunder, withdrew, taking with them some of the mules and horses.

Leavenworth soon persuaded the Arikaras to treat for peace. Pilcher, who had been appointed an Indian sub-agent, refused to draw up a treaty, for he wanted a signal crushing of the Indians, not a negotiated peace. Leavenworth himself drew up terms, the chief of which obligated the Arikaras to restore the property taken from Ashley in June.

The Indians restored very little, insisting that they could do no more. The alternatives were to accept the Indians' failure to comply or renew the attack. Leavenworth chose the first of the alternatives. The Indians were allowed to escape from their villages at night and were never overtaken, and Leavenworth ordered his command back down the Missouri. He had lost no men, except for a sergeant and six men who had drowned when their boat sank during the advance up the Missouri. As the force departed, men of the Missouri Fur Company set fire to the Arikara villages and destroyed them, an act hardly likely to encourage friendship. Leavenworth blamed Pilcher, but the trader, though he thought the destruction justified, had not given the order.

On his return to Fort Atkinson, Leavenworth announced the successful outcome of the expedition: "The blood of our countrymen have been honorably avenged, the Ricarees humbled, and in such a manner as will teach them and other Indian tribes to respect the American name and character." General Gaines, commanding the Western Department, praised Leavenworth for "the handsome and honorable result of the late expedition."[36]

Leavenworth, however, was stridently attacked by Pilcher, who wrote embittered letters condemning the colonel's failure to humble or destroy the Arikaras. To Indian agent Benjamin O'Fallon the trader wrote:

It is my sincere and candid opinion that the expedition against the Arikaras, from which so much service might have been rendered to this dwindling and bleeding commerce, will rather tend to increase, than diminish, the evil; that the situation of affairs in this country is worsted materially; that instead of raising the American character in the estimation of its inhabitants and impressing them with the power and spirit of our government, the contrary effect has been produced; and that the outrages of the Indians will increase in consequence. That a most unfavorable impression has been left upon the minds of our Indian allies is a fact that I am sorry to communicate.[37]

[36] Atkinson orders of August 29, 1823, and Gaines orders of September 21, 1823, *American State Papers: Military Affairs*, II, 594–595.
[37] Quoted in Chittenden, *American Fur Trade of the Far West*, II, 603.

Pilcher did not hesitate to address Leavenworth himself, whom he accused of closing off the upper Missouri "by the imbecility of your conduct and operations." The letters of recrimination passed back and forth in the western press, as critics and defenders of Leavenworth had their say.[38] Leavenworth himself calmly defended his decision in his final report of October 20 and laid the blame for future Indian hostilities on the traders who had burned the villages. "It will be impossible," he said, "for the military force of our Country to preserve peace between the Indians and our Citizens, (and there is nothing else to do it) if traders or citizens can with impunity burn the villages and towns of Indians whenever they choose to do so."[39]

General Atkinson was less sanguine about the outcome of the expedition than Leavenworth or Gaines. He feared that the Arikaras would recommence hostilities at the first opportunity and that the Sioux, disappointed that the Arikaras had not been exterminated, might themselves declare war on the Americans. He repeated with insistence his old refrain: additional troops must be sent to the Missouri, with a view to dispatching a force of 600–700 men up as far as the Yellowstone in the summer of 1824.[40]

☆

The action of Leavenworth against the Arikaras did not end agitation for more military protection of the upper Missouri fur trade. The criticisms of Leavenworth and what he accomplished stirred up public interest in the matter. Nor was congressional interest dead. The Senate Committee on Indian Affairs, chaired by that inveterate promoter of Missouri interests, Thomas Hart Benton, asked Secretary of War Calhoun on February 11, 1824, what it would cost to move a competent military force to some point between the mouth of the

[38] See letters and editorials printed in Frost, *Notes on General Ashley*, Appendix B.

[39] Report of October 20, 1823, Robinson, *South Dakota Historical Collections*, I, 232.

[40] Atkinson to Gaines, September 13, 1823, *American State Papers: Military Affairs*, II, 594–595. For accounts of Indian hostilities in 1823–1824 and the need for military action, see the letters and reports printed in Morgan, *The West of William H. Ashley*, pp. 61–87. Atkinson, after his own expedition up the Missouri in 1825, revised his opinion about the effects of Leavenworth's campaign against the Arikaras. He and O'Fallon in their report of November 7, 1825, spoke of the Arikaras as being "humbled and chastened" as a result of Leavenworth's operation. *American State Papers: Indian Affairs*, II, 607.

Yellowstone and the falls of the Missouri, what the expense would be for holding treaties with the Indians in the region, whether additional Indian agents were needed for those tribes, and what plan the executive preferred for "maintaining peace with the Indians, and preserving the fur trade within the United States to American citizens."[41]

Calhoun dutifully answered on February 23, supplying an estimate from the Quartermaster General for the cost of the troop movement (a modest $13,000), his own estimate of $10,000 for treaties of friendship, a recommendation for two additional sub-agents, and an explicit statement that he had not changed his mind about defense plans for the West since his earlier reports. "The exclusion of foreign traders from our territory is deemed to be indispensable to the security of our traders, and the establishing and maintaining relations of amity and peace with the numerous tribes of Indians on the Mississippi and Missouri," he said; "and it is believed that the extension of our posts, as formerly proposed, or occasional movements of our troops up the Missouri, as far as the Mandan villages, or the mouth of the Yellow Stone, present the only effectual mode of attaining these desirable objects."[42]

Benton's committee also questioned Richard Graham, Indian agent at St. Louis, and Joshua Pilcher, the fur trader, about the protection of the Indian trade in the West. The two men supplied similar information about the character of the Indians, and both indicated the need for a military post somewhere above the Mandan villages to prevent the rich Rocky Mountain fur trade from falling completely into the hands of the British.[43] More documents submitted to Benton by Calhoun at the end of April gave further evidence of Indian hostilities, and Calhoun concluded: "Every day's experience affords evidence that, unless effectual measures be taken to protect it, our trade on the upper part of the Missouri will be entirely cut off."[44]

Benton introduced a bill on March 18, 1824, embodying the recommendations received from the War Department. As finally passed on May 25, it provided $10,000 for making treaties of trade and friendship with the Indian tribes living beyond the Mississippi. It authorized the President to appoint commissioners to treat with the Indians and

[41] *Ibid.*, p. 448.

[42] Calhoun to Benton, February 23, 1824, *ibid.*, pp. 448–449.

[43] *Ibid.*, pp. 451–457.

[44] Calhoun to Benton, April 26, 1824, *Senate Document* No. 71, 18 Congress, 1 session, serial 91, p. 1.

supplied an additional $10,000 to enable him to furnish a competent military escort to the commissioners.[45]

Benton's original bill called for $13,100 to enable a military force "to be transported to, and stationed at" some suitable point on the upper Missouri, but the Senate substituted the weaker provision of the military escort for the treaty commissioners.[46] Although Benton argued strongly for the necessity of his original proposal, insisting that without it all the rest of the plans would be "vain and nugatory," opponents in the Senate, declaring that illegal hunting and trapping on the Indian lands ought to be stopped before protection of the fur trade was considered, forced the Missouri senator to agree to the amendment that gave no more than the military escort.[47]

President Adams appointed Henry Atkinson and Benjamin O'Fallon as commissioners, and Atkinson began at once to prepare. The act was passed too late to enable an expedition to be sent out to such remote points as the mouth of the Yellowstone in 1824, but Atkinson began to provide transportation and provisions and to concentrate the troops for the military escort at Council Bluffs in the fall, so that the advance up the Missouri from that point could begin early in the spring.[48] Atkinson and O'Fallon left Council Bluffs on May 16, 1825, with a military escort of 476 men, including forty mounted men who paralleled the course of the boats on land. Eight keelboats served as transports, equipped with ingenious paddle-wheel devices which the soldiers operated by their own power.[49]

[45] U. S. Statutes at Large, IV, 35–36.

[46] Senate Journal, 18 Congress, 1 session, serial 88, pp. 239, 281, 432.

[47] Annals of Congress, 18 Congress, 1 session, col. 443–445, 449–461, 505–507, 752–753.

[48] Summary accounts of the Atkinson-O'Fallon expedition appear in Nichols, General Henry Atkinson, pp. 90–108, and Chittenden, American Fur Trade of the Far West, II, 608–618. Copies of the treaties together with the official report of the commissioners are in American State Papers: Indian Affairs, II, 595–609. Nichols has edited Atkinson's report in "Report of the Yellowstone Expedition of 1825," Nebraska History, XLIV (June, 1963), 65–82. A supplementary report of Atkinson is in American State Papers: Indian Affairs, II, 656, and a personal letter describing the expedition in "Letter from General Atkinson to Colonel Hamilton," Nebraska History, V (January–March, 1922), 9–11. The journal of the expedition is in Russell Reid and Clell G. Gannon, eds., "Journal of the Atkinson-O'Fallon Expedition," North Dakota Historical Quarterly, IV (October, 1929), 5–56. Newspaper items about the expedition appear in Frost, Notes on General Ashley, pp. 134–142.

[49] Atkinson was enthusiastic about the scheme, which he had developed after considerable experimentation. His first attempts made use of an inclined treadmill to turn the paddle wheels, which he described to the Quartermaster General in 1823: "The machinery for a twenty five ton Boat (the size on which I made the experiement) consists of an inclined wheel twenty feet in diameter, attached

The commissioners and the troops moved by stages up the Missouri, meeting in council with the various tribes which came to meet them. On the way up the river to the Mandan villages between June 9 and August 4 nine treaties were concluded—with the Poncas, Teton, Yanktonai and Yanktonai bands of the Sioux, Oglalas, Cheyennes, Hunkpapa Sioux, Arikaras, Minitarees, Mandans, and Crows. The various councils were much alike. There was first a review of the troops drawn up in parade —a sight that never failed to awe the Indians. Then a formal council would be organized, the treaty approved, and presents distributed. Sometimes in the evening shells were fired from the howitzer, making a deep impression on the natives. The treaties themselves were statements of friendship and provided that all trade with the tribes was to be done at designated sites, that licensed American traders were to be admitted and protected by the tribes, and that foreign traders be apprehended and turned over to American authorities. For injuries done by individuals no private retaliation was to be taken, but due legal processes were to be used. Return of and indemnities for stolen horses or other property were agreed upon.[50]

On August 6 the party left the Mandan villages for the mouth of the Yellowstone with the hope of meeting the Blackfeet and the Assiniboines. In this the commissioners were disappointed. William Ashley, whom they met returning with furs from the Rocky Mountains, informed them that the Blackfeet were above the falls of the Missouri and at the mountain headwaters of the river, and hope of seeing them was given up. With the possibility that the Assiniboines might yet be

---

to a verticle shaft, to which is also attached below, a cog wheel eight feet in diameter; these wheels have an inclination of twelve degrees, and a motion of three and a half revolutions in a minute, and revolve a horizontal shaft that is cogged and to which the water wheel is attached, twenty times in a minute, giving a velocity to the boat sufficient to advance her ascent up the Missouri at the rate of 2½ to 3 miles an hour." With a crew of good men he expected to make 25 miles a day, twice the ordinary rate of keelboat travel, and save fatigue on the men and wear on the clothing. The cost of the equipment he figured as no more than supplying a mast and sails. Atkinson to Calhoun, October 11, 1823, quoted in Grant Foreman, "River Navigation in the Early Southwest," *Mississippi Valley Historical Review*, XV (June, 1928), 36. Frequent breakdowns, however, led him in 1824 to change the device. The treadmill was abandoned, and the men, instead, sat on benches along the sides of the boat and in unison pushed horizontal slides, which through a gear mechanism turned the paddle wheels. *Ibid.*, p. 37; Nichols, *General Henry Atkinson*, pp. 91–92. Atkinson attributed the great facility of his 1825 expedition "partly to the manner our transports were propelled, that is by wheels." Atkinson to Hamilton, December 21, 1825, *Nebraska History*, V, 11. The journal of the expedition, however, indicates a great many breakdowns in the machinery.

50 Kappler, *Treaties*, pp. 225–246.

located, five keelboats with 350 men proceeded up the Missouri 120 miles beyond the mouth of the Yellowstone, but they found no recent signs of Indians and turned around when low water made further advance difficult. On August 27 the expedition began its return, taking on board Ashley and his twenty-five men and their packs of beaver skins. An uneventful trip brought them back to Council Bluffs on September 19.

Messages were now sent out to the Otos, Pawnees, and Omahas, and when these tribes came in to Fort Atkinson, councils were held and treaties signed.[51] On October 7, their work successfully accomplished except for the Blackfeet and Assiniboines, the commissioners left Fort Atkinson on a barge for St. Louis.

The report of the commissioners included short sketches about the Indian tribes they had encountered, with a delineation of the country each inhabited, their numbers, manners of living, patterns of trade, and attitude toward the Americans. The picture they painted of American relations with the tribes was an unusually rosy one for two men who had so recently seen storm clouds on the upper Missouri with British lurking behind them:

> Notwithstanding the many rumors that the northwest traders were holding intercourse and exercising an injurious influence over the Indians on the Missouri, no such fact appears to exist; nor is it believed that any of their traders have been across to the Missouri, below Milk river, for several years. Mr. McKenzie (then a British trader) visited the Mandans in 1820. If the British have traded and trapped within our limits east of the Rocky Mountains latterly, it has been above the falls of Missouri, among the Blackfeet Indians; which we understand has been, and probably is now, the case. They can have no possible interest in coming to the Missouri, lower than Milk river, to trade, as the Indians below that point have little or nothing to barter but buffalo robes. . . . It is moreover believed (and the fact is not doubted) that none of the Indians residing on the Missouri ever visit the northwest establishments on Red river.[52]

Atkinson had been on the expedition in two capacities—as Indian commissioner and as army commander—and he could not refrain from voicing his opinion again on the question of a permanent military post

[51] *Ibid.*, pp. 256–262.
[52] *American State Papers: Indian Affairs*, II, 607–608.

above Council Bluffs. Because of the favorable Indian conditions on the Missouri below the falls, he believed that American traders could enter that region in safety without military protection. Where protection was needed against the hostile Blackfeet—that is, beyond the falls and on the headwaters of the river—no post was feasible because of the impossibility of supplying it. Atkinson asserted now that an "occasional show of an imposing military force in an Indian country" was more effective than a permanent garrison of troops among them, and he suggested an expedition of 300–400 troops every three or four years to the falls of the Missouri.[53]

☆

In 1823, while Colonel Leavenworth with his punitive expedition was moving up the Missouri against the Arikaras, Major Stephen H. Long was leading a peaceful exploratory party along the Minnesota and Red rivers, in a significant probe into an area long within the British sphere of influence. Under orders from Secretary of War Calhoun, Long traveled from Philadelphia via Fort Wayne, Fort Armstrong, and Fort Snelling to the source of the Minnesota River, then north to the 49th parallel, along the northern border of the United States to Lake Superior, and thence homeward by the Great Lakes.[54] The objects—to make a general survey of the country and submit a report on its topography, its flora and fauna, and the character and customs of the Indians—were scientific rather than military, but Long was authorized to call upon the post commanders for whatever supplies or assistance he needed; the guard of soldiers that set out with him for Fort Snelling on July 9 added a military cast to the expedition as it penetrated into regions not yet reached by officials of the American government. Long checked, too, on the activities of the British traders along the Red River, who rumors said were drawing off rich furs from the region, and on the settlers of Lord Selkirk at Pembina, and as a shrewd military man he looked at the whole region and its inhabitants from the viewpoint of national defense.

Long met few Indians, but he did encounter British traders and

---

[53] Atkinson to General Jacob Brown, November 23, 1825, *ibid.*, p. 656.

[54] The expedition is reported in William H. Keating, *Narrative of an Expedition to the Source of St. Peter's River, Lake Winnepeek, Lake of the Woods, &c. &c. Performed in the Year 1823* . . . (2 vols., Philadelphia, 1824). The London edition of 1825 has been reprinted in one volume, Minneapolis, 1959. There is a careful account in Wood, *Stephen Harriman Long*, pp. 121–141.

settlers. When the astronomer in the company determined the precise point of the 49th parallel, an oaken post with the letters "G.B." on one side and "U.S." on the other was driven into the ground. A salute was fired, and Major Long proclaimed that by virtue of the authority given him by the President, all the country on the Red River above that point was part of the territory of the United States. The inhabitants were assembled for the ceremony, and they appeared well satisfied that all but one of the sixty log houses at Pembina were found to be in United States territory.[55]

Long's party, unable to proceed directly east to Lake Superior as the orders had directed, traveled by canoe down the Red River to Lake Winnepeg, along the chain of lakes to Lake Superior, and then to Sault Ste. Marie, where they were hospitably received by the garrison at Fort Brady. At Mackinac Island the party divided. The military escort left for Green Bay, to return via the Fox, Wisconsin, and Mississippi rivers to Fort Snelling. Major Long and the scientists took ship for Detroit and the East. They reached Philadelphia on October 26, having covered over 5,400 miles in a period of about six months.

☆

The year 1827 brought a new Indian scare and a new military crisis to the northwest frontier, one that seemed almost inevitable as the lead miners pushed into Indian lands along the Fever River and in the region south and east of Prairie du Chien. The Winnebagos resented the encroachment; their patience was nearly gone, and they were ready to believe the rumors that floated into their villages about white injustices. Two Winnebagos, held in captivity at Fort Snelling for the murder of white settlers near Prairie du Chien in 1826, were reported to have been killed in prison by Colonel Snelling, and rumors circulated as well about white murders of Sioux. Stories that the United States and Great Britain were drifting again toward war gave further courage to the restless Indians. It was not long before violence broke out.[56]

[55] Keating, *Narrative of an Expedition*, II, 46–47. The Hudson's Bay Company, suspecting that the village lay south of the international line, earlier that year had moved its fort down the river.

[56] A recent, well-documented account of the outbreak is Nichols, *General Henry Atkinson*, pp. 119–136. It is very laudatory of Atkinson's handling of the affair. Bruce E. Mahan, *Old Fort Crawford and the Frontier* (Iowa City, 1926), pp. 100–119, tells the story in close paraphrases of the original accounts. Milo M. Quaife, *Chicago and the Old Northwest, 1673–1835: A Study of the Evolution of the Northwestern Frontier, Together with a History of Fort Dearborn* (Chicago,

Retaliation for the reputed white murders was determined upon by the Winnebago leaders, and the chief Red Bird was picked to do the deed. Although long a friend of the whites and reluctant to betray the respect in which he was held, Red Bird at last was driven by taunts of cowardice to proceed late in June to Prairie du Chien. Here he, We-Kau, and another companion murdered a settler named Gagnier and an old, discharged soldier living with the family and scalped an infant daughter. The mother wrestled with one of the attackers and when his gun misfired, escaped with her young son and ran to spread the alarm. Red Bird and his friends fled north to their village, where they displayed the scalps and urged an uprising against the whites. Soon after the Gagnier murders other Winnebagos attacked two army keelboats passing down the Mississippi from Fort Snelling, killed two of the crew, and wounded others. The arrival of the boats at Prairie du Chien with the story of the attack added greatly to the alarm, and as news of these happenings spread there was general panic along the frontier.[57]

Despite the growing tension in the area, Fort Crawford at Prairie du Chien had been evacuated in October, 1826, and its troops sent up river to Fort Snelling. The old fort, built on the bank of the Mississippi in 1816, had been severely weakened by repeated flooding from the river and had become so dilapidated that repair seemed unwise if not impossible. But withdrawal of the soldiers had encouraged the war-minded Winnebagos and had left the inhabitants of the village without a refuge. The settlers fixed up the deserted fort as well as they could as protection against a general Indian attack, but they knew that they would have to rely on military succor coming from outside if they were not to be destroyed by the avenging Indians. Help was not long in coming.

The outbreak had occurred just as a council was being prepared with the Winnebagos to settle their grievances. Governor Lewis Cass of Michigan Territory and Thomas L. McKenney, head of the Indian Office, had arrived on the Fox River as official commissioners to treat

---

1913), pp. 310–321, describes the outbreak from the standpoint of Chicago. Official documents are printed in Item M of the Report of the Secretary of War, 1827, in *House Executive Document* No. 2, 20 Congress, 1 session, pp. 146–158, serial 169. Views about the possibilities for peace on the northwestern frontier after the outbreak are given in documents printed in *House Document* No. 277, 20 Congress, 1 session, serial 175.

[57] Contemporary accounts of the outrages appear in James H. Lockwood, "Early Times and Events in Wisconsin," *Wisconsin Historical Collections*, II (1856), 161–168, and [William J. Snelling], "Early Days at Prairie du Chien, and the Winnebago Outbreak of 1827," *ibid.*, V (1868), 143–153.

with the Winnebagos and other tribes in adjusting the boundaries set by the Treaty of Prairie du Chien in 1825. When the commissioners reached Butte des Morts, the site picked for the council, they received word of the outrages on the Mississippi. Leaving McKenney at the council grounds, Governor Cass set off at once to pacify the Indians. He boldly passed up the Fox and down the Wisconsin through the Winnebago country and arrived at Prairie du Chien on July 4. He enrolled a local militia company, promised reinforcements to the frightened settlers, and proceeded at once down river to Galena to quiet the panic-stricken miners and to gather help for Prairie du Chien. He enrolled a rifle company and sent it north to Fort Crawford and continued on his rapid journey to St. Louis to carry the news of the troubles to the Indian superintendent, William Clark, and to the military commander at Jefferson Barracks, General Henry Atkinson.

While Clark wrote to his agents to do everything possible to keep their tribes at peace so that the Winnebagos would be isolated if war came, Atkinson prepared for an expedition up the Mississippi. On July 15 the general with 580 men steamed away from Jefferson Barracks. At Fort Armstrong he conferred with the Sacs and Foxes (failing to get their help against the Winnebagos) and on July 27 was at Galena. He checked the local defenses, left a supply of arms and ammunition, and pushed on to Prairie du Chien, where he arrived on July 29.

Meanwhile other forces had been converging on the region. Illinois militia, called up by Governor Ninian Edwards, rendezvoused at Peoria, ready to cooperate with Atkinson's regulars. Colonel Josiah Snelling, who had come into Prairie du Chien with four companies on July 12, discharged the unruly Galena militiamen who had been sent by Cass, and seized several Winnebagos as hostages.

Atkinson took no action against the Indians while he waited word from Cass, who had returned from St. Louis to Butte des Morts to further the plans for the council. He hoped by a firm display of force to keep the Winnebagos peaceful and induce them to turn over the murderers of the whites. He sent Snelling and his men back to Fort Snelling with necessary supplies and directed the colonel to send down four other companies under Major John Fowle with light boats that could be used to ascend the Wisconsin.[58]

Word finally reached Atkinson from Cass on August 19, indicating

[58] For Atkinson's report of his activity, see his letter to Gaines, September 28, 1827, *House Executive Document* No. 2, 20 Congress, 1 session, serial 169, pp. 155–158.

that agreement on boundaries had been reached with the Winnebagos but that the question of the murders had not been settled. The governor feared an attack on the miners at Galena, and he advised Atkinson to move up the Wisconsin to the portage. Atkinson started toward the portage on August 29, with the boats that had arrived from Fort Snelling a week earlier. As Atkinson, supported by militia cavalry under Henry Dodge, advanced into the heart of the Winnebago country, a detachment of regulars from Fort Howard under Major William Whistler and accompanied by McKenney arrived at the portage on September 1.

The Winnebagos realized the hopelessness of their position, and on September 3 Red Bird and We-Kau in solemn procession with a hundred braves, carrying a white flag and two American flags, turned themselves in to Major Whistler.[59] Two other murderers were surrendered after Atkinson arrived, and on September 9 a provisional treaty was drawn up which promised that the United States would appoint a commission to study the conflicting claims to the lead lands and stipulated that until an agreement was reached the Indians were not to molest the miners south of the Wisconsin River.[60] Atkinson received two more Indian fugitives at Prairie du Chien, and then on September 22 issued a proclamation of peace:

> Know ye, that the Winnebago Nation, having surrendered up all the offenders in the late transgressions, that have been demanded of them, and showing an entire submission to the authority of the United States, I have granted them peace.[61]

Later that day he and his troops boarded two steamboats and headed back to St. Louis. Major Fowle and his four companies of the Fifth Infantry were left to garrison Fort Crawford.

The quick action of Cass, Atkinson, and the subordinate army commanders had halted a movement that might have erupted into widespread terror and bloodshed. Atkinson's avowed policy of using the threat of force to end troubles peacefully instead of taking immediate punitive action against the whole tribe had succeeded in quieting the frontier once more, and General Brown's policy of concentrating troops

---

[59] An elaborate description of Red Bird and his surrender is given in Thomas L. McKenney, "The Winnebago War of 1827," *Wisconsin Historical Collections*, V (1868), 179–187.

[60] Provisional treaty, September 9, 1827, *House Executive Document* No. 2, 20 Congress, 1 session, serial 169, pp. 152–153.

[61] Proclamation, September 22, 1827, *ibid.*, p. 154.

at Jefferson Barracks to be used as crises arose on the frontier had proved itself.

Yet Atkinson's brave statement that the "frontier is in a state of tranquillity, that will not be shortly interrupted" was little more than military rhetoric.[62] In point of fact, the frontier fears had not been dissipated, and the War Department took immediate steps to strengthen its military hold on Winnebago country. In September, 1827, the War Department ordered the reestablishment of Fort Crawford as a military post, and a new fort on higher ground was constructed by the troops over a period of years. The next year Fort Dearborn, on one flank of the Indian disorders, was reoccupied by troops of the Fifth Infantry, and to make doubly sure that the Winnebagos would understand the value of peace, a new post (significantly called Fort Winnebago) was built at the portage between the Fox and the Wisconsin. The new fort, constructed by troops from Fort Howard under Major David E. Twiggs, became a vital link in the chain of northwest forts.[63] Alexander Macomb, Commanding General of the Army, reported with satisfaction in November, 1828, that "there is a complete cordon from Green Bay to the Mississippi, which must have a powerful influence over the Winnebagoes, and afford protection to the Indian trade which passes in that direction; and there is every reason to believe that neither the Winnebagoes nor their confederates will attempt any hostilities so long as the troops maintain their present positions."[64]

Under ordinary circumstances Macomb's prediction might well have been fulfilled. But he did not reckon with Black Hawk and his British band of the Sacs and Foxes, who soon entangled the army in a new Indian war.

[62] Atkinson to Gaines, September 28, 1827, *ibid.*, p. 158.
[63] See Andrew J. Turner, "The History of Fort Winnebago," *Wisconsin Historical Collections*, XIV (1898), 65–103.
[64] Macomb to the Secretary of War, November, 1828, *Senate Document* No. 1, 20 Congress, 2 session, serial 181, p. 26.

☆ NINE ☆

Attack upon the Wilderness

THE soldiers of the regular army in the West were more than guardians of American rights and promoters of American sovereignty. They also made a physical attack upon the wilderness and were in a very real sense among the advanced pioneers who opened up the frontier.[1] Part of the failure in discipline and the lack of military spirit noted by observers of the frontier army arose from the labors that the troops were expected to perform, work that had no direct bearing on drill in military tactics but that was necessary for the very survival of the garrisons in the wilderness. In the remote reaches of the new American empire the soldiers found no one to perform the necessary tasks of fort building and maintenance except themselves, and they took up the tools of the mechanic and the farmer. "The ax, pick, saw & trowel, has become more the implement of the American soldier," Zachary Taylor complained in 1820, "than the cannon, musket or sword."[2]

Respectable inactivity, which recruits may have looked for when they joined the army, had no place in the life of the frontier soldier. The disillusionment of the enlistee in 1838 who recorded the following sentiments shows not only the feelings of the soldiers but indicates with remarkable force the constructive functions of the troops:

I am deceived; I enlisted for a soldier; I enlisted because I preferred military duty to hard work; I never was given to understand

[1] I have discussed these activities of the army in *Broadax and Bayonet: The Role of the United States Army in the Development of the Northwest, 1815–1860* (Madison, Wis., 1953).
[2] Taylor to Thomas S. Jesup, September 18, 1820, Zachary Taylor Papers, Library of Congress.

that the *implements of agriculture and the mechanic's tools* were to be placed in my hands *before I had received a musket or drawn a uniform coat.* I never was told that I would be called on to *make roads, build bridges, quarry stone, burn brick and lime, carry the hod, cut wood, hew timber, construct it into rafts and float it to the garrisons, make shingles, saw plank, build mills, maul rails, drive teams, make hay, herd cattle, build stables, construct barracks, hospitals, &c.&c. &c., which takes more time for their completion than the period of my enlistment.* I never was given to understand that such duties were customary in the army, much less that I would be called on to perform them, *or I never would have enlisted.* I enlisted to avoid work, and here I am, compelled to perform three or four times the amount of labor I did before my enlistment.[3]

This cynical statement was not overdone. Inspector General George Croghan on his annual rounds of the frontier posts found the soldiers so busily engaged in manual labor that he was unable to hold the inspections and parades that were a traditional part of the visit of the inspector. The state of instruction in the "school of the soldier" was everywhere deficient because it was impossible to squeeze in the necessary practice. When Croghan came to Fort Snelling on his first tour he found the instruction "not very perfect," but he could not help but be impressed by the fort that he found. "Look at Fort Snelling as it now stands," he wrote, "be told that it was erected in six years by the soldiers themselves, who at the same time were tillers of the soil to the extent of many hundred acres, and you will feel disposed to give them credit if they have preserved even the proper *feelings* of the *soldier*, instruction in the duties justly appertaining to their situation out of the question." The officers were unhappy about the matter, but they were caught by the force of circumstances. "We have lost almost all that we once knew," they told Croghan, "but as our labours as farmers and builders are now comparatively closed we hope soon to recover our lost ground." The construction of the new Fort Crawford, begun when the post was reestablished after the Winnebago scare of 1827, stretched over a number of years and took practically the entire energies of the garrison. In July, 1831, Croghan called off the review and inspection because so many men were away on work details. He reported that at times since August 15, 1830, there had been not a single man available for military duty and that even during the winter the average of men

---

[3] *Army and Navy Chronicle,* VI (May 17, 1838), 314–315.

for duty was not more than one quarter of the number of men on extra duty. The only drills that the commander could give the troops came during the winter months whenever the weather would permit. When the Inspector General returned to Fort Crawford in 1833, he still found four-fifths of the garrison busy on working parties, and the inspection was again canceled. "The barracks erected here are certainly the best in the country," Croghan admitted, "but they have as certainly been built at the cost, I may say, of one of the best regiments that we have ever had."[4]

☆

The first posts built by the soldiers along the Ohio during the 1780's were simple stockade defenses, differing little from the outposts that pioneer settlers themselves built on the frontiers for protection against Indian depredations. Some were thrown up in a hurry and never intended for extended occupation. Others, where the garrisons were more permanent, gradually developed some of the amenities of more civilized living.

The posts constructed of logs by Colonel Harmar and his subordinates along the Ohio set a general pattern. Fort Steuben, down the Ohio from Pittsburgh, stood 120 yards from the river on a high bank of commanding ground. It was a square enclosure with large blockhouses at the corners and other buildings or pickets joining them. On each side of the main gate were the officers' houses, whose rear walls served as a row of pickets. The sally port was on the river side and over it was built the guardhouse. The blockhouses served as quarters for the men. Fort Finney, built at the mouth of the Great Miami in 1786 for the treaty with the Shawnees, was almost identical in design, with the addition of a small blockhouse close to the bank of the river to cover the landing place and the boats.[5] When posts were built for more troops or longer occupancy, barracks for the enlisted men lined the sides of the square. A well-protected magazine was placed in one corner, and shops of blacksmiths and other artisans appeared.

[4] George Croghan, *Army Life on the Western Frontier: Selections from the Official Reports Made Between 1826 and 1845 by Colonel George Croghan*, ed. Francis Paul Prucha (Norman, Okla., 1958), pp. 134, 138–140.

[5] "Diary of Major Erkuries Beatty, Paymaster of the Western Army, May 15, 1786, to June 5, 1787," *Magazine of American History*, I (March, 1877), 176, (June, 1877), 382.

Fort Harmar at the mouth of the Muskingum, for some time the headquarters for Harmar's regiment, was a bit more elaborate. It was located on a curve of the Ohio and controlled not only the mouth of the Muskingum but the Ohio too for some distance both up and down the river. The fort stood on an elevated bottom land beyond the reach of the floods of the river and was laid out as a pentagon, enclosing about three-fourths of an acre. The main walls of the fort, 120 feet in length, were constructed of large timbers laid horizontally, to a height of 12 or 14 feet. At each of the five corners, instead of the usual blockhouses, were pentagonal bastions made of logs set upright in the ground and mounted with cannon. The barracks for the enlisted men extended along the main walls, with their roofs sloping inward; they were divided into rooms about 30 feet long and were furnished with fireplaces. The officers' houses—of hewn logs and one and a half or two stories high—were set within the corner bastions. They had kitchens in back and good stone chimneys, and as Paymaster Beatty remarked in 1787, "These houses add much to the beauty of the fort, but rather crowd the Bastions too much." The barracks on the wall facing the Ohio were topped with a cupola that served as a post for the sentinel. From the cupola rose a flagstaff, and the room beneath served as a guardhouse. Behind the fort were gardens laid out by the commandant, and between the fort and the river were three large log buildings that served the blacksmith, carpenter, and other mechanics.[6] Fort Washington, which replaced Fort Harmar as headquarters, reverted to a square design, covering about an acre of ground, with traditional blockhouses and strongly built barracks.

The posts hastily thrown up by St. Clair and Wayne in their campaigns against the Indians were simpler versions of these forts. Fort Hamilton, which St. Clair's troops built in two weeks on the bank of the Great Miami, for example, was 150 feet square and constructed of log pickets 20 feet long fitted close together and stuck upright in a trench 3 feet deep. A bank of timber around the top held the pickets secure and the earth was packed tight at their base. On the inside between each two pickets, another was fastened tight, making a stout protection against Indian attack. At the four corners bastions were

[6] *Ibid.*, I, 382. There are detailed descriptions of Fort Harmar in Samuel P. Hildreth, *Pioneer History: Being an Account of the First Examinations of the Ohio Valley, and the Early Settlement of the Northwest Territory* (Cincinnati, 1848), pp. 317–318, and Hildreth, *Contributions to the Early History of the North-West, Including the Moravian Missions in Ohio* (Cincinnati, 1864), pp. 215–218.

built and two of them had platforms for cannon, which could sweep the approaches to the fort. Within the square, quarters for the troops and storehouses for supplies were built.[7]

The realization on the part of the War Department that the military frontier both north and south of the Ohio would continually advance and the deep concern for economy led to careful directions to the western commanders about what sort of posts should be built. "Being of opinion that for the general defence of our Country we ought not to rely on Fortifications but on men and steel," Secretary of War Dearborn wrote to General Wilkinson in 1804; "and that works calculated for resisting batteries of Cannon are necessary only for our principal seaposts, I cannot conceive it to be useful or expedient to construct expensive works for our interior military posts, especially such as are intended merely to hold the Indians in check." He sent sketches of forts to the frontier commanders, recommending a square stockade of 120 feet on a side, with two blockhouses, "so placed as to afford a flank fire from every part of the Post, which with a fire from other buildings would effectually annoy any number of Indians." The blockhouses were to be 20 feet square and two stories high, with portholes for small ordnance in the upper story and portholes for muskets in both.[8]

Dearborn's directions for the building of barracks and officers' quarters were sometimes given at great length. That the Secretary of War himself dealt with such details is an interesting insight into the levels of administrative operation in the early army. The instructions he sent to the commandant at Detroit in 1805 are a good example:

If clay, proper for making bricks, can be found in the neighborhood of the Post at Detroit, a sufficient quantity should be dug up this autumn, for manufacturing from two to three hundred thousand, as early next season as possible. But, if brick cannot be made in the vicinity of the Fort, other materials should be procured in the course of next autumn, winter and spring, for erecting two barracks, each sixty two feet in length, twenty in width, and one and a half story in heighth; each barrack to be divided into four rooms, exclusive of the half story, which should be occupied for lodging rooms. Each

[7] William Henry Smith, *The St. Clair Papers: The Life and Public Services of Arthur St. Clair* (2 vols., Cincinnati, 1882), II, 292–293n.

[8] Secretary of War to Hamtramck and Stoddard, March 9, 1803, National Archives, Records of the Secretary of War, Letters Sent, vol. 1, pp. 388–389; Secretary of War to Wilkinson, June 28, 1804, *ibid.*, vol. 2, p. 251.

lower room should have a large fire place, with a closet on one side, and a stair way on the other, to ascend to the lodging rooms; and should also have two windows of twenty squares of 7 by 9 glass each. To each upper room there should be one lutheran window [luthern] of twelve squares of like glass. The walls of the half story should not exceed 3½ feet in heighth. In front of each barracks, a piazza should be erected, seven feet wide, with a gravel floor, and benches to sit on. The buildings, when otherwise completed, should be painted, the roof, and walls if of wood, Spanish brown, the window and door frames, the corner and weather boards and the posts of the piazza, white. If the walls of the Barracks are built of wood, they should be frame works, well covered with boards and then shingled like the roofs. The joints of the roof should be covered with strips of white Birch or paper birch bark, previous to the Shingling; this will prevent either the snow or rain from blowing through. A building for the Officers' quarters should also be erected within the fort, forty two feet long, thirty two wide, and two stories high, the lower story nine feet in the clear, and the upper eight feet, with four stacks of chimnies; and an entry of eight feet in width, through the house, with one common stair way. A cellar with stone or brick walls should be made under the whole house. The base of each building should be at least two feet above the common surface. The whole of the work should be done in a plain, strong manner.

The officers' quarters should be divided into four rooms to each story. The front room should be larger than the back one;—the former may be 16 by 18 feet, and the latter 16 by 14.

A kitchen will be necessary—and a store house of one story, and about 20 by 16 feet on the ground;—a guard house also will be requisite, of one story, and about 15 feet square. The walls of the guard house should be built of square timber of nine inches thickness.

The Fort should be put into good repair, and may be called in future, Detroit.[9]

When the army began its advance into the Northwest after the War of 1812, the old patterns of frontier forts were relied upon. Fort Armstrong on the tip of Rock Island was a structure of blockhouses

[9] Dearborn to Commanding Officer at Detroit, August 5, 1805, *ibid.*, vol. 2, pp. 360–362.

and palisades that was reminiscent of the earlier Fort Washington. Fort Howard at Green Bay, Fort Crawford at Prairie du Chien, and the new Fort Dearborn were similarly constructed. But the increase in size of the posts and their greater longevity led little by little to much more elaborate stations, with an eye, it must be said, more to the comfort and convenience of the garrisons than to the essential needs of defense. Sawmills were built, and finished lumber replaced the rough hewn timbers of earlier days. Where quarrying was possible, stone construction appeared, and the posts took on a greater air of permanence. The conglomeration of sutlers' stores, Indian agency buildings, laundresses' quarters, post hospitals, quartermaster and commissary storehouses, barns for grain and stables for horses, gristmills, and workshops eventually made some of the western posts impressive installations.

Consider what the troops did to the wilderness landscape at Council Bluffs, where the ill-fated Yellowstone Expedition came to a halt in 1819. Clearing the ground on the bottom lands along the Missouri, the soldiers cut the cottonwoods that grew in thick groves in the area and with logs hewn with broadaxes and planks cut with handsaws began to erect a home for the large force. Stone for the fireplaces and lime for mortar were transported in from ten or twelve miles away, and barracks, storehouses, workshops, and a hospital were erected. A great enclosed square with four roofed gateways rose on the bank of the river.[10]

The lowlands proved unhealthy and 160 men succumbed to fever in the first winter; then in June, 1820, a flood washed the whole post away. A new site down the river on the bluffs, however, was soon abuilding, as the officers and their men reproduced the establishment that the river had destroyed.[11] When Paul Wilhelm, Duke of Württemberg, traveled up the Missouri in 1823, he visited the "good-looking, white washed buildings" of the new fort. The post was, he thought, a veritable town, and except for St. Charles and Franklin the most populous place on the Missouri. The duke's description of the fort conveys a sense of the busy activity of this remotest of outposts:

[10] Sally A. Johnson, "Cantonment Missouri, 1819–1820," *Nebraska History*, XXXVII (June, 1956), 121–133, describes the building of the cantonment in considerable detail.

[11] Sally A. Johnson, "The Sixth's Elysian Fields—Fort Atkinson on the Council Bluffs," *Nebraska History*, XL (March, 1959), 1–38; Marvin F. Kivett, "Excavations at Fort Atkinson, Nebraska: A Preliminary Report," *ibid.*, 39–66; Edgar B. Wesley, "Life at Fort Atkinson," *ibid.*, XXX (December, 1949), 348–358.

The fort itself was a square structure. Its sides were each 200 American yards long. There were eight log-houses, two on each side. There were three gates leading into this fort. On the side toward the river there was only a passage under the houses which here were set one against the other. Each house consisted of ten rooms, and was 25 feet wide and 250 feet long. The roof of the houses sloped toward an interior court. The doors and windows opened upon this court. On the outside each room has an embrasure or loophole, ten feet long. The interior court was a large grass-covered square, in the center of which stood the powder house, built of stone. Around the fort, at a distance of 50 paces ran a fence with three gates. Outside the fort, on the northwest side was situated a council house, about 50 feet long, consisting of a hall and a small room. Here the government agents negotiated with deputations of the Indian nations and their chiefs.

On the northwest side of the fort were also several small houses, intended for the supplies of the artillery. The gunsmith also had his smithy here. The remaining buildings which were around the fort were located on the banks of the Missouri, on a level lower than the fort. In these buildings were housed the store for the personal needs of the establishment, moreover, the bakery, and the smithy. Here was also the house for the cabinet-makers and the carpenters.

On the south side was the grist mill and a sawmill. They were driven by oxen, and said to be completely equipped for this region. A storehouse, consisting of three stories, housed on the lower floor the spirituous beverages, on the second the salt pork, and on the third the cereals. Another storehouse, two stories high, contained all the materials and hardware required in the agricultural under-takings at the fort. The agricultural enterprise near the fort was splendid. A considerable stretch of land along the Missouri, south of the fort, and separated from the prairie by a row of hills, had been converted into excellent garden land. Here the finest European vegetables were grown. I saw our common cabbage, beans, onions and melons of excellent quality.

The watermelons in this region are of unusually fine quality and size. On the border of the garden the soldiers grew Italian millet, the tops of which are used for making brooms in Italy. Large corn-fields and wheatfields surrounded the fort. There are also some farms in the neighborhood where livestock is raised. The fine prairie with its excellent grass encouraged the raising of horses. This grass also furnishes the finest kind of hay for winter feeding.

The manner in which the government handles the military posts seems very sensible to me. It not only pays, feeds and clothes its soldiers well, but also requires of them strict industriousness. The American military establishment must be looked upon as a great industrial center, which provides the post with all its requirements even beyond its needs, naturally excepting the raw material, as for example cloth, linen and leather. Many of the artisans are very clever and produce the finest kind of work. In 1823 it was still necessary for the government to supply the post with salt meat and brandy. In the following year the garrison had raised enough stock to supply fresh meat, which took the place of unwholesome salt meat, and a recently established distillery supplied the necessary brandy.[12]

There were a thousand men at Fort Atkinson in 1820, and even when the garrison was cut in half in subsequent years, it had one of the largest complements in the country. Yet the fort was too far away from the settlements, and the advanced position was deemed unnecessary. In 1827 the elaborate setup was abandoned and a new post down the river, Fort Leavenworth, began a similar mushroom growth.

Even more pretentious than Fort Atkinson was Fort Snelling. The troops who arrived in August, 1819, were set at once to construct quarters for the winter on the bottom lands at the mouth of the Minnesota River. By October they were procuring timber, making shingles, quarrying stone, and erecting barracks, and they had built a kiln to make lime for the construction of the chimneys.[13] Yet this was only a temporary encampment, for when Colonel Josiah Snelling replaced Henry Leavenworth in 1820, he began to construct on the bluff overlooking the confluence of the rivers a fort so solid and impressive that the War Department gave it his name in compliment. Through his dogged goading of the soldiers the fort arose in a massive array of towers and stonework. It held a striking position and its commodious arrangements and its superior construction impressed all who visited it. A large, diamond-shaped enclosure boasted stone towers at the corners and stone walls connecting these defenses. Within the walls were barracks, officers' quarters, and storehouses lining the parade ground; outside were the usual array of auxiliary buildings and the

12 Paul Wilhelm, Duke of Württemberg, "First Journey to North America in the Years 1822 to 1824," trans. William G. Bek, *South Dakota Historical Collections*, XIX (1938), 360–362.

13 Josiah H. Vose to Leavenworth, October, 1819, enclosed in Leavenworth to Macomb, October 24, 1819, National Archives, Records of the Secretary of War, Letters Received.

garden plots of the garrison. Some soldiers quarried Trenton lime-stone from the nearby bluffs and others set up a sawmill at the Falls of St. Anthony to supply the lumber that went into the construction of the fort's buildings.

☆

Striking as these posts might seem to visitors to the West, to whom they looked as welcome refuges in the wilderness, they were far from perfect as defense posts. They were primarily garrisons to house the troops, and the commanders cannot be blamed if they gave more atten-tion to the comforts of living than to plans to meet an attacking enemy, but it was fortunate that the forts never became the scenes of armed conflict. Frederick Marryat remarked that Fort Winnebago was "merely a square of barracks, connected together with palisades, to protect it from the Indians; and it is hardly sufficiently strong for even that purpose."[14] Charles Latrobe, who visited Fort Snelling in 1833, was struck with the dramatic appearance of the fort, but he noted, too:

> It has an appearance of strength which is hardly confirmed on a nearer survey; and the impression you carry away is, that for the purposes of Indian warfare it is far too strong and important a work, while its position would not avail it much in an attack from regular troops, as the interior is commanded from a rise on the land immediately behind. The idea is further suggested, that the strong stone wall was rather erected to keep the garrison in, than the enemy out. Though adapted for mounting cannon if needful, the walls were unprovided with those weapons; and the only piece of ordinance [sic] that I detected out of the magazine, was an old churn thrust gallantly through one of the embrasures. We were however far from complaining of the extra expense and taste which the worthy officer whose name it bears had expended on the erec-tion of Fort Snelling, as it is in every way an addition to the sub-lime landscape in which it is situated.[15]

But the really serious strictures came from the army inspectors, who not only deprecated the terrible state of military readiness, but

[14] Frederick Marryat, *A Diary in America, with Remarks on Its Institutions* (3 vols., London, 1839), II, 54.
[15] Charles J. Latrobe, *The Rambler in North America, MDCCCXXXII–MDCCCXXXIII* (2 vols., New York, 1835), II, 214.

frequently voiced great concern about the dilapidated conditions of quarters, storehouses, and other buildings of the forts. General Gaines, at the end of an inspection of the right wing of the Western Department in 1827, complained about the excessive size of Fort Snelling— its buildings were too large, too numerous, and too far apart, and the parade ground was five times as large as was necessary. He was worried that the main point of defense against an enemy had been sacrificed for the peacetime comfort and convenience of troops.[16] Inspector General Croghan found much to rail against in his twenty years of visits to the western posts. Of Fort Brady at Sault Ste. Marie he exclaimed, "Why this place is dignified with the name of fort I can not imagine, for it is fitted for neither offensive or defensive purposes. So badly is it designed for either that in the event of an attack the danger of troops composing its garrison would be lessened only when they had gained the open spot without the line of pickets." Of Fort Leavenworth he declared, "There is about as much propriety in calling this post *Fort* Leavenworth as there would be in calling an armed schooner a line of battle ship, for it is not only not a fort but is even devoid of the regularity of a common barrack. Of defences it has none."[17]

Such remarks were to be expected from the army inspectors, who thought in strictly military terms. But their comments and strictures were pretty much beside the point. The western forts for the most part did not need to serve as military fortresses awaiting attack from an enemy force. They were primarily stations to house and care for the soldiers, whose very presence served to convince the Indians that the United States government intended to exert its jurisdiction and to enforce its decisions on the western frontier. The forts were symbols of that determination, and the "men of steel" of Henry Dearborn were closer to the realities of the situation than the military bastions ready instantly to meet a hostile foe that Edmund Gaines and George Croghan wanted.

☆

The construction of the posts was only part of the soldier's work. Woodcutting, to supply the fireplaces for the long winters on the

[16] *American State Papers: Military Affairs* (7 vols., Washington, 1832–1861), IV, 122–123.
[17] Croghan, *Army Life on the Western Frontier*, pp. 24, 35.

northwestern frontier, was a time-consuming task, and it increased in severity as time progressed because of the necessity to go farther afield for wood. Fort Snelling in 1834 was cutting 800 to 1,000 cords of wood; by 1840 it was cutting 1,200 to 1,400 cords and bringing it in from a distance of five or six miles. In 1842 Croghan found the soldiers bringing in wood from eight to ten miles away, and in September of the following year he reported that "45 days have just been consumed in procuring 500 tons of hay and perhaps 90 more are now to be given towards the getting in of 1,200 cords of fire wood."[18]

Haying, to provide forage for the livestock, was a particularly onerous duty, yet the garrisons were expected to supply what was needed, and sites for military posts were chosen with a view to easily accessible prairie land that could supply the hay. When commanding officers sought to obtain permission to purchase the forage in order to relieve their men from the task, the War Department replied that it wanted the garrisons to be self-sufficient in the matter, and only reluctantly did it gradually relax its position and permit the quartermaster officers to buy hay from civilians in the neighborhood of the posts. At Fort Howard it took a strong statement from the post surgeons that the prairies were covered with mud and water and that the deleterious effects of poisonous plants and reptiles caused chronic infection and swellings that were decidedly prejudicial to the health of the soldiers.[19]

The almost incessant concern for economy that beset the War Department (reflecting a similar concern in Congress) led to experiments to see how self-sufficient the western garrisons could become. Instead of transporting the bulky provisions for the soldiers' rations from the East, adding to the expense of the supplies the heavy cost of transportation, why could not the posts supply a large part of their own subsistence? To supplement the beans and salt pork and bread that were the basic elements in the military diet, vegetable gardens were prescribed as an essential part of every post. Gardening became a familiar occupation for the soldiers. A profusion of vegetables was grown at the western posts, and the ability of the soldiers as gardeners was amply demonstrated.

The immemorial custom of growing vegetable gardens, however, supplemented the main staples of the diet and did not replace them. In an attempt to supply much of the basics, too, the War Department in 1818 directed an extensive field cultivation program. By general

18 *Ibid.*, pp. 143–144.
19 Prucha, *Broadax and Bayonet*, p. 130.

orders dated September 11, the western posts were told to initiate extensive farming operations in order to supply the wheat for the soldier's bread, peas and beans, turnips, potatoes, and cabbages for his table, and oats and corn for the forage of the livestock. The army officers and their men went at the work with great goodwill. Fort Snelling in 1823 had 210 acres under cultivation, half in wheat, 60 in corn, and the rest in oats, potatoes, and garden vegetables. Fort Dearborn in 1820 had 50 acres of corn and 35 acres of wheat, which yielded a crop estimated at 500–700 bushels of corn and 355–500 bushels of wheat.[20]

It was Fort Atkinson at Council Bluffs, however, that the farming became almost an obsession. It was a large post, but even for its size the farming activities were extensive. In the first season the soldiers harvested 8,839 bushels of potatoes and nearly 500 bushels of turnips, as well as other crops. In 1821 the corn crop amounted to 26,400 bushels, and in the subsequent years similar amounts of grain were raised. The main farm was on the bottom lands along the Missouri, but each company in addition was given a tract of land for gardens, from five to fourteen acres, and the staff officers were assigned garden plots as well. The post commander took the directives of the War Department seriously and appointed officers as Superintendent and Director of Agriculture and as Superintendent of Stock. Great numbers of horses and mules and at least sixty oxen were used in the farming operations. There were in addition the cattle that supplied the soldiers with beef and milk. A census of stock in 1823 indicated that there were 382 cattle at the post, exclusive of the work oxen, and hogs were numerous, since individual soldiers were allowed to keep a hog or two, provided they did not run free over the fields.[21]

It is no wonder that Inspector General Croghan nearly had apoplexy when he arrived at the fort in 1826 and saw the amount of energy devoted to the work of farming, and at the expense of military training. He found Fort Atkinson the weakest of the posts he had visited, and he pleaded for a return to a system that would not "sink the proud soldier into a menial and reduce him who may have gallantly led in the front of our enemies into the base overseer of a troop of awkward ploughmen." "Look at Fort Atkinson," Croghan exclaimed, "and you will see barn yards that would not disgrace a Pennsylvania farmer,

[20] *Ibid.*, pp. 122–123.
[21] Edgar B. Wesley, "Life at a Frontier Post: Fort Atkinson, 1823–1826," *Journal of the American Military Institute*, III (Winter, 1939), 205–206.

herds of cattle that would do credit to a Potomac grazier, yet where is the gain in this, either to the soldier or to the government? Ask the individual who boastingly shews you all this, why such a provision of hay and corn. His answer will be, to *feed* the *cattle*. But why so many *cattle?* Why—to eat the *hay and corn*." Croghan did not insist that the soldiers never be called upon to do nonmilitary duties, but he did want such work to be considered secondary to the main work. "I would have the soldier point to his garden in proof of the good provision he has made during the short intervals from military exercise," he said, "rather than boastingly talk of his proficiency as a farmer, of the advantages of the *broadcast* over the *drill*, or of the five bushels of corn per acre made by Company C more than by Company B from relying more upon the plough than upon the hoe."[22]

Not all the farming efforts were as successful as those at Fort Atkinson seemed to have been. Unduly wet seasons, flooding of the bottom lands where the crops were planted, and swarms of blackbirds that consumed the seed corn before it had a chance to sprout all contributed to seasons of failure. The erratic yields prevented the smooth operation of the commissary system in estimating and contracting for supplies, and the toll in military spirit was incalculable. Yet the farming program dragged on for fifteen years, until in 1833 the War Department released the posts from the obligation to engage in anything more than kitchen gardening. Not until after the Mexican War, when new territorial advances spread the army again over lands where no civilian supplies were readily available, did the farm program spring up anew.

☆

A significant contribution of the regular army to the West, both military and civilian, was the network of military roads, planned by army officers and to a large extent constructed by the troops.[23] Cutting roads through the wilderness was a part of nearly every campaign, and in areas east of the Mississippi where the forest and underbrush coverage was heavy and streams and swamp lands numerous, the task was almost overwhelming. The campaigns in the Northwest Territory

[22] Croghan, *Army Life on the Western Frontier*, pp. 6–7.
[23] An excellent survey of military roads in the West is Harold L. Nelson, "Military Roads for War and Peace—1791–1836," *Military Affairs*, XIX (Spring, 1955), 1–14. Included is a map showing all of the roads Nelson discusses.

in the 1790's were slowed considerably—in the cases of Harmar and St. Clair with disastrous results—because passageways had to be hewn out by the army as it invaded the Indian lands. Part of Wayne's success rested on the efficiency and speed of his movements, and whereas the East knew him as "Mad Anthony," the Indians called him "Whirlwind" because of his rapid road building and his consequent rush through the wilderness.[24] This road work, however, and similar operations in subsequent campaigns was strictly subordinate to military objectives. The roads were necessary for the movement of troops and supplies, and little thought was given to them as permanent highways to serve future defense needs or civilian interests.

It was not long before the value of regular overland routes to supplement the river transportation network in the West became obvious. Such routes would multiply the effectiveness of the small garrisons and reduce the costs of their supply, to be sure, but they would serve national expansionist purposes as well. The construction force was already on the spot in the form of peacetime regulars, although it was necessary to make sure that the Indians were willing to allow the building of roads through their territory, and frequently specific treaty provision was made for the construction of roads. In April, 1801, Secretary of War Dearborn directed the construction of a wagon road along the portage between Lakes Erie and Ontario. The work was to be done by the troops and given priority over the construction necessary at Fort Niagara.[25]

At the same time plans were made for soldier labor on the road from Nashville to Natchez, the old Natchez Trace, for the organization of Mississippi Territory in 1798 made necessary better communications between its capital at Natchez and the East. The Postmaster General appealed to the War Department for the use of troops stationed in the Southwest to build a usable wagon road from Natchez to Nashville.[26] The Indians' permission was obtained in treaties with the Chickasaws and Choctaws in October and December, 1801, and in the spring Dearborn sent specific directions about the construction of the road and the

[24] The road building of Harmar, St. Clair, and Wayne is discussed in Archer Butler Hulbert, *Military Roads of the Mississippi Basin: The Conquest of the Old Northwest* (Cleveland, 1904).

[25] Dearborn to Wilkinson, April 1, 1801, National Archives, Records of the Secretary of War, Letters Sent, vol. 1.

[26] Habersham to Dearborn, March 12, 1801, cited in J. P. Bretz, "Early Land Communication with the Lower Mississippi Valley," *Mississippi Valley Historical Review*, XIII (June, 1926), 7.

use of troops to build it.[27] When the French traveler, F. A. Michaux, visited Nashville in the late summer of 1802, he reported on the improvements in the road:

> The road that leads to the Natches was only a path that serpentined through these boundless forests, but the federal government have just opened a road, which is on the point of being finished, and will be one of the finest in the United States, both on account of its breadth and the solidity of the bridges constructed over the small rivers that cut through it; to which advantages it will unite that of being shorter than the other by a hundred miles.[28]

Unfortunately it is impossible to trace completely all the road building of the frontier army in the years before the War of 1812. Troops worked on the Georgia frontier from Fort Hawkins on the Ocmulgee River to Fort Stoddert on the Mobile, and no doubt elsewhere, but the report of Quartermaster General Jesup in 1831 on roads constructed by the army listed none before 1817 since he could find no records of them.[29] During the war itself the lack of suitable roads for the military movements undertaken was all too obvious. It was a matter, again, of building roads as the troops advanced, and the delay was costly.[30]

The wartime experience helped to promote the development of a positive policy of building roads by means of army troops. General Andrew Jackson proposed at the end of 1815 that a new military road be cut from Nashville to New Orleans, which by shortening the old route would enable men and supplies to be furnished the southwestern frontier and be "of incalculable consequence in our future operations." In answer Secretary of War Crawford directed the concentration of troops in the Southwest, in case dangers arose with Spain but also

---

[27] Charles J. Kappler, ed., *Indian Affairs: Laws and Treaties* (2 vols., Washington, 1904), II, *Treaties*, pp. 55, 56; Dearborn to Thomas Butler, April 16, 1802, National Archives, Records of the Secretary of War, Letters Sent, vol. 1.

[28] F. A. Michaux, *Travels to the West of the Alleghany Mountains, in the States of Ohio, Kentucky, and Tennessea* (London, 1805), printed in Reuben Gold Thwaites, ed., *Early Western Travels, 1748–1846* (32 vols., Cleveland, 1904–1907), III, 255.

[29] Bretz, *Mississippi Valley Historical Review*, XIII, 3; *American State Papers: Military Affairs*, IV, 625–630. Jesup wrote to the Secretary of War, January 7, 1831: "Roads required for the troops in their own operations were sometimes opened by them previous to and during the late war; but there are no data within the control of the government from which anything more can be ascertained in relation to them than the fact that they were actually made by the labor of the troops." *Ibid.*, p. 626.

[30] For a brief account of military road building during the War of 1812, see Nelson, *Military Affairs*, XIX, 4–5.

to permit the employment of the troops in cutting a military road from the Tennessee River to Mobile and New Orleans. "The employment of the troops in opening military roads, and in constructing fortifications," Crawford told Jackson, "has been determined upon by the President, after due deliberation. It is believed to be no less necessary to the discipline, health and preservation of the troops, than useful to the public interest."[31] With a small appropriation from Congress and directives from the War Department, "Jackson's Military Road" from the Tennessee border to Madisonville, Louisiana (on Lake Pontchartrain north of New Orleans) was built by the army between June, 1817, and January, 1820, a distance of almost 300 miles. The road ran east of the old Natchez Trace and reduced the route of communication between Nashville and New Orleans by more than 200 miles. With its 35 bridges and 392 causeways, the road was described as "well-opened and of ample breadth," and the popular acclaim of the road in the West was high.[32]

A similarly useful road, though of considerably shorter length, was that from Detroit to Fort Meigs, running from the Michigan capital to the rapids of the Maumee some seventy miles to the south. Noting the expediency of connecting the northwestern posts of the army with the settled areas of Ohio from which supplies must come in time of war, the Secretary of War in 1816 directed Major General Alexander Macomb, commanding the Fifth Military Department at Detroit, to open the road with soldier labor. Crawford sent Major John Anderson of the Corps of Engineers to survey the route and specifically ordered the payment of an extra ration of whiskey and fifteen cents a day extra pay for the soldiers while engaged in the construction. The Secretary of War also mentioned other roads to be built in Ohio and, perhaps to set Macomb's mind at rest, noted: "The troops under General Jackson are employed in the same service, and those stationed in the vicinity of the fortifications which are intended to be erected, will be employed in their construction."[33]

[31] Jackson to Crawford, December 17, 1815, and Crawford to Jackson, March 8, 1816, *Correspondence of Andrew Jackson*, ed. John Spencer Bassett (6 vols., Washington, 1926–1933), II, 222–223, 235.

[32] *U. S. Statutes at Large*, III, 315; *American State Papers: Military Affairs*, IV, 626–627; Bretz, *Mississippi Valley Historical Review*, XIII, 17–20. William A. Love, "General Jackson's Military Road," *Publications of the Mississippi Historical Society*, XI (1910), 402–417, gives a good many details on the history of the road, indicates the extent of the soldiers' work, and describes in detail the route of the road.

[33] Crawford to Macomb, May 29, 1816, Clarence E. Carter, ed., *The Territorial Papers of the United States* (26 vols., Washington, 1934–1962), X, 639–640.

Macomb responded with enthusiasm. "Every one is convinced of the vast importance of a military way which will connect this sequestered settlement with the inhabited parts of the State of Ohio," he wrote from Detroit; and he significantly added, "It will of itself form the best defence ever afforded to this frontier and moreover be the means of introducing a population which will forever hereafter secure it from the desolation and distress to which it has been so recently exposed." Macomb had already dispatched seven companies of the Third Infantry to Mackinac, Chicago, and Green Bay, but the entire Fifth Infantry and a company of artillery were still at Detroit, and with them and the company of the Third at Fort Wayne he began at once to construct the road, complaining only that he was ill-supplied with tools, since nearly everything available had been sent out with the troops to establish the new posts on the Lakes.[34]

Macomb was not disappointed with the results of the army's labors, as two years later he reported the completion of the road to within eight miles of the rapids of the Maumee. "The road is truly a magnificent one," he exclaimed. The roadway was cleared to a width of 80 feet, the low places causewayed, and the creeks and rivers crossed with substantial bridges. The general complimented the officers and men for their zeal and perseverance and remarked again how beneficial the road was proving both to the army and to the people of the country. The road opened the public lands and greatly increased their value.[35]

Meanwhile another military road was being built under War Department orders on the frontiers of New York state, from Plattsburg to Sackets Harbor. Colonel Henry Atkinson was directed in August, 1817, to employ the troops of the Sixth Infantry for improving the road from that post to Chateaugay, and in October, 1818, Colonel Hugh Brady at Sackets Harbor was instructed to detach troops from his command to work east in "the same excellent manner." About half the distance between the two points was constructed by the troops; then the road remained unfinished because of lack of appropriations.[36]

The question of "military roads" to be provided for the general welfare soon became a constitutional issue. On the day before he left office, President Madison vetoed on constitutional grounds the "Bonus Bill,"

---

[34] Macomb to Crawford, June 20, 1816, *ibid.*, p. 652.

[35] Macomb to Calhoun, November 2, 1818, *ibid.*, p. 785.

[36] *American State Papers: Military Affairs*, IV, 626–628. The military importance of the road is indicated in Major General Jacob Brown's letter to Calhoun, January 20, 1823, *American State Papers: Miscellaneous* (2 vols., Washington, 1832), II, 988.

which would have used profits from the Bank of the United States to build internal improvements, and Monroe similarly rejected general internal improvements.[37] Whether roads that would not be allowed directly could be constructed by the troops under the guise of military roads was the subject of long debate in the House of Representatives in January, 1819. Beset by worries about the prerogatives of Congress, Henry Clay noted that the Executive was able to employ the labor and money of the nation on internal improvements, while Congress was denied the same power, and he referred to the road being constructed from Tennessee to Lake Pontchartrain. He remarked sarcastically that "over this *military* road it was proposed very soon to march a detachment of stage coaches, proposals having been already made to the Post Office Department to avail itself of the services of this description of *military corps.*"[38]

Presidential scruples did not affect Secretary of War Calhoun nor deter him from drawing up a strong document on the need for the construction of military roads and their usefulness for national development.[39] On two points he convincingly showed the intimate relationship between the needs for military defense and the general development of the nation. First of all, the same network of roads would have to be constructed whether the object was strictly military defense or the promotion of the economic welfare of the country. "The road or canal can scarcely be designated, which is highly useful for military operations," Calhoun observed, "that is not equally required for the industry and political prosperity of the community." In the second place, the increased wealth and fiscal capacity of the nation that would result from internal improvements would themselves be resources in time of war. Military roads and canals that would make possible rapid troop movements were especially indispensable in the United States, Calhoun thought, because of the great expanse of territory with its sparce population, and because of the American opposition to a large standing army (which would have been able to stand guard at many places at once).

The use of troops to build the roads—at least in part—was well in

37 James D. Richardson, ed., *A Compilation of the Messages and Papers of the Presidents* (10 vols., Washington, 1896–1899), I, 584–585.

38 The debate, January 6, 1819, is in *Annals of Congress*, 15 Congress, 2 session, col. 446–463. The quotation from Clay is in col. 452.

39 Report on Roads and Canals, January 14, 1819, *The Works of John C. Calhoun*, ed. Richard K. Crallé (6 vols., New York, 1854–1857), V, 40–54. The quotations from Calhoun are from this report.

accord with Calhoun's mind. "The propriety of employing the army on works of public utility canot be doubted," he asserted. "Labor adds to its usefulness and health. A mere garrison life is equally hostile to its vigor and discipline; both officers and men become the subjects of its deleterious effects." But he proposed that the soldiers be rewarded for their labor by an increase in the rate of extra pay from fifteen cents to twenty-five cents a day, lest the hard work deter men from enlisting or lead to desertion. "Among the leading inducements to enlist," Calhoun candidly remarked, "is the exemption from labor; and if the life of a soldier should be equally subjected to it as that of other citizens in the same grade, he will prefer, if the wages are much inferior, to labor for himself instead of laboring for the public."

Calhoun dircted the use of soldier labor on the Detroit-Fort Meigs, Tennessee-New Orleans, and Sackets Harbor-Plattsburg roads, because of their military origin and use, but he was cautious about using the troops to build roads that were not clearly military until the constitutional principles could be settled.[40] Ultimately, however, Monroe abandoned his scruples about the constitutionality of federal roads when he signed the Survey Act of 1824, which called for surveys of routes for commercial and postal as well as military purposes. Within a month Congress had approved the survey and construction of a new road from Detroit to Ohio and authorized the President to employ troops of the United States in completing it.[41] Much of the agitation for this road came from Lewis Cass, Governor of Michigan Territory, who argued that there were plenty of troops at Detroit for the work and that the officers would be glad to be thus employed. Some of the troops had been intended for Green Bay, but Cass asserted that they could be much more usefully employed on the road building than at Green Bay. When Congress authorized the use of troops, Cass made specific request that they be so employed.[42]

The new federal interest in internal improvements was reflected in a series of military roads centering in Florida, Arkansas, and Michi-

---

[40] Report of Soldiers on Fatigue Duty, January 14, 1819, *American State Papers: Military Affairs*, I, 822. In a letter to Major General Brown, September 22, 1819, Calhoun instructed him not to employ troops in the construction of a road at Niagara unless in his opinion it was "decidedly of a Military character." National Archives, Records of the Secretary of War, Letters Sent, vol. 10.

[41] Acts of April 30, 1824, and May 26, 1824, *U. S. Statutes at Large*, IV, 22–23, 71.

[42] Cass to Joseph Vance, March 9, 1824, Carter, *Territorial Papers*, XI, 533; Cass to Jacob Brown, December 2, 1824, "Territorial Records Schoolcraft Papers," *Michigan Pioneer and Historical Collections*, XXXVI, 491–493.

gan Territories. Between 1824 and 1826 roads were built from Pensacola to Barrancas, to Fort Mitchell, Alabama, to St. Augustine, and
from Tampa Bay to Coleraine in southern Georgia. The first two were
done under War Department directives and were built completely by
the troops. For the others Congress made special appropriations, while
at the same time authorizing the use of soldiers in their construction.
Of these roads only a little more than half the length was completed
by the soldiers. At the end of 1827 a fifth Florida military road was
begun from the Georgia border south through St. Augustine to New
Smyrna.[43]

For Arkansas and neighboring regions Congress between 1824 and
1827 approved three military roads: from the Mississippi opposite
Memphis to Little Rock in 1824, from Little Rock to Fort Gibson in
1825, and in 1827 from Fort Towson to the northern boundary of
Louisiana, which was afterward extended to Natchitoches by the
Quartermaster General.[44] To these were added in the 1830's an additional series of roads, in some of which soldier labor was predominant.[45]

The call for additional roads in Michigan Territory was loud and
clear from both military and civilian leaders. In special reports on
the defense of the northwestern frontier in January, 1826, General
Brown and General Macomb stressed the importance of improved lines
of communication which would speed the movement of troops and by
encouraging settlement strengthen the means of self-defense.[46] Governor Lewis Cass at the same time provided a long and forceful memoir
on the state of affairs in the Territory and on the means to effect its
defense.[47] Essential was an adequate system of roads. He emphasized
the importance of the road from the settlements in Ohio to Detroit, but
he outlined as well three other roads, "commencing at Detroit, the
great depot of the country, passing through the most important parts
of the peninsula, and terminating at the borders of the great lakes
which almost entirely encircle it." One of these was a road from

[43] U. S. Statutes at Large, IV, 5–6, 132, 227–228; American State Papers:
Military Affairs, IV, 626–628. See also the report of Quartermaster General
Jesup, November 26, 1825, and attached reports on the surveys for the Florida
roads, ibid., III, 117–122.

[44] U. S. Statutes at Large, IV, 5, 135, 244; American State Papers: Military
Affairs, IV, 626–629.

[45] Nelson, Military Affairs, XIX, 2, 9.

[46] Brown to Secretary of War, January 11, 1826, and Macomb to Secretary
of War, January 10, 1826, House Report No. 42, 19 Congress, 1 session, serial
141, pp. 2–6.

[47] "Memoir of Governor Cass," January 11, 1826, ibid., pp. 6–18. The quotations following are from this report.

Detroit to Chicago, which had been surveyed the year before. This road would ensure safe communications with Lake Michigan at all times, would enable troops to penetrate the heart of the Potawatomi country, and would offer inducements to enterprising immigrants. A second road, from Detroit to Fort Gratiot at the entrance into Lake Huron, was a necessary substitute for the water passageway, which was unsafe if an enemy held the opposite shore. A third, from Detroit to Saginaw Bay, would keep open communications with Lake Huron and would effectively check and restrain the Chippewas of the area. Upon these roads depended the security and prosperity of the country.

Without them [Cass continued], the forts upon the upper lakes may fall, as they have already fallen; the Indians, removed from the reach of our troops, and feeling confident in their strength, may again descend upon us, as they have before done, and renew the scenes of the Miami and the river Raisin. With these roads, we shall be enabled to penetrate into every portion of the Indian country, to restrain or chastise them, as circumstances may require, and, by operating upon their fears, compel them to become spectators, and not actors, in any future hostilities with a civilized power: a state of quietude as much demanded by their interest, as by ours. We shall be enabled, under the most adverse circumstances, to reach the navigable waters to the North and West, and to preserve the necessary intercourse with the remote posts whose possession is essential, not only to the prosperity, but to the very existence of our power in these regions.

Cass pointed out that Michigan was too weak to construct the roads itself; only the federal government could do it. Lest the expense of such roads be a stumbling block, however, Cass hastened to show the general benefit that they would bring:

The construction of the roads herein recommended, would produce an immediate and decisive effect upon the migration to the territory. They would be lined with hardy and vigorous farmers, interested in the preservation of the country, and be able and willing to defend it. The physical strength of the frontier would be increased, and the supplies required for the subsistence of the troops, produced where they are to be consumed. Thus diminishing the force necessary to be brought from remote points, and reducing the heavy expenditures, always occasioned by long and distant transportation.

The committee was impressed and recommended the roads that Cass wanted, "not merely as a defensive measure, but as a measure of sound policy, calculated to build up, by proper encouragement, the settlement of that frontier with the sturdy yeomanry of the country." Congress authorized the roads, but troops entered little into their construction. The military roads in the Lower Peninsula were built largely by civilian contractors under the supervision of army engineers.[48]

The troops, however, were essential in the part of Michigan Territory that stretched west of Lake Michigan (to become Wisconsin Territory in 1836), where a road was constructed in 1835–1837 to replace the Fox-Wisconsin passage between the Lakes and the Mississippi.[49] This important waterway was one of the key channels of communication in the West, but it was not a satisfactory all-season highway from either military or civilian points of view. The Fox was unsatisfactory, for its serpentine course greatly lengthened the distance, and in the Wisconsin sandbars impeded navigation. In dry seasons, the rivers were scarcely navigable, while for several months of the year ice closed the rivers altogether. If Forts Howard, Winnebago, and Crawford were to guard the Northwest effectively, Cass (now Secretary of War) insisted that an overland route be built to connect them. That such a road would attract settlers as well as promote military ends was but another argument in its favor.[50]

In July, 1832, Congress appropriated $5,000 for laying out and opening the road and a survey was undertaken, but construction did not begin until 1835.[51] The road was then divided into three sections, each committed to the commandant of the nearest post. Three companies were to be employed from each fort. The western section, from Fort Crawford east, was completed with little difficulty by Colonel Zachery Taylor and his men, for this section crossed relatively open country, and it was ready by August, 1835. The rest of the road, run-

---

[48] *Ibid.*, p. 1; *U. S. Statutes at Large*, IV, 231–232; *American State Papers: Military Affairs*, IV, 39. See also George B. Catlin, "Michigan's Early Military Roads," *Michigan History Magazine*, XIII (Spring, 1929), 196–207, and Mrs. Bert Garner, "A Notable United States Military Road," *ibid.*, XX (Spring and Summer, 1936), 177–184.

[49] For details about this road, see Prucha, *Broadax and Bayonet*, pp. 134–143, and H. E. Cole, "The Old Military Road," *Wisconsin Magazine of History*, IX (September, 1925), 47–62.

[50] Cass report, January 4, 1832, and supporting documents, *American State Papers: Military Affairs*, IV, 815–816. Ten officers at Fort Winnebago petitioned the Secretary of War for such a road. *Ibid.*, p. 850.

[51] *U. S. Statutes at Large*, IV, 602. The report of the survey is in *American State Papers: Military Affairs*, V, 512–513.

ning through forested land with many streams to cross, proceeded slowly and was not even nominally completed until the end of 1837. Although there were valid grounds for complaint on the crude nature of the roadway, it was for many years the only overland route between Green Bay and Prairie du Chien.

The calls for roads built at federal expense continued, and many were argued for on military grounds, but the troops gradually passed from the scene as road builders. Settlements that were large enough to win their demands for the roads usually also had the means to construct them, provided Congress appropriated the necessary funds and army engineers were available to survey the routes and direct the construction.[52]

So intermingled were military and civilian uses of these roads that no one can disentangle them. Nor should we be concerned to do so. The army consciously considered itself a force for national development, and if its military preparations had beneficial economic and social effects, the men who directed the activities of the army were delighted.

[52] For the work of army officers in surveying and constructing internal improvements, see Forest G. Hill, *Roads, Rails and Waterways: The Army Engineers and Early Transportation* (Norman, Okla., 1957).

☆ TEN ☆

The Army and Indian Affairs

THE United States sought to maintain order on the Indian frontier
by the presence of the regular army, which would overawe the red
men and which in times of crisis could take military action against the
tribes. The threat of force and the use of force, however, were not the
only tools in the new nation's kit for dealing with the Indians. The federal government under the Constitution sincerely sought to remove the
need for military expedients in its relations with the aborigines. President Washington and Secretary of War Henry Knox were architects
of an Indian policy that had as its aim the well-being of the United
States while maintaining untarnished its honor. In the enforcement of
this policy the regular army of the United States played an official and
indispensable part.[1]

The first consideration was, of course, peace. Washington and Knox
were both military men, and they knew that peace with the Indians
could be attained by military defeat and subjugation. But the United
States could not stand the strain of a long war, nor were these leaders
willing to risk besmirching the honor of the republic by such a brutal
undertaking. The alternative was fair treatment of the red men by
negotiation, liberality, guarantees of protection from encroaching white
settlers, and the fostering of an honest trade. The program to attain
these ends included first of all the treaties that were negotiated with
the tribes when the Revolution ended.

[1] I have treated the development of American Indian policy at length in
*American Indian Policy in the Formative Years: The Indian Trade and Inter-
course Acts, 1790–1834* (Cambridge, Mass., 1962), and the army's part in the
enforcing of the policy in *Broadax and Bayonet: The Role of the United States
Army in the Development of the Northwest, 1815–1860* (Madison, Wis., 1953),
pp. 55–80, 91–94.

It soon became apparent that the treaties alone were not sufficient to ease the contacts between the Indians and the whites. Frontier disturbances arose because the treaties were not strictly adhered to by the aggressive American frontiersmen, who cared little that, according to the Constitution, treaties duly ratified by the Senate were the supreme law of the land. In answer to the pleas of the President, Congress enacted a series of laws that were intended originally to supplement the treaties and to enforce the provisions of the treaties against the lawless whites on the frontier. These laws, as they were gradually expanded to meet the problems of dealing with the Indians, came to embody the Indian policy of the United States. The first of the laws was passed on July 22, 1790; it was renewed and augmented from time to time, until in 1834 a codification of preceding laws and some new amendments became the basic legislation for Indian relations for the next century. These laws bore the significant title of acts "to regulate trade and intercourse with the Indian tribes, and to preserve peace on the frontier."

In peaceful dealings with the Indians under these laws, direct responsibility rested upon the Indian agents and sub-agents appointed for the various tribes. These men, initially authorized in a vague sort of way by the Indian intercourse law of 1793, gradually came to have a carefully spelled out set of duties, from issuing licenses to traders to promoting the progress of the Indians toward civilization. The agents came directly under the superintendents of Indian affairs (usually an *ex officio* duty of the territorial governors) and were civilian employees of the War Department. They had responsibility, but no force, and they relied upon the presence of military garrisons to accomplish their objectives. The agency house in most cases was established at a military post, and the agents and commanding officers were directed to cooperate with each other.[2]

The agents represented the government on a day-to-day basis, as Indians in small groups came for visits to the agency. In the absence of the agent, the post commander was frequently directed to assume

[2] Prucha, *American Indian Policy in the Formative Years*, pp. 53–57; Edgar B. Wesley, *Guarding the Frontier: A Study of Frontier Defense from 1815 to 1825* (Minneapolis, 1935), pp. 16–30; Ruth A. Gallaher, "The Indian Agent in the United States Before 1850," *Iowa Journal of History and Politics*, XIV (January, 1916), 3–55. The work of one agent is discussed in Merritt B. Pound, *Benjamin Hawkins—Indian Agent* (Athens, Ga., 1951). For a day-by-day account of the work of an agent on the northwestern frontier, see Henry R. Schoolcraft, *Personal Memoirs of a Residence' of Thirty Years with the Indian Tribes on the American Frontiers* (Philadelphia, 1851).

his duties. The act of 1834, which organized the Indian department, authorized the President to require any military officer to take over the work of the Indian agency, but long before that date army officers had been intimately involved in Indian affairs. Thus Lieutenant Colonel Henry Leavenworth, when he established Fort Snelling at the mouth of the Minnesota River in 1819, was directed to take charge of the Indian agency there until the arrival of Lawrence Taliaferro, the newly appointed agent. Taliaferro had instructions to consult with the commander and report to him regarding his duties as agent. "It is of the first importance," Secretary of War Calhoun had written him, "that, at such remote posts, there should be a perfect understanding between the officers, civil and military, stationed there, to give energy and effect to their operations." Taliaferro, a proud and high-strung Virginian, was often at odds with the post commanders, but it is hard to see how he could have succeeded in his long tenure at the St. Peter's Agency if there had been no military force at Fort Snelling. During Taliaferro's absences the work of his office fell directly upon the Fort Snelling commanders.[3]

Taliaferro's instructions were only an example of what was the established War Department policy. The principle was clearly set forth in an order of February 29, 1832:

> From the peculiar situation of Indian Agents on our exposed fron-
> tier, it is found that unless they are in some degree sustained in the
> execution of their duties by the Military force, their endeavors to
> conciliate the Indians and to keep order among them, must in many
> instances fail of success. It is therefore ordered that officers com-
> manding on the Indian frontiers or in the Indian country, will when
> in their opinion, circumstances may require it, lend their aid in fur-
> thering the views and intentions of the Indian Agents, residing near
> their respective posts and commands; and it is further ordered, that
> where there are no Indian Agents stationed in the vicinity of a post,
> the commandant will consider himself authorized to act as agent
> for Indian Affairs, and to attend to the interests of the Indians,

---

[3] *U. S. Statutes at Large,* IV, 736; Calhoun to Leavenworth, December 29, 1819, *Correspondence of John C. Calhoun,* ed. J. Franklin Jameson (*Annual Report of the American Historical Association for the Year 1899,* II, Washington, 1900), pp. 166–167; Calhoun to Taliaferro, December 27, 1819, National Archives, Records of the Secretary of War, Letters Sent, Indian Affairs, vol. D, p. 350. The Taliaferro Papers in the Minnesota Historical Society are a rich source of information on the agent's work and his relations with the personnel at Fort Snelling.

residing near their posts; and will also receive any deputations from other tribes which may desire to confer with him respecting their own affairs.[4]

Usually the officers' duties were only temporary, but at Fort Winnebago after 1834 there was no regular agent and the post commander was saddled with the extra work. The work of Indian agent was exceedingly irksome to the army officers, for it was often petty and always time-consuming, nor was there extra compensation for the extra duties. When Colonel Zachary Taylor was obliged to take up the agent's duties at Prairie du Chien in 1835, he wrote bitterly to the superintendent of Indian affairs at St. Louis: "I have in no way sought the duties of Indian Agent; on the contrary I have entered on them with great reluctance, with a fear of not being able to discharge them without neglecting those of my proper profession, in a manner to give satisfaction to the Department, and to do justice to those poor miserable and degraded creatures." He was most concerned, however, that the American Fur Company agents would attack his work as agent if he failed to conform to their interests.[5]

On more formal occasions—the drawing up of treaties, the payment of annuities, or moving Indians to new homes—the army was much more willing to aid the agents, for here the military aspects of the work were clearly discernible. The soldiers by their uniforms, parades, and military salutes furnished the necessary solemnity and ceremony to impress the Indians, and the immediate availability of military force more than once saved a conference from an otherwise disastrous ending. When negotiations were carried on at an established fort, the full panoply of ceremony was impressive even to the white participants. Caleb Atwater, one of the commissioners for the treaty with the Winnebagos at Fort Crawford in 1829, described the scene:

> The commissioners sat on a raised bench, facing the Indian chiefs; on each side of them stood the officers of the army in full dresses, while the soldiers, in their best attire, appeared in bright array, on the sides of the council shade. The ladies belonging to the officers' families, and the best families in the Prairie, were seated

4 Orders No. 19, Headquarters of the Army, Adjutant General's Office, February 29, 1832.

5 Elbert Herring to Enos Cutler, July 22, 1834, Clarence E. Carter, ed., *The Territorial Papers of the United States* (26 vols., Washington, 1934–1962), XII, 789; Taylor to William Clark, July 2, 1835, copy in State Historical Society of Wisconsin from original letter in Historical Department of Iowa, Des Moines.

directly behind the commissioners, where they could see all that passed, and hear all that was said. Behind the principal Indian chiefs sat the common people—first the men, then the women and children, to the number of thousands, who listened in breathless and deathlike silence, to every word that was uttered. The spectacle was grand and morally sublime in the highest degree, to the nations of red men, who were present.[6]

☆

The intercourse laws made explicit provision to protect the lands reserved for the Indians from illegal white encroachment, and from 1796 on the laws provided that the President of the United States could employ such military force as he judged necessary to remove illegal squatters on the Indian lands or to apprehend any person in the Indian country in violation of the provisions of the act that required licensing of all traders who entered the Indian lands. Persons apprehended by the army in such cases were not to be tried by courts-martial, as Henry Knox wanted, but were to be handed over to the civil authorities for trial and punishment. To quiet the fears of those who saw all military action as incipient despotism and tyranny, the law as reenacted in 1799 provided that the officers and soldiers having custody of a prisoner should treat him "with all the humanity which the circumstances will possibly permit; and every officer and soldier who shall be guilty of maltreating any such person, while in custody, shall suffer such punishment as a court-martial shall direct."[7]

A law of 1816 added provisions against foreigners in the Indian trade and authorized the President to direct the use of military force in seizing the goods brought in illegally by foreigners and the furs they had collected. And in 1822 the military officers were directed to search traders' stores suspected of harboring liquor, which in that year was prohibited from being introduced into the Indian country.[8]

The initiative in most cases was to come from the civilian agents, and the necessity of close and friendly cooperation between the two arms of the War Department was apparent. In the United States it

[6] Caleb Atwater, *Remarks Made on a Tour to Prairie du Chien, Thence to Washington City, in 1829* (Columbus, Ohio, 1831), p. 69.

[7] *U. S. Statutes at Large*, I, 470, 473, 748.

[8] *Ibid.*, III, 332–333, 682–683.

was clear that the civilians had to have the upper hand. The officers were not happy about taking orders from civilians, but when the orders came down from the President through proper channels, they usually responded eagerly and effectively. Army officers and Indian agents frequently enough clashed about action in given cases, but these disputes were more than balanced by the energy and zeal with which most of the military officers enforced the intercourse laws. In removing intruders, confiscating liquor, restraining Indian hostilities, and lending an element of force to treaty conferences, the army was an indispensable agent of national sovereignty. Indeed, it could be argued that the small garrisons on the frontier would have had their hands full if they had had nothing else to do than remove squatters and knock in the heads of whiskey barrels.

On all sections of the frontier the encroachments of white settlers into the lands still reserved to the Indians brought army action.[9] As intrusions on the Cherokee, Creek, and Chickasaw lands in Georgia, Alabama, and Mississippi threatened the peace, the Indian agents and the military commanders in the region were repeatedly directed to be vigilant in enforcing the laws against the "licentiousness of daring and unprincipled men" who paid little attention to the rights of the Indians or to the laws and treaties of the United States. In March, 1809, for example, the acting Secretary of War directed the Cherokee agent to disperse all intruders on the Indian lands. With a military detachment from Hiwassee Garrison, the agent removed 83 families from Cherokee lands and 201 from Chickasaw lands. The whites, who had begun to farm, pleaded for permission to gather in the crops they had planted, but to no avail. Yet the success of the expedition was not lasting. In October the agent was forced again to warn intruders who had reappeared and to call for another detachment from the commander at Hiwassee. The agent went out with the troops, who destroyed the cabins of the intruders. Similarly on the upper Mississippi federal troops from Fort Crawford made innumerable sorties into the lead regions on both sides of the Mississippi to disperse whites on Indian lands. Success was only temporary, despite the vigilance of the army officers. In Arkansas, in Iowa, in Missouri—wherever the rich lands of the Indians offered a prize for the avaricious whites—the lands were eroded away by the illegal entry of the settlers, who knew that the

[9] See Prucha, *American Indian Policy in the Formative Years*, pp. 139–187.

military arm of the government was insufficient to patrol all areas all the time, and who realized that ultimately the government would heed their cries for extinguishment of the Indian title and confirmation of the titles they themselves had sought to establish.

The smallness of the military force available to watch all avenues of entry into the forbidden lands was no doubt the primary cause of failure to enforce completely the prohibitions against settling in the Indian country. Yet behind the failure was a more fundamental issue. The government did not intend to stop westward advance for all time. Its aim was to regularize the advance and to prevent disorder and injustice as far as possible while the advanced culture of the whites irresistibly replaced that of the Indians. Despite the lack of full success, there can be little doubt that the military forces on the frontiers prevented much conflict. If the military commanders and their meager commands had done nothing else in the West than guard the Indian country from lawless whites, their maintenance there would have been more than justified.

☆

Still more frustrating than the attempt to prevent all encroachment on the Indian lands were the efforts to prevent the introduction of liquor into the Indian country. There was perhaps no greater disrupter of peace among the Indians than the white man's whiskey, which made madmen of the Indians and enabled the heartless white traders to cheat them of their furs. Yet to stanch the flow of the vicious liquor was almost beyond the capabilities of the government and its agents on the frontier. Little by little the federal laws clamped down on the whiskey dealers, and it was up to the military commanders along the channels of entry into the Indian country to enforce the prohibitions. The first aim of the officials of the War Department was to regulate the whiskey trade by regulating the traders—making sure that only men of integrity were licensed for trade and hedging their operations around with various restrictions to control their activities. Some, like Thomas L. McKenney, hoped to squeeze out the private traders altogether and let the Indians be supplied by the federal government's trading houses among the Indians, which could be directly controlled.

When the federal trading posts were quashed by the pressure of private interests in 1822, a more direct attack on whiskey was sub-stituted. By an amendment to the intercourse act of 1802, passed on May 6, 1822, the President was authorized to direct Indian agents, governors of territories acting as superintendents of Indian affairs, and military officers to cause the stores and packages of goods of all traders to be searched, in case of suspicion or information that ardent spirits were being carried into the Indian country. If such contraband liquor was found, all the goods of the traders were to be forfeited and their bonds put in suit. The commanders of the frontier posts were all sent copies of the legislation and given express instructions to follow the letter of the law. They were to search all the stores and packages of traders suspected of bringing in whiskey. Where whiskey was found, the goods were to be seized and libel proceedings begun.[10]

There were loopholes in the 1822 law, for the President was given discretionary authority to permit liquor if the exigencies of the trade demanded it, and a good deal of liquor was introduced under the guise of whiskey for the use of boatmen in the fur trade. These open channels prevented the absolute prohibition that was needed if the evils of the whiskey traffic were to be overcome. Finally in 1832 Congress decreed an absolute block: "No ardent spirits shall be hereafter introduced, under any pretence, into the Indian country."[11] The War Department sent new instructions to the Indian agents and directed the absolute adherence to the law, and the military officers were given new energy in searching out the forbidden commodity.

Against great odds the army officers went about their duty. At Fort Leavenworth, which monitored the important traffic up the Missouri River, the officers were especially alert. When the agent of the American Fur Company, Kenneth McKenzie, tried to take liquor up the river in the spring of 1833, it was all seized at the fort. McKenzie wrote: "We have been robbed of all our liquors. . . . They kicked and knocked about everything they could find and even cut through our bales of blankets which had never been undone since they were put up in Eng-land." On the same steamboat was the distinguished foreign naturalist, Maximilian, Prince of Wied, who noted of Fort Leavenworth: "We were stopped at this place, and our vessel searched for brandy, the importation of which, into the Indian territory, is prohibited; they

---

[10] *U. S. Statutes at Large*, III, 682–683; Gaines to post commanders, June 12, 1822, *American State Papers: Military Affairs* (7 vols., Washington, 1832–1861), V, 508.

[11] *U. S. Statutes at Large*, IV, 564.

would scarcely permit us to take a small portion to preserve our specimens of natural history."[12]

Captain John Stuart, commander of Fort Smith on the Arkansas, was equally zealous, but he faced a more difficult task, since not all the contacts between Arkansas and the Indian nations were funneled through Fort Smith. He explained the situation to the Secretary of War in May, 1833:

> I have now been here a Little more than one Month, And have made it my particular Duty, to prevent so far as practicable the Introduction of Ardent Spirits, into the Indian Country, And so far as relates to the passage of this river I Confidently beleive that I have Succeeded, but that will by no means put a final Stop to its Introduction. For the Situation of the Country is Such that although it be prevented from passing up the river, It can and will, be Introduced by means of Waggons Pack horses &ct., along the numerous by roads and Paths which cross the Line into the Indian Country, And I am well Convinced from the Knowledge that I have of the Country, And its Inhabitants, on both Sides of the Line, that it is not within the Scope of Human possibility to Entirely Prevent its Introduction among the Indians. In the first place, the Inhabitants of the Territory of Arkansas, Particularly Such of them as border on the Indian Country, are either adventurers from different Parts of the world, whose Purpose it is to make money in any way they can, without regard to Laws or they are such as have been all their Lives moving along in Advance of Civilization and good order, And who have for their Governing Principles Self Interest alone, Without regard to Law or honesty—[13]

But the difficulties did not stop Stuart from trying. He seized every drop of whiskey that he found in the Indian country—"except out of the bars of Steam Boats"—and by his constant alertness was able to end the whiskey traffic in the immediate area of Fort Smith. Yet overall he had not succeeded, for he wrote at the beginning of 1834 that the introduction of liquor among the Indians had increased.[14]

---

[12] Hiram M. Chittenden, *The American Fur Trade of the Far West* (3 vols., New York, 1902), I, 357–358; Maximilian, Prince of Wied, *Travels in the Interior of North America* (London, 1843), reprinted in Reuben Gold Thwaites, ed., *Early Western Travels, 1748–1846* (32 vols., Cleveland, 1904–1907), XXII, 253–254.

[13] Stuart to Cass, May 1, 1833, Carter, *Territorial Papers*, XXI, 710.

[14] Stuart to Cass, February 7 and 17, 1834, *ibid.*, pp. 896–898, 907–908.

On the upper Mississippi Captain William R. Jouett, the commander at Fort Snelling, armed with instructions from the War Department to enforce the laws strictly, set out to search for and seize whiskey coming up the river. The year 1832 was a critical one. The Black Hawk War was in progress, and the Sioux and Chippewas, longtime enemies, were threatening to break out into open conflict again. Abundant whiskey sources in such a circumstance could explode the frontier. Captain Jouett first tried to warn the traders of the danger of bringing in liquor, but, as he reported, "when he found that neither warnings nor persuasions could influence, nor danger deter the traders from violating the laws of the country at so critical a period, there was but one course left for him to pursue relative to the subject, and that was, faithfully to execute the orders and instructions he had received." Accordingly he seized two Mackinac boats at Lake Pepin. They were loaded with goods for the Indian trade, and among the goods Jouett found sixteen kegs of alcohol or high wines. These he seized and impounded at Fort Snelling.[15]

☆

The actions of the army officers to enforce the intercourse laws in regard to intrusions on the Indian lands and the prohibition against whiskey ran afoul of the frontier traders and settlers, who would brook no such interference with their schemes for aggrandizement. Army officers and Indian agents who removed intruders were charged with trespass and haled into the frontier courts to stand trial for their action. Thus Major David E. Twiggs, who in 1829 removed intruders seeking to cut timber on the Indian lands along the upper Wisconsin River, was charged with trespass by a Green Bay trader, arrested by the sheriff, and required to furnish $1,600 bail for his appearance at the district court in Green Bay. No judgment was pronounced against the officer, but the case was not finally settled until 1831, and Twiggs put in a bill for more than $1,000 of expenses incurred in attending court, for lawyer's fees, and for incidental expenses. When he in turn tried to prosecute the violaters of the intercourse law, he got nowhere.[16] The frontiersmen and the courts that represented them were hostile to

[15] Jouett petition to Congress, October 30, 1833, *American State Papers: Military Affairs*, V, 507.
[16] Prucha, *Broadax and Bayonet*, pp. 64–65.

military action, even when the laws were clearly on the side of the officers.

Major Stephen W. Kearny, when he was commander of Fort Crawford, acted with the Indian agent at Prairie du Chien, Joseph M. Street, to seize timber cut in the Indian country. For their zeal in enforcing the laws of the United States, they were fined by the United States circuit court on the ground that they had acted without specific authorization from the President, and Congress had to reimburse the officers for their loss. As Street later complained to the Secretary of War, "there is little prostpect [sic] of Justice from a Jury, on the part of an officer of the U.S."[17]

Captain Jouett for his action in seizing the liquor in 1832 was charged with illegal trespass and assault on the employees of the American Fur Company. He won his case, but the situation was not conducive to careful enforcement of the law, for the officer had to engage a lawyer to defend him and had to travel nearly 300 miles from his post at Fort Snelling to attend the court at Mineral Point. In the end he had to call upon Congress to reimburse him for $642.37 of expenses. Colonel Taylor, Jouett's immediate superior, chided the War Department for not standing firmly behind the officers of the army in their attempts to enforce the laws of the nation, instead of permitting them to be harassed by sheriffs and dragged from place to place to defend themselves as well as they could. It is little wonder that many officers, including Taylor himself, seriously considered leaving the military service for some more tranquil activity. As Street wrote Cass, "If something more effectual is not done to protect the officers of the Government against the *cupidity of the Traders*, they will be reduced to the *alternative* of deciding between pecuniary ruin, on the one hand, and disobedience of orders on the other."[18]

Whatever the outcome may have been in a given case, the threats of civil action against army officers was a deterrent to effective enforcement. The American Fur Company was powerful, it stood behind its traders, and it had the support of the local courts and judges, who did not take kindly to the army officers and what the frontiersmen considered their arbitrary, if not tyrannical, action. It was usually an uneven match. The army officers and Indian agents were isolated and

[17] *American State Papers: Military Affairs*, V, 9–10; *U. S. Statutes at Large*, VI, 515; Street to Cass, October 4, 1832, transcript in the Joseph M. Street Papers, State Historical Society of Wisconsin.

[18] Jouett case, *American State Papers: Military Affairs*, V, 506–511; Street to Cass, December 5, 1832, Carter, *Territorial Papers*, XII, 551.

ill-supported by far-off Washington, and whenever the interests of the American Fur Company were at stake, the officers suffered harassment, inconvenience, and often financial loss. It came to be the accepted thing that the officers would get into trouble by enforcing the acts, that the offenders brought to trial for violation of the laws would escape conviction in the frontier courts, and that the men apprehending them would be subjected to a civil prosecution for faithful discharge of their official duties. It is little wonder that Colonel Taylor concluded bitterly: "Take the American Fur Company in the aggregate, and they are the greatest scoundrels the world ever knew."[19]

A number of army officers recommended martial law for the Indian country, and some suggested a tightly regulated monopoly of the fur trade that would eliminate the evils arising from competition between traders for the furs and affections of the Indians, but this medicine was too strong for Americans to accept. Secretary of War Eaton in 1829 suggested that the local courts be bypassed and the cases from the frontier taken directly to the Supreme Court in order to prevent "those frequent suits with which our officers are annoyed," but this solution, too, was not feasible.[20]

The War Department was not completely hardhearted in the matter. It instructed district attorneys to defend the officers and authorized the officers to engage other counsel for their defense. But the action was not aggressive and did little to encourage the officers who were attacked on the frontier for their concern for the laws and for the rights of the Indians. The post commander at Fort Armstrong, Lieutenant Colonel William Davenport, declared in 1833 that it was "impossible to move out of the regular routine of garrison duty, even upon an order from the highest authority, without having a law suit upon your hands." And General Atkinson cautioned the commandant at Fort Des Moines in 1835, "You run some risk of being prosecuted for destroying the contents of the [whiskey] shops in your neighborhood. You should be cautious in this subject, for you know how utterly an officer is abandoned by the government under prosecutions of this sort."[21]

Such a situation weakened in large measure the effect of the military

[19] Quoted in Kenneth W. Porter, *John Jacob Astor, Business Man* (2 vols., Cambridge, Mass., 1931), II, 756.

[20] *American State Papers: Military Affairs*, IV, 153.

[21] Davenport to Atkinson, June 10, 1833, National Archives, Records of Army Commands, Department of the West, Letters Received; Atkinson to Kearny, February 18, 1835, National Archives Records of Army Commands, Right Wing Western Department, Letter Book.

as enforcers of the law on the frontier. Yet the officers continued to act out of a sense of duty and from an appreciation that the tranquility of the frontier was often in direct proportion to the legal protection given to the Indians against the whites. It is unfortunate that there were not more soldiers to guard the frontier and that they were not more firmly supported by the War Department, for wherever the army went into action the effect was salutary.

☆

The Indian trade and intercourse laws with their military enforcement were a direct attack upon the problem of preserving peace between the Indians and the whites on the frontier. At the same time the federal government sought by indirect means to eliminate some of the antagonisms that occurred because of unjust treatment of the Indians by the whites with whom they came most in contact in the initial stages of the frontier—the fur traders. There was no doubt that trade relations were fundamental in Indian affairs. With the advent of European goods, from guns to copper kettles, the Indian cultures underwent a change that made continued reliance upon the trade goods an absolute necessity. Peaceful relations with the tribes came to depend to a large extent upon satisfactory trade relations, and control of the tribes rested upon control of the trade. Colonial experience had clearly established the principles.

In the first decades of our national existence, many Indians residing in the United States were drawn into the diplomatic orbit of the British or the Spanish, and private American means seemed to be lacking to supply the goods the Indians depended upon, and which could draw them into American dominion. Furthermore, even when American traders appeared in sufficient numbers, they too frequently were an unsavory lot, who cheated and debauched the Indians in their rush for wealth. Restrictive laws did not adequately reach the traders, and their elimination became the goal of many who had the welfare of the Indians at heart and who were deeply concerned about the peaceful development of the West.

President Washington saw part of the answer in government trading houses among the Indians. Such enterprises would furnish the Indians with the goods they needed and desired under terms that were fair and honest. Because the government posts would not be interested in making profits, they could sell to the Indians at low prices and pay a reasonable rate for the furs of the natives. Each trading house (called a factory) would be in charge of a factor, an employee of the federal government, and subject to strict regulation. The factors could be prevented from introducing liquor into the trade and could be used, too, as positive agents in the civilizing of the aborigines. But most important, by means of the lower charges for goods and higher prices for the furs, these government factories would eventually drive out the private traders. When once in control of the fur trade, the government would have an effective means of controlling the Indians by threatening to cut off the supplies if the Indians became hostile or obstreperous.[22]

George Washington persuaded Congress of the wisdom of his plan, and in 1795 an appropriation was made to begin among the southern Indians. Factories were established in 1795 at Coleraine on the St. Mary's River in southern Georgia and at Tellico in eastern Tennessee. In the following year new appropriations were made to continue the system, and from then until 1822 the factory system was an essential part of American Indian policy. In 1806 a special office of Indian trade was created within the War Department, and the two men who headed the office—John Mason and his successor Thomas L. McKenney— became key figures in federal dealings with the Indians. The initial success of the program led to cautious expansion until, all told, twenty-eight factories had been in operation at one time or another. Their locations and relocations reflected the advance of the frontier.

The factory at Coleraine was moved to Fort Wilkinson in 1797, to Fort Hawkins in 1808, and finally to Fort Mitchell in 1817, as the Indians retreated before white settlement. The factory at Tellico was moved to Hiwassee in 1807 and four years later discontinued. At the same time factories were springing up in the West. In 1802 they appeared at Fort Wayne, Detroit, Chickasaw Bluffs, and Fort St. Stephens on the Tombigbee. In 1805 others were established at Chicago, Belle Fontaine, Natchitoches, Arkansas Post, and Sandusky. In 1808 the goods at Belle Fontaine were distributed between the two new factories at Fort Madison and Fort Osage, and in the same year a house was opened on Mackinac Island.

---

[22] The best brief history of the factory system is in Wesley, *Guarding the Frontier*, pp. 31–54. See also Royal B. Way, "The United States Factory System for Trading with the Indians, 1796–1822," *Mississippi Valley Historical Review*, VI (September, 1919), 220–235, and Prucha, *American Indian Policy in the Formative Years*, pp. 84–93. Ora Brooks Peake, *A History of the United States Indian Factory System, 1795–1822* (Denver, 1954), is the most complete published study, but it is poorly done.

FORT HARMAR. Established in 1785 on the Ohio at the mouth of the Muskingum River, this post gave notice to the Indians that the American government intended to protect its citizens moving into the Ohio valley. The drawing is from Samuel P. Hildreth's *Pioneer History*. (Courtesy of the National Archives)

FORT WASHINGTON. Built on the site of the future city of Cincinnati, this typical early army post was the headquarters from which the campaigns of Generals Harmar, St. Clair, and Wayne moved against the Indians in the 1790's. The engraving is from Benson J. Lossing's *The Pictorial Field-Book of the War of 1812*. (Courtesy of the National Archives)

HENRY KNOX. Gilbert Stuart's portrait of the first Secretary of War shows the portly figure and kindly face of a military man whose concern for just and humane treatment of the Indians greatly influenced early Indian policy. (Courtesy of the National Archives)

HENRY DEARBORN. Another Gilbert Stuart portrait shows Jefferson's Secretary of War, a physician turned soldier, who served during a crucial period in the expansion of the American national domain to the West. (Courtesy of the National Archives)

ANTHONY WAYNE. Edward Savage's portrait of "Mad Anthony" Wayne seems too mild for the fiery martinet, whose well-disciplined troops at the Battle of Fallen Timbers destroyed the Indians' hold on most of Ohio. (Courtesy of The New-York Historical Society)

(*below*) PITTSBURGH IN 1790. An army officer, Seth Eastman, made this drawing of the early city for Henry R. Schoolcraft's *Indian Tribes of the United States*. His source was a sketch by Lewis Brantz, the earliest pictorial record of Pittsburgh. (Courtesy of the National Archives)

Council with the Indians. This engraving from Sergeant Patrick Gass's *A Journal of the Voyages and Travels of a Corps of Discovery, under the Command of Capt. Lewis and Capt. Clarke of the Army of the United States,* the first published account of the great exploration, is based largely on the artist's imagination, since the Indians portrayed do not resemble any of those the explorers met. (Courtesy of the Library of Congress)

The Number of Officer & Men for to Protect the Indian and keep the savages in peace with the US. and each other

1806 of folyin at as Bonfmonds

Names of eligable stations of Establishments	Colonel	Major	Captain	Lieutenant	Ensign	Surjon mate	Interpreter	Sergeant	Corporal	Musick	Privats	Total
At St Louis	1	1	1	1	1	1		3	4	4	62	68
the Gorge, or Arkansaus			1	1	1	1		1	1	1	45	48
the mouth of Kanzes			1	1	1	1		1	2	1	23	28
the Council Bluff				1	1	1	2	2	2	2	30	36
Chien or Shar ha R.			1	1	1	1	3	4	4	4	75	88
Rochjohn river	1		1	1	1	1	4	3	3	3	45	54
Falls of Missourie			1	1	1		2	2	1		30	38
Head of Kanzes or Arkansas			1	1	1	1	2	4	4	4	75	87
the Mississippi Praira de Chien	1		1	1	1		2	4	4	4	70	82
Peten or Falls of St Anthoney				1	1	1	1	2	2	2	30	38
do do Sand Lake					1	1		2	2	2	40	48
the St Peters River			1	1	1	1	1	4	4	4	75	82
	3	1	8	9	8	12	22	30	29	32	600	700

WILLIAM CLARK. The Philadelphia painter, Charles Willson Peale, who sought to add the portraits of famous explorers to his gallery of distinguished citizens, made this portrait of the red-haired, blue-eyed Clark in 1810. Clark in his long service as Governor of Missouri Territory and Superintendent of Indian Affairs at St. Louis was responsible for Indian relations in much of the West. (Courtesy of the Independence National Historical Park)

MERIWETHER LEWIS. This calm portrait of the explorer was painted by Charles Willson Peale in 1807, shortly after Lewis had been appointed Governor of Louisiana Territory. Less successful in political office than in leading his party through the wilderness to the Pacific, the unfortunate Lewis died in 1809, probably by suicide. (Courtesy of the Independence National Historical Park)

(left) PLAN FOR WESTERN DEFENSE. Among the field notes of the explorer William Clark discovered in St. Paul in 1956 was this 1805 plan for western defense, in which the captain lists sites for military posts and indicates appropriate garrisons. The document is now in the Western American Collection of Yale University and was first published in Ernest S. Osgood's edition of *The Field Notes of Captain William Clark, 1803–1805*. (Courtesy of the Yale University Library and the Yale University Press)

ZEBULON MONTGOMERY PIKE. The young lieutenant, who boldly proclaimed American sovereignty over the upper Mississippi valley in 1805–1806 and westward over the Great Plains in the following year, was painted by Charles Willson Peale in 1808. (Courtesy of the Independence National Historical Park)

JAMES WILKINSON. As army commander at St. Louis, Wilkinson sent out Lieutenant Pike on his explorations. Charles Willson Peale's portrait of 1797 shows him as a brigadier general and senior officer in the army. (Courtesy of the Independence National Historical Park)

BATTLE OF THE THAMES. This fanciful representation of the battle on October 5, 1813, which restored American control in the Northwest, shows Colonel Robert M. Johnson killing Tecumseh. In the background the British commander, General Proctor, is shown escaping in his carriage. (Courtesy of the Library of Congress)

BATTLE OF HORSESHOE BEND. John A. Cheatham, a topographer with Jackson's Tennessee Volunteers, drew a map of the decisive battle on the Tallapoosa River, in which the power of the hostile Creeks was broken. This section of his map shows the sharp bend in the river where the Indians took their stand. (Courtesy of the National Archives)

PAWNEE COUNCIL. Samuel Seymour, official artist with Major Stephen H. Long's exploring expedition, painted a careful picture of the council held with the Pawnee Indians above present-day Omaha in October, 1819. The painting served as the basis for this engraving from Edwin James's *Account of an Expedition from Pittsburgh to the Rocky Mountains*. (Courtesy of the Library of Congress)

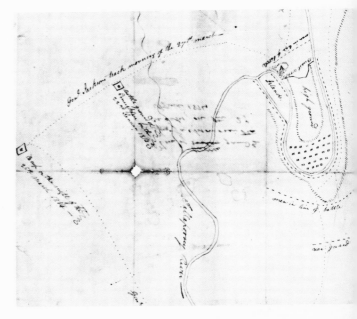

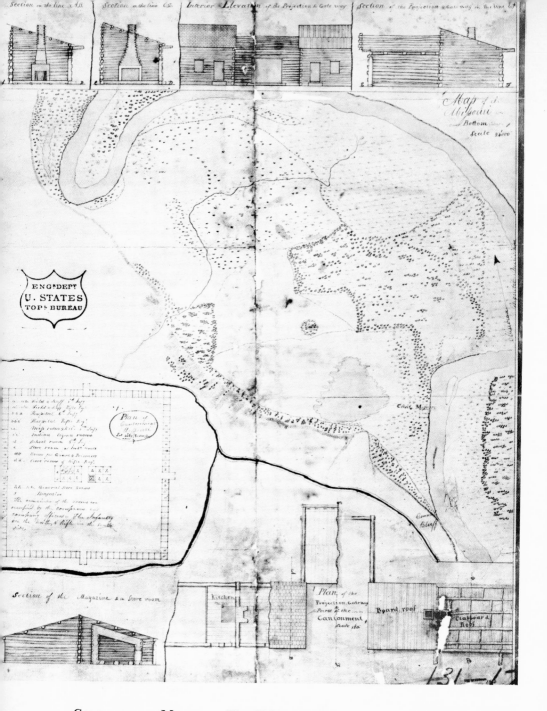

CANTONMENT MISSOURI. The ill-fated Yellowstone Expedition of 1819 built these winter quarters on the bank of the Missouri above present-day Omaha. In 1820 the post was flooded out, and a new post, Fort Atkinson, was built on the bluffs a short distance down river. (Courtesy of the National Archives)

STEPHEN H. LONG. Charles Willson Peale painted this portrait in 1819 shortly before Major Long left with his exploring party for the West. Peale's son Titian accompanied the expedition as an assistant naturalist. (Courtesy of the Independence National Historical Park)

(*below*) ENGINEER CANTONMENT. Titian Ramsay Peale made this watercolor at Long's winter quarters on the Missouri River. It shows the steamboat "Western Engineer" with its serpent figurehead spouting steam. (Courtesy of the American Philosophical Society)

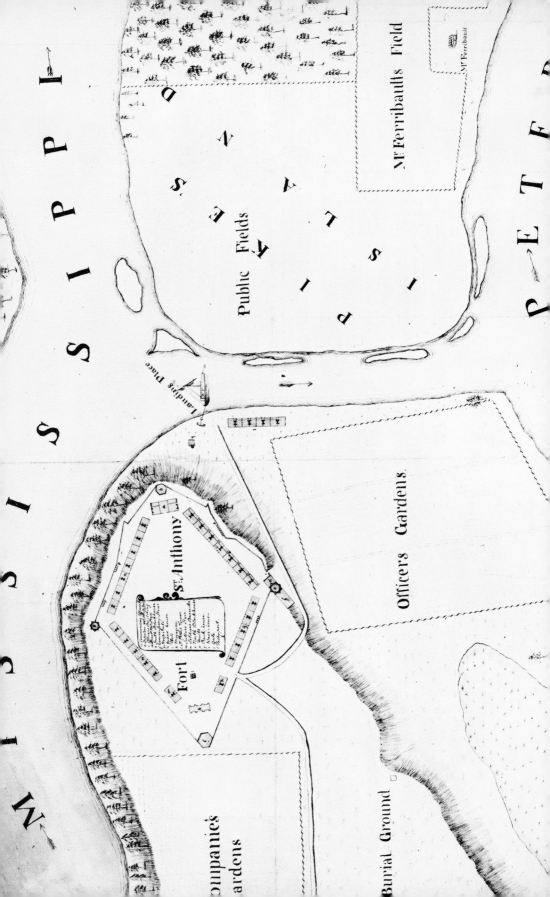

FORT SNELLING. Seth Eastman as a captain in the First Infantry was commander of Fort Snelling in the 1840's. A talented artist of western Indian scenes, Eastman was called upon in the 1870's to decorate the room of the House Committee on Military Affairs in the United States Capitol with a series of pictures of American forts, of which this is one. (Courtesy of the Library of Congress)

(*left*) FORT ST. ANTHONY. This plan of the fort that was soon to be renamed Fort Snelling was drawn about 1825. It shows the strategic location of the fort at the confluence of the Mississippi and the St. Peter's (Minnesota) rivers. (Courtesy of the National Archives)

(*right*) JOHN C. CALHOUN. As Secretary of War, Calhoun, with his vision of the nation expanding into the West, was responsible for the establishment of Fort Snelling in 1819. This portrait of the Secretary is by John Wesley Jarvis. (Courtesy of the National Archives)

BLACK HAWK. George Catlin's portrait of the Sac chieftain, who led his "British band" in a futile war with the United States, was part of Catlin's famous gallery of Indian paintings. (Courtesy of the National Collection of Fine Arts, Smithsonian Institution)

(*below*) BATTLE OF THE BAD AXE. This conception of the disastrous battle that ended the Black Hawk War was included by the artist, Henry Lewis, in his illustrated history of the Mississippi valley, which appeared in Düsseldorf in 1854 under the title *Das illustrirte Mississippithal*. (Courtesy of the Library of Congress)

FIRST DRAGOON REGIMENT. The dragoons, who brought to the army the mobility that was needed in dealing with the mounted Plains Indians, are shown here in dress uniform, 1836–1851. (Courtesy of Charles Mc-Barron and the Company of Military Historians)

(*right*) WINFIELD SCOTT. Entering the army in 1809 as a captain in the light artillery, Scott rose to be Commanding General of the Army in 1841, a post he held until the Civil War. This engraving by P. M. Whelpley was made from a Mathew Brady daguerreotype. (Courtesy of the National Archives)

(*lower right*) EDMUND P. GAINES. A rival of Scott and a man of quarrelsome temperament, Gaines was the commander in the West from 1821 until the Mexican War. This photograph by Mathew Brady captures some of the dramatic quality of the general. (Courtesy of the National Archives)

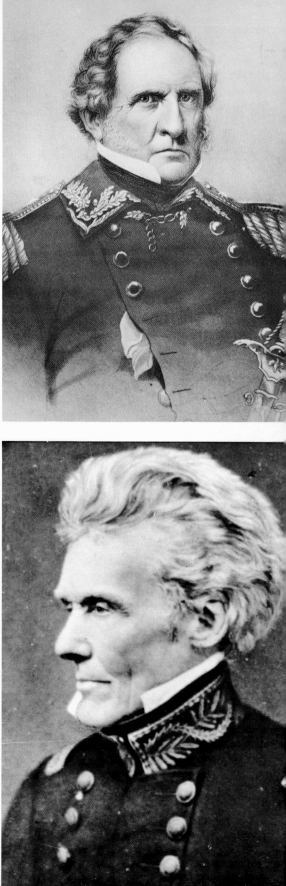

COMANCHE PARTY MEETING DRAGOONS. Colonel Henry Dodge's dragoon expedition of 1834 had this dramatic first encounter with the Comanches. The painting is by the artist George Catlin, who accompanied the soldiers on their march. (Courtesy of the National Collection of Fine Arts, Smithsonian Institution)

WICHITA (Pawnee Pict) VILLAGE. This village of the Wichita Indians in what is now southwestern Oklahoma was the goal of Colonel Dodge's 1834 expedition. The engraving, after a painting by George Catlin, is in Catlin's *Letters and Notes on the Manners, Customs, and Condition of the North American Indians*. (Courtesy of the Library of Congress)

FORT BROOKE. This lithograph, issued at Charleston, South Carolina, in 1837, is one of a series showing scenes of the Second Seminole War. Fort Brooke, established at the head of Tampa Bay in 1824, was a key post in the war against the Florida Indians. (Courtesy of the Library of Congress)

(*right*) OSCEOLA. George Catlin's portrait shows something of the nobility of this Seminole chief, who led his people in their violent resistance to removal. Osceola died in 1838, shortly after his capture and imprisonment. (Courtesy of the National Collection of Fine Arts, Smithsonian Institution)

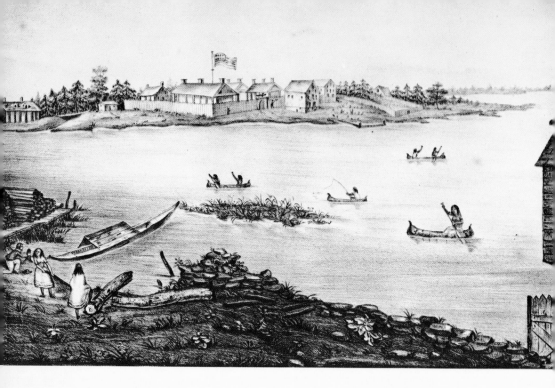

Captain   Private   First Sergeant

(*above*) FORT HOWARD. This post, established at the head of Green Bay in 1816, guarded the Fox-Wisconsin River waterway between the Great Lakes and the Mississippi. The lithograph appeared in Francis de Castelnau's *Vues et souvenirs de l'Amerique du nord*, published in Paris in 1842. (Courtesy of the Library of Congress)

(*left*) SECOND INFANTRY REGIMENT. Infantry soldiers bore the brunt of frontier defense, manning posts, chastising hostile Indians, and making visible United States authority in the West. Soldiers of the Second Infantry appear here in winter dress uniform, 1841–1851. (Courtesy of Charles McBarron and the Company of Military Historians)

A number of these factories were lost during the War of 1812, which struck a severe economic blow at the system, but with the end of the war a new push into the Northwest was begun, as factories were established at Green Bay, Prairie du Chien, and Fort Edwards on the Mississippi. The rise to prominence of the American Fur Company after the war and the failure to recover the economic losses quickly doomed the system, however, and in 1822, after a bitter conflict of views, it was abolished.

What success the system had can be attributed in part to the protection and aid given to the factories by the regular army garrisons in the West. The mere listing of the locations of the factories indicates how many were under the immediate shadow of an existing military post or were themselves the occasion for the building of a fort. Of the twenty-eight factories that operated during the existence of the system, all but four were closely connected with a military post. Fort Madison and Fort Osage were established in 1808 primarily to protect the factories that had been decided upon, and the expeditions to build the posts were dual affairs of factory and garrison. The setting-up of factories at Green Bay and Prairie du Chien in 1815 was followed almost immediately by the building of military posts.

The great work of the army in aiding the factories was the protection it supplied, but important too was the prestige that the presence of soldiers gave to the trading houses. The troops, moreover, were sometimes the only labor force available for building the factories, transporting goods, and on occasion beating and packing the furs.

☆

For the remote frontier, where the organization of civil government was rudimentary, the Indian intercourse laws provided a detailed code for dealing with crime in the Indian country.[23] Although the laws were not completely effective in preventing attacks upon the person or property of members of one race by those of the other, they were invoked in many cases of Indian criminals—murderers especially. Since the Indian tribes were considered quasi-sovereign nations, Indians who had murdered whites were demanded of the tribe. If the accused criminals were not turned over, military expeditions were sent to apprehend them or to seize and hold hostages until the criminals appeared. The

[23] See Prucha, *American Indian Policy in the Formative Years*, pp. 188–212.

culprits were guarded by the army troops before being transferred to a civil jurisdiction for trial according to established white procedures.[24]

In many cases the system worked well, for the Indian chiefs frequently enough cooperated by delivering up the criminals. Again and again, however, only the threat of military force accomplished the desired end, and the post commanders were aggressive in carrying out the law. In 1820, for example, when Winnebago Indians murdered two soldiers near Rock Island, Lieutenant Colonel Leavenworth immediately left his regimental headquarters at Fort Snelling and hastened to Fort Armstrong, where he made a formal demand for the murderers in a council with the Indians. He retained four chiefs as hostages until, sixteen days later, the criminals were turned in, and he guarded the prisoners until they were in the hands of the civil authorities. Leavenworth personally wanted to shoot the Indians on the spot, but he was persuaded to follow the provisions of the law and after a preliminary examination sent the Indians down the Mississippi for trial in the district court of Illinois, where they were convicted and sentenced to death. Such action was common all along the frontier, as detachments of troops were sent out at the request of the Indian agents or civilian authorities to apprehend Indians and as criminals turned in were confined in the post guardhouses until arrangements could be made for their trials.[25]

Such procedures did not always satisfy the military men, since the wheels of justice turned slowly, and too often the Indians, after languishing in prison for a long period, were finally freed because of the impossibility of proving their guilt. Leavenworth, after reluctantly turning over the Winnebago murderers, exclaimed, "It would have been better to have *executed* them & *then have tried them*—If they are *tried* they must be *executed* or we shall feel the weight of the Winnebago Tomahawk."[26] Other officers expressed the same sentiments, but

[24] The intercourse law of 1834, for example, declared that "it shall be the duty of superintendents, agents, and sub-agents, to endeavor to procure the arrest and trial of all Indians accused of committing any crime, offence, or misdemeanor, and all other persons who may have committed crimes or offences within any state or territory, and have fled into the Indian country, either by demanding the same of the chiefs of the proper tribe, or by such other means as the President may authorize; and the President may direct the military force of the United States to be employed in the apprehension of such Indians, and also, in preventing or terminating hostilities between any of the Indian tribes." *U. S. Statutes at Large*, IV, 732.

[25] Prucha, *Broadax and Bayonet*, pp. 85–87; Prucha, *American Indian Policy in the Formative Years*, p. 196.

[26] Leavenworth to Daniel Parker, June 10, 1820, National Archives, Records of the Secretary of War, Letters Received.

the War Department could not be moved from its policy of affording strict judicial procedures. The post commanders and their subordinate officers continued to police the frontier, despite what they considered serious limitation on the effectiveness of their work.

In dealing with hostilities between the Indian tribes—another serious threat to the peace of the frontier—the army was less successful. At first such intertribal conflicts were considered none of the government's business, but as they tended to catch white traders between hostile tribes or to spread into attacks on the white settlers, tranquility on the frontier seemed to necessitate some positive action by the United States. In treaties with the Indians, such as the Treaty of Prairie du Chien in 1825, the United States sought to persuade the Indians to stop private retaliation and let the American government see that justice was done by proper punishment of the guilty. Indians who attacked other tribes were demanded of the chiefs or arrested by military detachments and were placed in confinement at military posts awaiting trial. The intercourse law of 1834 specifically authorized the use of military force "in preventing or terminating hostilities between any of the Indian tribes," but practically the situation was almost impossible. The army officers could not set themselves up as referees for all intertribal disputes, nor was justice meted out quickly or surely enough to satisfy the Indians. Dispersal of war parties was no simpler, for they usually struck before a post commander was aware of their existence. Yet the presence of the troops at military posts along the frontier and their patrolling of the Indian country was an effective deterrent to serious intertribal hostilities.

ELEVEN

The Black Hawk War

THE conflict with Black Hawk was the one military engagement in the Northwest after the War of 1812 that was serious enough to warrant the designation "war."[1] This was one of the great ironies of American frontier history, for the war was not a planned aggression by either side nor a last-ditch stand of noble natives against Indian-hating frontiersmen. Misunderstandings were the key to the conflict. A disgruntled war chief, naïvely relying on the counsel of unreliable advisers who promised British aid and Indian allies and seeking ascendancy over a rival chief of saner mind, was opposed by reluctant and hesitant regular army commanders and undisciplined volunteer troops. Had the consequences not included so heavy a toll of death and misery, one might enjoy the comic opera aspect of the whole affair.

It was certainly not an unavoidable war. A wiser decision here, a tighter rein there, would have obviated the dangers and provided a peaceful settlement of the trouble. The Black Hawk War, neverthe-

[1] The story of the Black Hawk War has been told many times. The most complete is Frank E. Stevens, *The Black Hawk War, Including a Review of Black Hawk's Life* (Chicago, 1903). Stevens collected information on the war for more than thirty years and made use of interviews as well as published accounts and manuscripts reports. His work is more a collection of data than a well-wrought narrative and has been relied upon heavily by later historians. Of similar scope but less objective in tone and less carefully done is Perry A. Armstrong, *The Sauks and the Black Hawk War with Biographical Sketches, Etc.* (Springfield, Ill., 1887), a detailed account based largely upon the writings of participants. John A. Wakefield, *History of the War between the United States and the Sac and Fox Nations of Indians, and Parts of Other Disaffected Tribes of Indians, in the Years Eighteen Hundred and Twenty-seven, Thirty-one, and Thirty-two* (Jacksonville, Ill., 1834), is the story of the war by a member of the Illinois militia, who participated in much of the campaign and who filled in his story from newspaper and other reports. Wakefield reflects the pioneer's viewpoint of the war and considered the war justified

less, is a valuable case study of western frontier defense, illustrative of the problems and inefficiencies of the military philosophy of the American people. The inability of the regular army in the West to prevent unwarranted Indian movements, to protect Indian rights from lawless white squatters, or to satisfy the white settlers and politicians that adequate defense was provided permitted rumors of grave Indian threats to grow unchecked and led to a call for citizen volunteers who left a serious blot on the record of American-Indian relations.

Black Hawk, the chief protagonist, was a Sac warrior with a long history of anti-American views and actions.[2] Born, according to his own account, in 1767, he became a war leader though never a formal chief of the Sacs. During the War of 1812 the Sacs and Foxes had actively supported the British. British agents had successfully stirred up their resentment against the advancing Americans while at the same time supplying the trade goods needed by the Indians. Black Hawk, at first hesitant in his neutrality, decided to join actively with the British. "*I*

---

by the "many outrages and depredations committed by those lawless savages." His book was reprinted as *Wakefield's History of the Black Hawk War* (Chicago, 1908), edited with preface and notes by Frank E. Stevens. A very pro-Indian account, first published in 1838, is Benjamin Drake, *The Life and Adventures of Black Hawk: With Sketches of Keokuk, The Sac and Fox Indians, and the Late Black Hawk War* (7th ed., Cincinnati, 1846). An early historical narrative and appraisal of the war by a noted historian is Reuben Gold Thwaites, "The Story of the Black Hawk War," *Wisconsin Historical Collections*, XII (1892), 217–265. This is still probably the best short account of the conflict.

The story has been retold many times in more recent years, without the addition of significant new information. Cyrenus Cole, *I Am a Man—The Indian Black Hawk* (Iowa City, 1938), devotes most of its pages to the Black Hawk War. John H. Hauberg, "The Black Hawk War, 1831–1832," *Illinois State Historical Society Transactions for the Year 1932*, pp. 91–134, gives a brief survey of the facts. The best recent detailed retelling of the story is William T. Hagan, *The Sac and Fox Indians* (Norman, Okla., 1958), pp. 106–204. A popular account is Donald Jackson and William J. Petersen, "The Black Hawk War," *Palimpsest*, XLIII (February, 1962), 65–113. See also Roger L. Nichols, *General Henry Atkinson: A Western Military Career* (Norman, Okla., 1965), pp. 152–175.

[2] Of unrivaled importance is the autobiography of Black Hawk, dictated to the interpreter Antoine LeClaire soon after the war and prepared for publication by a young newspaperman, J. B. Patterson. The first edition, *Life of Ma-Ka-Tai-Me-She-Kia-Kiak or Black Hawk* (Cincinnati, 1833), was reissued in Boston in 1834. A new edition, somewhat augmented, was published by Patterson in 1882, *Autobiography of Ma-Ka-Tai-Me-She-Kia-Kiak, or Black Hawk* (Oquawka, Ill., 1882). Two modern reprintings of the first edition are valuable for the editors' introductions and notes: *Life of Black Hawk, Ma-Ka-Tai-Me-She-Kia-Kiak*, ed. Milo M. Quaife (Chicago, 1916), and *Ma-Ka-Tai-Me-She-Kia-Kiak—Black Hawk: An Autobiography*, ed. Donald Jackson, (Urbana, Ill., 1955). The problem of the authenticity and accuracy of the work is discussed in Jackson's introduction to his edition, pp. 31–38.

had not discovered one good trait in the character of the Americans that had come to the country," he asserted. "They made *fair promises* but *never fulfilled them!* Whilst the *British* made but few—but we could always *rely upon their word!"*[3] After the Treaty of Ghent the Sacs and Foxes resumed more or less peaceful relations with the Americans, but Black Hawk and those who followed him still bore a deep resentment against the United States and a proportionate attachment to the British. Periodic trips to the British at Malden reinforced the anti-American propensities of Black Hawk's followers, who became known as the British band.

What made the rancor fester in the heart of Black Hawk was the treaty of 1804, negotiated by William Henry Harrison with the Sacs and Foxes at St. Louis.[4] Here the tribes—or at least the chiefs on hand —agreed to cede to the United States their extensive holdings east of the Mississippi in western Illinois and southern Wisconsin.[5] In return they got a paltry annuity of $1,000, which was immediately eaten up by debts due to traders. They got also the right to continue living on the land thus ceded as long as it was held by the United States government and not surveyed and sold to actual white settlers. Black Hawk denied the legitimacy of the 1804 cession. He consistently asserted: "That *we* had never sold our country. *We* never received any annuities from our American father! And *we* are determined to hold on to our village!"[6] He contended that the Sacs and Foxes who had treated with Harrison had no right to speak for the tribe. The annual $1,000 that the tribe received he considered a gift in the British fashion, not a payment for land, since as a price for the land it was altogether insufficient. Although further treaties with the Sacs and Foxes had confirmed the 1804 cession and Black Hawk himself had signed at least one of them,[7] the chief and the British band were adamant in refusing to forsake their village, Saukenuk, and the lands and graves of their ancestors east of the Mississippi near the mouth of the Rock River.

There was no crisis as long as white settlement remained in the

3 *Black Hawk: An Autobiography*, ed. Jackson, p. 68.

4 Charles J. Kappler, ed. *Indian Affairs: Laws and Treaties* (2 vols., Washington, 1904), II, *Treaties*, pp. 74–77.

5 The area ceded is shown in Charles C. Royce, *Indian Land Cessions in the United States (Eighteenth Annual Report of the Bureau of American Ethnology*, Part II, Washington, 1899), Plates 17 and 65, Cession 50.

6 *Black Hawk: An Autobiography*, ed. Jackson, p. 125.

7 Treaties of St. Louis, May 13, 1816, Fort Armstrong, September 3, 1822, and Prairie du Chien, August 19, 1825, Kappler, *Treaties*, pp. 126–128, 202–203, 250–255.

southern part of Illinois. The census of 1820, however, showed a population of 55,221 for the new state, and early in the 1820's squatters began to appear on the 1804 cession. They moved into the rich lands along the Rock River and by the end of the decade began to threaten the village of Saukenuk itself. The removal of the Indians from Illinois became a political issue. Governor Ninian Edwards repeatedly called upon the federal government to move the Indians out of Illinois altogether, and his political existence seemed to depend on the success of his endeavors.[8]

Many of the Sacs and Foxes considered removal west of the Mississippi inevitable and, following the leadership of Keokuk, began to establish themselves in new villages along the Iowa River. Keokuk continually preached acquiescence in the demands of the United States, and he persuaded many to follow his counsel. Not so Black Hawk. The older leader set himself squarely against Keokuk. He refused to leave Saukenuk and rallied around himself the dissidents of like mind.

The Sac and Fox agent informed the Indians that they would not be allowed to return to Saukenuk in the spring of 1830, for the government intended to sell the land there to white settlers, thus bringing into effect the provisions of the treaty of 1804. Black Hawk determined to resist and led his followers back to their old lands at the end of the winter hunt. The whites were more numerous than before, and the women of Black Hawk's band were hard put to find free patches on which to plant their corn. Black Hawk protested his peaceful intentions, but incidents between the two races were inevitable, and open clashes were only narrowly avoided. Black Hawk revisited the British at Malden and was assured that the American government would not dispossess his band if they had not in fact sold the land to the whites.

Keokuk attempted to dissuade the old chief's followers from persisting in a course of action that would lead only to their destruction, but Black Hawk continued to hope for outside help and listened to more dangerous advisers. One of these was the Winnebago Prophet, a heavy, mustached chief who had a village on the Rock River some thirty miles above Black Hawk's village. The Prophet promised support from the Winnebagos and the Potawatomis in any conflict with the

[8] Correspondence on the matter can be found in *The Edwards Papers: Being a Portion of the Collection of the Letters, Papers, and Manuscripts of Ninian Edwards*, ed. E. B. Washburne (Chicago, 1884). See also the letters of Edwards and Reynolds in Evarts B. Greene and Clarence W. Alvord, eds., *The Governors' Letter-Books, 1818–1834* (*Collections of the Illinois State Historical Library*, IV, Springfield, Ill., 1909).

whites. Another was the Sac chief Neopope, Black Hawk's second in command; when the leader's spirits flagged, he was at hand to whisper into his ear exciting tales of promised British aid. Furthermore, in the fall of 1830 a party of Sacs, including Black Hawk's son, visited the Creeks, Cherokees, Osages, and other tribes to the south, seeking unsuccessfully to enlist their aid in a general war against the Americans, an act reminiscent of the earlier schemes of Tecumseh and his brother.

The pressures of white population on the Indian lands in Illinois did not abate. The census of 1830 showed 157,445 persons, and the cries for federal action to remove the Indians reached a new pitch. John Reynolds, elected governor in 1830 to succeed Ninian Edwards, was imbued with the frontier view that Indian claims to land were transcended by those of the whites, and he listened sympathetically to settlers' charges against the Indians.[9]

☆

Before the government took any action, Black Hawk in the spring of 1831 again led his band back to Saukenuk at the finish of the winter hunt. They were advised to remove, but the women instead began their corn planting, and the 300 warriors in the band, although not openly hostile, seemed determined to remain. The Indian agent and the army commander at Fort Armstrong on Rock Island took no action, and the settlers, drawing up reports of Indian hostility, petitioned the governor for assistance. Reynolds in turn informed the Indian superintendent at St. Louis, William Clark, of his intention to call out the militia to remove the Indians dead or alive. Clark told the governor that unless Black Hawk's band increased in size the regular army could handle the situation, and General Gaines, commander of the Western Department, moved up to Rock Island with new troops.[10]

Gaines summoned Black Hawk and his braves to meet in council with him and called in Keokuk and representatives of the peaceful fac-

[9] Governor Reynolds tells the story of the Black Hawk War and his part in it in *My Own Times, Embracing Also, the History of My Life* (Belleville, Ill., 1855), pp. 320–421.

[10] The correspondence between Reynolds and Clark and Gaines appears in "Papers relating to the disturbances in the State of Illinois, by a band of the Sac Indians, headed by a brave called Black Hawk," *House Executive Document* No. 2, 22 Congress, 1 session, serial 216, pp. 180–197. Much of it is printed also in Stevens, *Black Hawk War*, pp. 85–91.

tion as well. Black Hawk came in a spirit of defiance, insisting upon his intention to remain at his village. Keokuk pleaded with Black Hawk's followers 'to desert their leader for more peaceful policies and succeeded in winning over some of the band, but Black Hawk himself preferred the advice of the Winnebago Prophet, who assured him that the Americans were only bluffing.

Gaines meanwhile had decided to call upon Governor Reynolds for militia support and to await its arrival before taking any action against the recalcitrant Indians. Fourteen hundred militiamen prepared to move into the critical area, drilled and trained "with as much accuracy as if they were regulars, so far as raw troops were capable," as Reynolds described them. "The material was an energetic and efficient troop, possessing all the qualities except discipline, that were necessary in any army. This small army was composed of the flower of the country, and possessed strong sense and unbounded energy. They also entertained rather an excess of the *Indian ill-will;* so that it required much gentle persuasion to restrain them from killing indiscriminately all the Indians they met."[11]

The militiamen arrived at their rendezvous a few miles below the mouth of the Rock River on the afternoon of June 25, 1831. They rested from their march, cleaned their equipment, and drew fresh supplies of ammunition as their commanders prepared the attack. At sunrise on the 26th, while the regular troops with artillery moved up the river from Fort Armstrong, the mounted volunteers according to plan attacked from the south. The troops moved into the village, but there was no opposition. The Indians had quietly abandoned the village during the night, a few moving up the river to the Prophet's village, but the majority following Black Hawk across the Mississippi. Black Hawk declared that he would have "remained and been taken prisoner by the *regulars*, but was afraid of the multitude of *pale faces*, who were on horseback, as they were under no restraint of their chiefs."[12]

The volunteer "pale faces," finding no Indians to fight, satisfied themselves with burning the huts of the village and opening the graves of former inhabitants and scattering the remains. A heavy rain added another dismal aspect to the whole affair.

Gaines then called the Indians again to council. Black Hawk refused at first to attend, but threats of force and entreaties from Keokuk finally won his agreement. On June 30 he and some of his band went to the

11 Reynolds, *My Own Times*, pp. 334–337.
12 *Black Hawk: An Autobiography*, ed. Jackson, p. 129.

council house on Rock Island, and "Articles of Agreement and Capitulation" were read to them. The terms demanded that the British band
submit to the authority of the friendly chiefs and that they stay west
of the Mississippi, crossing over to the east side only with the express
permission of the President of the United States or the governor of
Illinois. The Sacs and Foxes were to abandon all communication with
the British and were to acknowledge the right of the United States
to establish military posts and roads in the Indian country for the protection of the frontier inhabitants. In return the United States government guaranteed to the Sacs and Foxes the integrity of their lands
west of the Mississippi. The friendly chiefs were bound to enforce the
agreement and were instructed to inform the nearest military post if
at any time they were unable to restrain their allies, the Potawatomis,
Kickapoos, or Winnebagos. By the final article of the agreement all
parties promised to maintain permanent peace and friendship.[13]

The agreement was signed by General Gaines and Governor Reynolds for the United States and by twenty-eight chiefs and warriors.
A young officer, aide-de-camp to General Gaines, recorded the dramatic
scene as Black Hawk was called to the table to sign:

> He arose slowly, and with great dignity, while in the expression of
> his fine face there was a deep-seated grief and humiliation that no
> one could witness unmoved. The sound of his heel upon the floor
> as he strode majestically forward was measured and distinct. When
> he reached the table where I sat, I handed him a pen, and pointed
> to the place where he was to affix the mark that would sunder the
> tie he held most dear on earth. He took the pen—made a large, bold
> cross with a force which rendered *that* pen forever unfit for further
> use; then returning it politely, he turned short upon his heel, and
> resumed his seat in the manner he had left it. It was an imposing
> ceremony, and scarcely a breath was drawn by any one present dur-
> ing its passage.[14]

"I touched the goosequill to this treaty," Black Hawk admitted, "and
was determined to live in peace."[15]

Gaines agreed to supply the Indians with corn equivalent to that

---

[13] *House Executive Document* No. 2, 22 Congress, 1 session, serial 216, pp.
187–189. The Articles are reprinted in Stevens, *Black Hawk War*, pp. 96–98.
[14] George A. McCall, *Letters from the Frontiers, Written During a Period
of Thirty Years' Service in the Army of the United States* (Philadelphia, 1868),
p. 241.
[15] *Black Hawk: An Autobiography*, ed. Jackson, p. 129.

left behind in their fields. The volunteers dispersed to their homes, disappointed in the anticlimactic ending to their campaign. "Our treaty was ridiculed by the volunteers," Governor Reynolds recalled. "It was called a *corn treaty*. It was said we gave them *food* when it ought to have been *lead*."[16] All was quiet as the Indians prepared for their winter hunts, but Governor Reynolds declared that if he had to muster the militia again, he would call out a force large enough to exterminate all the Indians who would not leave the people of Illinois alone.[17]

☆

The quiet was short-lived. Sacs who returned to Saukenuk to rebury the bodies dug up by the soldiers were hindered in their work of piety by the whites. When the supply of corn distributed by Gaines ran out, some of the Indians went back to their abandoned fields to harvest the grain, only to be fired upon by the white settlers and driven back empty-handed across the river. These dilatory activities might have quickly ended and the Indians adjusted to the new home west of the Mississippi had not a new disturbance electrified the frontier. On July 31 a body of Sac and Fox warriors surprised an unarmed camp of Menominees near Fort Crawford and slew twenty-eight of the camp in vengeance for the massacre of Fox chiefs by the Sioux and Menominees the year before. "This retaliation (which with us is considered lawful and right)," declared Black Hawk, "created considerable excitement among the whites!"[18]

The outrage convinced many whites that they would be the next victims, and the government moved quickly to demand the murderers from the tribes. Black Hawk, too, was re-energized by the massacre. He had resigned himself to passing the rest of his years in quiet obscurity, but the murder of the Menominees revived his hopes. He championed those who refused to surrender the guilty braves and thus

---

[16] Reynolds, *My Own Times*, p. 346.

[17] Governor Reynolds maintained a strongly anti-Black Hawk position. He speaks of "the utter fallacy of the positions taken by Black Hawk, and by many of his white hypocritical sympathizers. It was the want of sound judgment, in Black Hawk, and his malignant hostility to the whites, together with promises of support from the Indians residing on the frontiers of the country, that caused him to attempt to remain in his village in defiance of the power of the general government." To Reynolds, "Black Hawk was a treacherous and evil disposed Indian." *Ibid.*, pp. 325, 348.

[18] *Black Hawk: An Autobiography*, ed. Jackson, p. 130.

drew new elements into his depleted band and strengthened his position against his rival Keokuk, under whose domination he chafed. Then Neapope brought news from Canada that the British would assist their red brothers, and from the Winnebago Prophet that the Potawatomis, Chippewas, and Ottawas had agreed to aid the Sacs and Foxes and that the British had sent promises to the Prophet of guns, ammunition, and provisions to be landed at Milwaukee. During the hunting season Black Hawk, taken in by the false promises, gathered his band around him and prepared to return to the lands he had so recently agreed to abandon. He assembled his followers at the site of old Fort Madison and on April 6 crossed the Mississippi at the Yellow Banks (now Oquawki, Illinois) with about 500 mounted warriors, together with the old men, women, and children of his band, who swelled the total number to an estimated 2,000 persons.

The United States government, meanwhile, was more concerned about the intertribal hostilities than about the return of Black Hawk to Illinois. Fearing a massive retaliation by the Sioux and Menominees against the Sacs and Foxes if the perpetrators of the massacre were not delivered up for punishment, President Jackson had resolved to secure the murderers. In March, 1832, General Macomb ordered General Atkinson to proceed to Rock Island with whatever forces were available at Jefferson Barracks in order to restrain the Sioux and Menominees from an attack upon the Sacs and Foxes. By such chance, Atkinson arrived at Rock Island on April 11, five days after Black Hawk made his ill-fated reentry of the Rock River country.

Atkinson did not move at once against the British band. The 226 men he had brought from Jefferson Barracks, augmented by the available men at Fort Armstrong, he did not consider adequate to contest with Black Hawk. The Indians so far had acted peacefully enough, but Atkinson notified Macomb that if the situation became more serious the militia would again be needed.

The situation was already serious enough. Felix St. Vrain, the Indian agent for the Sacs and Foxes, and the traders considered Black Hawk hostile, and only the peaceful conduct of Keokuk and his followers encouraged Atkinson. The army commander met in council with the Keokuk band, made a quick trip to Galena and Prairie du Chien to confer with the men in those communities about defense plans, instructed the commanding officer at Fort Crawford to cut off Sioux and Menominee raiders, and ordered the troops at Fort Winnebago to keep alert for hostile signs among the Menominees.

Although Black Hawk was invited to a second council called at Rock Island, he refused to come, and General Atkinson prepared for a drawn-out campaign. He wanted a force of 3,000 mounted militia troops to augment his regulars and awaited orders from Macomb and Gaines to carry out his plans. Governor Reynolds, however, was not willing to delay. On April 16 he issued a call for about 1,600 men, proclaiming that the Indians were in possession of the Rock River country and that the settlers were in imminent danger. The volunteers were directed to rendezvous at Beardstown on the Illinois River and to march from there to the Yellow Banks on the Mississippi to meet supplies coming up the river from St. Louis. About 1,700 men eventually answered the governor's summons. They were organized into a brigade with three regiments under the command of General Samuel Whiteside. One of the volunteers was Abraham Lincoln, who was elected captain of his company.[19] In the north, having been directed by Atkinson to raise as many mounted volunteers as possible, Henry Dodge (a colonel in the militia of Michigan Territory, of which Wisconsin at the time was a part) organized a body of rangers for protection of the mining region.

Atkinson tried once more to persuade Black Hawk to depart peaceably. He sent a moderate message to the chief, urging him to pay no attention to those who promised British aid. But Black Hawk asserted that his "heart was bad" and that if Atkinson sent troops he would fight them. Atkinson then resolved to begin operations. On May 9 he ordered that on the following morning Whiteside and the mounted volunteers move up the Rock River by way of the Prophet's village. About 340 regulars, plus the unmounted militia, all under the command of Colonel Zachary Taylor, followed on foot. Boats brought up the river the ordnance stores and twenty or twenty-five days' rations for the whole army.

The regular army officers must have had qualms about the ability of the volunteers to carry on a disciplined operation. One lieutenant described the militia camp as a "multitude of citizen volunteers, who were as active as a swarming hive; catching horses, electioneering, drawing rations, asking questions, shooting at marks, electing officers, mustering in, issuing orders, disobeying orders, galloping about, 'cuss-

---

[19] Because of his later fame, Abraham Lincoln's small part in the war has received unwarranted emphasis. A reasonable account is Harry E. Pratt, "Abraham Lincoln in the Black Hawk War," in O. Fritiof Ander, ed., *The John E. Hauberg Historical Essays* (Rock Island, Ill., 1954), pp. 18–28. See also Stevens, *Black Hawk War*, pp. 277–289, and Alfred A. Jackson, "Abraham Lincoln in the Black Hawk War," *Wisconsin Historical Collections*, XIV (1898), 118–136.

Battle of Bad Axe

River

Fort Winnebago

Battle of
Wisconsin Heights

Four Lakes

Fort Crawford

Wisconsin

Blue Mounds

Fort Koshkonong

Battle of
Pecatonica River

Fort Hamilton

Galéna

Stillman's Run

Chicago

Rock River

Dixon's Ferry

Fort Armstrong

Prophet's Village

LAKE MICHIGAN

Iowa River

Saukenuk

Ottawa

Fort Wilbourn

River

Yellow Banks

Peoria

rt Madison

Illinois

ILLINOIS

Fort Edwards

Mississippi

Beardstown

•• Route of Black Hawk's Band

☆ Battles

Area in which route is
confused or unknown

The Black Hawk War

ing and discussing' the war, and the rumors thereof."[20] But the mounted troops had speed and mobility, which the regular infantrymen lacked, and Atkinson authorized Whiteside, if he considered it prudent when he arrived at the Prophet's village, to move ahead rapidly and either force Black Hawk's surrender or "coerce him into submission."

When Whiteside arrived at the Prophet's village, he learned that the British band was only two days' march up the river, and he decided to move ahead without waiting for the regulars. He burned most of the lodges of the village, and he abandoned his baggage wagons in order to speed his march. When he arrived at Dixon's Ferry on May 12, he discovered that Black Hawk was still about thirty miles ahead. Since his rations were low, he determined to encamp and wait for Atkinson and the supplies.

Two fresh groups with ample rations were at hand, however, and they were eager for action. These units pleaded with Governor Reynolds, who had accompanied the expedition, for permission to scout ahead of the main body of troops. The governor, as commander in chief of the Illinois militia, gave the command, and Major Isaiah Stillman, with 275 men, moved out in search of the Indians, making their camp just north of what was known as Old Man's Creek.

☆

Black Hawk had not fared well as he moved up the Rock River, for he did not find the aid promised by the Winnebagos, nor were the Potawatomis any more helpful. He soon discovered, too, that no British were coming to Milwaukee with ammunition and provisions. He realized at last that he had been deceived, that "all the fair promises that had been held out to us, through Ne-a-pope, were *false!*"[21] When he saw the hopelessness of the situation, Black Hawk decided that if Atkinson overtook him he would surrender and go back.

In the midst of a ceremonial feast with the Potawatomi chiefs, Black Hawk received word that 300 to 400 men on horseback had been sighted about eight miles away. He immediately dispatched three young men with a white flag to meet them and bring their leaders into camp for a council. If the Americans had already encamped, the young men

[20] Philip St. George Cooke, *Scenes and Adventures in the Army: or, Romance of Military Life* (Philadelphia, 1859), p. 158.
[21] *Black Hawk: An Autobiography*, ed. Jackson, p. 140.

were to return and Black Hawk himself would go to the whites' camp
for a conference. Black Hawk then sent five more warriors as scouts
to follow the peace party to see what would take place.

The three Indians with the flag of truce, appearing unexpectedly in
Stillman's disorganized camp, caused an uproar. The white flag was
suspected to be a ruse, a suspicion that seemed to be confirmed when
the group of five scouts was spotted. Excited volunteers mounted their
horses and rode out after the Indians, who turned in flight. Someone
opened fire and others joined in, and two of the scouts were killed.
The noise of the shooting increased the confusion back at the camp,
and the panic-stricken whites attacked the peace delegation and shot
down one of the three, while the other two escaped in the melee.

The surviving scouts raced back to Black Hawk. The treacherous
attack of the whites could mean only that the peace overtures had been
rejected. Black Hawk started off with the few braves in his immediate
company (about forty, he reported), concealed his men behind some
bushes until the oncoming mass of volunteers was within range, then
ordered a charge. In panic and confusion the volunteers wheeled about
in retreat before the yelling Indians and dashed headlong in flight.
Only a few brave men stood their ground and paid for their courage
with their lives. The rest did not stop even at their camp, an easily
defensible site, but hurried on to Dixon's Ferry, each one of the early
arrivals certain that he was one of the few survivors. It appeared at
first as though Stillman's entire company had been wiped out, but
slowly the recruits came in. By morning only fifty-two men were missing and of those forty-one were later accounted for. The sight of the
eleven dead when Whiteside's soldiers returned to bury them, however,
did little to calm the frontier, for the Indians had horribly mutilated
their bodies.

The demoralized militiamen were of little use after Stillman's rout.
They made a futile advance along what was thought to be the Indians'
line of retreat, but the great majority insisted on returning home, and
Governor Reynolds discharged the men at Ottawa on May 27 and 28.
Only 300 of the volunteers, among them Lincoln, remained in service
until a new levy could be mustered in.

The report of Stillman's defeat passed on in exaggerated form, plus
the news of a massacre at Indian Creek in which a band of nearly
forty Indians—mostly Potawatomis—had massacred fifteen settlers and
run off with two young girls, set the frontier in turmoil. Atkinson,
jarred by letters from his superiors, who demanded decisive action,

sent orders to Reynolds to issue a new call for 2,000 militiamen. He sent an officer to recruit auxiliaries and scouts from the Sioux and Menominees and called for two companies of regulars from Fort Winnebago. Volunteer companies were organized to defend Galena and the surrounding area. Women and children were sent down river by steamboat. Other families "forted in" and built stockades and block-houses or reinforced their cabins as defense spots.

Although a marauding war band of Winnebagos killed four men of a party carrying dispatches from Atkinson to Galena (including the Sac and Fox agent, Felix St. Vrain) and although the defeat of the militia encouraged some Kickapoos, Winnebagos, and Potawatomis to join the hostiles, there was in fact only limited danger from Black Hawk. He had decided not to risk another battle but to provide for the safety of his women and children by retreat. He would seek a refuge at the headwaters of the Rock River or in the vicinity of the Four Lakes, the site of present-day Madison, Wisconsin.

Atkinson, who rightly feared for his reputation if he did not pursue the campaign to a successful conclusion, was going to take no chances. After conferring with Governor Reynolds, he directed him to issue a call for an additional 1,000 troops, and he ordered two infantry com-panies from Fort Leavenworth to strengthen the regulars. While Atkin-son bided his time, waiting to organize the second levy of volunteers before beginning his pursuit, minor skirmishes occurred between vol-unteer bands and the Indians. In one of these, on June 15, Colonel Dodge and a body of troops from the mines killed a band of eleven hostiles at a bend of the Pecatonica River in southwestern Wisconsin. The news of the victory of the "Battle of Pecatonica" encouraged the whites; as a successful engagement it was blown up into an important event.

Organizing the new volunteers was a slow process, and the regular army officers continued to look with disdain upon the raw troops. "The more I see of the militia," Colonel Taylor commented, "the less confi-dence I have in their effecting any thing of importance; and therefore tremble not only for the safety of the frontiers; but for the reputations of those who command them."[22] But without the manpower of the militia Atkinson did not dare to attack, and the processing of the citi-zen soldiers continued at Fort Wilbourn, a supply depot set up on the

<hr>

22 Taylor to Atkinson, June 2, 1832, quoted in Hagan, *Sac and Fox Indians*, p. 166. The troubles that Atkinson and Taylor had with the militia throughout the war are treated in William T. Hagan, "General Henry Atkinson and the Militia," *Military Affairs*, XXIII (Winter, 1959–1960), 194–197.

Illinois river near present-day Peru. Three brigades of mounted troops were organized, headed by generals Alexander Posey, Milton K. Alexander, and James D. Henry, with each brigade having a spy battalion. Altogether these militia numbered more than 3,000, and with the regular infantry and Dodge's rangers the total army in the field was about 4,000.[23]

☆

The delay in operations against Black Hawk irked the War Department. It was an election year and failure to bring Black Hawk to terms would embarrass the administration. Expenses moved far beyond the original estimates, and the War Department wrote to Atkinson: "Some one is to blame in this matter, but upon whom it is to fall, is at present unknown to the Department."[24]

President Jackson was determined to force a successful conclusion to the war. To do so he moved over the head of Atkinson, who was commanding on the spot, and over the head of General Gaines, commanding the Western Department at Louisville, in whose department the conflict was raging, and on June 16, 1832, ordered Brevet Major General Winfield Scott to assume the general conduct of the war. At the same time he issued orders for the concentration in the theater of war of all the troops that could be spared from the seacoast, the lakes, and the lower Mississippi. Nine companies of artillery, equipped as infantry, were drawn from Fort Monroe and Fort McHenry and from the harbor defenses of New York. Nine more companies of infantry were ordered from the posts on the Great Lakes. To these were added a detachment of more than 200 recruits from the recruiting rendezvous in New York. In all about 1,000 troops were dispatched to Chicago. In addition, two companies from Baton Rouge moved up the Mississippi to Atkinson's headquarters.[25]

[23] The exploits of the Illinois militia are emphasized in Thomas Ford, *A History of Illinois from Its Commencement as a State in 1818 to 1847* (Chicago, 1854). This book called forth rebuttals by Wisconsin partisans, such as Peter Parkinson, "Strictures upon Gov. Ford's History of the Black Hawk War," and Charles Bracken, "Further Strictures on Gov. Ford's History of the Black Hawk War," *Wisconsin Historical Collections*, II (1856), 393–401, 402–414.

[24] Acting Secretary of War John Robb to Atkinson, June 12, 1832, quoted in Hagan, *Sac and Fox Indians*, p. 169.

[25] Report of Alexander Macomb, November, 1832, *House Executive Document* No. 2, 22 Congress, 2 session, serial 233, pp. 60–61. An excellent account of Scott's troop movement to Chicago with the difficulties encountered is in Charles W. Elliott, *Winfield Scott: The Soldier and the Man* (New York, 1937), pp. 259–273. See also Stevens, *Black Hawk War*, pp. 242–253.

Scott was an ideal man for the task set for him. He was an able soldier and an officer well fitted to win the respect and cooperation of regulars, volunteers, and settlers alike. President Jackson and Secretary of War Cass were confident that he would quickly bring the unsavory affair to a decisive and successful conclusion. Scott began at once with great speed to assemble the troops. The passage of the soldiers from Fort Monroe to Chicago, a travel distance of 1,800 miles, took only eighteen days, a speed, according to General Macomb, "which is believed unprecedented in military movements."

The rapid troop movement, unfortunately, was frustrated by forces beyond Scott's control, and none of the troops sent to Chicago saw action in the field against Black Hawk. They met instead another invader, an epidemic of the dread Asiatic cholera, which worked its way down from Canada and was spreading swiftly across the country as Scott and the troops started west. Two cases developed on Scott's ship at Detroit, and within days the command was incapacitated. Sick and dying were left at Detroit and at Fort Gratiot, as the expedition moved on. The attacks seemed to have subsided, but as the ships entered Lake Michigan another outbreak occurred, and by the time Chicago was reached on July 10, an officer and fifty-three privates were dead and eighty more seriously ill. In all more than 200 men succumbed to the cholera, and Scott dared not move into the field with his troops lest they carry the seeds of death with them. The war was carried to its conclusion by General Atkinson after all, who when notified of Scott's arrival at Chicago was eighty miles away at Lake Koshkonong.

☆

Atkinson had planned to march up the Rock River in pursuit of the British band as soon as the new levy of militia was organized, but diversionary operations by Black Hawk and 200 of his warriors near Galena delayed his start. Finally, on June 28, Atkinson moved out of his headquarters camp at Dixon's Ferry up the left bank of the Rock.

The retreating Indians continued to stay out of reach, leaving no clear indications of their goal. On July 2 the army arrived at the outlet of Lake Koshkonong. There were fresh signs of the Indians, but no one was found beyond a few stragglers. Black Hawk's band had disappeared into the wilderness, and the advancing army after two weeks of discomfort and with supplies running dangerously low had accomplished nothing. The campaign to all appearances was a failure, and Atkinson saw his army disintegrate as many of the volunteers, including Governor Reynolds, departed for home. If he could not soon overtake the British band, Atkinson realized that the campaign might well extend into the winter.

Black Hawk, however, was having troubles of his own. His supplies were exhausted. The old men and women and children, a serious impediment to a retreating army, fell by the wayside in increasing numbers. The weakhearted allies among the Winnebagos, Kickapoos, and the Potawatomis deserted. Black Hawk's position was growing desperate. "The great distance to any settlement, and the impossibility of bringing supplies therefrom, if any could have been obtained, deterred our young men from making further attempts," Black Hawk wrote. "We were forced to dig *roots* and *bark trees*, to obtain something to satisfy hunger and keep us alive! Several of our old people became so much reduced, as actually to *die with hunger!*"[26] With Atkinson's army again on the move, the Indian chief feared encirclement. He decided, thereupon, to head for the Wisconsin River, descend it to the Mississippi, and find refuge at last west of the Mississippi.

Black Hawk was not able to carry out his plan of escape without detection. On July 9, Atkinson had ordered the militia brigades of Henry and Alexander to Fort Winnebago for supplies and had sent Dodge with his troops on the same mission a day later. At the portage the commanders got word from a party of Winnebagos about the whereabouts of the fugitive band. Alexander decided to follow the letter of his orders from Atkinson and return directly to the general's headquarters. Henry and Dodge decided instead to seek out Black Hawk's location. On July 18 they came across the trail of the British band and the next day enthusiastically set out in pursuit. The Indians' trail ran west from the headwaters of the Rock River to the Four Lakes and then slightly northwest to the Wisconsin River, which was reached by the Americans on July 21.[27]

Here occurred the "Battle of Wisconsin Heights." The Indians, having been overtaken by the Americans, fired into their ranks in an

[26] *Black Hawk: An Autobiography*, ed. Jackson, p. 153.

[27] The relative importance of Dodge and Henry in these operations is discussed in William T. Hagan, "The Dodge-Henry Controversy," *Journal of the Illinois State Historical Society*, L (Winter, 1957), 377–384. Hagan concludes that "to Henry Dodge must go the greenest laurels." For more details on Henry, see Frank E. Stevens, "A Forgotten Hero: General James Dougherty Henry," *Illinois State Historical Society Transactions for the Year 1934*, pp. 77–120.

attempt to delay the pursuit as a crossing was made. Leaving their horses behind, the Americans forced the Indians down into the high grass of the river bottom, but as night was approaching and the Indians were sheltered by a rim of trees along the river, Dodge and Henry decided to break off action and rest their troops until morning.

The delay was all that Black Hawk needed. In a maneuver of great daring and skill he moved his warriors and their accompanying dependents, who were in a weakened and desperate condition, across the Wisconsin in makeshift rafts and canoes. Black Hawk had been dealt a heavy blow, but he won a tactical victory in crossing the river under such conditions in the face of a superior force.[28] If Henry and Dodge had crossed the river in pursuit the morning after the battle, they could undoubtedly have overtaken the Indians and ended the campaign. Instead they chose to recuperate for a day, and the Indians were spared to prolong the misery of their flight.

While the volunteer army rested fitfully through the night, Black Hawk made another attempt to surrender. He sent his lieutenant Neapope to describe the pitiful condition of the women and children and to propose that the band be permitted to retire to the west of the Mississippi, where they would remain at peace. Neapope appeared before the camp at dawn and in a loud voice proclaimed his message in the Winnebago tongue. Unfortunately, the Winnebago interpreters were no longer in the camp, and the whites failed to comprehend the surrender offer. They feared that the voice signaled another Indian onslaught.

In the morning after the surrender offer, Henry and Dodge marched their command about twenty miles south to the Blue Mounds, where they were joined in the evening by Atkinson and the regulars and part of Alexander's brigade. The next day the combined forces marched to Helena, where preparations were made for crossing the Wisconsin. Atkinson picked a command of 400 regulars under Colonel Taylor and detachments of the mounted volunteers of Henry, Dodge, Posey, and

[28] The number of casualties sustained by the Indians in the battle is not known, and the reports vary widely. Black Hawk himself claimed a "loss of only six men." *Black Hawk: An Autobiography*, ed. Jackson, p. 155. Henry Dodge, in his report to Atkinson on July 22, said: "Our loss was one man killed and eight wounded; from the scalps taken by the Winnebagoes, as well as those taken by the whites, and the Indians carried from the field of battle, we must have killed forty of them. The number of wounded is not known; we can only judge from the number killed that many were wounded." Quoted in Stevens, *Black Hawk War*, p. 219. John A. Wakefield asserted: "We have learned since the battle, that we killed sixty-eight of the enemy, and wounded a considerable number; twenty-five of whom, they report, died soon after the battle." Stevens, *Wakefield's History of the Black Hawk War*, p. 113.

Alexander, 1,300 men in all, for his final assault on the fleeing Indians. By noon of July 28 his column was across the river, but Black Hawk now had a five-day lead and was fleeing through difficult country that was entirely unknown to the whites.

The Indians were in increasingly serious condition. There was a desperate need of horses to speed their flight, yet they were forced to slaughter their mounts for food. Corpses of Indians found by the whites along the trail gave evidence of starvation, while discarded traps and kettles and blankets indicated that the retreat had become a rout. No delaying action was taken by the Indians to slow down their pursuers, and by evening of July 31, the army was only twenty miles behind the desperate Indians.

On August 1 the remnants of the British band, now numbering no more than 500, arrived at the Mississippi about two miles below the mouth of the Bad Axe River. No means were at hand for crossing the Mississippi, and Black Hawk advised going up the river to hide among the Winnebagos, but few paid attention to his counsel. Most busied themselves in an attempt to improvise rafts or canoes for the crossing of the river. A few managed to reach the western bank, when to the dismay of the Indians the steamboat "Warrior" appeared, returning from a mission to Wabasha's village to engage Sioux warriors for the campaign against the Sacs and Foxes. The Indians raised white flags and sought to surrender, but their actions were misinterpreted and, with both whites and Indians jittery and unable to communicate with each other, another battle ensued. The troops on the steamboat opened fire on the Indians, who scattered for shelter and returned the fire. Twenty-three Indians were lost during the two-hour exchange, when the "Warrior" withdrew to Prairie du Chien for more fuel.

Black Hawk with a few faithful followers moved out of the camp at night north along the Mississippi. Others managed to cross the river under cover of darkness, but most waited until dawn. Then Atkinson's regulars and the volunteer brigades caught up with them. The nearly defenseless Indians were driven to the river bottoms and in the confusion women and children were killed indiscriminately with the braves, since it was hard to distinguish the warriors from others in the band. The retreating Indians then were met by the "Warrior," back from the Prairie, and the battle became a massacre. An estimated 150 Indians were killed, thirty-nine women and children were taken prisoner. Atkinson's losses were comparatively small.

Atkinson loaded his prisoners and the wounded on the steamboat and moved down to Fort Crawford, electing not to pursue Black

Hawk. Some of the Sacs and Foxes made it across the Mississippi, but before they could reach a refuge with Keokuk, they were cut down by Wabasha and his Sioux warriors, who returned with sixty-eight scalps. It was a pathetic ending.

☆

General Scott, as soon as he was convinced that the cholera was subsiding, left the troops at Chicago under the command of Colonel Abraham Eustis, and on July 29 with his staff and a small escort set out across the prairies for Galena, which he reached on August 3. On the 7th he arrived at Fort Crawford and took over the command from Atkinson. He discharged the volunteers, sending them back to Dixon's Ferry to be mustered out. Then he moved his own headquarters to Rock Island and was joined there by Eustis and the remnants of his force. The regular troops who had been sent in for the campaign were ordered back to their respective posts.

Before Atkinson turned over his command to Scott and headed down for Jefferson Barracks and his family, he had posted rewards for the capture of Black Hawk and other leaders of the British band. Neapope was the first received, turned in by Keokuk at Rock Island. Black Hawk and the Prophet were captured by a party of Winnebagos near the Wisconsin Dells and delivered to the Indian agent at Prairie du Chien. Black Hawk asked to be released to join Keokuk, but he and his two sons and the Prophet and his son were turned over to Colonel Zachary Taylor at Fort Crawford, who sent them to Jefferson Barracks in charge of a young lieutenant named Jefferson Davis.[29]

General Atkinson was praised by General Scott at the conclusion of the war: "The persevering ardor both of the general & the troops under unusual difficulties & privations, richly merited the success which has been won."[30] But, in fact, the war had not been anything

[29] Black Hawk was kept in irons at Jefferson Barracks, but in the spring of 1833 he, his son, the Prophet, Neapope, and two others were taken east to see President Jackson. The Indians were imprisoned briefly at Fort Monroe, then returned to the West, making a somewhat triumphal tour of eastern cities in the process. Black Hawk lived out his life in peaceful retirement. He died on October 3, 1838. See Black Hawk: An Autobiography, ed. Jackson, Introduction, pp. 1–18, and Cole, I Am a Man—The Indian Black Hawk, pp. 234–274.

[30] Scott to Secretary of War Cass, August 10, 1832, quoted in Black Hawk: An Autobiography, ed. Jackson, p. 29. Zachary Taylor's judgment was less favorable; see "Zachary Taylor and the Black Hawk War," ed. Holman Hamilton, Wisconsin Magazine of History, XXIV (March, 1941), 305–315.

to be proud of. It need never have begun had there been honorable dealing with the Indians and a firm policy toward both Indians and whites. Squatters had been allowed to violate treaty obligations by invading the Sacs in their ancient lands before the area had been sold by the government. An earlier concentration of regular troops on the upper Mississippi might have kept the Indians better in check, and a less cautious commander than Atkinson might have successfully stopped the movement of Black Hawk's band up the Rock River before hostile acts had occurred. The shameful violation of the flag of truce by Stillman's volunteers precipitated open warfare just as Black Hawk had decided to surrender. Again at the Wisconsin and at the Bad Axe attempts of the Indians to surrender were misunderstood or rejected by the whites. It was "a bloody and costly contest, characterized on our part by heartlessness, bad faith, and gross mismanagement."[31]

The Black Hawk War was the last Indian war in Illinois or Wisconsin. The Sacs and Foxes were crushed, and a large block of their land west of the Mississippi was taken from them, "partly as indemnity for the expenses incurred, and partly to secure the future safety and tranquillity of the invaded frontier."[32] The lesson of the defeat was not lost on other tribes. The Winnebagos, especially, were humbled in spirit and never resumed the mischief-making and arrogant tone that had marked their existence east of the Mississippi.

The garrisons of regular troops on the lakes and the Mississippi were reduced to normal size and hardly an Indian scare disturbed the tranquility sought by the Black Hawk treaty. The attention of the army was directed to newer areas, and the rich lands of northern Illinois and southern Wisconsin, discovered and advertised by the soldiers of the Black Hawk War, were filled by pioneer farmers.

[31] This is the conclusion of Reuben Gold Thwaites, "The Story of the Black Hawk War," *Wisconsin Historical Collections*, XII (1892), 263–264. There seems little reason to amend it.

[32] Treaty of Rock Island, September 21, 1832, Kappler, *Treaties*, pp. 349–351. The land ceded is shown in Royce, *Indian Land Cessions*, Plate 24, Cession 175.

TWELVE

Mounted Troops for the West

IN THE decade of the 1820's, as American settlement pressed westward toward the prairies and as enterprising American traders began to venture out more boldly across the Great Plains, contacts with the western Indians multiplied, and a new element came to the fore in military planning—the need for a cavalry service. Responsible spokesmen in the army and in the War Department, frequently enough egged on by western frontiersmen and their elected representatives, began an ever-increasing cry for congressional authorization for mounted troops to cope with the mounted Indians of the expanding West. The United States had had no mounted regular troops since the War of 1812, and the guarding of the nation had been accomplished by infantry and artillery troops, stationed at strategic spots along the seaboard and the interior waterways, which served as the main channels of communication and troop movement.

The first concerted effort for a change in the defense arrangements came from Missouri, which entered the Union in 1821 and did not mean to let anything stand in the way of rapid economic development. A great part of the state's economic well-being came from the trade of its merchants in the West. The Missouri River and Rocky Mountain fur trade had already centered long at St. Louis, and in the 1820's new riches appeared on the western horizons, as Mexico, having won her independence from Spain at the same time that Missouri became a state, opened up Santa Fe for trade with the Americans.

Beginning with the party of William Becknell in 1821, who opened in that year the route from the Arkansas River through Raton Pass to Santa Fe and in the next year pioneered a shorter, 780-mile route along the Cimarron River, which became the chief artery of the trade, increasing numbers of wagons made the trip from Independence or some other jumping-off point on the Missouri River. The rich caravans on the prairies invited Indian attack, and the early parties were occasionally molested by the roving bands. By 1824 the Missourians had begun to think of military protection for the traders, nor were they loath to unite their personal economic concerns with ideas of national honor. Attacks by the Indians, one trader declared, would be considered not merely "private injury, but a *public wrong*, a *national insult*, and one which will bring down upon the heads of the guilty, the strong arm of national power."[1]

The first proposals were in terms of new military posts, to be established along the trail, since it was easier to envisage a mere extension of existing methods than a change to new. The Indian agent of the Osages and Delawares, Richard Graham, when interviewed by the Senate Committee on Indian Affairs early in 1824, recommended the establishment of a post at or near the mouth of the Little Arkansas River. Any position on the Arkansas below that point, he argued, would be too far from the trail to afford much protection.[2] In April of that year Fort Gibson was established some eighty miles up the Arkansas from Fort Smith, but it was too far from the route of the traders to give them any direct aid, and the War Department continued to consider the matter. General Atkinson in November, 1825, asserted that the great bend of the Arkansas would be the best site for a Santa Fe Trail post, but he did not recommend the erection of a fort there because of the expense of supplying the troops and the already overextended services of the small regular army. Under the existing military establishment, such a post anyway would be "limited and circumscribed, unless horses were provided and kept in readiness to mount eighty or one hundred men, to escort the caravans, and make fresh pursuit of depredating parties of Indians." He felt, further-

[1] *Missouri Republican*, February 28, 1825, quoted in Henry H. Goldman, "A Survey of Federal Escorts of the Santa Fe Trade, 1829–1843," *Journal of the West*, V (October, 1966), 505. F. F. Stephens, "Missouri and the Santa Fe Trade," *Missouri Historical Review*, X (July, 1916), 233–262, tells of the agitation in Missouri for federal protection of the Santa Fe trade. A recent study of defense of the Santa Fe trade is Leo E. Oliva, *Soldiers on the Santa Fe Trail* (Norman, Okla., 1967). See also the older work by Henry P. Beers, "Military Protection of the Santa Fe Trail to 1843," *New Mexico Historical Review*, XII (April, 1937), 113–133.

[2] Report of Richard Graham, February 10, 1824, *American State Papers: Indian Affairs* (2 vols., Washington, 1832–1834), II, 452.

more, that caravans of thirty or forty men should be able to protect themselves against the Indians.[3]

Very similar views were expressed in 1827, after further prodding by Missouri, by the commanding general, Jacob Brown, who reiterated the difficulties of supplying a post so far in advance of settlement. If the importance of the project was considered such that it had to be undertaken nevertheless, he recommended a post manned by two companies of infantry supported by two additional companies of mounted troops who could range out onto the prairies. "*Without* the full force which I have suggested, especially of the cavalry arm," he concluded, "I should judge it inexpedient to make the movement. *With* this force it is presumed that the trade might be secured and the garrison placed beyond the probable reach of disaster."[4] A proposal submitted to the Senate by Missouri Senator Thomas Hart Benton came to nothing, however.

The immediate need for such a post along the trail had not been convincingly demonstrated, but the erection of Fort Leavenworth as a replacement for Fort Atkinson provided in fact an important fort at the beginning of the trail. The site of the new fort, occupied in May, 1827, by Colonel Henry Leavenworth and a detachment of the Third Infantry, was an ideal one. Located on the border between the white settlements and the Indian country, the fort could offer not only escorts for the Santa Fe caravans but also a jumping-off point for fur traders and emigrants going into the Rockies and beyond.[5]

Agitation came also from other sections of the frontier. On March 25, 1828, Joseph Duncan, a veteran of the War of 1812 and a member of the House of Representatives from Illinois, wrote to General Gaines about a proposed resolution for an inquiry into the expediency of raising eight companies of "volunteer mounted gunmen, to be stationed on the western frontier of the United States." A single company of such troops on the western frontier, he asserted, "would be a surer protection to the inhabitants of that region against sudden attacks and depredations, and a greater terror to the savages, than an entire regiment on foot or stationed in forts upon the line." With true frontier

[3] Report of Henry Atkinson, November 23, 1825, *ibid.*, pp. 656–657.
[4] Report of Jacob Brown to Secretary of War Barbour, January 10, 1827, *American State Papers: Military Affairs* (7 vols., Washington, 1832–1861), III, 615.
[5] For the history of Fort Leavenworth, see Elvid Hunt, *History of Fort Leavenworth, 1827–1927* (Fort Leavenworth, Kan., 1926), and George C. Reinhardt, "Fort Leavenworth Is Born," *Military Review*, XXXIII (October, 1953), 3–8.

spirit, Duncan preferred volunteers rather than regular troops for his new corps—"Young men of vigor and enterprise, reared in the western country, acquainted with the Indian artifice and their mode of warfare, full of pride and patriotic spirit"—who could not only be formidable to the enemy but would be well received by the citizens among whom they would operate. Duncan was willing to disband one regiment of regular infantry to make way for his volunteers.[6]

Gaines's reply was sympathetic but cautious. He agreed about the usefulness of such troops but did not want to disband any infantry in place of them, preferring to keep the infantry at such centers as Jefferson Barracks "to take the field and co-operate with the mounted riflemen whenever the frontier is menaced by large bodies of Indians." He emphasized the importance of mounted men to keep the western Indians in check and liked Duncan's term "volunteers," making it plain, however, that he would want them to be subject to regular army discipline and to enlist for no less than a two- or three-year period.[7]

General Alexander Macomb, too, had listened sympathetically to the demands of the westerners for mounted protection, and in his annual report of November, 1828, he recognized the need for something more than the traditional infantry on the open plains that stretched from the western settlements to the Mexican frontier and to the Rocky Mountains. His suggestion was to mount some of the light infantry companies as rangers so that they could quickly overtake and punish the mounted Indians who inflicted depredations on the whites.[8]

☆

The happenings of the year on the Santa Fe Trail gave new emphasis to these recommendations, for 1828 marked an end to the relative peace on the plains between the Santa Fe traders and the Indians. In one party returning from New Mexico in August, two traders who separated from the main party were killed by the Indians while they slept. In retaliation, the trading party killed half a dozen Indians in the next band they encountered, without inquiring to see whether or not they were the guilty ones. When the train reached the Arkansas River,

[6] Joseph Duncan to Gaines, March 25, 1828, *American State Papers: Military Affairs*, III, 828.

[7] Gaines to Duncan, March 27, 1828, *ibid.*, pp. 828–829.

[8] Report of Alexander Macomb, November, 1828, *ibid.*, IV, 5–6.

Indians drove off nearly a thousand mules and horses. A second smaller train, leaving Santa Fe on September 1, lost one man killed by the Comanches and all its livestock. Abandoning their cargo, the men felt lucky to escape the rigors of the plains with their lives.

A new memorial of the Missouri legislature for military aid against such dangers[9] and attempts of Senator Benton to force some legislation through Congress failed, but the Missourians did not give up. They petitioned the new President, Andrew Jackson, for aid, and it was soon forthcoming, although not in just the form they wanted. Troops of the Sixth Infantry were ordered to escort the spring caravans as far as the international boundary at the Arkansas crossings and to await the return of the caravans in the fall.[10] They were not mounted troops, but perhaps they would quiet the agitation until Congress could act.

Four companies of the Sixth at Jefferson Barracks were detailed for the task. Embarking on the steamboat "Diana" on May 5, 1829, they arrived at Fort Leavenworth ten days later and were organized by Major Bennet Riley for their march to Round Grove, the place of rendezvous with the traders.[11] The caravan was assembled and waiting when Riley and his infantrymen arrived on June 11. It was a small caravan, only sixty men and thirty-six wagons under command of Charles Bent, the famous western trader, and with the troops marching ahead, it made an uneventful trip to the crossings. Here the troops stopped at the limits of American territory, as the traders proceeded to cross the Arkansas and make their way through Mexican territory to Santa Fe. Only a few miles beyond the Arkansas, however, the train

[9] Memorial of the Legislature of Missouri, December, 1828, *Senate Document No. 52*, 20 Congress, 2 session, serial 181.

[10] Major Bennet Riley's infantry expedition of 1829 on the Santa Fe Trail is the subject of Otis E Young, *The First Military Escort on the Santa Fe Trail, 1829: From the Journal and Reports of Major Bennet Riley and Lieutenant Philip St. George Cooke* (Glendale, Calif., 1952). An excellent brief account is in Otis E Young, *The West of Philip St. George Cooke* (Glendale, Calif., 1955), pp. 33–54. Major Riley's report is printed in *Senate Document No. 46*, 21 Congress, 1 session, serial 192, and in *American State Papers: Military Affairs*, IV, 277–280. A corrected version of the report and Riley's journal of the expedition are in Fred S. Perrine, ed., "Military Escorts on the Santa Fe Trail," *New Mexico Historical Review*, II (April, 1927), 178–192, III (July, 1928), 265–300. Young, *First Military Escort*, pp. 61–62, asserts that both documents were actually the work of Lieutenant Philip St. George Cooke.

[11] As an economy measure, Riley experimented with the use of oxen to haul the supply wagons of the command instead of the usual draft animals of the plains, horses and mules. As the wagons were lightened, the oxen then would be slaughtered for food, and some of them were paid for from subsistence rather than quartermaster funds. Riley allowed the commander of the caravan, Charles Bent, to take some of the oxen all the way to Santa Fe. The experiment worked out well, and the next year Bent went out on his own with oxen.

was attacked by Kiowas and Comanches, who killed one of the traders before being driven off by cannon fire. Messengers hastened back to Riley, beseeching him to come to the aid of the party. The major crossed the Arkansas and escorted the train deeper into Mexican territory, onto prairies where the Indian danger was less. On July 13 Riley again parted company with the traders and returned to the Arkansas.

Riley's weeks spent on the Arkansas waiting for the return of the traders were marked by several Indian forays; the red men in the course of the summer killed four soldiers and drove off stock. The inability of his infantrymen to cope with the mounted Indians gave considerable grief to the commander. "Think what our feelings must have been to see them going off with our cattle and horses, when if we had been mounted, we could have beaten them to pieces," he wrote in his report; "but we were obliged to content ourselves with whipping them from our camp."[12]

By the beginning of October Riley was planning for his return to Fort Leavenworth. There were no signs of the caravan, and the major decided not to wait any longer, for his troops were inadequately clothed for the cold weather. On October 11 the command began its march for home and had hardly gotten under way when advance riders from the caravan were sighted in the rear. Riley waited for the traders to pull up, listened to their tales of Indian harassment on their way to Santa Fe, exchanged hospitality with the commander of the Mexican troops who had escorted the train on its return from Santa Fe, and on October 14 continued his march with the caravan as far as the Little Arkansas. The troops reached Fort Leavenworth at seven o'clock in the evening on November 8, weary and cold, but with a military flourish. "The battalion marched into garrison in Column of Companies, by field music; it was received with a Salute of 15 guns."[13]

☆

Secretary of War Eaton had cautiously repeated the recommendation for mounted troops in the West in his report of November 30, 1829,[14] and the publication of Major Riley's report and the stir in the newspapers about the dangers on the trail began to awaken Congress. Move-

[12] Report of Riley, *New Mexico Historical Review*, II, 185.
[13] *Ibid.*, III, 300.
[14] Report of Secretary of War Eaton, November 30, 1829, *American State Papers: Military Affairs*, IV, 154.

ment, however, was very slow, as the Congress began to assemble opinions about the expediency of the move. General Macomb in a reply to an inquiry from the House reported in January, 1830, that there were sufficient troops on the borders of Louisiana, Arkansas, and Missouri, if only an appropriation could be obtained to mount eight companies of them as a "disposable force." This was the only way, he asserted, "by which the Indians can be properly punished, should they molest the inhabitants who are settled on the frontiers, or who may be engaged in the trade with Santa Fe."[15] In April Quartermaster General Thomas S. Jesup added his forceful argument for mounted troops with an analogy between the plains and the ocean that occurred to many of his contemporaries:

> As well might we leave the defence of our maritime frontier and the protection of our foreign commerce to the artillery stationed on our seaboard. The means of pursuing rapidly and punishing promptly those who aggress, whether on the ocean or on the land, are indispensable to a complete security; and if ships-of-war are required in one case, a mounted force is equally so in the other. Were we without a navy, piracies might be committed with entire impunity, not only on the high seas, but in our very harbors, and within view of our forts. So, without a mounted force on the frontier south of the Missouri, the Indian, confident in the capacity of his horse to bear him beyond the reach of pursuit, despises our power, chooses his point of attack, and often commits the outrages to which he is prompted either by a spirit-of-revenge or a love of plunder in the immediate vicinity of our troops; and the impunity of the first act invariably leads to new aggressions.[16]

The Senate passed a bill in 1830, but the bill died in the House, and further information and opinions were sought. In his annual report of November 21, 1831, Secretary of War Cass called for mounted troops to prevent such disturbances as had occurred in the upper Mississippi valley between the Sacs and Foxes and the Menominees and such agitation as that caused by Black Hawk's British band.[17] Then in February, 1832, Cass supplied the Senate with a massive dossier of reports from Indian traders, Indian agents, and other knowledgeable men in the West about the needs for military protection of the western trade. He himself summed up the testimony in no uncertain terms:

[15] Macomb to Eaton, January 4, 1830, *ibid.*, p. 219.
[16] Jesup to A. H. Sevier, April 5, 1830, *ibid.*, p. 371.
[17] Report of Secretary of War Cass, November 21, 1831, *ibid.*, p. 716.

It is quite time that the United States should interpose, efficaciously, to put a stop as well to the depredations of the Indians against our own citizens, as to their hostilities among themselves. If this be not soon done, the evil will increase, and it will be more and more felt as the Indians east of the Mississippi migrate to the country west of that river. We shall be bound by every principle of duty to protect them; and as they will be placed in juxtaposition with the savage tribes of the plains, unless we restrain the latter, a perpetual border warfare will be the consequence.[18]

☆

Congress hesitated to satisfy these demands by instituting a full-fledged regular cavalry. The old bugaboo of a standing army was not easily dispelled, and an aristocratic mounted arm seemed a special threat to American democratic life. There was, too, the almost perpetual need for economy in the service, which precluded the heavy expenses supposed to attend the outfitting and maintaining of mounted troops. It was part of the American republican myth that if swift moving soldiers were ever needed on the frontier, they could be quickly supplied as citizen volunteers.

The myth was made of sturdy stuff, and the annual pleadings of the secretaries of war had fallen largely on deaf ears in Congress. Little by little, however, the realization came that mounted troops were absolutely essential in dealing with the Indians. The futile attempts of infantry to cope with the Indians of the Great Plains was manifested by the experience of escorts on the Santa Fe Trail in 1829, and the growing restlessness of the Indians in the upper Mississippi valley that culminated in the Winnebago outbreak of 1827 and the Black Hawk War of 1832 helped drive the point home. A conclusion much harder to swallow was that militia troops, mounted or not, were unsatisfactory.

Congress breached the barrier of prejudice against a regular cavalry by a half-way measure—the formation of a battalion of 600 mounted rangers.[19] These troops, authorized on June 15, 1832, were to be organ-

[18] Report of Cass, February 8, 1832, *Senate Document* No. 90, 22 Congress, 1 session, serial 213, p. 4.

[19] The definitive account of the Mounted Ranger Battalion is Otis E Young, "The United States Mounted Ranger Battalion, 1832–1833," *Mississippi Valley Historical Review*, XLI (December, 1954), 453–470. A briefer and less satisfactory story is found in Louis Pelzer, *Henry Dodge* (Iowa City, 1911), 67–79. Grant Foreman, *Pioneer Days in the Early Southwest* (Cleveland, 1926), pp. 85–108, tells of the activities of the ranger companies at Fort Gibson.

ized as six companies, made up of one-year volunteers who were to arm
and equip themselves and provide their own horses. One dollar a day
was set as the full compensation for their services and the use of their
arms and horses. Each company was to have a captain and three lieutenants, ten noncommissioned officers, and one hundred privates, which
made the units larger than those of the regular army.[20] The short term
of enlistment and the provision that each man furnish his own arms
and mount made the rangers really a special class of militia rather than
regular troops.

To head the rangers with the rank of major, President Jackson
appointed Henry Dodge, issuing the commission on June 21, while
Dodge was adding to his military fame in the campaign against Black
Hawk. Neither the men nor the officers were men of regular army
experience. Only Dodge, and two of the captains, Jesse Bean and
Nathan Boone, had ever experienced military command before, and the
ranks were filled with sturdy sons of pioneer families, for whom the
discipline of military life had to be a rather relaxed sort. Charles J.
Latrobe, who accompanied an expedition of rangers west from Fort
Gibson in 1832, praised the men, with a somewhat ambiguous compliment:

> To keep the file, when on march; never to leave the camp without
> express permission, and to obey the general orders, was all that the
> captain required: and considering this to have been the case, I am
> astonished at the almost unbroken good conduct of such a number
> of young men, brought together with no very definite idea of what
> it was to submit their will to that of a superior, or of the necessity
> which teaches men the value of discipline. As it was, we heard and
> saw nothing bordering on either insubordination or coercion. They
> were for the most part sons of substantial farmers and settlers, and
> some certainly accustomed from their earliest years to study the craft
> of a backwoodsman.[21]

The lack of military finesse showed most plainly in their dress. The
"uniform" was the responsibility of each soldier, and the motley appearance struck all who saw them. Washington Irving, who viewed the
rangers at Fort Gibson, found them "a heterogeneous crew; some in
frock coats made of green blankets; others in leathern hunting shirts,

[20] "An Act to authorize the President to raise mounted volunteers for the
defence of the frontier," June 15, 1832, *U. S. Statutes at Large*, IV, 533.
[21] Charles J. Latrobe, *The Rambler in North America, MDCCCXXXII–
MDCCCXXXIII* (2 vols., New York, 1835), I, 149–150.

but the most part in marvellously ill cut garments, much the worse for wear, and evidently put on for rugged service."[22]

The first companies organized—those of Captains Boone, Lemuel Ford, Benjamin V. Beekes, and Jesse B. Browne—were directed to Fort Armstrong, where Dodge was located following the Battle of the Bad Axe. They arrived at the end of August, too late to aid in the campaign against the Sacs and Foxes, and just in time to be hit by the cholera epidemic that had followed Scott's troops from Chicago. Fifteen men of the batallion lost their lives from the disease, and the morale of the new organization was severely impaired. Dodge ordered his troops from the stricken area, while he himself set up headquarters at Dodgeville. The companies of Browne and Beekes were assigned to the Eastern Department and were given the task of patrolling the frontiers in Illinois and Wisconsin, but they passed several uneventful months in winter quarters at Danville, Illinois.[23]

The Winnebagos, despite the lesson of Black Hawk's defeat, were restive, and the rangers were directed to overawe them and force them to move from the Rock River country to north of the Wisconsin River, as they had agreed to do in the treaty at Rock Island in September.[24] When Dodge held a council with the Winnebagos in June, 1833, the presence of the rangers gave force to the major's words, and the Indians handed over the murderers of a party of whites and prepared to cross the Wisconsin.

The year of enlistment for these troops was now about up, and the rangers clamored to be mustered out. Most of Browne's company was discharged at Dodgeville on July 23, 1833. A few men whose enlistments had not yet run out patrolled northern Illinois against the Potawatomis, and then they, too, were mustered out. On July 7 Captain Beekes's men had already departed unceremoniously for their homes in Indiana.

The rangers sent to the southwestern frontier played a more active role. There the peaceful relations that had existed between the plains Indians and the Santa Fe traders had been upset, and the infantry escort of 1829 had not secured a permanent peace. So Captain Matthew Duncan's company of rangers was directed to report at Fort Leaven-

[22] *A Tour on the Prairies (The Crayon Miscellany* No. 1, Philadelphia, 1835), pp. 28–29.

[23] "Reminiscences of Wisconsin in 1833," *Wisconsin Historical Collections*, X (1888), 231–234, written by a member of Captain Browne's company.

[24] Charles J. Kappler, ed., *Indian Affairs: Laws and Treaties* (2 vols., Washington, 1904), II, *Treaties*, pp. 345–348.

worth to take part in a new escort expedition. The rangers arrived at the post in February, 1833, and in May were united with a company of the Sixth Infantry under the command of Captain William N. Wickliffe. The escort troops, all commanded by Wickliffe, moved out of Fort Leavenworth on May 22 to rendezvous with the traders at Council Grove. The escort marched ahead of the caravan, which was carrying goods of an estimated value of $100,000, as far as the Arkansas River. There the parties separated, the traders continuing on to Santa Fe, the soldiers returning directly to Fort Leavenworth. The march had been uneventful and the rangers had performed their duty satisfactorily, but they were assigned no more tasks and quietly waited out the end of their enlistment at the fort.

The best publicized of the rangers' exploits were those that centered at Fort Gibson. Captain Bean's company, which arrived at the post on September 14, was quickly put to work by Colonel Matthew Arbuckle, the post commander, who had been directed to keep the new unit busy. He ordered Bean to take his company on an exploratory junket through the lands to be used for Indians removed from east of the Mississippi. "The principal object of your command," Arbuckle directed, "is to preserve peace between the different Tribes on this Frontier with which the United States have Treaties: and between these and our Citizens: and you will, as far as may be in your power, protect our Citizens and the Indian Tribes referred to, from injury from the Pawnee and Commanchee Indians." If possible Captain Bean was to entice the Pawnees and Comanches to a council at Fort Gibson in the spring. Armed with these directives and a suggested route of travel, the rangers left Fort Gibson on October 6, 1832.[25]

They had been gone only two days when a whole new dimension to the expedition opened up unexpectedly. There arrived at Fort Gibson, on October 8, Henry L. Ellsworth, one of the three commissioners appointed by Secretary of War Cass to examine the lands provided for the removal of the eastern Indians.[26] Ellsworth had in tow a distinguished companion, whom he had met enroute and whom he had invited to join him in his tour—Washington Irving. Arbuckle arranged

[25] Documents dealing with the expedition are printed in the introduction to *The Western Journals of Washington Irving*, ed. John Francis McDermott (Norman, Okla., 1944).
[26] Secretary of War Cass's instructions to these commissioners, July 14, 1832, are in *House Executive Document* No. 2, 22 Congress, 2 session, serial 233, pp. 32–37. The report of the commissioners, February 10, 1834, is in *House Report* No. 474, 23 Congress, 1 session, serial 263, pp. 78–103.

to send Ellsworth and his guest with a detachment of rangers to overtake Bean's main company and accompany them on their tour of the prairies, and on October 10 the party departed from Fort Gibson. When they arrived at the Verdigris Trading Post, just west of the fort, they were joined by Charles Latrobe, who was also interested in touring the West and who would be another witness to give an account of the expedition to the public.[27] The party returned to Fort Gibson without mishap, and the men built themselves winter quarters six miles from the fort.

The companies of Boone and Ford, which had been assigned to the Western Department, delayed their departure from Fort Armstrong until September 24, after the cholera epidemic had subsided, and they did not reach Fort Gibson until November 22. They built winter quarters for themselves a half mile below the fort.

In the spring of 1833 a new expedition into the Southwest was set on foot. Lieutenant Colonel James B. Many of the Seventh Infantry detachment at Fort Gibson was ordered to march through the territory between the north fork of the Canadian River and the Red River, to drive out any Comanche or Wichita Indians found there, and to persuade the chiefs to come to Fort Gibson to treat concerning the safety of the Indians emigrating from the East to this new land. Colonel Many organized the three ranger companies and two infantry companies from the post, and the groups assembled on May 7. The expedition was marked by the kidnapping of George B. Abbay, a private from Boone's company, by a band of Wichita Indians near the Red River. The detachment went in pursuit for twelve days, but to no avail, and the unfortunate soldier was later killed by his captors.[28] Thus the march ended in failure. Instead of impressing the Indians with the strength of the United States Army, the troops had shown their impotence in the face of Indian impertinence.

When the rangers returned to Fort Gibson in July, their thoughts turned to their discharge, not to further Indian escapades. By September all three companies were dissolved. It was the end of the experiment.

[27] All three of the civilian travelers left accounts of the trip: Henry L. Ellsworth, *Washington Irving on the Prairie, or A Narrative of a Tour of the Southwest in the Year 1832*, ed. Stanley T. Williams and Barbara D. Simison (New York, 1937); Irving, *A Tour on the Prairies;* Latrobe, *Rambler in North America*, I, 136–190.

[28] An account of the affair, together with a pathetic letter written to the Secretary of War by the murdered private's father, is found in Foreman, *Pioneer Days in the Early Southwest*, pp. 105–107.

The one-year provision had proved inefficient. The cooperation between rangers and regulars did not work well because of the different spirit of the two groups toward military discipline. Even the cost factor seemed to come out wrong, for the Adjutant General reported that the rangers cost $153,942.50 more than the estimated cost of a regular regiment of dragoons.[29] But the rangers should not be written off as a failure. They softened congressional opposition to regular mounted regiments by demonstrating that mounted troops were absolutely necessary in the West, while at the same time disclosing the weaknesses of volunteer service. The rangers were the essential step toward the dragoons.[30]

☆

Pressed on by Secretary of War Cass and unable to ignore any longer the exigencies of western defense, the House Committee on Military Affairs reported a bill on December 28, 1832, to change the corps of rangers into a regiment of dragoons, and on March 2, 1833, the "Act for the more perfect defense of the frontiers" became law.[31]

Henry Dodge, the major of the rangers, was to be commander of the dragoons with the rank of colonel. Stephen Watts Kearny of the Third Infantry was commissioned lieutenant colonel, and Richard B. Mason, major. Captains Boone, Browne, and Duncan were transferred from the rangers, while a number of other officers came from the infantry service, among them Captain Clifton Wharton, Captain Edwin V.

[29] Adjutant General Roger Jones submitted a comparative tabulation in the Report of the Secretary of War for 1832. The dragoon regiment had only 502 men, compared with the 660 men of the ranger battalion. *American State Papers: Military Affairs*, V, 40.

[30] Young, *Mississippi Valley Historical Review*, XLI, 470.

[31] Report of House Committee on Military Affairs, December 28, 1832, *American State Papers: Military Affairs*, V, 126; *U. S. Statutes at Large*, IV, 652. There are accounts of the recruitment and organization of the dragoons and the first winter at Fort Gibson in Young, *The West of Philip St. George Cooke*, pp. 67–74; Louis Pelzer, *Marches of the Dragoons in the Mississippi Valley: An Account of Marches and Activities of the First Regiment United States Dragoons in the Mississippi Valley between the Years 1833 and 1850* (Iowa City, 1917), pp. 13–33; and Pelzer, *Henry Dodge*, pp. 80–89. Full personal accounts are in Philip St. George Cooke, *Scenes and Adventures in the Army: or, Romance of Military Life* (Philadelphia, 1859), pp. 197–225, and [James Hildreth], *Dragoon Campaigns to the Rocky Mountains: Being a History of the Enlistment, Organization, and First Campaigns of the Regiment of United States Dragoons; Together with Incidents of a Soldier's Life, and Sketches of Scenery and Indian Character* (New York, 1836), pp. 2–212. Both Cooke and Hildreth, however, have a very critical tone.

Sumner, and the irrepressible recorder of dragoon scenes, Lieutenant Philip St. George Cooke. This had been an obvious arrangement and followed the specific recommendation of Dodge, who wrote to the Adjutant General: "I wish the regiment to be efficient and useful to the country; and taking a part of the officers from the regular army, who understand the first principles of their profession, and uniting them with the Ranging officers, who understand the woods' service, would promote the good of the service."[32]

Dodge was responsible for dissolving the rangers, while Kearny and other officers attended to the recruiting of the dragoons. There were to be ten companies, each with a captain and two lieutenants, four noncommissioned officers, two buglers, a farrier, a blacksmith, and sixty privates. The law provided that the regiment of dragoons be recruited in the same manner and be given the same provisions and allowances as the other soldiers making up the peace establishment, but it was clear from the start that the new regiment was considered to be and expected to be something special. The recruits were to be native citizens, between the ages of twenty and thirty-five, "whose size, figure, and early pusuits may best qualify them for mounted soldiers."[33] The recruits were to be sought from all parts of the country so that there would be no sectional tone, and since the corps was to be elite, their own regimental officers were detailed to recruiting duty.

There can be no doubt that the regiment attracted especially good men compared with the regular infantry and artillery troops of the day. The spirit of adventure summoned forth by the enthusiasm of the officers played its part. Lieutenant Cooke, on recruiting duty in western Tennessee, engaged "some hardy recruits, whose imaginations inflamed them with the thoughts of scouring the far prairies on fine horses, amid buffalo and strange Indians," and he could not dissuade them from their romantic views of dragoon life by relating discouraging particulars of the service.[34] Captain Sumner's recruits in New York State were described in the press as "the finest looking raw recruits we ever saw; all New Yorkers, selected by capt. S himself from the northern and western counties of the state, within the age of 25 years, and as nearly as possible 5 feet 8 inches in height. All possessing a good English education and men of strictly correct habits." The demo-

[32] Dodge to Roger Jones, August 28, 1833, in William Salter, "Henry Dodge: Part IV, Colonel, U. S. Dragoons, 1833–6," *Iowa Historical Record*, VII (April, 1891), 103.

[33] *Ibid.*, p. 102.

[34] Cooke, *Scenes and Adventures in the Army*, p. 201.

cratic atmosphere of the age crept into the notice, however, as the item continued: "Such youth, with such a commander, who permits of no menial service from any member of his detachment, and fares as they fare, cannot fail to prove useful and become an ornament to the service."[35]

The traveler Charles J. Latrobe, who saw a good deal of the military in his roaming through the country, looked upon the dragoon recruits most favorably; they were, he wrote, "distinguished from the rag-tag-and-bob-tail herd drafted into the ranks of the regular army, by being for the most part picked, athletic young men of decent character and breeding. They were all Americans, whereas the ordinary recruits consist either of the scum of the population of the older states, or of the worthless German, English, or Irish emigrants."[36] One of the first dragoons described the earliest recruits as men who "in point of talent, appearance and respectability, perhaps never were surpassed in the history of military affairs." Many expected to be treated as cadets at West Point; others thought they would not have to submit to the regular army discipline; and the recruits were told that "it would disgrace a dragoon even to speak with an infantry soldier."[37]

The new recruits gathered during the summer and early fall at Jefferson Barracks.[38] Here the officers hoped to whip them into shape, but it was not an easy task. Cooke spoke of the "amount of labor, care, and vexation, attendant upon the task of enlisting, organizing, disciplining, and instructing a new corps,—of producing order from chaos." But the difficulties were multiplied with the mounted troops, for whom no manuals existed and whose officers themselves had to learn the tactics before they could instruct the troops.[39]

Unfortunately, things just did not measure up. Many of the high-minded "elite" corps did not appreciate the drudgery of camp life and the necessity of military discipline. The clothing and equipment that the recruits expected to receive did not arrive on time, and the men who had left their own clothes at home began to suffer from the cold.

[35] *Niles' Weekly Register*, XLIV (August 24, 1833), 422.
[36] Latrobe, *Rambler in North America*, II, 317–318. See also the favorable comments in [Charles F. Hoffman], *A Winter in the West* (2 vols., New York, 1835), II, 106–108.
[37] Hildreth, *Dragoon Campaigns*, pp. 44–45.
[38] See Pelzer, *Marches of the Dragoons*, pp. 13–22, for an account of the travels to Jefferson Barracks and the first days there. There are valuable first-hand accounts in Cooke, *Scenes and Adventures in the Army*, and Hildreth, *Dragoon Campaigns*.
[39] Cooke, *Scenes and Adventures in the Army*, pp. 204–205.

It was a normal tangle, which exasperated the officers, but it led many of the new men to desert.[40]

Then in November came the order for the transfer of the first five companies to Fort Gibson. The march in the winter and the establishment of a cantonment, Camp Jackson, at Fort Gibson, where sufficient supplies and equipment were unavailable, did little to improve the morale of the men. Lieutenant Cooke excoriated the motives behind the move. Just when there had been some hope of training the corps before it would be assigned to duty, half of it was marched out to some impossible station. He blamed the order on political considerations—*"that the corps having been raised for the defence of the frontier, would be disbanded if it remained inactive so far in the interior as Jefferson Barracks"*—and began to wonder whether the government had "constancy of purpose equal to the creation of a single regiment of dragoons."[41] The remaining companies, enlisted during the course of the winter and organized at Jefferson Barracks, were then marched to Fort Gibson, where they arrived in June.

The dragoons, despite the problems of their initial organization, proved their value at once. The regular cavalry arm made it possible for the United States to patrol the prairies and the plains and thus to make effective American authority in the West.

[40] Hildreth, *Dragoon Campaigns*, pp. 44–51, is especially strong on the disaffection of the men.

[41] Cooke, *Scenes and Adventures in the Army*, pp. 220–221. Pelzer, *Marches of the Dragoons*, pp. 23–33, describes the winter quarters at Camp Jackson.

THIRTEEN

Indian Removal from the Southern States

CHANGING government policy toward the Indians directly affected the deployment of military troops in the West. Changes that came gradually could be met by similar adjustments in army plans, but major or sudden shifts profoundly altered the task of the army and led to unforeseen and sometimes shattering results. Of such a fundamental nature was the policy known as Indian Removal, adopted in the 1820's and carried out in the 1830's. Indian Removal forced a rethinking of defense plans for the western frontier, the establishment of new military posts in regions once thought too far afield, the unsavory task of removing peaceful Indians from their ancestral homes by military force, the demand for a new cavalry arm of the service, and ultimately a drawn-out war in the wilderness of Florida, which seriously drained the resources as well as the patience of the army and the nation.

The whites had from the first contacts with the Indians pushed the red men back. The European view, set forth with conviction by such eminent and widely followed jurists as Emmerich de Vattel, was that nature intended the lands to be used. The fact that the Indians move "their habitations through these immense regions, cannot be taken for a true and legal possession," according to Vattel; "and the people of Europe, too closely pent up, finding land of which these nations are in no particular want, and of which they make no actual and constant use, may lawfully possess it, and establish colonies there."[1] Such theories of outright dispossession of Indian claims, however shadowy, did not

---

[1] Emmerich de Vattel, *The Law of Nations; or Principles of the Law of Nature, Applied to the Conduct and Affairs of Nations and Sovereigns* (Northampton, Mass., 1820), chapter XVIII, paragraph 209, pp. 158–159.

persist in United States policy. The tribes were treated as Indian "nations," and negotiations were held between government commissioners and Indian chiefs for matters of war and peace, trade, and extinguishment of land titles. The Indians after the Revolution were briefly told that they had been on the losing side and should expect to give up territory as reparations, but the Indians did not seem to heed, and Secretary of War Knox, rather than risk a renewal of open conflict, which the infant nation could ill afford, agreed to a new policy, in which the Indians were paid for the lands they had been forced to part with. There was a steady reduction of Indian holdings as the line dividing the Indian country from white lands was edged to the West in successive treaties.[2]

This sort of continual restriction of Indian holdings caused no special crisis at first. The West was a limitless expanse in the direction of the setting sun, with plenty of room for the Indians to continue their way of life undisturbed if they did not choose to be absorbed immediately by the white man's civilization.

The serious frontier disturbances in the Northwest Territory and in the region south of the Ohio River in the 1790's, however, were clear indications that the aborigines were going to be a hindrance to white advance into the garden lands of the Ohio and Mississippi valleys. Moreover, despite the sanguine view of humanitarians that the Indians would quickly assume the white man's culture when they learned about it and saw its advantages, the Indians were slow to come around. Indeed it seemed as though, perversely, the Indians took on the vices of the whites—notably a vicious attachment to strong liquor—without enthusiastically accepting Christian civilization. The deleterious effects of white contacts on the Indians appeared more and more to outweigh the benefits, and it was not long before prudent men were suggesting that perhaps, after all, the contacts should be restricted if not completely ended until the Indians were better able to withstand the onslaught of civilization.

To both groups—those avid for Indian lands and those genuinely concerned for Indian welfare—the Louisiana Purchase of 1803 appeared as a godsend. If all the lands east of the Mississippi could be opened up for white settlement, the vast lands west of the great river could be

_____

[2] For a discussion of the formation of American Indian policy, see Francis Paul Prucha, *American Indian Policy in the Formative Years: The Indian Trade and Intercourse Acts, 1790–1834* (Cambridge, Mass., 1962), and William T. Hagan, *American Indians* (Chicago, 1961), pp. 1–91.

reserved for the Indians. Instead of just gradually pushing the Indians back, dispossessing them without any exchange beyond the niggardly annuities provided in the treaties of cession, the talk now turned to "removal." The term signified an exchange of lands; the Indians in return for their eastern lands would be given equal lands in the West, and the government would in addition pay the moving expenses, take care of the Indians for a set period in their new homes, and protect them from white contacts and their evil effects.[3]

This noble dream of moving the Indians to a permanent reservation west of the Mississippi originated with Thomas Jefferson in 1803, and before the end of his administration gentle pressure was put upon the Cherokees to exchange their lands for others in the West. Some of the Cherokees did go west, at first only to hunt but then to settle, and by 1816 more than 2,000 of them had emigrated. In 1817 the Cherokees agreed to exchange some of their lands in North Carolina for land in Arkansas, and by 1819 6,000 of them had moved west.

Even this minor relocation caused military problems. The warlike Osages made the occupation of the Arkansas region dangerous for both whites and incoming eastern Indians, and a state of perpetual warfare developed as the Osages stole the cattle of the emigrant Indians, who in turn defended their possessions by force. The United States had guaranteed to protect the Indians in their new western homes, and petitions from the frontiersmen for protection forced the extension of the western military frontier into this new Southwest. The treaty of 1817 with the Cherokees had given the United States the right to establish military posts, roads, and trading factories, and General Jackson, commander of the Division of the South, was directed to establish a fort on the Arkansas River where the boundary of the Osage country crossed the river. Major Stephen H. Long and Major William Bradford, to whom the work was assigned, left Fort Belle Fontaine late in September, 1817, ascended the Arkansas River 450 miles to the mouth

[3] The fullest account of the origin and development of the policy of Indian removal is Annie H. Abel, "The History of Events Resulting in Indian Consolidation West of the Mississippi," *Annual Report of the American Historical Association for the Year 1906* (Washington, 1908), I, 233–450. A briefer discussion is in Prucha, *American Indian Policy in the Formative Years*, pp. 224–249. The story of the actual emigration of the eastern Indians is told thoroughly, but with perhaps too critical a tone, in Grant Foreman, *Indian Removal: The Emigration of the Five Civilized Tribes of Indians* (Norman, Okla., 1932), and Foreman, *The Last Trek of the Indians* (Chicago, 1946). A very readable account, which emphasizes the injustices done to the Indians, is Dale Van Every, *Disinherited: The Lost Birthright of the American Indian* (New York, 1966).

of the Poteau River, and selected a site there for a new garrison, which was named Fort Smith. The new fort brought a measure of peace. Warnings from the military commander quieted the Indians, but periodically raids and killings occurred. Detachments of troops from Fort Smith were frequently sent out to remove white intruders from Indian lands or to prevent Indian threats from turning into full-scale hostilities.[4]

In 1821 serious war broke out between the western Cherokees and the Osages. While Governor James Miller of Arkansas Territory was willing to let the Indians fight it out among themselves as long as the whites were not endangered by the conflict, Major Bradford tried earnestly but unsuccessfully to prevent the outbreak. Additional troops were ordered into the area by General Gaines, and 250 men of the Seventh Infantry under Colonel Matthew Arbuckle arrived at Fort Smith on February 26, 1822. With this augmented force on the ground, renewed efforts were undertaken to establish peace between the tribes and to end the depredations on the white settlers. With the combined efforts of Governor Miller, Colonel Arbuckle, and the Indian agent, a treaty between the two tribes was signed on August 9, 1822. Even this formal agreement was short-lived, however, and the frontier continued in turmoil, as the influx of whites increased the chances of Indian-white conflicts. The settlers spilled over the western boundary of Arkansas Territory, and to catch up with them the western boundary of the Territory on May 26, 1824, was moved to a line running due south from a point forty miles west of the southwest corner of Missouri.

The War Department found it expedient to move as well the military garrison standing guard on the boundary. In April, 1824, the garrison of Fort Smith moved up the Arkansas to a new site, on the east side of the Neosho or Grand River about three miles from its confluence with the Arkansas. The new post, named Fort Gibson, had an immediate effect on the Osages, who surrendered members of the tribe accused

---

[4] The founding of Fort Smith is described in Edwin C. Bearss, "In Quest of Peace on the Indian Border: The Establishment of Fort Smith," *Arkansas Historical Quarterly*, XXIII (Summer, 1964), 123–153. For the interaction of emigrant Indians, plains Indians, and white settlers in the West and the relations of the army with all three, see Grant Foreman, *Indians & Pioneers: The Story of the American Southwest before 1830* (New Haven, 1930), and the same author's *Advancing the Frontier, 1830–1860* (Norman, Okla., 1933). The latter work gives good information on the establishment of the military posts in the Southwest. See also Carolyn Thomas Foreman, "William Bradford," *Arkansas Historical Quarterly*, XIII (Winter, 1954), 231–241, which describes Bradford's activities at Fort Smith, 1817–1824.

of murders of whites and who undertook to organize a form of government under the guidance of Colonel Arbuckle and the Osage agent. Fort Gibson remained the key military establishment in the Southwest as the eastern Indians in the 1830's moved into the lands beyond the Mississippi in large numbers.[5]

At the same time Fort Towson was established in the Red River country near the mouth of the Kiamichi River.[6] The situation was in some respects similar to that which had led to Fort Gibson. The Choctaws of Mississippi on October 18, 1820, had ceded a large part of their lands in Mississippi in exchange for a tract of land in Arkansas Territory and what is now Oklahoma, stretching from the Arkansas and Canadian rivers to the Red River. The Choctaws, as had the Cherokees, tangled with the Plains Indians and were considered a threat by the white settlers who were on the Indian lands. In addition, an investigation of the Red River region by Lieutenant Richard Wash in the fall of 1823 had supplied information about the smuggling of slaves on the border and the flagrant violations of the laws governing trade with the Indians. In March, 1824, General Scott ordered one company of infantry from Fort Jesup and the one that had been stationed at Sulphur Fork to protect the factory there to move to a site near the mouth of the Kiamichi River. The troops, under the command of Major Alexander Cummings, reached the area in May and established Fort Towson on a site about six miles north of the Red River and about the same distance east of the Kiamichi. The troops were actively engaged in maintaining peace among the tribes and in attempting to enforce the laws against squatters and whiskey dealers, until the post was temporarily abandoned in 1829 because of quieting of Indian dangers and problems with the supply line up the Red River—but to the cries of indignation, of course, from the white settlers.

☆

Meanwhile in the East the agitation for Indian removal gathered momentum. The wish of eastern states to be freed of the embarrass-

[5] For the history of Fort Gibson and the military activities there in the early days, see Grant Foreman's works, *Fort Gibson: A Brief History* (Norman, Okla., 1936); *Advancing the Frontier*, pp. 35–76; *Indians & Pioneers, passim;* and "The Centennial of Fort Gibson," *Chronicles of Oklahoma,* II (June, 1924), 119–128.

[6] On Fort Towson, see Foreman, *Advancing the Frontier*, pp. 83–93; Foreman, *Indians & Pioneers*, pp. 202–212; and William B. Morrison, "Fort Towson," *Chronicles of Oklahoma,* VIII (June, 1930), 226–232.

ment of having independent groups of natives within their boundaries was added to the selfish drive of whites who coveted the rich lands of the Indians. Over all was the ever louder voice of humanitarians, who looked upon removal as the last hope of survival for the tribes, who were rapidly degenerating under white pressures.[7]

When James Monroe became President in 1817, he and Secretary of War John C. Calhoun began to work for a full-scale removal policy. The large groups of aboriginal tribes surrounded by growing white settlements appeared to them to be a striking anomaly, which could be solved in only two ways, either by a full adoption by the Indians of the American culture or removal to the open West, where the Indians could work out their destiny unimpeded by white problems and machinations. Monroe in his message to Congress of December 2, 1817, asserted his belief that "the earth was given to mankind to support the greatest number of which it is capable, and no tribe or people have a right to withhold from the wants of others more than is necessary for their own support and comfort."[8] Problems of land tenure could be solved only if the Indians would move to the Trans-Mississippi vastnesses, and Monroe and Calhoun were sure that the ultimate good of the Indians demanded an end to their independent status within the states. They urged Congress to take some action.

These theoretical speculations were strengthened by practical developments in Georgia, Alabama, and Mississippi. The Cherokees in Georgia had well-developed farms, able political leadership, and a government modeled on that of the United States. They had, furthermore, the abiding attachment of Indians for their ancestral lands, and they were determined not to be dislodged by the force of Georgia or by the inducements of the federal government. The Georgians insisted that the Indian titles be extinguished, as the United States had agreed to do in a compact signed with Georgia in 1802, and the governor of Georgia censured the federal government for having been so slow to fulfill its part of the bargain. President Monroe refused to be intimidated and declared that the United States had no obligation to remove the Indians against their will, but his own opinion grew more set that only wholesale removal would solve the difficulties.

In a special message to Congress on January 27, 1825, Monroe made a new plea, based largely on a report drawn up by Calhoun. The Sec-

---

[7] Prucha, *American Indian Policy in the Formative Years*, pp. 224–249.

[8] James D. Richardson, ed., *A Compilation of the Messages and Papers of the Presidents* (10 vols., Washington, 1896–1899), II, 16.

retary of War had divided the eastern Indians into two groups. Those living in the northern parts of Indiana and Illinois, in Michigan, New York, and Ohio he wanted to move into the region west of Lake Michigan and north of Illinois. The southern tribes and those in southern Illinois and Indiana—the great bulk of the eastern Indians—he would grant "a sufficient tract of country west of the State of Missouri and Territory of Arkansas." The exact locations would be determined only after consultation with the Indians.[9] Accepting these proposals, Monroe asked Congress for "a well-digested plan" which would satisfy both the Cherokees and the Georgians, one that would shield the Indians from impending ruin and advance their happiness. The essence of Monroe's proposal was the institution of a government in the West for the Indians that would preserve order, prevent the encroachment of whites, and further the process of civilization. "It is not doubted," Monroe asserted, "that this arrangement will present considerations of sufficient force to surmount all their prejudices in favor of the soil of their nativity, however strong they may be." He asked Congress to pledge the solemn faith of the United States to fulfill the arrangements he suggested.[10] But despite considerable support the bills introduced in Congress failed to pass, and Monroe ended his term without any of the legislation he had called for. John Quincy Adams, adopting the removal scheme for want of a better solution, fared no better.[11]

When Andrew Jackson became President, the advocates of removal took on new life, for Jackson was convinced that if the Indians did not move west they should be made subject to the states in which they resided. His views gave courage to the Georgians, who extended the laws of the state over the Cherokee lands, as did Alabama and Missis-

[9] Calhoun report of January 24, 1825, *American State Papers: Indian Affairs* (2 vols., Washington, 1832–1834), II, 542–544.

[10] Richardson, *Messages and Papers of the Presidents*, II, 280–283.

[11] I have avoided using the term "Permanent Indian Frontier" to describe the line marking off the Indian country west of Arkansas and west and north of Missouri, where the Indians from the East were ultimately settled. Many historians have adopted the term, apparently from Frederick L. Paxson's *History of the American Frontier, 1763–1893* (Boston, 1924), which has a chapter so entitled and a map on which the "Permanent Indian Frontier" is boldly inscribed with a dotted line. It is doubtful, however, if the men who originated and carried out the removal policy thought specifically in such terms. A "Western Territory" for the Indians was proposed by some, but Congress refused to establish it. See Annie H. Abel, "Proposals for an Indian State, 1778–1878," *Annual Report of the American Historical Association for the Year 1907* (Washington, 1908), I, 87–104. The army men who drew up plans for western defense in the 1830's seem to have had a much vaguer (or perhaps broader) notion about what the "frontier" was than Paxson's line would suggest.

sippi later over those of the Choctaws and Creeks. A new removal bill stirred up bitter debate in Congress and in the press. The advocates of removal met strong opposition from men who supported the rights of the Indians to their present lands, but on May 28, 1830, the bill became law by a small margin.[12] The legislation did not threaten to remove the Indians by force but merely gave the President authority and money to negotiate treaties of removal with the tribes. Jackson's views were known, however, and pressure to negotiate treaties with the southern tribes began at once.

By September 27, 1830, the United States commissioners, Secretary of War Eaton and John Coffee, had negotiated a treaty with the Choctaws (the Treaty of Dancing Rabbit Creek).[13] The Choctaws ceded to the United States the entire country owned by them east of the Mississippi and were given three years to move to the domain designated for them west of Arkansas. Amid considerable dissension from members of the nation who opposed the cession and crowded in upon by unscrupulous whites who prematurely entered the ceded lands, the Choctaws prepared to emigrate. They sent out an exploring party to look over the new land and were supplied an escort of twelve men by Colonel Arbuckle at Fort Gibson to protect them from roving Plains Indians.[14]

The army now began to play its role in the removal process. The military posts in the West became focal points for the protection and assistance of the emigrating bands. In 1831 the entire Seventh Infantry was concentrated at Fort Gibson and four companies of the Third Infantry under Major Stephen W. Kearny reestablished Fort Towson. These positions, General Macomb noted, "are favorable to the affording of facilities to the Indians emigrating . . . and at the same time to the protection of them in their new abodes from the attacks of unfriendly tribes, and those wild hordes with whom they are as yet unacquainted. The troops there stationed will also, by their presence and force, exert a beneficial influence over the conduct of the various

[12] *U. S. Statutes at Large*, IV, 411–412.

[13] Charles J. Kappler, ed., *Indian Affairs: Laws and Treaties* (2 vols., Washington, 1904), II, *Treaties*, pp. 310–319.

[14] Foreman, *Indian Removal*, pp. 19–104; Muriel H. Wright, "The Removal of the Choctaws to the Indian Territory, 1830–33," *Chronicles of Oklahoma*, VI (June, 1928), 103–128. A basic source for the Indian removal of 1831–1833 is the five-volume *Senate Document* No. 512, 23 Congress, 1 session, serials 244–248, a collection of correspondence and disbursing records supplied to Congress by the Commissary General of Subsistence.

tribes, and be instrumental in maintaining harmony and peace among them."[15]

President Jackson placed the responsibility for removal on the Commissary General of Subsistence, George Gibson, but since the enterprise was looked upon as essentially a civilian undertaking, civilian superintendents of emigration were appointed. It was not intended that the military force of the nation should be employed to carry out the removal, yet it was taken for granted that much of the work and the responsibility in the area west of the Mississippi would fall to army officers. There were few others to whom General Gibson could turn for directing the movement of the tribes in that relatively unknown and unmarked area or for the burdensome duty of disbursing the funds and supplies that the United States government had promised the Indians.

Soon after the treaty with the Choctaws had been signed, Gibson ordered Lieutenant Lawrence F. Carter at Fort Gibson to the Kiamichi River, where it was supposed the Indians would settle, and the officer was directed to investigate the resources of the area for furnishing grain and livestock. Another lieutenant at the fort, J. R. Stephenson, was directed to the same area later to meet the emigrants and to procure and issue food to them. He arrived at the Kiamichi in March, 1831, and set about to get supplies, contract for grain, and establish stations from which to issue the rations to the incoming bands.

The Choctaws had requested that a friend of the tribe, George S. Gaines, be allowed to conduct them west, and he was appointed to superintend the collection and removal of the Choctaws as far as the west bank of the Mississippi. There they were to be delivered to Captain J. B. Clark of the Third Infantry, who would lead them the rest of the way. A detachment was ordered to Fort Smith to repair the abandoned buildings, with the idea of making the old fort the principal supply station for the Choctaws. Clark resigned when he foresaw the difficulties attendant on the whole business and was replaced by Captain Jacob Brown of the Sixth Infantry, who supervised the emigration from Little Rock. Lieutenant Gabriel J. Rains was appointed disbursing agent for the Choctaws at Fort Smith.

The emigration of the Choctaws was not without suffering and mismanagement, though the army officers did what they could to ease the

[15] Report of Alexander Macomb, November, 1831, *American State Papers: Military Affairs* (7 vols., Washington, 1832–1861), IV, 717.

journey of the Indians. The settlers in Arkansas were intent on stretching to the limit their profits from the sale of stores, and the supply routes to the Choctaw country were tenuous.

The reopening of Fort Towson had added another reason for improving communications with the region. In answer to the citizens and Indians on the Red River, who were clamoring for a road to connect them with the Arkansas, the War Department authorized the commander at Fort Gibson to furnish troops to build one. Captain John Stuart with a detachment of the Seventh Infantry was assigned to the work and in three months constructed a road from Fort Smith 147 miles to Horse Prairie, some distance above Fort Towson, following the route blazed through the country by a local woodsman.[16]

The mass of Choctaw emigration was completed by the summer of 1833, and by 1834, 12,800 had moved to Indian territory. More than 5,000 of the tribe still remained in Mississippi, but most of these gradually joined their brothers in the West.

☆

The next to be removed were the Creeks, and they caused considerably more trouble for the army.[17]

Some Creeks were already in the West before the Removal Bill of 1830. A treaty of January 24, 1826, had provided for the cession of Creek lands in Georgia for the payment of $217,600 and a perpetual annuity of $20,000.[18] It had provided further that those who wanted to migrate to the West could go out to investigate the land and the government would assign an agreeable piece to them. An exploring party returned with favorable reports, and about 2,400 Creeks moved to the area beyond the Verdigris River.

The Creeks remaining in the East did not want to remove and protested to Washington the operation of Alabama laws over their territory and the intrusion of white settlers on their lands. But their condition steadily worsened and they ultimately agreed to part with their lands, in a treaty of March 24, 1832.[19] The tribe ceded all its lands

16 "Report of Capt. John Stuart on the Construction of the Road from Fort Smith to Horse Prairie on Red River," ed. Carolyn Thomas Foreman, *Chronicles of Oklahoma*, V (September, 1927), 333–347.

17 Foreman, *Indian Removal*, pp. 107–190.

18 Kappler, *Treaties*, pp. 264–268.

19 *Ibid.*, pp. 341–343.

east of the Mississippi. The lands were to be surveyed and each head of a family was allowed to select a half section for use for five years unless he wished to sell it earlier. At the end of five years he could receive a deed for the land if he did not choose to emigrate. The treaty, however, stated bluntly: "The United States are desirous that the Creeks should remove to the country west of the Mississippi, and join their countrymen there," and the government agreed to pay the cost of emigration and subsistence for the Indians for a year. The United States also agreed to "defend them from the unjust hostilities of other Indians."

The provisions of the treaty made it possible for whites to defraud the Indians of their allotments, and the United States' pledge to keep intruders off the lands until the Indians sold their half-sections was not kept. The Creeks soon found themselves beset at every turn by the whites, for whom the treaty was a simple signal to invade the Indians' lands.[20] The whites intimidated the Indians, who looked in vain for the promised protection. The whole Creek nation was in a state of turmoil and bitterness resulting from the premature and illegal action of the whites, and a government attempt to get the Creeks to sign a new treaty that would provide for immediate removal came to nothing. Only a small number migrated in 1834.

Investigation of the frauds was undertaken, and the Indians, hoping that everything would be adjusted satisfactorily, continued their preparations for removal. Prospects looked good until the Indians discovered that the contract for their removal had been let to a company of men who had been active in defrauding them of their lands. The tension on both sides mounted, as destitute Indians sought refuge wherever they could find it, some moving into Cherokee country in Alabama and Georgia. The smoldering situation broke into open fire in the spring of 1836. Georgia militia attacked Creeks who had encamped on Georgia soil, and roving bands of Creeks began to attack and kill the whites and destroy their property.

As the alarming reports reached Washington, Secretary of War Cass issued orders to remove the Creeks as a military measure. He ordered General Thomas S. Jesup to inaugurate a military operation against

---

[20] The story of the frauds is told in Foreman, *Indian Removal*, pp. 129–139. For a detailed study of the Choctaw, Creek, and Chickasaw allotments, see Mary E. Young, *Redskins, Ruffleshirts and Rednecks: Indian Allotments in Alabama and Mississippi, 1830–1860* (Norman, Okla., 1961).

the Indians, subdue them, and force their removal to the West.[21] In this "Creek War" of 1836 several thousand troops were ordered into the Creek country, including 1,103 regulars, 4,755 Georgians, and 4,300 Alabamans. General Winfield Scott, leaving behind his Seminole difficulties in Florida, arrived at Savannah on May 22 and assumed general command of the war. He conferred with the governor of Georgia and with General Jesup and outlined his plan of campaign, which sought to prevent the Creeks from escaping into Florida while the white forces swept the Indians northward to utter defeat.

Scott insisted that no movement begin until he had completed all preparations and had received necessary supplies and equipment. He sent Jesup to Alabama to direct, at the proper moment, the operations of the Alabama militia toward the Creeks on the Chattahoochee River, while he himself would advance toward the same objective from the east. Between them, the two forces would find and defeat the Indians. Before Scott could perfect his preparations, however, Jesup acted on his own against the hostiles. Fearing that he could no longer restrain the militia, who were eager for action as reports of new Indian ravages came in, he moved directly into the heart of the Indian country. In a few days he had located the principal Creek camp and had captured the leader, Eneah Micco, and 300 or 400 of the warriors. The success of the whites quieted the Indians, and Jesup wrote to Scott that he had brought tranquility once more to the frontier. Scott was furious at Jesup's precipitate action and continued with his own plans to round up the Indians who had escaped Jesup's troops. Georgia cavalry met and defeated the fleeing Creeks, and on June 24 Scott reported to the Adjutant General that the war could be considered terminated, although mopping-up operations against scattered bands continued for two weeks in Alabama and Georgia.

The subdued Creeks were now removed to the West. Dejected warriors, handcuffed, chained, and guarded by soldiers, left Fort Mitchell on July 2, followed by wagons and ponies carrying the children and old women and the sick. On July 14 almost 2,500 of the

---

[21] The causes of the Creek War of 1836 and subsequent removal of the Creeks are discussed in Foreman, *Indian Removal*, pp. 140–165. The military strategy and campaign are treated in Charles W. Elliott, *Winfield Scott: The Soldier and the Man* (New York, 1937), pp. 310–321. Letters and reports dealing with the operation are printed in "Proceedings of a Court of Inquiry in the Case of Major General Scott—Delay in Opening and Prosecuting the Creek Campaign," *American State Papers: Military Affairs*, VII, 168–365.

Indians, including 800 warriors, were embarked at Montgomery and conveyed down the Alabama River to Mobile, thence to New Orleans and up the rivers to the western lands of the Creeks. The remainder of the hostiles left Montgomery on August 2. The western Indians, uneasy as the eastern Creeks approached, called for aid from Colonel Arbuckle, who turned to the governor of Arkansas Territory for ten companies of volunteers.

The friendly Creeks soon followed their "hostile" brothers west. One contingent of 2,700, under the leadership of the friendly chief Opothley-holo and in charge of Lieutenant M. W. Batman, began its march on August 1, moving overland from Tallassee to Memphis. A second detachment of over 3,000, conducted by Lieutenant R. B. Screven, followed on August 6. A third group of about 2,000 under Lieutenant Edward Deas moved north to Gunter's Landing and then through Huntsville to Memphis. Deas returned for another party of 2,300, who marched on the south side of the Tennessee River and then west to the Mississippi. A final detachment under Lieutenant J. T. Sprague left Tallassee early in September. In all, 14,609 Creeks had been removed in 1836, including 2,495 enrolled as hostile.[22] A number of Creek warriors, who had enlisted for service in Florida against the Seminoles, were released too late to emigrate in 1836 and followed the next year.

The Chickasaws were the next of the Five Civilized Tribes to sign a removal treaty.[23] The government endeavored to induce this tribe to share lands in the West with the Choctaws, but the Chickasaws refused, since they were outnumbered three to one by the more powerful tribe. A provisional treaty, negotiated September 1, 1830, was never ratified because of this stumbling block, but it served as an opening for whites in Alabama and Mississippi to press into the Chickasaw country. Finally on October 20, 1832, a new treaty was signed.[24] By it the tribe ceded all its lands to the United States and was to decide on a location in the West. A number of exploring expeditions were necessary before a final agreement was made in January, 1837, to purchase land from the Choctaws for the western home of the Chickasaws. The bulk of the Chickasaws emigrated in 1837, and others followed in succeeding

[22] "Statements of the Probable Number of Creek Warriors Engaged in Hostilities Against the United States during the Years 1836 and 1837," *ibid.*, pp. 951–952.

[23] For Chickasaw removal, see Foreman, *Indian Removal*, pp. 193–226.

[24] Kappler, *Treaties*, pp. 356–362.

years. Compared with the Creek war and with the Cherokee troubles to follow, the Chickasaw removal was a comparatively quiet affair.

☆

Of the southern tribes, the Cherokees were the most advanced, the best organized, and (if one excepts the Seminoles) the most determined to resist removal. As they were the focal point of agitation that brought the removal policy into play with the Removal Bill of 1830, so they furnished the most striking example of forced removal.[25] Here the United States Army—regulars and militia—played a significant role.

Jackson's administration hoped to persuade all the Indians to move west by liberal inducements in the way of annuities, financial help in emigrating, schools and other civilization aids, and promises of protection in the West, and Jackson and his Secretary of War were embarrassed by the failure of the Indians to accept the offers. Secretary of War Cass, who replaced Eaton in 1831, repeatedly met with Cherokee delegations and reasserted the President's desire to aid them, pointing out, however, that if the Indians elected to remain in the East they would have to accept submission to state laws. Cass was clearly exasperated by the unwillingness of the Cherokees to depart. "Some strange infatuation seems to prevail among these Indians," he wrote in December, 1832. "That they cannot remain where they are and prosper is attested as well by their actual condition as by the whole history of our aboriginal tribes. Still they refuse to adopt the only course which promises a cure or even an alleviation for the evils of their present condition."[26] Little by little he lost patience with the Cherokees until he told them curtly in 1834 that new discussion with them was useless since the government had not changed its position. A few parties of Indians enrolled for emigration, but the main body of the nation remained adamant.

As conditions among the Cherokees worsened and the government showed no signs of weakening its stand, a group of the Cherokees

[25] Foreman, *Indian Removal*, pp. 229–312; Charles C. Royce, "The Cherokee Nation of Indians: A Narrative of Their Official Relations with the Colonial and Federal Governments," *Fifth Annual Report of the Bureau of Ethnology, 1883–1884* (Washington, 1887), pp. 121–378; James Mooney, *Myths of the Cherokee (Nineteenth Annual Report of the Bureau of American Ethnology, 1897–1898*, Part 1, Washington, 1900), pp. 99–143.

[26] Quoted in Prucha, *American Indian Policy in the Formative Years*, p. 247.

headed by the sub-chief Major John Ridge began to despair of successful resistance and prepared to negotiate for removal. The Cherokees thus split into two factions, that of Ridge and that of John Ross, who led the anti-removal diehards. Delegates from the two rival groups appeared in Washington in February, 1835.

The United States commissioner, the Reverend J. F. Schermerhorn, negotiated a treaty with the Ridge party, which provided for the cession of all the Cherokee eastern holdings. When the treaty was considered by the full council of the nation in October, however, it was rejected. The Cherokees were then directed to appear at New Echota, their capital, in December to negotiate another treaty. They were informed by circulars that all who did not appear for the negotiations would be considered in favor of any treaty drawn up. Despite such threats, only 300 to 500 men, women, and children out of a total population of about 17,000 appeared, yet the treaty making went ahead as scheduled, and on December 29, 1835, a treaty was signed by the Ridge party.[27] Over the protests of the unrepresented majority of the nation, the Senate ratified the treaty by a majority of one vote.

The government at last had a removal treaty with the Cherokees, and a number of treaty Indians began the movement west. But opposition to the treaty from John Ross and his followers did not slacken, and many of them said they preferred to die rather than leave the country.

The general air of dissension within the Cherokee country and the fear that the treaty of New Echota would not be carried out by the mass of the Cherokee nation caused Secretary of War Cass to assign Brevet Brigadier General John E. Wool to the Cherokee country on June 20, 1836.[28] Wool was ordered to ascertain the designs of the Cherokees and to take command of the Tennessee volunteers raised by the governor of Tennessee, who were due to rendezvous at Athens, Tennessee, on July 7. Cass directed him to reduce the Cherokees to submission if they should begin any hostilities and if necessary to call for more troops from the governors of Tennessee, Georgia, and North Carolina.

Wool, whose sympathies lay with the Indians, did not find his task an appealing one. "The whole scene since I have been in this country

[27] Kappler, *Treaties*, pp. 439–449.
[28] Documents concerning Wool's activities in the Cherokee country appear in "Proceedings of a Court of Inquiry Relating to Transactions of Brevet Brigadier General John E. Wool, and Those Under His Command in the Cherokee Country, in Alabama," *American State Papers: Military Affairs*, VII, 532–571.

has been nothing but a heart-rending one, and such a one as I would be glad to get rid of as soon as circumstances will permit," he wrote on September 10, 1836.[29] He anxiously hoped for a force of regular troops to be sent to him that fall, but he received only a curt note from the War Department that "there is no portion of the regular army that can be placed at your disposal." He was told to make use of the volunteers.

When Wool attempted to protect the Indians in the Cherokee country in Alabama, where the oppression of the Indians was particularly notorious, he was charged by the governor and legislature of Alabama with having usurped the powers of the civil tribunals, disturbed the peace of the community, and trampled upon the rights of the citizens. The President referred the charges to a military court of inquiry, which met in Knoxville in September, 1837. The court completely vindicated Wool, but such maneuverings to protect the reputation of the general did nothing to ease the tense situation in the Cherokee country.

Very few Cherokees had departed by May 23, 1838, the ultimate date set for voluntary removal. Nathaniel Smith, as civilian superintendent of emigration, managed to collect and send off a few parties as the deadline neared, a final group embarking on April 5 under the charge of Lieutenant Deas. But it was all too obvious to the War Department that voluntary removal under the terms of the 1835 treaty had failed. Only about 2,000 had gone west, leaving some 15,000 behind. The next step, since John Ross and his chiefs who continued to seek a stay of execution on removal had won no ground, was force.

On April 6, 1838, the Commanding General of the Army ordered General Scott, commanding the Eastern Division, to the Cherokee country "with a view to the fulfillment of the treaty."[30] Orders were issued for the Fourth Artillery and the Fourth Infantry and six companies of dragoons to move from Florida to the agitated area as soon as possible. Scott was authorized, furthermore, to call on the governors of Tennessee, North Carolina, Georgia, and Alabama for militia and volunteer forces not to exceed 3,000 men.

When Scott arrived at the Cherokee agency on the Hiwassee River on May 8, he found a good bit of the groundwork already done, for Colonel William Lindsay with a company of the Fourth Infantry and thirty-one companies of militia (twenty-one of them mounted) had col-

[29] Letter of September 10, 1836, quoted in Mooney, *Myths of the Cherokee*, p. 127.

[30] Scott's part in the removal is treated in Elliott, *Winfield Scott*, pp. 345–355. The documents appear in *House Document* No. 453, 25 Congress, 2 session, serial 331.

lected subsistence in depots and had established twenty-three military posts for the militia, preparatory to rounding up the Indians.[31] Two days after his arrival Scott issued an address to the assembled Cherokee chiefs. "The President of the United States has sent me, with a powerful army, to cause you, in obedience to the Treaty of 1835, to join that part of your people who are already established in prosperity on the other side of the Mississippi," he told them bluntly. He stressed his determination to carry out his orders and pointed to the troops already occupying the Indian country and the "thousands and thousands . . . approaching from every quarter." He urged them to move with haste, thus to spare him "the horror of witnessing the destruction of the Cherokees."[32]

On the 17th Scott issued Order No. 25, a long directive to his troops. He announced his staff and set up three military districts to expedite the collecting of the Indians, and in the remainder of the order instructed the soldiers (still largely militia at the time) about the humanity and mercy with which they were to carry out their duties:

> Considering the number and temper of the mass to be removed, together with the extent and fastnesses of the country occupied, it will readily occur that simple indiscretions, acts of harshness, and cruelty on the part of our troops, may lead, step by step, to delays, to impatience, and exasperation, and in the end, to a general war and carnage; a result, in the case of these particular Indians, utterly abhorrent to the generous sympathies of the whole American people. Every possible kindness, compatible with the necessity of removal, must, therefore, be shown by the troops; and if, in the ranks, a despicable individual should be found, capable of inflicting a wanton injury or insult on any Cherokee man, woman, or child, it is hereby made the special duty of the nearest good officer or man instantly to interpose, and to seize and consign the guilty wretch to the severest penalty of the laws. . . .

> By early and persevering acts of kindness and humanity, it is impossible to doubt that the Indians may soon be induced to confide in the army, and, instead of fleeing to mountains and forests, flock to us for food and clothing. . . .

> It may happen that Indians will be found too sick, in the opinion

[31] Mooney, *Myths of the Cherokee*, p. 221, identifies and gives the location of thirteen stockaded "forts"—five in Georgia, six in North Carolina, and one each in Tennessee and Alabama.

[32] *House Document* No. 453, 25 Congress, 2 session, serial 331, pp. 11–12.

of the nearest surgeon, to be removed to one of the depots. . . .
In every such case, one or more of the family or the friends of the
sick person will be left in attendance, with ample subsistence and
remedies, and the remainder of the family removed by the troops.
Infants, superannuated persons, lunatics, and women in a helpless
condition, will all, in the removal, require peculiar attention, which
the brave and humane will seek to adapt to the necessities of the
several cases. . . .[33]

The soldiers were to be stationed at the centers set up by Colonel
Lindsay, going out daily in squads to bring in the Indians. When large
groups had been collected, they were forwarded under guard to the
main collecting points at the Cherokee agency on the Hiwassee (Calhoun, Tennessee), and on the Tennessee River at Ross's Landing
(present-day Chattanooga) and Gunter's Landing (Guntersville, Alabama), whence they would proceed under the direction of the superintendent of emigration to the west.

Scott began operations in Georgia on May 26, and by the 30th he
reported an estimated 2,500 persons brought in. The Indians, he said,
"finding that they have been approached kindly, begin to come in
voluntarily." Five days later 4,000 Georgia Indians had been collected
and were on their way to Ross's Landing. Within another week Scott
expected Georgia to be clear of Indians except for a few families or
refugees who had fled to the mountains. The operations that were to
have begun in North Carolina, Tennessee, and Alabama on June 5
were now postponed for a week—to encourage voluntary emigration
and to prevent too rapid an accumulation of emigrants at the depots.

The regular troops of the infantry and artillery were reporting in
little by little, although a serious shortage of company officers irked the
general, and on June 17 Scott gave orders for discharging the volunteer troops. He praised the work of the soldiers, including the state
volunteers, in the distressing job of removing the often-destitute Indians from their homes. He did not seem to be aware of any serious
breaches of the high code of behavior he had set in his Order No. 25,
and he asserted that removal was carried out in a considerate manner.

But, inevitably, another side of the story also appeared. An anonymous letter of July 24, 1838, published in *Niles' Register* asserted:
*"In most cases the humane injunctions of the commanding general were
disregarded.* The captors sometimes drove the people with whooping

[33] *Ibid.*, pp. 8–11.

and hallowing, like cattle through rivers, allowing them no time even to take off their shoes and stockings. Many, when arrested, were not so much as permitted to gather up their clothes. The scenes of distress exhibited at Ross's Landing defy all description."[34] An oft-quoted account, set down more than half a century after the events on the basis of the reminiscence of participants, gives a picture of grief and pathos:

> Families at dinner were startled by the sudden gleam of bayonets in the doorway and rose up to be driven with blows and oaths along the weary miles of trail that led to the stockade. Men were seized in their fields or going along the road, women were taken from their wheels and children from their play. In many cases, on turning for one last look as they crossed the ridge, they saw their homes in flames, fired by the lawless rabble that followed on the heels of the soldiers to loot and pillage.[35]

The whole affair, of course, was not a happy one, and Scott did what he could to relieve the misery of the Indians gathered in the concentration areas awaiting embarkation west.

As the Indians were marched to the river landings, they were organized into detachments, each accompanied by a military officer, a corps of assistants, and two physicians. The first party of about 800, under Lieutenant Deas, left Ross's Landing on June 6; a second party of 875 under Lieutenant R. H. K. Whiteley departed on the 13th; on the 17th a third contingent of 1,070 started out. These initial groups were joined by other small bands brought in along the early stages of the journey. About 3,000 of the captive Indians had departed when Scott called a halt to the exodus for the rest of the hot summer season. The remaining Indians were held in the concentration camps, the largest camp being at the agency on the Hiwassee. Here the Cherokee leaders gave active cooperation and helped maintain order. Scott retained only two regiments of regular troops (the Fourth Infantry and the Third Artillery), as protection for the camps rather than to guard the captives, and the rest of the regulars were sent back to Florida or ordered to the posts on the Canadian border.

The Indian leaders made an agreement with Scott whereby they themselves would take charge of the emigration when it began again in the fall, and the operation became a project of the Cherokee nation.

---

[34] *Niles' National Register*, LIV (August 18, 1838), 385.
[35] Mooney, *Myths of the Cherokee*, p. 130.

Officers were appointed by the Cherokee Council, and a quasi-military order was maintained on the march. When the drought that had further delayed the departure was broken in October, the caravan began its march overland to Nashville and Memphis. They numbered about 13,000, including Negro slaves, and carried along whatever of their belongings they had managed to save. The Indian leaders themselves were responsible for the good behavior of the nation. No military escort was deemed necessary. The journey, with its late start, occurred during the hardest months of the year, and this "Trail of Tears" reaped a heavy harvest of deaths.

The removal of the Cherokees was an unpleasant episode in the history of the army on the frontier, yet it was not of the army's making, and the officers and the soldiers acquitted themselves well. The foremost historian of Indian removal, Grant Foreman, who on the whole strongly condemns the treatment of the Indians in the removal process, evaluates the army's part in the most laudatory terms:

> A conspicuous saving grace of this sorrowful story is the fidelity and skill with which the regular army officers and soldiers in the field discharged their unwelcome duties in connection with the removal. In nearly all instances they devoted themselves indefatigably and sympathetically to the sad task of removing the Indians with as much expedition and comfort as possible within the provisions made by their superiors in Washington. In this they contrasted sharply with the volunteer soldiers and a large class of political, civilian employees and especially those of local attachments and prejudices, and the contractors whose purpose was to realize as much profit as possible from their contracts, thereby excluding considerations of comfort for the emigrants.[36]

The unfortunate lot of the Cherokees could be forgotten by the nation, for the Indians passed to the West, beyond immediate contact with most white Americans. With the last of the southern tribes, the Seminoles, the story did not end so quietly. Their refusal to accept migration brought the nation the longest, the most costly, and the most frustrating Indian conflict in its history.

[36] Foreman, *Indian Removal*, Preface.

FOURTEEN

The Florida War

THE Seminoles, an amalgam of Creeks who had gradually drifted down into Florida and the native tribes there with whom they mixed, were few in number. All told, they numbered no more than 5,000 souls, but they showed a resistance to the removal policy of the government that kept the army occupied for seven years and that was never completely broken. Defense plans for the frontier, so carefully worked out in theory, had to be cast aside, for the demands of the war against the Seminoles drained of their manpower not only the seaboard fortifications but the western garrisons as well. One commander after another tried his hand at bringing the embarrassing affair to a successful conclusion, yet the war dragged on, despite optimistic announcements from the commanding generals and the War Department, which periodically proclaimed that the war had finally been brought to an end. It was a sad and distressing affair. The United States government had made a decision that the Seminoles were to be removed, and then it tried with main force to carry it out—even though it soon became clear that the land that was thus to be freed of the Indians was not of significant value to the whites and that if the Seminoles had been left alone, the expense and grief of the conflict might well have been avoided.[1]

[1] A full treatment of the war appears in John K. Mahon, *History of the Second Seminole War, 1835–1842* (Gainesville, Fla., 1967); it was published too late, however, for use in the writing of this chapter. An older general history of the war is John T. Sprague, *The Origin, Progress, and Conclusion of the Florida War* (New York, 1848; facsimile ed., Gainesville, Fla., 1964). Sprague took part in the last phases of the war and gives a detailed account of the campaigns from 1841 on, but he gives also a survey of the whole war, and the many documents he prints in his narrative make the book an important source. Later writers rely heavily on him. Published works by participants other than

The removal of the Seminoles had complications that were not present in the removal of the other tribes. It was not simply a matter of exchanging the lands that the Indians claimed in Florida for lands in the Trans-Mississippi West—although indeed this might be matter enough for dispute. The Seminole problem was also a problem of the Negroes. For many years Negro slaves from the southern states had fled as fugitives to the Indian settlements in Florida. They often became slaves of the Seminoles, and the Indians may have augmented the number by purchase of slaves in the white manner, but whatever the source, the Negroes enjoyed a less restrictive existence among the Seminoles than with white masters of Georgia or Alabama. They lived in a kind of semibondage, more like allies than slaves of the Indians. They lived in their own villages as vassals of the chief whose protection they enjoyed, contributing shares of the produce from their own fields rather than labor on the lands of the chief.

The demands of the white masters of the fugitives became increasingly insistent. Claims were presented which the Seminoles, who kept no legal records of their slaves, could not easily refute in court. More and more frequently raiding parties from the north invaded the Seminole lands and attempted to carry off by force Negroes who were claimed as slaves. The Seminole War was perhaps as much a move-

Sprague, are limited in scope and often have some special point of view to advance. Examples, which are very critical of the war, are M. M. Cohen, *Notices of Florida and the Campaigns* (Charleston, 1836; facsimile ed., Gainesville, Fla., 1964) and [Woodburne Potter], *The War in Florida: Being an Exposition of Its Causes, and an Accurate History of the Campaigns of Generals Clinch, Gaines and Scott* (Baltimore, 1836). Journals and diaries of other participants in the war have been published by later editors. Among these are W. A. Croffut, *Fifty Years in Camp and Field: Diary of Major-General Ethan Allen Hitchcock, U.S.A.* (New York, 1909); Jacob Rhett Motte, *Journey into Wilderness: An Army Surgeon's Account of Life in Camp and Field During the Creek and Seminole Wars, 1836–1838*, ed. James F. Sunderman (Gainesville, Fla., 1953); and a number of briefer items published from time to time in the *Florida Historical Quarterly*.

The printed government documents dealing with the Second Seminole War are voluminous, touching on all aspects of the conflict. As the war dragged on and the promised terminations did not materialize, Congress repeatedly called for explanations from the President and the Secretary of War. The reports, often with extensive reprinting of correspondence, orders, and other documents, make it possible for the historian to reconstruct the war in great detail. The annual reports of the Secretary of War give excellent information from the government's viewpoint. *The American State Papers: Military Affairs* (7 vols., Washington, 1832–1861), V–VII, are very rich, and there are many special documents in the Serial Set of Congressional Documents, too numerous to list individually. Many valuable documents on the war are printed in Clarence E. Carter, ed., *The Territorial Papers of the United States* (26 vols., Washington, 1934–1962), XXV and XXVI.

ment on the part of the slave owners to recover the property they claimed as it was a war to acquire Indian land for white use. And the Negroes clearly sensed that fact. Although about a tenth of the Seminoles sided with the United States in the conflict over removal, acting as guides and interpreters against their blood brothers, the Negroes almost to a man fought bitterly against the whites until assurance was given that turning oneself in for removal to the West did not mean placing oneself within the clutches of some white slave owner, who stood by waiting to enforce his claims. As tension over removal mounted, the people of Florida seemed not overly concerned, considering the Seminoles as essentially peaceful and little likely to put up an aggressive resistance. But this complacency overlooked the Negroes—the free Negroes in Florida, the Indian Negroes in loose bondage to the Seminoles, and the plantation Negroes of Florida.[2]

The removal issue proper can be traced in three treaties between the Seminoles and the United States government. The first of these was the Treaty of Camp Moultrie, signed on September 18, 1823, on Moultrie Creek, a few miles south of St. Augustine. The Florida Indians here were induced to give up their claims to all of Florida, and in return were granted a reservation of land in central Florida, which by executive proclamation was slightly increased at the north in 1824 and 1826 to include more tillable land. By the treaty the Indians agreed to prevent runaway slaves from entering their country and to aid in the return of slaves who had escaped from their white masters. They were granted $6,000 worth of livestock and an annuity of $5,000 for twenty years.[3]

[2] All the serious accounts of the war call attention to the importance of the Negro element. The best consideration of the problem is in three articles by Kenneth W. Porter: "Florida Slaves and Free Negroes in the Seminole War, 1835–1842," *Journal of Negro History*, XXVIII (October, 1943), 390–421; "Osceola and the Negroes," *Florida Historical Quarterly*, XXXIII (January–April, 1955), 235–239; and "Negroes and the Seminole War, 1835–1842," *Journal of Southern History*, XXX (November, 1964), 427–450. See also Mark F. Boyd, "The Seminole War: Its Background and Onset," *Florida Historical Quarterly*, XXX (July, 1951), 3–115. The abolitionist Joshua R. Giddings claimed: "One feature was most obvious, in the commencement and prosecution of this war: we allude to the very respectful, almost obsequious obedience of the Executive to the popular feeling in favor of slavery, in every part of the country where that institution existed. This war had been commenced at the instance of the people of Florida." *The Exiles of Florida: or, The Crimes Committed by Our Government against the Maroons, Who Fled from South Carolina and Other Slave States, Seeking Protection under Spanish Laws* (Columbus, Ohio, 1858; facsimile ed., Gainesville, Fla., 1964), pp. 270–271.
[3] Charles J. Kappler, ed., *Indian Affairs: Laws and Treaties* (2 vols., Washington, 1904), II, *Treaties*, pp. 203–207; Charles C. Royce, *Indian Land Cessions*

Much of the land thus reserved for the Indians was not well suited for cultivation, and the Indians did not abide by the reservation lines. The Seminoles were irritated by whites who were allowed to invade the reservation in search of slaves, and they retaliated by raids upon white settlements outside the reservation boundaries. Many of the Indians remained in their old homes when whites came into the area to settle, and there was increasing agitation for the removal of the Indians altogether from Florida. Secretary of War Calhoun, however, in his report on Indian removal in 1825, saw no special problem in regard to the Indians in Florida. "It is believed that immediate measures need not be taken with regard to the Indians of Florida," he stated. "By the treaty of the 18th of September, 1823, they ceded the whole northern portion of Florida, with the exception of a few small reservations, and have had allotted to them the southern part of the peninsula; and it is probable that no inconvenience will be felt, for many years, either by the inhabitants of Florida, or the Indians, under the present arrangement."[4] But Calhoun lacked his usual perceptiveness here, and when the Removal Act of 1830 made provision for removal treaties, the Florida Indians were also pressured into moving. In 1832 Colonel James Gadsden was sent to Florida to negotiate with the Seminoles for their removal with the rest of the southern Indians to the region west of Arkansas.

A treaty was signed with the Indians on May 9, 1832, at Payne's Landing. The Indians were near destitution and the promises of food and clothing in the treaty eased the negotiations. The Seminoles, however, insisted that they would not agree to removal until they themselves had had an opportunity to inspect the land and determine its suitability for their new homes. The treaty, accordingly, provided that the government would send out a party of the Indians to the West, where they could themselves judge the land that would be set aside for them.[5]

The Seminole delegation arrived at Fort Gibson in November, 1832, and they were shown the territory that was to be theirs in the Creek country. They were persuaded to sign an agreement, stating that they

---

in the United States (Eighteenth Annual Report of the Bureau of American Ethnology, Part II, Washington, 1899), Plate 14, Cession 173. For a detailed, reasonable account of the treaty and its background, which is less condemnatory of the treaty than most accounts, see John K. Mahon, "The Treaty of Moultrie Creek, 1823," Florida Historical Quarterly, XL (April, 1962), 350–372.

[4] Report of Calhoun, January 24, 1825, American State Papers: Indian Affairs (2 vols., Washington, 1832–1834), II, 543.

[5] Kappler, Treaties, pp. 344–345. The treaty was not ratified and proclaimed until April 12, 1834.

approved of the land. This Treaty of Fort Gibson, March 28, 1833, although it was not accepted by the Seminole nation, was considered by the government as fulfilling the provisions of the Payne's Landing Treaty, and the government began to demand that the Indians carry out that treaty and move out of Florida.[6]

The Seminoles did not think that the agreement made by the delegation expressed the approval of the whole nation, and they did not want to go west as an integral part of the Creek nation, as the United States desired. The usual impasse had arrived. The government pointed to the treaty and insisted that it be fulfilled; the Indians denied that they had made the agreements specified and refused to move. As the impasse tightened and tension increased, the stage was set for the Seminole War. One's views on the justice of the war depend upon one's views on the legality and justice of the Payne's Landing and Fort Gibson treaties. It is easy, under the circumstances, to see these treaties as the "cause" of the war and to condemn them as frauds upon the Indians. Many army officers, upon whom fell the onerous duty of carrying out removal by force, were sympathetic toward the Seminoles. Major Ethan Allen Hitchcock, for example, recorded in his diary: "The treaty of Payne's Landing was a fraud on the Indians: They never approved of it or signed it. They are right in defending their homes and we ought to let them alone." Others echoed this opinion.[7]

☆

The United States made efforts to negotiate removal with the Seminoles through the Indian agent, Wiley Thompson, and Brevet Brigadier General Duncan L. Clinch, who commanded regular troops in Florida. Clinch operated from three posts in central Florida—Fort King, established in 1827 near present-day Ocala; Fort Drane, about 20 miles

---

[6] *Ibid.*, pp. 394–395.

[7] Journal entry at Fort King, November 4, 1840, Croffut, *Fifty Years in Camp and Field*, p. 122. Woodburne Potter declared: "I cannot but regard the treaty of Payne's Landing as having been the main cause of all those excesses which have led to the present war. . . ." *The War in Florida*, p. 38. See also Sprague, *The Florida War*, pp. 94–95. John K. Mahon, "Two Seminole Treaties: Payne's Landing, 1832, and Ft. Gibson, 1833," *Florida Historical Quarterly*, XLI (July, 1962), 1–21, makes a very careful analysis of the treaties and the charges of fraud. Because the evidence is "fragmentary and often contradictory," he is unable to arrive at apodictic judgments. He concedes, however, that the Seminoles did not regard the treaties as just and that their refusal to abide by them led to war.

northwest of Fort King on a plantation owned by General Clinch; and Fort Brooke, established in 1824 on Tampa Bay. While the officials of the War Department were optimistic about the willingness of the Seminoles to leave Florida, Clinch on the spot was more realistic. "The more I see of this tribe of Indians," he wrote, "the more fully am I convinced that they have not the least intention of fulfilling their treaty stipulations, unless compelled to do so by a stronger force than *mere* words."[8]

Additional companies of troops were sent to Fort King, and Clinch attempted throughout 1835 to come to terms with the Seminole chiefs about removal. The Indians' tactics were dilatory, but plans were slowly matured by Agent Thompson for concentrating the Indians who agreed to move at Fort King and other points and then moving them to Tampa Bay for transportation to New Orleans and new western homes. A date was set for their assembling, and General Clinch notified the Indians that if they did not come in voluntarily, he would bring them in by force. Routine notice of the operation was given in Secretary of War Cass's annual report on November 30, 1835: "Fourteen companies have been placed under the command of General Clinch, in Florida, with a view to impose a proper restraint upon the Seminole Indians, who have occasionally evinced an unquiet spirit, and to insure the execution of the treaty stipulations providing for the removal of these Indians. As soon as this takes place these troops will resume their proper positions."[9] Little did Cass realize how long it would be before the task that had been given so routinely to Clinch would be completed.

As the army closed in to force removal, the Indians struck. Wiley Thompson and Lieutenant Constantine Smith were murdered by a band of Indians under the leadership of Osceola on December 28, 1835, as they walked outside the fortification at Fort King. On the same day, six or seven miles north of the Withlacoochee River near the Great Wahoo swamp, a party of Indians and Negroes ambushed the company of troops under Major Francis L. Dade, who were proceeding from Fort Brooke to Fort King to compel the Indians to remove. All but three of the company of eight officers and 102 noncommis-

---

[8] Clinch to the Adjutant General, January 22, 1835, quoted in Rembert W. Patrick, *Aristocrat in Uniform: General Duncan L. Clinch* (Gainesville, Fla., 1963), p. 71.

[9] *American State Papers: Military Affairs*, V, 627. Documents on the negotiations in 1835 are found in *Senate Document* No. 152, 24 Congress, 1 session, serial 281.

sioned officers and privates were killed. These defiant acts opened the second Seminole War. Three days later the first pitched battle of the war took place at the Withlacoochee River, where General Clinch and 200 regulars from Fort Drane and General Richard K. Call with Florida volunteers (some 400 strong) engaged the warriors of Osceola in a bitter battle. Although a few of Call's command crossed the river and participated in the actual fighting, the mass of the volunteers were mere spectators of the conflict, a fact that did not boost the reputation of the militia.[10]

The murder of Thompson and the Dade Massacre electrified the Florida frontier, and the War Department hastened to act. On January 21, 1836, Winfield Scott, commanding general of the Eastern Department, was ordered to move at once to Florida to take charge of the operations against the hostile Indians. Florida at the time, however, was divided between the Eastern Department and the Western Department by a line drawn from the tip of the peninsula (Cape Sable) to the head of Lake Superior at Fond du Lac, and the massacre of Dade's command had been on the western side of the line and properly in the command of General Edmund P. Gaines, the archenemy of Scott. In an effort to avoid conflict between the two department commanders when unified command was needed in a war that would undoubtedly pay little attention to the niceties of army protocol, the War Department instructed Scott: "The line dividing your own department from that of General Gaines is at present an imaginary one, and probably would, if run, actually pass through the scene of hostilities. You will pursue your operations, therefore, without regard to any such divisionary line." On the following day the Adjutant General sent a letter to Gaines informing him of the authority conferred on Scott, and directing Gaines to await orders in New Orleans, since "the state of affairs *west* of the Mississippi may soon require your attention, if not presence, in that quarter."[11]

General Clinch, although he resented being superseded by Scott with the imputation that he was unable to conduct the campaign successfully himself, loyally submitted to Scott's command.[12] Not so General

[10] See Samuel E. Cobb, "The Florida Militia and the Affair at Withlacoochee," *Florida Historical Quarterly*, XIX (July, 1940), 128–139, for documents on both sides.

[11] Cass to Scott, January 21, 1836, *American State Papers: Military Affairs*, VII, 217; Jones to Gaines, January 22, 1836, *ibid.*, p. 423.

[12] After participation in the initial campaign of the war, Clinch submitted his resignation on April 26, 1836, and in May he left Florida. Patrick, *Aristocrat in Uniform*, p. 136.

Gaines. The Western Department commander heard the ill news of the Indian uprising at New Orleans in early January, as he was making an inspection tour of the southern part of his command. News of Scott's appointment was slower in arriving, and as rumors of disasters in Florida filtered into New Orleans, there was no doubt in Gaines's mind that he had to repair immediately to Florida to take charge.

Without waiting for any orders from Washington he asked the governor of Louisiana to have ready for immediate movement a regiment of eight companies of volunteers, while he himself went to Pensacola to secure naval aid. By January 29 he was back in New Orleans and on February 3 ready to embark with 1,100 troops, made up of six companies of the Fourth Infantry and the regiment of Louisiana volunteers. On February 10 Gaines and his soldiers landed at Tampa. The general proceeded almost at once against the Indians, marching toward Fort King, where he expected to find suitable stores. On the 20th he came upon the scene of Dade's defeat. No one had visited the site in the nearly two months since the disaster, and a grim sight awaited Gaines. The men still lay where they had been killed, mostly no more than skeletons now, and the soldiers took time to give the remains appropriate burial. Two more days of march brought them to Fort King, but the rations had not arrived, and Gaines had to move quickly to provide for his men. Clinch was at Fort Drane, twenty-two miles away, and Gaines sent part of his troops there. But Fort Drane, too, was short of supplies, and Gaines, after requisitioning 12,000 of the 20,000 rations at the post, directed his troops back to Fort Brooke. So far no Indians had been encountered, and the return journey was by a different route, west of the outward march, in the hope that the enemy might be encountered.[13]

When Gaines attempted to cross the Withlacoochee River at a spot pointed out by the friendly Indians as fordable, he was met with fire from the opposite bank. Finding the river farther down unfordable, Gaines prepared to operate from his position. He constructed a fortified camp, called Camp Izard, and asked Clinch to come down with his troops and additional stores and ammunition. The Indians repeatedly attacked the camp, but they were driven off, and although supplies ran so low that horses were killed for food, the soldiers maintained their position.

[13] Gaines's part in the war is well told in James W. Silver, *Edmund Pendleton Gaines, Frontier General* (Baton Rouge, 1949), pp. 167–190.

Meanwhile General Scott had belatedly arrived in Florida. Leaving Washington on January 21, he stopped briefly at Columbia, South Carolina, and Augusta, Georgia, to send requisitions to the state governors for troops, conferred with Governor Schley of Georgia at Milledgeville about mobilization, and then established himself at Savannah until February 20, making arrangements for the shipment of munitions and provisions to Florida. He finally arrived in Florida on the 22d and set up his general headquarters at Picolata, a village on the St. Johns River west of St. Augustine. Here he delayed for more than two weeks, embarrassed by a lack of troops, supplies, and means of transportation for any campaign into the interior. He was also furious to find that Gaines was on hand and had started a campaign against the Indians. He considered Gaines's action as an intrusion into his own proper sphere of action and fired off letters of complaint to the War Department. He accused Gaines of using up supplies that should have been Clinch's and thwarting his own campaign plans by engaging the enemy prematurely. The only service Gaines had rendered, said Scott, was the burial of Dade's command.[14]

Scott considered Gaines responsible for his own movements and ordered Clinch not to succor him at Camp Izard on the Withlacoochee, but Clinch on his own accord had escorted a small supply of food and ammunition to Gaines. Gaines meanwhile had held a conference with the Indians on the Withlacoochee, which resulted in no formal agreement but which did bring about a certain state of peace, allowing the troops to move without harassment. On March 9 Gaines turned over the command to Clinch, claiming that the enemy had been "met, beaten, and forced to sue for peace." On the following day his troops marched toward Fort Drane and were there when Scott, having hastened toward the fort on what he thought was a rescue mission, arrived.

The old rivals passed a day together at Fort Drane. "The meeting between the two generals was cold in the extreme," a junior officer reported. "No civilities or courtesies passed between them. They sat opposite to each other at table without any salutations on either side."[15]

---

[14] For Scott's operations in Florida, see Charles W. Elliott, *Winfield Scott: The Soldier and the Man* (New York, 1937), pp. 286–310. Both Elliott and Silver treat of the conflict between Scott and Gaines. See also the extensive documentation in the "Proceedings of the Military Court of Inquiry, in the Case of Major General Scott and Major General Gaines," *Senate Document* No. 224, 24 Congress, 2 session, serial 299.

[15] Croffut, *Fifty Years in Camp and Field*, pp. 95–96.

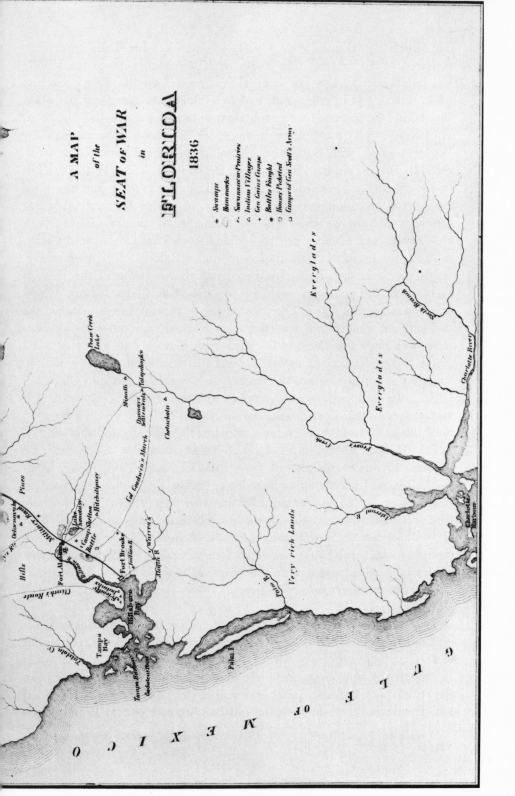

A Map of the Seat of War in Florida, 1836

On March 14, Gaines with a party of four left for Tallahassee, unmolested by Indians on their route, and then took a stage for Mobile and points west, where the general was needed on the Texas frontier.

Scott was left in command, and he was free to carry out his plans "to reduce the enemy to unconditional submission." He had proposed to converge upon the Indians in the Cove, a swamp area south of the Withlacoochee, with three separate columns coming from different directions. One would march from Fort Drane south to the Withlacoochee to cut off any northward flight of the Indians or their juncture with the Creeks in southern Georgia. A second under General Abraham Eustis would march from St. Augustine, cross the St. Johns River at Volusia, and advance on the Indians from Pilaklakaha at the east. A third, made up of Alabama troops under Colonel William Lindsay, would proceed north from Fort Brooke on the west side of the Withlacoochee. If the advances could be properly timed, the Indians would be ensnared in the Cove. The plan on paper appeared excellent, but the problems of supply and transportation through a roadless wilderness were well-nigh insurmountable. And then Gaines had appeared with 1,100 unexpected men, to upset the calculations on supplies and to engage the Indians before the master plan could be put into effect.

Still, the campaign went forward as well as it could. Scott and Clinch moved down from Fort Drane, crossed the Withlacoochee and pursued the Indians without much success through the swamps and then retired to Fort Brooke. Eustis, short of supplies and constantly harassed by the Indians, led his troops directly from Pilaklakaha to Tampa Bay. Lindsay had moved according to plan from Tampa Bay but seeing nothing of the other forces had retraced his steps to Fort Brooke. Thus by the first week of April, 1836, all the Florida army was at Tampa Bay. "It will be seen," Scott reported to the Adjutant General, "that, although no general battle has been fought, many combats and sharp affairs have taken place; that the boast of Major General Gaines that *he had beaten the enemy, and compelled him to sue for peace*, was but a vain imagination."[16]

Scott's problems were far from over, as he more and more clearly realized. The volunteers, who had enlisted in January for three months of service, were eagerly awaiting their discharge, and the concentration of the troops at Tampa Bay left much of Florida unprotected from the still-defiant Indians. Clinch was sent back to Fort Drane, while Scott and Eustis returned to Picolata and St. Augustine, and Lindsay was

[16] Scott to Jones, April 12, 1836, *American State Papers: Military Affairs*, VII, 267.

left at Fort Brooke. The summer season made a campaign impossible, and the discharge of the volunteers weakened the forces. The settlers cried out in alarm and fled their farms as scattered Indian depredations continued, only to be castigated by Scott for their lack of courage and determination. Such panic, he told them, was "infinitely humiliating," and he warned them that "no general, even with extensive means, can cure a disease in the public mind, so general and so degrading, without some little effort on the part of the people themselves."[17] Such statements did little to endear Scott to the people of Florida, whom he had already enraged by a report to the Adjutant General asking for 3,000 troops and urging that they be *"good troops, (not volunteers)."*[18]

Scott was much disturbed by the hostility he had aroused and was weakened by illness, and although he declared, "If I can be convicted of having committed one serious blunder, in theory or practice, since I left Washington to conduct the war in Florida, let me be shot," he was quite willing to leave the war to someone else.[19] When he received orders from Cass to quit Florida and look into the Creek disturbances in Georgia, he promptly departed St. Augustine on May 21.

☆

With Clinch resigning, Gaines busy once more in the West, and Scott called to take charge of the disturbances among the Creeks, the command of the Florida war fell upon Governor Richard Keith Call. Call was a protégé of Andrew Jackson, with whom he had fought in the Creek war of 1813 and with whom he had maintained the closest of friendly ties. He had resigned his army commission in 1821 and had set up law practice in Pensacola. From 1823 to 1825 he had served as Florida's delegate in Congress, and he had been brigadier general in the Florida militia since 1823. In that latter position he was directly concerned with the defense of the territory against the hostile Seminoles and had tasted battle against them with Clinch at Withlacoochee in the last days of 1835.[20]

[17] Orders No. 48, May 17, 1836, *ibid.*, p. 294.
[18] Scott to Jones, April 30, 1836, *ibid.*, p. 278.
[19] Scott to Jones, May 20, 1836, *ibid.*, p. 298.
[20] For Call's part in the war, see Herbert J. Doherty, Jr., *Richard Keith Call, Southern Unionist* (Gainesville, Fla., 1961), pp. 93–108. A rich collection of documents on Call and the war is in *Senate Document* No. 278, 26 Congress, 1 session, serial 358. See also *Senate Document* No. 100, 24 Congress, 2 session,

Call had been appointed governor of Florida Territory by his old friend Jackson on March 16, 1836, and he longed for a more active role in the war. Finally on May 18, 1836, Jackson sent word to the governor that he would be placed in command of the regular army, the 1,500 Tennessee mounted volunteers, and the Florida militia. "I accept, with great pleasure, of the trust you have conferred on me," Call wrote exultantly to Jackson; "and I promise you that I will soon put an end to the war in Florida, or perish in the attempt."[21]

Call knew Florida well, and he had had long experience with the Indians in the Territory. Although he had never commanded a full-scale campaign, he worked out a plan of operations that won the approval of both Jesup and Jackson and began to pursue it with vigor. But he worked against great odds. The regular troops resented being under the command of a civilian and looked back bitterly to the inactivity of Call's volunteers at the battle of the Withlacoochee. The naval forces cooperating with him likewise were not enthusiastic about his command, and the Florida militia, who at least could not object to being under a militia general, fretted about their uncertain pay. Call found, in addition, that the officers of the regular troops were in extremely short supply; among eleven artillery companies there were only six officers, and eight infantry companies had no officers at all.

Call's plan called for a concentrated attack upon the Indians in the area south of the Withlacoochee, with supply bases set up on three sides of the region upon which the troops could fall back when necessary. He set out from Tallahassee on September 19 and reported on October 10 that the region north of the Withlacoochee had been cleared of Indians and that he was preparing for a drive south of the river. His plans to cross the river did not work out, and he fell back toward a supply base that was to have been established near the mouth of the river. The base, however, had not been set up, and Call was forced to retire to Fort Drane. His reports indicating that the withdrawal would be only temporary did not reach Washington, and before he could show any success in the campaign, orders had been issued by Jackson for his removal.

---

serial 298; Herbert J. Doherty, Jr., "Richard K. Call vs. the Federal Government on the Seminole War," *Florida Historical Quarterly*, XXXI (January, 1953), 163–180; Caroline Mays Brevard, "Richard Keith Call," *ibid.*, I (July, 1908), 3–12, (October, 1908), 8–20; Sidney Walter Martin, "Richard Keith Call, Florida Territorial Leader," *ibid.*, XXI (April, 1943), 332–351.

[21] Call to Jackson, May 30, 1836, *Senate Document* No. 278, 26 Congress, 1 session, serial 358, p. 54.

Before the orders reached him, he had reorganized his forces and successfully crossed the Withlacoochee. In three battles he had engaged the Indians and driven them back before withdrawing to the supply base at Volusia. It was here that he received word of his removal. He considered the action unjustified, and his friendship with Jackson was severely strained. It is perhaps true that the recall was unduly hasty and that Call was not given time to show what he could do once the supplies and men were available for his operations. He had a clearer grasp of the problems faced in Florida than the men who were directing the affair from Washington, and none of the regular army generals who fought in the Florida war succeeded much better than he did. But the conduct of the war was subject to much criticism in the nation, and the President could not afford to delay. Call was known to have been ill throughout the campaign, and a replacement was already on the scene.[22]

Call was replaced by General Thomas S. Jesup, who had been relieved temporarily of his duties as Quartermaster General to take command in the Creek campaign and who had then been ordered to Florida to replace Scott. He arrived in Florida on September 25 and at first voluntarily placed himself under Call's command until the governor's campaign could be completed. On December 8, however, he relieved Call and it was now his turn to see what could be done to bring the war to a quick close.[23]

☆

Jesup immediately began his pursuit of the elusive Indians. He pushed his campaign with energy and commanded a force of considerable size—with regulars and volunteers it exceeded 8,000 men. From headquarters set up on the Withlacoochee he sent men in pursuit of Osceola and other leaders. He reported: "The campaign will be tedious, but I hope successful in the end. I am not, however, very sanguine; the difficulty is not to fight the enemy, but to find him. . . . The difficulties in regard to transportation are such that every officer is obliged to carry seven days' rations in his haversack. I often carry

[22] I follow here the evaluation of Call in Doherty, *Richard Keith Call*, p. 107.
[23] Correspondence dealing with Jesup's operations appears in *House Document* No. 78, 25 Congress, 2 session, serial 323, pp. 1–118. See also *Senate Document* No. 507, 25 Congress, 2 session, serial 319.

subsistence for six days."[24] For three months he sought out the enemy under conditions that he only little by little came to realize in their full import. It was a war of attrition upon the Indians and their Negro allies, a strike here, a quick march through the difficult terrain there, keeping the Indians on edge and capturing or killing a few. This was not the kind of war the army knew or that the officers looked forward to. In a report to the Adjutant General at the beginning of February, 1837, Jesup commented in unfeigned humility:

> As an act of justice to all my predecessors in command, I consider it my duty to say, that the difficulties attending military operations in this country can be properly appreciated only by those acquainted with them. I have had advantages which neither of them possessed, in better preparations, and more abundant supplies; and I found it impossible to operate with any kind of success, until I had established a line of depots across the country.
>
> This is a service which no man would seek with any other view than the mere performance of his duty: distinction, or increase of reputation, is out of the question; and the difficulties are such, that the best concerted plans may result in absolute failure, and the best established reputation be lost without a fault.
>
> If I have, at any time, said aught in disparagement of the operations of others in Florida, either verbally or in writing, officially or unofficially, knowing the country as I now know it, I consider myself bound, as a man of honor, solemnly to retract it.[25]

Jesup's pressure upon the Indians, his widely extended and continuous movement of troops, induced the Indians to sue for some sort of abatement. They needed to plant their crops and were unable to provide for their subsistence with the incessant hammering of the troops. The Indians asked that peace be granted so that those inclined to surrender might come in and prepare for migration to the west. After considerable delay and careful stipulations between the parties, large numbers of Indians assembled under their chiefs at Fort Dade on the Withlacoochee River, where a capitulation was signed by most of the important chiefs on March 6, 1837.

The chiefs agreed to cease hostilities immediately and bound themselves with their bands to emigrate at once to the country assigned them by the President west of the Mississippi. As an earnest of their

[24] Jesup to Jones, January 12, 1837, Sprague, *The Florida War*, p. 167.
[25] Jesup to Jones, February 7, 1837, *ibid.*, p. 173.

good faith, they agreed to place hostages with Jesup, one of whom was to be the chief Micanopy. Jesup's side of the agreement showed that the American negotiators had learned the importance of the Negro element in the opposition to removal. Instead of demanding the surrender of the Negroes claimed by white owners as slaves, the capitulation explicitly protected the Seminole Negroes, providing that "the Seminoles and their allies, who come in and emigrate to the west, shall be secure in their lives and property; that their negroes, their bona fide property, shall accompany them to the west; and that their cattle and ponies shall be paid for by the United States at a fair valuation." The expenses of the movement west, subsistence at Tampa Bay while awaiting transportation, and subsistence for twelve months in their new homes were to be provided by the United States.[26]

The Indians began to assemble under the direction of Micanopy at a designated spot ten miles from Fort Brooke in preparation for emigration. By the middle of May there were many Indians in camp, and the chiefs Alligator, Holatoochee, Jumper, and Cloud, and occasionally Coacoochee (Wild Cat) came into the fort in good spirits and apparently satisfied with the way things were going. Twenty-six vessels were on hand to transport the Indians to New Orleans, and the Indians were enrolled and issued provisions and clothing as they came in to surrender. From time to time, however, the chiefs asked for postponement of the sailing, until expected friends or relatives could come in. Even Osceola sent messages intimating that he too agreed with the terms of capitulation.

The peaceful preparations for emigration convinced Jesup that the war was at an end. The volunteers and militia were sent home, and orders came from the Secretary of War to redistribute the regular troops to healthful garrisons where they might recruit their strength after the debilitating duty in the swamps and hammocks of central Florida. The citizens of Florida, too, rejoiced in the new peace. The surrender of so many chiefs and sub-chiefs boded well for permanent peace, and good times seemed to have returned. It was all in vain.

On June 5 Jesup had to inform the War Department that the Indians, who had so peacefully gathered at Fort Brooke and had spent the summer quietly consuming the supplies given them by the government, had all fled. The indisposition to emigrate was more strongly

[26] The capitulation is printed in *House Document* No. 78, 25 Congress, 2 session, serial 323, pp. 79–80. See also Jesup to Jones, March 6, 1837, *ibid.*, pp. 78–79.

imbedded than Jesup realized, and among the young chiefs especially there was a determination never to leave their homes. Osceola and Coacoochee came 'to camp at midnight and forced Micanopy to follow them. The old man gave in, and finding the other chiefs in sympathy with the move, was led away. The entire camp, numbering some 700 Indians, fled the camp and were out of reach by dawn. They had been well fed, their crops were well along, and the summer months precluded any serious military operation against them.

This treacherous act and the subsequent criticism which the public and the press rained upon Jesup discouraged the commander, and he asked to be relieved of command and returned to his quartermaster duties. But his request for relief also met criticism, and he agreed to stay on until he was positively ordered to relinquish the command. The secret escape of the Indians undoubtedly made a deep impression on Jesup's mind and influenced his later dealings with Osceola and other chiefs.

A new campaign was planned for autumn, when operations were again possible. Jesup reported to the Secretary of War that he needed more than 6,000 regular troops—almost 1,700 to garrison the forts set up in Florida, 750 to escort and protect supply trains, and the remainder to take the field against the hostile Indians.[27] There was little that the War Department could do in its increasing desire to be rid of the strange war in the south but comply with the general's requests. The western forts were stripped of their garrisons and every available regular soldier was speeded to Florida. In addition, 4,000 volunteers were mustered into service from Kentucky, Tennessee, Louisiana, Georgia, Alabama, and Florida and required to be in the field by the beginning of October.

Jesup himself took direct command of operations in the eastern part of Florida. He continued to scour the country for hostile Indians and Negroes and gradually accumulated a sizable number of captives. In his report filed after he had been relieved of his command in Florida, Jesup summarized his accomplishments: 2,400 Indians and Negroes had been taken, including those who surrendered voluntarily, over 700 of whom were warriors; the villages of the Indians had been destroyed, and their cattle, horses, and other stock had been taken or destroyed; the whole country had been gone over, until only small dispersed groups

---

[27] Jesup to Poinsett, July 15, 1837, *American State Papers: Military Affairs*, VII, 872–874. Joel R. Poinsett had succeeded Lewis Cass as Secretary of War in March, 1837.

were still at large. Yet after all this was added up, the general was conscious of how small the numbers must seem to anyone acquainted with more significant wars. He hastened to justify the seeming triviality of his operations:

> These results, trifling as they are compared with those of the Creek campaign, and with public expectation, are greatly beyond what we had any right to hope, when we consider the nature and extent of the country which has been the theatre of operations, and our utter ignorance of the greater part of it, even when we commenced the last campaign. Nothing but the untiring devotion of both officers and soldiers to their duties, and the energy and efficiency of the different branches of the staff, could have enabled me to overcome the difficulties which surrounded me, so far as to accomplish what has been done.
>
> If our operations have fallen short of public expectation, it should be remembered that we were attempting that which no other armies of our country had ever before been required to do. I, and my predecessors in command, were not only required to fight, beat, and drive the enemy before us, but to go into an unexplored wilderness and catch them. Neither Wayne, Harrison, nor Jackson, was required to do this; and unless the objects to be accomplished be the same, there can be no just comparison as to the results.[28]

Jesup was extremely sensitive to public opinion. He maintained that "the moment the public confidence is withdrawn from a general, the executive is bound to remove him; for, no matter what may be his merits, or how transcendent his abilities, his private and personal interests should not be put in competition with the interests of the nation," and he had asked to be relieved when public opinion turned against him after his first campaign in Florida.[29] His pique, however, was quieted, and he stayed on in command. But he did not escape further public censure. The most notable case was his capture of Osceola.[30]

In September General Joseph M. Hernandez of the Florida volunteers captured two Seminole chiefs, King Philip and Uchee Billy, with their followers and imprisoned them at Fort Marion. News of the capture was sent back to the tribe, and Philip's son, Coacoochee, came back

[28] Jesup to Poinsett, July 6, 1838, Sprague, *The Florida War*, p. 197.
[29] *Ibid.*, p. 185.
[30] Osceola, the most famous of the Seminole leaders, has been given considerable attention. A double issue of the *Florida Historical Quarterly*, XXXIII (January–April, 1955), was devoted entirely to him.

with the messenger to offer surrender of his band. On October 17 Coacoochee returned once more to General Hernandez and told him that Osceola was ready for a conference. After some negotiations Osceola proposed that General Hernandez come to his camp near Fort Peyton without a military escort for a talk. Jesup directed Hernandez to make the visit but to take along enough soldiers to meet any attack. Osceola came to the conference under a white flag, indicating that he considered it a truce, not a surrender. When it became clear that the Indians did not intend to turn themselves in, General Hernandez (following the orders of Jesup) seized Osceola and his party on October 22, 1837. There were thirteen chiefs in addition to Osceola and ninety-five persons altogether. The captives were marched to St. Augustine and imprisoned in Fort Marion. Coacoochee and a number of others escaped from their cell through a small window high in the wall, but Osceola asserted that he had nothing to be ashamed of and would not sully his cause by an attempt to escape.[31]

Whether Jesup violated one of the sacred principles of civilized warfare and seized the Indians under a flag of truce or whether he was justified in the seizure on the grounds that the Indian treachery of the past might well have been repeated has divided historians to the present day.[32] Pro-Indian advocates have excoriated Jesup in unbelievably harsh terms. The general was severely criticized at the time, and Osceola became a great hero in the minds of many. As time passed and Indian questions became the great humanitarian topic of the day, the story of Osceola and his white flag became a classic example of the white man's inhumanity to the Indian. At this extreme was a story of the Seminoles published in 1898. Of Osceola's capture the author finds "nothing that can palliate this treachery—no circumstance or event that transpired previous to the act lessens its enormity." He concludes: "If the painter of the world-famed picture, 'Christ before Pilate,' should seek in American history a subject worthy of his brush, we would commend to him, 'Osceola before General Jesup': Osceola, the despised Seminole, a captive and in chains—Jesup, in all the pomp and circumstance of an American Major-General; Osceola, who had 'done nothing

---

[31] The capture is reported in Sprague, *The Florida War*, pp. 216–219. For a critical examination of the traditional story of Coacoochee's escape and a new reconstruction of what happened, see Kenneth W. Porter, "Seminole Flight from Fort Marion," *Florida Historical Quarterly*, XXII (January, 1944), 113–133.

[32] Contemporary documents illustrating both sides are presented by Julien C. Yonge in "The White Flag," *ibid.*, XXXIII (January–April, 1955), 218–234.

to be ashamed of,' calmly confronting his captor, who cowers under the steady gaze of a brave and honorable man!"[33]

Jesup's own defense of his action is moderate and understandable. He insisted that he clearly had made known that he would not communicate with the Seminoles unless they determined to emigrate and came with the intention of remaining for that purpose, that many of the captured Indians were hostages who had violated their parole and had violated a recent truce entered into at Fort King, that the white flag had been allowed "for no other purpose than to enable them to communicate and come in without danger of attack from our parties." Since the Indians had not come to give themselves up but intended to return to their wilderness hideouts, Jesup felt that it was his duty to secure them.[34] Given his experience with the Seminoles, especially the coup of Osceola in June, it is hard to judge Jesup's action severely.[35]

While the Seminoles were imprisoned at St. Augustine, a deputation of Cherokees arrived, sent by their principal chief, John Ross, in an attempt to bring the war to an end. Jesup objected to the message they brought to the Seminoles, since it held out the promise of a treaty, and the general insisted that they change their message before presenting it, since he was required "to enforce the provisions of an *existing treaty*, not to make a *new treaty*." The Cherokee commissioners met with the prisoners in St. Augustine and made excursions to the south to meet with leaders of the hostile bands. But in the end nothing was accomplished. The Cherokees were sympathetic with the Seminole position and expected a change in the government's that was not forthcoming.[36]

Jesup faced the situation in Florida realistically, and he came to the

[33] Charles H. Coe, *Red Patriots: The Story of the Seminoles* (Cincinnati, 1898), pp. 89, 91.

[34] Jesup's letter of justification of November 17, 1837, and related documents are in *House Document* No. 327, 25 Congress, 2 session, serial 329. See also Jesup's report to Poinsett, July 6, 1838, Sprague, *The Florida War*, p. 188.

[35] Mark F. Boyd in his sketch of Osceola says: "It would be difficult to understand how, given the opportunity, Jesup could have done otherwise than to seize Osceola and the other Indians, and not have been derelict in his duty." "Asi-Yaholo or Osceola," *Florida Historical Quarterly*, XXXIII (January–April, 1955), 297.

[36] Jesup recounts the mission in his report to Poinsett, July 6, 1838, Sprague, *The Florida War*, pp. 191–192. An extended discussion of the mission is in Edwin C. McReynolds, *The Seminoles* (Norman, Okla., 1957), pp. 197–206. Documents on the mission are in *House Document* No. 285, 25 Congress, 2 session, serial 328. The report of the commissioners to Ross is in "Report of Cherokee Deputation into Florida," *Chronicles of Oklahoma*, IX (December, 1931), 423–438.

conclusion that the removal of the Seminoles was not practicable, that to insist upon it would prolong a useless war without any hope of a satisfactory conclusion. "In regard to the Seminoles," he told the Secretary of War in February, 1838, "we have committed the error of attempting to remove them when their lands were not required for agricultural purposes; when they were not in the way of the white inhabitants; and when the greater portion of their country was an unexplored wilderness, of the interior of which we were as ignorant as of the interior of China. We exhibit, in our present contest, the first instance, perhaps, since the commencement of authentic history, of a nation employing an army to explore a country (for we can do little more than explore it), or attempting to remove a band of savages from one unexplored wilderness to another." While admitting that as a soldier, it was his duty to carry out the government's policy and not to comment upon it, he nevertheless expressed his frank opinion that "unless *immediate* emigration be abandoned, the war will continue for years to come, and at a constantly accumulating expense." He questioned "whether, even if the wilderness we are traversing could be inhabited by the white man (which is not the fact), the object we are contending for would be worth the cost? I certainly do not think it would; indeed, I do not consider the country south of Chickasa-Hatchee worth the medicines we shall expend in driving the Indians from it." He proposed that the Indians be allowed to remain in the south of Florida behind specified boundaries, where they would be allowed to live unmolested if they did not commit depredations upon the whites to the north. A trading post and agency at Charlotte Harbor and military posts there and at Tampa, he judged, would be enough to keep the Indians in line. He concluded with a reiteration of his initial assertion: "I respectfully recommend the measure to your consideration, and that of the president, as the only means of terminating, immediately, a most disastrous war, and leaving the troops disposable for other service."[37]

The answer from the Secretary of War dashed Jesup's hopes completely to the ground. The government was not yet willing to budge an inch in its intransigence.

In the present stage of our relations with the Indians residing within the states and territories east of the Mississippi, including the

[37] Jesup to Poinsett, February 11, 1838, Sprague, *The Florida War*, pp. 200–201.

Seminoles, it is useless to recur to the principles and motives which induced the government to determine their removal to the west. The acts of the executive and the laws of congress evince a determination to carry out the measure, and it is to be regarded as the settled policy of the country. In pursuance of this policy, the treaty of Payne's Landing was made with the Seminoles, and the character of the officer employed on the part of the government is a guarantee of the perfectly fair manner in which that negotiation was conducted and concluded. Whether the government ought not to have waited until the Seminoles were pressed upon by the white population, and their lands became necessary to the agricultural wants of the community, is not a question for the executive now to consider. The treaty has been ratified, and is the law of the land; and the constitutional duty of the president requires that he should cause it to be executed. I cannot, therefore, authorize any arrangement with the Seminoles, by which they will be permitted to remain, or assign them any portion of the Territory of Florida as their future residence.[38]

All that the Secretary of War would allow, in case the war could not be prosecuted to a successful conclusion in that season, was a temporary arrangement with the Seminoles "by which the safety of the settlements and the posts will be secured throughout the summer."

☆

While Jesup was involved in the campaigns in the northeast, the operations southeast of Tampa Bay were placed in the hands of Colonel Zachary Taylor, who had arrived with the First Infantry in the fall.[39] After organizing his troops, consisting of several regiments of regulars, volunteers from Florida, Louisiana, and Missouri, and a group of Delaware and Shawnee Indians, Taylor in the middle of December headed his command east from Tampa Bay to search out the enemy. As he proceeded, some chiefs and their followers gave themselves up and were sent back to Tampa Bay while Taylor continued his march. He

[38] Poinsett to Jesup, March 1, 1838, *ibid.*, pp. 201–202. For a similar statement, see Poinsett to Jesup, July 25, 1837, *House Document* No. 78, 25 Congress, 2 session, serial 323, pp. 32–33.

[39] For Taylor's operations, see the excellent account in Brainerd Dyer, *Zachary Taylor* (Baton Rouge, 1946), pp. 100–127, and also the presentation in Holman Hamilton, *Zachary Taylor, Soldier of the Republic* (Indianapolis, 1941), pp. 122–141.

established a temporary depot on the banks of the Kissimmee, then pressed on with a reduced force of 800 men through the tortuous terrain of cypress swamps and dense hammocks, passing hastily abandoned camps of the hostiles, until finally on the morning of December 25 he caught up with the enemy.[40]

The Indians had chosen a position in a swamp, which Taylor described as "three-fourths of a mile in breadth, being totally impassable for horse, and nearly so for foot, covered with a thick growth of sawgrass, five feet high and about knee deep in mud and water." Taylor ordered his men to dismount, and the horses and baggage were left under guard at the edge of the swamp. He placed the Missouri volunteers in the front line with instructions to fall back to the rear if hard pressed, and with troops of the Fourth and Sixth Infantry in the second line and those of the First held in reserve, he led his army through the swamp to meet the enemy. The troops were met by heavy fire, and although the volunteers held their ground briefly, when their commander, Colonel Richard Gentry, fell mortally wounded, they fled back across the swamp to their baggage and horses; "nor could they be again brought into action as a body," Taylor reported, "although efforts were made repeatedly by my staff to induce them to do so."

As the volunteers fell back, the regulars of the Fourth and Sixth Infantry moved into the face of the fire from the Indians but continued to advance. After three hours of heavy fighting the Seminoles were driven back to the shores of Lake Okeechobee, completely routed. Taylor then turned his attention to his own casualties—26 dead and 112 wounded officers and men—who had to be conveyed back through the swamps and hammocks.

The large number of casualties made the Battle of Okeechobee one of the most disastrous of the war. The Seminole losses were probably less than those of Taylor's army, for the known dead totaled only fourteen. But the battle had been one of the few times when the Indians had been aggressively pursued into their interior hiding places and fought on their own ground. Taylor continued to harass the Indians in the Everglade country, but he fought no further battles. The power of the Americans was not lost upon the Indians, and in the following months additional groups, including Alligator and his whole band of 360, surrendered to the general.

Taylor's success at Lake Okeechobee won for him a brevet brigadier-

[40] Taylor to Jones, January 4, 1838, *American State Papers: Military Affairs*, VII, 986–989. The quotations in the paragraphs following are from this report.

generalcy, but his remarks about the Missouri volunteers in his official report plagued him for many years. Taylor was severely criticized by Senator Thomas Hart Benton and other Missourians, but his demand for a court of inquiry to clear his name was turned down by the War Department. Secretary of War Poinsett declared that his reputation was secure.[41]

On May 15, 1838, General Jesup relinquished command of the army in Florida to Taylor, who considered the war "pretty much at an end" as far as the main body of the Seminoles was concerned. By the time he took command, more than 2,000 Seminoles had been captured or had surrendered and had been sent to the West. If the estimate of 5,000 Seminoles at the beginning of the hostilities was correct, Taylor now faced no more than 3,000 and possibly a considerably smaller number. But the prediction of the end of the war was unduly optimistic. Small parties of Indians dispersed all over the Territory would suddenly appear to attack a settlement or a detachment of soldiers and then quickly disappear into the wilderness again. For two years Taylor faced the recalcitrant warriors, who could not be met in force and defeated by the superior American army, but who instead had to be ferreted out almost one at a time, keeping the army on constant patrol and large numbers of soldiers tied up in the seemingly never-ending campaign.

Taylor took his duties seriously and was willing to attempt any reasonable means of bringing the war to a close. He insisted that it was necessary to encourage settlers to migrate to Florida so that an increased population could provide its own protection, and to that end

[41] Dyer, *Taylor*, pp. 111–113. Poinsett, in transmitting Taylor's report on the battle to the Senate, February 20, 1838, attempted to soften the general's strictures on the volunteers: "As it has been supposed that some expressions contained in that report cast unmerited censure upon the Missouri volunteers, I avail myself of the occasion to remove so erroneous an impression. The patriotic feelings which led these brave men to volunteer their services in Florida, and leave their homes to engage in a campaign against the Indians, were duly appreciated by the President and by this department; and, in their opinion, the pledge thus given to the country has been amply redeemed. The fact that they broke and retired in disorder under the murderous fire of an enemy as advantageously posted as if they had been behind regular entrenchments, is not stated to disparage the character or the efforts of the young soldiers. The heavy loss they sustained, in killed and wounded, affords sufficient proof of the firmness with which they advanced upon the enemy under a galling fire. It was not expected that their unaided efforts could drive the enemy from his strong hold; and the gallant manner in which they led the attack contributed, no doubt, to the success of the day." *Senate Document* No. 277, 25 Congress, 2 session, serial 316, p. 1.

Statements of officers of the Missouri volunteers repudiating Taylor's remarks are printed in *Senate Document* No. 356, 25 Congress, 2 session, serial 317.

he urged that militia not be called from Florida, since the departure of the men from their homes weakened the settlements and the possibility of military service was hardly an inducement for new settlers to come in.

He also approved the use of Cuban bloodhounds to track down the Indians. "I am decidedly in favor of the measure," he wrote to the Adjutant General in July, 1838, "and beg leave again to urge it as the only means of ridding the country of the Indians who are now broken up into small parties that take shelter in swamps and hammocks as the army approaches, making it impossible for us to follow or overtake them, without the aid of such auxiliaries."[42] Secretary of War Poinsett approved the measure, arguing that the "cold blooded and inhuman murders lately perpetrated upon helpless women and children by these ruthless savages" made any means expedient to track down the Indians.[43] Although Taylor himself never ordered any bloodhounds, a supply of dogs was acquired by territorial officials of Florida. Initial trials seemed to indicate success, and dogs were delivered to the First Infantry and to the Second Dragoons. But further experiments proved the dogs much less successful. The dogs had little interest in following Indian trails, and the swamps, bogs, lakes, and streams of Florida in which they had to work prevented their following the trails for any distance.[44]

When word got out, however, that the scheme had been proposed, there was an immediate howl of protest from humanitarians in the North. Objection to the use of bloodhounds was raised in Congress, and angry citizens sent in petition after petition against the use of the animals.[45] The matter had to be quieted by the Secretary of War, who assured Senator Benton that the critics were deceived about the dogs "when they suppose that their employment will degrade the character of the country, or render its officers obnoxious to the charge of cruelty." The purpose, he asserted, had been merely to use the bloodhounds as guides in discovering the lurking places of the Indians, not to worry or destroy them. And he pointed to his earlier order to General Taylor directing that if the dogs were employed their use be limited to merely tracking the Indians; whenever they were in the field they were to be

[42] Taylor to Jones, July 28, 1838, *Senate Document* No. 187, 26 Congress, 1 session, serial 357, p. 3.

[43] Adjutant General to Taylor, August 31, 1838, quoted in Dyer, *Taylor*, pp. 116–117.

[44] A general account of the use of bloodhounds in the war is James W. Covington, "Cuban Bloodhounds and the Seminoles," *Florida Historical Quarterly*, XXXIII (October, 1954), 111–119.

[45] Dyer, *Taylor*, p. 117n, cites references to numerous memorials.

muzzled and held on a leash.[46] It was a tempest in a teapot, but it showed the sensitiveness of the nation to what was going on in Florida. The use of the bloodhounds, indeed, could be treated lightly, as John Quincy Adams did in the House of Representatives when he introduced a resolution calling upon the Secretary of War to report on the "natural, political, and martial history of bloodhounds, showing the peculiar fitness of that class of warriors to be associates of the gallant army of the United States . . . and whether he deems it expedient to extend to the said bloodhounds and their posterity the benefits of the pension laws."[47] But the dragging-out of the war was increasingly embarrassing. As the number of hostile Indians decreased, it was more and more difficult to show any striking victories. Forcing Indians out of their hiding places in as vast and wild an area as Florida was not a very glamorous task. It is to Taylor's credit that he went about the work in an orderly and businesslike way.

In his winter campaign of 1838–1839, Taylor's object was to drive the Indians from the vicinity of the settlements north of Tampa Bay. He proceeded to construct a line of forts across Florida from the bay to New Smyrna on the Atlantic and to force the Indians south of that line. He and his troops pursued the work with great diligence, with efforts that Taylor regarded as "amounting to recklessness" and as "unparalled in the annals of Indian Warfare."[48] The results were meager. Taylor in this campaign had built or rebuilt fifty-three forts, constructed nearly 4,000 feet of bridges and opened almost 1,000 miles of new roads. Yet the army could not seem to catch the elusive Indians, who fled from one swamp to another but who could not be captured or brought into open battle.

General Taylor then proposed another plan. Despairing of driving all the hostiles out of the northern part of the Florida Territory by moving his troops in columns and detachments, he proposed instead to divide the whole area north of the Withlacoochee River into military districts, twenty miles square. In the center of each square he would garrison a post with an officer and twenty to thirty men, who would scour the district every other day to be sure it was clear of Indians. Thus would the settlers be able to return to their homes. The project moved ahead rapidly under the direction of skilled officers, and the

[46] Poinsett to Benton, February 17, 1840, *Senate Document* No. 187, 26 Congress, 1 session, serial 357, p. 1; Poinsett to Taylor, January 26, 1840, *ibid.*, p. 5.
[47] Quoted in Dyer, *Taylor*, pp. 117–118.
[48] *Ibid.*, pp. 118–119.

maps of the Florida war prepared under Taylor's direction show the squares marked off with a "fort" in each.[49]

Meanwhile a new effort for peace was undertaken. Congress appropriated $5,000 to pay the cost of special negotiations with the Seminoles, and the administration after the frustrations of the war was willing to make peace short of absolute removal. Jesup's proposals, which had been flatly turned down the year before, were now to be given a trial. General Alexander Macomb, the Commanding General of the Army, himself undertook the peace mission. Macomb left Washington on March 22, 1839, and arrived at Garey's Ferry on April 7. By the end of the month he had moved his headquarters to Fort King, where the meetings with the Indians were to be held. Macomb approached his mission with a high sense of humanity and justice, and great hopes were entertained for the success of the conclave. Two meetings were held with the Seminoles, one on May 18 and a second on May 22, and a general agreement—a non-written treaty—was reached. Macomb optimistically announced the cessation of hostilities and the return of peace, for the Indians agreed to withdraw to the region south of Pease Creek, and they were given sixty days to remove their families into the designated district. The troops of the United States were to see that the Indians were not molested there by intruders and that the Indians did not pass the limits assigned to them.[50]

But the end was not yet. The whites in Florida denounced the agreement, since they saw no peace until all the Indians had been exterminated or removed. And events quickly showed that the treaty of Macomb was not the beginning of permanent peace that he had supposed. In June scattered depredations were reported, and on July 22 the war began again with the murder of a detachment of troops on the Caloosahatchee River east of Charlotte Harbor.

[49] The "Map of the Seat of War in Florida, compiled by order of Bvt Brigr Genl Z. Taylor, principally from the surveys & reconnaissances of the Officers of the U. S. Army, by Capt John Mackay and Lieut J. E. Blake, U. S. Topographical Engineers . . . 1839," National Archives, Cartographic Branch, Record Group 77, shows the numbered squares marked out, with a fort—named or unnamed—within each one. The number of named forts in the Florida War was very large, somewhere in the neighborhood of 150, plus 14 on the southern Georgia frontier. Most of these were temporary fortifications or depots. See the list in Francis Paul Prucha, A Guide to the Military Posts of the United States, 1789–1895 (Madison, Wis., 1964), Appendix A, pp. 139–141.

[50] Macomb's General Orders of May 18, 1839, announcing the termination of the war, and his report of May 22, 1839, to Poinsett, are in Sprague, The Florida War, pp. 228–232. See also "Macomb's Mission to the Seminoles: John T. Sprague's Journal Kept during April and May, 1839," ed. Frank F. White, Jr., Florida Historical Quarterly, XXXV (October, 1956), 130–193.

General Taylor complained about the shortage of officers for the army under his command and noted the hostility of the people of Florida toward the regular army and toward himself, and he requested to be relieved of his command. But Poinsett denied his request, and the general prepared for another campaign. This time his instructions were to drive the Indians out of the settlements into the region south of a line from the mouth of the Withlacoochee to Pilatka on the St. Johns River, a line nearly one hundred miles north of the line from Tampa Bay to New Smyrna, along which Taylor's troops had been building a line of forts the year before. The campaign was quieter than those of previous years, for there were few encounters with the Indians, and the settlers were able to do their planting with less danger than at any time since the beginning of the war. Again Taylor requested to be relieved of command, and Poinsett finally agreed. Brigadier General W. K. Armistead was directed to assume command of the army in Florida.[51]

☆

General Armistead assumed command on May 6, 1840, but he made no appreciable headway in the campaign. The war dragged on through the summer, and the excessive heat and the summer sickness took the usual toll of the troops. By the next spring Armistead had had enough and on April 30 asked to be relieved of the command. One month later the command of the Florida army was once again turned over to a new officer, this time to Colonel William Jenkins Worth of the Eighth Infantry, who had arrived in Florida the previous October and had taken over direction of the operations. Worth aggressively pursued the war, deciding upon a summer campaign, something that had been considered impossible because of the heat. He led his men into the swamps of the Everglades, destroying the settlements and crops of the Seminoles. Through the heat of the summer he harried the Indians, and despite the sickness of his troops succeeded in his expedi-

---

[51] Dyer, *Taylor*, pp. 124–125. The two recent biographies of Taylor give seemingly contradictory evaluations of Taylor's part in the Florida War. Dyer, *Taylor*, p. 126, says: ". . . whether he contributed more to the winning of the war [than his predecessors] is not easy to determine. Probably he did not." Hamilton, *Zachary Taylor, Soldier of the Republic*, p. 141, says: ". . . he had contributed more substantially than any other individual in shaping it toward a successful termination." But the story of Taylor's efforts told by the two biographers is substantially the same.

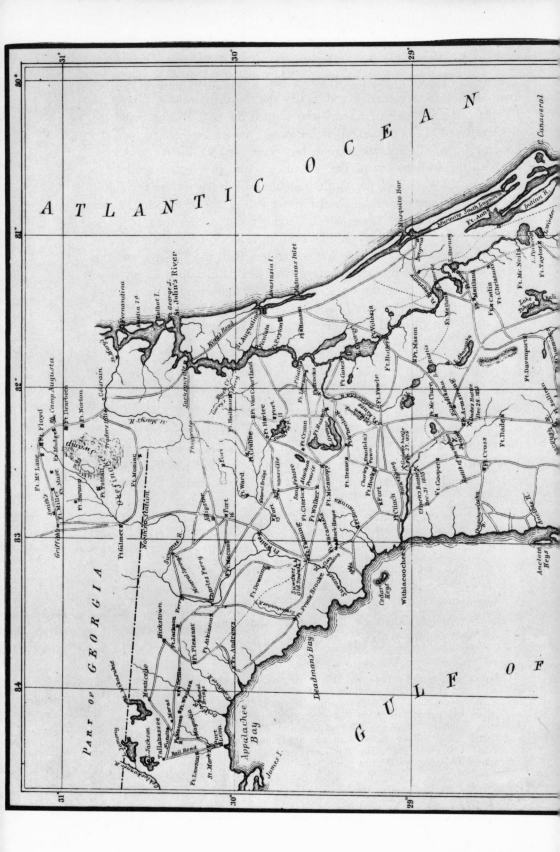

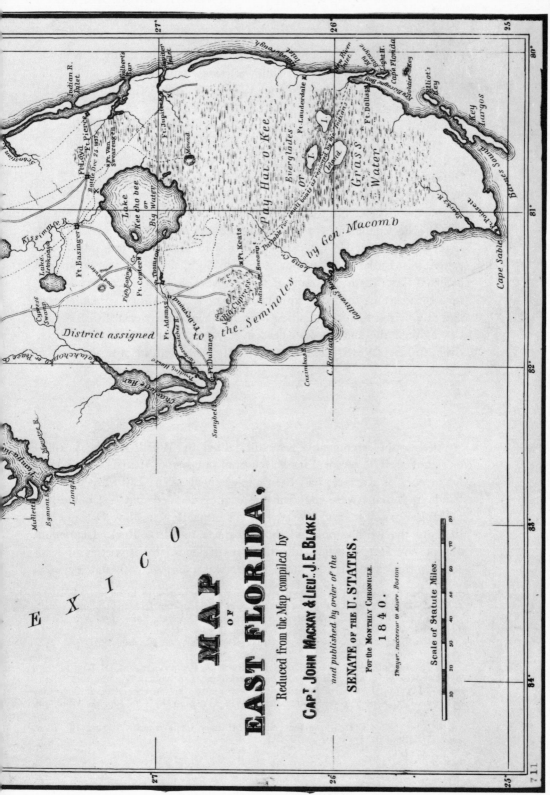

Map of East Florida, 1840

tion. Chief Wild Cat and his followers submitted peacefully to removal to Arkansas and other bands followed this example.[52]

On February 14, 1842, Colonel Worth wrote to Winfield Scott, who had succeeded Macomb as Commanding General of the Army in the summer of 1841, suggesting that a halt be called to the hostilities. "I believe there has been no instance," he began, "in which, in the removal of Indians, some, more or less, have not been left." And he declared the "utter impracticability" of securing by force the few Seminoles still left in Florida.[53] His observations were heeded, after some hestitation lest the honor of the country and the gallantry of the army be compromised, and the President on May 10 announced the decision in a special message to Congress. He noted the presence in Florida of only about 240 remaining Indians, of whom 80 were judged to be warriors, and asserted that "further pursuit of these miserable beings by a large military force seems to be as injudicious as it is unavailing." He therefore had authorized the commanding officer in Florida to declare that hostilities against the Indians had ceased.[54] In accordance with these directives, Colonel Worth on August 14, 1842, declared the war at an end.[55]

☆

All but the irremovable remnant tallied by Worth had been killed or removed. The removal itself, the final purpose of the treaties and the long years of warfare, had been a piecemeal affair. Little by little the bands of Indians were rounded up, as they decided that resistance was no longer possible, and moved from Tampa Bay to New Orleans and then up the Mississippi and the Arkansas to Little Rock. Lieutenant Joseph W. Harris, who had already experienced the anxieties of leading Cherokees to their western home, was charged with the responsi-

[52] A brief account of Worth's participation in the war is in Edward S. Wallace, *General William Jenkins Worth, Monterey's Forgotten Hero* (Dallas, 1953), pp. 53–55. Colonel Worth's correspondence on the Florida campaign is in *House Document* No. 262, 27 Congress, 2 session, serial 405.

[53] Worth to Scott, February 14, 1842, Sprague, *The Florida War*, pp. 441–444.

[54] Message of Tyler, May 10, 1842, James D. Richardson, ed., *A Compilation of the Messages and Papers of the Presidents* (10 vols., Washington, 1896–1899), IV, 154. Details of handling the termination are in the letter of Secretary of War J. C. Spencer to Scott, May 10, 1842, Sprague, *The Florida War*, pp. 477–479.

[55] Order No. 28, Headquarters Ninth Military Department, August 14, 1842, *ibid.*, p. 486.

bility of transporting the willing Indians from Tampa Bay. On April 11 and 12, 1836, he embarked 407 of the friendly Indians and on the 23d arrived with them at New Orleans. On a steamboat and keelboat in tow, they arrived at Little Rock on May 5, numbering then 382, for 25 had died on the way. Harris was too ill to accompany them farther, but under Lieutenant George G. Meade the Indians made their way on to the West. By the time they reached their destination, only 320 of the original band were left. As the war progressed, additional bands of Indians were secured and sent from Tampa Bay to New Orleans, to join their brothers west of Arkansas.[56]

By May 1, 1838, a thousand Indians and Negroes were at New Orleans, waiting to be transported up the Mississippi and Arkansas rivers. On May 14 Lieutenant John G. Reynolds reached the city from Tampa Bay with another party of captives, which brought the total to 1,160. As these moved up the Mississippi, others arrived at New Orleans—117 from Charleston on May 28 and on June 14, 335 more from Tampa Bay. Throughout the year captives were slowly assembled at Tampa Bay and sent on as circumstances permitted. The years 1839, 1840, and 1841 saw the same kinds of movements. By March 21, 1842, according to the estimate of General Taylor, then stationed at Fort Smith, Arkansas, 2,833 Seminole Indians had been removed from Florida and located on new lands in the vicinity of Fort Gibson.

So ended this bitterest episode in the annals of the frontier army. After more than six years of fighting under conditions that no soldier was trained or equipped to meet, the futile contest was declared over. More than 1,500 soldiers had lost their lives and the costs of the war reached the staggering total of $20 million. The soldiers who were left, departing from the treacherous climate of Florida to new and hopefully more healthful posts in the north and west, might well have wondered if it was all worthwhile. The troops and their officers had acquitted themselves well. The Secretary of War and the President lauded them for the success of their efforts, but the Florida war was for the soldiers themselves in retrospect a time of sadness, as they watched the fate of a doomed people.

The inadequacies of the military arm had again been made apparent. Having stubbornly determined upon a course of fulfilling the letter of

---

[56] The fullest account of the removal, and that on which I have relied, is Grant Foreman, *Indian Removal: The Emigration of the Five Civilized Tribes of Indians* (Norman, Okla., 1932), pp. 315–386. See also McReynolds, *The Seminoles*, pp. 169–173, 208–242.

the treaties of removal at all cost, the government discovered too late that it did not have on hand the means to execute effectively what it had so strongly resolved upon. The regular army, gallant and dutiful as it may have been, was clearly unequal to the task, and the militia called to duty from Florida and from nearby states was little more valuable than the militia had been in other frontier campaigns, and the volunteers frequently caused more trouble than their aid was ultimately worth.

☆

At the end of the war in 1842 Colonel Worth had made an agreement with the Seminoles remaining in Florida, by which the Indians were allowed lands on which to plant and hunt. It was a temporary arrangement, which, though not formally repudiating the title of the United States to the lands acquired by the Treaty of Payne's Landing, nevertheless reserved for the remaining Seminoles lands on which no white settlements were to be made. This *modus vivendi* did not guarantee a lasting peace. After Florida became a state in 1845, there was increasing dissatisfaction among her people with the agreement of Colonel Worth, and the cries became more strident for a final expulsion of the Seminole remnants, who numbered no more than 500 individuals.[57]

In 1849, when a small party of Seminoles murdered a white man fishing on Indian River, Florida was immediately aroused. The legislature called for the federal government to put down the Indian uprising, and the government made another attempt to effect the removal of the remaining Seminoles. Colonel Joseph Plympton was ordered with the Seventh Infantry from Jefferson Barracks to Tampa, to report there to General David E. Twiggs, commander of the Western Division. And the Secretary of War reported the assembling of more than 1,700 officers and men in Florida. The Indians meanwhile had surrendered three men accused of the murder, but the chiefs refused to consider emigration. A delegation of Seminoles from the West headed by Halleck Tustenuggee, which arrived in November, 1849, had little success in persuading their brethren to move; nor did General Twiggs, who held a meeting with the chiefs on January 19, 1850, in which he placed

[57] Secretary of the Interior Alexander H. H. Stuart to the President, January 14, 1853, *House Document* No. 19, 32 Congress, 2 session, serial 676, p. 3.

before the Seminoles a more attractive offer than had been made to any other emigrating Indians. Only eighty-five Indians could be assembled, and the western delegation gave up and went home.[58]

Then the Commissioner of Indian Affairs, working with the Secretary of the Interior, on April 18, 1851, appointed Luther Blake as a special agent "for the purpose of endeavoring, by judicious arrangements and efforts" to remove the remaining Indians from Florida and establish them with their kinsmen west of Arkansas.[59] Blake, a former Creek agent, who held conferences with the Indians in Florida and at first reported encouragingly on the prospect of removal, soon despaired of a voluntary emigration. The Seminole chief, Billy Bowlegs, and other Seminoles who visited Washington to confer with the commissioner in September, 1852, agreed to use their influence among the Indians for removal, but Blake reported in December that they had not complied with their agreement. He recommended that the whole Indian region be surveyed for white settlement at once, under military protection.[60] Further hostilities occurred between the Indians and the settlers, and the Florida legislature announced to the President in January, 1853, that Florida was bound "to enforce her rights, under the treaty of Payne's Landing, by expelling the Seminole Indians."[61]

President Fillmore passed the matter on to Congress, offering only the alternatives of continuing the arrangement of 1842 (which he described as "a serious injury to the State of Florida") or compelling the Indians to move by force. The latter alternative would entail an enlarged military force, he noted, for owing to the great extent of the area occupied by the small number of Indians and its adaptation to the Indian mode of fighting, "a force very disproportioned to their numbers would be necessary to capture or expel them, or even to protect the white settlements from their incursions."[62] The tension continued until force was again the arbiter.

The situation came to a head in 1856 as efforts for peaceful removal

[58] McReynolds, *The Seminoles*, pp. 264–267. See also the report of Secretary of War George W. Crawford, November 30, 1849, *Senate Executive Document* No. 1, 31 Congress, 1 session, serial 549, pp. 93–94, and documents in "Operations in Florida," *ibid.*, pp. 116–137.

[59] Luke Lea to Luther Blake, April 18, 1851, *Senate Executive Document* No. 71, 33 Congress, 1 session, serial 702, pp. 2–4. This entire document contains letters and reports dealing with the Florida troubles.

[60] See the documents in *House Executive Document* No. 19, 32 Congress, 2 session, serial 676.

[61] *Senate Miscellaneous Document* No. 51, 32 Congress, 2 session, serial 670.

[62] Message of January 18, 1853, *House Executive Document* No. 19, 32 Congress, 2 session, serial 676, pp. 1–2.

failed and outrages along the frontier continued, and the War Department sent more regular troops to Florida. The ten companies of the First and Second Artillery that made up the Department of Florida on June 30, 1856, were transferred to the Department of Texas and the Department of the East, and a whole new force manned the posts in the Florida peninsula—four companies of the Fourth Artillery, and the Fifth Infantry—twenty-four companies in all. Brevet Brigadier General William S. Harney was given command of the department.[63]

The Indians disappeared into the swamps, but their occasional raids and engagements with scouting parties kept the "war" alive. On March 5, 1857, a reconnoitering party of the Fifth Infantry under Lieutenant Edmund Freeman was attacked by the Indians near Bowlegs' town in Big Cypress Swamp. The Indians in turn were attacked and put to flight by a supporting party from Fort Keais. Four of the whites were killed and five wounded; the Indians carried their casualties uncounted into the impenetrable hammocks. A month later, on April 7, a large force of Seminoles attacked a detachment of artillery. The regulars suffered seven casualties in driving the Indians back into the swamps.[64] These were small engagements, but the threat they posed was enough to tie down large numbers of troops.

The troops could ill be spared for Florida, for the whole West was smoldering or aflame, and the Fifth Infantry was withdrawn from Florida and dispatched to take part in the expedition to Utah organized in June, 1857. Only the ten companies of artillery remained when the Adjutant General submitted his strength reports on June 30; in the fall of the year even these were cut to four companies when the Fourth Artillery was sent to Kansas.[65] The military service in Florida devolved upon mounted Florida volunteers, who were mustered into federal service. Under Colonel Gustavus Loomis of the Fifth Infantry, who had replaced Harney in command of the Department of Florida on April 27, 1857, they carried on the same tactics that the regulars had used. Their operations were duly recorded as they scouted out the Seminoles, killing

---

[63] Report of Secretary of War Jefferson Davis, December 1, 1856, *Senate Executive Document* No. 5, 34 Congress, 3 session, serial 876, p. 5.

[64] General Orders No. 4, Headquarters of the Army, March 30, 1857, *Senate Executive Document* No. 11, 35 Congress, 1 session, serial 920, p. 50; General Orders No. 14, Headquarters of the Army, November 13, 1857, *ibid.*, pp. 52–53; William S. Harney to Lorenzo Thomas, Assistant Adjutant General, March 8, 1857, *ibid.*, p. 142.

[65] *Senate Executive Document* No. 11, 35 Congress, 1 session, serial 920, pp. 70–71.

a few warriors and capturing women and children.[66] It was a type of conflict that frustrated the War Department. "The country is a perpetual succession of swamps and morasses, almost impenetrable," Secretary of War John B. Floyd reported in December, 1857, "and the Indians partake rather of the nature of beasts of the chase than of men capable of resisting in fight a military power. Their only strength lies in a capacity to elude pursuit."[67]

Although it was reported that the Seminoles were receiving supplies from the Bahamas, the steady attrition on their small fighting force and the destruction of their fields began to tell. The volunteers overran Billy Bowlegs' village (identified by a daguerreotype found there of Billy's group taken on its peace mission to Washington), and prisoners reported that Billy himself was entreating the Indians to turn themselves in but that more belligerent members of the tribe threatened anyone who talked of peace. Colonel Loomis talked of an "active prosecution of the campaign" and of anticipating "some important results in a few weeks."[68]

The denouement began as a new peace delegation from the western Seminoles and Creeks was set on foot to attempt once more to convince the Florida Seminoles to emigrate. Elias Rector, superintendent of the southern Indians, accompanied by the Seminole and Creek agents and a group of Seminoles and Creeks, arrived at Fort Brooke on January 19, 1858. On January 27 Colonel Loomis went with the delegation to Fort Myers; he directed Captain John M. Brannan, in charge of the military district there, to call in his scouting parties and to cease hostilities, and he did all in his power to bring the Indians and the delegation into communication. "I am satisfied," he reported optimistically, "that there never has been a more favorable time for peaceful communication than the present." The delegation succeeded in making contact with the chiefs and arranged a council at Fort Myers on March 15, which promised well, and another for the 27th to make final arrangements for removal.[69]

[66] General Orders No. 22, Headquarters of the Army, November 10, 1858, *Senate Executive Document* No. 1, 35 Congress, 2 session, serial 975, pp. 20–21.

[67] *Senate Executive Document* No. 11, 35 Congress, 1 session, serial 920, p. 5.

[68] Gustavus Loomis to Irvin McDowell, Assistant Adjutant General, December 2, December 6, December 13, 1857, *Senate Executive Document* No. 1, 35 Congress, 2 session, serial 975, pp. 224–225, 229–230.

[69] Loomis to Brannan, January 29, 1858; Loomis to McDowell, January 30, March 6, March 22, 1858, *ibid.*, pp. 236–238, 241. See McReynolds, *The Seminoles*, pp. 286–287, for an account of the delegation.

A party of 125 were assembled at Fort Myers and carried on May 4 to Egmont Key at the entrance to Tampa Bay. Here they were joined by 40 more, who'had been concentrated on the key for safekeeping by the Florida volunteers. As the full party prepared to leave for New Orleans on the steamer "Grey Cloud," Rector reported his charges: 123 Indians, including 38 warriors and 85 women and children, who had consented to emigrate voluntarily; 41 hostiles who had been captured; and the Indian woman "Polly," a niece of Bowlegs who had been used to effect contact between the parties—a total of 165 being moved to new homes away from Florida. There still remained scattered groups that had not been rounded up: 17 men under the centenarian Sam Jones, 12 warriors in the "Boat party," and a small group (perhaps 8 warriors) of Tallahassees.[70]

Colonel Loomis could now declare the war at an end, which he hastened to do on May 8, 1858. The widely scattered warriors remaining, he proclaimed, were no longer a threat and the people could lead their lives without fear of further molestation. He ordered the entire volunteer force mustered out and thanked his troops for their zeal and energy. When the Adjutant General next reported the distribution of troops (June 30, 1858), there was only one company of artillery with 104 officers and men of the regular army left in Florida, and most of them were at Key West.[71]

[70] Rector to Loomis, May 6, 1858; Loomis to Samuel Cooper, Adjutant General, May 8, 1858, *Senate Executive Document* No. 1, 35 Congress, 2 session, serial 975, pp. 241–242; Foreman, *Indian Removal*, pp. 384–385. In December, 1858, Rector and a group of eight Seminoles including Bowlegs were back in Florida on another mission. This time a total of seventy-five Seminoles were persuaded to move to the west, and they sailed for New Orleans on February 15, 1859. McReynolds, *The Seminoles*, p. 287.

[71] General Orders No. 4, Headquarters Department of Florida, May 8, 1858, *Senate Executive Document* No. 1, 35 Congress, 2 session, serial 975, p. 244; Adjutant General's report, *ibid.*, serial 976, pp. 772–773.

FIFTEEN

New Threats on the Frontiers

WHILE the troubles in Florida were engaging the major attention of the army, the United States was faced with two new claims upon its limited military forces, one on the Louisiana-Texas frontier, the other along the Canadian border from Michigan to Vermont.

The Texas agitation began almost simultaneously with the Florida war. When Secretary of War Cass sent General Scott in January, 1836, to take command of the operations against the Seminoles, he at the same time directed General Gaines to await orders in New Orleans for attending to affairs west of the Mississippi, which threatened to come to a crisis as the Texans staged their revolution against Mexico. Although Gaines in his energetic fashion had managed to stick his oar into the troubled Florida waters, he was shortly back at New Orleans, ready to safeguard American neutrality along the Sabine River and to protect the frontier population from Indian dangers.[1]

On January 23, 1836, the Secretary of War had sent instructions to Gaines to proceed to the western frontier of the State of Louisiana and there to assume personal command of the troops in the area adjoining the Mexican boundary. Gaines was informed that the Sixth Infantry was being ordered to Fort Jesup and that he was to use these troops

---

[1] The story of General Gaines's activities on the Texas frontier in 1836 is told in Eugene C. Barker, "The United States and Mexico, 1835–1837," *Mississippi Valley Historical Review*, I (June, 1914), 3–30; Thomas Maitland Marshall, *A History of the Western Boundary of the Louisiana Purchase, 1819–1841* (Berkeley, Calif., 1914), pp. 141–185; and James W. Silver, *Edmund Pendleton Gaines, Frontier General* (Baton Rouge, 1949), pp. 191–215. See also J. Fair Hardin, "Fort Jesup—Fort Selden—Camp Sabine—Camp Salubrity: Four Forgotten Frontier Army Posts of Western Louisiana," *Louisiana Historical Quarterly*, XVI (April, 1933), 279–292, (July, 1933), 441–453.

and all those in the country west of the Mississippi and south of the Missouri. "The state of affairs in Texas," Cass said, "calls for immediate measures on the part of the Government." Gaines was to prevent belligerents of either side from crossing the boundary and to make sure that Indians from the United States did not make hostile incursions into Texas.[2]

These orders reached Gaines on March 28, after he had returned to New Orleans, and the general immediately turned over the troops he was collecting for the Seminole War and started on his way to the frontier. From Baton Rouge on the next day he wrote to the War Department of his plans—a forthright intention to take aggressive action if necessary: "Should I find any disposition on the part of the Mexicans, or their red allies, to menace our frontier, I cannot but deem it to be my duty not only to hold the troops of my command in readiness for action in defence of our slender frontier, but to anticipate their lawless movements, by crossing our supposed or imaginary national boundary, and meeting the savage marauders wherever to be found in their approach towards our frontier." To accomplish his purpose, he would need mounted forces equal to the estimated strength of the enemy, some 8,000 to 12,000 men.[3]

Gaines reached Natchitoches on April 4 and began to recruit and organize his forces. He ordered the commanders at Fort Towson and Fort Gibson to prevent both Texans and Mexicans from passing the border in arms and to stop Indians from joining in the conflict. He became concerned that United States Indians had already crossed into Texas and would join with Santa Anna, who was moving north determined to wipe out his adversaries, and he considered it his duty "to prepare for action." He therefore called upon the governors of Louisiana, Mississippi, and Tennessee for a brigade of volunteers each, and on the governor of Louisiana for an additional battalion.[4]

Gaines was stirred to action by the reports of turmoil on the frontier when he arrived at Natchitoches. Texan forces had been repeatedly defeated by Santa Anna, and panic set in among the border settlers, who fled eastward in great numbers seeking security across the Sabine under the protection of United States troops. Rumors of Indian uprising increased the panic, and Gaines believed that agents were attempt-

---

[2] *House Executive Document* No. 256, 24 Congress, 1 session, serial 291, pp. 40–41.
[3] *Ibid.*, p. 43.
[4] Gaines to Cass, April 8, 1836, and to governors, April 8, 1836, *ibid.*, pp. 46–48.

ing to incite the Indians to join the Mexican forces. The settlers at Nacogdoches, painting a picture of impending doom from the Indians, appealed to Gaines for aid.

The Battle of San Jacinto changed the entire situation. By April 28 Gaines received word of the Texas victory, and at the same time he learned that the United States Indians who had gone into Texas were returning peaceably to their homes. In accord with this turn of events, Gaines withdrew his call for volunteers, who in any case had not yet been enrolled.

The sudden quieting of fears on the frontier and the fact that none of the fears had indeed been realized made Gaines's rapid movement of troops to the frontier and his plans for action seem precipitous. Yet it is hard to judge how much the very presence of Gaines's force contributed to the peaceful outcome, and the evidence he possessed, whatever its validity, certainly pointed to the need for preparations to meet serious trouble.

The initial hopes for peace after San Jacinto were soon dispelled, as Mexican recognition of Texan independence was withheld and the war renewed. Gaines soon had reason to fear a renewed restlessness on the part of the Indians. He called again for volunteers, but their movement to the Sabine was suspended by the President. Regular troops, however, moved in force to the southwest frontier, and the report of the Adjutant General showed 360 men at Fort Jesup, 124 men at a camp seventy miles from Fort Jesup, and 447 men at Camp Sabine, twenty-five miles west of the fort.[5]

As a precautionary measure Gaines had ordered a squadron of dragoons and six companies of the Seventh Infantry from Fort Gibson to Fort Towson, and on July 10 he ordered these troops to occupy Nacogdoches.[6] Gaines sent to Lieutenant Colonel Whistler, commanding these troops, a copy of Cass's instructions of May 12, which cautiously authorized such a movement. "If the Indians are not employed immediately upon the borders," Cass had directed, "there will be no need of your advancing beyond the territory heretofore in the actual occupation of the United States, unless armed parties should approach our frontiers so near as manifestly to show that they mean to violate our territory." The Secretary of War expected no such problems from the Texans or Mexicans, but the Indians he knew were less inclined to be

[5] Report of the Secretary of War, 1836, *American State Papers: Military Affairs*, VI, 819, 825.

[6] *House Executive Document* No. 190, 25 Congress, 2 session, serial 327, p. 98.

restrained by boundary lines, and if they threatened trouble Gaines was authorized "to cross the line dividing the country actually in the occupation of the 'United States, from that heretofore in the possession of Mexico." Under no circumstances was he to cooperate in any way with the belligerents, and he was to withdraw as soon as the safety of the frontier would permit.[7]

This movement of American forces into territory claimed by a foreign state, although it could be justified by conflicting and unsettled boundary definitions and the failure of the Mexican government to control the Indians of the border, caused sharp diplomatic protestations from the Mexican Minister in Washington.[8] As it turned out, the crossing of the border was probably an unnecessary move. The War Department and the President repeatedly sent Gaines counsels of prudence—"Unless the necessity exists, unless there are actual disturbances of the peace of the frontier, or a moral certainty that the Indians are in hostile array for the purpose and are drawing the means of operation from the territory of Mexico, the occupation of an advanced post in that territory, by our troops, must be avoided."[9] Colonel Whistler at Nacogdoches reported no disposition on the part of the Indians to attack our frontiers and complained of the hardships of an unnecessary 400-mile march.[10]

[7] Cass to Gaines, May 12, 1836, *House Executive Document* No. 256, 24 Congress, 1 session, serial 291, pp. 54–55.

[8] See *House Executive Document* No. 190, 25 Congress, 2 session, serial 291.

[9] Quoted in Barker, *Mississippi Valley Historical Review*, I, 21.

[10] Gaines has generally fared well with the historians for his Nacogdoches episode. Silver, *Gaines*, p. 215, says: "It is impossible to pass final judgment on Gaines's actions in the spring and summer of 1836. On the one hand he may simply have involved the United States in a bitter diplomatic dispute, while on the other he may possibly have saved the whole frontier from a devastating Indian war. His aid to the cause of Texan independence is problematical; what might have happened had the Mexicans marched to the Sabine in the spring or seriously invaded Texas will, of course, never be known. It is true that Gaines was an efficient and cautious general and that while he may have been overzealous in the performance of what he regarded as his duty, he attempted conscientiously to carry out his orders in the light of his remarkable past experience." Barker, *Mississippi Valley Historical Review*, I, 26, says: "While his sympathy for the Texans caused him to exaggerate the danger, it seems to the writer that he was sincere in his belief that it did exist, and that his conscious purpose was solely to protect the frontier of the United States from a devastating Indian war." Samuel Flagg Bemis, *A Diplomatic History of the United States* (New York, 1936), p. 224, concludes: "Gaines had loose instructions from the Secretary of War which he interpreted to allow him, in case a confused situation on the frontier should threaten an Indian outbreak, to cross the 'imaginary boundary line.' The territory he invaded was at least under dispute between Mexico and the United States; and the treaty of 1832 might be interpreted to justify such a step as Gaines' 'invasion' at a moment when Mexican forces were unable forcibly to keep the Indians pacified."

Sometime in October Gaines left the frontier for duty on a military court of inquiry in the East, passing the command in the Southwest to Colonel Arbuckle. Since there seemed to be no reason for the continued occupation of Nacogdoches, the troops were withdrawn on December 19, the dragoons marching to Fort Coffee and the Seventh Infantry to Fort Gibson. Seven companies of the Sixth Infantry left Fort Jesup for Florida, but the guard on the Sabine was maintained until 1838.

Threats of attacks from Indians inhabiting Texas (believed to have been incited by Mexican authorities) led to a request for a new call for militia in 1838, but the War Department withheld approval. The United States Indians, however, were warned not to take any part in Texas-Mexico conflicts under pain of losing their annuities.[11] From time to time detachments of troops moved into the upper Red River area to protect emigrant Indians from raids across the Texas border, until Fort Washita was built in 1842 to give continued protection to the area.

☆

Of greater potential danger was the excitement that suddenly burst upon the nation along the Canadian frontier. Here was a peculiar and unexpected situation. Growing discontent in both Upper and Lower Canada finally erupted in late 1837 into open rebellion. The frontier population of the United States along the border reacted strongly and immediately. These people, many of whom eked out a precarious existence and now suffered still more from the depression of 1837 and who were already touched with a radical spirit, rallied in support of the Canadians, whose oppression and rebellion they likened to the experience of the Americans in 1776. Public meetings of sympathy at Buffalo and other towns along the border attracted large crowds, who were inflamed by such speakers as William Lyon Mackenzie, the leader of the rebellion in Upper Canada. Many refugees from Canada drifted across the border and together with American sympathizers formed a pool of recruits for a "Patriot army" which sought to aid the rebellion by filibustering raids into Canada from the United States. By the end of 1837 the whole border was in ferment.[12]

[11] Report of Poinsett, November 28, 1838, *Senate Document* No. 1, 25 Congress, 3 session, serial 338, p. 112.

[12] The most satisfactory account of Patriot disturbances along the American-Canadian frontier is Albert B. Corey, *The Crisis of 1830–1842 in Canadian-American Relations* (New Haven, 1941), although the book is based chiefly on

The United States marshal of the northern district of New York hastened to Buffalo, which was the immediate focus of the infection, and wrote in alarm to President Van Buren: "This frontier is in a state of commotion. . . . I learned, on my arrival, that some 200 or 300 men, mostly from the district of country adjoining this frontier, and from this side of the Niagara, had congregated upon Navy island (Upper Canada), and were then in arms, with Rensselaer Van Rensselaer, of Albany, at their head as commander-in-chief. From that time to the present they have received constant accessions of men, munitions of war, provisions, &c., from persons residing within the States." He estimated that the total force of the Patriot army was 1,000 men and that they were well supplied with arms.[13]

To meet this challenge the Canadian authorities relied upon the civil and military power of the United States, which was expected to prevent such military activities originating on American soil. But the United States was ill-prepared. The civil authorities in New York, Vermont, and Michigan were powerless to stem such a popular movement, and the state militia, had it been called out, would have been of little help, since the men would have been recruited from the same border population that sympathized so strongly with the Patriot cause. The reliance should have been upon the regular military forces of the United States, but the northern frontier had been neglected in favor of the West and the South, and regular army troops at the key trouble spots in the north were nonexistent. As population increased along the St. Lawrence-Great Lakes frontier, the War Department had allowed the military defenses to disintegrate, on the theory that the populace itself was the only defense needed against such a weak neighbor as Canada.

State Department records and makes little use of War Department materials. Older or briefer accounts are Edwin C. Guillet, *The Lives and Times of the Patriots: An Account of the Rebellion in Upper Canada, 1837–1838, and the Patriot Agitation in the United States, 1837–1842* (Toronto, 1938); Wilson Porter Shortridge, "The Canadian-American Frontier During the Rebellion of 1837–1838," *Canadian Historical Review*, VII (March, 1926), 13–26; and Orrin Edward Tiffany, "The Relations of the United States to the Canadian Rebellion of 1837–1838," *Publications of the Buffalo Historical Society*, VIII (1905), 1–118. Robert B. Ross, "The Patriot War," *Michigan Pioneer and Historical Collections*, XXI (1894), 509–609, presents an undocumented account of the Patriot activities in the Detroit area, based apparently on reminiscences.

For official government reports, see the annual reports of Secretary of War Poinsett and Commanding General Macomb for 1838, *Senate Document* No. 1, 25 Congress, 3 session, serial 338, pp. 103, 117–119; and *House Executive Documents* Nos. 73 and 74, 25 Congress, 2 session, serial 323.

[13] N. Garrow to Van Buren, December 28, 1837, *House Executive Document* No. 64, 25 Congress, 2 session, serial 322, p. 2.

The theory that there should be no standing army in peacetime in the republic was carried to the ultimate conclusion along the Canadian frontier, and the Adjutant General's report of November, 1837, showed the three traditional locations of garrisons along that border—Fort Gratiot at the outlet of Lake Huron, Fort Niagara at the mouth of the Niagara River, and Madison Barracks at Sackets Harbor at the eastern end of Lake Ontario—as "abandoned."[14]

The slightest show of military force might well have restrained the poorly led Patriots on Navy Island, and they no doubt in time would have dispersed. But the failure of anyone to act gave the Patriots a chance to grow and led to the most celebrated act of the border troubles—the destruction of the steamboat "Caroline." This American-owned boat had been used by the forces on Navy Island as a supply boat, transporting supplies and recruits, as well as sightseers and visitors, to Navy Island. The Canadian authorities determined to put a stop to this activity, and Colonel Allan MacNab, commander of the Upper Canadian militia, commissioned Commander Andrew Drew of the Royal Navy to destroy the "Caroline." On the night of December 29, 1837, Drew's force set out for Navy Island, where they expected to find the steamboat. They did not find it there but discovered it instead moored at a dock across the river at Schlosser, New York. Drew and his men boarded the boat, and in the general disturbance that followed, one American was killed. The "Caroline" was set on fire and set free into the current of the Niagara River to float down over the Falls, but it sank in the river before it reached the Falls.[15]

The destruction of the "Caroline" threw the frontier and indeed the whole nation into an uproar, and until Britain finally apologized for the affair in 1841, it threatened to lead to war between the two nations, as the emotions of the Patriot sympathizers flared. Fear and indignation gripped the entire border, and the United States government could no longer ignore the dangers.[16]

The news of the destruction of the "Caroline" reached Washington on January 4. Immediately Secretary of War Poinsett took action

[14] *American State Papers: Military Affairs* (7 vols., Washington, 1832–1861), VII, 596.

[15] Corey, *Crisis of 1830–1842*, p. 37.

[16] *House Executive Document* No. 302, 25 Congress, 2 session, serial 329; *House Executive Document* No. 183, 25 Congress, 3 session, serial 347; *House Executive Document* No. 33, 26 Congress, 2 session, serial 383; *House Document* No. 162, 26 Congress, 2 session, serial 388; *Senate Document* No. 99, 27 Congress, 3 session, serial 415.

to protect American rights and yet calm the troubled area. On January 5 he gave orders to General Scott to "repair, without delay, to the Canada frontier of the United States, and assume the military command there." Scott was instructed to call for militia from New York and Vermont, since few regular troops would be available to draw upon, but he was cautioned to see that the troops called into service in those states were "exempt from the state of excitement which the late violation of our territory has created," and he was instructed to impress upon the governors the necessity of drawing the militia troops from areas of the states farthest removed from the scenes of the disturbances along the border. As to specific details about his work, Scott was left free to exercise his own discretion. He was to do what seemed necessary to maintain order in the region, to enforce the neutrality laws of the United States, and to prevent the border population from counterattacks that might lead to the outbreak of war.[17]

☆

Scott was on the way at once. He went first to Albany to meet Governor William L. Marcy and his adjutant general, and the three hastened to Buffalo, picking up whatever regular army recruits they could find at stations along the way. Scott found the region greatly upset, with war expected momentarily, and the few troops at his command could hardly have quelled a serious outbreak. Fortunately, Scott had been sent less as a field commander than as a statesman, and as he himself said, "rhetoric and diplomacy" were his chief weapons.[18]

He arranged for public meetings at which he addressed the crowds, seeking to quiet their excitement, and such was his reputation that his very appearance seemed to bring a return of sanity. "I shall never forget," one citizen wrote in later years, "the feeling of security that this yellow-plumed, gold-laced hero inspired everyone with."[19] But

[17] Poinsett to Scott, January 5, 1838, *House Executive Document* No. 73, 25 Congress, 2 session, serial 323, pp. 4–5. Scott's part in the border troubles is well told in Charles W. Elliott, *Winfield Scott: The Soldier and the Man* (New York, 1937), pp. 335–344. Scott's own account of his activities on the northern frontier appears in *Memoirs of Lieut.-General Scott, LL.D., Written by Himself* (2 vols., New York, 1864), but this transcribes almost verbatim a section from Edward D. Mansfield, *Life and Services of General Winfield Scott* (New York, 1852).
[18] Scott, *Memoirs*, I, 308.
[19] Quoted in Elliott, *Winfield Scott*, p. 340.

Scott did not hesitate to harangue the more radical assemblies with dramatic rhetoric, telling one group, "I stand before you without troops and without arms, save for the blade by my side. I am, therefore, in your power. Some of you have known me in other scenes, and all of you know that I am ready to do what my country and what duty demands. I tell you, then, except it be over my body, you shall *not* pass this line—you shall *not* embark."[20]

Scott was indefatigable in the cause of peace. He corresponded and conferred with Canadian officers and officials, impressing them with the desire of the Americans for peace. He traveled up and down the length of the frontier, observing the activities of the Patriots and encouraging and advising his military subordinates, until the immediate dangers seemed to have passed away.

The general was seconded by equally able lieutenants. In charge of the northern district with headquarters at Buffalo was Major William J. Worth, a man who was no less esteemed on the frontier than Scott himself and who later assumed command in the Seminole War. His name was frequently associated with that of Scott in the official reports and in the press, and the *Buffalo Commercial Advertiser* declared that "the names of Scott and Worth alone have contributed more to arrest the border difficulties than the combined civil authorities of the country."[21]

On the Vermont frontier was Colonel John E. Wool, called from his duties as inspector general to preserve the peace on a part of the frontier where the local feeling was strong in favor of the Patriots. He arrived at Buffalo on January 12 and four days later was ordered to the Lake Champlain region to check the activity of the Patriots. He mustered volunteers into the federal service and sent them to patrol the highways to intercept men and ammunition moving toward Canada. He worked earnestly and effectively to support the civil authorities and to frustrate the Patriot designs in northern Vermont.[22]

At Detroit, the key area in the West, was General Hugh Brady, commanding the Seventh Military Department. The Detroit area was little less crucial than Buffalo, for the inhabitants were strongly favorable to the Patriot cause and the location was a favorite one

---

[20] Scott, *Memoirs*, I, 312.
[21] Issue of February 9, 1838, cited in Corey, *Crisis of 1830–1842*, p. 62.
[22] Harwood P. Hinton, "The Military Career of John Ellis Wool, 1812–1863." Unpublished Ph.D. dissertation, University of Wisconsin, 1960, pp. 140–170.

for the invasion of Canada. The militia were disaffected and could not be relied upon, and Brady complained to Scott: "I have been upwards of thirty five years in the Military Service of my Country and never before, felt so much the want of a regular force, to aid the Civil authority, in the execution of the laws of the country and the protection of public property: —"[23] Brady continued to call for more troops, writing on June 29: "More officers and men are absolutely required on this part of our frontier—We have a frontier of more than a hundred miles to guard, an arsenal and magazine at different points to protect and for the performance of these duties I have a force consisting of only four officers and about ninety recruits, a vast disproportion truly between the duties to be performed and the means available for that purpose—."[24]

Brady was equal to the task despite the difficulties of his position. He was a man of long army experience and beloved by the community in which he lived. He was able to maintain a correct diplomatic attitude on behalf of the United States government while at the same time energetically curbing the illegal operations of the Patriots.

The initial activities of the Patriots met with little success, and the agitation for a time quieted down. Peace seemed to have returned to the northern frontier. General Brady wrote on March 14 that "perfect tranquillity pervades this part of our frontier and that with our usual vigilance, we are unable to discover any preparations making to disturb it."[25] By the end of March Scott had returned to New York City, and all danger of serious disturbances with Canada appeared to have ended. But the fire had by no means been stamped out. There was turbulence underneath the surface, and some special cause could easily make it explode again into the open. While on high diplomatic levels the British and American governments were proceeding smoothly enough, the lower classes along the border were still smoldering and only a spark was needed to ignite them.

The British army officer, Lieutenant Colonel Charles Grey (brother-in-law of Lord Durham, Governor-General of Canada), had been sent on a special diplomatic mission to Washington and on June 13 had a private conversation with President Van Buren. He came away convinced of the goodwill of the American government in its efforts

[23] Brady to Scott, January 14, 1838, "Reports of General Brady on the Patriot War," ed. Francis Paul Prucha, *Canadian Historical Review*, XXXI (March, 1950), 59.
[24] Brady to Roger Jones, June 29, 1838, *ibid.*, p. 64.
[25] Brady to Scott, March 14, 1838, *ibid.*, p. 63.

to prevent war or any further disturbances between the United States and Canada. On his way back to Canada, however, Grey got quite a different impression from the people he met. He wrote to his father:

> Great numbers of the Refugees are scattered about the frontier villages of Vermont and New York and talk pretty openly of fresh attempts. If they could organize anything, which I do not believe from the total want of Leaders, there is no doubt that the *whole* of that American population would join them. A very large proportion of the labouring population in Vermont is originally French Canadian and would of course join, and the Americans, without entering into the merits of the case, would assist them from the general principle that a distant country has no right to any dominion in Canada and from the bitter feelings, not at all yet subsided, created by the last war. It was impossible to come up, as I did, by the Canal boat from Albany to Whitehall and in the Steamer up and down the Lake Champlain without being convinced of this. There was but one language used and that most hostile to England. This feeling, however, certainly does not extend to the higher Classes and is otherwise confined to the frontier Provinces, but there it exists to a degree that, as the President himself told me, makes it impossible for them to call out the Militia with any security—and we know how little power the general Government possess of restraining their People.[26]

At the same time General Brady reported a "feverish state of excitement" along his border, a sharp change from the tranquility noted just a few weeks earlier.[27] The Patriots, in fact, had begun to organize in secret societies to keep the agitation going. The chief of these, the so-called Hunters' Lodges, soon became the central rallying point for the renewed attempts to invade Canada. For some time they remained quiet as their organization was perfected, but the army commanders feared that they were only experiencing the calm before the storm.[28]

[26] Grey to his father, June 25, 1838, *Crisis in the Canadas, 1838–1839: The Grey Journals and Letters*, ed. William Ormsby (London, 1965), p. 53.

[27] Brady to Jones, June 27, 1838, *Canadian Historical Review*, XXXI, 64.

[28] The organization and activities of the Hunters are discussed in Oscar A. Kinchen, *The Rise and Fall of the Patriot Hunters* (New York, 1956). For General Scott's views at the beginning of 1839, see "A Private Report of General Winfield Scott on the Border Situation in 1839," ed. C. P. Stacey, *Canadian Historical Review*, XXI (December, 1940), 407–414.

The continued agitation and renewed disturbances along the northern frontier led to a demand for an expansion of the regular army. It was evident that the available forces under the current authorization were insufficient and that the goodwill of the government would come to naught if the troublemakers along the northern border could not be controlled. The Canadian authorities were convinced of the good intentions of the American President and Secretary of War, but they scoffed at the inability of the federal government to carry out its will. Colonel Grey recorded in his journal after his visit to Washington that the British Minister to Washington had little faith in the real exertions of the American government. "The fact is, he says and I believe it, they have not the power," Grey wrote. "*Their whole Army is under 6,000* men, and they are fully employed elsewhere."[29] This was the matter in a nutshell, and the Canadians were not the only ones to realize it. From many sources demands were made upon Washington for a strengthening of the regular army forces in the north. Brady's concern has already been noted, and Colonel Wool on the Vermont frontier proceeded to Washington early in June to ask for a larger force. Congressman Isaac Bronson of New York asked for the transfer of a regiment from Florida to the New York frontier, and the newspapers of Washington and New York called for the augmentation of the troops on the Canadian border.[30]

Secretary of War Poinsett's hands were tied until he could get more troops to distribute. Fortunately no serious outbreak occurred, and when Congress in July, 1838, authorized a new regiment (the Eighth Infantry), the newly recruited troops were stationed along the northern frontier. They provided the force necessary to discourage and restrain the secret societies and their sympathizers. Thus closely watched, the Patriots and their agitation finally disappeared in 1841 and 1842, and the soldiers of the Eighth Infantry joined the troops of their sister regiments in the general defense of the western frontier.

[29] Grey, *Crisis in the Canadas*, p. 35.
[30] Corey, *Crisis of 1830–1842*, p. 98n.

☆ SIXTEEN ☆

Agents of Empire

THE demand for additional troops and for improvements in the service which grew out of the Patriot crisis along the Canadian border in 1838 put a temporary spotlight upon serious problems of long standing in the American army. The regular army that proclaimed and defended the American empire in the years between the Revolution and the Mexican War, unfortunately, did so with less than ideal composition. Nearly always suspect and seldom if ever extolled, the army did not receive support to match its significant role.

It was, first of all, always too small. Congress refused to authorize regular troops in numbers commensurate with the duties with which they were charged on the frontier. Republican principles called for reliance upon the militia, the citizen soldiery who were to be the bulwark of defense. Whether a regular army or militia and volunteers should have been the basis for military action in foreign or civil wars has been seriously debated by followers and opponents of Emory Upton,[1] but (except for the War of 1812) that was not of immediate concern between 1783 and 1846. It is clear that on the Indian frontier, where the chief work of the army lay, a reliance on militia was unsatisfactory.

The militia were seldom well organized, never well disciplined,

---

[1] Brevet Major General Emory Upton held that only by entrusting war primarily to professionals of a regular army could the United States have military security. Before his death in 1884, he had written a history of American military policy up to 1862, which persuasively argued his position. The book was first published in 1904, as *The Military Policy of the United States*, and both before and after its publication Upton's ideas gained wide acceptance. Opponents of Upton, however, argued for a reliance on a citizen soldiery. An able exposition of both viewpoints appears in Russell F. Weigley, *History of the United States Army* (New York, 1967), though Weigley himself favors the anti-Upton position.

and frequently not turned out in the numbers called for. There was continual agitation to regularize the militia organization, to get states to train the citizen troops and to send in returns, and to make adequate provision for equipment and supplies. Had these problems been solved, a more troublesome one would have remained. The militiamen, reflecting the attitude of the frontier communities from which they were called, were a dangerous tool for handling Indians and an ineffective one for restraining whites. They had little sense of justice toward the Indians, tended to get trigger-happy and unable to distinguish friendly Indians from hostile ones, and in general made it almost impossible to carry on normal war-and-peace measures with the Indians.

As a result of its size the army was forced to perform a task on the frontier that was almost beyond its means. The strategic planning for the western frontier reflected this inadequacy. The problem was always how to spread the too-few troops to the best advantage over a long line of frontier. Plans for concentrations of troops, for military roads on the line of the frontier, or alternately, as spokes radiating from the center, for railroads built by the soldiers—all these were premised on the idea that the troops had to be kept to the barest minimum. If there had been a few more troops available this sort of "economy of scarcity" would have been unnecessary and the effectiveness of the army's work immeasureably improved.

The difficulty of maintaining an army of sufficient size to accomplish the duties incumbent upon it was compounded by the problem of recruiting men of adequate quality. If Americans opposed in principle the idea of a standing army in peacetime, the same republican spirit made the army unattractive to individuals of ability and substance. From its very first days, when Congress pleaded with the states to supply small quotas of troops for the "First American Regiment," recruiting difficulties more than once threatened to halt or enfeeble the work of the army if not destroy the regiments altogether. One marvels that the army accomplished what it did under such circumstances. The "sword of the Republic," alas, was often made of inferior steel.[2]

The problems of the Congress under the Articles of Confederation are perhaps understandable enough. A federal army was feared as a

[2] I have discussed the quality of the army men in *Broadax and Bayonet: The Role of the United States Army in the Development of the Northwest, 1815–1860* (Madison, Wis., 1953), pp. 34–54, and in "The United States Army as Viewed by British Travelers, 1825–1860," *Military Affairs*, XVII (Fall, 1953), 113–124. See also Norman W. Caldwell, "The Enlisted Soldier at the Frontier Post, 1790–1814," *Mid-America*, XXXVII (October, 1955), 195–204.

threat to liberty, but men recruited and supplied by the states were far from satisfactory in either number or ability. Colonel Harmar's first recruiting efforts in Pennsylvania resulted in a "very considerable" number of deserters, whose attachments in Philadelphia kept them there when the corps moved west. So great was Harmar's dependence on them to fill out his complement of men, however, that he recommended advertising a general pardon for them if they would show up within a specified time. When the first year's enlistments ran out, Harmar reported that more than a fifth of the men were not fit to be reenlisted.[3]

The small regular army continued under the new national government of the Constitution (a professional army, in the mind of Hamilton, which would consider war a science and prepare accordingly) was little improvement. The defeats of Harmar and St. Clair by the Indians in Ohio were due in large measure to the raw and undisciplined militia who made up such a large part of their commands. But it is clear that the regular troops recruited for their armies were not of much better stock, nor did men rush to enlist. Part of the militia problem was the need to rely on the citizen troops because even the small number of authorized regular soldiers could not be enlisted.

"Mad Anthony" Wayne's task should have been easier. The offensive name of "regular army" was dropped in favor of the more romantic Roman "legion"; Wayne as Commanding General should have stirred some excitement; and the need to defend the honor of the nation against the Indian tribes was manifest. Yet all the reports on recruiting were disappointing, and the quality of the men who got to Wayne without deserting on the route from the recruiting rendezvous demanded heroic efforts to whip into shape. Knox wrote to Wayne in August, 1792: "The recruiting service still languishes—the Officers expect better things after the hurry of farming is over." Two weeks later he reported that the recruiting service was almost at a standstill, nor did he see any way to stimulate it without authorization for higher pay, and his halfhearted hopes that the fall and winter would bring better results were not fulfilled. The small numbers arriving disappointed Wayne, for without more men "*real* encampments of Manoeuvre & discipline" were impossible.[4]

[3] Harmar to Dickinson, December 5, 1784, and August 1, 1785, Consul W. Butterfield, ed., *Journal of Capt. Jonathan Heart . . .* [and] *Dickinson-Harmar Correspondence of 1784–5* (Albany, 1885), pp. 48, 82.

[4] Knox to Wayne, August 17, and September 1, 1792, and Wayne to Knox, November 9, 1792, Richard C. Knopf, ed., *Anthony Wayne, A Name in Arms: The Wayne-Knox-Pickering-McHenry Correspondence* (Pittsburgh, 1960), pp. 71, 82–83, 130.

Knox did not give up. He wrote letters to the recruiting officers urging them to the highest exertions, but the personal endeavors of the officers were not enough, and no pay raises were forthcoming. Thus there developed a situation at the beginning of the regular army's existence that was to plague it through much of its history. Knox wrote to Wayne at the end of November, 1793: "[T]he objects of pursuit in the Country generally are so profitable that I apprehend that not more than three or four hundred recruits at most could be obtained from this time until the first of May next upon the present pay." A year later he had given up. "The recruiting for the legion, upon the present encouragements has almost terminated," he told Wayne. "The general prosperity of the Country and the high price of labour of all sorts precludes the expectation of any considerable augmentation of the legion." These failures to supply men for the regular army made it necessary to fall back upon militia—an expedient apparently quite agreeable to many members of Congress, but which drove Wayne to distraction. And what men did appear for the legion were hardly the sort of raw material Wayne needed to keep up an efficient military force. In desperation Wayne complained to the Secretary of War about the recruits sent to him in Ohio from the Atlantic states: "One third of them have neither size nor Stamina—Nor did god or Nature ever intend them for Soldiers—a considerable number have already been discharged—for being under size—& over age. In fact they were not only an incumbrance to the *public* but a disgrace to the *Legion.*" As evidence Wayne cited one case of an "old infirm man . . . five feet & one half an inch high—aged Fifty Nine years & decript [decrepit]—this old *dwarf* was called by the Magistrate before whom he was sworn, *an able bodied man.*"[5]

Conditions did not materially improve. Wayne's successor as Commanding General, James Wilkinson, described the army in 1797:

> The condition of that part of the army stationed in this quarter is truly deplorable; and at this moment presents a frightful picture to the scientific soldier; ignorance & licentiousness have been fostered, while intelligence and virtue have been persecuted & exiled; the consequences were that factions have been generated to sanction enormity, & it followed that all ideas of system, economy, order,

5 Knox to Wayne, January 26, 1793, November 25, 1793, and December 5, 1794; Wayne to Knox, May 30, 1794; Wayne to Pickering, September 2, 1795; *ibid.*, pp. 178–179, 286, 335, 366–367, 452–453.

subordination & discipline were banished, & that disorder, vice, absurdity, & abuse infested every member of the *corps militaire*.[6]

Even if much of this can be attributed to Wilkinson's pique against Wayne, the picture is not a pretty one. Nor did the pacific mentality of the Jeffersonian Era cause a great rush of able men to the recruiting centers.

From the War of 1812 to the Mexican War, when the principle of a *small* standing army for the defense of the frontiers was not seriously challenged, the problems of quality were paramount. In the surge of westward expansion that followed the Treaty of Ghent and the spirit of enterprise that marked the Age of Jackson, the army simply was not attractive to able and energetic young Americans. The fact was noted by visitors to the West, who could not escape contact with the army garrisons as they toured the frontier. James E. Alexander, a somewhat dyspeptic Englishman, wrote in 1833: "The great extent of territory in the states, with the scanty population, causes wages to be high, while provisions are also cheap; generally, speaking, therefore, the most worthless characters enter the army, which consists of a *melange* of English deserters, Dutch, French, Americans, &c. Five dollars are the monthly pay of a private, and many labourers in the States earn a dollar per day, so that it is obvious there is no great inducement to belong to an army which is held in no great estimation by the citizens generally, and has no pension list, or asylum for disabled soldiers."[7] The Frenchman Guillaume Tell Poussin, long a resident in the United States, came to the same conclusion. "The recruits," he wrote, "are generally men, who, as laborers and mechanics, receive much higher compensation than in the military service. They must, therefore, be infected with some moral infirmity, which renders them unfit for a useful and laborious life."[8] "Where employment is sure and wages high," observed still another traveler, "men are not very willing to subject themselves to the hardships and rigid discipline of a soldier's life."[9] More than one foreign observer

[6] Quoted in Thomas R. Hay and M. R. Werner, *The Admirable Trumpeter: A Biography of General James Wilkinson* (Garden City, N.Y., 1941), pp. 163–164.

[7] James E. Alexander, *Transatlantic Sketches, Comprising Visits to the Most Interesting Scenes in North and South America and the West Indies, with Notes on Negro Slavery and Canadian Emigration* (2 vols., London, 1833), II, 281.

[8] Guillaume Tell Poussin, *The United States: Its Power and Progress*, trans. Edmund L. DuBarry (Philadelphia, 1851), p. 393.

[9] Alexander Mackay, *The Western World: or, Travels in the United States in 1846–47* (2 vols., Philadelphia, 1849), II, 221.

noted that the American enlisted man had no chance to advance through the ranks to officer status, since all the officers came from West Point.[10]

The officers commanding the army and the secretaries of war, of course, were not unmindful of the deficiencies.[11] They deplored the fact and made strong recommendations for improving conditions but generally without avail, for Congress was reluctant to authorize the kind of inducements upon which a better quality of recruits depended.

The statements of critics from abroad, who frequently enough liked to probe for weak spots in the American republic, and the complaints of army commanders, who might be expected to keep up a chorus of demands for a better army, could perhaps be discounted did not incontrovertible evidence of desertion and drunkenness among the troops speak so loudly of the low character of the enlisted soldiers. In both of these cases the aversion of the Americans to strict military discipline was painfully evident.

☆

The rate of desertion was no less than phenomenal, and the drain on the regular army was almost more than it could bear. The work and effectiveness of the military force on the frontier must be evaluated in the light of these frightening statistics. In 1823 desertions equaled one-fourth the number of enlistments for that year and in 1825 nearly one-half. A large share of these left the recruiting stations or rendezvous before they had even had a fair taste of military service, and desertions in the first year of service were very heavy.[12] The Adjutant General at the beginning of 1826 described the situation:

The season of probation in the army, as in most other vocations, is the one which presents the greatest trial for the soldier. The

[10] See Mackay, *The Western World*, II, 220; Arthur Cunyngham, *A Glimpse at the Great Western Republic* (London, 1851), pp. 169–170.

[11] See, for example, the report of the Adjutant General, January 11, 1826, *American State Papers: Military Affairs* (7 vols., Washington, 1832–1861), III, 228; and General Jacob Brown to the Secretary of War, January 7, 1827 [1828], National Archives, Records of the Adjutant General's Office, Special Reports to the Secretary of War, vol. 1, p. 98.

[12] Figures on desertion are given in *American State Papers: Military Affairs*, III, 193–199, 228, 273–277, 686–689, IV, 287–289; *House Document* No. 47, 19 Congress, 1 session, serial 133; *House Document* No. 140, 19 Congress, 1 session, serial 138.

spirit of restless inquietude which not unfrequently induces him to enlist, but too often stimulates him to desert, in its influence is more powerful than any moral restraint derived from the force of his oath to serve "honestly and faithfully" the full period of his engagement. The class from whence a majority of private soldiers are drawn scarcely regards the circumstance of desertion as an act of turpitude. Whenever, therefore, the enlisted man *deserts*, he most commonly reverts to his original society, or to associates of kindred morality, who, so far from condemning him as a faithless, perjured citizen, choose rather to unite in rejoicing in his successful escape. This erroneous appreciation of crime, superadded to the restless spirit incident to that ordeal, common almost to every recruit, probably constitutes the primary cause of desertion.[13]

The record for the rest of the decade was no better. Secretary of War Cass in his annual report of 1831 presented the following data:[14]

	Number deserting	Monetary loss
1826	636	$54,393
1827	848	61,344
1828	820	63,137
1829	1115	98,345
1830	1251	102,087
1831 (estimated)	1450	118,321

When one considers that the authorized strength of the army in these years was only 6,000 men, and that the actual strength fell considerably below this figure, the statistics are staggering.

Some remedy was absolutely necessary. The Committee on Military Affairs in the House of Representatives in December, 1831, declared that it was necessary "to recur to rewards and punishments, the motives by which the mass of mankind is ordinarily influenced." To this end it recommended ameliorating the condition of the soldier so as to induce those who were in "respectable situations" to enlist. To punish those who deserted, the committee urged the reestablishment of corporal punishment. Noting that the estimated number of desertions for 1831 would equal one-fourth of the total army, the committee concluded: "It is evident, unless a check be interposed to

[13] Report of Roger Jones, January 11, 1826, *American State Papers: Military Affairs*, III, 228.
[14] *Ibid.*, IV, 708.

the progress of this evil, that the purposes for which the military peace establishment was organized, will be utterly frustrated."[15]

Congress finally attempted to correct the evils in March, 1833, with an act "to improve the condition of the non-commissioned officers and privates of the army and marine corps of the United States and to prevent desertion." It cut the term of enlistment from five years to three, increased the pay of the private soldier from five to six dollars a month (with the provision that one dollar a month be withheld for the first two years of service and paid in a lump sum at the end of that time if the soldier had served faithfully), granted a bounty for reenlistment of two months' pay, and restored whipping as a punishment for men convicted of desertion by a general court-martial.[16]

The remedies at first seemed to promise well. Cass asserted that they would bring "important meliorations in the character of the army," and in 1834 the Commanding General, Alexander Macomb, reported a decrease in drunkenness, less desertion, and fewer other crimes. But the evils did not disappear.[17]

☆

Because native Americans would not enter the army in sufficient numbers to maintain the small peace establishment, recruiting officers resorted to the enlistment of foreign immigrants. These foreigners in the ranks were noticed immediately by all who came in contact with the army, and they generally were viewed critically. When Inspector General George Croghan visited Fort Brady in 1838, he complained about the poor state of drill. "It might be well in this place to remark," he added by way of extenuation, "that not only are most of the men of the company recruits, but they are moreover not naturalized citizens of the United States—out of 52 composing the company, there are 32 foreigners, some of whom speak the English language so imperfectly as scarcely to be understood." At Fort Leavenworth in 1840 he found twenty men out of a detachment of one hundred and ten recruits who could neither understand nor speak a word of English. They were either Dutch or German. "It is no pleasant task to instruct raw recruits," Croghan wrote in his report, "but when those

[15] *House Report* No. 63, 22 Congress, 1 session, serial 224, pp. 1–2.
[16] *U. S. Statutes at Large*, IV, 647–648.
[17] Reports of the Secretary of War, 1833 and 1834, *American State Papers: Military Affairs*, V, 169, 362.

recruits are ignorant of your language, the task becomes ten times more tedious and disagreeable. I would suggest the propriety of forbidding the enlistment of all such persons for the future, taking care at the same time to issue a like interdict against the Irish, who (a few honourable exceptions to the contrary) are the very bane of our garrisons."[18]

The increasing numbers of foreign-born entering the army made patriotic Americans wonder about the propriety of an army manned by a smaller and smaller percentage of citizens. The *General Regulations for the Army* drawn up by Major General Scott in 1820 described acceptable recruits as follows: "All free white male persons, above eighteen and under thirty-five years, who are able bodied, active, and free from disease." Of men enlisting between June, 1821, and December, 1823, roughly one-quarter were of foreign birth, and this large percentage undoubtedly led to the restriction on foreigners appearing in the *General Regulations* of 1825, which declared: "No foreigner shall be enlisted in the army without special permission from general head-quarters." Since the diminution of enlistments in 1825 and 1826 was blamed in part upon this restriction, in 1828 all citizens were accepted no matter what their place of birth, and in 1842 the Secretary of War proposed taking immigrants who had taken the first steps toward naturalization. It seems clear, moreover, that foreigners were enlisted in large numbers even when the regulations made no provision for them.[19]

The picture was not all black, of course. Answers to a special questionnaire sent to the officers superintending the recruiting service in 1827 showed that the foreign soldiers were no less efficient in military duties than the Americans and were less likely to desert. Although many were men of "turbulent character and intemperate habits," others were decent men, to whom the army was attractive for one reason or another.[20] Many new arrivals, apparently, were attracted to the security

[18] George Croghan, *Army Life on the Western Frontier: Selections from the Official Reports Made Between 1826 and 1845 by Colonel George Croghan*, ed. Francis Paul Prucha (Norman, Okla., 1958), pp. 141–142, 148.

[19] *General Regulations for the Army* (Philadelphia, 1821), Art. 74, Par. 13; *General Regulations for the Army* (Washington, 1825), Art. 74, Par. 1287; Order No. 43, Adjutant General's Office, August 13, 1828; *Senate Document* No. 1, 27 Congress, 3 session, serial 413, p. 180. For statistics on foreign enlistment, see Prucha, *Broadax and Bayonet*, pp. 41–42 and references cited there.

[20] Enos Cutler to the Adjutant General, November 14, 1827, National Archives, Records of the Adjutant General's Office, Letters Received; William Davenport to the Adjutant General, November 23, 1827, National Archives, Records of Army Commands, Western Department Recruiting Service, Letter Book.

of the army, at least as a temporary expedient in a new country, and for others enlistment was a way to get free transportation to the West. Even Croghan had a good word for the appearance of the Germans he found at Fort Winnebago in 1842: "men of homely, stolid-looking visages but of stout frame well becoming the dress and equipments of the soldier."[21] When all is said and done, the paradox remained: the American regular army could hardly have survived without this heavy non-American infusion.

☆

On a par with desertion as a disruptive force in the army was intemperance. It was all-pervasive, and at times the effective force of a military post would be seriously curtailed because of the numerous drunkards languishing in the guardhouse. Croghan's inspection reports are filled with observations of the evil. From Fort Winnebago he reported in 1834, for example, that there were sixteen privates in confinement, most of them for drunkenness. At Detroit in 1842 out of a force of 245 enlisted men he found 41 in confinement, again primarily for drunkenness. The large number of courts-martial—the Adjutant General reported 7,058 for the years 1823–1828—was due in great part to intemperance, as is obvious from any perusal of court-martial orders. "I must say," one traveler remarked, "that I have seen more cases of drunkenness than ever I saw among any troops in the world." The effect on the health of the army, of course, was deleterious. The Surgeon General reported in 1825, "The deaths from intemperance and its various consequences have been numerous. Out of the whole number (116) forty may be traced to this pest of the army, under the different forms of Liver disease, Dropsy, Consumption, Appoplexy, Palsey, &c."[22]

The ease with which the troops could get liquor was a primary factor in the heavy rates of drunkenness. Unscrupulous whiskey dealers considered the soldiers fair game, and they appeared at some posts in large numbers. The commander at Fort Howard reported in 1824 that "the facility of disposing of, and exchanging their clothing and stolen goods for whiskey, afforded by the Horde of Hucksters settled

[21] Croghan, *Army Life on the Western Frontier*, p. 149.
[22] *Ibid.*, pp. 121, 124; *American State Papers: Military Affairs*, IV, 288; Charles A. Murray, *Travels in North America during the Years 1834, 1835 & 1836* (2 vols., New York, 1839), II, 67–68; Joseph Lovell to Barbour, May 1, 1825, National Archives, Records of the Surgeon General's Office, Report Book, vol. 1.

in our vicinity, induces the men to be more vicious than they would probably be under other circumstances." Colonel Taylor at Fort Crawford in 1836 described the post as "completely surrounded with whiskey establishments occupied by individuals of the most dissolute habits and character, whose object and business is to debauch the Soldiers, and to which in great measure may be attributed the desertions which are constantly occurring as well as the large number of those who are annually discharged on Surgeon's certificate of disability." No post was free if there were citizens within reach. At Fort Snelling the post surgeon in 1839 reported, "Since the middle of winter we have been completely inundated with ardent spirits, and consequently the most beastly scenes of intoxication among the soldiers of the garrison and the Indians in its vicinity." Wherever the commanders were able by one means or another to reduce the liquor traffic, good discipline flourished. Croghan was quick to comment on the connection of the two circumstances. The good discipline he found at Fort Armstrong in 1826, for example, he ascribed in a great measure to the almost entire exclusion of whiskey from the post.[23]

Attempts were made to correct the evil on the spot. Military reservations were enlarged and settlers forced to withdraw from the neighborhood of the posts. Temperance societies had a brief flurry of existence at some of the forts. But the evil persisted in all too virulent a form, and some striking at the roots of the problem seemed necessary.

Drunkenness among the soldiers was attributed by many to the ration of whiskey allowed the troops. Calhoun in 1818 condemned the regular issue of whiskey to the soldiers, for he believed that it perpetuated habits of intemperance, and strong opposition to the provision developed. Finally in 1830 a War Department regulation ended the daily ration of liquor because "the habitual use of ardent spirits by the troops, has a pernicious effect upon their health, morals, and discipline," and a sum of money was allowed instead. Two years later the commutation in money was ended, and instead sugar and coffee were substituted in the ration for whiskey.[24]

[23] Prucha, *Broadax and Bayonet*, pp. 47–48; Croghan, *Army Life on the Western Frontier*, p. 110.

[24] Report of Calhoun, December 11, 1818, *American State Papers: Military Affairs*, I, 781; Order No. 72, Adjutant General's Office, December 8, 1830; Order No. 100, Headquarters of the Army, Adjutant General's Office, November 5, 1832. Secretary of War Cass reported in 1831: "There were issued to the army in 1830 72,537 gallons of whiskey, at the cost of $22,132. If this sum were applied to the purchase of tea, coffee, and sugar, for the use of the soldiers, their habits and morals would be greatly improved, and the discipline and respectability of the army promoted." *American State Papers: Military Affairs*, IV, 709.

Others sought some deeper cause than the daily gill of whiskey in the ration. Surgeon General Joseph Lovell and Secretary of War Peter B. Porter laid the blame upon the community from which the enlisted men came, the laboring classes among whom heavy drinking was prevalent. The solution was to improve army conditions so as to attract a better class of citizens. At the very least the practice of enlisting and reenlisting confirmed drunkards would have to stop. This was not an easy matter. A surgeon connected with one of the recruiting stations spoke out strongly against the constant habit of reenlisting known drunkards, yet he asserted, "The officers gravely tell me that we might as well disband the army as to exclude these men." On the basis of such reports the Secretary of War issued orders prohibiting the enlistment of any man when intoxicated, but the effect of such an order cannot be determined. Certainly the sots were a minority among the soldiery and they should not be allowed to give the whole army a bad name, but the problem was not satisfactorily solved. The best that could be done was to keep the wayward in line by strict discipline and to continue the efforts to lessen the sources of supply.[25]

One group of soldiers, the dragoons, escaped the general opprobrium, and the weakness of the rest of the army did not completely vitiate military operations on the frontier, as has certainly been evident in the preceding chapters. Rough as the raw material was and uncommitted as many of the recruits proved to be, there was a core of men with integrity and dedication to duty who prevented collapse. In many cases, moreover, the mere presence of the army in a strategic spot served the purpose of overawing the Indians and proclaiming American sovereignty over a crucial area. At no posts did discipline completely break down, and the commanding officers in the West constructed posts and cut roads and planted crops and maintained the discipline and subordination that are essential in a military establishment. Inspector General Croghan, despite his unhappiness about the lack of military spirit, reported again and again that military discipline was proper.

☆

The credit for the success in asserting American sovereignty on the frontier and in its frontal attack upon the wilderness belongs, without doubt, chiefly to the corps of officers. In contradistinction to

[25] *Ibid.*, pp. 83–85.

the enlisted men, the officers formed an elite group. Some early officers, like Wayne and Wilkinson and a good many of their contemporaries, began their military careers in the Revolution. Others, like
Jackson and Brown, were catapulted into prominence from militia
commands by the War of 1812. A few received direct commissions
when periods of lesser crisis brought brief augmentations to the regular
army. Thus Macomb entered the army in 1799 during the period of
French hostilities, Atkinson was appointed captain in the infantry
when fear of England led to an increase in the army in 1808, and
Scott accepted a captaincy in the light artillery in 1809. But the
Military Academy established at West Point in 1802 eventually became the major source of the officers of the regular army. West Point
provided these men with a common viewpoint and spirit, inculcated
them with ideals of military discipline and procedure, and trained
them not only in the strategy and tactics of war, but also (and probably most successfully) in engineering science.[26]

The officers were able representatives of the nationalistic spirit of
the age, and they were an outstanding expression of the romantic
impulse which marked so much of early nineteenth-century America.[27]
They rose, moreover, above the dominant selfishness (not to say
avarice) that controlled the outlook of many frontiersmen, whose attacks upon the rights of the Indians and whose unconcern about violations of federal laws regarding land and trade were forcefully blocked
by the army. It is true, of course, that some army officers were enthusiastic speculators in western lands, that others were politically
ambitious, that many were overly conscious of their rights and prerogatives, that quarrels between high-ranking officers were frequently
a public scandal, and that a few officers were as confirmed drunkards
as any of the privates, but by and large they were a tremendous force
for order on the frontier. They were conscious and conscientious agents
of American empire and nationalism and zealous supporters of the attempts of the federal government to proceed with justice and humanity in its dealings with both the Indians and the frontiersmen.

Perceptive observers who came in contact with the American army

---

[26] Sidney Forman, *West Point: A History of the United States Military Academy*
(New York, 1950); Stephen E. Ambrose, *Duty, Honor, Country: A History of
West Point* (Baltimore, 1966). Some of the activities of the army officers are
described in Norman W. Caldwell, "The Frontier Army Officer, 1794–1814,"
Mid-America, XXXVII (April, 1955), 101–128.

[27] William H. Goetzmann, *Army Exploration in the American West, 1803–
1863* (New Haven, 1959), pp. 17–18, speaks of the Corps of Topographical
Engineers as an expression of romanticism. The same applies, to some extent,
to the army officers as a whole.

in the West seldom failed to be impressed with the character of the officers who were their hosts. One Englishman wrote in 1839 that he had found the officers of the army and navy "more favourable specimens both in respect to manners and attainments" than the average of young men who entered business, and he attributed the fact to their training at West Point. Another foreign visitor found the American officer corps "remarkable for its military knowledge, its moral character, its spirit of discipline, and its sentiment of honor and patriotism." Caleb Atwater, who visited the posts on the upper Mississippi in 1829, found the young West Point graduate "a gentleman and man of science, brave, active, vigorous, energetic, high minded, honorable, strictly honest and correct in all his deportment." The good effects that would result from the dispersal of trained men along the uncultured frontier was not lost on these observers. The graduates of West Point, as one writer phrased it, were scattered "like productive corn" over the whole country.[28]

Such praise, it is true, was not universal. The army officers were an obvious target for democratic critics who saw in them a dangerous aristocratic influence, if not an actual source of tyranny. In the egalitarian upsurge of the era of Andrew Jackson, the Military Academy at West Point was accused of breeding a clique of officers who were inimical to the country's democratic spirit.[29] But the essential work done by the army could not be abandoned, and the skills of the graduates of West Point could not be supplied easily by others.

Many officers got a popular reputation as martinets, for enlisted men who felt the force of military discipline were quick to cry out, and their cries were sympathetically received on the frontier, where a certain contempt of authority was not unknown. Occasionally the popular attacks brought some rebuttal, as when Colonel Leavenworth wrote an open letter to the editors of the *St. Louis Enquirer:* "I wish to say in your paper that the report going the rounds in the different news-papers, as to *cutting off Soldiers* ears, &c. as far as relates to the posts on the upper Mississippi, is wholly unfounded. From my knowl-

---

[28] Murray, *Travels in North America,* II, 212; Poussin, *The United States,* pp. 391–392; Caleb Atwater, *Remarks Made on a Tour to Prairie du Chien, Thence to Washington City, in 1829* (Columbus, Ohio, 1831), p. 179; C. D. Arfwedson, *The United States and Canada, in 1832, 1833, and 1834* (2 vols., London, 1834), I, 63–64.

[29] For a perceptive essay on American antimilitarism and antiprofessionalism in the army, see Marcus Cunliffe, "The American Military Tradition," in H. C. Allen and C. P. Hill, eds., *British Essays in American History* (New York, 1957), pp. 207–224.

edge of General Atkinson, I feel assured that nothing of that kind has been permitted under his command."[30]

Such attacks were the least of the officers' hardships. Isolated for long periods at the small western posts, beyond the reach of relatives and friends and the eastern culture that many relished, the officers and their families had to create their own social world. For many it was too much to ask. The low pay, the uncertain future, the problems of unruly soldiers, and the rigors of pioneer life drove many officers from the service.[31]

☆

In 1838 the inadequacies of the regular army service once again became the subject for a full-scale debate in Congress. The Patriot disturbances along the northern frontier, which were of immediate concern, in fact only gave added impetus to the continuing agitation for a larger regular army. The expanding frontiers in the West—to say nothing of the Florida war—seemed clearly to demand more regular troops. While lip service continued to be given to the principle that the bulwark of the republic was the citizen-soldiery of the militia, the exigencies of the moment pointed to the need for at least a limited addition to the standing army. Senator Benton, the great spokesman for the western interests, introduced a bill "to increase the military establishment of the United States" two days before word of the "Caroline" affair had reached Washington. Benton's bill provided for an increase of army strength to more than 14,000, thus more than doubling the authorization provided by the army bill of 1821. His bill would have instituted changes in the organization of the army and added to the pay of both officers and men. The Senate, with little debate, amended the bill in some small details, passed the measure on January 25, and sent it to the House.[32] There was some desultory action in the House in February, but not until June 26 did serious debate on the bill take place. From that date until the passage

---

[30] *St. Louis Enquirer*, October 21, 1820.

[31] See Charles J. Latrobe, *The Rambler in North America, MDCCCXXXII–MDCCCXXXIII* (2 vols., New York, 1835), II, 152; Francis Wyse, *America, Its Realities and Resources* (3 vols., London, 1846), II, 97; E. T. Coke, *A Subaltern's Furlough* (2 vols., New York, 1833), II, 163–164; *Army and Navy Chronicle*, II (May 19, 1836), 313, III (November 17, 1836), 313, IV (January 4, 1838), 8.

[32] *Senate Journal*, 25 Congress, 2 session, serial 313, pp. 121, 170, 174.

of an emasculated bill on July 2, the measure was one of the chief matters before the House. Many Congressmen spoke at length on the bill and the whole issue of the standing army and its optimum size was fully aired.[33]

The spokesmen for the bill pointed to the dangers on the frontiers. The northern frontier, as Isaac Bronson pointed out, was in ferment and the civil authorities were incapable of preventing the disturbances. In the West, the Indian dangers had been augmented by the emigration of the eastern Indians. Archibald Yell of Arkansas spoke for his section:

Mr. YELL was as much opposed to a needless increase of the army as anyone, or to an overgrown standing army, and would be the first to resist it when it shall be shown to be dangerous to the liberties of the country; yet the condition of the country, and the Western frontier in particular, imperiously demanded it. The same arguments now urged were used against the measure two years ago, when there was no more prospect of a war in Florida than there was at present on the frontier. It was well known that the Indians were making preparations for hostilities, and, as in Florida, we should get into a war before we were prepared for it, unless the army was increased with a sufficient force to keep the Indians in awe. He was not, however, in favor of a very large increase, nor of an augmentation of the staff; but he did desire to see the rank and file, the musketry, the bone and sinew, increased. This was indispensable; for the Government had placed between sixty and seventy thousand Indian warriors on the Western frontier, well armed with rifles and ammunition; and it now became the duty, the duty both of the Administration and the Opposition, to devise means for protecting its own citizens.[34]

The proponents of the bill needed to show that *regular* troops were necessary, and they brought forth arguments against reliance upon the militia. Congressman Bronson, the *Globe* reported, "went into a mass of minute details contrasting the expenses of militia or volunteers and regular soldiers, being a difference of about from four (or perhaps six) to one, without reference to the question of efficiency, and the more indirect loss to the country from taking men suddenly from

[33] The debates in the House are reported in *Congressional Globe*, 25 Congress, 2 session, pp. 482–489.
[34] *Ibid.*, p. 483.

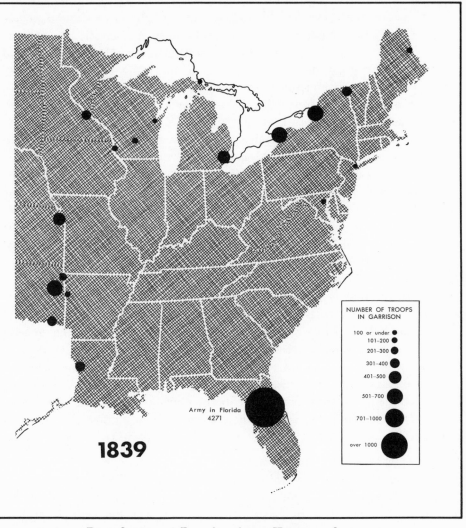

NUMBER OF TROOPS
IN GARRISON

100 or under ●
101–200 ●
201–300 ●

301–400 ●

401–500 ●

501–700 ●

701–1000 ●

over 1000 ●

Army in Florida
4271

1839

Distribution of Regular Army Troops, 1839

their ordinary pursuits." And the western advocates of the bill, not wanting to imply that their countrymen were incapable of their own defense, asserted that they were able to protect themselves, "but could they devote all their time to watch a vigilant and cautious enemy? . . . It would be too late, as in the Florida war, to send an army when half the citizens were butchered."[35]

The opponents of the bill came forth in strength. They argued

[35] *Ibid.*, pp. 482, 484.

principally that no great increase, such as the Senate bill proposed, was necessary, but every possible excuse was brought forth. Some speakers urged postponement of the measure because it was too late anyway to recruit a large increase in the current year. Horace Everett of Vermont argued that "any increase of the army must be made up chiefly from an enlistment of foreigners, and he never hoped to see that day when Irishmen, Englishmen, and other aliens should be organized and armed to keep the citizens of his State in order." John Robertson of Virginia ridiculed the idea that New York with upwards of two million people could not enforce the civil law but needed a "military police." "As to the Western frontier," he said, "let all the superfluous military from the interior be sent there, and appropriate some money to keep the Indians from starving, instead of expending $3,000,000 a year, which the proposed increase would cost." Samson Mason of Ohio irritated the western Congressmen by insisting that the danger on the western frontier was the fault of the Americans and that the Indians were the oppressed party.[36]

As the debate went on, it became clear that the increases in Benton's bill or even those in the substitute bill proposed by the House Committee on Military Affairs would not be approved. The general feeling that some increase was necessary to satisfy the demands of the western sections was matched by opposition to any increase that would strengthen the officer corps of the regular army. The deep-seated resentment or opposition to the regular army was aimed principally, as is understandable, against the officers and not against the rank and file. The views of David Petrikin of Pennsylvania were perhaps typical:

> Although his constituents were opposed to a standing army in time of peace, they were always ready and willing to enable the Government to defend the distant and weaker parts of the frontier when threatened by hostile invasion, as was the case at present on the Western and Southwestern frontier of the States of Arkansas, Missouri, and Louisiana; but they were opposed to creating a large number of unnecessary officers and they were opposed to raising the salaries of officers whose salaries were already quite large enough to pay them well for all the services they rendered to the country.
>
> He would vote for the first section of the bill, filling up the skeleton of the present army, and also for the additional regiment proposed

[36] *Ibid.*, pp. 484, 486.

to be raised for the defence of the Northern frontier, believing that the present exigencies of the country required this addition to the regular army, and which added but a small number to the officers already in commission, under the present army establishment; but he should not vote for the amendments increasing the number of officers in the staff and other departments, nor would he vote to increase the salaries of officers who lounged about the cities, already enjoying very high salaries, much larger in proportion than those who did duty in the Army, and endured the hardships of field and fort.[37]

Although some increases were allowed, it was a severely amended bill that finally passed the House on July 2. The Senate concurred in the House amendments on the 4th, and on July 5 President Van Buren signed the bill. The law provided for the addition of 38 privates to each infantry company and 16 privates to each artillery company and for the addition of one company to each of the four artillery regiments. The only additional unit authorized was the Eighth Infantry. The period of enlistment was once again set at five years, and the pay of the soldiers was raised, that of the privates (as the act was amended two days later) to seven dollars a month, with the provision that one dollar per month be retained until the expiration of the term of service. Officers were allowed an extra ration for each five years of service, some increase of officers was allowed in staff departments, and a separate Corps of Topographical Engineers was authorized.[38]

These measures, helpful as they were, fell short of what was needed to provide an adequate army. The small pay raises, the House Committee on Military Affairs concluded in 1841, were still not enough to encourage the enlistment of American citizens, and the committee supported a plan proposed by General Macomb in 1832 to train young boys for the army in a kind of apprenticeship program.[39] The men responsible for the manning of the frontier defenses had to make their plans with the uncomfortable realization that the implementation of their proposals would suffer from inadequate men and insufficient means.

---

[37] *Ibid.*, p. 486.
[38] *U. S. Statutes at Large*, V, 256–260, 308.
[39] *House Report* No. 125, 26 Congress, 2 session, serial 388. Macomb's original proposal is in *House Document* No. 16, 22 Congress, 2 session, serial 233.

SEVENTEEN

Plans and Counterplans

THE addition of mounted troops to the forces on the western frontier in 1832 and the augmented numbers that came with the army bill of 1838 helped to establish the military presence that was necessary to overawe and constrain the Indian tribes. But the new troops were merely part of the larger plans for western defense that engaged the attention of the Secretary of War and of high-ranking army officers. The basic planning continued to rest upon the concept of a line or cordon of military posts stretched along the frontier between the settlements of the whites and the Indian country. The posts were primarily garrisons for troops, both infantry and dragoons, which would place within sight of the Indians (and within striking distance if need be) the military arm of the American government, and which in some cases might serve as refuges for settlers in time of Indian uprisings. The object of the planning was to distribute the limited number of regular army men in the most efficient and most economical manner possible, but what this arrangement should be was not easily agreed upon.

The removal of the eastern Indians, which poured thousands of tribesmen into the region west of Missouri and Arkansas, upset the haphazard system of establishing one fort at a time as local conditions required. It necessitated now a more comprehensive, coordinated plan for the whole western frontier that would both maintain peace and fulfill the obligations, which the federal government had assumed, to protect the emigrating Indians. The decade before the Mexican War was a time of plans and counterplans, as the War Department sought to uphold the government's authority in the West and thus preserve tranquility on the frontier.

The first full-scale plan came from Secretary of War Lewis Cass shortly before he left that office to become Minister to France. When both the House and Senate committees on military affairs asked early in 1836 for his views on the subject of western defense, Cass drew up a detailed and well-thought-out plan, which he presented to the chairmen of the committees on February 19, 1836.[1] He wanted a long-term plan that would not change with every change of personnel in the War Department and one that would not excite the Indians by alternate advance and then withdrawal of posts. He was especially concerned, too, about the concentration of Indians on the borders of white settlement, which came as a result of the Indian removal policy. He estimated that when the removal of the eastern Indians was completed, about 93,500 emigrants would have been added to the indigenous tribes of the plains, making a total of 244,870 between the Mississippi and the Rocky Mountains. These numbers were bound to increase the difficulties between the tribes themselves and augment the likelihood of conflicts between the Indians and the whites. Having no conception of the actual power of the United States, the Indians judged only by what they could see; this fact necessitated arrangements of a sufficient military force along the frontier to overawe them, to intercept any bands that might attempt raids upon the white settlements, and to provide the means of concentrating troops wherever they might be needed in the shortest possible time.

To accomplish these ends, Cass proposed the building of a military road along the frontier, running from the Red River near Fort Towson in the south to the Mississippi near Fort Snelling in the north. Along this line he proposed to construct stockaded posts. At the terminuses of the road and at some midpoint he planned to station dragoons, while infantry could garrison the intermediate stations. Posts east of the line would be abandoned as quickly as possible and their troops transferred to the western line. During the summer months the dragoons would continually patrol the road and make side excursions to the Indian villages. Concentration of infantry troops could easily be effected along this line of communication, but Cass believed that the use of dragoons alone would fulfill his purposes. The few Indians

<hr>

[1] Report of Cass, February 19, 1836, and accompanying papers, *American State Papers: Military Affairs* (7 vols., Washington, 1832–1861), VI, 149–155. The documents also appear in *House Report* No. 401, 24 Congress, 1 session, serial 294.

who might be caught east of the line would most likely be emigrants from the East, who would cause little trouble.[2]

Cass counted on the troops to do much of the work on the defenses, and he submitted an estimate of $100,000 for the construction of the road and the necessary posts that had not already been planned and provided for.

His plan met immediate approval, and on July 2, 1836, Congress passed "An Act to provide for the better protection of the western frontier," which embodied his proposals and appropriated the $100,000 he had asked for to carry them out.[3] The President was authorized to survey and open a military road from the Mississippi to the Red River and to have military posts constructed along the road wherever they would be judged most proper for the protection of the frontier. The act itself specified the mode of construction of the road: "The timber shall be cut down to a reasonable width, and the wet and marshy places shall be causewayed or otherwise rendered passable; cheap bridges shall be erected over the small streams, not having good fords across them; and, where it may be found necessary, the road may be thrown up in the centre." The law specified that the army troops were to be used to construct the road to the extent that the labor did not interfere with their other duties.

Two weeks later Cass sent instructions to the commission of army officers selected to lay out the road and determine the posts.[4] But then the whole project bogged down, for new councils in the War Department rejected the plan as an inadequate answer to western defense problems.

Benjamin F. Butler, who replaced Cass as Secretary of War, expressed only reserved approval of the line of posts along a military road, noting that "though it will be sufficient, if well garrisoned, to protect our own frontier, [it] will not be all that caution and good faith will require." Butler had in mind the solemn pledges given to the emi-

[2] Cass counted on the retention of Forts Snelling, Leavenworth, and Towson along the western line and judged that not more than four or five others would be necessary. East of the line Fort Armstrong was already set for abandonment, and Forts Gratiot, Dearborn, and Howard could soon be given up. Forts Brady, Mackinac, Winnebago, and Crawford would be maintained only as long as they were necessary to control the Indians in the vicinity. Quartermaster General Thomas S. Jesup, whose recommendations Cass appended to his report, gave more specific details—including Forts Jesup, Leavenworth, Gibson, Towson, and Snelling, with four new posts built between these existing ones. Jesup also wanted the reoccupation of Council Bluffs.

[3] *U. S. Statutes at Large*, V, 67.

[4] Cass to Commissioners, July 16, 1836, *House Document* No. 278, 25 Congress, 2 session, serial 328, pp. 9–12.

grating Indians that they would be protected in their new homes, and he penned an eloquent appeal for the fulfillment of those promises. To preserve peace among the different tribes of emigrant Indians and to protect them from their savage neighbors would require posts in the interior of the country as well as on the exterior line. But Butler's greatest concern was to protect the Indians from the encroachments of the whites. The pledges given by the government to prevent the whites from intruding on the Indian lands had been given in the utmost sincerity, he said, and they could not be fulfilled without a strong military force—"a force adequate to repress the encroachments of the civilized and more powerful race."[5]

☆

Butler served only an interim term and was not in office long enough to carry on a successful fight for his highly honorable proposals. He was succeeded by Joel R. Poinsett, whose primary concern was once again the protection of whites from hostile Indians and who shortly drew up a plan for western defense based on principles that he considered diametrically opposed to the underpinnings of Cass's proposal.

On December 30, 1837, the new Secretary of War submitted his plan to the Senate, together with detailed proposals written by the Chief Engineer, General Charles Gratiot, and by the Acting Quartermaster General, Colonel Trueman Cross.[6] Gratiot's plan was a detailed consideration of points for defense works along the exterior line, with a concentration of reserve forces to be maintained at Baton Rouge and Jefferson Barracks. Much attention was given to the lines of supply, both by water and by land. The Chief Engineer stipulated the number of troops that would be required for each section of the frontier, arriving at a total of two regiments of dragoons, ten regiments of infantry, and ten companies of artillery—a grand total of 12,940 men. The estimate was clearly too high to be acceptable, and Gratiot's work is little reflected in Poinsett's own statement.[7]

[5] Report of Benjamin F. Butler, December 3, 1836, *American State Papers: Military Affairs*, VI, 815.

[6] Poinsett's plan of December 30, 1837, and accompanying documents are in *American State Papers: Military Affairs*, VII, 777–786, and *House Document No. 59*, 25 Congress, 2 session, serial 322.

[7] Gratiot's plan, October 31, 1837, *American State Papers: Military Affairs*, VII, 778–781.

Poinsett instead relied heavily on the recommendations and views of Cross. The Acting Quartermaster General minced no words in his criticism of the Cass plan for a great military road, which originated, he said, "in a very erroneous estimate of its importance for purposes of defence." The idea of the road running from north to south along the edge of settlement, Cross insisted, violated a fundamental principle of military science. He wrote:

The lines of communication should be diverging or *perpendicular* to the frontier, not *parallel* with it. The resources of an army are always presumed to be in its rear, from whence it can draw supplies and reinforcements under cover of its own protection and by lines of communication which are secured from interruption by the enemy. It is clear that no army can maintain its position long under any other circumstances. Roads between the posts on the frontier might be found convenient for occasional passing and repassing in time of peace; but as routes of communication they would be wholly useless in time of war. Exposed as they would be to constant interruption by the enemy, it is evident that nothing short of a force competent to take the field for offensive operations could expect to march upon them with safety.

But I do not perceive the necessity of keeping open these communications between the posts on the line of the frontier at so much hazard. It could only result from the error of making posts occupying a very extended front dependent on each other for support, which would be inverting a plain military principle. If reinforcements are required, they should be drawn from a corps of reserve posted in the rear, by means of rapid water conveyance and by roads leading to the frontier, not by flank marches through the enemy's country, on a line parallel with the frontier.[8]

Cross recommended two lines of posts, each with its own purpose— an *exterior* line of advanced positions in the Indian country and an *interior* line within the boundary for the special protection of the settlements. For the first line he proposed Fort Snelling, Fort Leavenworth, Fort Gibson, and Fort Towson, with the addition of a post at the upper forks of the Des Moines River. He saw no need for intermediate posts on this line, but urged the reoccupation of Council Bluffs, relegating Fort Leavenworth to the interior line. His interior line of posts, chosen

[8] Cross's report, November 7, 1837, *ibid.*, pp. 782–785.

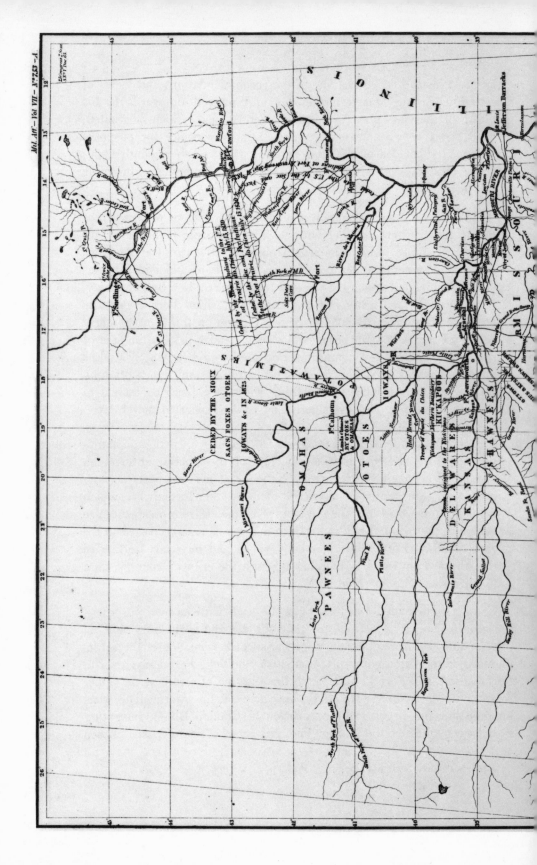

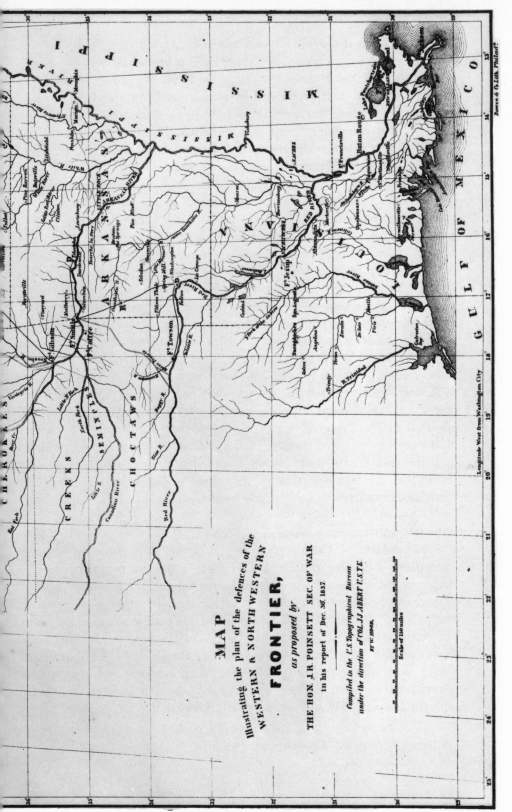

Plan for Defense of the Frontier, 1837

with reference to protection of the settlements rather than to the military features of the frontier, would be posts of refuge for the settlers in times of alarm and garrisoned by only a small regular force. Since the location of these posts would depend upon settlement rather than upon military principles, Cross was hesitant to locate them exactly. He suggested two between the Red and Arkansas rivers, four between the Arkansas and the Missouri, and two between the Missouri and the Mississippi. As a central reserve post from which a large force could quickly move to any trouble spot he selected Jefferson Barracks.

With a view both to protecting the border settlements from incursions of savage tribes and to fulfill the obligations toward the emigrant Indians, Cross asserted that "a military force of thirty thousand men on the western frontier would scarcely be adequate to enable the government to discharge its duties to its own citizens, and redeem these pledges of protection to the Indians." Realizing that "political expediency" would not permit such a figure to be seriously considered, Cross settled for 7,000 men to protect the border settlements, including large disposable forces at Fort Leavenworth, Fort Gibson, and Fort Towson, and a reserve of 1,500 men at Jefferson Barracks.

Poinsett gave support to this proposal and asserted its superiority over the previous plans. In his annual report of December 2, 1837, he adverted to the $100,000 appropriation of the year before for Cass's military road and noted that the road could not be surveyed and opened until the sites for the posts it was supposed to connect had been determined and that the selection of these sites would depend on lines of communication from interior to the frontier, not along the exterior line itself.[9]

In transmitting the reports of Gratiot and Cross, Poinsett added his own restatement of Cross's plan, remarking that he would have considered his obligation fulfilled by the mere submission of the reports, "had not other plans been previously recommended, which I regard as entirely inefficient, but which have received, in some measure, the sanction of Congress." Poinsett asked for 5,000 men to man the exterior and interior lines of posts, plus "a competent reserve at Jefferson Barracks, and an effective force at Baton Rouge" which he thought would "both insure the safety of the western frontier, and enable the government to fulfill all its treaty stipulations, and preserve its faith with the Indians." He added a proposal, however, for an auxiliary force

---

[9] Report of Poinsett, December 2, 1837, *ibid.*, p. 575.

of volunteer troops, to be instructed a certain number of days each year by regular army officers at regular army posts, in order to have on hand a trained reserve force.[10]

☆

Poinsett discovered that he could not escape some responsibility for the great military road of his predecessor Cass, for Congress had authorized the plan in its 1836 legislation and made inquiries from time to time to see how the work was progressing. A report made by the Acting Quartermaster General in March, 1838, nearly two years after the law had been passed, was not encouraging; Cross reported bluntly that "nothing has been done towards those objects, beyond the survey of the middle section of the road from the Missouri river to the Arkansas river."[11] The first commissioners appointed to the task had declined to serve, and it was not until November, 1836, that the board had been organized, and then it was too late in the season to begin the survey. The next years were no more fruitful.

Poinsett, since he was explicitly opposed to the whole theory behind the road, could not be expected to expedite matters. He explained the delay in getting the road surveyed by the fact that sites for the permanent posts in the West had to be decided upon first, and he directed Commanding General Macomb to have a reconnaissance made to determine the most eligible locations, with reference "to the facilities with which they can be approached from the interior, and also from the posts on either side, or from the Indian country in front." Once the sites were established, the survey of the road would "merely consist in choosing the best ground for connecting them."[12]

In 1838, however, things went considerably better. Poinsett reported at the end of that year that the southern section from the Red River to the Arkansas (140 miles) and a middle section from Fort Leavenworth to the Marais des Cygnes River (72 miles) had been completed and that measures had been taken to continue the road another 86 miles to

[10] *Ibid.*, pp. 777–778.

[11] This survey of 286 miles was completed between September 27 and October 8 by United States Civil Engineer Charles Dimmock and an assistant, accompanied by Commissioners Kearny and Boone and a detachment of dragoons. Timber was blazed in the wooded areas and mounds of earth erected at mile intervals in the prairie country. *House Document* No. 278, 25 Congress, 2 session, serial 328, pp. 6–7.

[12] Poinsett to Macomb, October 13, 1837, *ibid.*, p. 5.

Spring River—leaving only 128 miles to the Arkansas. The survey of the route from Fort Leavenworth to Fort Snelling, furthermore, had been carried out, and in that area of rolling prairies, which could be traveled over with no difficulty, Poinsett intended only to mark out the most direct route.[13]

Quartermaster General Jesup in the following year reported the completion of the section from Leavenworth to Spring River and predicted that with further appropriations and availability of soldier labor the final section might be finished in 1841.[14] But at the end of 1841, Jesup found it necessary to repeat his recommendation for a small appropriation to complete the western military road from Spring River to the Arkansas at Fort Smith or Fort Gibson.[15] No further report on the completion of the road appears, but the whole work was apparently completed by 1845. Sections of the military road meanwhile were much used. In 1844 new appropriations were asked to repair the section between Fort Leavenworth and Fort Scott. "This road," Jesup reported, "is highly important as a military communication; and, being the only direct route from the northwestern part of Missouri and Iowa to Arkansas and Texas, it has been much travelled, and those accustomed to use it will be put to great inconvenience by its present condition." He recommended that troops be assigned to rebuild bridges and repair the road.[16]

☆

While Poinsett was reluctantly carrying out the Cass plan, with which he disagreed, he had in hand another plan, which he did not like either. His order for a reconnaissance of the western frontier relative to the proper selection of the exterior outposts had been handed down by General Macomb to General Gaines, who commanded the Western Division at St. Louis.[17] This was just the sort of opportunity

[13] Report of Poinsett, November 30, 1839, *Senate Document* No. 1, 26 Congress, 1 session, serial 354, p. 47.

[14] Report of Jesup, November 28, 1840, *Senate Document* No. 1, 26 Congress, 2 session, serial 375, p. 88.

[15] Report of Jesup, November 15, 1841, *Senate Document* No. 1, 27 Congress, 2 session, serial 395, p. 109.

[16] Report of Jesup, November 11, 1844, *Senate Document* No. 1, 28 Congress, 2 session, serial 449, p. 147.

[17] Poinsett to Macomb, October 13, 1837, *House Document* No. 278, 25 Congress, 2 session, serial 328, p. 5; Macomb to Gaines, October 17, 1837, *House Document* No. 357, 25 Congress, 2 session, serial 330, pp. 2–3.

Gaines must have been waiting for, and he submitted on February 28, 1838, a full analysis of western defense needs and a detailed system of forts and communications to meet them.[18]

Gaines prided himself on his military experience in the West and especially on his special interest and knowledge of frontier topography. He considered himself the one man who was fully qualified to draw up a system of defense, and other men, he thought, had a duty to listen. He had first proposed a line of advanced posts to General Macomb on July 6, 1833.[19] Then, in reply to an inquiry from Missouri members of Congress in August, 1837, he offered another list of positions for defense of the frontier and added the recommendation that a full township of land be reserved at each post in order to keep out whiskey vendors and that the western posts be converted into military schools for "aspiring youths of the neighboring States, unable to obtain admission into the Military Academy at West Point."[20]

It was his 1838 report, however, that gave complete scope to Gaines's far-reaching and imaginative suggestions. His plan fundamentally called for eleven military posts, stretching from the mouth of the Sabine River on the Gulf of Mexico to the tip of Lake Superior, and he plotted them out with red dots on the map he submitted with his proposal. Forts in the Indian country, however, were only one part of Gaines's defense system. The second was a system of railroads, radiating from the protected interior states of Kentucky and Tennessee to what he called the five grand divisions of the national frontier, by which an army and supplies could be moved quickly and cheaply to any point of attack. His plan included, too, a special system of seven western railroads to supply the eleven frontier garrisons. The railroads were to be constructed primarily by the labor of the troops.[21] Nor was Gaines satisfied with these defense proposals. He added to them a special pet project of floating batteries to defend the seacoast, to the promotion of which he devoted many years.[22]

[18] Gaines's plan appears as *House Document* No. 311, 25 Congress, 2 session, serial 329. His defense plans are discussed at length in James W. Silver, *Edmund Pendleton Gaines: Frontier General* (Baton Rouge, 1949), pp. 216–257.

[19] *House Document* No. 311, 25 Congress, 2 session, serial 329, pp. 18–26.

[20] Gaines to L. F. Linn and A. G. Harrison, August 14, 1837, *American State Papers: Military Affairs*, VII, 959.

[21] An article by Gaines explaining the military advantages of railroads is in *Niles' Weekly Register*, L (August 13, 1836), 403. Gaines further amplified his proposal for railroads in a memorial of December 31, 1839, addressed over the heads of his military superiors to Congress, *House Document* No. 206, 26 Congress, 1 session, serial 368, pp. 118–143.

[22] Silver, *Gaines*, pp. 223–235.

Gaines's proposals won no approval despite his long and persistent advocacy, although they must have helped to heighten interest in defense plans. His system of western forts did not differ radically from the lists of posts advocated in other plans, and some of the sites indicated by Gaines later had military posts. But his transportation system and floating batteries were flatly rejected. To a large extent his statements were ignored, and when Secretary of War Poinsett was asked point-blank by the House of Representatives for his views on Gaines's plans, he declared that despite "every respect for the experience of the gallant author," he did not agree that the system of permanent defenses should be abandoned and the defenses of the nation based upon "the expedients of vast floating batteries and extensive lines of railroads."[23]

☆

Poinsett continued to speak in terms of his plan of 1837, and he was in office long enough—from March, 1837, to March, 1841—to give some continuity to plans for the defense of the western frontier, which was so much in the minds of national legislators and the western public. The Senate and the House kept pushing him with requests for plans, and the Secretary took the task seriously. In November, 1839, he convened a board of officers, composed of Colonel Joseph G. Totten, Chief Engineer, Lieutenant Colonel Sylvanus Thayer of the Engineers, Colonel Trueman Cross, and Lieutenant Colonel George Talcott of Ordnance, to take into consideration the whole defense of the United States. The board submitted its report on March 14, 1840. The third section dealt with the western frontier, and the recommendations coincided closely with Poinsett's earlier proposals.[24]

The most important defense segment in the West, in the minds of the board members, was that extending from the Red River to the Missouri. The board was mindful of a dual responsibility of the govern-

[23] Report of Poinsett, May 12, 1840, *House Document* No. 206, 26 Congress, 1 session, serial 368, pp. 1–2.

[24] The full report of the board, covering more than 100 pages, is in *Senate Document* No. 451, 26 Congress, 1 session, serial 360. The section of the report dealing with the western frontier is on pages 106–109. The report appears also, with some additional material, in *House Document* No. 206, 26 Congress, 1 session, serial 368, pp. 5–117. The western section of this report with special letters of transmittal from Poinsett is in *Senate Document* No. 379, 26 Congress, 1 session, serial 359, and in *House Document* No. 161, 26 Congress, 1 session, serial 366.

ment growing out of Indian removal and set forth this responsibility as the basis of their specific defense proposals:

It is along this line that the numerous tribes of Indians who have emigrated from the east have been located; thus adding to the indigenous force already in that region, an immense mass of emigrants, some of whom have been sent thither by coercion, with smothered feelings of hostility rankling in their bosoms, which, probably, waits but for an occasion to burst forth in all its savage fury. These considerations alone would seem to call for strong precautionary measures; but an additional motive will be found in our peculiar relations with those Indians.

We are bound, by solemn treaty stipulations, to interpose force, if necessary, to prevent domestic strife among them, preserve peace between the several tribes, and to protect them against any disturbance at their new homes, by the wild Indians who inhabit the country beyond. The Government has thus contracted the two-fold obligation of intervention among, and protection of, the emigrant tribes, in addition to the duty which it owes to its own citizens of providing for their safety.[25]

The board was convinced that these obligations could be properly fulfilled only by "an adequate restraining military force" stationed at advanced positions in the Indian country. In addition, it recommended an interior line of posts along the western borders of Arkansas and Missouri, "as auxiliaries to the advanced positions, and to restrain the intercourse between the whites and the Indians, and to serve as rallying-points for the neighboring militia in times of alarm."

The advanced posts should be Fort Towson on the Red River, Fort Gibson on the Arkansas, a new post at the head of navigation on the Kansas River, and one on the Missouri at Table Creek below the mouth of the Platte. The secondary posts should be those proposed by the officers who examined the country in connection with the laying out of the military road authorized in 1836—Fort Smith on the Arkansas, Fort Wayne on the Illinois, a post on Spring River, one on the Marais des Cygnes, and finally at Fort Leavenworth on the Missouri. The board recommended in addition one or two intermediate posts between the Arkansas and Red Rivers, near the state line rather than on the military road, which they considered too far in advance of the settlements to be good locations for the interior posts.

[25] *Senate Document* No. 451, 26 Congress, 1 session, serial 360, pp. 106–107.

For the northern segments of the frontier, the board repeated previous recommendations—a post near the upper forks of the Des Moines, Fort Snelling, and the ultimate establishment of a post on the western tip of Lake Superior, in order to influence the Indians in that northern area and protect the traders of that region. No interior line from the Missouri to the Mississippi was recommended, since the Indians of that region were likely to be removed farther west, but retention of Fort Crawford, Fort Winnebago, and Fort Howard was advised to protect the line of communication between the Great Lakes and the Mississippi.

☆

One of the basic principles in the thinking of the army men who drew up plans for frontier defense was the "disposable force." The frontier outposts were to be simple affairs, not permanent fortifications such as were constructed along the eastern seaboard.[26] And they were to be so built that they could be defended and maintained by a small force, say a company or two of infantry or artillery, leaving the rest of the troops free to move from place to place on short notice as threats of trouble or actual outbreaks demanded. Cass's plan for the great western military road was premised on forces free to march along it from section to section. Colonel Cross's plan of 1837, which Poinsett largely adopted, called for a permanent garrison of 200 men at Fort Leavenworth with a disposable force there of 1,000. At Fort Gibson Cross recommended a permanent garrison of 300, "leaving a disposable force of 1,200 that might take the field at a moment's warning, and march in the direction of the alarm." At Fort Towson a disposable force of 600 would be added to a regular garrison of 200.[27] Forts Atkinson and

[26] There was considerable argument about just what the nature of these western forts should be. General Gaines, in his plan for posts, recommended that each work "be built of stone or brick, flat-roofed, covered with sheet-lead of the thickest kind, and the whole work to be made fire-proof throughout; to be enclosed with a strong stone or brick wall. . . ." Gaines to Macomb, July 6, 1833, *House Document* No. 311, 23 Congress, 2 session, serial 329, p. 20. Quartermaster General Jesup in 1839, for the posts between Fort Leavenworth and Fort Snelling, recommended that "the ordinary log cabins and block houses of the frontiers alone be constructed and with as little expense as practicable." *Senate Document* No. 1, 26 Congress, 1 session, serial 354, p. 114. Secretary of War Poinsett urged construction of "permanent materials, and in a manner to insure the health and comfort of the soldier." *Senate Document* No. 1, 25 Congress, 3 session, serial 338, p. 100. Secretary of War Spencer in 1841 decided in favor of temporary "stockaded forts with log-block houses." *Senate Document* No. 1, 27 Congress, 2 session, serial 395, p. 61.

[27] Cross's figures are in *American State Papers: Military Affairs*, VII, 784.

Des Moines in Iowa had a company of infantry as part of their garrisons, so that the dragoons would be free to leave the posts for extended patrols into the Indian country.

In addition to these disposable troops on the frontier itself a concentration of larger reserves at central barracks was advocated, a principle that received more and more emphasis as transportation facilities improved. The concentration of reserves was an essential part of Poinsett's concept of western defense, with the lines of communication radiating out from the points of concentration, and his plan of 1837 called for a major reserve of troops at Jefferson Barracks. "The line of the frontier, especially if it be extended to include Council Bluffs," Colonel Cross had remarked, "describes an arc of a circle, whose chord would pass nearly through that point. From its central position, and its proximity to the mouths of the great rivers leading to the frontier, reinforcements may, by means of steam transports, be thrown, with great rapidity and nearly equal facility, up the Missouri, the Arkansas, and the Mississippi, as circumstances shall require."[28] Gaines's plan, too, looked for central depots of men and supplies at Jefferson Barracks and Memphis.

Poinsett came to emphasize the principle of the reserve of troops more and more. In his annual report of 1838 he recommended that the places and manner of quartering and stationing the troops be changed, in order to concentrate an effective striking force and at the same time provide for adequate military discipline and skill in military maneuvers. Troops should be stationed where they could form a center around which the citizen's militia could rally, with the combined forces then marching to the relief of any point that was threatened or attacked. This principle was to be applied to the whole frontier of the United States, east, north, south, and west, with one center on Lake Champlain in New York for the northern frontier, another at Carlisle in Pennsylvania for the east coast north of the Chesapeake, and a third near the headwaters of the Savannah River for the southeast. The fourth point, for the entire western frontier, was to be Jefferson Barracks. Small garrisons of regulars (aided by volunteers and militia) would occupy the forts and defend them until the *corps d'armée* nearest the point of attack could march to their relief. "In no other way," he concluded, "can an extensive line of frontier, like that of the United States, be defended by a small army such as ours."[29]

---

[28] *Ibid.*, pp. 782–783.
[29] Report of Poinsett, November 28, 1838, *Senate Document* No. 1, 25 Congress, 3 session, serial 338, pp. 98–99.

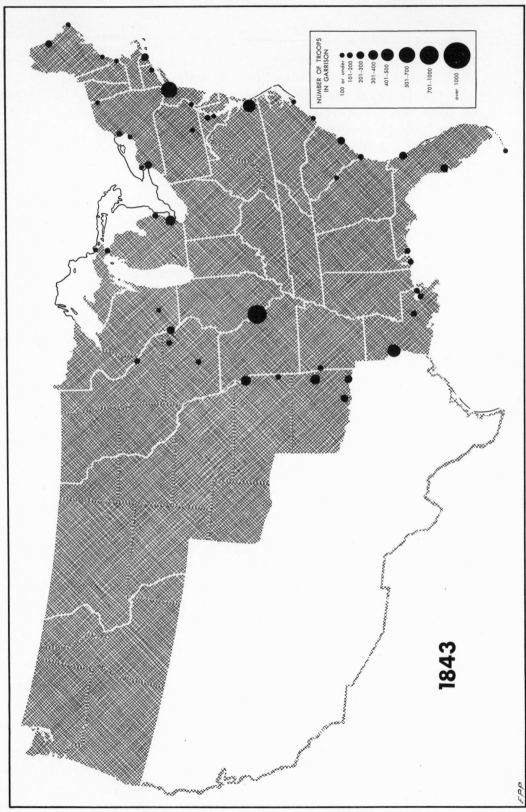

1843

Distribution of Regular Army Troops, 1843

Legend:

NUMBER OF TROOPS
IN GARRISON

100 or under
101–200
201–300
301–400
401–500
501–700
701–1000
over 1000

But the drain of troops to the Florida war and the immediate demands of the western and northern frontiers made it impossible to build up any reserve at Jefferson Barracks. When the troops from Florida were redistributed after the war, the reserve idea became feasible again, and Poinsett's words were echoed by General Scott, who in 1843 described Jefferson Barracks as the "western reserve," making it possible to maintain the western frontier from Lake Superior to the Gulf of Mexico with a small army. "To give to so extended a line of frontier (in length about 1700 miles) reasonable security, *without a reserve*," Scott asserted, "would require at least five additional regiments." The small size of the army necessitated concentration for adequate defense, but Scott offered another observation, "not likely to occur even to the intelligent, without military experience; small garrisons, scattered along a wild frontier, always, after a time, deteriorate in morals and military efficiency."[30]

When Scott wrote, the reserve at Jefferson Barracks was sixteen companies of the Third and Fourth Infantry, each regiment having detached two companies to serve on the frontier, but it was difficult to maintain in practice the reserve that was preached in principle. The needs of the frontier were so continually demanding that the reserve could not long be maintained. In 1844, in fact, the reserve troops at Jefferson Barracks were sent south to Fort Jesup and Natchitoches, where they built themselves huts for winter shelter.[31]

The doctrines of disposable forces and reserves of troops at central depots were based upon adequate transportation means to move the forces to endangered points. General Gaines's plan for a system of railroads to furnish the supply lines for the posts of the western military frontier having been dismissed by Poinsett as inefficient and too costly, it remained for the Secretary to give his own analysis of practicable means of communication to fasten the outer line of defense to the interior.[32]

Poinsett's first reliance was upon natural lines of communication, the great river networks that interlaced the middle United States. When their navigation was improved by removing rafts, snags, and sawyers, they would furnish an adequate cheap water highway. Droughts in the

[30] Report of Scott, November 24, 1843, *Senate Document* No. 1, 28 Congress, 1 session, serial 431, pp. 63–64.

[31] Report of Macomb, November 23, 1844, *Senate Document* No. 1, 28 Congress, 2 session, serial 449, p. 131.

[32] Report of Poinsett, March 21, 1840, *Senate Document* No. 379, 26 Congress, 1 session, serial 359, pp. 1–5.

summer and ice in the winter obstructed navigation during parts of the year, but careful planning to ship the annual stock of supplies for the stations during the spring floods, Poinsett observed, would obviate all inconveniences.

In the south was the Red River, a good supply line to Fort Towson once the great raft had been removed, and from which a short road would lead to the Sabine. The Arkansas River penetrated the central sector, supplying Fort Smith and Fort Gibson. From it in flood times the Neosho led to its tributary, the Spring River, on which a new post was contemplated. Then, as one moved north to the right flank of the central frontier, came the mighty Missouri, on which was located Fort Leavenworth and the new post proposed for the mouth of the Platte. The tributaries of the Missouri, the Kansas and Osage rivers, would furnish communication to the new forts which the board of officers had recommended for the head of navigation of the Kansas and for the Marais des Cygnes. The Mississippi and its tributaries had long borne supplies to the northern posts.

These natural waterways needed to be supplemented, however, with overland communications, which could be resorted to if weather or an enemy cut off the rivers and over which troop movements might be made at any time. To fill out his proposed network, Poinsett pointed out, not many new roads would be required, since the repair of those already built would be nearly sufficient.

There was already a military road from Natchitoches on the Red River to Fort Towson and one from the same place toward the Sabine, via Fort Jesup. Another stretched from the Mississippi opposite Memphis to Little Rock, and then had been extended by the soldiers to Fort Smith and Fort Gibson. These two roads, Poinsett said, "establish *a great central line of communication* by land, from a point on the Mississippi, abounding in resources of men and supplies, to our remotest frontier post." From the Arkansas River at Little Rock, an important road led to the town of Washington near the Red River, where it intersected the Natchitoches-Fort Towson road. This interior line would be of great importance, "since the frontier road, lately opened under the law of 1836, runs far beyond the boundary, through the Indian country, and is wholly unfit for a line of communication in time of war." (Poinsett could not resist this sly criticism of Cass's plan for defense.) Here was a fine alternate channel to supply the upper Red River country. The Arkansas was seldom so low that boats could not reach Little Rock, and if that should ever happen, the Memphis-Little

Rock road was still available. From Little Rock north to the southern boundary of Missouri still another military road joined the state and county road system of Missouri. Roads already in use from St. Louis and Boonville to the west and southwest would tie the interior with Fort Leavenworth and the new posts proposed at the west of the Missouri settlement. The only new road the Secretary recommended was one from the Arkansas River to Fort Wayne, a post which could not be supplied by water transportation. The other roads could be repaired as needed—nothing very expensive, no "attempt to give them what would be called a complete finish," just enough to make them passable to troops and to reestablish bridges and ferries to cross the streams.

☆

The plans for western defense worked out in the War Department were reasonable proposals, following a pattern developed by practical experience as well as theoretical speculations of military science over a number of years, yet the implementation of the plans was piecemeal. Establishment of individual posts often was the result of local pressures rather than the deliberate carrying out of an accepted over-all plan. Perhaps it was enough to ask that the new forts built on the western frontier should at least fit roughly into the broad general blueprints.

The circumstances involved in the location of specific forts can be seen in the cases of new forts built along the borders of Arkansas and Missouri, a vital region in all the defense plans. One of these posts was Fort Coffee, built on the Arkansas River to foil, if possible, the whiskey vendors of the region. These rascals were a constant menace to the peace of the Indian country, and the army officers were unsuccessful in outwitting them. Despite valiant efforts on the part of the military, the violations of the law prohibiting the liquor trade were flagrant. In an attempt to staunch the flow of whiskey, Captain John Stuart and his company of the Seventh Infantry were ordered in March, 1833, to station themselves at abandoned Fort Smith, where it was hoped they could intercept intruders into the Indian country. It was soon decided that a position farther up the Arkansas might be a better spot to catch the lawbreakers and at the same time offer a more healthful location for the troops. On June 16, 1834, therefore, the troops stationed at Fort Smith moved to a point about fifteen miles above that site on a bluff that commanded a view of the river for several miles in each direction. The new fort was near the Choctaw agency and was an important post as the emigrant Indians settled in their new homes. When Fort Smith was reestablished in 1838, Fort Coffee was no longer necessary, and during August and September the ordnance and stores were removed. On October 19, 1838, the troops left the post.[33]

Captain Stuart's company from Fort Coffee moved north to the Illinois River (a tributary of the Arkansas) to establish a new post in the Cherokee country, where conflict between the factions of the tribe seemed to call for closer watch. Work was begun on the new post, called Fort Wayne, on October 29, 1838, but the location chosen on the Illinois proved unhealthful, and a number of men and officers died, among them Captain Stuart. In June, 1840, work on the post was halted and the troops were ordered to a more satisfactory spot. A new site was selected north of the original location, near Spavinaw Creek, which flows into the Neosho. Fort Wayne became one of the links in the western chain of posts, and during the troubles within the Cherokee nation the fort was of some importance. In March, 1840, it had a garrison of 335 men.[34]

The Cherokees, however, objected to the presence of the fort within their country, and Major Ethan Allen Hitchcock, who was sent by the Secretary of War in 1841 to inspect the Indian territory, recommended the removal of the fort, which he did not consider necessary. Orders were issued for the evacuation of Fort Wayne, and some other site for a post between Fort Leavenworth and Fort Gibson was sought. The troops left Fort Wayne on May 26, 1842, and four days later arrived at the location for the new work, where the military road crossed the Marmaton River just west of the Missouri boundary. The new fort was named Fort Scott; it served as an intermediate post on the military road and satisfied the demands of Missourians for added military protection on their western border until its abandonment in 1853.[35]

---

[33] Grant Foreman, *Advancing the Frontier, 1830–1860* (Norman, Okla., 1933), pp. 29–33, 55.

[34] *Ibid.*, pp. 77–81; Henry P. Beers, *The Western Military Frontier, 1815–1846* (Philadelphia, 1935), p. 133; *Senate Document* No. 136, 28 Congress, 1 session, serial 433.

[35] Louise Barry, "The Fort Leavenworth-Fort Gibson Military Road and the Founding of Fort Scott," *Kansas Historical Quarterly*, XI (May, 1942), 115–129. In January, 1841, the Senate requested of the Secretary of War his opinion whether "a military post between Fort Leavenworth and Fort Wayne, on the borders of Arkansas, be not important to the protection of the State of Missouri from Indian incursions and aggressions." There is a hint of impatience in the reply of Poinsett and the officers to whom he referred the request. Colonels Totten and Cross referred to the board's report of 1840, which had precisely rec-

The location of Fort Gibson was a matter of greater controversy. Troops had been moved to the site of the Neosho in 1824 when the western boundary of Arkansas was pushed to the west. But in 1828, with the establishment of the Cherokee reservation, the boundary was set back at its original location, leaving Fort Gibson deep in the Indian country. This did not satisfy the residents of Arkansas, who memorialized Congress on October 23, 1833, to move the fort back to the vicinity of the white settlements and who suggested the old site of Fort Smith or some other spot near by.[36] The House Committee on Military Affairs supported the appeal with the statement that "such a disposition of our troops would more effectually protect our citizens, and, at the same time, bring the troops nearer to the point from which they draw their subsistence and support."[37] No action was taken, however, until May 14, 1836, when Congress appropriated $50,000 for the removal of troops "from Fort Gibson to some eligible point on or near the western frontier line of Arkansas," and for the erection of a fort at that site.[38]

The location of Fort Gibson then became immeshed in the sticky problem of the grand plan for western defense. Cass, in giving directions to the commissioners for laying out the road and determining sites for the posts, referred to the act of Congress ordering relocation of Fort Gibson and instructed the commissioners to select a suitable site for the fort and then use that as one of the defense works on the military road.[39] But when the commissioners made their report on December 11, 1836, they recommended the location of Fort Coffee as a suitable defense spot for the western boundary of Arkansas, but they could not recommend the abandonment of Fort Gibson, which they considered "indispensable for the preservation of peace amongst the Indians themselves."[40] On the basis of further investigations made in 1837, Secretary of War Poinsett concluded flatly that the act of Congress providing for the removal of Fort Gibson could not be carried out, if the solemn guarantees to the Cherokees to protect them in their western home were

---

ommended *two* posts between Fort Wayne and Fort Leavenworth, and declared that they saw no reason to change their opinion. Poinsett, too, said that he added his concurrence to the plan of defense proposed in 1840. *Senate Document* No. 104, 26 Congress, 2 session, serial 377.

[36] *American State Papers: Military Affairs*, V, 242–243.

[37] *Ibid.*, p. 261.

[38] *U. S. Statutes at Large*, V, 30.

[39] Cass to Commissioners, July 16, 1836, *House Document* No. 278, 25 Congress, 2 session, serial 328, p. 11.

[40] *Ibid.*, pp. 14–15.

to be honored.[41] The upshot of the matter was that Fort Gibson continued at its old site and Fort Smith was reestablished, a superfluous post that was erected to satisfy the inhabitants of Arkansas rather than to fulfill any military need.[42]

A more useful installation was the new fort erected west of Fort Towson in the Red River country. The Chickasaw emigrants in that region were frequently molested on their new reservation by bands of other Indians who had used the lands for common hunting grounds and by the usual frontier ruffians. Appeals to Colonel Arbuckle at Fort Gibson brought detachments of dragoons in 1841 to restore order, but when the troops departed, the old difficulties returned. Orders were finally given for the establishment of a new military post in the troubled area. The region near the mouth of the Washita River was examined in 1841 and a site selected on the east side of the Washita, fifteen miles from the Red River. In April of the following year troops of the Second Dragoons were sent to the location to construct the fort, which was called Fort Washita. At the end of the year a company of the Sixth Infantry was added to the garrison.[43]

☆

The emigration of Americans to Oregon added still another dimension to western defense plans.[44] As early as 1840, in reply to a resolution from the Senate, Secretary of War Poinsett asserted that a chain of posts from the Missouri to the Columbia "would facilitate the intercourse between the valley of the Mississippi, and the great Western ocean; would aid and protect trading caravans; and hold in check the various Indian tribes that occupy the country around them," and he suggested appropriate sites for such military posts.[45]

In the following year Poinsett's successor, John C. Spencer, advo-

[41] Poinsett report, February 20, 1838, and appended reports of Lieutenant Colonel William Whistler and Captain John Stuart of the Seventh Infantry, *American State Papers: Military Affairs*, VII, 974–985.

[42] Foreman, *Advancing the Frontier*, pp. 51–53.

[43] *Ibid.*, pp. 96–106; William B. Morrison, "Fort Washita," *Chronicles of Oklahoma*, V (June, 1927), 251–258.

[44] See Henry P. Beers, "The Army and the Oregon Trail to 1846," *Pacific Northwest Quarterly*, XXVIII (October, 1937), 339–362.

[45] Report of Poinsett, February 24, 1840, *Senate Document* No. 231, 26 Congress, 1 session, serial 358.

cated a similar proposal. The western territory, extending from the Lakes to the Gulf of Mexico, he noted, was "in immediate contact with numerous wild and warlike Indians, who are capable of bringing into the field a number of warriors estimated at from twenty to thirty thousand. From the intercourse which subsists between them and the traders, and emissaries of foreign nations, they may be rendered as formidable as any description of force that could be brought against us." To control these Indians in peace and counteract them in war, to secure American territory, and to protect its traders, Spencer recommended as indispensable the establishment of a chain of posts from Council Bluffs on the Missouri to the mouth of the Columbia on the Pacific, both to command the avenues by which the Indians traveled from north to south and to "maintain a communication with the territories belonging to us in the Pacific."[46]

President Tyler strongly recommended the plan to Congress, and in the following year Spencer spelled out his proposal in more detail. He was willing to begin slowly, however, with the establishment of a post at some point on the Missouri, from which supplies could be collected and parties sent out to explore and to protect the emigrants.[47] In his annual message to Congress in December, 1845, after heavy travel on the plains had been experienced for a number of years, President Polk urged the erection of a "suitable number of stockades and blockhouse forts . . . along the usual route between our frontier settlements on the Missouri and the Rocky mountains." He wanted, too, a force of mounted riflemen to protect the emigrants on their way.[48] These stirrings of Manifest Destiny, however, would have to wait until more was known about the West and until more insistent demands for protection were forthcoming.

The year 1844, in fact, had marked the culmination of defense arrangements in the West before the Mexican War. In that year Fort Wilkins was established at Copper Harbor on the extremity of Keweenaw Peninsula in Lake Superior, to meet the particular local defense needs arising from the influx of miners into that copper region. To the Secretary of War, for whom the post was named, however, the new

[46] Report of Spencer, December 1, 1841, *Senate Document* No. 1, 27 Congress, 2 session, serial 395, pp. 61–62.

[47] Report of Spencer, November 26, 1842, *Senate Document* No. 1, 27 Congress, 3 session, serial 413, pp. 188–189.

[48] Message of Polk, December 2, 1845, *Senate Document* No. 1, 29 Congress, 1 session, serial 470, pp. 12–13.

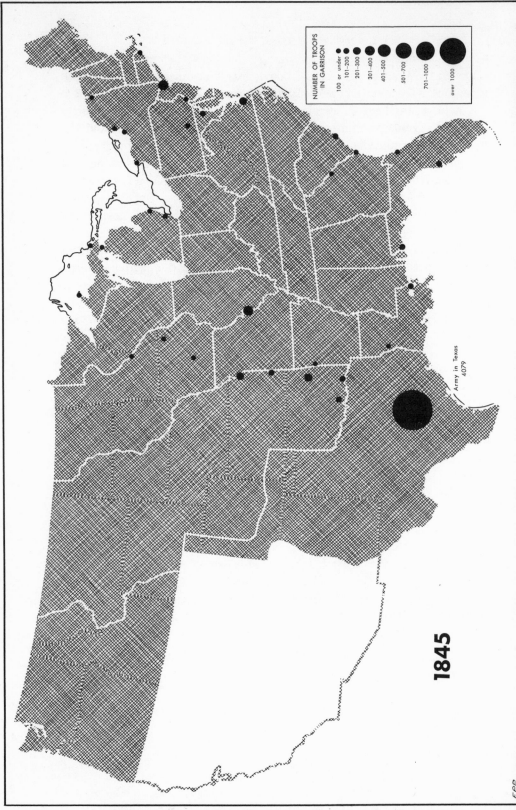

NUMBER OF TROOPS
IN GARRISON

100 or under
101-200
201-300
301-400
401-500
501-700
701-1000
over 1000

Army in Texas
4079

1845

Distribution of Regular Army Troops, 1845

FPP

fort formed "one point in a new cordon, which the general extension of our settlements and the enlargement of our territories by Indian treaties are about rendering necessary to be established."[49]

With Fort Wilkins the top link in the chain, the exterior line of posts in that year comprised Fort Snelling, Fort Leavenworth, Fort Scott, Fort Gibson, Fort Towson, and Fort Washita. The interior posts were Fort Mackinac and Fort Brady on the Lakes, Fort Winnebago at the portage, Fort Crawford at Prairie du Chien, and Forts Atkinson and Des Moines in Iowa. In the south Fort Smith and Fort Jesup also served the Indian frontier.

The impending Mexican War called for a massive concentration of troops, knocked complete links out of this chain that had been so laboriously constructed, and wiped out much of the eastern defense line as well. Secretary of War William L. Marcy reported in November, 1845, in a tone tinged with dismay:

> On our northern borders along the line of the British provinces, from Maine to Lake Superior, an extent of two thousand miles, there is now stationed but a single regiment. From the Falls of Saint Anthony, on the Upper Mississippi, along the western and southwestern frontier, bordering on the Indian country fifteen hundred miles, and extending south to New Orleans, only one regiment of dragoons and two of infantry are stationed. The artillery regiments, reduced in strength by having four companies detached from each, now garrison a few of the fortifications upon the seaboard, from Newport, in Rhode Island, to New Orleans, the exigencies of the public service having required the withdrawment of all the troops from Massachusetts, New Hampshire, and Maine. The residue of the army, consisting of one regiment of dragoons, sixteen companies of artillery, and five regiments of infantry, constituting more than half of the whole military force of the United States, is now serving in Texas. This important change in the position of our military force was made in the course of the last summer.[50]

The plans of the decade had been made with great seriousness of purpose. The concern for the West was genuine, and the cordon of

---

[49] Report of Wilkins, November 30, 1844, *Senate Document* No. 1, 28 Congress, 2 session, serial 449, p. 114. Wilkins recommended in addition two intermediate posts between Fort Wilkins and Fort Snelling, which were not established.

[50] Report of Marcy, November 29, 1845, *Senate Document* No. 1, 29 Congress, 1 session, serial 470, p. 193.

posts, despite differences of opinion about where it should be, had maintained peace and order on the frontier, for the troops who manned them had not sat quietly in their garrisons but summer after summer had marched deep into the Indian country to parley with the tribes and convince them of the authority and power of the United States.

EIGHTEEN

The Dragoons on the Prairies and Plains

THE dragoons were very much in evidence in the West in the dozen years between their organization and the Mexican War. The mounted troops appeared in the country of the mounted Indians without the feeling of impotence that had frequently accompanied the foot soldiers. They in fact significantly impressed the remote tribes with the power of the United States, and their mobility promised quick reprisal to tribes who molested emigrants crossing the plains or who otherwise disturbed the peace.

The first expedition of the dragoons in the summer of 1834, however, was a near disaster. Although it carried out an important mission, it moved west onto the plains in the heat of high summer, and the soldiers and the horses succumbed in large numbers. The goal was the Pawnee Pict village in what is now southwestern Oklahoma, as the government determined once again to make a show of strength in the country of the Comanches, Kiowas, and Pawnees.[1] These tribes had

[1] A detailed account of Colonel Henry Dodge's expedition to the Pawnee Pict village in the summer of 1834 is in Louis Pelzer, *Marches of the Dragoons in the Mississippi Valley: An Account of Marches and Activities of the First Regiment United States Dragoons in the Mississippi Valley between the Years 1833 and 1850* (Iowa City, 1917), pp. 34–48, which repeats the material from the same author's *Henry Dodge* (Iowa City, 1911), pp. 94–112. The story is told more briefly in Otis E Young, *The West of Philip St. George Cooke* (Glendale, California, 1955), pp. 74–82. The official journal of the expedition by Lieutenant Thompson B. Wheelock accompanies the Report of the Secretary of War for 1834, *House Executive Document* No. 2, 23 Congress, 2 session, serial 271, pp. 70–91. Wheelock's journal was edited by Edgar B. Harlan, "Colonel Henry Dodge and His Regiment of Dragoons on the Plains in 1832," *Annals of Iowa*, Third Series, XVIII (January, 1930), 173–197, and by George H. Shirk, "Peace on the Plains," *Chronicles of Oklahoma*, XXVIII (Spring, 1950), 2–41. A narrative firsthand report on the expedition by a soldier of Company I is in Louis

not yet treated with the United States, and they were a continual danger to the Santa Fe traders and to the emigrant Indians from the East. Secretary of War Cass believed that the dragoons would excite in the Indians a deeper respect for the United States.[2]

General Henry Leavenworth took command of the Western Division in April, 1834, and he prepared to direct the operations in the Southwest. He arrived at Fort Gibson on April 23 and began preparations for an expedition to visit the Comanche and Pawnee Pict (Wichita) villages on the Mexican frontier, some 250 miles to the west of Fort Gibson. Roads were laid out to the Washita River and advance bases for the dragoon expedition set up.

The expedition, which should have gotten under way at the beginning of May, was delayed because it had to wait for the five additional companies of dragoons ordered from Jefferson Barracks, the last of whom arrived at Camp Jackson on June 2 after their march of 450 miles,[3] and because low water on the Arkansas River caused supplies to be late.

On June 15, with about 500 men in his command, Colonel Dodge moved out of Camp Jackson, across the Arkansas about twenty miles to Camp Rendezvous, where the final preparations for the journey were made. In the company were two young Indian girls, a Kiowa of about fifteen years and a Pawnee of about eighteen, who had been recovered from the Osages and who were taken along in the hope of exchanging them for Private George B. Abbay, kidnapped from the ranger expe-

---

Pelzer, ed., "A Journal of Marches by the First United States Dragoons, 1834–1835," *Iowa Journal of History and Politics*, VII (July, 1909), 341–360. Sergeant Hugh Evans kept a journal of the march, which appears in Fred S. Perrine and Grant Foreman, eds., "The Journal of Hugh Evans, Covering the First and Second Campaigns of the United States Dragoon Regiment in 1834 and 1835: Campaign of 1834," *Chronicles of Oklahoma*, III (September, 1925), 175–215. [James Hildreth], *Dragoon Campaigns to the Rocky Mountains: Being a History of the Enlistment, Organization, and First Campaigns of the Regiment of United States Dragoons; Together with Incidents of a Soldier's Life, and Sketches of Scenery and Indian Character* (New York, 1836), describes the expedition. George Catlin, who accompanied the dragoons until he became ill, describes the activities of the troops, the Indians, and the country in *Letters and Notes on the Manners, Customs, and Condition of the North American Indians* (2 vols., New York, 1841), II, 45–75. Colonel Dodge's personal reactions can be seen in "Letters of Henry Dodge to Gen. George W. Jones," ed. William Salter, *Annals of Iowa*, Third Series, III (October, 1897), 220–223.

[2] Report of Cass, November 27, 1834, *House Executive Document* No. 2, 23 Congress, 2 session, serial 271, pp. 33–34.

[3] A journal of this march appears in Pelzer, *Iowa Journal of History and Politics*, VII, 335–341. Pelzer gives a brief account of the trip in *Marches of the Dragoons*, pp. 30–33. See also Hamilton Gardner, "The March of the First Dragoons from Jefferson Barracks to Fort Gibson in 1833–1834," *Chronicles of Oklahoma*, XXXI (Spring, 1953), 22–36.

dition of the previous year, and a boy, Matthew Wright Martin, who were supposedly held by the Pawnees. Also on hand were Montford Stokes, one of the Indian commissioners sent out by Cass, the Prussian botanist Carl Beyrich, and the Indian artist George Catlin, the last of whom looked forward with anticipation to "the first grand *civilized foray*, into the country of the wild and warlike Camanchees."[4]

On June 21, joined by small bands of Senecas, Osages, Cherokees, and Delawares to serve as guides and interpreters, the expedition began its march toward the Washita. The tremendous heat of the summer quickly took its toll, as the temperature passed 105° in the shade. Twenty-three men were sent back to Fort Gibson as unfit even before the march began, and on July 1, forty-five men and three officers were reported on the sick list from the excessive heat. Each day that the march continued saw further depletion of the ranks.

On July 4 the Washita River was crossed, a camp made, and reorganization of the expedition initiated. General Leavenworth, who had joined the expedition on June 26, was himself ill and ordered Dodge to take the healthy men and press on. Six companies of forty-two men each were organized under Dodge. One hundred and nine men were left for duty at the camp, together with eighty-six sick. On the 7th Dodge and his column marched forward, furnished with only ten days' rations and eighty rounds of ammunition apiece, for the baggage wagons were left behind. More of the men fell by the wayside, but the expedition could not well be called off without disastrous loss of face before the Indians and troublesome explaining to do to the public.

The troops moved on across the rolling prairies. They observed roving bands of Indians and large herds of wild horses and buffaloes, but not until July 16 did they reach a Comanche village, where they were met by 100 mounted Indians. The chief was absent, and not able to delay more than a day, Dodge headed on toward the Pawnee Pict village. By July 19 the expedition had been reduced to 183, as the men suffered from the forced march, the heat, and the shortage of provisions, but two days later they reached their goal. Dodge held a grand council with the Pawnee chiefs and with bands of Comanches and Kiowas who arrived at the camp. On July 22 he spoke in council with the Indians:

We are the first American offcers who have ever come to see the Pawnees; we meet you as friends, not as enemies, to make peace with you, to shake hands with you. The great American captain is at

4 Catlin, *North American Indians*, II, 44.

peace with all the white men in the world; he wishes to be at peace with all the red men of the world; we have been sent here to view this country, and to invite you to go to Washington, where the great American chief lives, to make a treaty with him, that you may learn how he wishes to send among you traders, who will bring you guns and blankets, and every thing that you want.[5]

After initial denials on the part of the Pawnees, Dodge recovered the Martin boy and turned over the Indian girls, but the expedition came too late to rescue the unfortunate Abbay. The chiefs were impressed with Dodge and his mounted troops, and overcoming their hesitation, a deputation of chiefs agreed to return with the colonel to Fort Gibson.

The return march began on July 25, and 100 miles were covered in the first week despite the continuing heat and the large number of sick. When the troops reached the Cross Timbers on August 5, they learned of the death of General Leavenworth on July 21. Ten days later Dodge and the main party once again were at Fort Gibson. The group that had encamped at the Cross Timbers returned under Colonel Kearny on the 24th with both men and horses in serious condition.

Catlin was sick and Beyrich the botanist had died. Deaths among the troops continued to occur daily; altogether more than 100 enlisted men succumbed. A hundred of the dragoon horses had been killed or broken by the extreme heat. "Perhaps their [sic] never has been in America a campaign that operated more severely on men and horses," was Dodge's summary of the expedition to a friend.[6]

Despite the decimation this first operation of the dragoons had been a success. The plains Indians, accustomed to look with scorn upon the infantry, had been impressed by the new regiment, which demonstrated effectively the might of the American government. The delegation of Indian chiefs met in council at Fort Gibson from September 1 to September 4. Choctaws, Cherokees, Osages, and Senecas met with the Pawnees, Comanches, and Kiowas, and Colonel Dodge believed that he had laid the foundations for lasting peace among these frontier tribes.

☆

[5] Lieutenant Wheelock's journal, *House Executive Document* No. 2, 23 Congress, 2 session, serial 271, p. 79.
[6] Dodge to Jones, October 1, 1834, *Annals of Iowa*, Third Series, III, 222.

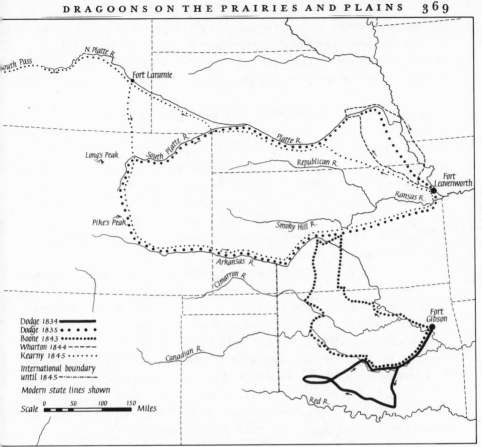

The Dragoons on the Plains, 1834–1845

Before Dodge left on the disastrous expedition to the Pawnee Pict village, he detached Company A, commanded by Captain Clifton Wharton, as an escort for the Santa Fe trains of that year.[7] Wharton marched out of Fort Gibson on May 13 and hit the Santa Fe Trail on June 3 at the south fork of the Neosho River. He sent two men to try to locate the caravan and waited at the site until June 8, when the caravan of about one hundred wagons under the leadership of Josiah Gregg arrived. The traders accepted Wharton's proffered escort, and the train moved to the Arkansas crossings without mishap.

At this point a band of peaceful Comanches appeared, but Wharton was unable to hold a council with them, for the traders threatened the

[7] Wharton's report and documents relating to his expedition are printed in Fred S. Perrine, ed., "Military Escorts on the Santa Fe Trail," *New Mexico Historical Review*, II (July, 1927), 269–285, 296–304.

Indians and forced them to depart. Wharton refused the requests of the traders for escorts through the Mexican territory, and on June 28 he left the traders to their own devices and returned to Fort Gibson, having issued the last flour the day before and with his horses broken down.

Captain Wharton reported that he saw little necessity for an escort of the traders while they were in American territory as long as the Indians were at peace among themselves and with the United States. In fact, such escorts, he thought, were more of a detriment than an advantage, for they lulled the traders into a sense of security that might prove dangerous when they encountered hostile Indians in the Mexican part of their journey beyond the reach of the United States army.

Wharton's judgment was apparently correct, for several years passed without any serious encounters between the Indians and the Santa Fe trains. In 1839 Josiah Gregg again applied for an escort, but he was told that the troops were needed elsewhere because of troubles with the Cherokees. Gregg, choosing a route west from Van Buren, Arkansas, along the north bank of the Canadian River, started out with his small train unescorted. He was overtaken in the middle of May, however, at the edge of the Cross Timbers by a detachment of forty dragoons led by Lieutenant James M. Bowman. The troops accompanied the train until west of the international boundary at the 100th meridian, and on June 7 Bowman returned to Fort Gibson.[8] Not until 1843 did the military escorts appear again on the regular Santa Fe Trail.

☆

The heavy toll of sickness in the regiment as it operated out of Fort Gibson in the hot summer of 1834 undoubtedly confirmed the prudence of sending the dragoons to more hospitable latitudes. Four companies under Colonel Dodge were marched to Fort Leavenworth, three more under Major Mason moved to a point on the Arkansas River about eighty miles above Fort Gibson, and the rest (Sumner's, Boone's, and Browne's companies) under Lieutenant Colonel Kearny followed out earlier orders to establish a post within the Indian country on the right bank of the Mississippi near the mouth of the Des Moines River.[9]

---

[8] Henry P. Beers, "Military Protection of the Santa Fe Trail to 1843," *New Mexico Historical Review*, XII (April, 1937), 126–127.

[9] An article prepared by the War Department, "Fort Des Moines (No. 1), Iowa," *Annals of Iowa*, Third Series, III (April–July, 1898), 351–363, provides a general history of the post and reprints pertinent documents. See also Pelzer,

Leaving Fort Gibson on September 3, 1834, the men of Kearny's command moved north across the state of Missouri. They crossed the Missouri River at Boonville on September 19 and six days later arrived at the mouth of the Des Moines, the site for the new fort. The quarters were already being constructed by civilian laborers under the direction of Lieutenant George H. Crosman, who had engaged forty-five mechanics and laborers at the beginning of the summer and at one time had as many as seventy men employed. Sickness caused a rapid turnover, however, and seven times between July and September Crosman had to send into the interior of Illinois to recruit workmen. Altogether about 170 men were employed for longer or shorter periods.[10] Yet when Kearny arrived, he found the work not as far along as he had expected, and no provision at all had been made to quarter the horses.

The soldiers were set to work to finish the construction without much hope of fancy living. Kearny judged that the result would be buildings "less comfortable and of meaner appearance, than those occupied by any other portion of the Army." The winter was unusually severe, and the commander complained frequently about the uncomfortable quarters and insufficient supplies for his men.

The War Department did not intend Fort Des Moines to be a permanent post. It was to serve as winter quarters for the troops, who could patrol the country to the west until a permanent fort farther within the Indian country could be established. In the spring of 1835 Kearny received orders to reconnoiter the Des Moines River up to the Raccoon Fork in search of a site for a military post and then to march his command up into the Sioux country in what is now southern Minnesota.

With 150 men Kearny marched out of the post on June 7, moving northwest across the "handsome prairies" east of the Des Moines River.[11] On June 23, having missing the Raccoon Fork on his way up, Kearny

---

Marches of the Dragoons, pp. 49–63. A journal of the trip from Fort Gibson to Fort Des Moines appears in Pelzer, *Iowa Journal of History and Politics*, VII, 361–364. For a general biography of Kearny, see Dwight L. Clarke, *Stephen Watts Kearny: Soldier of the West* (Norman, Okla., 1961).

[10] Francis Paul Prucha, *Broadax and Bayonet: The Role of the United States Army in the Development of the Northwest, 1815–1860* (Madison, Wis., 1953), p. 167.

[11] A journal account of the expedition is in Pelzer, *Iowa Journal of History and Politics*, VII, 364–378. A map showing the route of travel is included in Albert M. Lea, *Notes on the Wisconsin Territory: Particularly with Reference to the Iowa District, or Black Hawk Purchase* (Philadelphia, 1836), which is reprinted as *The Book That Gave to Iowa Its Name* (Iowa City, 1935). A memoir by Lea, which describes the expedition, is in "The Expedition of 1835," ed. John Ely Briggs, *Palimpsest*, XVI (April, 1935), 105–136.

turned his march to the northeast, direct toward the Sioux village of Chief Wabasha on the Mississippi, which was reached on July 8. For two weeks the troops remained encamped in the vicinity, the chronicler of the expedition finding Wabasha's band "a dirty thieving race living in the most abominable filthy manner." On July 19 Wabasha visted the camp to treat with the army commander. Two days later the men began their return trip, heading due west to the headwaters of the Des Moines, then down the west bank of the river. They encamped on August 8 at the Raccoon Fork, where Kearny examined the country carefully with a view to establishing a military post.

He was not impressed. The navigation on the Des Moines for bringing in supplies was at all times uncertain. The Sacs and Foxes of the area, furthermore, were peaceful, and if it were considered necessary to build a fort to restrain the more warlike Sioux, the location should be another hundred miles up the river. The Sacs, too, Kearny learned, were opposed to the erection of a post at the Raccoon, for the entrance of the whites would drive off what little game was left. Lieutenant Albert M. Lea, with a dragoon and an Indian guide, descended the Des Moines in a canoe, while the rest of the troops continued their march along the river. They returned to their post on August 19, after a pleasant summer campaign without sickness or Indian hostility.

The subsequent history of Fort Des Moines was equally uneventful. The barracks life was monotonous during the winter, the lack of purposefulness of the post impaired morale, and desertions were numerous. When Inspector General George Croghan visited the post on December 3, 1835, he found the quarters more comfortable than in the previous winter, but he was very critical of the post as a whole and of its site.

The summer of 1836 was spent in another routine expedition, this time to the northeast. Beginning on June 6, a detachment of about 100 men under Captain Sumner marched across Illinois to Chicago, then north along the lake through the beginnings of Milwaukee to Green Bay, returning via the Fox-Wisconsin waterway and down the Mississippi to the fort.

The fort was now set for dissolution. The poor location of the post, both from the standpoint of health and of distance from the Indian country that needed patrolling, made abandonment only a question of time. The white settlers, too, were a nuisance as they encroached on the lands surrounding the garrison, and Lieutenant Colonel Mason, who had succeeded Kearny in command of the post when the latter was promoted to command of the regiment and departed for Fort Leavenworth, continually urged the abandonment of the post. Orders were issued on October 20, 1836, for the post to be broken up and the garrison moved to Fort Leavenworth, but not until the following summer were the arrangements completed. On July 1, 1837, the few remaining troops took up their march for Fort Leavenworth, the headquarters of the regiment.

☆

As Kearny was moving his companies of dragoons to garrison Fort Des Moines, Dodge was exercising the companies of Captains Lupton, Duncan, and Ford on a march of 1,600 miles from Fort Leavenworth to the Rockies.[12] The expedition was the most extensive military campaign yet undertaken in the West and duplicated in part the famous journey of Major Long in 1820. With about 120 men Dodge marched out of Fort Leavenworth on May 29, 1835, accompanied by Major Dougherty, the Indian agent, and Captain Gantt, an Indian trader, who were to act as interpreters and guides. On June 9 the force reached the Platte River and encamped near the Oto village, where they were greeted by Jutan, the principal chief. On the 11th Dodge met with the chiefs and warriors of the tribe. He spoke of the President's desire for peace and deplored the sale of whiskey to the Otos. After a brief reply by Jutan, presents were distributed to the Indians.

Dodge waited a week at the Oto village, for he wished to speak too with the Omaha Indians, and on the 17th about fifty of the headmen of that tribe appeared. Dodge talked to them as he had to the Otos, and Big Elk, the principal chief, replied with words of friendship. The scene was repeated again and again as the dragoons moved toward the Rockies.

[12] The expedition of Dodge to the Rocky Mountains in the summer of 1835 is treated in Pelzer, *Marches of the Dragoons*, pp. 64–75, and in his *Henry Dodge*, pp. 113–127. The official journal, kept by Lieutenant Gaines P. Kingsbury, together with a brief report by Dodge, appears in *House Document* No. 181, 24 Congress, 1 session, serial 289, and in *American State Papers: Military Affairs*, VI, 130–146. A map showing the route of the expedition accompanies the journal. A journal of the march kept by Captain Lemuel Ford is printed as "Captain Ford's Journal of an Expedition to the Rocky Mountains," ed. Louis Pelzer, *Mississippi Valley Historical Review*, XII (March, 1926), 550–579. A narrative expanded from this journal appeared in the *Army and Navy Chronicle*, 1836, and is reprinted as "A Summer Upon the Prairie," in Archer Butler Hulbert, ed., *The Call of the Columbia: Iron Men and Saints Take the Oregon Trail* (Denver, 1934), pp. 227–305. Sergeant Hugh Evans's journal of the expedition (up to August 19) is in "Hugh Evans' Journal of Colonel Henry Dodge's Expedition to the Rocky Mountains in 1835," ed. Fred S. Perrine, *Mississippi Valley Historical Review*, XIV (September, 1927), 192–214.

The Grand Pawnee village was the next stop. Here Dodge spoke with Chief Angry Man and then sent out runners to bring in chiefs from the other Pàwnee villages, whom he offered to help make peace with their old enemies, the Arapahos and Cheyennes. "They are already impressed with a high opinion of the United States," wrote Lieutenant Kingsbury, the journalist of the expedition, "and it will not be difficult for the Government in a short time, to exert a controlling influence over them."[13]

The column continued up the Platte River and on June 29 passed the head of Grand Island. On July 5 the warriors and chiefs of the Arikaras, who had been rounded up by Captain Gantt, heard the words of the "great father," warning them of the evils of intertribal wars and threatening the power of the American army. The council dispersed after the usual exchange of presents. Dodge continued his march west along the South Platte until within sight of the Rockies, then turned south toward the Arkansas River, which he reached on July 30. The dragoons followed the Arkansas down to Bent's Fort, where another council was held, this time with Arapahos, Gros Ventres, and a few Blackfeet who had been collected by Gantt and with the Cheyennes whose villages were nearby. As the troops continued down the river new groups of Indians were encountered—Cheyennes, Pawnees, and Arikaras—and Dodge endeavored to induce them to become friends among themselves. On August 23 the detachment hit the Santa Fe Trail and returned quickly to Fort Leavenworth along its well-worn path. By September 16 the men were at the fort.

By all counts it had been a successful enterprise. "Since leaving the fort," Kingsbury concluded his journal, "the command had marched upwards of 1,600 miles, over an interesting country; had visited all the Indians between the Arkansas and Platte, as far west as the mountains, had made peace between several tribes, and established friendly relations with them all, and returned to Fort Leavenworth in a perfect state of health, with the loss of but one man. Our provisions lasted until the day of our arrival; and our horses, most of them returned in good order. The expedition had exceeded in interest and success the most sanguine anticipations."[14]

The impression made on the Indians of the "*justice, magnanimity, humanity*, and *power* of our Government and country" was hailed by General Gaines, who recommended that special rewards be given Dodge,

---

[13] *House Document* No. 181, 24 Congress, 1 session, serial 289, p. 9.
[14] *Ibid.*, pp. 32–33.

his officers, and his men for the extraordinary and unprecedented results of the expedition.[15] The arguments in favor of mounted troops were proving their worth.

☆

The dragoons at Fort Leavenworth were at the edge of the Indian country, where white settlement began to exert pressure. They served, too, as guardians of the Missouri River, and from year to year they went out on patrols among the nearby Indian tribes, holding councils with the chiefs, exhorting the warriors to good behavior, and in general keeping an eye open for threats of trouble. It was deliberate policy of the War Department to let the mounted soldiers be seen. Their very presence would serve to keep the Indians in order, and expeditions into the Indian country would relieve the soldiers of the monotony of routine garrison duties.

In July, 1839, a company of dragoons traveled from Fort Leavenworth to Bellevue, on the Missouri a few miles below present-day Omaha, to return to their tribe some Omaha Indians recovered from the Sacs.[16] On September 5 Colonel Kearny with 200 men under Captains Boone and Allen set out for the country of the Otos between Bellevue and the Platte, whence rumors came of unfriendly dispositions and an arrogant attitude toward the agent at Council Bluffs. In a council on the 16th with the chiefs of the tribe, Kearny demanded that the wrongdoers be delivered up for punishment. Three braves were surrendered, but the agent promised to guarantee their future good behavior and they were released. The Indians were impressed by the firm attitude of the army commander.[17] The next day the command crossed the Missouri for a brief meeting with a group of Potawatomi chiefs and then returned to Fort Leavenworth on September 25. In 1840 similar brief expeditions occurred, although the year was generally quiet on the western frontier.

☆

In the summer of 1843 Captain Boone with a detachment of dragoons made a reconnaissance of the western prairies between the Arkansas and

[15] Gaines to R. Jones, November 12, 1835, *ibid.*, pp. 36–37.
[16] Pelzer, *Marches of the Dragoons*, p. 82.
[17] *Ibid.*, pp. 82–84.

Canadian rivers.[18] Leaving Fort Gibson on May 14 with two lieutenants
and sixty men, Boone proceeded along the north side of the Arkansas
River for about seventy-five miles, where he was joined on May 21 by
Lieutenant A. S. Johnston and Company D. The next day he crossed
the Arkansas and continued up the river until he struck the Santa Fe
Trail on June 8, which he followed westward. On June 10 he crossed
the Arkansas again to the south side and on the 13th came up with
Captain Philip St. George Cooke, who had come out from Fort Leavenworth with Companies A, F, and H to protect the traders on the trail.
For ten days Boone remained encamped, then move southwest to inspect
the salt plains. He headed next for the Canadian River and traveled
down between that stream and the Washita until July 14, when Lieutenant Johnston's detachment left Boone's column for Fort Washita, while
the main body again crossed the Canadian and returned to Fort Gibson,
which it reached on July 31.

A few Osages had been encountered along the way, but nothing
notable occurred. The results of the expedition lay largely in the increased knowledge it brought of this segment of the West. Boone in
both his report and his journal described the resources of the country
through which he passed and his account of the salt region on the red
fork of the Arkansas was noted as especially significant by General
Zachary Taylor, to whom Boone submitted his report.

☆

Detachments of the dragoons under Captain Cooke made two expeditions in the summer of 1843 to protect the traders on the Santa Fe Trail.
The first resulted in an international incident, as Cooke tangled with the
Texas freebooter, Jacob Snively; the second was a routine march, hardly
noted in the annals of the regiment, so accustomed had it become to
such duties.[19]

As the independent Republic of Texas and her mother state, Mexico,

[18] *Ibid.*, pp. 97–102. Boone's report and his journal of the march are printed
in the Appendix to Pelzer's book, pp. 181–237. These documents are reprinted
in "Captain Nathan Boone's Journal," ed. W. Julian Fessler, *Chronicles of Oklahoma*, VII (March, 1929), 58–105, with a map of the route and extensive
footnotes.

[19] Young, *The West of Philip St. George Cooke*, pp. 109–135. For Cooke's
journal of the march, see "A Journal of the Santa Fe Trail," ed. William E.
Connelley, *Mississippi Valley Historical Review*, XII (June, 1925), 72–98,
(September, 1925), 227–255.

continued in no more than a fitful peace, clashes between Texans and Mexicans threatened to involve the United States, for the boundaries in the West were not clearly marked out. The dragoons, as policemen of the plains, eventually became involved. The *cause célèbre* centered on one Jacob Snively, who conceived the daring plan of preying upon the rich caravans of the Santa Fe trade, many of which were owned by Mexican merchants. A blow at them would at once enrich the adventures and further the Texan cause against Mexico. Snively received from the Texas government a commission that authorized him to organize a private company of soldiers not to exceed 300 men "for the purpose of intercepting and capturing the property of the Mexican traders who may pass through the territory of the republic to and from Santa Fe." He could operate anywhere in Texas north of the line of settlements. Half the booty was to go to the state, the other half to be divided among the members of the company.[20]

The news of the enterprise leaked out, and both the Santa Fe traders and the Mexican Minister in Washington requested an army escort for the caravans. Colonel Kearny ordered three companies from Fort Leavenworth and one company from Fort Scott to protect the traders from attack, and Captain Cooke was placed in command of the expedition. Cooke reached Council Grove on June 3, and on the next day was joined by the company from Fort Scott. The escort of the traders began at this point, but there were no difficulties as they moved toward the Arkansas River.

At Walnut Creek Cooke met Captain Boone's company, out on its patrol from Fort Gibson. He also got word of Texas scouts in the area. On June 25 the caravan began to cross Walnut Creek and move forward on its way, escorted by Cooke's dragoons. On June 30 the Texas scouts were discovered, and soon the camp of the Texans was sighted on the south side of the Arkansas.

Cooke halted, called a council of his officers, and under flags of truce conferred with Snively. Although there was considerable question about the matter, since the meeting was very close to the 100th meridian, which marked the international border, Cooke announced to Snively that the Texas group was on United States soil and demanded to see Snively's commission. Cooke insisted that the Texans must be disarmed, and despite their cry that disarmament was a death sentence on the Indian-infested plains, carried out his decision. Some of the

[20] The commission is printed in Cooke's journal, *ibid.*, pp. 228–229.

Texans were escorted eastward to the edge of the buffalo range, given a few rifles, and dismissed. The rest, with Snively, elected to return to Texas. They were ordered to get out of the United States by sundown.[21]

The caravan continued unmolested on its way, accompanied by Cooke's troops as far as the crossing of the Arkansas, at which point the traders left United States soil. When the wagons were out of sight, Cooke began to retrace his steps. He reached Council Grove on July 15 and reentered Fort Leavenworth on the 21st, having encountered two more small caravans enroute to Santa Fe.

Cooke's affair with Snively and the Texans soon became big news. The Texas government termed Cooke's action an "enormous outrage" of Texan soil, and Cooke was accused of savage cruelty toward the Snively company. Snively's own report of the affair voiced indignation at Cooke's high-handed action. Secretary of State A. P. Upshur politely refused satisfaction to the Texans, noting that Snively had had no legitimate business on United States soil. Texas would be paid for the weapons confiscated and a court of inquiry would be called to investigate Cooke's actions.[22] The court, which met on April 24, 1844, with Colonel Kearny presiding, completely vindicated Cooke.

General Gaines's support of the dragoon captain had been emphatic. In a letter to General Zachary Taylor he asserted: "We must *destroy, arrest,* or *disarm* all such lawless combinations whenever found within or near our *unmarked boundary.*" He approved specifically "the conduct of that excellent officer, Capt. Cooke."[23]

Actions speak louder than words, and when an escort was sent back to the Santa Fe Trail late in the summer of 1843, Cooke was again placed in command.[24] He left Fort Leavenworth on August 24, joined a company from Fort Scott at Council Grove, and began his escort of

[21] A valuable account of the Snively affair, which is very favorable to the Snively party, is H. Bailey Carroll, "Steward A. Miller and the Snively Expedition of 1843," *Southwestern Historical Quarterly,* LIV (January, 1951), 261–286. It is based largely on a diary kept by one of Snively's men.

[22] "Texas Documents Referring to the Red River Case and the Disarming of Snively's Command," *Senate Document* No. 1, 28 Congress, 2 session, serial 449, pp. 91–112.

[23] Gaines to Taylor, July 27, 1843, printed in *Niles' National Register,* LXIV (August 19, 1843), 386.

[24] Cooke's report of this second march is in *Mississippi Valley Historical Review,* XII, 249–255. Cooke also reports on the expedition in his *Scenes and Adventures in the Army: or, Romance of Military Life* (Philadelphia, 1859), pp. 236–282. Accounts of the march are in Pelzer, *Marches of the Dragoons,* pp. 102–107, and Otis E Young, "Dragoons on the Santa Fe Trail in the Autumn of 1843," *Chronicles of Oklahoma,* XXXII (Spring, 1954), 42–51.

the numerous wagons, nearly all owned by Mexicans. He accompanied them as far as the crossing of the Arkansas and was debating whether to accompany them farther or turn back, when he was informed that a Mexican escort had arrived from Santa Fe to protect the traders on the last leg of the journey. His problem thus resolved, Cooke turned back toward Fort Leavenworth on October 12 and was safe in quarters on October 25.

☆

The intertribal wars among the plains Indians were an incessant annoyance to the United States government, for they endangered everyone within range, and the increasing movement of whites across the plains to the Pacific slope emphasized the necessity of overawing the tribes into peace among themselves and with the whites. To that end a detachment of dragoons under Major Wharton was sent out in the late summer of 1844 to the Pawnee villages on the Platte.[25] The multiple purposes of the expedition were set forth by the commander: "to impress upon such Indian tribes as we may meet the importance of their friendly treatment of all white persons in their country, to convince them of the power of the U. S. Government to punish them for aggressions on such persons, to urge upon them the policy of peace among themselves & their neighbors, and to endeavour to effect a reconciliation between the Pawnees and the Sioux, between whom a most ferocious war has been carried on for many years."[26]

The detachment, with the men well equipped and the horses in fine condition, left Fort Leavenworth on August 12. Fifteen supply wagons

[25] Major Clifton Wharton's expedition to the Pawnees in the summer of 1844 is described briefly in Young, *The West of Philip St. George Cooke*, pp. 137–151. The chief source for this march is the journal kept by Major Wharton, printed in "The Expedition of Major Clifton Wharton in 1844," *Collections of the Kansas State Historical Society*, XVI (1925), 272–305. A map showing the route is included. Of this journal Young asserts: "Although this report is signed by Clifton Wharton, the style is so palpably that of Philip St. G. Cooke that it is likely Wharton copied his report almost verbatim from Cooke's diary." *Cooke*, p. 139n. A parallel source is the narrative written by Lieutenant James Henry Carleton, which appeared anonymously in *The Spirit of the Times* (New York), from November 9, 1844, to April 12, 1845. This has been reprinted in *The Prairie Logbooks: Dragoon Campaigns to the Pawnee Villages in 1844, and to the Rocky Mountains in 1845*, ed. Louis Pelzer (Chicago, 1943), pp. 3–152.

[26] Wharton journal, *Collections of the Kansas State Historical Society*, XVI, 273.

were in the train to see that the needs of the squadrons were well attended to, and two 12-pound howitzers added to the formidable appearance of the command. The painter of the West, Charles Deas, was also in the company.

Seeking a shortcut toward the Pawnee villages, Wharton turned off the Council Bluffs trail which the troops had been following in a generally northwest direction between the Missouri and Kansas rivers. The shortcut proved difficult, and for two weeks the men struggled forward, until on August 27 they broke into the open valley of the Platte somewhat below the Pawnee villages they sought. Wharton convened a council with the Grand Pawnees on August 30. The commander pointed out the strength of the dragoons and how quickly they had covered the distance from their headquarters. He spoke of the President's desire for peace with the Indians and of the evils of wars between the tribes, and he urged the end of horse stealing, a major cause of the conflicts. "A great many of your Great Father's white children are now going to the big water which lies beyond the Stony mountains," he said. "He expects that when you meet such of his children and others you will treat them kindly and afford them aid, if they require it, and that you will act in like manner to his children who may pass down the river which now flows at our feet." Wharton reminded the Pawnees of their treaty of 1833, in which they had agreed to move north of the Platte, and he strongly urged them to carry out that agreement. The reply of Cunning Chief was not very encouraging, and the major resorted to a display of military prowess, as he put the dragoons through their drills and fired a few shells from the howitzers. With the Indians thus awed, the dragoons crossed the Platte and headed for another village on the Loup Fork of the Platte, where a second council was held.

The next morning Wharton departed eastward, marching his command toward Bellevue on the Missouri. At the Missouri he held a conference on September 7 with the Otos, whom he scolded for their raids upon nearby whites and upon the Omahas. "Such conduct will not be suffered," he warned, "and I tell you, that if thus your hand be raised against every man every man's hand will be raised against you. You will be then like the lone tree in a far spreading prairie, upon which every storm spends its fury until some blast more powerful than the rest prostrates it upon the earth there to lie and rot." He remonstrated with the chiefs to restrain the young men from wrongdoing, and he shot off some rockets to impress the camp.

Wharton ferried his troops across the Missouri at this point, and conferences were held with the Potawatomis. On September 18 the command recrossed the Missouri, held councils with small bands of Sacs and Iowas, and then headed for home, which they reached on the 21st. The expedition by no means brought permanent peace to the plains, but there is no doubt that the Indians Wharton visited were impressed by his military displays, which helped to keep the tribes quiet during the critical years when the lines of communication across the plains were developed.

☆

Much of the activity of the dragoons in the early 1840's centered in Iowa Territory, where the Indians were pushed westward by advancing settlers with startling rapidity. At short intervals, beginning with the Black Hawk Purchase of 1832, sizable sections of Iowa were acquired from the Indians. Some areas were assigned for a time to tribes removed from east of the Mississippi, others were opened immediately to white settlement, still others were kept for the temporary use of the resident tribes until they could arrange to depart. In all of this the presence of a military force was absolutely essential to prevent, or at least reduce, conflicts between the several Indian tribes and to restrain the eager white settlers who, unmindful of Indian rights, rushed into the rich prairies before they were legally entitled to do so. Dragoon patrols operated out of new military posts established in Iowa Territory. It was humdrum work without any of the glory of military combat, but it was important in the orderly development of Iowa.[27]

The first of the new forts was Fort Atkinson, established on the Turkey River west of Prairie du Chien on May 31, 1840, by a detachment of the Fifth Infantry from Fort Crawford. The post was built to watch over the Neutral Ground, a strip of territory forty miles wide running between the Mississippi and Des Moines rivers, which had been ceded by the Sacs and Foxes and the Sioux tribes in 1830 as a sort of buffer between the two groups of Indians. In 1833 the strip was assigned to the Winnebagos, who had been persuaded to cede their lands east of the Mississippi and move across that river. A new treaty in 1837

[27] Pelzer, *Marches of the Dragoons*, pp. 88–96; Jacob Van der Zee, "Forts in the Iowa Country," *Iowa Journal of History and Politics*, XII (April, 1914), 163–204.

with the tribe confirmed the arrangement, but it was not until the summer of 1840 that the last band of Winnebagos took up their new home. The soldiers of Fort Atkinson were to protect the miserable remnants of this tribe from their warlike neighbors and to overcome, if possible, their disturbing habit of wandering back to their old haunts. To do this effectively mounted troops were necessary, and on June 24, 1841, a company of dragoons arrived at the post, which continued to be garrisoned by a company of dragoons and one of infantry.[28]

A second fort was a new post on the Des Moines River, to protect the Sacs and Foxes, whose agent called for military protection for his charges:

I know of no point upon our Indian frontier where the permanent presence of a military force is more essentially requisite than at this. Within a period of less than two years, it has been necessary three times to call for a detachment, whose march on each occasion has been attended with much expense and inconvenience; while requisition for another to attend the approaching payment has been sent. No obstructions, no means of prevention, here exist to the continual passage to and fro in the Indian country of the most lawless and desperate characters, who can at any time commit outrages against order, morality, and the laws, with perfect impunity; and many of whom, feeling themselves aggrieved by their recent expulsions from the Indian country, are the more ready to avenge themselves by acts of violence.[29]

To meet this serious situation and in response to the pleas of the governor of Iowa Territory, a force of dragoons set up camp near the Sac and Fox agency on October 12, 1842, making use of some cabins of the American Fur Company and temporary huts and stables. The post, called Fort Sanford, was occupied only until May, 1843, when the troops moved up the Des Moines to the mouth of the Raccoon Fork, to build a new Fort Des Moines.[30] They were joined by a company of in-

---

[28] "Fort Atkinson, Iowa," *Annals of Iowa*, Third Series, IV (July, 1900), 448–453; Bruce E. Mahan, "Old Fort Atkinson," *Palimpsest*, II (November, 1921), 333–350; Roger L. Nichols, "The Founding of Fort Atkinson," *Annals of Iowa*, Third Series, XXXVII (Spring, 1965), 589–597.

[29] John Beach to John Chambers, September 1, 1842, *Senate Document* No. 1, 27 Congress, 3 session, serial 413, p. 426.

[30] "Fort Sanford, Iowa," *Annals of Iowa*, Third Series, IV (January, 1900), 289–293.

fantry from Fort Crawford, and Fort Des Moines for all its temporary nature became a considerable establishment.[31]

These Iowa forts were established to protect not the white settlers but the Indians. The American pioneers and white speculators, who were eager to overflow into the Indian lands, and the unscrupulous whiskey dealers who flooded the Indian country with their vile concoctions, were restrained as well as could be by the troops. The post commanders at Fort Atkinson and Fort Des Moines as well as at Fort Crawford were continually receiving from the Indian agents or the governor of Iowa Territory requisitions for troops to apprehend and remove the intruders. The War Department instructed the officers to follow these requests to the letter, and they were rebuked if they failed to do so. The mounted patrols were the only effective force that prevented the immigrants who swarmed into the Des Moines valley from seizing prematurely the lands that the Indians still occupied.[32]

The limitation of the whiskey trade was an even more frustrating chore, but the vigilance of the dragoon commanders at the Iowa posts seems to have had some success. Captain Sumner at Fort Atkinson was praised especially by the Indian agents for his effective checking of the smuggling of whiskey into the Indian country, even though he was unable to stop the Indians from going to the white settlements to procure the liquor.[33]

Still another Iowa post came into being in the 1840's. The Potawatomis, who had been removed with associated bands of Chippewas and Ottawas from their lands near Lake Michigan in 1833 and settled in western Iowa, were in constant danger from the Sioux, and the dragoons from Fort Leavenworth kept an eye upon their villages. Detachments of troops sent to Council Bluffs from time to time restrained the Sioux, but in the spring of 1842, when Sioux threats of war seemed dangerous, a post was established among the Potawatomis for their protection. Captain J. H. K. Burgwin, with a company from Fort Leavenworth, built a post near present-day Council Bluffs, Iowa, a site

[31] "Fort Des Moines, No. 2," *Annals of Iowa*, Third Series, IV (October, 1899), 161–178.

[32] By the treaty of October 11, 1842, the Sacs and Foxes ceded all their remaining lands in Iowa. They were allowed to remain on the western section for three years. Charles J. Kappler, ed., *Indian Affairs: Laws and Treaties* (2 vols., Washington, 1904), II, *Treaties*, pp. 546–548.

[33] J. E. Fletcher to John Chambers, September 20, 1845, *Senate Document No. 1*, 29 Congress, 1 session, serial 470, pp. 487–488.

he reached on May 31, 1842. The post was first called Camp Fenwick, but it was renamed Fort Croghan in November. Spring floods forced the abandonment of the fort buildings, but troops stayed in the vicinity until the fall of 1843, when they returned to Fort Leavenworth.[34]

☆

In the summer of 1844, Captain Allen, commander of the dragoon company at Fort Des Moines, was ordered to proceed "up the Des Moines river, to the sources of the Blue Earth river of the St. Peter's [Minnesota]; thence to the waters of the Missouri; and thence returning through the country of the Pottowatomies."[35] The march was ordered primarily as part of what General Scott that year described as "standing policy, *to prevent Indian hostilities by the exhibition of military force on and beyond our frontiers*."[36] But Captain Allen was concerned as well to bring back a detailed account of the geographical features and natural resources of the country.

Leaving Fort Des Moines on August 11, 1844, with a company of fifty dragoons, Captain Allen moved up the Des Moines River on the west side for about one hundred miles, then crossed the river a few miles above its forks and proceeded up between the forks to the source of the west fork. Leaving Lieutenant Patrick Noble and twenty-five men encamped in that vicinity, Allen and the other half of the command made a side trip north to the Minnesota River, returning to Noble's camp in six days. The reunited command marched west to the Big Sioux River and down that river to its juncture with the Missouri, then headed directly back to Fort Des Moines, where they arrived on October 3, after a journey of about 740 miles.

Allen saw few Indians on his march—only two roving bands of Sioux along the Big Sioux River—but he judged the effects of the expedition

---

[34] Henry P. Beers, *The Western Military Frontier, 1815–1846* (Philadelphia, 1935), p. 140; "Fort Croghan," *Annals of Iowa*, Third Series, III (April–July, 1898), 471.

[35] Pelzer, *Marches of the Dragoons*, pp. 108–114. Allen's official report and journal appear in "Captain James Allen's Dragoon Expedition from Fort Des Moines, Territory of Iowa, in 1844," ed. Jacob Van der Zee, *Iowa Journal of History and Politics*, XI (January, 1913), 68–108, and in *House Executive Document* No. 168, 29 Congress, 1 session, serial 485. See also Robert Rutland, ed., "A Journal of the First Dragoons in the Iowa Territory, 1844," *Iowa Journal of History*, LI (January, 1953), 57–78. Rutland furnishes a map of the route, p. 64.

[36] *Senate Document* No. 1, 28 Congress, 2 session, serial 449, p. 130.

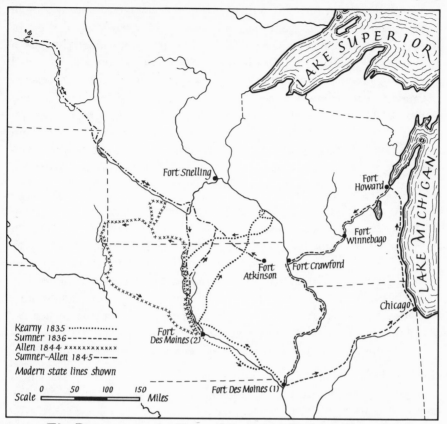

The Dragoons in the Upper Mississippi Valley, 1835–1845

to be significant nevertheless, for he suspected that the Indians were deliberately keeping out of his way. The expedition, he thought, "must have produced a great moral effect upon these wild Indians, as showing them conclusively that we can easily throw cavalry enough into the heart of their country to chastise them for any wrong they may do to our people and government."[37] His judgment on the value of the country through which he passed was less optimistic. "The whole country is good for nothing," he wrote about the lake country he found in the upper reaches of the Des Moines River, and most of the other areas he passed were criticized for lack of fertile soil or lack of timber. He was a poor prophet.

[37] Allen's report, *Iowa Journal of History and Politics*, XI, 81.

The following summer a similar expedition engaged the dragoons in Iowa.[38] They were to continue the process of overawing the often-hostile Sioux, but the campaign in this summer had an added dimension furnished by the British half-breeds of the Canadian border. The Red River half-breeds, or Metis, continued to cross the border established between Great Britain and the United States in 1818 to carry on their buffalo hunts in the Pembina country. The explorer-cartographer Joseph N. Nicollet, who had visited the area in 1839, met the Metis, whom he had heard were considered "the best hunters, the most expert horse-men, and the bravest warriors of the prairies." In his official report Ni-collet described them and their activities:

> They are called Metis, or half breeds, being descendants of Cana-dians, English, and Scotch, crossed with Chippeways, Kristinaux, Assiniboins, Sioux, &c., &c. . . . It is their usage to come twice a year upon the territory of the United States where the buffalo abounds: each family has its cart or wagon drawn by oxen; each hunter has his horse, which is remarkably fleet. They are accompanied by mis-sionaries, who regulate both their temporal and spiritual concerns. Their first campaign is made at the setting in of summer; their sec-ond in the fall of the year; and they remain about two months.[39]

Surplus hides were sold to the Hudson's Bay Company. The meat was made into pemmican and a year's supply was laid in during the summer hunts.[40]

These activities had gone on undisturbed for many years, but the numbers of Metis increased, and the Sioux began to resent this invasion of their hunting lands. The Indian agent at St. Peter's, Amos J. Bruce, remonstrated with the government to take some action in the matter lest

---

[38] Pelzer, *Marches of the Dragoons*, pp. 115–119. Captain Sumner's official report is in *Senate Document* No. 1, 29 Congress, 1 session, serial 470, pp. 217–220. It has been reprinted in "Captain Edwin V. Sumner's Dragoon Expedition in the Territory of Iowa in the Summer of 1845," ed. Jacob Van der Zee, *Iowa Journal of History and Politics*, XI (April, 1913), 258–267. A recently discovered anonymous journal of the march, which adds considerable information, appears in Robert Rutland, ed., "The Dragoons in the Iowa Territory, 1845," *Iowa Journal of History*, LI (April, 1953), 156–182. See also Nancy L. Woolworth, "Captain Edwin V. Sumner's Expedition to Devil's Lake in the Summer of 1845," *North Dakota History*, XXVIII (April–July, 1961), 79–98.

[39] Joseph N. Nicollet, *Report Intended to Illustrate a Map of the Hydro-graphical Basin of the Upper Mississippi River (House Document* No. 52, 28 Congress, 2 session, Washington, 1843), p. 49.

[40] A detailed account of the buffalo hunt of 1840 is in Alexander Ross, *The Red River Settlement: Its Rise, Progress, and Present State* (London, 1856; facsimile ed., Minneapolis, 1957), pp. 241–274.

armed conflict break out between the half-breeds and the Sioux. Captain Sumner's brief excursion to the Minnesota River valley in the summer of 1844 was partly in response to the agent's reports, but Bruce continued his appeals. He described the Metis as coming to hunt "in large bands, well armed, and in too much force to fear the Indians; and as to the threatened interference of our Government, they laugh at the idea." He recommended specifically that the government order some of the dragoons to that frontier "to keep those foreigners from intruding upon our territory."[41]

Such an expedition was set on foot on June 3, 1845, as a company of dragoons under Captain Sumner left Fort Atkinson to penetrate the Sioux country. Ten days later Captain Allen with another company from Fort Des Moines joined Sumner's troops, and the combined forces proceeded to Traverse des Sioux, where they arrived on June 22. Marching from Traverse des Sioux on the 25th, they arrived on July 1 at Lac qui Parle, a widening of the Minnesota River. Here Sumner held council with the Wahpeton Sioux, giving them presents and trying to impress them that any crimes against the whites would be severely punished.

Sumner sensed that he was not making much impression upon the Indians:

I do not think the disposition of the upper Sioux toward us is very friendly. They receive no annuities, and are not connected with us in any way, and they have always had a strong partiality for the British; I believe, principally, because that government has been more liberal in their presents to them. One thing I observed particularly—they seemed unwilling that we should interfere with the "half-breeds" from the British settlements; and I am convinced that the Indians would prefer that that people should continue to hunt upon their lands, than that our government should send troops through the country to keep them out. I asked them who had made the complaints about the inroads of the half-breeds, and they all professed their ignorance on the subject, disclaiming it entirely for themselves.[42]

At Big Stone Lake on July 6 the dragoon captain met with a large band of Sisseton Sioux and gave them what presents he had left, but

[41] Report of Amos J. Bruce, September 15, 1842, *Senate Document* No. 1, 27 Congress, 3 session, serial 413, p. 430; Report of Bruce, September 1, 1844, *Senate Document* No. 1, 28 Congress, 2 session, serial 449, pp. 422–423.

[42] Sumner report, *Iowa Journal of History and Politics*, XI, 261.

with some reluctance, for he thought that "the small presents we make to the Indians do more harm than good, for they serve as a contrast to the very liberal presents they formerly received from the English agents." Among the Sissetons Sumner seized three Indian criminals wanted for the murder of a party of whites. When the Indians boldly walked into his presence, Sumner had them arrested and carried them with him until he could send them down river to Dubuque for civil trial.

Devils Lake was reached on July 18. Here Sumner came upon the half-breeds. In a council with about 180 men, including some Indians who were in the party, Sumner explained the position of the United States. He found them "a shrewd and sensible people" and "by no means as formidable as they have been represented to be." Sumner was convinced that, undisciplined as they were, without capable leaders, and hampered by their families, they posed no military threat to the United States. They had no thought of resisting American authority and crossed the boundary to the old hunting grounds of their Indian forebears because they could not find enough subsistence on the Canadian side. The Metis asked about the possibility of having a few years' grace to change their living habits, which Sumner could not promise. He admitted in his report, however, that it would be impossible to prevent their incursions, for as soon as the troops left, parties who had been ordered out would return. He was somewhat encouraged by reports that the half-breeds might become United States citizens and thus solve the problem. He estimated that there were 600 men in the whole band of half-breeds and that the number was rapidly increasing.[43]

More Sioux, decidedly unfriendly in appearance but attempting no acts of hostility, were encountered on the return to Traverse des Sioux. Here on August 11 Sumner broke up the party, sending Allen back to Fort Des Moines while he himself returned with his company to Fort Atkinson.

☆

The expansionist dreams of the mid-1840's could never be fulfilled without increasing protection for those who ventured west, and in the

---

[43] The Metis continued their annual buffalo hunts in the United States for a number of years, until threatened by American officials and facing the enmity of the Indians on the American side, they gradually gave up their hunts south of Pembina.

spring of 1845 dragoons under Colonel Kearny were sent out along the Oregon Trail.[44] The protection of the emigrants was the governing purpose of the expedition, but Lieutenant W. B. Franklin of the Corps of Topographical Engineers was attached to the troops to map the territory through which they traveled, and Kearny was directed to return by way of the Santa Fe Trail, to protect the rich caravans that were expected to move out of Santa Fe that year.

The five companies, numbering some 250 men, which Kearny prepared for the task were the best in the regiment, accustomed for two years to marching together in the West, and they were officered by men who then and later proved themselves able leaders. They left Fort Leavenworth on May 18 for the Blue River, where they picked up the Oregon Trail. It was a busy year on the trail as the tempo of emigration continued after the great migrations of 1843 and 1844. Kearny reported that his command overtook 850 men, 475 women, 1,000 children, 7,000 cattle, 400 horses and mules, and 460 wagons—so many trains that the herds and teams cropped the grass short and consumed the forage that Kearny needed for his own command. He was forced to speed ahead of the emigrants in order to obtain adequate grazing for his horses. Encounters with the emigrant trains were almost daily affairs as the dragoons followed the trail to the Platte and then up that river toward Fort Laramie, which they reached on June 14.

Kearny encamped two and one-half miles up the Laramie River above the post and sent out runners to call in the Indians for a council, so that he might convince the Sioux not to disturb the emigrant trains. On the 16th Kearny addressed the assembled chiefs with the standard message: The Great Father was determined to keep the Oregon Trail open, peacefully if possible, if not, by force of arms. Presents were distributed, and the howitzers fired to impress the red men. Again the uniformed troops on horseback had made their mark, and one of the lieutenants reported:

[44] A good description of the expedition of Kearny to South Pass in 1845 is in Young, *The West of Philip St. George Cooke*, pp. 153–171. The official report of Kearny, dated September 15, 1845, abstracts of the journals kept by Lieutenant Turner and Lieutenant Franklin, as well as Franklin's map of the itinerary, appear with the Secretary of War's report for 1845, *House Executive Document* No. 2, 29 Congress, 1 session, serial 480, pp. 210–217. More detailed narratives are in Cooke, *Scenes and Adventures in the Army*, pp. 282–432, and Carleton, *The Prairie Logbooks*, pp. 155–280. A detailed account of the expedition based largely on the manuscript journal of Lieutenant Turner is Hamilton Gardner, "Captain Philip St. George Cooke and the March of the 1st Dragoons to the Rocky Mountains in 1845," *Colorado Magazine*, XXX (October, 1953), 246–269.

The traders at the Forts, who could converse perfectly well with the Indians, informed us, that previous to our having come, the Dahcotahs [Sioux] were of the opinion the emigrants were all the white people there were. But that, when they saw the Dragoons, they were so terrified they hardly knew which way to turn. They told the traders when they first discovered us—and while we were yet a long way off upon the prairies—that our numbers were so great we blackened the land.

Such were their fears, no doubt they magnified our force at least tenfold. And in their account of our coming, transmitted from one to the other of the bands that did not see us—their alarm and wonder will, in all probability, exaggerate our power still more and more, as the intelligence spreads.[45]

Captain William Eustis was left at the Fort Laramie camp with one company to watch the Sioux, while the rest of the command continued the journey up the North Platte. The march became more difficult, but on June 30 the men discovered a branch of the Green River—they had crossed the continental divide without realizing it, for South Pass proved to be an open plain, not a sharp cut through the mountains.

Kearny had reached his objective and immediately turned around for the return journey toward Fort Laramie. Joined again by Eustis and his company, he directed his march south from the trading post; guiding by Long's Peak and Pike's Peak, he skirted the mountain wall and headed for Bent's Fort and the supplies he expected to find there for him. The dragoons were welcomed by Bent and St. Vrain on July 29, fifteen days out of Fort Laramie. There was no delay here, and Kearny moved down the Arkansas to the Santa Fe Trail, where the traders he met were experiencing no difficulty with the Indians, and then past the familiar landmarks back to Fort Leavenworth on August 24. They had marched 2,200 miles in ninety-nine days.

This reconnaissance was an experiment to test the value of sending out occasional patrols of mounted troops in order to keep the Indians at peace as an alternative to a chain of posts. Kearny, with a pessimistic view of the West and imbued with military considerations only, opposed the establishment of posts far from sources of supply. Near Fort Laramie, where a site for a military post had been proposed, Kearny sent out Captain Cooke to inspect the location, but he kept to his own convictions:

[45] Carleton, *Prairie Logbooks*, p. 250.

I am of the opinion that the establishment of a post there, at this time, would be very injudicious, and the little advantage to be derived from it not in the least commensurate with the enormous expense which would necessarily be incurred in maintaining it. . . .

In lieu of the establishment of a military post in that upper country, I would suggest that a military expedition, similar to the one of this season, be made every two or three years. They would serve to keep the Indians perfectly quiet, reminding them of (as this one proved) the facility and rapidity with which our dragoons can march through any part of their country, and that there is no place where they can go but the dragoons can follow; and, as we are better mounted than they are, overtake them.[46]

☆

The explorations of the Trans-Mississippi West that the dragoons accomplished in the 1840's, as they marched out into the Indian country to keep the Indians aware of the American presence, were augmented by the scientific explorations of the army officers who belonged to the Corps of Topographical Engineers. The Corps, organized as a separate unit within the army by the army bill of 1838, was composed of officers only, thirty-six in number. It served as a body of scientific explorers for mapping the West, and it performed important civilian tasks as well in marking national boundaries, laying out roads, and improving rivers and harbors.[47] In the period from its founding until the beginning of the Mexican War, members of the Corps directed four expeditions in the West, which complemented the pattern of exploration begun by the troops stationed on the Indian frontier. Three of these were the work of Lieutenant John Charles Frémont, the controversial son-in-law of Senator Benton.[48]

[46] Kearny's report, *House Executive Document* No. 2, 29 Congress, 1 session, serial 490, p. 212.

[47] A detailed history of the explorations carried on by the Corps of Topographical Engineers is William H. Goetzmann, *Army Exploration in the American West, 1803–1863* (New Haven, 1959); a short survey of the corps is Henry P. Beers, "A History of the U. S. Topographical Engineers, 1813–1863," *Military Engineer*, XXXIV (June, 1942), 287–291, (July, 1942), 348–352.

[48] Frémont was a literary man as well as an explorer, and his reports are important writings of his era. They popularized his own exploits and became the guides for many emigrants to the Far West. See Frémont's *Report of the Exploring Expedition to the Rocky Mountains in the Year 1842, and to Oregon and North California in the Years 1843–'44* (Washington, 1845), a reprinting

Frémont had become a member of the Corps at its inception and had served an apprenticeship in 1838–1839 as an assistant to the immigrant French scientist, Joseph N. Nicollet, in his travels up the Minnesota and Missouri rivers. Then in 1842 Frémont mounted an exploratory expedition of his own to the Rocky Mountains. The head of the Topographical Engineers, Colonel John J. Abert, had suggested to the Secretary of War in January, 1842, that the territory between the Missouri and the mountains be examined to determine sites for military posts, and when Nicollet became ill, Frémont was chosen to carry on.[49] With a band of experienced voyageurs recruited at St. Louis and accompanied by the German topographer Charles Preuss and the veteran mountain man Kit Carson, Frémont set out on June 10, 1842, from Pierre Chouteau's trading station near the mouth of the Kansas River. The party followed the regular Oregon Trail to the forks of the Platte. Here Frémont divided his men. One group continued along the trail to Fort Laramie, while Frémont, Preuss, and four others followed the South Platte toward Long's Peak. Frémont wrote of his purpose: "In a military point of view, I was desirous to form some opinion of the country relative to the establishment of posts on a line connecting the settlements with the South Pass of the Rocky Mountains, by way of the Arkansas and the South and Laramie Forks of the Platte."[50] From St. Vrain's Fort, a trading post on the South Platte, Frémont turned his group north toward Fort Laramie, where he rejoined the main body. The united expedition moved up the Platte and the Sweetwater and on August 8 reached South Pass. After a short diversion into the Wind River Mountains, where Frémont climbed what he thought to be the highest peak of the range (called Frémont's Peak), the party headed directly home.

Frémont quickly prepared a report of his expedition, which described the West in much more glowing terms than had Pike or Long.[51] As

---

of his official reports of which there were numerous editions, and his *Memoirs of My Life* (New York, 1887), which gives detailed accounts of his explorations. Allan Nevins has edited Frémont's various reports in *Narratives of Exploration and Adventure* (New York, 1956). A biography is Allan Nevins, *Frémont: Pathmarker of the West* (New York, 1939; new ed., 1955). Goetzmann, *Army Exploration*, gives good brief accounts of the expeditions.

[49] Henry P. Beers, "The Army and the Oregon Trail to 1846," *Pacific Northwest Quarterly*, XXVIII (October, 1937), 355.

[50] Frémont, *Memoirs*, p. 92.

[51] "A Report on an Exploration of the Country Lying Between the Missouri River and the Rocky Mountains, on the Line of the Kansas and Great Platte Rivers," *Senate Document* No. 243, 27 Congress, 3 session, serial 416.

far as military considerations went, Frémont strongly asserted his position: "If it is in contemplation to keep open the communications with
Oregon Territory, a show of military force in this country is absolutely
necessary." He thought in terms of permanently established posts, and
the neighborhood of Fort Laramie he considered the most suitable place
on the Platte. With small posts at St. Vrain's Fort on the South
Platte and at Bent's Fort on the Arkansas, a fort there could hold
the troublesome tribes in check.[52] Such conclusions, of course, were
most pleasing to Benton and other Oregon expansionists. Indeed,
Frémont's next tour originated more as a Bentonian scheme than as
an army operation.

In the spring of 1843 Frémont and a new party set out on a "great
reconnaissance." It was, says William H. Goetzmann, "above everything else a chronicle of heroic adventure. In this quality lay its value
as a means of inspiring western emigration and settlement, as well
as capturing national attention."[53] It was in its conception and in its
report a far cry from the more prosaic expeditions of the dragoons, a
more flamboyant expression of the Manifest Destiny of the age, but
which the regular army garrisons in the West could not help but
reflect. Frémont moved west along the Kansas River toward St. Vrain's
Fort, north to South Pass, then on to the Snake River, the Columbia,
and Fort Vancouver. He then turned south along the eastern edges
of the Sierra Nevadas, crossed west through the mountains into the
great interior valley of California, following it south to the Spanish
Trail, which took him across the desert to the Colorado River. The
party then marched northeast to Utah Lake, through the Colorado
Rockies to the Arkansas, and back home along the Smoky Hill Fork
of the Kansas. Frémont reached St. Louis on August 6, 1844, after
"the most spectacular official reconnaissance of the American West
since Lewis and Clark."[54]

In 1845 Frémont headed west for the third time. His instructions
were to survey the Arkansas and Red rivers and to explore the region
around Bent's Fort. The trading post was reached in late July, but
Frémont did not tarry there. Instead, for motives that are not yet

---

[52] Goetzmann contrasts Frémont's views with those of Kearny, the former
interested in advancing settlement, the latter (professionally military) focusing
on frontier defense alone. *Army Exploration*, p. 115.

[53] *Ibid.*, p. 86. Goetzmann gives a detailed account of the exploration, pp. 87–
101.

[54] *Ibid.*, p. 101. See the extended evaluation of the significance of Frémont's
expedition, pp. 101–108.

clear, he led his party on into California, where his presence caused political and military complications.[55]

More closely allied to the marches of the western army across the plains was the exploration of the Comanche country along the Canadian River undertaken by Lieutenant James W. Abert, the son of the colonel who commanded the Topographical Engineers. While Frémont led his unauthorized expedition into California, Lieutenant Abert was detached to command a party that carried out much of the exploration Frémont had been directed to do. With a party of thirty-three, only two of whom were soldiers, he moved down into New Mexico through Raton Pass, struck the Canadian River and followed it toward Fort Gibson, gathering information about the Comanches and the Kiowas and collecting specimens of flora and fauna.[56]

The dragoons' expeditions and those of the Corps of Topographical Engineers, crisscrossing the Indian country west of the Mississippi, cast a web of American authority over the West that the Indians could not shake off. Less significant, to be sure, than the work of the army in protecting the Trans-Mississippi West in later decades, these operations of the soldiers nevertheless served their more limited purposes well. The Indians met and respected these agents of the United States government, and the knowledge of new country that the officers brought back, as was inevitably the case, made significant openings for the wedges of settlement to enter.

☆

The army in the six decades between the Revolutionary War and the Mexican War marched with the expanding nation to the West. The child of the frontier, whose exigencies called it into being, the army grew as the nation grew (although never quite enough), and it devoted its energies to national development. In the north and south and west, as the agent of a government that sought to exert its authority in the lands over which it claimed jurisdiction, the army upheld American sovereignty. For a nation whose leaders struggled to find a humane solution to the difficult problem of providing for

[55] *Ibid.*, pp. 116–123.

[56] *Ibid.*, pp. 123–127. Abert's report is in "Journal of Lieutenant J. W. Abert, from Bent's Fort to St. Louis, in 1845," *Senate Document* No. 438, 29 Congress, 1 session, serial 477.

the orderly advance of a rapidly growing population over lands tenaciously held by thinly spread tribes, the army served as the weapon to hold back lawless frontiersmen as well as to chastise Indians for savage incursions against white settlements. In searching out the secrets of unknown areas within the vast domain of the young nation, army officers and their detachments skillfully explored the land, until American presence was everywhere experienced and respected. To be sure, not all the visions of national grandeur were fulfilled, not all the laws whose enforcement rested so largely upon the army were properly enforced.

The inadequacies of the army in size and in quality of personnel were regrettable, most profoundly so in the matter of contacts and conflicts between the whites and Indians on the frontier. But Americans of the period were unwilling to give unstinted support to a regular military force. Here was a serious flaw in the American experience, which marred the period of early national development. The need for order on the frontier was clear. The only available means to maintain that order was a regular army of reasonable size, to act for national not local interests. The character of the American republic, unfortunately, would not allow this means to be developed. American democratic ideals themselves thus paradoxically permitted conflicts that every honest American can only lament.

Yet if the mission of the regular army on the frontier is seen primarily as the upholding of American dominion within the territorial limits of the United States—against foreign encroachment and against the Indian nations—the army successfully fulfilled its role. Here the "sword of the Republic," despite its weakness, served the nation honorably and well.

Bibliography of Printed Sources

THE footnotes include brief bibliographical essays as well as specific references to sources of quotations and other data. They contain some references not listed specifically in this bibliography.

Primary Sources

The resources of the National Archives are of great importance for any study of the army. For the period before 1800, when a fire destroyed most of the War Department records, the files are nearly barren, but from that date on the records are very rich. The Records of the Adjutant General's Office (Record Group 94), Records of Army Commands (Record Group 98), Records of the Headquarters of the Army (Record Group 108), Records of the Office of Indian Affairs (Record Group 75), Records of the Inspector General (Record Group 92), Records of the Secretary of War (Record Group 107), and Records of the Surgeon General's Office (Record Group 112) provide letters sent and received, records of recruiting and enlistment, general orders, inspection reports, medical histories of posts, and various records on supply, construction, and transportation. Detailed information on a given installation or operation must often be sought in these records. For the general account presented in this book, however, extensive new research in these materials was not undertaken, but notes taken over a period of twenty years from these records were a basic ingredient in the study. The same is true of other unpublished manuscripts indicated in the notes.

Printed government documents are voluminous and are not listed item by item in the bibliography, although specific references are given fully in the footnotes. Of primary importance are the documents compiled in *American State Papers: Military Affairs* (7 vols., Washington, 1832–1861) and *American State Papers: Indian Affairs* (2 vols., Washington, 1832–1834). For the period of the Articles of Confederation the *Journals of the Continental Congress* (34 vols., Washington, 1904–1937) are essential.

In addition there are numerous documents and reports published in the Serial Set of Congressional Documents, which have been drawn upon heavily.

Other primary sources are listed below. The books and articles are listed under the author of the work whenever authorship is clear. If the author is unknown or the item contains writings of several authors, the work is listed under the editor. Many of the works listed as secondary sources below also contain valuable primary materials.

Alexander, James E. *Transatlantic Sketches, Comprising Visits to the Most Interesting Scenes in North and South America and the West Indies, with Notes on Negro Slavery and Canadian Emigration.* 2 vols. London, 1833.

Allen, James. "Captain James Allen's Dragoon Expedition from Fort Des Moines, Territory of Iowa, in 1844," ed. Jacob Van der Zee, *Iowa Journal of History and Politics,* XI (January, 1913), 68–108.

Anderson, Robert. "Reminiscences of the Black Hawk War," *Wisconsin Historical Collections,* X (1888), 167–176.

Andrews, Joseph Gardner. *A Surgeon's Mate at Fort Defiance: The Journal of Joseph Gardner Andrews for the Year 1795,* ed. Richard C. Knopf. Columbus, Ohio, 1957.

Arfwedson, C. D. *The United States and Canada, in 1832, 1833, and 1834.* 2 vols. London, 1834.

Armstrong, John. *Notices of the War of 1812.* 2 vols. New York, 1836–1840.

Atkinson, Henry. "Letter from General Atkinson to Colonel Hamilton," *Nebraska History,* V (January–March, 1922), 9–11.

————. "Report of the Yellowstone Expedition of 1825," ed. Roger L. Nichols, *Nebraska History,* XLIV (June, 1963), 65–82.

Atwater, Caleb. *Remarks Made on a Tour to Prairie du Chien, Thence to Washington City, in 1829.* Columbus, Ohio, 1831.

Barr, James. *A Correct and Authentic Narrative of the Indian War in Florida, with a Description of Maj. Dade's Massacre.* New York, 1836.

Beatty, Erkuries. "Diary of Major Erkuries Beatty, Paymaster of the Western Army, May 15, 1786, to June 5, 1787," *Magazine of American History,* I (March, 1877), 175–179; (April, 1877), 235–243; (May, 1877), 309–315; (June, 1877), 380–384; (July, 1877), 432–438.

Bell, John R. *The Journal of Captain John R. Bell, Official Journalist for the Stephen H. Long Expedition to the Rocky Mountains, 1820,* ed. Harlin M. Fuller and LeRoy R. Hafen. Glendale, Calif., 1957.

Black Hawk. *Autobiography of Ma-Ka-Tai-Me-She-Kia-Kiak, or Black Hawk.* Oquawka, Ill., 1882.

————. *Life of Ma-Ka-Tai-Me-She-Kia-Kiak or Black Hawk.* Cincinnati, 1833.

————. *Life of Black Hawk, Ma-Ka-Tai-Me-She-Kia-Kiak,* ed. Milo M. Quaife. Chicago, 1916.

————. *Ma-Ka-Tai-Me-She-Kia-Kiak—Black Hawk: An Autobiography,* ed. Donald Jackson. Urbana, Ill., 1955.

Boone, Nathan. "Captain Nathan Boone's Journal," ed. W. Julian Fessler, *Chronicles of Oklahoma*, VII (March, 1929), 58–105.

[Boyer, John]. "Daily Journal of Wayne's Campaign, From July 28th to November 2d, 1794, Including an Account of the Memorable Battle of 20th August," *The American Pioneer*, I (September, 1842), 315–322; (October, 1842), 351–357. Reprinted as *A Journal of Wayne's Campaign*, Cincinnati, 1866.

Bradley, Daniel. *Journal of Capt. Daniel Bradley: An Epic of the Ohio Frontier*, ed. Frazer E. Wilson. Greenville, Ohio, 1935.

Brady, Hugh. "Reports of General Brady on the Patriot War," ed. Francis Paul Prucha, *Canadian Historical Review*, XXXI (March, 1950), 56–68.

Brannan, John, ed. *Official Letters of the Military and Naval Officers of the United States, During the War with Great Britain in the Years, 1812, 13, 14, & 15*. Washington, 1823.

Briggs, John Ely, ed. "The Expedition of 1835," *Palimpsest*, XVI (April, 1935), 105–136.

Brown, Everett S., ed. "The Senate Debate on the Breckinridge Bill for the Government of Louisiana, 1804," *American Historical Review*, XXII (January, 1917), 340–364.

Buchanan, Robert C. "A Journal of Lt. Robert C. Buchanan during the Seminole War," ed. Frank F. White, Jr., *Florida Historical Quarterly*, XXIX (October, 1950), 132–151.

———. "A Scouting Expedition along Lake Panasoffkee," ed. Frank F. White, Jr., *Florida Historical Quarterly*, XXXI (April, 1953), 282–289.

Bunn, Matthew. *A Journal of the Adventures of Matthew Bunn*. Providence, 1796. Facsimile ed., Chicago, 1962.

Burton, Clarence M., ed. "General Wayne's Orderly Book," *Michigan Pioneer and Historical Collections*, XXXIV (1904), 341–733.

Butterfield, Consul W., ed. *Journal of Capt. Jonathan Heart . . .* [and] *Dickinson-Harmar Correspondence of 1784–5*. Albany, 1885.

Calhoun, John C. *Correspondence of John C. Calhoun*, ed. J. Franklin Jameson. (*Annual Report of American Historical Association for the Year 1899*, II.) Washington, 1900.

———. *The Works of John C. Calhoun*, ed. Richard K. Crallé. 6 vols. New York, 1854–1857.

Callan, John F. *The Military Laws of the United States, Relating to the Army, Volunteers, Militia, and to Bounty Lands and Pensions, from the Foundation of the Government to the Year 1863*. Philadelphia, 1863.

Carleton, James Henry. *The Prairie Logbooks: Dragoon Campaigns to the Pawnee Village in 1844, and to the Rocky Mountains in 1845*, ed. Louis Pelzer. Chicago, 1943.

Carter, Clarence E., ed. *The Territorial Papers of the United States*. 26 vols. Washington, 1934–1962.

Catlin, George. *Letters and Notes on the Manners, Customs, and Condition of the North American Indians*. 2 vols. New York, 1841.

[Chew, John]. "The Diary of an Officer in the Indian Country in 1794," *American Historical Magazine*, III (November, 1908), 639–643; IV (January, 1909), 69–71.

Claiborne, William C. C. *Official Letter Books of W. C. C. Claiborne, 1801–1816*, ed. Dunbar Rowland. 6 vols. Jackson, Miss., 1917.

Clark, William. *The Field Notes of Captain William Clark, 1803–1805*, ed. Ernest Staples Osgood. New Haven, 1964.

———. "William Clark's Journal of General Wayne's Campaign," ed. R. C. McGrane, *Mississippi Valley Historical Review*, I (December, 1914), 418–444.

Coffee, John. "Letters of General John Coffee to His Wife, 1813–1815," ed. John H. DeWitt, *Tennessee Historical Magazine*, II (December, 1916), 264–295.

Cohen, M. M. *Notices of Florida and the Campaigns*. Charleston, 1836. Facsimile ed., Gainesville, Fla., 1964.

Coke, E. T. *A Subaltern's Furlough*. 2 vols. New York, 1833.

Cooke, Jacob E., ed. *The Federalist*. Middletown, Conn., 1961.

Cooke, John. "General Wayne's Campaign in 1794 & 1795: Captain John Cooke's Journal," *American Historical Record*, II (July, 1873), 311–316; (August, 1873), 339–345.

Cooke, Philip St. George. "A Journal of the Santa Fe Trail," ed. William E. Connelley, *Mississippi Valley Historical Review*, XII (June, 1925), 72–98; (September, 1925), 227–255.

———. *Scenes and Adventures in the Army: or, Romance of Military Life*. Philadelphia, 1859.

"Copies of Papers on File in the Dominion Archives at Ottawa, Canada, Pertaining to the Relations of the British Government with the United States During the Period of the War of 1812," *Michigan Pioneer and Historical Collections*, XV (1889).

Coues, Elliott, ed. *History of the Expedition Under the Command of Lewis and Clark*. 4 vols. New York, 1893.

Croghan, George. *Army Life on the Western Frontier: Selections from the Official Reports Made Between 1826 and 1845 by Colonel George Croghan*, ed. Francis Paul Prucha. Norman, Okla., 1958.

Cruikshank, E. A., ed. *Documents Relating to the Invasion of Canada and the Surrender of Detroit, 1812*. Ottawa, 1913.

Cunyngham, Arthur. *A Glimpse at the Great Western Republic*. London, 1851.

Debate in the House of Representatives of the United States, on the Seminole War, in January and February, 1819. Washington, 1819.

Denny, Ebenezer. "Military Journal of Major Ebenezer Denny," *Memoirs of the Historical Society of Pennsylvania*, VII (1860), 237–409.

Dodge, Henry. "Letters of Henry Dodge to Gen. George W. Jones," ed. William Salter, *Annals of Iowa*, Third Series, III (October, 1897), 220–223; (January, 1898), 290–296; (April–July, 1898), 384–400.

Doty, James Duane. "Official Journal, 1820, Expedition with Cass and Schoolcraft," *Wisconsin Historical Collections*, XIII (1895), 163–219.

Dunbar, William. *Journal of a Voyage . . .*, printed in *Documents Relating to the Purchase and Exploration of Louisiana*. Boston, 1904.

Edwards, Ninian. *The Edwards Papers: Being a Portion of the Letters*,

Papers, and Manuscripts of Ninian Edwards, ed. E. B. Washburne. Chicago, 1884.

Ellsworth, Henry Leavitt. *Washington Irving on the Prairie, or A Narrative of a Tour of the Southwest in the Year 1832*, ed. Stanley T. Williams and Barbara D. Simison. New York, 1937.

Evans, Hugh. "Hugh Evans' Journal of Colonel Henry Dodge's Expedition to the Rocky Mountains in 1835," ed. Fred S. Perrine, *Mississippi Valley Historical Review*, XIV (September, 1927), 192–214.

————. "The Journal of Hugh Evans, Covering the First and Second Campaigns of the United States Dragoon Regiment in 1834 and 1835: Campaign of 1834," ed. Fred S. Perrine and Grant Foreman, *Chronicles of Oklahoma*, III (September, 1925), 175–215.

Flint, Timothy. *Recollections of the Last Ten Years, Passed in Occasional Residences and Journeyings in the Valley of the Mississippi*. Boston, 1826. Reprint, New York, 1932.

Ford, Lemuel. "Captain Ford's Journal of an Expedition to the Rocky Mountains, 29 May to 16 September, 1835," ed. Louis Pelzer, *Mississippi Valley Historical Review*, XII (March, 1926), 550–579.

[Ford, Lemuel]. "A Summer Upon the Prairie," in Archer B. Hulbert, ed., *The Call of the Columbia; Iron Men and Saints Take the Oregon Trail*. Denver, 1934. Pp. 227–305.

Forsyth, Thomas. "Journal of a Voyage from St. Louis to the Falls of St. Anthony, in 1819," *Wisconsin Historical Collections*, VI (1872), 188–219.

Frémont, John Charles. *Memoirs of My Life*. Chicago, 1887.

————. *Narratives of Exploration and Adventure*, ed. Allan Nevins. New York, 1956.

————. *Report of the Exploring Expedition to the Rocky Mountains in the Year 1842, and to Oregon and North California in the Years 1843–'44*. Washington, 1845.

"General Wayne's Campaign of 1794 and the Battle of Fallen Timbers," *Historical Society of Northwestern Ohio Quarterly Bulletin*, I (April, 1929), 9–16.

Greene, Evarts Boutell, and Alvord, Clarence Walworth, eds. *The Governors' Letter-Books, 1818–1834 (Collections of the Illinois State Historical Library, IV)*. Springfield, Ill., 1909.

Grey, Charles. *Crisis in the Canadas, 1838–1839: The Grey Journals and Letters*, ed. William Ormsby. Toronto, 1964.

Guion, Isaac. "Military Journal of Captain Isaac Guion, 1797–1799," *Seventh Annual Report of the Director of the Department of Archives and History of the State of Mississippi* (Nashville, Tenn., 1909), pp. 25–112.

Hamer, Philip M., ed. "The British in Canada and the Southern Indians, 1790–1794," *East Tennessee Historical Society's Publications*, II (1930), 107–134.

Hamilton, Alexander. *The Papers of Alexander Hamilton*, ed. Harold C. Syrett and Jacob E. Cooke. 11 vols. to date. New York, 1961–.

Harmar, Josiah. "Letters of General Josiah Harmar and Others," *Memoirs of the Historical Society of Pennsylvania*, VII (1860), 413–477.

Harrison, William Henry. *Messages and Letters of William Henry Harrison*, ed. Logan Esarey. 2 vols. Indianapolis, 1922.

[Hildreth, James]. *Dragoon Campaigns to the Rocky Mountains: Being a History of the Enlistment, Organization, and First Campaigns of the Regiment of United States Dragoons; Together with Incidents of a Soldier's Life, and Sketches of Scenery and Indian Character.* New York, 1836.

[Hoffman, Charles F.]. *A Winter in the West.* 2 vols. New York, 1835.

Hull, William. *Memoirs of the Campaign of the North Western Army of the United States, A.D. 1812.* Boston, 1824.

Irving, Washington. *A Tour on the Prairies (The Crayon Miscellany, No. 1).* Philadelphia, 1835.

————. *The Western Journals of Washington Irving*, ed. John Francis McDermott. Norman, Okla., 1944.

Jackson, Andrew. *Correspondence of Andrew Jackson*, ed. John Spencer Bassett. 6 vols. Washington, 1926–1933.

Jackson, Donald, ed. *Letters of the Lewis and Clark Expedition with Related Documents, 1783–1854.* Urbana, Ill., 1962.

Jackson, James. "The Letter Book of General James Jackson, 1788–1796," *Georgia Historical Quarterly*, XXXVII (September, 1953), 220–249; (December, 1953), 299–329.

James, Edwin. *An Account of an Expedition from Pittsburgh to the Rocky Mountains, Performed in the Years, 1819, 1820.* 2 vols. and atlas, Philadelphia, 1822–1823; 3 vols., London, 1823, reprinted in Reuben Gold Thwaites, ed., *Early Western Travels, 1748–1846* (32 vols., Cleveland, 1904–1907), XIV, XV, XVI, XVII.

Jefferson, Thomas. *The Works of Thomas Jefferson*, ed. Paul Leicester Ford. 12 vols. New York, 1904–1905.

————. *The Writings of Thomas Jefferson*, ed. Andrew A. Lipscomb. 20 vols. Washington, 1903–1904.

Jones, Roger. "Gen. Brown's Inspection Tour Up the Lakes in 1819," *Publications of the Buffalo Historical Society*, XXIV (1920), 295–323.

Kappler, Charles J., ed. *Indian Affairs: Laws and Treaties.* 2 vols. Washington, 1904.

Kearny, Stephen Watts. "Journal of Stephen Watts Kearny: Part I, The Council Bluff-St. Peter's Exploration (1820)," ed. Valentine Mott Porter, *Missouri Historical Society Collections*, III (January, 1908), 8–29; (April, 1908), 99–131.

Keating, William H. *Narrative of an Expedition to the Source of St. Peter's River, Lake Winnepeek, Lake of the Woods, &c. &c. Performed in the Year 1823, by Order of the Hon. J. C. Calhoun, Secretary of War, under the Command of Stephen H. Long, Major U.S.T.E.* 2 vols. Philadelphia, 1824. Reprint of London ed., of 1825, Minneapolis, 1959.

Kennerly, James. "Diary of James Kennerly, 1823–1826," ed. Edgar B. Wesley, *Missouri Historical Society Collections*, VI (October, 1928), 41–97.

Knopf, Richard C., ed. *Anthony Wayne, A Name in Arms: The Wayne-Knox-Pickering-McHenry Correspondence.* Pittsburgh, 1960.

———, ed. *Document Transcriptions of the War of 1812 in the Northwest.* 6 vols. Columbus, Ohio, 1957–1959.

———, ed. "A Precise Journal of General Wayne's Last Campaign," *Proceedings of the American Antiquarian Society,* LXIV (October 20, 1954), 273–302.

———, ed. "Two Journals of the Kentucky Volunteers, 1793 and 1794," *The Filson Club History Quarterly,* XXVII (July, 1953), 247–281.

Latrobe, Charles Joseph. *The Rambler in North America, MDCCCXXXII–MDCCCXXXIII.* 2 vols. New York, 1835.

Lea, Albert M. *Notes on the Wisconsin Territory; Particularly with Reference to the Iowa District, or Black Hawk Purchase.* Philadelphia, 1836. Reprinted as *The Book That Gave to Iowa Its Name,* Iowa City, 1935.

Lockwood, James H. "Early Times and Events in Wisconsin," *Wisconsin Historical Collections,* II (1856), 98–196.

McCall, George A. *Letters from the Frontiers, Written During a Period of Thirty Years' Service in the Army of the United States.* Philadelphia, 1868.

McKenney, Thomas L. "The Winnebago War of 1827," *Wisconsin Historical Collections,* V (1868), 178–204.

Mackay, Alexander. *The Western World; or, Travels in the United States in 1846–1847.* 2 vols. Philadelphia, 1849.

Manning, William R., ed. *Diplomatic Correspondence of the United States: Canadian Relations, 1784–1860.* 3 vols. Washington, 1940–1943.

Marryat, Frederick. *A Diary in America, with Remarks on Its Institutions.* 3 vols. London, 1839.

Michaux, F. A. *Travels to the West of the Alleghany Mountains, in the States of Ohio, Kentucky, and Tennessea.* London, 1805. Reprinted in Reuben Gold Thwaites, ed., *Early Western Travels, 1748–1846* (32 vols., Cleveland, 1904–1907), III, 105–306.

Miller, Hunter, ed. *Treaties and Other International Acts of the United States of America.* 8 vols. Washington, 1931–1948.

Miller, John. "The Military Occupation of Green Bay," *Mississippi Valley Historical Review,* XIII (March, 1927), 549–553.

Monroe, James. *The Writings of James Monroe,* ed. Stanislaus Murray Hamilton. 7 vols. New York, 1898–1903.

Motte, Jacob Rhett. *Journey into Wilderness: An Army Surgeon's Account of Life in Camp and Field during the Creek and Seminole Wars, 1836–1838,* ed. James F. Sunderman. Gainesville, Fla., 1953.

Murray, Charles A. *Travels in North America during the Years 1834, 1835, & 1836.* 2 vols. New York, 1839.

Newman, Samuel. "A Picture of the First United States Army: The Journal of Captain Samuel Newman," ed. Milo M. Quaife, *Wisconsin Magazine of History,* II (September, 1918), 40–73.

Nichols, Roger L., ed. "The Black Hawk War: Another View," *Annals of Iowa,* XXXVI (Winter, 1963), 525–533.

Nicollet, Joseph N. *Report Intended to Illustrate a Map of the Hydrographi-*

cal Basin of the Upper Mississippi River (*House Document* No. 52, 28 Congress, 2 session). Washington, 1843.

Paul Wilhelm, Duke of Württemberg. "First Journey to North America in the Years 1822 to 1824," trans. William G. Bek, *South Dakota Historical Collections*, XIX (1938), 7–462.

Pelzer, Louis, ed. "A Journal of Marches by the First United States Dragoons 1834–1835," *Iowa Journal of History and Politics*, VII (July, 1909), 331–378.

Perrine, Fred S., ed. "Military Escorts on the Santa Fe Trail," *New Mexico Historical Review*, II (April, 1927), 175–193; (July, 1927), 269–304.

Pike, Zebulon Montgomery. *The Expeditions of Zebulon Montgomery Pike*, ed. Elliott Coues. 3 vols. New York, 1895.

———. *The Journals of Zebulon Montgomery Pike with Letters and Related Documents*, ed. Donald Jackson. 2 vols. Norman, Okla., 1966.

[Potter, Woodburne]. *The War in Florida: Being an Exposition of Its Causes, and an Accurate History of the Campaigns of Generals Clinch, Gaines and Scott*. Baltimore, 1836.

Poussin, Guillaume Tell. *The United States: Its Power and Progress*, trans. Edmund L. DuBarry. Philadelphia, 1851.

Putnam, Rufus. *The Memoirs of Rufus Putnam and Certain Official Papers and Correspondence*, ed. Rowena Buell. Boston, 1903.

Quaife, Milo M., ed. "Fort Knox Orderly Book, 1793–97," *Indiana Magazine of History*, XXXII (June, 1936), 137–169.

———, ed. "Journals and Reports of the Black Hawk War," *Mississippi Valley Historical Review*, XII (December, 1925), 392–409.

———, ed. *The Journals of Captain Meriwether Lewis and Sergeant John Ordway Kept on the Expedition of Western Exploration, 1803–1806*. Madison, Wis., 1916.

Reid, Russell, and Gannon, Clell G., eds. "Journal of the Atkinson-O'Fallon Expedition," *North Dakota Historical Quarterly*, IV (October, 1929), 5–56.

"Reminiscences of Wisconsin in 1823," *Wisconsin Historical Collections*, X (1888), 231–234.

"Report of Cherokee Deputation into Florida," *Chronicles of Oklahoma*, IX (December, 1931), 423–438.

Reynolds, John. *My Own Times, Embracing Also, the History of My Life*. Belleville, Ill., 1855.

Robertson, James. "The Correspondence of General James Robertson," *American Historical Magazine*, II–V (1897–1900), *passim*.

Robinson, Doane, ed. "Official Correspondence Pertaining to the Leavenworth Expedition of 1823 into South Dakota for the Conquest of the Ree Indians," *South Dakota Historical Collections*, I (1902), 179–256.

Rowland, Dunbar, ed. *The Mississippi Territorial Archives, 1798–1803*. Nashville, Tenn., 1905.

Rutland, Robert, ed. "The Dragoons in the Iowa Territory, 1845," *Iowa Journal of History*, LI (April, 1953), 156–182.

———, ed. "A Journal of the First Dragoons in the Iowa Territory, 1844," *Iowa Journal of History*, LI (January, 1953), 57–78.

St. Clair, Arthur. *A Narrative of the Manner in Which the Campaign Against the Indians, in the Year One Thousand Seven Hundred and Ninety-one, Was Conducted, Under the Command of Major General St. Clair.* Philadelphia, 1812.

Sargent, Winthrop. *Diary of Col. Winthrop Sargent, Adjutant General of the United States' Army, During the Campaign of MDCCXCI.* Wormsloe, Ga., 1851. Reprinted as "Winthrop Sargent's Diary While with General Arthur St. Clair's Expedition against the Indians," in *Ohio Archaeological and Historical Quarterly,* XXXIII (July, 1924), 237–273.

Schaumburgh, Bartholomew. "Fort Stoddart [sic] in 1799: Seven Letters of Captain Bartholomew Schaumburgh," ed. Jack D. L. Holmes, *Alabama Historical Quarterly,* XXVI (Fall–Winter, 1964), 231–252.

Schoolcraft, Henry R. *Narrative Journal of Travels through the Northwestern Region of the United States Extending from Detroit through the Great Chain of American Lakes to the Sources of the Mississippi River in the Year 1820,* ed. Mentor L. Williams. East Lansing, Mich., 1953.

————. *Personal Memoirs of a Residence of Thirty Years with the Indian Tribes on the American Frontiers.* Philadelphia, 1851.

Scott, Winfield. *Memoirs of Lieut.-General Scott, LL.D., Written by Himself.* 2 vols. New York, 1864.

————. "A Private Report of General Winfield Scott on the Border Situation in 1839," ed. C. P. Stacey, *Canadian Historical Review,* XXI (December, 1940), 407–414.

Smith, Dwight L., ed. "From Greene Ville to Fallen Timbers: A Journal of the Wayne Campaign, July 28–September 14, 1794," *Indiana Historical Society Publications,* XVI (1952), 239–333.

Smith, Henry. "Indian Campaign of 1832," *Wisconsin Historical Collections,* X (1909), 150–166.

[Snelling, William J.]. "Early Days at Prairie du Chien, and the Winnebago Outbreak of 1827," *Wisconsin Historical Collections,* V (1868), 123–153.

Sprague, John T. "Macomb's Mission to the Seminoles: John T. Sprague's Journal Kept during April and May, 1839," ed. Frank F. White, Jr., *Florida Historical Quarterly,* XXXV (October, 1956), 130–193.

Stuart, John. "Report of Capt. John Stuart on the Construction of the Road from Fort Smith to Horse Prairie on Red River," ed. Carolyn Thomas Foreman, *Chronicles of Oklahoma,* V (September, 1927), 333–347.

Sumner, Edwin V. "Captain Edwin V. Sumner's Dragoon Expedition in the Territory of Iowa in the Summer of 1845," ed. Jacob Van der Zee, *Iowa Journal of History and Politics,* XI (April, 1913), 258–267.

Symmes, John Cleves. "John Cleves Symmes to Elias Boudinot," *Quarterly Publication of the Historical and Philosophical Society of Ohio,* V (July–September, 1910). 93–101.

Tait, James A. "Journal of James A. Tait for the Year 1813," ed. Peter A. Brannon, *Georgia Historical Quarterly,* VIII (September, 1924), 229–239. Reprinted in *Alabama Historical Quarterly,* II (Winter, 1940), 430–440.

Taylor, Zachary. "Zachary Taylor and the Black Hawk War," ed. Holman Hamilton, *Wisconsin Magazine of History*, XXIV (March, 1941), 305–315.

Thornbrough, Gayle, ed. *Outpost on the Wabash, 1787–1791 (Indiana Historical Society Publications*, No. 19), Indianapolis, 1957.

Thwaites, Reuben Gold, ed. *Original Journals of the Lewis and Clark Expedition, 1804–1806*. 8 vols. New York, 1904–1905.

"Transfer of Upper Louisiana," *Glimpses of the Past*, II (May–September, 1935), 78–122.

Trowbridge, Charles C. "With Cass in the Northwest in 1820," ed. Ralph H. Brown, *Minnesota History*, XXIII (June, 1942), 126–148; (September, 1942), 233–252; (December, 1942), 328–348.

Twiggs, John. "The Creek Troubles of 1793," ed. E. Merton Coulter, *Georgia Historical Quarterly*, XI (September, 1927), 274–280.

Underwood, Thomas Taylor. *Journal, Thomas Taylor Underwood, March 26, 1792 to March 18, 1800, an Old Soldier in Wayne's Army*, ed. Lee Shepard. Cincinnati, 1945.

Van Cleve, Benjamin. "Memoirs of Benjamin Van Cleve," ed. Beverley W. Bond, Jr., *Quarterly Publication of the Historical and Philosophical Society of Ohio*, XVII (January–June, 1922), 1–71.

Washington, George. *The Writings of George Washington from the Original Manuscript Sources, 1745–1799*, ed. John C. Fitzpatrick. 39 vols. Washington, 1931–1944.

Wharton, Clifton. "The Expedition of Major Clifton Wharton in 1844," *Collections of the Kansas State Historical Society*, XVI (1925), 272–305.

Wheelock, Thompson B. "Colonel Henry Dodge and His Regiment of Dragoons on the Plains in 1834," ed. Edgar B. Harlan, *Annals of Iowa*, Third Series, XVIII (January, 1930), 173–197. The same journal appears in "Peace on the Plains," ed. George H. Shirk, *Chronicles of Oklahoma*, XXVIII (Spring, 1950), 2–41.

"The White Flag," *Florida Historical Quarterly*, XXXIII (January–April, 1955), 218–234.

Wilkinson, James. "General James Wilkinson's Narrative of the Fallen Timbers Campaign," ed. Milo M. Quaife, *Mississippi Valley Historical Review*, XVI (June, 1921), 81–90.

———. *Memoirs of My Own Times*. 3 vols. Philadelphia, 1816.

Wyse, Francis. *America, Its Realities and Resources*. 3 vols. London, 1846.

Secondary Sources

Abel, Annie Heloise. "The History of Events Resulting in Indian Consolidation West of the Mississippi," *Annual Report of the American Historical Association for the Year 1906* (Washington, 1908), I, 233–450.

———. "Proposals for an Indian State, 1778–1878," *Annual Report of the*

American Historical Association for the Year 1907 (Washington, 1908), I, 87–104.

Abernethy, Thomas P. *The Burr Conspiracy.* New York, 1954.

———. *The South in the New Nation, 1789–1819.* Baton Rouge, 1961.

Adams, Henry. *History of the United States During the Administration of Jefferson and Madison.* 9 vols. New York, 1889–1891.

———. *The War of 1812,* ed. H. A. DeWeerd. Washington, 1944.

Adams, Randolph G. "The Harmar Expedition of 1790," *Ohio State Archaeological and Historical Quarterly,* L (January–March, 1941), 60–62.

Adams, Randolph G., and Peckham, Howard H. *Lexington to Fallen Timbers, 1775–1794.* Ann Arbor, Mich., 1943.

Ambrose, Stephen E. *Duty, Honor, Country: A History of West Point.* Baltimore, 1966.

Armstrong, Perry A. *The Sauks and the Black Hawk War with Biographical Sketches, Etc.* Springfield, Ill., 1887.

Bakeless, John. *Lewis & Clark, Partners in Discovery.* New York, 1947.

Bald, F. Clever. "Colonel John Francis Hamtramck," *Indiana Magazine of History,* XLIV (December, 1948), 335–354.

Barker, Eugene C. "The United States and Mexico, 1835–1837," *Mississippi Valley Historical Review,* I (June, 1914), 3–30.

Barry, Louise. "The Fort Leavenworth-Fort Gibson Military Road and the Founding of Fort Scott," *Kansas Historical Quarterly,* XI (May, 1942), 115–129.

Bassett, John Spencer. *The Life of Andrew Jackson.* 2 vols. Garden City, N. Y., 1911.

Bearss, Edwin C. "In Quest of Peace on the Indian Border: The Establishment of Fort Smith," *Arkansas Historical Quarterly,* XXIII (Summer, 1964), 123–153.

Beers, Henry P. "The Army and the Oregon Trail to 1846," *Pacific Northwest Quarterly,* XXVIII (October, 1937), 339–362.

———. "A History of the U.S. Topographical Engineers, 1813–1863," *Military Engineer,* XXXIV (June, 1942), 287–291; (July, 1942), 348–352.

———. "Military Protection of the Santa Fe Trail to 1843," *New Mexico Historical Review,* XII (April, 1937), 113–133.

———. *The Western Military Frontier, 1815–1846.* Philadelphia, 1935.

Beirne, Francis F. *The War of 1812.* New York, 1949.

Bemis, Samuel Flagg. *Jay's Treaty: A Study in Commerce and Diplomacy.* Revised ed., New Haven, 1962.

———. *Pinckney's Treaty: A Study of America's Advantage from Europe's Distress, 1783–1800.* Baltimore, 1926.

Bernardo, C. Joseph, and Bacon, Eugene H. *American Military Policy: Its Development Since 1775.* Second ed., Harrisburg, Pa., 1961.

Berry, Jane M. "The Indian Policy of Spain in the Southwest, 1783–1795," *Mississippi Valley Historical Review,* III (March, 1917), 462–477.

Bond, Beverley W., Jr. "William Henry Harrison in the War of 1812," *Mississippi Valley Historical Review,* XIII (March, 1927), 499–516.

Boyd, Mark F. "Asi-Yaholo or Osceola," *Florida Historical Quarterly*, XXXIII (January–April, 1955), 249–305.

———. "The Seminole War: Its Background and Onset," *Florida Historical Quarterly*, XXX (July, 1951), 3–115.

Boyd, Thomas. *Mad Anthony Wayne*. New York, 1929.

Bracken, Charles. "Further Strictures on Gov. Ford's History of the Black Hawk War," *Wisconsin Historical Collections*, II (1856), 402–414.

Brackett, Albert G. *History of the United States Cavalry, from the Formation of the Federal Government to the 1st of June, 1863*. New York, 1865.

Bretz, J. P. "Early Land Communication with the Lower Mississippi Valley," *Mississippi Valley Historical Review*, XIII (June, 1926), 3–29.

Brevard, Caroline Mays. "Richard Keith Call," *Florida Historical Society Quarterly*, I (July, 1908), 3–12; (October, 1908), 8–20.

Brooks, Noah. *Henry Knox: A Soldier of the Revolution*. New York, 1900.

Brown, Everett S. *The Constitutional History of the Louisiana Purchase, 1803–1812*. Berkeley, Calif., 1920.

Burt, A. L. *The United States, Great Britain, and British North America, from the Revolution to the Establishment of Peace after the War of 1812*. New Haven, 1940.

Burton, Clarence M. "Anthony Wayne and the Battle of Fallen Timbers," *Michigan Pioneer and Historical Collections*, XXXI (1901), 472–489.

Caldwell, Norman W. "Cantonment Wilkinsonville," *Mid-America*, XXXI (January, 1949), 3–28.

———. "Civilian Personnel at the Frontier Military Post (1790–1814)," *Mid-America*, XXXVIII (April, 1956), 101–119.

———. "The Enlisted Soldier at the Frontier Post, 1790–1814," *Mid-America*, XXXVII (October, 1955), 195–204.

———. "Fort Massac: The American Frontier Post, 1778–1805," *Journal of the Illinois State Historical Society*, XLIII (Winter, 1950), 265–281.

———. "Fort Massac: Since 1805," *Journal of the Illinois State Historical Society*, XLIV (Spring, 1951), 47–60.

———. "The Frontier Army Officer, 1794–1814," *Mid-America*, XXXVII (April, 1955), 101–128.

Callahan, North. *Henry Knox: General Washington's General*. New York, 1958.

Carroll, H. Bailey. "Steward A. Miller and the Snively Expedition of 1843," *Southwestern Historical Quarterly*, LIV (January, 1951), 261–286.

Catlin, George B. "Michigan's Early Military Roads," *Michigan History Magazine*, XIII (Spring, 1929), 196–207.

Caughey, John W. *McGillivray of the Creeks*. Norman, Okla., 1938.

Chittenden, Hiram Martin. *The American Fur Trade of the Far West*. 3 vols. New York, 1902.

Clarke, Dwight L. *Stephen Watts Kearny: Soldier of the West*. Norman, Okla., 1961.

Cleaves, Freeman. *Old Tippecanoe: William Henry Harrison and His Time*. New York, 1939.

Cobb, Samuel E. "The Florida Militia and the Affair at Withlacoochee," *Florida Historical Quarterly*, XIX (July, 1940), 128–139.

Coe, Charles H. "The Parentage and Birthplace of Osceola," *Florida Historical Quarterly*, XVII (April, 1939), 304–311.

———. *Red Patriots: The Story of the Seminoles.* Cincinnati, 1898.

Cole, Cyrenus. *I Am a Man—The Indian Black Hawk.* Iowa City, 1938.

Cole, H. E. "The Old Military Road," *Wisconsin Magazine of History*, IX (September, 1925), 47–62.

Coleman, Christopher B. "The Ohio Valley in the Preliminaries of the War of 1812," *Mississippi Valley Historical Review*, VII (June, 1920), 39–50.

Coleman, Kenneth. "Federal Indian Relations in the South, 1781–1789," *Chronicles of Oklahoma*, XXXV (Winter, 1957–1958), 435–458.

Coles, Harry L. *The War of 1812.* Chicago, 1965.

Corey, Albert B. *The Crisis of 1830–1842 in Canadian-American Relations.* New Haven, 1941.

Cotterill, R. S. "Federal Indian Management in the South, 1789–1825," *Mississippi Valley Historical Review*, XX (December, 1933), 333–352.

Covington, James W. "Cuban Bloodhounds and the Seminoles," *Florida Historical Quarterly*, XXXIII (October, 1954), 111–119.

Cox, Isaac J. "The Exploration of the Louisiana Frontier, 1803–1806," *Annual Report of the American Historical Association for the Year 1904* (Washington, 1905), pp. 151–174.

———. "The Indian as a Diplomatic Factor in the History of the Old Northwest," *Ohio Archaeological and Historical Quarterly*, XVIII (October, 1909), 542–565.

———. "The Louisiana-Texas Frontier: Part II, The American Occupation of the Louisiana-Texas Frontier," *Southwestern Historical Quarterly*, XVII (July, 1913), 1–42; (October, 1913), 140–187.

———. "The Louisiana-Texas Frontier During the Burr Conspiracy," *Mississippi Valley Historical Review*, X (December, 1923), 274–284.

———. "Opening the Santa Fe Trail," *Missouri Historical Review*, XXV (October, 1930), 30–66.

———. *The West Florida Controversy, 1798–1813: A Study in American Diplomacy.* Baltimore, 1918.

Croffut, W. A. *Fifty Years in Camp and Field: Diary of Major-General Ethan Allen Hitchcock, U.S.A.* New York, 1909.

Cunliffe, Marcus. "The American Military Tradition," in H. C. Allen and C. P. Hill, eds., *British Essays in American History.* New York, 1957. Pp. 207–224.

Dale, Harrison Clifford. *The Ashley-Smith Explorations and the Discovery of a Central Route to the Pacific, 1822–1829.* Revised ed., Glendale, Calif., 1941.

Davis, T. Frederick. "The Seminole Council, October 23–25, 1834," *Florida Historical Society Quarterly*, VII (April, 1929), 330–350.

DeRosier, Arthur H., Jr. "William Dunbar, Explorer," *Journal of Mississippi History*, XXV (July, 1963), 165–185.

Dillon, Richard H. *Meriwether Lewis, A Biography.* New York, 1965.

————. "Stephen Long's Great American Desert," *Proceedings of the American Philosophical Society*, CXI (April, 1967), 93–108.

Doherty, Herbert J., Jr. *Richard Keith Call, Southern Unionist*. Gainesville, Fla., 1961.

————. "Richard K. Call *vs*. the Federal Government on the Seminole War," *Florida Historical Quarterly*, XXXI (January, 1953), 163–180.

Downes, Randolph C. "Cherokee-American Relations in the Upper Tennessee Valley, 1776–1791," *East Tennessee Historical Society's Publications*, VIII (1936), 35–53.

————. 'Creek-American Relations, 1782–1790," *Georgia Historical Quarterly*, XXI (June, 1937), 142–184.

————. "Creek-American Relations, 1790–1795," *Journal of Southern History*, VIII (August, 1942), 350–373.

————. *Council Fires on the Upper Ohio: A Narrative of Indian Affairs in the Upper Ohio Valley until 1795*. Pittsburgh, 1940.

————. *Frontier Ohio, 1788–1803 (Ohio Historical Collection, III)*. Columbus, Ohio, 1935.

————. "Indian Affairs in the Southwest Territory, 1790–1796," *Tennessee Historical Magazine*, Second Series, III (January, 1937), 240–268.

Downey, Fairfax. *Indian Wars of the U. S. Army, 1776–1865*. New York, 1963.

Drake, Benjamin. *The Life and Adventures of Black Hawk: With Sketches of Keokuk, the Sac and Fox Indians, and the Late Black Hawk War*. Seventh ed., Cincinnati, 1846.

Dungan, James R. "'Sir' William Dunbar of Natchez, Planter, Explorer, and Scientist, 1792–1810," *Journal of Mississippi History*, XXIII (October, 1961), 211–228.

Dupuy, Richard Ernest. *The Compact History of the United States Army*. New York, 1956.

Dyer, Brainerd. *Zachary Taylor*. Baton Rouge, 1946.

Elliott, Charles Winslow. *Winfield Scott: The Soldier and the Man*. New York, 1937.

Fairbanks, George R. *History of Florida, from Its Discovery by Ponce de Leon, in 1512, to the Close of the Florida War, in 1842*. Philadelphia, 1871.

Fisher, Robert L. "The Treaties of Portage des Sioux," *Mississippi Valley Historical Review*, XIX (March, 1933), 495–508.

————. "The Western Prologue to the War of 1812," *Missouri Historical Review*, XXX (April, 1936), 267–281.

Fisher, Vincent J. "Mr. Calhoun's Army," *Military Review*, XXXVII (September, 1957), 52–58.

Flagler, Daniel W. *A History of the Rock Island Arsenal from Its Establishment in 1863 to December, 1876; and of the Island of Rock Island, the Site of the Arsenal, from 1804 to 1863*. Washington, 1877.

Fletcher, Mildred Stahl. "Louisiana as a Factor in French Diplomacy from 1763 to 1800," *Mississippi Valley Historical Review*, XVII (December, 1930), 367–376.

Ford, Thomas. *A History of Illinois from Its Commencement as a State in 1818 to 1847*. Chicago, 1854. Reprinted, 2 vols., Chicago, 1945–1946.

Foreman, Carolyn Thomas. "General Philip St. George Cooke," *Chronicles of Oklahoma*, XXXII (Summer, 1954), 195–213.

———. "William Bradford," *Arkansas Historical Quarterly*, XIII (Winter, 1954), 341–351.

Foreman, Grant. *Advancing the Frontier, 1830–1860*. Norman, Okla., 1933.

———. "The Centennial of Fort Gibson," *Chronicles of Oklahoma*, II (June, 1924), 119–128.

———. *Fort Gibson: A Brief History*. Norman, Okla., 1936.

———. *Indian Removal: The Emigration of the Five Civilized Tribes of Indians*. Norman, Okla., 1932.

———. *Indians & Pioneers: The Story of the American Southwest before 1830*. New Haven, 1930.

———. *The Last Trek of the Indians*. Chicago, 1946.

———. *Pioneer Days in the Early Southwest*. Cleveland, 1926.

———. "River Navigation in the Early Southwest," *Mississippi Valley Historical Review*, XV (June, 1928), 34–55.

Forman, Sidney. *West Point: A History of the United States Military Academy*. New York, 1950.

"Fort Atkinson, Iowa," *Annals of Iowa*, Third Series, IV (July, 1900), 448–453.

"Fort Croghan," *Annals of Iowa*, Third Series, III (April–July, 1898), 471–472.

"Fort Des Moines (No. 1), Iowa," *Annals of Iowa*, Third Series, III (April–July, 1898), 351–363.

"Fort Des Moines, No. 2," *Annals of Iowa*, Third Series, IV (October, 1899), 161–178.

"Fort Sanford, Iowa," *Annals of Iowa*, Third Series, IV (January, 1900), 289–293.

Fortier, Alcée. *A History of Louisiana*. 4 vols. New York, 1904.

Frost, Donald McKay. *Notes on General Ashley, the Overland Trail, and South Pass*. Worcester, Mass., 1945.

Gaines, William H., Jr. "The Forgotten Army: Recruiting for a National Emergency (1799–1800)," *Virginia Magazine of History and Biography*, LVI (July, 1948), 267–279.

Gallaher, Ruth A. *Fort Des Moines in Iowa History*. Iowa City, 1919.

———. "The Indian Agent in the United States Before 1850," *Iowa Journal of History and Politics*, XIV (January, 1916), 3–55.

———. "The Military-Indian Frontier 1830–1835," *Iowa Journal of History and Politics*, XV (July, 1917), 393–428.

Ganoe, William Addleman. *The History of the United States Army*. New York, 1924.

Gardner, Hamilton. "Captain Philip St. George Cooke and the March of the 1st Dragoons to the Rocky Mountains in 1845," *Colorado Magazine*, XXX (October, 1953), 246–269.

———. "The March of the First Dragoons from Jefferson Barracks to Fort

Gibson in 1833–1834," *Chronicles of Oklahoma*, XXXI (Spring, 1953), 22–36.

Garner, Mrs. Bert. "A Notable United States Military Road," *Michigan History Magazine*, XX (Spring and Summer, 1936), 177–184.

Gavarré, Charles. *History of Louisiana*. 4 vols. Third ed., New Orleans, 1885.

Giddings, Joshua R. *The Exiles of Florida: or, The Crimes Committed by Our Government against the Maroons, Who Fled from South Carolina and Other Slave States, Seeking Protection under Spanish Laws*. Columbus, Ohio, 1858. Facsimile ed., Gainesville, Fla., 1964.

Gilpin, Alec R. *The War of 1812 in the Old Northwest*. East Lansing, Mich., 1958.

Godfrey, Carlos E. "Organization of the Provisional Army of the United States in the Anticipated War with France, 1789–1800," *Pennsylvania Magazine of History and Biography*, XXXVIII (April, 1914), 129–182.

Goebel, Dorothy Burne. *William Henry Harrison: A Political Biography* (*Indiana Historical Collections*, XIV). Indianapolis, 1926.

Goetzmann, William H. *Army Exploration in the American West, 1803–1863*. New Haven, 1959.

———. *Exploration and Empire: The Explorer and the Scientist in the Winning of the American West*. New York, 1966.

Goldman, Henry H. "A Survey of Federal Escorts of the Santa Fe Trade, 1829–1843," *Journal of the West*, V (October, 1966), 504–516.

Goodpasture, Albert V. "Indian Wars and Warriors of the Old Southwest, 1730–1807," *Tennessee Historical Magazine*, IV (March, 1918), 3–49; (June, 1918), 106–145; (September, 1918), 161–210; (December, 1918), 252–289.

Goodwin, Cardinal L. "Early Explorations and Settlements of Missouri and Arkansas, 1803–1822," *Missouri Historical Review*, XIV (April–July, 1920), 385–424.

———. "A Larger View of the Yellowstone Expedition, 1819–1820," *Mississippi Valley Historical Review*, IV (December, 1917), 299–313.

Graham, Louis E. "Fort McIntosh," *Western Pennsylvania Historical Magazine*, XV (May, 1932), 93–119.

Gregg, Kate L. "Building of the First American Fort West of the Mississippi," *Missouri Historical Review*, XXX (July, 1936), 345–364.

———. "The History of Fort Osage," *Missouri Historical Review*, XXXIV (July, 1940), 439–488.

Guillet, Edwin C. *The Lives and Times of the Patriots: An Account of the Rebellion in Upper Canada, 1837–1838, and the Patriot Agitation in the United States, 1837–1842*. Toronto, 1938.

Hagan, William T. *American Indians*. Chicago, 1961.

———. "The Dodge-Henry Controversy," *Journal of the Illinois State Historical Society*, L (Winter, 1957), 377–384.

———. "General Henry Atkinson and the Militia," *Military Affairs*, XXIII (Winter, 1959–1960), 194–197.

————. *The Sac and Fox Indians*. Norman, Okla., 1958.

Halbert, H. S., and Ball, T. H. *The Creek War of 1813 and 1814*. Chicago, 1895.

Hall, Arthur H. "The Red Stick War: Creek Indian Affairs During the War of 1812," *Chronicles of Oklahoma*, XII (September, 1934), 264–293.

Hamilton, Holman. *Zachary Taylor: Soldier of the Republic*. Indianapolis, 1941.

Hansen, Marcus L. *Old Fort Snelling, 1819–1858*. Iowa City, 1918. Reprint, Minneapolis, 1958.

Hardin, J. Fair. "Fort Jesup—Fort Selden—Camp Sabine—Camp Salubrity: Four Forgotten Frontier Army Posts of Western Louisiana," *Louisiana Historical Quarterly*, XVI (January, 1933), 5–26; (April, 1933), 279–292; (July, 1933), 441–453; (October, 1933), 670–680; XVII (January, 1934), 139–168.

Hauberg, John H. "The Black Hawk War, 1831–1832," *Illinois State Historical Society Transactions for the Year 1932*, pp. 91–134.

Hay, Thomas Robson. "General James Wilkinson—The Last Phase," *Louisiana Historical Quarterly*, XIX (April, 1936), 407–435.

————. "Some Reflections on the Career of General James Wilkinson," *Mississippi Valley Historical Review*, XXI (March, 1935), 471–494.

Hay, Thomas Robson, and Werner, M. R. *The Admirable Trumpeter: A Biography of General James Wilkinson*. Garden City, N. Y., 1941.

Helderman, Leonard C. "The Northwest Expedition of George Rogers Clark, 1786–1787," *Mississippi Valley Historical Review*, XXV (December, 1938), 317–334.

Hildreth, Samuel P. *Contributions to the Early History of the North-West, Including the Moravian Missions in Ohio*. Cincinnati, 1864.

————. *Pioneer History: Being an Account of the First Examinations of the Ohio Valley, and the Early Settlement of the Northwest Territory*. Cincinnati, 1848.

Hill, Forest G. *Roads, Rails & Waterways: The Army Engineers and Early Transportation*. Norman, Okla., 1957.

Hill, Jim Dan. *The Minute Man in Peace and War: A History of the National Guard*. Harrisburg, Penn., 1964.

Hinton, Harwood Perry. "The Military Career of John Ellis Wool, 1812–1863." Unpublished Ph.D. dissertation, University of Wisconsin, 1960.

Hollon, W. Eugene. *The Lost Pathfinder, Zebulon Montgomery Pike*. Norman, Okla., 1949.

Horsman, Reginald. "The British Indian Department and the Resistance to General Anthony Wayne, 1793–1795," *Mississippi Valley Historical Review*, XLIX (September, 1962), 269–290.

————. "British Indian Policy in the Northwest, 1807–1812," *Mississippi Valley Historical Review*, XLV (June, 1958), 51–66.

————. "The Role of the Indian in the War," in Philip P. Mason, ed., *After Tippecanoe: Some Aspects of the War of 1812*. East Lansing, Mich., 1963. Pp. 60–77.

———. "Wisconsin and the War of 1812," *Wisconsin Magazine of History*, XLVI (Autumn, 1962), 3–15.

Hosmer, James K. *The History of the Louisiana Purchase.* New York, 1902.

Houck, Louis. *A History of Missouri, from the Earliest Explorations and Settlements until the Admission of the State into the Union.* 3 vols. Chicago, 1908.

Hulbert, Archer Butler. *Military Roads of the Mississippi Basin: The Conquest of the Old Northwest.* Cleveland, 1904.

Hunt, Elvid. *History of Fort Leavenworth, 1827–1927.* Fort Leavenworth, Kan., 1926.

Hunt, Samuel F. "General Anthony Wayne and the Battle of 'Fallen Timbers,'" *Ohio Archaeological and Historical Quarterly*, IX (October, 1900), 214–237.

———. "The Treaty of Greenville," *Ohio Archaeological and Historical Society Publications*, VII (1899), 218–240.

Ingersoll, L. D. *A History of the War Department of the United States, with Biographical Sketches of the Secretaries.* Washington, 1879.

Jackson, Alfred A. "Abraham Lincoln in the Black Hawk War," *Wisconsin Historical Collections*, XIV (1898), 118–136.

Jackson, Donald. "Old Fort Madison—1808–1813," *Palimpsest*, XXXIX (January, 1958), 1–64.

Jackson, Donald, and Petersen, William J. "The Black Hawk War," *Palimpsest*, XLIII (February, 1962), 65–113.

Jacobs, James Ripley. *The Beginning of the U. S. Army, 1783–1812.* Princeton, 1947.

———. *Tarnished Warrior, Major-General James Wilkinson.* New York, 1938.

James, Marquis. *Andrew Jackson, The Border Captain.* New York, 1933.

Johnson, Sally A. "Cantonment Missouri, 1819–1820," *Nebraska History*, XXXVII (June, 1956), 121–133.

———. "Fort Atkinson at Council Bluffs," *Nebraska History*, XXXVIII (September, 1957), 229–236.

———. "The Sixth's Elysian Fields—Fort Atkinson on the Council Bluffs," *Nebraska History*, XL (March, 1959), 1–38.

Kellogg, Louise Phelps. *The British Regime in Wisconsin and the Northwest.* Madison, Wis., 1935.

———. "The Capture of Mackinac in 1812," *Proceedings of the State Historical Society of Wisconsin* (1912), pp. 124–145.

———. "Old Fort Howard," *Wisconsin Magazine of History*, XVIII (December, 1934), 125–140.

Kinchen, Oscar A. *The Rise and Fall of the Patriot Hunters.* New York, 1956.

Kivett, Marvin F. "Excavations at Fort Atkinson, Nebraska: A Preliminary Report," *Nebraska History*, XL (March, 1959), 39–66.

Knopf, Richard C. "Crime and Punishment in the Legion, 1792–1793," *Bulletin of the Historical and Philosophical Society of Ohio*, XIV (July, 1956), 232–238.

————. "Fort Miamis: The International Background," *Ohio State Archaeological and Historical Quarterly*, LXI (April, 1952), 146–166.

Kreidberg, Marvin A., and Henry, Merton G. *History of Military Mobilization in the United States Army, 1775–1945*. Washington, 1955.

Lambert, Joseph I. "The Black Hawk War: A Military Analysis," *Journal of the Illinois State Historical Society*, XXXII (December, 1939), 442–473.

Love, William A. "General Jackson's Military Road," *Publications of the Mississippi Historical Society*, XI (1910), 402–417.

McAfee, Robert B. *History of the Late War in the Western Country*. Lexington, Ky., 1816. Reprint, Bowling Green, Ohio, 1919.

McCaleb, Walter Flavius. *The Aaron Burr Conspiracy*. Expanded ed., New York, 1936.

McReynolds, Edwin C. *The Seminoles*. Norman, Okla., 1957.

Mahan, Bruce E. "Old Fort Atkinson," *Palimpsest*, II (November, 1921), 333–350.

————. *Old Fort Crawford and the Frontier*. Iowa City, 1926.

Mahon, John K. "Anglo-American Methods of Indian Warfare, 1676–1794," *Mississippi Valley Historical Review*, XLV (September, 1958), 254–275.

————. *History of the Second Seminole War, 1835–1842*. Gainesville, Fla., 1967.

————. "Military Relations Between Georgia and the United States, 1789–1794," *Georgia Historical Quarterly*, XLIII (June, 1959), 138–155.

————. "Pennsylvania and the Beginnings of the Regular Army," *Pennsylvania History*, XXI (January, 1954), 33–44.

————. "The Treaty of Moultrie Creek, 1823," *Florida Historical Quarterly*, XL (April, 1962), 350–372.

————. "Two Seminole Treaties: Payne's Landing, 1832, and Ft. Gibson, 1833," *Florida Historical Quarterly*, XLI (July, 1962), 1–21.

Mansfield, Edward D. *Life and Services of General Winfield Scott*. New York, 1852.

Marshall, Thomas Maitland. *A History of the Western Boundary of the Louisiana Purchase, 1819–1841*. Berkeley, Calif., 1914.

Martin, François-Xavier. *The History of Louisiana from the Earliest Period*. 2 vols. New Orleans, 1827–1829.

Martin, Sidney Walter. *Florida during the Territorial Days*. Athens, Ga., 1944.

————. "Richard Keith Call, Florida Territorial Leader," *Florida Historical Quarterly*, XXI (April, 1943), 332–351.

Masterson, William H. *William Blount*. Baton Rouge, 1954.

Mattison, Ray H. "The Indian Frontier on the Upper Missouri to 1865," *Nebraska History*, XXXIX (September, 1958), 241–266.

————. "The Military Frontier on the Upper Missouri," *Nebraska History*, XXXVII (September, 1956) 159–182.

Meek, Basil. "General Harmar's Expedition," *Ohio Archaeological and Historical Quarterly*, XX (January, 1911), 74–108.

Millis, Walter. *Arms and Men: A Study in American Military History.* New York, 1956.

Mohr, Walter H. *Federal Indian Relations, 1774–1788.* Philadelphia, 1933.

Mooney, James. *Myths of the Cherokee (Nineteenth Annual Report of the Bureau of American Ethnology, 1897–1898,* Part 1), Washington, 1900.

Morgan, Dale L. *The West of William H. Ashley: The International Struggle for the Fur Trade of the Missouri, the Rocky Mountains, and the Columbia, with Explorations Beyond the Continental Divide, Recorded in the Diaries and Letters of William H. Ashley and His Contemporaries, 1822–1838.* Denver, 1964.

Morris, Ralph C. "The Notion of a Great American Desert East of the Rockies," *Mississippi Valley Historical Review,* XIII (September, 1926), 190–200.

Morrison, William B. "Fort Towson," *Chronicles of Oklahoma,* VIII (June, 1930), 226–232.

——. "Fort Washita," *Chronicles of Oklahoma,* V (June, 1927), 251–258.

——. *Military Posts and Camps in Oklahoma.* Oklahoma City, 1936.

Nelson, Harold L. "Military Roads for War and Peace—1791–1836," *Military Affairs,* XIX (Spring, 1955), 1–14.

Nettels, Curtis. "The National Cost of the Inland Frontier, 1820–1830," *Transactions of the Wisconsin Academy of Science,* XXV (1930), 1–37.

Nevins, Allan. *Frémont: Pathmarker of the West.* New York, 1939. New ed., 1955.

Nichols, Roger L. "The Founding of Fort Atkinson," *Annals of Iowa,* Third Series, XXXVII (Spring, 1965), 589–597.

——. *General Henry Atkinson: A Western Military Career.* Norman, Okla., 1965.

Norton, W. T. "Old Fort Belle Fontaine," *Journal of the Illinois State Historical Society,* IV (October, 1911), 334–339.

Oliva, Leo E. *Soldiers on the Santa Fe Trail.* Norman, Okla., 1967.

Osgood, Howard L. "The British Evacuation of the United States," *Rochester Historical Society Publication Fund Series,* VI (1927), 55–63.

Palmer, John McAuley. *America in Arms.* New Haven, 1941.

Parkinson, Peter. "Strictures upon Gov. Ford's History of the Black Hawk War," *Wisconsin Historical Collections,* II (1856), 393–401.

Parton, James. *Life of Andrew Jackson.* 3 vols. New York, 1860.

Patrick, Rembert W. *Aristocrat in Uniform: General Duncan L. Clinch.* Gainesville, Fla., 1963.

Peake, Ora Brooks. *A History of the United States Indian Factory System.* Denver, 1954.

Peckham, Howard H. "Josiah Harmar and His Indian Expedition," *Ohio State Archaeological and Historical Quarterly,* LV (July–September, 1946), 227–241.

Pelzer, Louis. "A Frontier Officer's Military Order Book," *Mississippi Valley Historical Review,* VI (September, 1919), 260–267.

——. *Henry Dodge.* Iowa City, 1911.

——. *Marches of the Dragoons in the Mississippi Valley: An Account of*

Marches and Activities of the First Regiment United States Dragoons in the Mississippi Valley between the Years 1833 and 1850. Iowa City, 1917.

Philbrick, Francis S. *The Rise of the West, 1754–1830.* New York, 1965.

Phillips, Ulrich B. *Georgia and State Rights: A Study of the Political History of Georgia from the Revolution to the Civil War, with Particular Regard to Federal Relations* (*Annual Report of the American Historical Association for the Year 1901,* II). Washington, 1902.

Phinney, A. H. "The Second Spanish-American War," *Florida Historical Society Quarterly,* V (October, 1926), 103–111.

Pirtle, Alfred. *The Battle of Tippecanoe.* Louisville, 1900.

Poesch, Jessie. *Titian Ramsay Peale, 1799–1885, and His Journals of the Wilkes Expedition* (*Memoirs of the American Philosophical Society,* vol. 52). Philadelphia, 1961.

Porter, Kenneth Wiggins. "Florida Slaves and Free Negroes in the Seminole War, 1835–1842," *Journal of Negro History,* XXVIII (October, 1943), 390–421.

———. *John Jacob Astor, Business Man.* 2 vols. Cambridge, Mass., 1931.

———. "Negro Guides and Interpreters in the Early Stages of the Seminole War, Dec. 28, 1835–Mar. 6, 1837," *Journal of Negro History,* XXXV (April, 1950), 174–182.

———. "Negroes and the Seminole War, 1835–1842," *Journal of Southern History,* XXX (November, 1964), 427–450.

———. "Osceola and the Negroes," *Florida Historical Quarterly,* XXXIII (January–April, 1955), 235–239.

———. "Seminole Flight from Fort Marion," *Florida Historical Quarterly,* XXII (January, 1944), 113–133.

Pound, Merritt B. *Benjamin Hawkins—Indian Agent.* Athens, Ga., 1951.

Pratt, Fletcher. *Eleven Generals: Studies in American Command.* New York, 1949.

Pratt, Harry E. "Abraham Lincoln in the Black Hawk War," in O. Fritiof Ander, ed., *The John H. Hauberg Historical Essays.* Rock Island, Ill., 1954. Pp. 18–28.

Pratt, Julius W. "Fur Trade Strategy and the American Left Flank in the War of 1812," *American Historical Review,* XL (January, 1935), 246–273.

Priddy, O. W. "Wayne's Strategic Advance from Fort Greenville to Grand Glaize," *Ohio Archaeological and Historical Publications,* XXXIX (January, 1930), 42–76.

Prucha, Francis Paul. *American Indian Policy in the Formative Years: The Indian Trade and Intercourse Acts, 1790–1834.* Cambridge, Mass., 1962.

———. *Broadax and Bayonet: The Role of the United States Army in the Development of the Northwest, 1815–1860.* Madison, Wis., 1953.

———. "Distribution of Regular Army Troops Before the Civil War," *Military Affairs,* XVI (Winter, 1952), 169–173.

————. *A Guide to the Military Posts of the United States, 1789–1895.* Madison, Wis., 1964.

————. "Indian Removal and the Great American Desert," *Indiana Magazine of History*, LIX (December, 1963), 299–322.

————. "The United States Army as Viewed by British Travelers, 1825–1860," *Military Affairs*, XVII (Fall, 1953), 113–124.

Putnam, Herbert Everett. *Joel Roberts Poinsett: A Political Biography.* Washington, 1935.

Quaife, Milo M. *Checagou: From Indian Wigwam to Modern City, 1673–1835.* Chicago, 1933.

————. *Chicago and the Old Northwest, 1673–1835: A Study of the Evolution of the Northwestern Frontier, Together with a History of Fort Dearborn.* Chicago, 1913.

————. "From Detroit to the Mississippi in 1820," *Burton Historical Collection Leaflet*, VIII (March, 1930), 49–64.

————. "General William Hull and His Critics," *Ohio State Archaeological and Historical Quarterly*, XLVII (April, 1938), 168–182.

Reinhardt, George C. "Fort Leavenworth Is Born," *Military Review*, XXXIII (October, 1953), 3–8.

Risch, Erna. *Quartermaster Support of the Army: A History of the Corps, 1775–1939.* Washington, 1962.

Rippy, J. Fred. *Joel R. Poinset, Versatile American.* Durham, N.C., 1935.

Rodenbough, Theophilus F. *From Everglade to Cañon with the Second Dragoons.* New York, 1875.

Rooney, Elizabeth B. "The Story of the Black Hawk War," *Wisconsin Magazine of History*, XL (Summer, 1957), 274–283.

Roosevelt, Theodore. *The Winning of the West.* 4 vols. New York, 1889–1896.

Ross, Alexander. *The Red River Settlement: Its Rise, Progress, and Present State.* London, 1856. Facsimile ed., Minneapolis, 1957.

Ross, Robert B. "The Patriot War," *Michigan Pioneer and Historical Collections*, XXI (1894), 509–609.

Rossiter, Clinton. *Alexander Hamilton and the Constitution.* New York, 1964.

Rowland, Mrs. Dunbar. *Andrew Jackson's Campaign Against the British, or the Mississippi Territory in the War of 1812: Concerning the Military Operations of the Americans, Creek Indians, British, and Spanish.* New York, 1926.

————. *Life, Letters and Papers of William Dunbar, of Elgin, Morayshire, Scotland, and Natchez, Mississippi: Pioneer Scientist of the Southern United States.* Jackson, Miss., 1930.

Royce, Charles C. "The Cherokee Nation of Indians: A Narrative of Their Official Relations with the Colonial and Federal Governments," *Fifth Annual Report of the Bureau of Ethnology, 1883–1884* (Washington, 1887), pp. 121–378.

————. *Indian Land Cessions in the United States (Eighteenth Annual*

Report of the Bureau of American Ethnology, Part II), Washington, 1899.

Ryan, Harold W. "Daniel Bissell—His Story," *Bulletin of the Missouri Historical Society*, XII (October, 1955), 32–44.

———. "Daniel Bissel—'Late General,' " *Bulletin of the Missouri Historical Society*, XV (October, 1958), 20–28.

Salter, William. "Henry Dodge: Part IV, Colonel U. S. Dragoons, 1833–6," *Iowa Historical Record*, VII (April, 1891), 101–119; VIII (April, 1892), 251–267.

Scanlan, Peter L. "The Military Record of Jefferson Davis in Wisconsin," *Wisconsin Magazine of History*, XXIV (December, 1940), 174–182.

———. *Prairie du Chien: French, British, American*. Menasha, Wis., 1937.

Shortridge, Wilson Porter. "The Canadian-American Frontier during the Rebellion of 1837–1838," *Canadian Historical Review*, VII (March, 1926), 13–26.

Shreve, Royal Ornan. *The Finished Scoundrel: General James Wilkinson, Sometime Commander-in-Chief of the Army of the United States, Who Made Intrigue a Trade and Treason a Profession*. Indianapolis, 1933.

Silver, James W. *Edmund Pendleton Gaines, Frontier General*. Baton Rouge, 1949.

Slocum, Charles Elihu. *The Ohio Country Between the Years 1783 and 1815*. New York, 1910.

Smith, Dwight L. "Provocation and Occurrence of Indian-White Warfare in the Early American Period in the Old Northwest," *Northwest Ohio Quarterly*, XXXIII (Summer, 1961), 132–147.

———. "Wayne and the Treaty of Greene Ville," *Ohio State Archaeological and Historical Quarterly*, LXIII (January, 1954), 1–7.

———. "Wayne's Peace with the Indians of the Old Northwest, 1795," *Ohio State Archaeological and Historical Quarterly*, LIX (July, 1950), 239–255.

Smith, William Henry. *The St. Clair Papers: The Life and Public Services of Arthur St. Clair*. 2 vols. Cincinnati, 1882.

Smith, William L. G. *The Life and Times of Lewis Cass*. New York, 1856.

Spaulding, Oliver Lyman. *The United States Army in War and Peace*. New York, 1937.

Sprague, John T. *The Origin, Progress, and Conclusion of the Florida War*. New York, 1848. Facsimile ed., Gainesville, Fla., 1964.

Stafford, Robert Charles. "The Bemrose Manuscript on the Seminole War," *Florida Historical Quarterly*, XVIII (April, 1940), 285–292.

Stanley, George F. G. "The Indians in the War of 1812," *Canadian Historical Review*, XXXI (June, 1950), 145–165.

Steiner, B. C. *The Life and Correspondence of James McHenry*. Cleveland, 1907.

Stephens, F. F. "Missouri and the Santa Fe Trade," *Missouri Historical Review*, X (July, 1916), 233–262.

Stevens, Frank E. *The Black Hawk War, Including a Review of Black Hawk's Life.* Chicago, 1903.

———. "A Forgotten Hero: General James Dougherty Henry," *Illinois State Historical Society Transactions for the Year 1934*, pp. 77–120.

Thian, Raphael P. *Notes Illustrating the Military Geography of the United States.* Washington, 1881.

Thoburn, Joseph B. "The Dragoon Campaigns to the Rocky Mountains," *Chronicles of Oklahoma*, VII (March, 1930), 35–41.

Thwaites, Reuben Gold. "The Story of the Black Hawk War," *Wisconsin Historical Collections*, XII (1892), 217–265.

Tiffany, Orrin Edward. "The Relations of the United States to the Canadian Rebellion of 1837–1838," *Publications of the Buffalo Historical Society*, VIII (1905), 1–118.

Tohill, Louis Arthur. "Robert Dickson, British Fur Trader on the Upper Mississippi," *North Dakota Historical Quarterly*, III (October, 1928), 5–49; (January, 1929), 83–128; (April, 1929), 182–203.

Tucker, Glenn. *Poltroons and Patriots: A Popular Account of the War of 1812.* 2 vols. Indianapolis, 1954.

———. *Tecumseh: Vision of Glory.* Indianapolis, 1956.

Tucker, John M. "Major Long's Route from the Arkansas to the Canadian River, 1820," *New Mexico Historical Review*, XXXVIII (July, 1963), 185–219.

Turner, Andrew J. "The History of Fort Winnebago," *Wisconsin Historical Collections*, XIV (1898), 65–103.

Turner, Frederick Jackson. "The Policy of France toward the Mississippi Valley in the Period of Washington and Adams," *American Historical Review*, X (January, 1905), 249–279.

United States, Department of the Army. *American Military History, 1607–1953* (ROTC Manual 145–20). Washington, 1956.

Upton, Emory. *The Military Policy of the United States.* Washington, 1917.

Van der Zee, Jacob. *The Black Hawk War.* Iowa City, 1918

———. "Forts in the Iowa Country," *Iowa Journal of History and Politics*, XII (April, 1914), 163–204.

———. *Old Fort Madison.* Iowa City, 1918.

Van Every, Dale. *Disinherited: The Lost Birthright of the American Indian.* New York, 1966.

Wakefield, John A. *History of the War between the United States and the Sac and Fox Nations of Indians, and Parts of Other Disaffected Tribes of Indians, in the Years Eighteen Hundred and Twenty-seven, Thirty-one, and Thirty-two.* Jacksonville, Ill., 1834. Reprinted, with preface and notes by Frank E. Stevens, as *Wakefield's History of the Black Hawk War*, Chicago, 1908.

Wallace, Edward S. *General William Jenkins Worth, Monterey's Forgotten Hero.* Dallas, 1953.

Ward, Harry M. *The Department of War, 1781–1789.* Pittsburgh, 1962.

Watson, Richard L., Jr. "Congressional Attitudes Toward Military Preparedness, 1829–1835," *Mississippi Valley Historical Review*, XXXIV (March, 1948), 611–636.

Way, Royal B. "The United States Factory System for Trading with the Indians, 1796–1822," *Mississippi Valley Historical Review*, VI (September, 1919), 220–235.

Weigley, Russell F. *History of the United States Army*. New York, 1967.

——. *Towards an American Army: Military Thought from Washington to Marshall*. New York, 1962.

Wesley, Edgar Bruce. *Guarding the Frontier: A Study of Frontier Defense from 1815 to 1825*. Minneapolis, 1935.

——. "Life at a Frontier Post: Fort Atkinson, 1823–1826," *Journal of the American Military Institute*, III (Winter, 1939), 203–209.

——. "Life at Fort Atkinson," *Nebraska History*, XXX (December, 1949), 348–358.

——. "The Military Policy of the Critical Period," *Coast Artillery Journal*, LXVIII (April, 1928), 281–290.

——. "A Still Larger View of the So-Called Yellowstone Expedition," *North Dakota Historical Quarterly*, V (July, 1931), 219–238.

Wheat, Carl I. *Mapping the Transmississippi West*. 5 vols. San Francisco, 1957–1963.

Whitaker, Arthur Preston. "Alexander McGillivray, 1783–1789," *North Carolina Historical Review*, V (April, 1928), 181–203.

——. "Alexander McGillivray, 1789–1793," *North Carolina Historical Review*, V (July, 1928), 289–309.

——. *The Mississippi Question, 1795–1803: A Study in Trade, Politics, and Diplomacy*. New York, 1934.

——. "Spain and the Cherokee Indians, 1783–1798," *North Carolina Historical Review*, IV (July, 1927), 252–269.

——. *The Spanish-American Frontier, 1783–1795: The Westward Movement and the Spanish Retreat in the Mississippi Valley*. Boston, 1927.

Wildes, Harry Emerson. *Anthony Wayne, Trouble Shooter of the American Revolution*. New York, 1941.

Williams, Mentor L. "John Kinzie's Narrative of the Fort Dearborn Massacre," *Journal of the Illinois State Historical Society*, XLVI (Winter, 1953), 343–362.

Williams, T. Harry. *Americans at War*. Baton Rouge, 1960.

Wilson, Frazer Ells. "St. Clair's Defeat," *Ohio Archaeological and Historical Quarterly*, XI (July, 1902), 30–43.

——. *The Treaty of Greenville*, Piqua, Ohio, 1894.

Wiltse, Charles M. *John C. Calhoun, Nationalist, 1782–1828*. Indianapolis, 1944.

Winger, Otho. "The Indians Who Opposed Harmar," *Ohio State Archaeological and Historical Quarterly*, L (January–March, 1941), 55–59.

Wood, Richard G. *Stephen Harriman Long, 1784–1864: Army Engineer, Explorer, Inventor*. Glendale, Calif., 1966.

——. "Stephen H. Long at Belle Point," *Arkansas Historical Quarterly*, XIII (Winter, 1954), 338–340.

Woolworth, Nancy L. "Captain Edwin V. Sumner's Expedition to Devil's Lake in the Summer of 1845," *North Dakota History*, XXVIII (April–July, 1961), 79–98.

Wright, Muriel H. "The Removal of the Choctaws to the Indian Territory, 1830–33," *Chronicles of Oklahoma*, VI (June, 1928), 103–128.

Young, Mary E. *Redskins, Ruffleshirts, and Rednecks: Indian Allotments in Alabama and Mississippi, 1830–1860.* Norman, Okla., 1961.

Young, Otis E "Dragoons on the Santa Fe Trail in the Autumn of 1843," *Chronicles of Oklahoma*, XXXII (Spring, 1954), 42–51.

————. *The First Military Escort on the Santa Fe Trail, 1829: From the Journal and Reports of Major Bennet Riley and Lieutenant Philip St. George Cooke.* Glendale, Calif., 1952.

————. "Military Protection of the Santa Fe Trail and Trade," *Missouri Historical Review*, XLIX (October, 1954), 19–32.

————. "The United States Mounted Ranger Battalion, 1832–1833," *Mississippi Valley Historical Review*, XLI (December, 1954), 453–470.

————. *The West of Philip St. George Cooke, 1809–1895.* Glendale, Calif., 1955.

Young, Rogers W. "Fort Marion During the Seminole War, 1835–1842," *Florida Historical Society Quarterly*, XIII (April, 1935), 193–223.

INDEX

Index

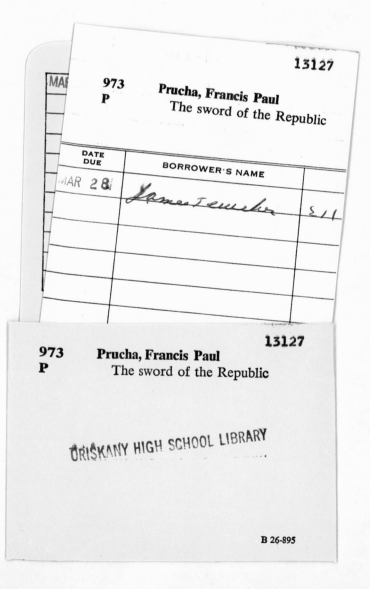

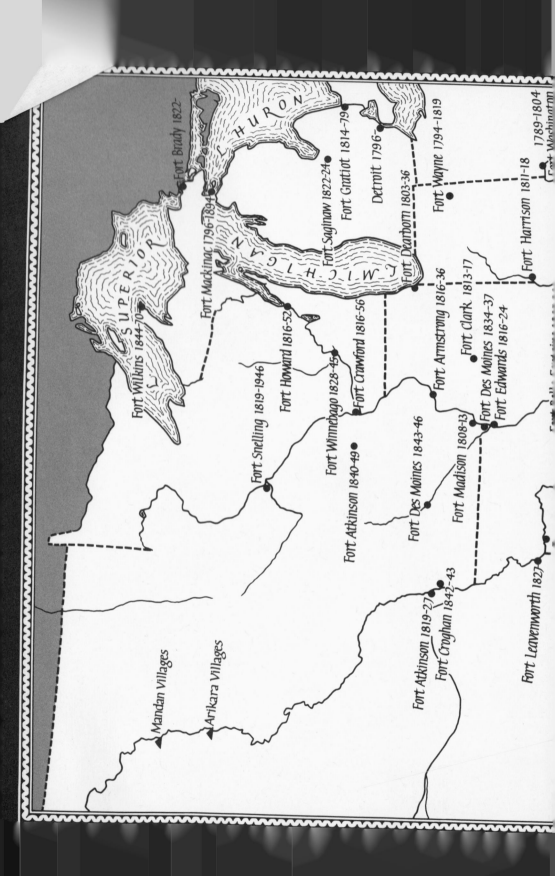